D0857208

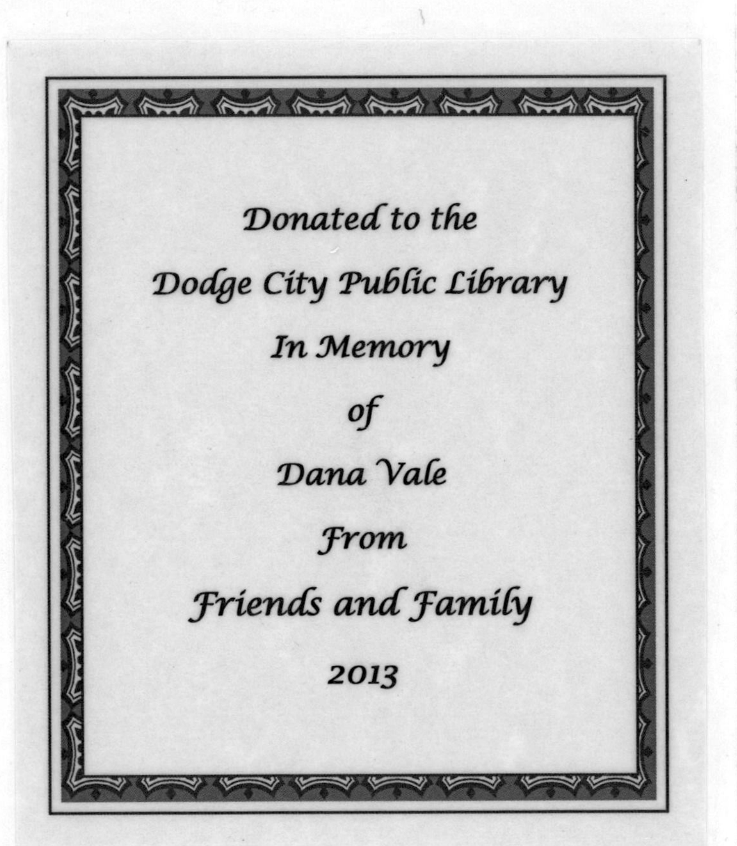
Donated to the
Dodge City Public Library
In Memory
of
Dana Vale
From
Friends and Family
2013

THE STARDANCE TRILOGY

Baen Books
by Spider Robinson

⁎ ⁎ ⁎

Callahan's Lady
Lady Slings the Booze
The Stardance Trilogy (with Jeanne Robinson)
Lifehouse
User Friendly
Telempath
Very Bad Deaths

THE STARDANCE TRILOGY

by

SPIDER & JEANNE ROBINSON

THE STARDANCE TRILOGY

A Baen Book Original

Baen Publishing Enterprises
P.O. Box 1403
Riverdale, NY 10471
www.baen.com

ISBN 10: 1-4165-2082-1
ISBN 13: 978-1-4165-2082-2

Cover art by Kurt Miller

First Baen printing, September 2006

Library of Congress Cataloging-in-Publication Data
Robinson, Spider.
The stardance trilogy / by Spider & Jeanne Robinson.
p. cm.
"A Baen Books original."
ISBN-13: 978-1-4165-2082-2
ISBN-10: 1-4165-2082-1
1. Science fiction, American. I. Robinson, Jeanne. II. Title.

PS3568.O3156S725 2006
813'.54--dc22
2006012263

Distributed by Simon & Schuster
1230 Avenue of the Americas
New York, NY 10020

Printed in the United States of America

10 9 8 7 6 5 4 3 2 1

CONTENTS

* * *

STARDANCE

This one's for Luanna Mountainbourne,
who may well make prophets of us one day. . .

"In order to find one's place in the infinity of being,
one must be able both to separate and unite."

—I Ching

Acknowledgments

What we'd like to do here is thank all the people without whom this book could not have been finished, as opposed to, but not excluding, that general gang of friends and relatives who kept us alive during its writing; they would have done so anyway, book or no book, and should be thanked in different ways.

Among the former and sometimes the latter are: Ben Bova, Gordon R. Dickson, our agent Kirby McCauley, our editor and friend Jim Frenkel, Joe W. Haldeman, Jerry Pournelle, Ph.D., and Laurence Janifer, all of whom donated information, advice, and assistance above and beyond the call of friendship, all at the cost of working time or leisure or both. It should be clearly understood that none of the above people are to blame for what we have done with their information and aid: any errors are ours.

On a less personal but just as basic level, this book could also never have become what it is without *A House In Space,* Henry S.F. Cooper's fascinating account of zero-gee life in Skylab; G. Harry Stine's *The Third Industrial Revolution,* which built Skyfac in our minds; the recent works of John Varley and Frank Herbert, who roughly simultaneously pioneered (at least as far as we know) the concept on which the ending of this book depends; Murray Louis's exquisite and moving columns in *Dance Magazine*; the books, past advice and present love of Stephen Gaskin; the inspirational dance of Toronto Dance Theatre, Murray Louis, Pilobolus, the Contact Improv Movement, and all of our dancing buddies in Nova Scotia; the lifework of Robert Heinlein, Theodore Sturgeon, Edgar Pangborn, and John D. MacDonald; the whiskey of Mr. Jameson, the coffee of Jamaica, and the music of Frank Zappa, Paul Simon, and Yes.

I

I can't really say that I knew her, certainly not the way Seroff knew Isadora. All I know of her childhood and adolescence are the anecdotes she chanced to relate in my hearing—just enough to make me certain that all three of the contradictory biographies on the current best-seller list are fictional. All I know of her adult life are the relatively few hours she spent in my presence and on my monitors—more than enough to tell me that every newspaper account I've seen is fictional. Carrington probably believed he knew her better than I, and in a limited sense he was correct—but he would never have written about it, and now he is dead.

But I was her video man, since the days when you touched the camera with your hands, and I knew her backstage: a type of relationship like no other on Earth or off it. I don't believe it can be described to anyone not of the profession—you might think of it as somewhere between co-workers and combat buddies. I was with her the day she came to Skyfac, terrified and determined, to stake her life upon a dream. I watched her work and worked with her for that whole two months, through endless rehearsals, and I have saved every tape and they are not for sale.

And, of course, I saw the Stardance. I was there. I taped it.

I guess I can tell you some things about her.

To begin with, it was not, as Cahill's *Shara* and Von Derski's *Dance Unbound: The Creation of New Modern* suggest, a lifelong fascination with space and space travel that led her to become her race's first zero-gravity dancer. Space was a means to her, not an end, and its vast empty immensity scared her at first. Nor was it, as Melberg's hardcover tabloid *The Real Shara Drummond* claims, because she lacked the talent to make it as a dancer on Earth. If you think free-fall dancing is easier than conventional dance, you try it. Don't forget your dropsickness bag.

But there is a grain of truth in Melberg's slanders, as there is in all the best slanders. She could *not* make it on Earth—but not through lack of talent.

I first saw her in Toronto in July 1989. I headed Toronto Dance Theater's video department at that time, and I hated every minute of it. I hated everything in those days. The schedule that day called for spending the entire afternoon taping students, a waste of time and tape that I hated more than anything except the phone company. I hadn't seen the new year's crop yet, and was not eager to. I love to watch dance done well—the efforts of a tyro are usually as pleasing to me as a first-year violin student in the next apartment is to you.

My leg was bothering me more than usual as I walked into the studio. Norrey saw my face and left a group of young hopefuls to come over. "Charlie . . . ?"

"I know, I know. They're tender fledglings, Charlie, with egos as fragile as an Easter egg in December. Don't bite them, Charlie. Don't even bark at them if you can help it, Charlie."

She smiled. "Something like that. Leg?"

"Leg."

Norrey Drummond is a dancer who gets away with looking like a woman because she's small. There's about a hundred and fifteen pounds of her, and most of it is heart. She stands about five-four, and is perfectly capable of seeming to tower over the tallest student. She has more energy than the North American Grid, and uses it as efficiently as a vane pump (do you know the principle of a standard piston-type pump? Go look up the principle of a vane pump.) There's a signaturelike uniqueness to her dance, the only reason I can see why she got so few of the really juicy parts in company productions until Modern gave way to New Modern. I liked her because she didn't pity me. We lived together once, but it didn't work out.

"It's not only the leg," I admitted. "I hate to see the tender fledglings butcher your choreography."

"Then you needn't worry. The piece you're taping today is by . . . one of the students."

"Oh fine. I knew I should have called in sick." She made a face. "What's the catch?"

"Eh?"

"Why did the funny thing happen to your voice just as you got to 'one of my students'?"

She blushed. "Dammit, she's my sister."

Norrey and I go back a *long* way together, but I'd never met a sister—not unusual these days, I suppose. My eyebrows rose. "She must be good then."

"Why, thank you, Charlie."

"Bullshit. I give compliments right-handed or not at all—I'm not talking about heredity. I mean that you're so hopelessly ethical you'd bend over backward to avoid nepotism. For you to give your own sister a feature like that, she must be *terrific*."

"Charlie, she is," Norrey said simply.

"We'll see. What's her name again?"

"Shara." Norrey pointed her out, and I understood the rest of the catch. Shara Drummond was ten years younger than her sister—and a good eighteen centimeters taller, with fifteen or eighteen more kilos. I noted absently that she was stunningly beautiful, but it didn't lessen my dismay—in her best years, Sophia Loren could never have become a Modern dancer. Where Norrey was small, Shara was big, and where Norrey was big, Shara was bigger. If I'd seen her on the street I might have whistled appreciatively—but in the studio I frowned.

"My God, Norrey, she's enormous."

"Mother's second husband was a football player," she said mournfully. "She's awfully good."

"If she *is* good, that *is* awful. Poor girl. Well, what do you want me to do?"

"What makes you think I want you to do anything?"

"You're still standing here."

"Oh. I guess I am. Well . . . have lunch with us, Charlie?"

"Why?" I knew perfectly well why, but I expected a polite lie.

Not from Norrey Drummond. "Because you two have something in common, I think."

I paid her honesty the compliment of not wincing. "I suppose we do."

"Then you will?"

"Right after the session."

She twinkled and was gone. In a remarkably short time she had organized the studio full of wandering, chattering young people into something that resembled a dance ensemble if you squinted. They warmed up during the twenty minutes it took me to set up and check out my equipment. I positioned one camera in front of them, one behind, and kept one in my hands for walk-around closeup work. I never triggered it.

There's a game that you play in your mind. Every time someone catches or is brought to your attention, you begin making guesses about them. You try to extrapolate their character and habits from their appearance. Him? Surly, disorganized—leaves the cap off the toothpaste and drinks boilermakers. Her? Art-student type, probably uses a diaphragm and writes letters in a stylized calligraphy of her own invention. Them? They look like schoolteachers from Miami, probably here to see what snow looks like, attend a convention. Sometimes I come pretty close. I don't know how I typecast Shara Drummond, in those first twenty minutes. The moment she began to dance, all preconceptions left my mind. She became something elemental, something unknowable, a living bridge between our world and the one the Muses live in.

I know, on an intellectual and academic level, just about all there is to know about dance, and I could not categorize or classify or even really comprehend the dance she danced that afternoon. I saw it, I even appreciated it, but I was not equipped to understand it. My camera dangled from the end of my arm, next to my jaw. Dancers speak of their "center," the place their motion centers around, often quite near the physical center of gravity. You strive to "dance from your center," and the "contraction-and-release" idea which underlies so much of Modern dance depends on the center for its focus of energy. Shara's center seemed to move about the room under its own power, trailing limbs that attached to it by choice rather than necessity. What's the word for the outermost part of the sun, the part that still shows in an eclipse? Corona? That's what her limbs were: four lengthy tongues of flame that followed the center in its eccentric, whirling orbit, writhing fluidly around its surface. That the lower two frequently contacted the floor seemed coincidental—indeed the other two touched the floor nearly as regularly.

There were other students dancing. I know this because the two automatic videocameras, unlike me, did their job and recorded the piece as a whole. It was called *Birthing*, and depicted the formation of a galaxy that ended up resembling Andromeda. It was not an accurate literal portrayal, but it wasn't intended to be. Symbolically, it felt like the birth of a galaxy.

In retrospect. At the time I was aware only of the galaxy's heart: Shara. Students occluded her from time to time, and I simply never noticed. It hurt to watch her.

If you know anything about dance, this must all sound horrid to you. A dance about a nebula? I know, I know. It's a ridiculous notion. And it worked. In the most gut-level, cellular way it worked—save only that Shara was too good for those around her. She did not belong in that eager crew of awkward, half-trained apprentices. It was like listening to the late Steveland Wonder trying to work with a pickup band in a Montreal bar.

But that wasn't what hurt.

Le Maintenant was Shabby, but the food was good and the house brand of grass was excellent. Show a Diner's Club card in there and Fat Humphrey'd show you a galley full of dirty dishes. It's gone now. Norrey and Shara declined a toke, but in my line of work it helps. Besides, I needed a few hits. How to tell a lovely lady her dearest dream is hopeless?

I didn't need to ask Shara to know that her dearest dream was to dance. More: to dance professionally. I have often speculated on the motives of the professional artist. Some seek the narcissistic assurance that others will actually pay cash to watch or hear them. Some are so incompetent or disorganized that they can support themselves in no other way. Some have a message which they feel needs expressing. I suppose most artists combine aspects of all three. This is not complaint—what they do for us is necessary. We should be grateful that there *are* motives.

But Shara was one of the rare ones. She danced because she simply needed to. She needed to say things which could be said in no other way, and she needed to take her meaning and her living from the saying of them. Anything else would have demeaned and devalued the essential statement of her dance. I knew this, from watching that one dance.

Between toking up and keeping my mouth full and then toking

again (a mild amount to offset the slight down that eating brings), it was over half an hour before I was required to say anything beyond an occasional grunted response to the luncheon chatter of the ladies. As the coffee arrived, Shara looked me square in the eye and said, "Do you talk, Charlie?"

She was Norrey's sister, all right.

"Only inanities."

"No such thing. Inane people, maybe."

"Do you enjoy dancing, Ms. Drummond?"

She answered seriously. "Define enjoy."

I opened my mouth and closed it, perhaps three times. You try it.

"And for God's sake tell me why you're so intent on not talking to me. You've got me worried."

"Shara!" Norrey looked dismayed.

"Hush. I want to know."

I took a crack at it. "Shara, before he died I had the privilege of meeting Bertram Ross. I had just seen him dance. A producer who knew and liked me took me backstage, the way you take a kid to see Santa Claus. I had expected him to look older offstage, at rest. He looked younger, as if that incredible motion of his was barely in check. He talked to me. After a while I stopped opening my mouth, because nothing ever came out."

She waited, expecting more. Only gradually did she comprehend the compliment and its dimension. I had assumed it would be obvious. Most artists *expect* to be complimented. When she did twig, she did not blush or simper. She did not cock her head and say, "Oh, come on." She did not say, "You flatter me." She did not look away.

She nodded slowly and said, "Thank you, Charlie. That's worth a lot more than idle chatter." There was a suggestion of sadness in her smile, as if we shared a bitter joke.

"You're welcome."

"For heaven's sake, Norrey, what are you looking so upset about?"

The cat now had Norrey's tongue.

"She's disappointed in me," I said. "I said the wrong thing."

"That was the wrong thing?"

"It should have been 'Ms. Drummond, I think you ought to give up dancing.'"

"It should have been '*Shara*, I think you ought'. . . *what*?"

"Charlie—" Norrey began.

"I was supposed to tell you that we can't all be professional dancers, that they also surf who only sand and wade. Shara, I was supposed to tell you to dump the dance—before it dumps you."

In my need to be honest with her, I had been more brutal than was necessary, I thought. I was to learn that bluntness never dismayed Shara Drummond. She demanded it.

"Why you?" was all she said.

"We're inhabiting the same vessel, you and I. We've both got an itch that our bodies just won't let us scratch."

Her eyes softened. "What's your itch?"

"The same as yours."

"Eh?"

"The man was supposed to come and fix the phone on Thursday. My roommate Karen and I had an all-day rehearsal. We left a note. Mister telephone man, we had to go out, and we sure couldn't call you, heh heh. Please get the key from the concierge and come on in; the phone's in the bedroom. The phone man never showed up. They never do." My hands seemed to be shaking. "We came up the back stairs from the alley. The phone was still dead, but I never thought to take down the note on the front door. I got sick the next morning. Cramps. Vomiting. Karen and I were just friends, but she stayed home to take care of me. I suppose on a Friday night the note seemed even more plausible. He slipped the lock with a piece of plastic, and Karen came out of the kitchen as he was unplugging the stereo. He was so indignant he shot her. Twice. The noise scared him; by the time I got there he was halfway out the door. He just had time to put a slug though my hip joint, and then he was gone. They never got him. They never even came to fix the phone." My hands were under control now. "Karen was a damned good dancer, but I was better. In my head I still am."

Her eyes were round. "You're not Charlie . . . Charles *Armstead.*"

I nodded.

"Oh my God. So *that's* where you went."

I was shocked by how shocked she looked. It brought me back from the cold and windy border of self-pity. I began a little to pity her again. I should have guessed the depth of her empathy. And in the way that really mattered, we were too damned alike—we *did* share the same bitter joke. I wondered why I had wanted to shock her.

"They couldn't repair the joint?" she asked softly.

"I can walk splendidly if asymmetrically. Given a strong enough motivation, I can even run short distances. I can't dance worth a damn."

"So you became a video man."

"Three years ago. People who know both video and dance are about as common as hen's teeth these days. Oh, they've been taping dance since the '70s—usually with the imagination of a network news cameraman. If you film a stage play with two cameras in the orchestra pit, is it a movie?"

"You try to do for dance what the movie camera did for drama?"

"It's a pretty fair analogy. Where it breaks down is that dance is more analogous to music than to drama. You can't stop and start it easily, or go back and retake a scene that didn't go in the can right, or reverse the chronology to get a tidy shooting schedule. The event happens and you record it. What I am is what the record industry pays top dollar for: a mixman with savvy enough to know which ax is wailing at the moment and mike it high—and the sense to have given the heaviest dudes the best mikes. There are few others like me. I'm the best."

She took it the way she had the compliment to herself—at face value. Usually when I say things like that, I don't give a damn what reaction I get, or I'm being salty and hoping for outrage. But I was pleased at her acceptance, pleased enough to bother me. A faint irritation made me go brutal again, *knowing* it wouldn't work. "So what all this leads to is that Norrey was hoping I'd suggest some similar form of sublimation for you. Because I'll make it in dance before you will."

She stubborned up. "I don't buy that, Charlie. I know what you're talking about, I'm not a fool, but I think I can beat it."

"Sure you will. *You're too damned big, lady.* You've got tits like both halves of a prize honeydew melon and an ass that any actress in Hollywood would sell her parents for and in Modern dance that makes you d-e-d dead, you haven't got a chance. Beat it? You'll beat your head in first, how'm I doing, Norrey?"

"For Christ's sake, Charlie!"

I softened. I can't work Norrey into a tantrum—I like her too much. It almost kept us living together, once. "I'm sorry, hon. My leg's giving me the mischief, and I'm stinkin' mad. She *ought* to make it—and she won't. She's your sister, and so it saddens you. Well I'm a total stranger, and it enrages me."

"How do you think it makes me feel?" Shara blazed, startling us both. I hadn't known she had so much voice. "So you want me to pack it in and rent me a camera, huh, Charlie? Or maybe sell apples outside the studio?" A ripple ran up her jaw. "Well I'll be damned by all the gods in southern California before I'll pack it in. God gave me the large economy size, but there is not a surplus pound on it and it fits me like a glove and I can by Jesus *dance* it and I will. You may be right—I may beat my head in first. But I will get it done." She took a deep breath. "Now I thank you for your kind intentions, Char . . . Mister Armst . . . oh shit." The tears came and she left hastily, spilling a quarter-cup of cold coffee on Norrey's lap.

"Charlie," Norrey said through clenched teeth, "why do I like you so much?"

"Dancers are dumb." I gave her my handkerchief.

"Oh." She patted at her lap awhile. "How come you like me?"

"Video men are smart."

"Oh."

I spent the afternoon in my apartment, reviewing the footage I'd shot that morning, and the more I watched, the madder I got.

Dance requires intense motivation at an extraordinarily early age—a blind devotion, a gamble on the as-yet-unrealized potentials of heredity and nutrition. The risk used to be higher in ballet, but by the late '80s Modern had gotten just as bad. You can begin, say, classical ballet training at age six—and at fourteen find yourself broad-shouldered, the years of total effort utterly wasted. Shara had set her childhood sights on Modern dance—and found out too late that God had dealt her the body of a woman.

She was not fat—you have seen her. She was tall, big-boned tall, and on that great frame was built a rich, ripely female body. As I ran and reran the tapes of *Birthing*, the pain grew in me until I even forgot the ever present aching of my own legs. It was like watching a supremely gifted basketball player who stood four feet tall.

To make it in Modern dance nowadays, it is essential to get into a big company. You cannot be seen unless you are visible. (Government subsidy operates on the principle that Big Is Better—a sadly self-fulfilling prophecy. The smaller companies and independents have always had to knife each other for pennies—but since the early '80s there haven't *been* any pennies.)

"Merce Cunningham saw her dance, Charlie. Martha Graham saw her dance, just before she died. Both of them praised her warmly, for her choreography as much as for her technique. Neither offered her a position. I'm not even sure I blame them—I can sort of understand, is the hell of it."

Norrey could understand all right. It was her own defect magnified a hundredfold: uniqueness. A company member must be capable of excellent solo work—but she must also be able to blend into group effort, in ensemble work. Shara's very uniqueness made her virtually useless as a company member. She could not help but draw the eye.

And once drawn, the male eye at least would never leave. Modern dancers must sometimes work nude these days, and it is therefore meet that they have the bodies of fourteen-year-old boys. We may have ladies dancing with few or no clothes on up here, but by God it is Art. An actress or a musician or a singer or a painter may be lushly endowed, deliciously rounded—but a dancer must be nearly as sexless as a high fashion model. Perhaps God knows why. Shara could not have purged her dance of her sexuality even if she had been interested in trying, and as I watched her dance on my monitor and in my mind's eye, I knew she was not.

Why did her genius have to lie in the only occupation besides model and nun in which sexiness is a liability? It broke my heart, by empathic analogy.

"It's no good at all, is it?"

I whirled and barked. "Dammit, you made me bite my tongue."

"I'm sorry." She came from the doorway into my living room. "Norrey told me how to find the place. The door was ajar."

"I forgot to shut it when I came home."

"You leave it open?"

"I've learned the lesson of history. No junkie, no matter how strung out he is, will enter an apartment with the door ajar and the radio on. Obviously there's someone home. And you're right, it's no damn good at all. Sit down."

She sat on the couch. Her hair was down, now, and I liked it better that way. I shut off the monitor and popped the tape, tossing it on a shelf.

"I came to apologize. I shouldn't have blown up at you at lunch. You were trying to help me."

"You had it coming. I imagine by now you've built up quite a head of steam."

"Five years worth. I figured I'd start in the States instead of Canada. Go farther faster. Now I'm back in Toronto and I don't think I m going to make it here either. You're right, Mr. Armstead—I'm too damned big. Amazons don't dance."

"It's still Charlie. Listen, something I want to ask you. That last gesture, at the end of *Birthing*—what was that? I thought it was a beckoning, Norrey says it was a farewell, and now that I've run the tape it looks like a yearning, a reaching out."

"Then it worked."

"Pardon?"

"It seemed to me that the birth of a galaxy called for all three. They're so close together in spirit it seemed silly to give each a separate movement."

"Mmm." Worse and Worse. Suppose Einstein had had aphasia? "Why couldn't you have been a rotten dancer? That'd just be irony. This"—I pointed to the tape—"is high tragedy."

"Aren't you going to tell me I can still dance for myself?"

"No. For you that'd be worse than not dancing at all."

"My God, you're perceptive. Or am I that easy to read?"

I shrugged.

"Oh Charlie," she burst out, "what am I going to do?"

"You'd better not ask me that." My voice sounded funny.

"Why not?"

"Because I'm already two-thirds in love with you. And because you're not in love with me and never will be. And so that is the sort of question you shouldn't ask me."

It jolted her a little, but she recovered quickly. Her eyes softened, and she shook her head slowly. "You even know why I'm not, don't you?"

"And why you won't be."

I was terribly afraid she was going to say, "Charlie, I'm sorry," but she surprised me again. What she said was, "I can count on the fingers of one foot the number of grown-up men I've ever met. I'm grateful for you. I guess ironic tragedies come in pairs?"

"Sometimes."

"Well, now all I have to do is figure out what to do with my life. That should kill the weekend."

"Will you continue your classes?"

"Might as well. It's never a waste of time to study. Norrey's teaching me things."

All of a sudden my mind started to percolate. Man is a rational animal, right? Right? "What if I had a better idea?"

"If you've got another idea, it's better. Speak."

"Do you have to have an audience? I mean, does it have to be *live*?"

"What do you mean?"

"Maybe there's a back way in. Look, they're building video facilities into all the TVs nowadays, right? And by now everybody has collected all the old movies and Ernie Kovacs programs and such that they always wanted, and now they're looking for new stuff. Exotic stuff, too esoteric for network or local broadcast, stuff that—"

"The independent video companies, you're talking about."

"Right. TDT is thinking of entering the market, and the Graham company already has."

"So?"

"So suppose we go freelance? You and me? You dance it and I'll tape it: a straight business deal. I've got a few connections, and I can get more. I could name you ten acts in the music business right now that never go on tour—just record and record. Why don't you bypass the structure of the dance companies and take a chance on the public? Maybe word of mouth could—"

Her face was beginning to light up like a jack-o-lantern. "Charlie, do you think it could work? Do you really think so?"

"I don't think it has a snowball's chance." I crossed the room, opened up the beer fridge, took out the snowball I keep there in the summer, and tossed it to her. She caught it, but just barely, and when she realized what it was, she burst out laughing. "I've got just enough faith in the idea to quit working for TDT and put my time into it. I'll invest my time, my tape, my equipment and my savings. Ante up."

She tried to get sober, but the snowball froze her fingers and she broke up again. "A snowball in July. You madman. Count me in. I've got a little money saved. And . . . and I guess I don't have much choice, do I?"

"I guess not."

II

The next three years were some of the most exciting years of my life, of both our lives. While I watched and taped, Shara transformed herself from a potentially great dancer into something truly awesome. She did something I'm not sure I can explain.

She became dance's analogue of the jazzman.

Dance was, for Shara, self-expression, pure and simple, first, last, and always. Once she freed herself from the attempt to fit into the world of company dance, she came to regard choreography per se as an *obstacle* to her self-expression, as a preprogrammed rut, inexorable as a script and as limiting. And so she devalued it.

A jazzman may blow *Night in Tunisia* for a dozen consecutive nights, and each evening will be a different experience, as he interprets and reinterprets the melody according to his mood of the moment. Total unity of artist and his art: spontaneous creation. The melodic starting point distinguishes the result from pure anarchy.

In just this way Shara devalued preperformance choreography to a starting point, a framework on which to build whatever the moment demanded and then jammed around it. She learned in those three busy years to dismantle the interface between herself and her dance. Dancers have always tended to sneer at improv dancing, even while they practiced it, in the studio, for the looseness it gave. They failed to see that *planned* improv, improv around a theme fully thought out in advance, was the natural next step in dance. Shara took the step. You must be very, very good to get away with that much freedom. She was good enough.

There's no point in detailing the professional fortunes of Drumstead Enterprises over those three years. We worked hard, we made some magnificent tapes, and we couldn't sell them for paperweights. A home video-cassette industry indeed grew—and they knew as much about Modern dance as the record industry knew about the blues when *they* started. The big outfits wanted credentials, and the little outfits wanted cheap talent. Finally we even got desperate enough to try the schlock houses—and learned what we already knew. They didn't have the distribution, the prestige, or the technical specs for the critics to pay any attention to them. Word-of-mouth advertising is like a gene pool—if it isn't a certain minimum size to start with, it doesn't get anywhere. "Spider" John Koerner is an incredibly talented musician and songwriter who has been making and selling his own records since 1972. How many of you have ever heard of him?

In May of 1992 I opened my mailbox in the lobby and found the letter from VisuEnt Inc., terminating our option with deepest sorrow and no severance. I went straight over to Shara's apartment, and my leg felt like the bone marrow had been replaced with thermite and ignited. It was a very long walk.

She was working on *Weight Is A Verb* when I got there. Converting her big living room into a studio had cost time, energy, skullsweat, and a fat bribe to the landlord, but it was cheaper than renting time in a studio considering the sets we wanted. It looked like high mountain country that day, and I hung my hat on a fake alder when I entered.

She flashed me a smile and kept moving, building up to greater and greater leaps. She looked like the most beautiful mountain goat I ever saw. I was in a foul mood and I wanted to kill the music (McLaughlin and Miles together, leaping some themselves), but I never could interrupt Shara when she was dancing. She built it gradually, with directional counterpoint, until she seemed to hurl herself into the air, stay there until she was damned good and ready, and then hurl herself down again. Sometimes she rolled when she hit and sometimes she landed on her hands, and always the energy of falling was transmuted into some new movement instead of being absorbed. It was total energy output, and by the time she was done I had calmed down enough to be almost philosophical about our mutual professional ruin.

She ended up collapsed in upon herself, head bowed exquisitely humbled in attempt to defy gravity. I couldn't help applauding. It felt corny, but I couldn't help it.

"Thank you, Charlie."

"I'll be damned. Weight *is* a verb. I thought you were crazy when you told me the title."

"It's one of the strongest verbs in dance—the strongest, I guess—and you can make it do *anything.*"

"Almost anything."

"Eh?"

"VisuEnt gave us our contract back."

"Oh." Nothing showed in her eyes, but I knew what was behind them. "Well, who's next on the list?"

"There is no one left on the list."

"Oh." This time it showed. "Oh."

"We should have remembered. Great artists are never honored in their own lifetime. What we ought to do is drop dead—then we'd be all set."

In my way I was trying to be strong for her, and she knew it and tried to be strong for me.

"Maybe what we should do is go into death insurance, for artists," she said. "We pay the client premiums against a controlling interest in his estate, and we guarantee that he'll die."

"We can't lose. And if he becomes famous in his lifetime he can buy out."

"Terrific. Let's stop this before I laugh myself to death."

"Yeah."

She was silent for a long time. My own mind was racing efficiently, but the transmission seemed to be blown—it wouldn't *go* anywhere. Finally she got up and turned off the music machine, which had been whining softly ever since the tape ended. It made a loud *click.*

"Norrey's got some land in Prince Edward Island," she said, not meeting my eyes. "There's a house."

I tried to head her off with the punchline from the old joke about the kid shoveling out the elephant cage in the circus whose father offers to take him back and set him up with a decent job. "What? And leave show business?"

"Screw show business," she said softly. "If I went to PEI now, maybe I could get the land cleared and plowed in time to get a garden in." Her expression changed. "How about you?"

"Me? I'll be okay. TDT asked me to come back."

"That was six months ago."

"They asked again. Last week."

"And you said no. Moron."

"Maybe so, maybe so."

"The whole damn thing was a waste of time. All that time. All that energy. All that work. I might as well have been farming in PEI—by now the soil'd be starting to bear well. What a waste, Charlie. What a stinking waste."

"No, I don't think so, Shara. It sounds glib to say that 'nothing is wasted,' but—well, it's like that dance you just did. Maybe you can't beat gravity—but it surely is a beautiful thing to *try*."

"Yeah, I know. Remember the Light Brigade. Remember the Alamo. They tried." She laughed bitterly.

"Yes, and so did Jesus of Nazareth. Did you do it for material reward, or because it needed doing? If nothing else we now have several hundred thousand meters of the most magnificent dance recordings on tape, commercial value zero, real value incalculable, and by me that is no waste. It's over now, and we'll both go do the next thing, but it was *not a waste*." I discovered that I was shouting, and stopped.

She closed her mouth. After a while she tried a smile. "You're right, Charlie. It wasn't a waste. I'm a better dancer than I ever was."

"Damn right. You've transcended choreography."

She smiled ruefully. "Yeah. Even Norrey thinks it's a dead end."

"It is *not* a dead end. There's more to poetry that haiku and sonnets. Dancers don't *have* to be robots, delivering memorized lines with their bodies."

"They do if they want to make a living."

"We'll try it again in a few years. Maybe they'll be ready then."

"Sure. Let me get us some drinks."

I slept with her that night, for the first and last time. In the morning I broke down the set in the living room while she packed. I promised to write. I promised to come and visit when I could. I carried her bags down to the car, and stowed them inside. I kissed her and waved goodbye. I went looking for a drink, and at four o'clock the next morning a mugger decided I looked drunk enough and I broke his jaw, his nose and two ribs, and then sat down on him and cried. On

Monday morning I showed up at the studio with my hat in my hand and a mouth like a bus-station ashtray and crawled back into my old job. Norrey didn't ask any questions. What with rising food prices, I gave up eating anything but bourbon, and in six months I was fired. It went like that for a long time.

I never did write to her. I kept getting bogged down after "Dear Shara . . . ."

When I got to the point of selling my video equipment for booze, a relay clicked somewhere and I took stock of myself. The stuff was all the life I had left, and so I went to the local AA instead of the pawnshop and got sober. After a while my soul got numb, and I stopped flinching when I woke up. A hundred times I began to wipe the tapes I still had of Shara—she had copies of her own—but in the end I could not. From time to time I wondered how *she* was doing, and I could not bear to find out. If Norrey heard anything, she didn't tell me about it. She even tried to get me my job back a third time, but it was hopeless. Reputation can be a terrible thing once you've blown it. I was lucky to land a job with an educational TV station in New Brunswick.

It was a long couple of years.

Vidphones were coming out by 1995, and I had breadboarded one of my own without the knowledge or consent of the phone company, which I still hated more than anything. When the peanut bulb I had replaced the damned bell with started glowing softly off and on one evening in June, I put the receiver on the audio pickup and energized the tube, in case the caller was also equipped. "Hello?"

She was. When Shara's face appeared, I got a cold cube of fear in the pit of my stomach, because I had quit seeing her face everywhere when I quit drinking, and I had been thinking lately of hitting the sauce again. When I blinked and she was still there, I felt a very little better and tried to speak. It didn't work.

"Hello, Charlie. It's been a long time."

The second time it worked. "Seems like yesterday. Somebody else's yesterday."

"Yes, it does. It took me *days* to find you. Norrey's in Paris, and no one else knew where you'd gone."

"Yeah. How's farming?"

"I . . . I've put that away, Charlie. It's even more creative than dancing, but it's not the same."

"Then what *are* you doing?"

"Working."

"Dancing?"

"Yes. Charlie, I need you. I mean, I have a job for you. I need your cameras and your eye."

"Never mind the qualifications. Any kind of need will do. *Where are you?* When's the next plane there? Which cameras do I pack?"

"New York, an hour from now, and none of them. I didn't mean 'your cameras' literally unless you're using GLX-5000s and a Hamilton Board lately."

I whistled. It hurt my mouth. "Not on my budget. Besides, I'm old-fashioned—I like to hold 'em with my hands."

"For this job, you'll use a Hamilton, and it'll be a twenty-input Masterchrome, brand new."

"You grew poppies on that farm? Or just struck diamonds with the roto-tiller?"

"You'll be getting paid by Bryce Carrington."

I blinked.

"Now will you catch that plane so I can tell you about it? The New Age, ask for the Presidential Suite."

"The hell with the plane, I'll walk. Quicker." I hung up.

According to the *Time* magazine in my dentist's waiting room, Bryce Carrington was the genius who had become a multibillionaire by convincing a number of giants of industry to underwrite Skyfac, the great orbiting complex that kicked the bottom out of the crystals market—and seventy-'leven other markets besides. As I recalled the story, some rare poliolike disease had wasted both his legs and put him in a wheelchair. But the legs had lost strength, not function—in lessened gravity they worked well enough. So he created Skyfac, established mining crews on Luna to supply it with cheap raw materials, and spent most of his time in orbit under reduced gravity. His picture made him look like a reasonably successful author (as opposed to writer). Other than that I knew nothing about him. I paid little attention to news and none at all to space news.

The New Age was *the* hotel in New York in those days, built on the ruins of the Sheraton. Ultraefficient security, bulletproof windows, carpet thicker than the outside air, and a lobby of an architectural persuasion that John D. MacDonald once called "Early Dental Plate." It stank of money. I was glad I'd made the effort to locate a necktie, and I wished I'd shined my shoes. An incredible man blocked my way as I came in through the airlock. He moved and was built like the toughest, fastest bouncer I ever saw, and he dressed and acted like God's butler. He said his name was Perry, as if he didn't expect me to believe it. He asked if he could help me, as though he didn't think so.

"Yes, Perry. Would you mind lifting up one of your feet?"

"Why?"

"I'll bet twenty dollars you've shined your soles."

Half his mouth smiled, and he didn't move an inch. "Whom did you wish to see?"

"Shara Drummond."

"Not registered."

"The Presidential Suite."

"Oh." Light dawned. "Mister Carrington's lady. You should have said so. Wait here, please." While he phoned to verify that I was expected, keeping his eye on me and his hand near his pocket, I swallowed my heart and rearranged my face. So that was how it was. All right then. That was how it was.

Perry came back and gave me the little button-transmitter that would let me walk the corridors of the New Age without being cut down by automatic laser-fire, and explained carefully that it would blow a largish hole in me if I attempted to leave the building without returning it. From his manner I gathered that I had just skipped four grades in social standing. I thanked him, though I'm damned if I know why.

I followed the green fluorescent arrows that appeared on the bulbless ceiling, and came after a long and scenic walk to the Presidential Suite. Shara was waiting at the door, in something like an angel's pajamas. It made all that big body look delicate. "Hello, Charlie."

I was jovial and hearty. "Hi, babe. Swell joint. How've you been keeping yourself?"

"I haven't been."

"Well, how's Carrington been keeping you, then?" Steady, boy.

"Come in, Charlie."

I went in. It looked like where the Queen stayed when she was in town, and I'm sure she enjoyed it. You could have landed an airplane in the living room without waking anyone in the bedroom. It had two pianos. Only one fireplace, barely big enough to barbecue a buffalo—you have to scrimp somewhere, I guess. Roger Kellaway was on the quadio, and for a wild moment I thought he was actually in the suite, playing some unseen third piano. So this was how it was.

"Can I get you something, Charlie?"

"Oh, sure. Hash Oil, Citrolli Supreme. Dom Perignon for the pipe."

Without cracking a smile she went to a cabinet that looked like a midget cathedral, and produced precisely what I had ordered. I kept my own features impassive and lit up. The bubbles tickled my throat, and the rush was exquisite. I felt myself relaxing, and when we had passed the narghile's mouthpiece a few times I felt her relax. We looked at each other then—really looked at each other—then at the room around us and then at each other again. Simultaneously we roared with laughter, a laughter that blew all the wealth out of the room and let in richness. Her laugh was the same whooping, braying belly laugh I remembered so well, an unselfconscious and lusty laugh, and it reassured me tremendously. I was so relieved I couldn't stop laughing myself, and that kept *her* going, and just as we might have stopped she pursed her lips and blew a stuttered arpeggio. There's an old audio recording called the *Spike Jones Laughing Record*, where the tuba player tries to play "The Flight Of The Bumblebee" and falls down laughing, and the whole band breaks up and horselaughs for a full two minutes, and every time they run out of air the tuba player tries another flutter and roars and they all break up again, and once when Shara was blue I bet her ten dollars that she couldn't listen to that record without at least giggling and I won. When I understood now that she was quoting it, I shuddered and dissolved into great whoops of new laughter, and a minute later we had reached the stage where we literally laughed ourselves out of our chairs and lay on the floor in agonies of mirth, weakly pounding the floor and howling. I take that laugh out of my memory now and then and rerun it—but not often, for such records deteriorate drastically with play.

At last we dopplered back down to panting grins, and I helped her to her feet.

"What a perfectly dreadful place," I said, still chuckling.

She glanced around and shuddered. "Oh God, it *is*, Charlie. It must be awful to need this much front."

"For a horrid while I thought *you* did."

She sobered, and met my eyes. "Charlie, I wish I could resent that. In a way I do need it."

My eyes narrowed. "Just what do you mean?"

"I need Bryce Carrington."

"This time you can trot out the qualifiers. *How* do you need him?"

"I need his money," she cried.

How can you relax and tense up at the same time?

"Oh, *damn* it, Shara! Is *that* how you're going to get to dance? Buy your way in? What does a critic go for, these days?"

"Charlie, stop it. I need Carrington to get seen. He's going to rent me a hall, that's all."

"If that's all, let's get out of this dump right now. I can bor—get enough cash to rent you any hall in the world, and I'm just as willing to risk my money."

"Can you get me Skyfac?"

"Uh?"

I couldn't for the life of me imagine why she proposed to go to Skyfac to dance. Why not Antarctica?

"Shara, you know even less about space than I do, but you must know that a satellite broadcast doesn't have to be made from a satellite?"

"Idiot. It's the setting I want."

I thought about it. "Moon'd be better, visually. Mountains. Light. Contrast."

"The visual aspect is secondary. I don't want one-sixth gee, Charlie. I want zero gravity."

My mouth hung open.

"And I want you to be my video man."

God, she was a rare one. What I needed then was to sit there with my mouth open and think for several minutes. She let me do just that, waiting patiently for me to work it all out.

"Weight isn't a verb anymore, Charlie," she said finally. "That dance ended on the assertion that you can't beat gravity—you said so yourself. Well, that statement is incorrect—obsolete. The dance of the twenty-first century will have to acknowledge that."

"And it's just what you need to make it. A new kind of dance for a new kind of dancer. Unique. It'll catch the public eye, and you should have the field entirely to yourself for years. I like it, Shara. I like it. But can you pull it off?"

"I thought about what you said: that you can't beat gravity but it's beautiful to try. It stayed in my head for months, and then one day I was visiting a neighbor with a TV and I saw newsreels of the crew working on Skyfac Two. I was up all night thinking, and the next morning I came up to the States and got in Skyfac One. I've been up there for nearly a year, getting next to Carrington. I can do it, Charlie, I can make it work." There was a ripple in her jaw that I had seen before—when she'd told me off in Le Maintenant. It was a ripple of determination.

Still I frowned. "With Carrington's backing."

Her eyes left mine. "There's no such thing as a free lunch."

"What does he charge?"

She failed to answer, for long enough to answer me. In that instant I began believing in God again, for the first time in years, just to be able to hate Him.

But I kept my mouth shut. She was old enough to manage her own finances. The price of a dream gets higher every year. Hell, I'd half expected it from the moment she'd called me.

But only half.

"Charlie, don't just sit there with your face all knotted up. Say something. Cuss me out, call me a whore, *something*."

"Nuts. You be your own conscience; I have trouble enough being my own. You want to dance, you've got a patron. So now you've got a video man."

I hadn't intended to say that last sentence at all.

Strangely, it almost seemed to disappoint her at first. But then she relaxed and smiled. "Thank you, Charlie. Can you get out of whatever you're doing right away?"

"I'm working for an educational station in Shediac. I even got to shoot some dance footage. A dancing bear from the London Zoo. The amazing thing was how well he danced." She grinned. "I can get free."

"I'm glad. I don't think I could pull this off without you."

"I'm working for you. Not for Carrington."

"All right."

"Where is the great man, anyway? Scuba diving in the bathtub?"

"No," came a quiet voice from the doorway. "I've been sky diving in the lobby."

His wheelchair was a mobile throne. He wore a five-hundred-dollar suit the color of strawberry ice cream, a powder-blue turtleneck and one gold earring. The shoes were genuine leather. The watch was the newfangled bandless kind that literally tells you the time. He wasn't tall enough for her, and his shoulders were absurdly broad, although the suit tried to deny both. His eyes were like twin blueberries. His smile was that of a shark wondering which part will taste best. I wanted to crush his head between two boulders.

Shara was on her feet. "Bryce, this is Charles Armstead. I told you. . . ."

"Oh yes. The video chap." He rolled forward and extended an impeccably manicured hand. "I'm Bryce Carrington, Armstead."

I remained in my seat, hands in my lap. "Ah yes. The rich chap."

One eyebrow rose an urbane quarter inch. "Oh my. Another rude one. Well, if you're as good as Shara says you are, you're entitled."

"I'm rotten."

The smile faded. "Let's stop fencing, Armstead. I don't expect manners from creative people, but I have far more significant contempt than yours available if I need any. Now I'm tired of this damned gravity and I've had a rotten day testifying for a friend and it looks like they're going to recall me tomorrow. Do you want the job or don't you?"

He had me there. I did. "Yeah."

"All right, then. Your room is 2772. We'll be going up to Skyfac in two days. Be here at eight A.M."

"I'll want to talk with you about what you'll be needing, Charlie," Shara said. "Give me a call tomorrow."

I whirled to face her, and she flinched from my eyes.

Carrington failed to notice. "Yes, make a list of your requirements by tonight, so it can go up with us. Don't scrimp—if you don't fetch it, you'll do without. Good night, Armstead."

I faced him. "Good night, Mr. Carrington." Suh.

He turned toward the narghile, and Shara hurried to refill the chamber and bowl. I turned away hastily and made for the door. My leg hurt so much I nearly fell on the way, but I set my jaw and made it. When I reached the door I said to myself, you will now open the door and go through it, and then I spun on my heel. "Carrington!"

He blinked, surprised to discover I still existed. "Yes?"

"Are you *aware* that she doesn't love you in the slightest? Does that matter to you in any way?" My voice was high, and my fists were surely clenched.

"Oh," he said, and then again, "Oh. So that's what it is. I didn't think success alone merited that much contempt." He put down the mouthpiece and folded his fingers together. "Let me tell you something, Armstead. No one has ever loved me, to my knowledge. This suite does not love me." His voice took on human feeling for the first time. "But it is *mine*. Now get out."

I opened my mouth to tell him where to put his job, and then I saw Shara's face, and the pain in it suddenly made me deeply ashamed. I left at once, and when the door closed behind me I vomited on a rug that was worth slightly less than a Hamilton Masterchrome board. I was sorry then that I'd worn a necktie.

The trip to Pike's Peak Spaceport, at least was aesthetically pleasurable. I enjoy air travel, gliding among stately clouds, watching the rolling procession of mountains and plains, vast jigsaws of farmland, and intricate mosaics of suburbia unfolding below.

But the jump to Skyfac in Carrington's personal shuttle, *That First Step*, might as well have been an old Space Commando rerun. I *know* they can't put portholes in space ships—but dammit, a shipboard video relay conveys no better resolution, color values, or presence than you get on your living room tube. The only differences are that the stars don't "move" to give the illusion of travel, and there's no director editing the POV to give you dramatically interesting shots.

Aesthetically speaking. The *experiential* difference is that they do not, while you are watching the Space Commando sell hemorrhoid remedies, trap you into a couch, batter you with thunders, make you weigh better than half a megagram for an unreasonably long time, and then drop you off the edge of the world into weightlessness.

Body fluids began rising into my upper half: my ears sang, my nose flooded, and I "blushed" deep red. I had been prepared far nausea, but what I got was even more shocking: the sudden, unprecedented, total absence of pain in my leg. Shara got the nausea for both of us, barely managing to deploy her dropsickness bag in time. Carrington unstrapped and administered an antinausea injection with sure movements. It seemed to take forever to hit her, but when it did there was an enormous change—color and strength returned rapidly, and she was apparently fully recovered by the time the pilot announced that we were commencing docking and would everyone please strap in and shut up? I half expected Carrington to bark manners into him, but apparently the industrial magnate was not that sort of fool. He shut up and strapped himself down.

My leg didn't hurt in the slightest. Not at all.

The Skyfac complex looked like a disorderly heap of bicycle tires and beach balls of various sizes. The one our pilot made for was more like a tractor tire. We matched course, became its axle, and matched spin, and the damned thing grew a spoke that caught us square in the airlock. The airlock was "overhead" of our couches, but we entered and left it feet first. A few yards into the spoke, the direction we traveled became "down," and handholds became a ladder. Weight increased with every step, but even when we had emerged into a rather large cubical compartment it was far less than Earth normal. Nonetheless my leg resumed nibbling at me.

The room tried to be a classic reception room, high-level ("Please be seated. His Majesty will see you shortly"), but the low gee and the p-suits racked along two walls spoiled the effect. Unlike the Space Commando's armor, a real pressure suit looked like nothing so much as a people-shaped baggie, and they look particularly silly in repose. A young dark-haired man in tweed rose from behind a splendidly gadgeted desk and smiled. "Good to see you, Mr. Carrington. I hope you had a pleasant jump."

"Fine thanks, Tom. You remember Shara, of course. This is Charles Armstead. Tom McGillicuddy." We both displayed our teeth and said we were delighted to meet one another. I could see that beneath the pleasantries, McGillicuddy was upset about something.

"Nils and Mr. Longmire are waiting in your office, sir. There's . . . there's been another sighting."

"God *damn* it," Carrington began, and cut himself off. I stared at him. The full force of my best sarcasm had failed to anger this man. "All right. Take care of my guests while I go hear what Longmire has to say." He started for the door, moving like a beach ball in slow motion but under his own power. "Oh yes—the *Step* is loaded to the gun'ls with bulky equipment, Tom. Have her brought round to the cargo bays. Store the equipment in Six." He left, looking worried. McGillicuddy activated his desk and gave the necessary orders.

"What's going on, Tom?" Shara asked when he was through.

He looked at me before replying. "Pardon my asking, Mr. Armstead, but are you a newsman?"

"Charlie. No, I'm not. I am a video man, but I work for Shara."

"Mmmm. Well, you'll hear about it sooner or later. About two weeks ago an object appeared within the orbit of Neptune, just appeared out of nowhere. There were . . . certain other anomalies. It stayed put for half a day and then vanished again. The Space Command slapped a hush on it, but it's common knowledge on board Skyfac."

"And the thing has appeared again?" Shara asked.

"Just beyond the orbit of Saturn."

I was only mildly interested. No doubt there was an explanation for the phenomenon, and since Isaac Asimov wasn't around I would doubtless never understand a word of it. Most of us gave up on intelligent nonhuman life when Project Ozma came up empty. "Little green men, I suppose. Can you show us the Lounge, Tom? I understand it's just like the one we'll be working in."

He seemed to welcome this change of subject. "Sure thing."

McGillicuddy led us through a p-door opposite the one Carrington had used, through long halls whose floors curved up ahead of and behind us. Each was outfitted differently, each was full of busy, purposeful people, and each reminded me somehow of the lobby of the New Age, or perhaps of the old movie 2001. Futuristic Opulence, so understated as to fairly shriek. Wall Street lifted bodily into orbit—the *clocks* were on Wall Street time. I tried to make myself believe that cold, empty space lay a short distance away in any direction, but it was impossible. I decided it was a good thing spacecraft didn't have portholes—once he got used to the low gravity, a man might forget and open one to throw out a cigar.

I studied McGillicuddy as we walked. He was immaculate in every respect, from necktie knot to nail polish, and he wore no jewelry at all. His hair was short and black, his beard inhibited, and his eyes surprisingly warm in a professionally sterile face. I wondered what he had sold his soul for. I hoped he had gotten his price.

We had to descend two levels to get to the Lounge. The gravity on the upper level was kept at one-sixth normal, partly for the convenience of the Lunar personnel who were Skyfac's only regular commuters, and mostly (of course) for the convenience of Carrington. But descending brought a subtle increase in weight, to perhaps a fifth or a quarter normal. My leg complained bitterly, but I found to my surprise that I preferred the pain to its absence. It's a little scary when an old friend goes away like that.

The Lounge was a larger room than I had expected, quite big enough for our purposes. It encompassed all three levels, and one whole wall was an immense video screen, across which stars wheeled dizzily, joined with occasional regularity by a slice of mother Terra. The floor was crowded with chairs and tables in various groupings, but I could see that, stripped, it would provide Shara with entirely adequate room to dance. From long habit my feet began to report on the suitability of the floor as a dancing surface. Then I remembered how little use the floor was liable to get.

"Well," Shara said to me with a smile, "this is what home will look like for the next six months. The Ring Two Lounge is identical to this one."

"Six?" McGillicuddy said. "Not a chance."

"*What do you mean?*" Shara and I said together.

He blinked at our combined volume. "Well, *you'd* probably be good for that long, Charlie. But Shara's already had a year of low gee, while she was in the typing pool."

"So what?"

"Look, you expect to be in free fall for long periods of time, if I understand this correctly?"

"Twelve hours a day," Shara agreed.

He grimaced. "Shara I hate to say this . . . but I'll be surprised if you last a month. A body designed for a one-gee environment doesn't work properly in zero gee."

"But it will adapt, won't it?"

He laughed mirthlessly. "Sure. That's why we rotate all personnel Earthside every fourteen months. Your body will adapt. One way. No return. Once you've fully adapted, returning to Earth will stop your heart—if some other major systemic failure doesn't occur first. Look, you were just Earthside for three days—did you have any chest pains? Dizziness? Bowel trouble? Dropsickness on the way up?"

"All of the above," she admitted.

"There you go. You were close to the nominal fourteen-month limit when you left. And your body will adapt even faster under no gravity at all. The successful free-fall endurance record of about eighteen months was set by a Skyfac construction gang with bad deadline problems—and they hadn't spent a year in one-sixth gee first, *and* they weren't straining their hearts the way you will be. Hell, there are four men in Luna now, from the original mining team, who will never see Earth again. Eight of their teammates tried. Don't you two know *any*thing about space? *Didn't Carrington tell you?*"

I had *wondered* why Carrington had gone to the trouble of having our preflight physicals waived.

"But I've got to have at least four months. Four months of solid work, every day. I *must*." She was dismayed, but fighting hard for control.

McGillicuddy started to shake his head, and then thought better of it. His warm eyes were studying Shara's face. I knew exactly what he was thinking, and I liked him for it.

He was thinking, *How to tell a lovely lady her dearest dream is hopeless?*

He didn't know the half of it. I *knew* how much Shara had already—irrevocably—invested in this dream, and something in me screamed.

And then I saw her jaw ripple and I dared to hope.

Doctor Panzella was a wiry old man with eyebrows like two fuzzy caterpillars. He wore a tight-fitting jump-suit which would not foul a p-suit's seals should he have to get into one in a hurry. His shoulder-length hair, which should have been a mane on that great skull, was clipped securely back against a sudden absence of gravity. A cautious man. To employ an obsolete metaphor, he was a suspender-*and*-belt type. He looked Shara over, ran tests on the spot, and gave her just under a month and a half. Shara said some things. I said some things. McGillicuddy said some things. Panzella shrugged, made further, very careful tests, and reluctantly cut loose of the suspenders. Two months. Not a day over. Possibly less, depending on subsequent monitoring of her body's reactions to extended weightlessness. Then a year Earthside before risking it again. Shara seemed satisfied.

I didn't see how we could do it.

McGillicuddy had assured us that it would take Shara at least a month simply to learn to handle herself competently in zero gee, much less dance. Her familiarity with one-sixth gee would, he predicted, be a liability rather than an asset. Then figure three weeks of choreography and rehearsal, a week of taping and just maybe we could broadcast one dance before Shara had to return to Earth. Not good enough. She and I had calculated that we would need three successive shows, each well received, to make a big enough dent in the dance world for Shara to squeeze into it. A year was far too big a spacing to be effective—and *who knew how soon Carrington might tire of her?* So I hollered at Panzella.

"Mr. Armstead," he said hotly, "I am specifically contractually forbidden to allow this young lady to commit suicide." He grimaced sourly. "I'm told it's terrible public relations."

"Charlie, it's okay," Shara insisted. "I can fit in three dances. We may lose some sleep, but we can do it."

"I once told a man nothing was impossible. He asked me if I could ski through a revolving door. You haven't got . . ."

My brain slammed into hyperdrive, thought about things, kicked itself in the ass a few times, and returned to realtime in time to hear my mouth finish without a break: ". . . much choice, though. Okay Tom, have that damned Ring Two Lounge cleaned out, I want it naked and spotless and have somebody paint over that damned video wall, the same shade as the other three and I mean the *same*. Shara, get out of those clothes and into your leotard. Doctor, we'll be seeing you in twelve hours; quit gaping and *move*, Tom—we'll be going over there at once; *where the hell are my cameras?*"

McGillicuddy spluttered.

"Get me a torch crew—I'll want holes cut through the walls, cameras behind them, one-way glass, six locations, a room adjacent to the Lounge for a mixer console the size of a jetliner cockpit, and bolt a Norelco coffee machine next to the chair. I'll need another room for editing, complete privacy and total darkness, size of any efficiency kitchen, another Norelco."

McGillicuddy finally drowned me out. "Mister *Armstead*, this is the Main Ring of the Skyfac One complex, the administrative offices of one of the wealthiest corporations in existence. If you think this whole Ring is going to stand on its head for you. . . ."

So we brought the problem to Carrington. He told McGillicuddy that henceforth Ring Two was *ours*, as well as any assistance whatsoever that we requested. He looked rather distracted. McGillicuddy started to tell him by how many weeks all this would put off the opening of the Skyfac Two complex. Carrington replied very quietly that he could add and subtract quite well, thank you, and McGillicuddy got white and quiet.

I'll give Carrington that much. He gave us a free hand.

Panzella ferried over to Skyfac Two with us. We were chauffeured by lean-jawed astronaut types, on vehicles looking for all the world like pregnant broomsticks. It was as well that we had the doctor with us—Shara fainted on the way over. I nearly did myself, and I'm sure that broomstick has my thigh-prints on it yet. Falling through space is a scary experience the first time. Some people never get used to it. Most people. Shara responded splendidly once we had her inboard again, and fortunately her dropsickness did not return. Nausea can be a nuisance in free fall, a disaster in a p-suit. By the time my cameras and mixer had arrived, she was on her feet and sheepish. And while I browbeat a sweating crew of borrowed techs into installing them faster than was humanly possible, Shara began learning how to move in zero gee.

We were ready for the first taping in three weeks.

III

Living quarters and minimal life support were rigged for us in Ring Two so that we could work around the clock if we chose, but we spent nearly half of our nominal "off-hours" in Skyfac One. Shara was required to spend half of three days a week there with Carrington, and spent a sizable portion of her remaining nominal sack time out in space, in a p-suit. At first it was a conscious attempt to overcome her gut-level fear of all that emptiness. Soon it became her meditation, her retreat, her artistic reverie—an attempt to gain from contemplation of cold black depths enough insight into the meaning of extraterrestrial existence to dance of it.

I spent my own time arguing with engineers and electricians and technicians and a damn fool union legate who insisted that the second lounge, finished or not, belonged to the hypothetical future crew and administrative personnel. Securing his permission to work there wore the lining off my throat and the insulation off my nerves. Far too many nights I spent slugging instead of sleeping. Minor example: Every interior wall in the whole damned second Ring was painted the identical shade of turquoise—and they couldn't duplicate it to cover that godforsaken video wall in the Lounge. It was McGillicuddy who saved me from gibbering apoplexy—at his suggestion I washed off the third latex job, unshipped the outboard camera that fed the wall-screen, brought the camera inboard and fixed it to scan an interior wall in an adjoining room. That made us friends again.

It was all like that: jury-rig, improvise, file to fit and paint to cover. If a camera broke down, I spent sleep time talking with off-shift engineers, finding out what parts in stock could be adapted. It was simply too expensive to have anything shipped up from Earth's immense gravity well, and Luna didn't have what I needed.

At that, Shara worked harder than I did. A body must totally recoordinate itself to function in the absence of weight—she literally had to forget everything she had ever known or learned about dance and acquire a whole new set of skills. This turned out to be even harder than we had expected. McGillicuddy had been right: what Shara had learned in her year of one-sixth gee was an exaggerated attempt to *retain* terrestrial patterns of coordination. Rejecting them altogether was actually easier for me.

But I couldn't keep up with her—I had to abandon any thought of handheld camera work and base my plans solely on the six fixed cameras. Fortunately GLX-5000s have a ball-and-socket mount: even behind that damned one-way glass I had about forty degrees of traverse on each one. Learning to coordinate all six simultaneously on the Hamilton Board did a truly extraordinary thing to me: It lifted me that one last step to unity with my art. I found that I could learn to be aware of all six monitors with my mind's eye, to perceive almost spherically, to—not share my attention among the six—to *encompass* them all, seeing like a six-eyed creature from many angles at once. My mind's eye became holographic, my awareness multilayered. I began to really understand, for the first time, three-dimensionality.

It was that fourth dimension that was the kicker. It took Shara two days to decide that she could not possibly become proficient enough in free-fall maneuvering to sustain a half-hour piece in the time required. So she rethought her work plan too, adapting her choreography to the demands of her situation. She put in six hard days under normal Earth weight.

And for her, too, the effort was that one last step toward apotheosis.

On Monday of the fourth week we began taping *Liberation*.

Establishing shot:

A great turquoise box, seen from within. Dimensions unknown, but the color somehow lends an impression of immensity, of vast distances. Against the far wall a swinging pendulum attests that this is a standard-gravity environment; but the pendulum swings so slowly and is so featureless in construction that it is impossible to estimate its size and so extrapolate that of the room.

Because of this trompe-l'oeil effect, the room seems rather smaller than it really is when the camera pulls back and we are wrenched into proper perspective by the appearance of Shara, inert, face down on the floor, her head toward us.

She wears beige leotard and tights. Hair the color of fine mahogany is pulled back into a loose ponytail which fans across one shoulder blade. She does not appear to breathe. She does not appear to live.

Music begins. The aging Mahavishnu, on obsolete nylon acoustic, establishes a minor E in no hurry at all. A pair of small candles in simple brass holders appear inset on either side of the room. They are larger than life, though small beside Shara. Both are unlit.

Her body . . . there is no word. It does not move, in the sense of motor activity. One might say that a ripple passes through it, save that the motion is clearly all outward from her center. She *swells* as if the first breath of life were being taken by her whole body at once. She lives.

The twin wicks begin to glow, oh, softly. The music takes on quiet urgency.

Shara raises her head to us. Her eyes focus somewhere beyond the camera yet short of infinity. Her body writhes, undulates, and the glowing wicks are coals (that this brightening takes place in slow motion is not apparent).

A violent contraction raises her to a crouch, spilling the ponytail across her shoulder. Mahavishnu begins a cyclical cascade of runs, in increasing tempo. Long questing tongues of yellow-orange flame begin to blossom *downward* from the twin wicks, whose coals are turning to blue.

The contraction's release flings her to her feet. The twin skirts of flame about the wicks curl up over themselves, writhing furiously, to become conventional candleflames, flickering now in normal time. Tablas, tambouras, and a bowed string bass join the guitar, and they segue into an energetic interplay around a minor seventh that keeps trying, fruitlessly, to find resolution in the sixth. The candles stay in perspective, but dwindle in size until they vanish.

Shara begins to explore the possibilities of motion. First she moves only perpendicular to the camera's line of sight, exploring that dimension. Every motion of arms or legs or head is clearly seen to be a defiance of gravity—of a force as inexorable as radioactive decay, as entropy itself. The most violent surges of energy succeed only for a time—the outflung leg falls, the outthrust arm drops. She must struggle or fall. She pauses in thought.

Her hands and arms reach out toward the camera, and at the instant they do we cut to a view from the lefthand wall. Seen from the right side, she reaches out into this new dimension, and soon begins to move in it. (As she moves backward out of the camera's field, its entire image shifts right on our screen, butted out of the way by the incoming image of a second camera, which picks her up as the first loses her without a visible seam.)

The new dimension too fails to fulfill Shara's desire for freedom from gravity. Combining the two, however, presents so many permutations of movement that for a while, intoxicated, she flings herself into experimentation. In the next fifteen minutes Shara's entire background and history in dance are recapitulated, in a blinding tour de force that incorporates elements of jazz, Modern, and the more graceful aspects of Olympic-level mat gymnastics. Five cameras come into play, singly and in pairs on splitscreen, as the "bag of tricks" amassed in a lifetime of study and improvisation are rediscovered and performed by a superbly trained and versatile body, in a pyrotechnic display that would shout of joy if her expression did not remain aloof, almost arrogant. *This is the offering,* she seems to say, *which you would not accept. This, by itself, was not good enough.*

And it is not. Even in its raging energy and total control her body returns again and again to the final compromise of mere erectness, that last simple refusal to fall.

Clamping her jaw, she works into a series of leaps, ever longer, ever higher. She seems at last to hang suspended for full seconds, straining to fly. When, inevitably, she falls, she falls reluctantly, only at the last possible instant tucking and rolling back onto her feet. The musicians are in a crescendoing frenzy. We see her now only with the single original camera, and the twin candles have returned, small but burning fiercely.

The leaps begin to diminish in intensity and height, and she takes longer to build to each one. She has been dancing flat out for nearly twenty minutes; as the candle flames begin to wane, so does her strength. At last she retreats to a place beneath the indifferent pendulum, gathers herself with a final desperation, and races forward toward us. She reaches incredible speed in a short space, hurls herself into a double roll and bounds up into the air off one foot, seeming a full second later to push off against empty air for a few more centimeters of height. Her body goes rigid, her eyes and mouth gape wide, the flames reach maximum brilliance, the music peaks with the tortured wail of an electric guitar and—she falls, barely snapping into a roll in time, rising only as far as a crouch. She holds there for a long moment, and gradually her head and shoulders slump, defeated, toward the floor. The candle flames draw in upon themselves in a curious way and appear to go out. The string bass saws on alone, modulating down to D.

Muscle by muscle, Shara's body gives up the struggle. The air seems to tremble around the wicks of the candles, which have now grown nearly as tall as her crouching form.

Shara lifts her face to the camera with evident effort. Her face is anguished, her eyes nearly shut. A long beat.

All at once she opens her eyes wide, squares her shoulders, and contracts. It is the most exquisite and total contraction ever dreamed of, filmed in realtime but seeming almost to be in slow motion. She holds it. Mahavishnu comes back in on guitar, building in increasing tempo from a downtuned bass string to a D chord with a flatted fourth. Shara holds.

We shift for the first time to an overhead camera, looking down on her from a great height. As Mahavishnu's picking speed increases to the point where the chord seems a sustained drone, Shara slowly lifts her head, still holding the contraction, until she is staring directly up at us. She poises there for an eternity, like a spring wound to the bursting point . . .

. . . and explodes upward toward us, rising higher and faster than she possibly can in a soaring flight that *is* slow motion now, coming closer and closer until her hands disappear to either side and her face fills the screen, flanked by two candles which have bloomed into gouts of yellow flame in an instant. The guitar and bass are submerged in an orchestra.

Almost at once she whirls away from us, and the POV switches to the original camera, on which we see her fling herself down ten meters to the floor, reversing her attitude in mid-flight and twisting. She comes out of her roll in an absolutely flat trajectory that takes her the length of the room. She hits the far wall with a crash audible even over the music, shattering the still pendulum. Her thighs soak up the kinetic energy and then release it, and once again she is racing toward us, hair streaming straight out behind her, a broad smile of triumph growing larger on the screen.

In the next five minutes all six cameras vainly try to track her as she caroms around the immense room like a hummingbird trying to batter its way out of a cage using the walls, floor and ceiling the way a jai alai master does, *existing in three dimensions*. Gravity is defeated. The basic assumption of all dance is transcended.

Shara is transformed.

She comes to rest at last at vertcal center in the forefront of the cube, arms-legs-fingers-toes-face straining outward, her body turning gently end over end. All four cameras that bear on her join in a four-way splitscreen, the orchestra resolves into its final E major, and—fade out.

I had neither the time nor the equipment to create the special effects that Shara wanted. So I found ways to warp reality to my need. The first candle segment was a twinned shot of a candle being blown out from above—in ultraslow motion, and in reverse. The second segment with a simple recording of linear reality. I had lit the candle, started taping—and had the Ring's spin killed. A candle behaves oddly in zero gee. The low-density combustion gases do not rise up from the flame, allowing air to reach it from beneath. The flame does not go out: it becomes dormant. Restore gravity within a minute or so, and it blooms back to life again. All I did was monkey with speeds a bit to match in with the music and Shara's dance. I got the idea from Harry Stein, Skyfac's construction foreman, who was helping me design things Shara would need for the next dance.

I piped it to the video wall in the Ring One Lounge, and everyone in Skyfac who could cut work crowded in for the broadcast. They saw exactly what was being sent out over worldwide satellite hookup—(Carrington had arranged twenty-five minutes without commercial interruption) almost a full half second before the world did.

I spent the broadcast in the Communications Room, chewing my fingernails. But it went without a hitch, and I slapped my board dead and made it to the Lounge in time to see the last half of the standing ovation. Shara stood before the screen, Carrington sitting beside her, and I found the difference in their expressions instructive. Her face showed no embarrassment or modesty. She had had faith in herself throughout, had approved this tape for broadcast—she was aware, with that incredible detachment of which so few artists are capable, that the wild applause was only what she deserved. But her face showed that she was deeply surprised—and deeply grateful—to be given what she deserved.

Carrington, on the other hand, registered a triumph strangely admixed with relief. He too had had faith in Shara, and had backed it with a large investment—but his faith was that of a businessman in a gamble he believes will pay off, and as I watched his eyes and the glisten of sweat on his forehead, I realized that no businessman ever takes an expensive gamble without worrying that it may be the fiasco that will begin the loss of his only essential commodity: face.

Seeing his kind of triumph next to hers spoiled the moment for me, and instead of thrilling for Shara I found myself almost hating her. She spotted me, and waved me to join her before the cheering crowd, but I turned and literally flung myself from the room. I borrowed a bottle from Harry Stein and got stinking.

The next morning my head felt like a fifteen-amp fuse on a forty-amp circuit, and I seemed to be held together only by surface tension. Sudden movements frightened me. It's a long fall off that wagon, even at one-sixth gee.

The phone chimed—I hadn't had time to rewire it—and a young man I didn't know politely announced that Mr. Carrington wished to see me in his office. At once. I spoke of a barbed-wire suppository, and what Mr. Carrington might do with it, at once. Without changing expression he repeated his message and disconnected.

So I crawled into my clothes, decided to grow a beard, and left. Along the way I wondered what I had traded my independence for, and why?

Carrington's office was oppressively tasteful, but at least the lighting was subdued. Best of all, its filter system would handle smoke—the sweet musk of pot lay on the air. I accepted a macrojoint of "Maoi-Zowie" from Carrington with something approaching gratitude, and began melting my hangover.

Shara sat next to his desk, wearing a leotard and a layer of sweat. She had obviously spent the morning rehearsing for the next dance.

I felt ashamed, and consequently snappish, avoiding her eyes and her hello. Panzella and McGillicuddy came in on my heels, chattering about the latest sighting of the mysterious object from deep space, which had appeared this time in the Asteroid Belt. They were arguing over whether or not it displayed signs of sentience, and I wished they'd shut up.

Carrington waited until we had all seated ourselves and lit up, then rested a hip on his desk and smiled. "Well, Tom?"

McGillicuddy beamed. "Better than we expected, sir. All the ratings agree we had about 74 percent of the world audience. . . ."

"The hell with the Nielsens," I snapped. "*What did the critics say*?"

McGillicuddy blinked. "Well, the general reaction so far is that Shara was a smash. The *Times*. . . ."

I cut him off again. "What was the less-than-general reaction?"

"Well, nothing is ever unanimous."

"Specifics. The dance press? Liz Zimmer? Migdalski?"

"Uh. Not as good. Praise yes—only a blind man could've panned that show. But guarded praise. Uh, Zimmer called it a magnificent dance spoiled by a gimmicky ending."

"And Migdalski?" I insisted.

"He headed his review, 'But What Do You Do for An Encore?'" McGillicuddy admitted. "His basic thesis was that it was a charming one-shot. But the *Times*. . . ."

"Thank you, Tom." Carrington said quietly. "About what we expected, isn't it, my dear? A big splash, but no one's willing to call it a tidal wave yet."

She nodded. "But they will, Bryce. The next two dances will sew it up."

Panzella spoke up. "Ms. Drummond, may I ask you why you played it the way you did? Using the null-gee interlude only as a brief adjunct to conventional dance—surely you must have expected the critics to call it gimmickry."

Shara smiled and answered. "To be honest, Doctor, I had no choice. I'm learning to use my body in free fall, but it's still a conscious effort, almost a pantomime. I need another few weeks to make it second nature, and it *has* to be if I'm to sustain a whole piece in it. So I dug a conventional dance out of the trunk, tacked on a five-minute ending that used every zero-gee move I knew, and found to my extreme relief that they made thematic sense together. I told

Charlie my notion, and he made it work visually and dramatically—the whole business of the candles was his, and it underlined what I was trying to say better than any set we could have built."

"So you have not yet completed what you came here to do?" Panzella asked her.

"Oh, no. Not by any means. The next dance will show the world that dance is more than controlled falling. And the third . . . the third will be what this has all been for." Her face lit, became animated. "The third dance will be the one I have wanted to dance all my life. I can't entirely picture it, yet—but I know that when I become capable of dancing it, I will create it, and it will be my greatest dance."

Panzella cleared his throat. "How long will it take you?"

"Not long," she said. "I'll be ready to tape the next dance in two weeks, and I can start on the last one almost at once. With luck, I'll have it in the can before my month is up."

"Ms. Drummond," Panzella said gravely, "I'm afraid you don't have another month."

Shara went white as snow, and I half rose from my seat. Carrington looked intrigued.

"How much time?" Shara asked.

"Your latest tests have not been encouraging. I had assumed that the sustained exercise of rehearsal and practice would tend to slow your system's adaptation. But most of your work has been in total weightlessness. And I failed to realize the extent to which your body is accustomed to sustained exertion—in a terrestrial environment. There are already signs of Davis's Syndrome in—"

"How much time?"

"Two weeks. Possibly three, if you spend three separate hours a day at hard exercise in two gravities. We can arrange that by—"

"That's ridiculous." I burst out. "Don't you understand about dancers' spines? She could ruin herself in two gees."

"I've got to have four weeks," Shara said.

"Ms. Drummond, I am very sorry."

"I've got to have four weeks."

Panzella had that same look of helpless sorrow that McGillicuddy and I had had in our turn, and I was suddenly sick to death of a universe in which people had to keep looking at Shara that way. "Dammit," I roared, "she needs four weeks."

Panzella shook his shaggy head. "If she stays in zero gee for four working weeks, she may die."

Shara sprang from her chair. "Then I'll die," she cried. "I'll take that chance. I *have* to."

Carrington coughed. "I'm afraid I can't permit you to, darling."

She whirled on him furiously.

"This dance of yours is excellent PR for Skyfac," he said calmly, "but if it were to kill you it might boomerang, don't you think?"

Her mouth worked, and she fought desperately for control. My own head whirled. Die? Shara?

"Besides," he added, "I've grown quite fond of you."

"Then I'll stay up here in space," she burst out.

"Where? The only areas of sustained weightlessness are factories, and you're not qualified to work in one."

"Then for God's sake give me one of the new pods, the smaller spheres. Bryce, I'll give you a higher return on your investment than a factory pod, and I'll. . . ." Her voice changed. "I'll be available to you always."

He smiled lazily. "Yes, but I might not *want* you always, darling. My mother warned me strongly against making irrevocable decisions about women. Especially informal ones. Besides, I find zero-gee sex rather too exhausting as a steady diet."

I had almost found my voice, and now I lost it again. I was glad Carrington was turning her down—but the way he did it made me yearn to drink his blood.

Shara too was speechless for a time. When she spoke, her voice was low, intense, almost pleading. "Bryce, it's a matter of timing. If I broadcast two more dances in the next four weeks, I'll have a world to return to. If I have to go Earthside and wait a year or two, that third dance will sink without a trace—no one'll be looking, and they won't have the memory of the first two. This is my only option, Bryce—*let me take the chance*. Panzella can't guarantee four weeks will kill me."

"I can't guarantee your survival," the doctor said.

"You can't guarantee that any of us will live out the day," she snapped. She whirled back to Carrington, held him with her eyes. "Bryce, *let me risk it.*" Her face underwent a massive effort, produced a smile that put a knife through my heart. "I'll make it worth your while."

Carrington savored that smile and the utter surrender in her voice like a man enjoying a fine claret. I wanted to slay him with my hands and teeth, and I prayed that he would add the final cruelty of turning her down. But I had underestimated his true capacity for cruelty.

"Go ahead with your rehearsal, my dear," he said at last. "We'll make a final decision when the time comes. I shall have to think about it."

I don't think I've ever felt so hopeless, so . . . impotent in my life. Knowing it was futile, I said, "Shara, I can't let you risk your life—"

"I'm going to do this, Charlie," she cut me off, "with or without you. No one else knows my work well enough to tape it properly, but if you want out I can't stop you." Carrington watched me with a detached interest. "Well?" she prodded.

I said a filthy word.

"You know the answer."

"Then let's get to work."

Tyros are transported on the pregnant broomsticks. Old hands hang outside the airlock, dangling from handholds on the outer surface of the spinning Ring (not hard in less than half a gee). They face in the direction of their spin, and when their destination comes under the horizon, they just drop off. Thruster units built into gloves and boots supply the necessary course corrections. The distances involved are small. Still, there are very few old hands.

Shara and I were old hands, having spent more hours in weightlessness than some technicians who'd been working in Skyfac for years. We made scant and efficient use of our thrusters, chiefly in canceling the energy imparted to us by the spin of the Ring we left. We had throat mikes and hearing-aid-sized receivers, but there was no conversation on the way across the void. Being without a local vertical—a defined "up" and "down"—is more confusing and distressing than can possibly be imagined by anyone who has never left Earth. For that very reason, all Skyfac structures are aligned to the same imaginary "ecliptic," but it doesn't help very much. I wondered if I would ever get used to it—and even more I wondered whether I would ever get used to the cessation of pain in my leg. It even seemed to hurt less under spin these days.

We grounded, with much less force than a skydiver does, on the surface of the new studio. It was an enormous steel globe, studded with sunpower screens and heat losers, tethered to three more spheres in various stages of construction on which Harry Stein's boys were even now working. McGillicuddy had told me that the complex when completed would be used for "controlled density processing," and when I said, "How nice," he added, "Dispersion foaming and variable density casting," as if that explained everything. Perhaps it did. Right at the moment, it was Shara's studio.

The airlock led to a rather small working space around a smaller interior sphere some fifty meters in diameter. It too was pressurized, intended to contain a vacuum, but its locks stood open. We removed our p-suits, and Shara unstrapped her thruster bracelets from a bracing strut and put them on, hanging by her ankles from the strut while she did so. The anklets went on next. As jewelry they were a shade bulky—but they had twenty minutes' continuous use each, and their operation was not visible in normal atmosphere and lighting. Zero-gee dance without them would have been enormously more difficult.

As she was fastening the last strap I drifted over in front of her and grabbed the strut. "Shara. . . ."

"Charlie, I can beat it. I'll exercise in *three* gravities, and I'll sleep in two, and I'll make this body last. I know I can."

"You could skip *Mass Is A Verb* and go right to the *Stardance*."

She shook her head. "I'm not ready yet—and neither is the audience. I've to lead myself and them through dance in a sphere first—in a contained space—before I'll be ready to dance in empty space, or they to appreciate it. I have to free my mind, and theirs, from just about every preconception of dance, change all the postulates. Even two stages is too few—but it's the irreducible minimum." Her eyes softened. "Charlie—I must."

"I know," I said gruffly and turned away. Tears are a nuisance in free fall—they don't *go* anywhere, just form silly-looking expanding spherical contact lenses, in which the world swims. I began hauling myself around the surface of the inner sphere toward the camera emplacement I was working on, and Shara entered the inner sphere to begin rehearsal.

I prayed as I worked on my equipment, snaking cables among the bracing struts and connecting them to drifting terminals. For the first time in years I prayed, prayed that Shara would make it. That we both would.

The next twelve days were the toughest half of my life. Shara worked as hard as I did. She spent half of every day working in the studio, half of the rest in exercise under two and a quarter gravities (the most Dr. Panzella would permit), and half of the rest in Carrington's bed, trying to make him contented enough to let her stretch her time limit. Perhaps she slept in the few hours left over. I only know that she never looked tired, never lost her composure or her dogged determination. Stubbornly, reluctantly, her body lost its awkwardness, took on grace even in an environment where grace required enormous concentration. Like a child learning how to walk, Shara learned how to fly.

I even began to get used to the absence of pain in my leg.

What can I tell you of *Mass*, if you have not seen it? It cannot be described, even badly, in mechanistic terms, the way a symphony could be written out in words. Conventional dance terminology is by its built-in assumptions, worse than useless, and if you are at all familiar with the new nomenclature you *must* be familiar with *Mass Is A Verb*, from which it draws *its* built-in assumptions.

Nor is there much I can say about the technical aspects of *Mass*. There were no special effects; not even music. Raoul Brindle's superb score was composed *from the dance*, and added to the tape with my permission two years later, but it was for the original, silent version that I was given the Emmy. My entire contribution, aside from editing and installing the two trampolines, was to camouflage batteries of wide-dispersion light sources in clusters around each camera eye, and wire them so that they energized only when they were out-of-frame with respect to whichever camera was on at the time—ensuring that Shara was always lit from the front, presenting two (not always congruent) shadows. I made no attempt to employ flashy camera work; I simply recorded what Shara danced, changing POV only as she did.

No, *Mass Is A Verb* can be described only in symbolic terms, and then poorly. I can say that Shara demonstrated that mass and inertia are as able as gravity to supply the dynamic conflict essential to dance. I can tell you that from them she distilled a kind of dance that could only have been imagined by a group-head consisting of an acrobat, a stunt-diver, a skywriter and an underwater ballerina. I can tell you that she dismantled the last interface between herself and utter freedom of motion, subduing her body to her will and space itself to her need.

And still I will have told less than nothing. For Shara sought more than freedom—she sought meaning. *Mass* was, above all, a spiritual event—its title pun reflecting its thematic ambiguity between the technological and the theological. Shara made the human confrontation with existence a transitive act, literally meeting God halfway. I do not mean to imply that her dance at any time addressed an exterior God, a discrete entity with or without white beard. Her dance addressed reality, gave successive expression to the Three Eternal Questions asked by every human being who ever lived.

Her dance observed her *self*, and asked, "*How have I come to be here*?"

Her dance observed the universe in which *self* existed, and asked, "*How did all this come to be here with me*?"

And at last, observing her *self* in relation to its universe, "*Why am I so alone*?"

And having asked these questions with every muscle and sinew she possessed, she paused hung suspended in the center of the sphere, her body and soul open to the universe, and when no answer came, she contracted. Not in a dramatic, coiling-spring sense as she had in *Liberation*, a compressing of energy and tension. This was physically similar, but an utterly different phenomenon. It was an act of introspection, a turning of the mind's (soul's?) eye in upon itself, to seek answers that lay nowhere else. Her body too, therefore, seemed to fold in upon itself, compacting her mass, so evenly that her position in space was not disturbed.

And reaching within herself, she closed on emptiness.

The camera faded out leaving her alone, rigid, encapsulated, yearning. The dance ended, leaving her three questions unanswered, the tension of their asking unresolved. Only the expression of patient waiting on her face blunted the shocking edge of the non-ending, made it bearable, a small, blessed sign whispering, "To be continued."

By the eighteenth day we had it in the can, in rough form. Shara put it immediately out of her mind and began choreographing *Stardance*, but I spent two hard days of editing before I was ready to release the tape for broadcast. I had four days until the half-hour of prime time Carrington had purchased—but that wasn't the deadline

I felt breathing down the back of my neck.

McGillicuddy came into my workroom while I was editing, and although he saw the tears running down my face he said no word. I let the tape run, and he watched in silence, and soon his face was wet too. When the tape had been over for a long time he said, very softly, "One of these days I'm going to have to quit this stinking job."

I said nothing.

"I used to be a karate instructor. I was pretty good. I could teach again, maybe do some exhibition work, make ten percent of what I do now."

I said nothing.

"The whole damned Ring's bugged, Charlie. The desk in my office can activate and tap my vidphone in Skyfac. Four at a time, actually."

I said nothing.

"I saw you both in the airlock, when you came back the last time. I saw her collapse. I saw you bringing her around. I heard her make you promise not to tell Dr. Panzella."

I waited. Hope stirred.

He dried his face. "I came in here to tell you I was going to Panzella, to tell him what I saw. He'd bully Carrington into sending her home right away."

"And now?" I said.

"I've seen that tape."

"And you know that the *Stardance* will probably kill her?"

"Yes."

"And you know we have to let her do it?"

"Yes."

Hope died. I nodded. "Then get out of here and let me work."

He left.

On Wall Street and aboard Skyfac it was late afternoon when I finally had the tape edited to my satisfaction. I called Carrington, told him to expect me in half an hour, showered, shaved, dressed, and left.

A major of the Space Command was there with him when I arrived, but he was not introduced and so I ignored him. Shara was there too, wearing a thing made of orange smoke that left her breasts bare. Carrington had obviously made her wear it, as an urchin writes filthy words on an altar, but she wore it with a perverse and curious dignity that I sensed annoyed him. I looked her in the eye and smiled. "Hi, kid. It's a good tape."

"Let's see," Carrington said. He and the major took seats behind the desk and Shara sat beside it.

I fed the tape into the video rig built into the office wall, dimmed the lights, and sat across from Shara. It ran twenty minutes, uninterrupted, no soundtrack, stark naked.

It was terrific.

"Aghast" is a funny word. To make you aghast, a thing must hit you in a place you haven't armored over with cynicism yet. I seem to have been born cynical; I have been aghast three times that I can remember. The first was when I learned, at the age of three, that there were people who could deliberately hurt kittens. The second was when I learned, at age seventeen, that there were people who could actually take LSD and then hurt other people for fun. The third was when *Mass Is A Verb* ended and Carrington said in perfectly conversational tones, "Very pleasant; very graceful. I like it," when I learned, at age forty-five, that there were men, not fools or cretins but intelligent men, who could watch Shara Drummond dance and fail to *see*. We all, even the most cynical of us, always have some illusion which we cherish.

Shara simply let it bounce off her somehow, but I could see that the major was as aghast as I, controlling his features with a visible effort.

Suddenly welcoming a distraction from my horror and dismay, I studied him more closely, wondering for the first time what he was doing here. He was my age, lean and more hard bitten than I am, with silver fuzz on top of his skull and an extremely tidy mustache on the front. I'd taken him for a crony of Carrington's, but three things changed my mind. Something indefinable about his eyes told me that he was a military man of long combat experience. Something equally indefinable about his carriage told me that he was on duty at the moment. And something quite definable about the line his mouth made told me that he was disgusted with the duty he had drawn.

When Carrington went on, "What do you think, Major?" in polite tones, the man paused for a moment, gathering his thoughts and choosing his words. When he did speak, it was not to Carrington.

"Ms. Drummond," he said quietly, "I am Major William Cox, commander of S.C. *Champion*, and I am honored to meet you. That was the most profoundly moving thing I have ever seen."

Shara thanked him most gravely. "This is Charles Armstead, Major Cox. He made the tape."

Cox regarded me with new respect. "A magnificent job, Mister Armstead." He stuck out his hand and I shook it.

Carrington was beginning to understand that we three shared a thing which excluded him. "I'm glad you enjoyed it, Major," he said with no visible trace of sincerity. "You can see it again on your television tomorrow night, if you chance to be off duty. And eventually, of course, cassettes will be made available. Now perhaps we can get to the matter at hand."

Cox's face closed as if it had been zippered up, became stiffly formal. "As you wish, sir."

Puzzled, I began what I thought was the matter at hand. "I'd like your own Comm Chief to supervise the actual transmission this time, Mr. Carrington. Shara and I will be too busy to—"

"My Comm Chief will supervise the broadcast, Armstead," Carrington interrupted, "but I don't think you'll be particularly busy."

I was groggy from lack of sleep; my uptake was slow.

He touched his desk delicately. "McGillicuddy, report at once," he said, and released it. "You see, Armstead you and Shara are both returning to Earth. At once."

"*What?*"

"Bryce, you *can't*," Shara cried. "You *promised.*"

"Did I? My dear, there were no witnesses present last night. Altogether for the best, don't you agree?"

I was speechless with rage.

McGillicuddy entered. "Hello, Tom," Carrington said pleasantly. "You're fired. You'll be returning to Earth at once, with Ms. Drummond and Mr. Armstead, aboard Major Cox's vessel. Departure in one hour, and don't leave anything you're fond of." He glanced from McGillicuddy to me. "From Tom's desk you can tap any vidphone in Skyfac. From my desk you can tap Tom's desk."

Shara's voice was low. "Bryce, two days. God damn you, name your price."

He smiled slightly. "I'm sorry, darling. When informed of your collapse, Dr. Panzella became most specific. Not even one more day. Alive you are a distinct plus for Skyfac's image—you are my gift to the world. Dead you are an albatross around my neck. I cannot allow you to die on my property. I anticipated that you might resist leaving, and so I spoke to a friend in the," he glanced at Cox, "higher echelons of the Space Command, who was good enough to send the Major here to escort you home. You are not under arrest in the legal sense—but I assure you that you have no choice. Something like protective custody applies. Goodbye, Shara." He reached for a stack of reports on his desk, and I surprised myself considerably.

I cleared the desk entirely, tucked head catching him squarely in the sternum. His chair was bolted to the deck and so it snapped clean. I recovered so well that I had time for one glorious right. Do you know how, if you punch a basketball squarely, it will bounce up from the floor? That's what his head did, in low gee slow motion.

Then Cox had hauled me to my feet and shoved me into the far corner of the room. "Don't," he said to me, and his voice must have held a lot of that "habit of command" they talk about because it stopped me cold. I stood breathing in great gasps while Cox helped Carrington to his feet.

The multibillionaire felt his smashed nose, examined the blood on his fingers, and looked at me with raw hatred. "You'll never work in video again, Armstead. You're through. Finished. Un-em-ployed, you got that?"

Cox tapped him on the shoulder, and Carrington spun on him. "What the hell do you want?" he barked.

Cox smiled. "Carrington, my late father once said, 'Bill, make your enemies by choice, not by accident.' Over the years I have found that to be excellent advice. You suck."

"And not particularly well," Shara agreed.

Carrington blinked. Then his absurdly broad shoulders swelled and he roared, "Out all of you! *Off my property at once!*"

By unspoken consent, we waited for Tom, who knew his cue. "Mister Carrington, it is a rare privilege and a great honor to have been fired by you. I shall think of it always as a Pyrrhic defeat." And he half-bowed and we left, each buoyed by a juvenile feeling of triumph that must have lasted ten seconds.

IV

The sensation of falling that you get when you first enter zero gee is literal truth—but it fades rapidly as your body learns to treat it as illusion. Now, in zero gee for the last time, for the half hour or so before I would be back in Earth's gravitational field, I felt like I was falling. Plummeting into some bottomless gravity well, dragged down by the anvil that was my heart, the scraps of a dream that should have held me aloft fluttering overhead.

The *Champion* was three times the size of Carrington's yacht, which childishly pleased me until I recalled that he had summoned it here without paying for either fuel or crew. A guard at the airlock saluted as we entered. Cox led us aft to the compartment where we were to strap in. He noticed along the way that I used only my left hand to pull myself along, and when we stopped, he said, "Mr. Armstead, my late father also told me, 'Hit the soft parts with your hand. Hit the hard parts with a utensil.' Otherwise I can find no fault with your technique. I wish I could shake your hand."

I tried to smile, but I didn't have it in me. "I admire your taste in enemies, Major."

"A man can't ask for more. I'm afraid I can't spare time to have your hand looked at until we've grounded. We begin reentry immediately."

"Forget it. Get Shara down fast and easy."

He bowed to Shara, did *not* tell her how deeply sorry he was to et cetera, wished us all a comfortable journey, and left. We strapped into our acceleration couches to await ignition. There ensued a long and heavy silence, compounded of a mutual sadness that bravado could only have underlined. We did not look at each other, as though our combined sorrow might achieve some kind of critical mass. Grief struck us dumb, and I believe that remarkably little of it was self-pity.

But then a whole lot of time seemed to have gone by. Quite a bit of intercom chatter came faintly from the next compartment, but ours was not in circuit. At last we began to talk desultorily, discussing the probable critical reaction to *Mass Is A Verb*, whether analysis was worthwhile or the theater really dead, anything at all except future plans. Eventually there was nothing else to talk about, so we shut up again. I guess I'd say we were in shock.

For some reason I came out of it first. "What the hell is taking them so long?" I barked irritably.

Tom started to say something soothing, then glanced at his watch and yelped. "You're right. It's been over an hour."

I looked at the wall clock, got hopelessly confused until I realized it was on Greenwich time rather than Wall Street, and realized he was correct. "Chrissakes," I shouted, "the whole bloody *point* of this exercise is to protect Shara from overexposure to free fall! I'm going forward."

"Charlie, hold it." Tom, with two good hands, unstrapped faster than I. "Dammit, stay right there and cool off. I'll go find out what the holdup is."

He was back in a few minutes, and his face was slack. "We're not going anywhere. Cox has orders to sit tight."

"What? Tom, what the *hell* are you talking about?"

His voice was all funny. "Red fireflies. More like bees, actually. In a balloon."

He simply *could not* be joking, which meant he flat out *had* to have gone completely round the bend, which meant that somehow I had blundered into my favorite nightmare, where everyone but me goes crazy and begins gibbering at me. So I lowered my head like an enraged bull and charged out of the room so fast the door barely had time to get out of my way.

It just got worse. When I reached the door to the bridge I was going much too fast to be stopped by anything short of a body block, and the crewmen present were caught flatfooted. There was a brief flurry at the door, and then I was on the bridge, and then I decided that I had gone crazy too, which somehow made everything all right.

The forward wall of the bridge was one enormous video tank—and just enough off center to faintly irritate me, standing out against the black deep as clearly as cigarettes in a darkroom, there truly did swarm a multitude of red fireflies.

* * *

The conviction of unreality made it okay. But then Cox snapped me back to reality with a bellowed, "*Off* this bridge, Mister." If I'd been in a normal frame of mind it would have blown me out the door and into the farthest corner of the ship; in my current state it managed to jolt me into acceptance of the impossible situation. I shivered like a wet dog and turned to him.

"Major," I said desperately, "what is going on?"

As a king may be amused by an insolent varlet who refuses to kneel, he was bemused by the phenomenon of someone failing to obey him. It bought me an answer. "We are confronting intelligent alien life," he said concisely. "I believe them to be sentient plasmoids."

I had never for a moment believed that the mysterious object which had been leap-frogging around the solar system since I came to Skyfac was *alive*. I tried to take it in, then abandoned the task and went back to my main priority. "I don't care if they're eight tiny reindeer; you've got to get this can back to Earth *now*."

"Sir, this vessel is on Emergency Red Alert and on Combat Standby. At this moment the suppers of every one in North America are getting cold unnoticed. I will consider myself fortunate if I ever see Earth again. Now get off my bridge."

"But you don't *understand*. Shara's right on the edge: farting around like this'll kill her. That's what you came up here to prevent, dammit—"

"MISTER ARMSTEAD! This is a military vessel. We are facing more than fifty intelligent beings who appeared out of hyperspace near here twenty minutes ago, beings who therefore use a drive beyond my conception with no visible parts. If it makes you feel any better I am aware that I have a passenger aboard of greater intrinsic value to my species than this ship and everyone else aboard her and if it is any comfort to you this knowledge already provides a distraction I need like an auxiliary anus, and I can no more leave this orbit than I can grow horns. Now will you get off this bridge or will you be dragged?"

I didn't get a chance to decide; they dragged me.

On the other hand, by the time I got back to our compartment, Cox had put our vidphone screen in circuit with the tank on the bridge. Shara and Tom were studying it with rapt attention. Having nothing better to do, I did too.

Tom had been right. They *did* act more like bees, in the swarming rapidity of their movement. I couldn't get an accurate count: about fifty. And they *were* in a balloon—a faint, barely visible thing on the fine line between transparency and translucence. Though they darted like furious red gnats, it was only within the confines of the spheroid balloon—they never left it or seemed to touch its inner surface.

As I watched, the last of the adrenalin rinsed out of my kidneys, but it left a sense of frustrated urgency. I tried to grapple with the fact that these Space Commando special effects represented something that was—more important that Shara. It was a primevally disturbing notion, but I could not reject it.

In my mind were two voices, each hollering questions at the top of their lungs, each ignoring the other's questions. One yelled: *Are those things friendly? Or hostile? Or do they even use those concepts? How big are they? How far away? From where?* The other voice was less ambitious, but just as loud; all it said, over and over again was: *How much longer can Shara remain in free fall without dooming herself?*

Shara's voice was full of wonder. "They're . . . they're *dancing.*"

I looked closer. If there was a pattern to the flies-on-garbage swarm they made, I couldn't detect it. "Looks random to me."

"Charlie, look. All that furious activity, and they never bump into each other or the walls of that envelope they're in. They must be in orbits as carefully choreographed as those of electrons."

"Do atoms dance?"

She gave me all odd look. "Don't they, Charlie?"

"Laser beam," Tom said.

We looked at him.

"Those things have to be plasmoids—the man I talked to said they show on deepspace radar. That means they're ionized gases of some kind—the kind of thing that used to cause UFO reports." He giggled, then caught himself. "If you could slice through that envelope with a laser, I'll bet you could deionize them pretty good—besides, that envelope has to hold their life support, whatever it is they metabolize."

I was dizzy. "Then we're not defenseless?"

"You're both talking like soldiers," Shara burst out. "I tell you, they're dancing. Dancers aren't fighters."

"Come on, Shara," I barked. "Even if those things happened to be remotely like us, that's not true. T'ai chi, karate, kung fu—they're dance." I nodded to the screen. "All we know about these animated embers is that they travel interstellar space. That's enough to scare me."

"Charlie, *look* at them," she commanded.

I did.

By God, they didn't look threatening; and they did, the more I watched, seem to move in a dancelike way, whirling in mad adagios just too fast for the eye to follow. Not at all like conventional dance—more analogous to what Shara had begun with *Mass Is A Verb*. I found myself wanting to switch to another camera for contrast of perspective, and that made my mind start to wake up at last. Two ideas surfaced, the second one necessary in order to sell Cox the first.

"How far do you suppose we are from Skyfac?" I asked Tom.

He pursed his lips. "Not far. There hasn't been much more than maneuvering acceleration. The damned things were probably attracted to Skyfac in the first place—it must be the most easily visible sign of intelligent life in this system." He grimaced. "Maybe they don't use planets."

I reached forward and punched the audio circuit. "Major Cox."

"Get off this circuit."

"How would you like a closer view of those things?"

"We're staying put. Now stop jiggling my elbow and get off this circuit or I'll—"

"Will you listen to me? I have four mobile cameras in space, remote control, self-contained power and light, and better resolution than you've got. They were set up to tape Shara's next dance."

He shifted gears at once. "Can you patch them into my ship?"

"I think so. But I'll have to get back to the master board in Ring One."

"No good, then. I can't tie myself to a top—what if I have to fight or run?"

"Major—how far a walk is it?"

It startled him a bit. "A couple of klicks, as the crow flies. But you're a groundlubber."

"I've been in free fall for most of two months. Give me a portable radar and I can ground on Phobos."

"Mmmm. You're a civilian—but dammit, I need better video. Permission granted."

Now for the first idea. "Wait—one thing more. Shara and Tom must come with me."

"Nuts. This isn't a field trip."

"Major Cox—Shara *must* return to a gravity field as quickly as possible. Ring One'll do—in fact, it'd be ideal, if we enter through the 'spoke' in the center. She can descend very slowly and acclimatize gradually, the way a diver decompresses in stages, but in reverse. Tom will have to come along and stay with her—if she passes out and falls down the tube, she could break a leg even in one-sixth gee. Besides, he's better at EVA than either of us."

He thought it over. "Go."

We went.

The trip back to Ring One was longer than any Shara or I had ever made, but under Tom's guidance we made it with minimal maneuvering. Ring, *Champion* and aliens formed an equiangular triangle about five or six klicks on a side. Seen in perspective, the aliens took up about twice as much volume as a sphere the diameter of Ring One—one hell of a big balloon. They did not pause or slacken in their mad gyration, but somehow they seemed to watch us cross the gap to Skyfac. I got the impression of a biologist studying the strange antics of a new species. We kept our suit radios off to avoid distraction, and it made me just a little bit more susceptible to suggestion.

I failed to even notice the absence of a local vertical. I was too busy.

I left Tom with Shara and dropped down the tube six rungs at a time. Carrington was waiting for me in the reception room, with two flunkies. It was plain to see that he was scared silly, and trying to cover it with anger. "God damn it, Armstead those are my bloody cameras."

"Shut up, Carrington. If you put those cameras in the hands of the best technicians available—me—and if I put their data in the hands of the best strategic mind in space—Cox—we *might* be able to save your damned factory for you. And the human race for the rest of us." I moved forward, and he got out of my way. It figured. Putting all humanity in danger might just be bad PR.

After all the practicing I'd done it wasn't hard to direct four mobile cameras through space simultaneously by eye. The aliens ignored their approach. The Skyfac comm crew fed my signals to the *Champion*, and patched me in to Cox on audio. At his direction I bracketed the balloon with the cameras, shifting POV at his command. Space Command Headquarters must have recorded the video, but I couldn't hear their conversation with Cox, for which I was grateful. I gave him slow-motion replay, close ups, splitscreens—everything at my disposal. The movements of individual fireflies did not appear particularly symmetrical, but patterns began to repeat. In slow motion they looked more than ever as though they were dancing, and although I couldn't be sure, it seemed to me that they were increasing their tempo. Somehow the dramatic tension of their dance began to build.

And then I shifted POV to the camera which included Skyfac in the background, and my heart turned to hard vacuum and I screamed in pure primal terror—halfway between Ring One and the swarm of aliens, coming up on them slowly but inexorably, was a p-suited figure that had to be Shara.

With theatrical timing, Tom appeared in the doorway beside me, leaning heavily on Harry Stein, his face drawn with pain. He stood on one foot, the other plainly broken.

"Guess I can't . . . go back to exhibition work . . . after all," he gasped. "Said . . . 'I'm sorry, Tom'. . . knew she was going to swing on me . . . wiped me out anyhow. Oh dammit, Charlie, I'm sorry." He sank into an empty chair.

Cox's voice came urgently. "What in hell is going on? Who is that?"

She *had* to be on our frequency. "Shara!" I screamed "Get your ass back in here!"

"I can't Charlie." Her voice was startlingly loud, and very calm. "Halfway down the tube my chest started to hurt like hell."

"Ms. Drummond," Cox rapped, "if you approach any closer to the aliens I will destroy you."

She laughed, a merry sound that froze my blood. "Bullshit, Major. You aren't about to get gay with laser beams near those things. Besides, you need me as much as you do Charlie."

"What do you mean?"

"These creatures communicate by dance. It's their equivalent of speech, a sophisticated kind of sign language, like hula."

"You can't know that."

"I *feel* it. I know it. Hell, how else do you communicate in airless space? Major Cox, I am the only qualified interpreter the human race has at the moment. Now will you kindly shut up so I can try to learn their language?"

"I have no authority to. . . ."

I said an extraordinary thing. I should have been gibbering, pleading with Shara to come back, even racing for a p-suit to bring her back. Instead I said, "She's right. Shut up, Cox."

"But—"

"Damn you, don't *waste her last effort.*"

He shut up.

Panzella came in, shot Tom full of painkiller, and set his ankle right there in the room, but I was oblivious. For over an hour I watched Shara watch the aliens. I watched them myself, in the silence of utter despair, and for the life of me I could not follow their dance. I strained my mind, trying to suck meaning from their crazy whirling, and failed. The best I could do to aid Shara was to record everything that happened, for a hypothetical posterity. Several times she cried out softly, small muffled exclamations, and I ached to call out to her in reply, but did not. With the last exclamation, she used her thrusters to bring her closer to the alien swarm, and hung there for a long time.

At last her voice came over the speaker, thick and slurred at first as though she were talking in her sleep. "God, Charlie. Strange. So strange. I'm beginning to read them."

"How?"

"Every time I begin to understand a part of the dance, it . . . it brings us closer. Not telepathy, exactly, I just . . . know them better. Maybe it is telepathy. I don't know. By dancing what they feel, they give it enough intensity to make me understand. I'm getting about one concept in three. It's stronger up close."

Cox's voice was gentle but firm. "What have you learned, Shara?"

"That Tom and Charlie were right. They are warlike. At least, there's a flavor of arrogance to them—a conviction of superiority. Their dance is a challenging, a dare. Tell Tom I think they do use planets."

"What?"

"I think at one stage of their development they're corporeal, planet-bound. Then when they have matured sufficiently, they . . . become these fireflies, and head out into space."

"Why?" from Cox.

"To find spawning grounds. They want Earth."

There was a silence lasting perhaps ten seconds. Then Cox spoke up quietly. "Back away, Shara. I'm going to see what lasers will do to them."

"No!" she cried, loud enough to make a really first-rate speaker distort.

"Shara, as Charlie pointed out to me, you are not only expendable, you are for all practical purposes expended."

"No!" this time it was me shouting.

"Major," Shara said urgently, "that's not the way. Believe me, they can dodge or withstand anything you or Earth can throw at them. I *know.*"

"Hell and damnation, woman," Cox said. "What do you want me to do? Let them have the first shot? There are vessels from four countries on their way right now, but they won't—"

"Major, wait. Give me time."

He began to swear, then cut off. "How much time?"

She made no direct reply. "If only this telepathy thing works in reverse . . . it must. I'm no more strange to them than they are to me. Probably less so; I get the idea they've been around. Charlie?"

"Yeah."

"This is a take."

I knew. I had known since I first saw her in open space on my monitor. And I knew what she needed now, from the faint trembling of her voice. It took everything I had, and I was only glad I had it to give. With extremely realistic good cheer, I said, "Break a leg, kid," and killed my mike before she could hear the sob that followed.

And she danced.

It began slowly, the equivalent of one-finger exercises, as she sought to establish a vocabulary of motion that the creatures could comprehend. *Can you see,* she seemed to say, *that this movement is a reaching, a yearning? Do you see that* this *is a spurning, this an unfolding, that a graduated elision of energy? Do you feel the ambiguity in the way I distort this arabesque, or that the tension can be resolved so?*

And it seemed that Shara was right, that they had infinitely more experience with disparate cultures than we, for they were superb linguists of motion. It occurred to me later that perhaps they had selected motion for communication because of its very universality. Man danced before he spoke. At any rate, as Shara's dance began to build, their own began to slow down perceptibly in speed and intensity, until at last they hung motionless in space, watching her.

Soon after that, Shara must have decided that she had sufficiently defined her terms, at least well enough for pidgin communication—for now she began to dance in earnest. Before she had used only her own muscles and the shifting masses of her limbs. Now she added thrusters, singly and in combination, moving within as well as in space. Her dance became a true dance: more than a collection of motions, a thing of substance and meaning. It was unquestionably the *Stardance*, just as she had prechoreographed it, as she had always intended to dance it. That it had something to say to utterly alien creatures, of man and his nature, was not at all a coincidence: it was the essential and ultimate statement of the greatest artist of her age, and it had something to say to God Himself.

The camera lights struck silver from her p-suit, gold from the twin air tanks on her shoulders. To and fro against the black backdrop of space, she wove the intricacies of her dance, a leisurely movement that seemed somehow to leave echoes behind it. And the meaning of those great loops and whirls became clear, drying my throat and clamping my teeth.

For her dance spoke of nothing more and nothing less than the tragedy of being alive, and being human. It spoke, most eloquently, of despair. It spoke of the cruel humor of limitless ambition yoked to limited ability, of eternal hope invested in an ephemeral lifetime, of the driving need to try to create an inexorably predetermined future. It spoke of fear, and of hunger, and, most clearly, of the basic loneliness and alienation of the human animal. It described the universe through the eyes of man: a hostile embodiment of entropy into which we are all thrown alone, forbidden by our nature to touch another mind save secondhand, by proxy. It spoke of the blind perversity which forces man to strive hugely for a peace which, once attained, becomes boredom. And it spoke of folly, of the terrible paradox by which man is capable simultaneously of reason and unreason, forever unable to cooperate even with himself.

It spoke of Shara and her life.

Again and again cyclical statements of hope began, only to collapse into confusion and ruin. Again and again cascades of energy strove for resolution, and found only frustration. All at once she launched into a pattern that seemed familiar, and in moments I recognized it: the closing movement of *Mass Is A Verb* recapitulated—not repeated but reprised, echoed, the Three Questions given a more terrible urgency by this new context. And as before, it segued into that final relentless contraction, that ultimate drawing inward of all energies. Her body became derelict, abandoned, drifting in space, the essence of her being withdrawn to her center and invisible.

The quiescent aliens stirred for the first time.

And suddenly she exploded, blossoming from her contraction not as a spring uncoils, but as a flower bursts from a seed. The force of her release flung her through the void as though she were tossed, like a gull in a hurricane, by galactic winds. Her center appeared to hurl itself through space and time, yanking her body into a new dance.

And the new dance said, *This is what it is to be human: to see the essential existential futility of all action, all striving—and to act, to strive. This is what it is to be human: to reach forever beyond your grasp. This is what it is to be human: to live forever or die trying. This is what it is to be human: to perpetually ask the unanswerable questions, in the hope that the asking of them will somehow hasten the day when they will be answered. This is what it is to be human: to strive in the face of the certainty of failure.*

This is what it is to be human: to persist.

It said all this with a soaring series of cyclical movements that held all the rolling majesty of grand symphony, as uniquely different from each other as snowflakes, and as similar. And the new dance laughed, as much at tomorrow as at yesterday, and most of all at today.

For this is what it means to be human: to laugh at what another would call tragedy.

The aliens seemed to recoil from the ferocious energy, startled, awed, and perhaps a little frightened by Shara's indomitable spirit. They seemed to wait for her dance to wane, for her to exhaust herself, and her laughter sounded on my speaker as she redoubled her efforts, became a pinwheel, a catherine wheel. She changed the focus of her dance, began to dance around them, in pyrotechnic spatters of motion that came ever closer to the intangible spheroid which contained them. They cringed inward from her, huddling together in the center of the envelope, not so much physically threatened as cowed.

This, said her body, *is what it means to be human: to commit hari-kiri, with a smile, if it becomes needful.*

And before that terrible assurance, the aliens broke. Without warning fireflies and balloon vanished, gone, *elsewhere.*

I know that Cox and Tom were still alive, because I saw them afterwards, and that means they were probably saying and doing things in my hearing and presence, but I neither heard them nor saw them then; they were as dead to me as everything except Shara. I called out her name, and she approached the camera that was lit, until I could make out her face behind the plastic hood of her p-suit.

"We may be puny, Charlie," she puffed, gasping for breath. "But by Jesus we're tough."

"Shara—come on in now."

"You know I can't."

"Carrington'll *have* to give you a free-fall place to live now."

"A life of exile? For what? To dance? Charlie, *I haven't got any more to say.*"

"Then I'll come out there."

"Don't be silly. Why? So you can hug a p-suit? Tenderly bump hoods one last time? Balls. It's a good exit so far—let's not blow it."

"Shara!" I broke completely, just caved in on myself and collapsed into great racking sobs.

"Charlie, listen now," she said softly, but with an urgency that reached me even in my despair. "Listen now, for I haven't much time. I have something to give you. I hoped you'd find it for yourself, but . . . will you listen?"

"Y—yes."

"Charlie, zero-gee dance is going to get awful popular all of a sudden. I've opened the door. But you know how fads are, they'll bitch it all up unless you move fast. I'm leaving it in your hands."

"What . . . what are you talking about?"

"About you. Charlie. You're going to dance again."

Oxygen starvation, I thought. But she can't be that low on air already. "Okay. Sure thing."

"For God's sake stop humoring me—I'm straight, I tell you. You'd have seen it yourself if you weren't so damned stupid. Don't you understand? *There's nothing wrong with your leg in free fall!*"

My jaw dropped.

"Do you hear me, Charlie? You can dance again!"

"No," I said, and searched for a reason why not. "I . . . you can't . . . it's . . . dammit, the leg's not strong enough for inside work."

"Forget for the moment that inside work'll be less than half of what you do. Forget it and remember that smack in the nose you gave Carrington. Charlie, when you leaped over the desk: *you pushed off with your right leg.*

I sputtered for a while and shut up.

"There you go, Charlie. My farewell gift. You know I've never been in love with you . . . but you must know that I've always loved you. Still do."

"I love you, Shara."

"So long, Charlie. Do it right."

And all four thrusters went off at once. I watched her go down. A while after she was too far to see, there was a long golden flame that arced above the face of the globe, waned, and then flared again as the airtanks went up.

THE STARDANCERS

I

The flight from Washington was miserable. How can a man who's worked in free fall get airsick? Worse, I had awakened that morning with the same stinking cold I had had ever since returning Earthside, and so I spent the whole flight anticipating the knives that would be thrust through my ears when we landed. But I turned down the proffered drink as well as the meal.

I was not even depressed. Too much had happened to me in the last few weeks. I was wrung out, drained, just sort of . . . on standby, taking disinterested notes while my automatic pilot steered my body around. It helped to be in a familiar place—why, come to think, hadn't I once thought of Toronto, about a thousand years ago, as "home?"

There were reporters when I got through Customs, of course, but not nearly as many as there had been at first. Once, as a kid, I spent a summer working in a mental hospital, and I learned an extraordinary thing: I learned that anyone, no matter how determined, whom you *utterly* ignore will eventually stop pestering you and go away. I had been practicing the technique so consistently for the last three weeks that the word had gone out, and now only the most Skinnerian newstapers even troubled to stick microphones in my face. Eventually there was a cab in front of me and I took it. Toronto cabbies can be relied upon not to recognize anybody, thank God.

I was "free" now.

Reentering the TDT studio was a strong déjá vu experience, strong enough almost to penetrate my armor. Once, geologic ages ago, I had worked here for three years, and briefly again thereafter. And once, in this building, I had seen Shara Drummond dance for the first time. I had came full circle.

I felt nothing.

Always excepting, of course, the god damned leg. After all the time in free fall it hurt much worse than I'd remembered, more than it had hurt since the original days of its ruining, unimaginably far in the past. I had to pause twice on the way upstairs, and I was soaking with sweat by the time I made the top. (Ever wonder why dance studios are *always* up at least one flight of stairs? Did you ever try to rent that much square footage on ground level?) I waited on the landing, regularizing my breathing, until I decided that my color had returned, and then a few seconds more. I knew I should feel agitated now, but I was still on standby.

I opened the door, and déjá vu smacked at me again. Norrey was across the old familiar room, and just as before she was putting a group of students through their paces. They might have been the same students. Only Shara was missing. Shara would always be missing. Shara was air pollution now, upper atmosphere pollution, much more widely distributed than most corpses get to be.

She had been cremated at the *top* of the atmosphere, and by it.

But her older sister was very much alive. She was in the midst of demonstrating a series of suspensions on half-toe as I entered, and I just had time to absorb an impression of glowing skin, healthy sweat, and superb muscle tone before she glanced up and saw me. She stiffened like a stop-frame shot, then literally fell out of an extension. Automatically her body tucked and rolled, and she came out of it at a dead run, crying and swearing as she came, arms outstretched. I barely had time to brace the good leg before she cannoned into me, and then we were rocking in each other's arms like tipsy giants, and she was swearing like a sailor and crying my name. We hugged for an endless time before I became aware that I was holding her clear of the floor and that my shoulders were shrieking nearly as loud as my leg. *Six months ago it would have buckled,* I thought vaguely, and set her down.

"All right, are you all right, are you all right?" her voice was saying in my ear.

I pulled back and tried to grin. "My leg is killing me. And I think I've got the flu."

"Damn you, Charlie, don't you dare misunderstand me. *Are you all right*?" Her fingers gripped my neck as if she intended to chin herself.

My hands dropped to her waist and I looked her in the eyes, abandoning the grin. All at once I realized I was no longer on standby. My cocoon was ruptured, blood sang in my ears, and I could feel the very air impinging on my skin. For the first time I thought about why I had come here, and partly I understood. "Norrey," I said simply, "I'm okay. Some ways I think I'm in better shape than I've been in twenty years."

The second sentence just slipped out, but I knew as I said it that it was true. Norrey read the truth in my eyes, and somehow managed to relax all over without loosing her embrace. "Oh, thank *God,*" she sobbed, and pulled me closer. After a time her sobs lessened, and she said, almost petulantly, her voice tiny, "I'd have broken your *neck,*" and we were both grinning like idiots and laughing aloud. We laughed ourselves right out of our embrace, and then Norrey said "Oh!" suddenly and turned bright red and spun around to her class.

It seemed that we were occupying the only portion of the room that was not intensely fascinating. They knew. They watched TV, they read the papers. Even as we watched, one of the students stepped out in front of the rest. "All right," she said to them, "let's take it from the top, I'll give you three for nothing and—*one,*" and the whole group resumed their workout. The new leader would not meet Norrey's eyes, refused to accept or even acknowledge the gratitude there—but she seemed to be smiling gently, as she danced, at nothing in particular.

Norrey turned back to me. "I'll have to change."

"Not much, I hope."

She grinned again and was gone. My cheeks itched, and when I absently scratched them I discovered that they were soaking wet.

The afternoon outdoors struck us both with wonder. New colors seemed to boil up out of the spectrum and splash themselves everywhere in celebration of fall. It was one of those October days of which, in Toronto anyway, one can say either "Gee, it's chilly" or "Gee, it's warm" and be agreed with. We walked through it together arm in arm, speaking only occasionally and then only with our eyes. My stuffed head began to clear; my leg throbbed less.

Le Maintenant was still there then, but it looked shabbier than ever. Fat Humphrey caught sight of us through the kitchen window as we entered and came out to greet us. He is both the fattest happy man and the happiest fat man I've ever seen. I've seen him outdoors in February in his shirt sleeves, and they say that once a would-be burglar stabbed him three times without effect. He burst through the swinging doors and rushed toward us, a mountain with a smile on top. "Mist' Asmstead, Miz Drummond! Welcome!"

"Hey there, Fat," I called out, removing my filters, "God bless your face. Got a good table?"

"Sure thing, in the cellar somewheres, I'll bring it up."

"I'm sorry *I* brought it up."

There's certainly *some*thing wrong with your upbringing," Norrey agreed drily.

Fat Humphrey laughing aloud is like an earthquake in the Canadian Rockies. "Good to see you, good to see you both. You been away to long, Mist' Armstead."

"Tell you about it later, Fat, okay?"

"Sure thing. Lemme see: you look like about a pound of sirloin, some bake' potato, peas Italian hold the garlic and a bucket of milk. Miz Drummond, I figure you for tuna salad on whole wheat toast, side of slice' tomatoes and a glass of skim milk. Salad all around. Eh?"

We both burst out laughing. "Right again, as usual. Why do you bother to print menus?"

"Would you believe it? There's a law. How would you like that steak cooked?"

"Gee, that'd be terrific," I agreed, and took Norrey's coat and filtermask. Fat Humphrey howled and slapped his mighty thigh, and took my own gear while I was hanging Norrey's. "Been missin' you in this joint, Mist' Armstead. None of these other turkeys know a straight line when they hear it. This way." He led us to a small table in the back, and as I sat down I realized that it was the same table Norrey and Shara and I had shared so long ago. That didn't hurt a bit: it felt right. Fat Humphrey rolled us a joint by hand from his personal stash, and left the bag and a packet of Drums on the table. "Smoke hearty," he said and returned to the kitchen, his retreating buttocks like wrestling zeppelins.

I had not smoked in weeks; at the first taste I started to buzz. Norrey's fingers brushed mine as we passed the digit, and their touch was warm and electric. My nose, which had started to fill as we came indoors, flooded, and between toking and honking the joint was gone before a word had been spoken. I was acutely aware of how silly I must look, but too exhilarated to fret about it. I tried to review mentally all that must be said and all that must be asked, but I kept falling into Norrey's warm brown eyes and getting lost. The candle put highlights in them, and in her brown hair. I rummaged in my head for the right words.

"Well, here we are," is what I came up with.

Norrey half smiled. "That's a hell of a cold."

"My nose clamped down twenty hours after I hit dirt, and I've never properly thanked it. Do you have any *idea* how rotten this planet smells?"

"I'd have thought a closed system'd smell worse."

I shook my head. "There's a smell to space, to a space station I mean. And a p-suit can get pretty ripe. But Earth is a *stew* of smells, mostly bad."

She nodded judiciously. "No smokestacks in space."

"No garbage dumps."

"No sewage."

"No cow farts."

"How did she die, Charlie?"

Oof. "Magnificently."

"I read the papers. I *know* that's bullshit, and . . . and you were *there*."

"Yeah." I had told the story over a hundred times in the last three weeks—but I had never told a *friend,* and I discovered I needed to. And Norrey certainly deserved to know of her sister's dying.

And so I told her of the aliens' coming, of Shara's intuitive understanding that the beings communicated by dance, and her instant decision to reply to them. I told her of Shara's slow realization that the aliens were hostile, territorially aggressive, determined to have our planet for a spawning ground. And I told her, as best I could, of the *Stardance*.

"She danced them right out of the solar system, Norrey. She danced everything she had in her—and she had all of us in her. She danced what we are, what she was, and she scared them silly. They weren't afraid of military lasers, but she scared 'em right the hell back to deep space. Oh, they'll be back some day—I don't know why, but I feel it in my bones. But it might not be in our lifetime. She told them what it is to be human. She gave them the *Stardance*."

Norrey was silent a long time, and then she nodded. "Uh huh." Her face twisted suddenly. "But why did she have to die, Charlie?"

"She was done, honey," I said and took her hand. "She was acclimated all the way to free fall by then, and it's a one-way street. She could never have returned to Earth, not even to the one-sixth gee in Skyfac. Oh, she could have lived in free fall. But *Carrington* owns everything in free fall except military hardware—and she didn't have any more reason to take anything from him. She'd danced her *Stardance,* and I'd taped it, and she was done."

"Carrington," she said, and her fingers gripped my hand fiercely. "Where is he now?"

"I just found out myself this morning. He tried to grab all the tapes and all the money for Skyfac Incorporated, i.e., him. But he'd neglected to have Shara sign an actual contract, and Tom McGillicuddy found an airtight holograph will in her effects. It leaves everything fifty-fifty to you and me. So Carrington tried to buy a probate judge, and he picked the wrong judge. It would have hit the news this afternoon. The thought of even a short sentence in one gee was more than he could take. I think at the last he convinced himself that he had actually loved her, because he tried to copy her exit. He bungled it. He didn't know anything about leaving a rotating Ring, and he let go too late. It's the most common beginner's error."

Norrey looked puzzled.

"Instead of becoming a meteorite like her, he was last seen heading in the general direction of Betelgeuse. I imagine it's on the news by now." I glanced at my watch. "In fact, I would estimate that he's just running out of air about now—if he had the guts to wait."

Norrey smiled, and her fingers relaxed. "Let's hold that thought," she purred.

If captured—don't let them give you to the women.

The salad arrived then. Thousand Islands for Norrey and French for me, just as we would have ordered if we'd thought of it. The portions were unequal, and each was *precisely* as much as the recipient felt like eating. I don't know how Fat Humphrey does it. At what point does that kind of empathy become telepathy?

There was further sporadic conversation as we ate, but nothing significant. Fat Humphrey's cuisine demanded respectful attention. The meal itself arrived as we were finishing the salad, and when we had eaten our fill, both plates were empty and the coffee was cool enough to drink. Slices of Fat's fresh apricot pie were produced warm from the oven, and reverently dealt with. More coffee was poured. I took some pseudoephedrine for my nose. The conversation reawoke groggily, and there was only one question left for her to ask now so I asked her first.

"So what's happening with you, Norrey?"

She made a face. "Nothing much."

Lovely answer. Push.

"Norrey, on the day there is nothing much happening in your life, there'll be honest government in Ottawa. I hear you stood still, once, for over an hour—but the guy that said it was a famous liar. Come on, you know I've been out of touch."

She frowned, and that was it for me, that was the trigger. I had been thinking furiously ever since I came off standby in Norrey's arms back at the studio, and I had already figured out a lot of things. But the sight of that frown completed the process; all at once the jumble in my subconscious fell into shape with an almost audible click. They can come that way, you know. Flashes of insight. In the middle of a sentence, in a microsecond, you make a quantum jump in understanding. You look back on twenty years of blind stupidity without wincing, and perceive the immediate future in detail. Later you will marvel—at that instant you only accept and nod. The Sicilians have a thing like it, that they call *the thunder bolt*. It is said to bring deep calm and great gravity. It made me break up.

"What's so funny?"

"Don't know if I can explain it, hon. I guess I just figured out how Fat Humphrey does it."

"Huh?"

"Tell you later. You were saying. . . ."

The frown returned. "Mostly I wasn't saying. What's happening with me, in twenty-five words or less? I haven't asked myself in quite a while. Maybe too long." She sipped coffee. "Okay. You know that John Koerner album, the last commercial one he made? *Running Jumping Standing Still?* That's what I've been doing, I think. I've been putting out a lot of energy, doing satisfying things, and I'm not satisfied. I'm . . . I'm almost bored."

She floundered, so I decided to play devil's advocate. "But you're right where you've always wanted to be," I said, and began rolling a joint.

She grimaced. "Maybe that's the trouble. Maybe a life's ambition shouldn't be something that can be achieved—because what do you do then? You remember Koerner's movie?"

"Yeah. *The Sound of Sleep.* Nutball flick, nice cherries on top."

"Remember what he said the meaning of life was?"

"Sure. 'Do the next thing.'" I suited action to the word, licked it, sealed it and twisted the ends, then lit it. "Always thought it was terrific advice. It got me through some tough spots."

She toked, held it and exhaled before replying. "I'm ready to do the next thing—but I'm not sure what that *is.* I've toured with the company, I've soloed in New York, I've choreographed, I've directed the whole damn school and now I'm an artistic director. I've got full autonomy now; I can even teach a class again if I feel like it. Every year from now until Hell freezes TDT's repertoire will include one of my pieces, and I'll always have superb bodies to work with. I've been working on childhood dreams all my life, Charlie, and I *hadn't thought ahead any farther than this when I was a kid.* I don't know what 'the next thing' is. I need a new dream."

She toked again, passed it to me. I stared at the glowing tip conspiratorially, and it winked at me. "Any clues? Directions at least?"

She exhaled carefully, spoke to her hands. "I thought I might like to try working one of those commune-companies, where everybody choreographs every piece. I'd like to try working with a group-head. But there's really no one here I could start one with, and the only existing group-head that suits me is New Pilobolus—and for that I'd have to live in *America.*"

"Forget that."

"Hell, yes. I . . . Charlie, I don't know, I've even thought of chucking it all and going out to PEI to farm. I always meant to, and never really did. Shara left the place in good shape, I could . . . oh, that's crazy. I don't really want to farm. I just want *something new.* Something different. Unmapped territory, something that—Charlie Armstead, what the hell are you grinning about?"

"Sometimes it's purely magical."

"What?"

"Listen. Can you hear them up there?"

"Hear who?"

"I oughta tell Humphrey. There's gonna be reindeer shit all over his roof."

"Charlie!"

"Go ahead, little girl, tug on the whiskers all you want—they're real. Sit right here on my lap and place your order. Ho ho ho. Pick a number from one to two."

She was giggling now; she didn't know why but she was giggling. "Charlie. . . ."

"Pick a number from one to two."

"Two."

"That's a very good number. A very good number. You have just won one perfectly good factory-fresh dream, with all accessories and no warranty at all. This offer is not available through the stores. A very good number. How soon can you leave town?"

"Leave town! Charlie. . . ." She was beginning to get a glimmer. "You can't mean—"

"How would you like a half interest in a lot of vacuum, baby? I got *plenty* o' nuttin', or at least the use of it, and you're welcome to all you want. Talk about being on top of the world!"

The giggle was gone. "Charlie, you can't mean what I think you—"

"I'm offering you a simple partnership in a commune company—a *real* commune company. I mean, we'll all have to live together for the first season at least. *Lots* of real estate, but a bit of a housing shortage at first. We'll spring for expenses, and it's a free fall."

She leaned across the table, put one elbow in her coffee and the other in her apricot pie, grabbed my turtleneck and shook me. "Stop babbling and tell me straight, dammit."

"I am, honey, I am. I'm proposing a company of choreographers, a true commune. It'll have to be. Company members will live together, share equally in the profits, and I'll put up all the expenses just for the hell of it. Oh yeah, we're rich, did I tell you? About to be, anyway."

"Charlie—"

"I'm straight, I tell you. I'm starting a company. And a school. I'm offering you a half interest and a full-time, year-round job, dead serious, and I'll need you to start right away. Norrey, I want you to come dance in free fall."

Her face went blank. "How?"

"I want to build a studio in orbit and form a company. We'll alternate performing with school like so: three months of classes dirtside—essentially auditions—and the graduates get to come study for three months in orbit. Any that are any good, we work into the next three months of performance taping. By then we've been in low or no gee for a long time, our bodies are starting to adapt, so we take three months vacation on Earth and then start the process over again. We can use the vacations to hunt out likely talent and recruit 'em—go concert-hopping, in other words. It'll be *fun*, Norrey. We'll make history and money both."

"*How*, Charlie? How are you going to get the backing for all this? Carrington's dead, and I won't work for his associates. Who else but Skyfac and the Space Command have space capacity?"

"Us."

"?"

"You and me. We *own* the *Stardance* tape, Norrey. I'll show it to you later, I have a dub in my pouch. At this point maybe a hundred people on Earth and a few dozen in space have seen that tape in its entirety. One of them was the president of Sony. He offered me a blank check."

"A blank—"

"Literally. Norrey, the *Stardance* may be the single most magnificent artistic utterance of man—irrespective of its historical importance and news value. I would estimate that within five years every sighted person in the solar system will know it. And we own the only tape. *And*, I own the only existing footage of Shara dancing on Earth, commercial value incalculable. Rich? Hell, *we're powerful*! Skyfac Incorporated is so anxious to come out of this looking good that if I phone up to Ring One and ask Tokugawa for the time, he'll take the next elevator down and give me his watch."

Her hands dropped from my sweater. I wiped apricot from one limp elbow, dried the other.

"I don't feel squeamish about profiting from Shara's death. We made the *Stardance*, together, she and I; I earned my half and she left you hers. The only thing wrong with that is that it leaves me filthy rich, and I don't want to be rich—not on *this* planet. The only way I can think of to piss away that kind of money in a way Shara would have approved is to start a company and a school. We'll specialize in misfits, the ones who for one reason or another don't fit into the mold here on Earth. Like Shara. The less than classically perfect dancer's bodies. That stuff is just irrelevant in space. More important is the ability to open yourself, to learn a whole new kind of dance, to . . . I don't know if this will make any sense . . . to encompass three hundred and sixty degrees. We'll be making the rules as we go along—and we'll employ a lot of dancers that aren't working now. I figure our investment capital is good for about five years. By that time the performing company should be making enough to cover the nut, underwrite the school, and still show a profit. All the company members share equally. Are you in?"

She blinked, sat back, and took a deep breath. "In what? What have you got?"

"Not a damn thing," I said cheerily. "But I know what I need. It'll take us a couple of years to get started at the very least. We'll need a business manager, a stage manager, three or four other dancers who can teach. A construction crew to get started, of course, and an elevator operator, but they're just employees. My cameras run themselves, by Christ, and I'll be my own gaffer. I can do it, Norrey—if you'll help me. Come on—join my company and see the world—from a decent perspective."

"Charlie, I . . . I don't even know if I can *imagine* free fall dance, I mean, I've seen both of Shara's shows several times of course, and I liked them a *lot*—but I still don't know where you could go from there. I can't picture it."

"Of course not! You're still hobbled with 'up' and 'down,' warped by a lifetime in a gravity well. But you'll catch on as soon as you can get up there, believe me." (A year from now my blithe confidence would haunt me.) "You can learn to think spherically, I know you can, the rest is just recoordination, like getting sea legs. Hell, if I can do it at my age, anybody can. You'll make a *good* dancing partner."

She had missed it the first time. Now her eyes enlarged.

"A good what?"

Norrey and I go back a long time, and I'd have to tell you about most of it to explain how I felt just then. Remember when Alistair Sim, as Scrooge, has just awakened from his nightmare and vowed to make amends? And the more nice things he does, and the more people gape at him in bafflement, the more he giggles? And finally he slaps himself in the face and says, "I don't deserve to be this happy," and tries to get properly chastened? And then he giggles again and says, "but I just can't help myself," and breaks up all over again? *That's* how I felt. When a hangup of yours has been a burden to a friend for so many years, and all at once you not only realize that, but know that the burden is lifted, for both of you, there is an exquisite joy in sharing the news.

Remember how Scrooge sprung it on Bob Cratchit, by surprise? ". . . leaving me no alternative—but to raise your salary!" In the same childish way I had saved this, my *real* surprise Santa Claus announcement, for last. I intended to savor the moment.

But then I saw her eyes and I just said it flat out.

"The leg is functional in free fall, Norrey. I've been working out, hard, every day since I got back dirtside. It's a little stiff, and I'll—we'll—always have to choreograph around it to some extent. But it does everything a weightless dancer needs it to. *I can dance again.*"

She closed her eyes, and the lids quivered. "Oh my God." Then she opened them and laughed and cried at once, "Oh my God, Charlie, oh my God, oh my God," and she reached across the table and grabbed my neck and pulled me close and I got apricot and coffee on my own elbows, and oh her tears were hot on my neck.

The place had gotten busy while we talked; no one seemed to notice us. I held her head in the hollow of my throat, and marveled. The only true measure of pain is relief—only in that moment, as layers of scar tissue sloughed off my heart, did I perceive their true weight for the first time.

Finally we were both cried out, and I pulled back and sought her eyes. "I can dance again, Norrey. It was Shara who showed me, I was too damn dumb to notice, too blocked to see it. It was about the last thing she ever did. I can't throw that away now; I've got to dance again, you see? I'm going to go back to space and dance, on my own property and on my own terms and fucking dance again.

"And I want to dance with *you,* Norrey. I want you to be my partner. I want you to come dance with me. Will you come?"

She sat up straight and looked me in the eye. "Do you know what you are asking me?"

Hang on—here we go! I took a deep breath. "Yes. I'm asking for a full partnership."

She sat back in her chair and got a faraway look. "How many years have we known each other, Charlie?"

I had to think. "I make it twenty-four years, off and on."

She smiled. "Yeah. Off and on." She retrieved the forgotten joint and relit it, took a long hit. "How much of that time do you estimate we've spent living together?"

More arithmetic; I toked while I computed. "Call it six or seven years." Exhale. "Maybe eight."

She nodded reflectively and took the joint back. "Some pretty crumby times."

"Norrey—"

"Shut up, Charlie. You waited twenty-four years to propose to me, you can shut up and wait while I give you my answer. How many times would you estimate I came down to the drunk tank and bailed you out?"

I didn't flinch. "Too many."

She shook her head. "One less than too many. I've taken you in when you needed it and thrown you out when you needed it and never once said the word 'love,' because I knew it would scare you away. You were so damned afraid that anyone might love you, because then they'd have to pity you for being a cripple. So I've sat by and watched you give your heart only to people who wouldn't take it—and then picked up the pieces every time."

"Norrey—"

"Shut up," she said. "Smoke this digit and shut up. I've loved you since before you knew me, Charlie, before your leg got chopped up, when you were still dancing. I knew you before you were a cripple. I loved you before I ever saw you offstage. I knew you before you were a lush, and I've loved you all the years since in the way that you wanted me to.

"Now you come before me on two legs. You still limp, but you're not a cripple anymore. Fat Humphrey the telepath doesn't give you wine with your meal, and when I kiss you at the studio I notice you didn't have a drink on the plane. You buy me dinner and you babble about being rich and powerful and you try to sell me some crack-brained scheme for dancing in space, you have the goddam *audacity* to lay all this on me and *never once say the word 'love' with your mouth* and ask me to be your other half again." She snatched the roach out of my hand. "God dammit, Cratchit, you leave me no alternative. . . ."

And she actually paused and toked and held it and exhaled before she let the smile begin.

". . . but to raise your fucking salary."

And we were both holding hands in the apricots and grinning like gibbons. Blood roared in my ears; I literally shuddered with emotion too intense to bear. I groped for a cathartic wisecrack. "Who said I was buying dinner?"

A high, nasal voice from nearby said, "I'm buying, Mr. Armstead."

We looked up, startled to discover that the world still existed around us, and were further startled.

He was a short, slight young man. My first impression was of cascades of ringlets of exceedingly curly black hair, behind which lurked a face like a Brian Froud drawing of a puckish elf. His glasses were twin rectangles of wire and glass, thicker than the glass in airlock doors, and at the moment they were on the end of his nose. He squinted down past them at us, doing his best to look dignified. This was considerably difficult, as Fat Humphrey was holding him a clear foot off the floor, one big sausage-plate fist clutching his collar. His clothes were expensive and in excellent taste, but his boots were splendidly shabby. He was trying, unsuccessfully, not to kick his feet.

"Every time I pass your table I keep steppin' on his ears," Humphrey explained, bringing the little guy closer and lowering his voice. "So I figure him for a snoop or a newsie and I'm just givin' him the bum's rush. But if he's talkin' about buyin', it's your decision."

"How about it, friend? Snoop or newsie?"

Insofar as it was possible, he drew himself up. "I am an artist."

I queried Norrey with my eyes and was answered.

"Set that man down and get him a chair, Fat. We'll discuss the check later."

This was done, and the kid accepted the last of the roach, hitching his tunic into shape and pushing his glasses back up.

"Mr. Armstead, you don't know me, and I don't know this lady here, but I've got these terrific ears and no shame at all. Mr. Pappadopolous is right, I was eavesdropping just great. My name is Raoul Brindle, and—"

"I've heard of you," Norrey said. "I have a few of your albums."

"I do too," I agreed. "The next to the last one was terrific."

"Charlie, that's a terrible thing to say."

Raoul blinked furiously. "No, he's right. The last one was trash. I owed a pound and paid."

"Well, I liked it. I'm Norrey Drummond."

"You're Norrey *Drummond*?"

Norrey got a familiar look. "Yes. Her sister."

"Norrey Drummond of TDT, that choreographed *Shifting Gears* and danced the *Question An Dancer* variations at the Vancouver conference, that—" He stopped, and his glasses slid down his nose. "Ohmigod. Shara Drummond is your *sister*? Ohmigod, of course. Drummond. Drummond, sisters, imbecile." He sat on his excitement and hitched up his glasses and tried to look dignified some more.

For my money he pulled it off. I knew something about Raoul Brindle, and I was impressed. He'd been a child-genius composer, and then in his college days he'd decided music was no way to make a living and became one of the best special effects men in Hollywood. Right after *Time* did a half-page sidebar on his work of *Children of the Lens*—which I mightily admired—he released a video-cassette album composed entirely of extraordinary visuals, laser optics and color effects, with synthesizer accompaniment of his own. It was sort of *Yellow Submarine* cubed, and it had sold like hell and been followed by a half dozen more occasionally brilliant albums. He had designed and programmed the legendary million-dollar lightshow system for the Beatles' reunion as a favor for McCartney, and one of his audio-only tapes followed my deck everywhere it went. I resolved to buy *his* dinner.

"So how do you know me well enough to spot me in a restaurant, Raoul, and why have you been dropping eaves?"

"I didn't spot you here. I followed you here."

"Sonofabitch, I never saw you. Well, what did you follow me for?"

"To offer you my life."

"Eh?"

"I've seen the *Stardance*."

"You *have*?" I exclaimed, genuinely impressed. "How did you pull that off?"

He looked up at the ceiling. "Large weather we're having, isn't it? So I saw the *Stardance* and I made it my business to find you and follow you, and now you're going back to space to dance and I'm going with you. If I have to walk."

"And do what?"

"You said yourself, you're going to need a stage manager. But you haven't thought it through. I'm going to create a new art form for you. I'm going to beat my brains to peanut butter for you. I'm going to design free-fall sets and visuals and do the scores, and they'll both work integrally together and with the dances. I'll work for coffee and cakes, you don't even have to use my music if you don't want to, but I *gotta* design those sets."

Norrey cut him off with a gentle, compassionate hand over his month. "How do you mean, free-fall sets?" She took her hand away.

"It's free fall, don't you understand? I'll design you a sphere of trampolines, with cameras at the joints, and the framework'll be tubes of colored neon. For free-space work I'll give you rings of laser-lit metal flakes, loops of luminous gas, modified fireworks, giant blobs of colored liquid hanging in space to dance around and through—singing Jesus, as a special effects man I've been waiting all my *life* for zero gravity. It—it makes the Dykstraflex obsolete, don't you see?"

He was blinking hard enough to keep the insides of his glasses swept, glancing rapidly back and forth from Norrey to me. I was flabbergasted, and so was she.

"Look, I've got a microcasssette deck here. I'll give it to you, Mister Armstead—"

"Charlie," I corrected absently.

"—and you take it home and listen. It's just a few tracks I cut after I saw the *Stardance*. It's just audio, just first impressions. I mean, it's not even the frame of a score, but I thought it . . . I mean, I thought maybe you'd . . . it's completely shitful, here, take it."

"You're hired," I said.

"Just promise me you'll—hired?"

"Hired. Hey, Fat! You got a VCR in the joint somewhere?"

So we went into the back room where Fat Humphrey Pappadopolous lives, and I fed the *Stardance* tape into his personal television, and the four of us watched it together while Maria ran the restaurant, and when it was over it was half an hour before any of us could speak.

II

So of course there was nothing to do then but go up to Skyfac.

Raoul insisted on paying for his own passage, which startled and pleased me. "How can I ask you to buy a pig in a poke?" he asked reasonably. "For all you know I may be one of those permanently spacesick people."

"I anticipate having at least some gravity in the living units, Raoul. And do you have any *idea* what an elevator costs a civilian?"

"I can afford it," he said simply. "You know that. And I'm no good to you if I have to stay in the house all day. I go on your payroll the day we know I can do the job."

"That's silly," I objected. "I plan to take carloads of student dancers up, with no more warranty than you've got, and they sure as hell won't be paying for their tickets. Why should I discriminate against you for not being poor?"

He shook his head doggedly, his eyeglasses tattooing the sides of his nose. "Because I want it that way. Charity is for those that need it. I've taken a lot of it, and I bless the people who gave it to me when I needed it, but I don't need it any more."

"All right," I agreed. "But after you've proved out, I'm going to rebate you, like it or not."

"Fair enough," he said, and we booked our passage.

Commercial transportation to orbit is handled by Space Industries Corp., a Skyfac subsidiary, and I have to congratulate them on one of the finest natural puns I've ever seen. When we located the proper gate at the spaceport, after hours of indignity at Customs and Medical, I was feeling salty. I still hadn't fully readapted after the time I'd spent in free fall with Shara, and the most I could pry out of the corporation medicos was three months—my "pull" with the top brass meant nothing to the Flight Surgeon in charge. I was busy fretting that it wasn't enough time and tightening my guts in anticipation of takeoff when I rounded the last corner and confronted the sign that told me I was in the right place.

It said:

S.I.C. TRANSIT
(gloria mundi)

I laughed so hard that Norrey and Raoul had to help me aboard and strap me in, and I was still chuckling when acceleration hit us.

Sure enough, Raoul got spacesick as soon as the drive cut off—but he'd been sensible enough to skip breakfast, and he responded rapidly to the injection. That banty little guy had plenty of sand: by the time we were docked at Ring One he was trying out riffs on his Soundmaster. White as a piece of paper and completely oblivious, eyes glued to the outboard video, fingers glued to the Soundmaster's keyboard, ears glued to its earplugs. If elevator-belly ever troubled him again, he kept it to himself.

Norrey had no trouble at all. Neither did I. Our appointment with the brass had been set for an hour hence, just in case, so we stashed Raoul in the room assigned to him and spent the time in the Lounge, watching the stars wheel by on the big video wall. It was not crowded; the tourist trade had fallen off sharply when the aliens came, and never recovered. The New Frontier was less attractive with New Indians lurking in it somewhere.

My attempts to play seasoned old spacehound to Norrey's breathless tourist were laughably unsuccessful. No one *ever* gets jaded to space, and I took deep satisfaction in being the one who introduced Norrey to it. But if I couldn't pull off nonchalance, at least I could be pragmatic.

"Oh, Charlie! How soon can we go outside?"

"Probably not today, hon."

"Why *not*?"

"Too much to do first. We've got to insult Tokugawa, talk to Harry Stein, talk to Tom McGillicuddy, and when all that's done you're going to take your first class in EVA 101—indoors."

"Charlie, you've taught me all that stuff already."

"Sure. I'm an old spacehound, with all of six months experience. You dope, you've never even touched a real p-suit."

"Oh, welfare checks! I've memorized every word you've told me. I'm not scared."

"There in a nutshell is why I refuse to go EVA with you."

She made a face and ordered coffee from the arm of her chair.

"Norrey. Listen to me. You are not talking about putting on a raincoat and going to stand next to Niagara Falls. About six inches beyond that wall there is the most hostile environment presently available to a human. The technology which makes it possible for you to live there at all is not as old as you are. I'm not going to let you within ten meters of an airlock until I'm convinced that you're scared silly."

She refused to meet my eyes. "Dammit, Charlie, I'm not a child and I'm not an idiot."

"Then stop acting like both." She jumped at the volume and looked at me. "Or is there any other kind of person who believes you can acquire a new set of reflexes by being told about them?"

It might have escalated into a full-scale quarrel, but the waiter picked that moment to arrive with Norrey's coffee. The Lounge staff like to show off for the tourists; it increases the tip. Our waiter decided to come to our table the same way George Reeves used to leap tall buildings, and we were a good fifteen meters from the kitchen. Unfortunately, after he had left the deck, committing himself, a gaunt tourist decided to change seats without looking, and plotted herself an intersecting course. The waiter never flinched. He extended his left arm sideways, deploying the drogue (which looks just like the webbing that runs from Spiderman's elbow to his ribs); tacked around her; brought his hand to his chest to collapse the drogue; transferred the coffee to that hand; extended the other arm and came back on course; all in much less time than it has taken you to read about it. The tourist squawked and tumbled as he went by, landing on her rump and bouncing and skidding a goodly distance thereon; the waiter grounded expertly beside Norrey, gravely handed her a cup containing every drop of coffee he had started out with, and took off again to see to the tourist.

"The coffee's fresh," I said as Norrey goggled. "The waiter just grounded."

It's one of the oldest gags on Skyfac, and it always works. Norrey whooped and nearly spilled hot coffee on her hand—only the low gee gave her time to recover. That cut her laughter short; she stared at the coffee cup, and then at the waiter, who was courteously pointing out one of the half dozen *LOOK BEFORE YOU LEAP* signs to the outraged tourist.

"Charlie?"

"Yeah."

"How many classes will I need before I'm ready?"

I smiled and took her hand. "Not as many as I thought."

The meeting with Tokugawa, the new chairman of the board, was low comedy. He received us personally in what had been Carrington's office, and the overall effect was of a country bishop on the Pope's throne. Or perhaps "tuna impersonating a piranha" is closer to the image I want. In the vicious power struggle which followed Carrington's death, he had been the only candidate ineffectual enough to satisfy everyone. Tom McGillicuddy was with him, to my delight, the cast already gone from his ankle. He was growing a beard.

"Hi, Tom. How's the foot?"

His smile was warm and familiar. "Hello, Charlie. It's good to see you again. The foot's okay—bones knit faster in low gee."

I introduced Norrey to him, and to Tokugawa as an afterthought. The most powerful man in space was short, gray, and scrutable. In deference to the custom of the day he wore traditional Japanese dress, but I was willing to bet that his English was better than his Japanese. He started when I lit up a joint, and Tom had to show him how to turn up the breeze and deploy the smoke filter. Norrey's body language said she didn't like him, and I trust her barometer even more than my own; she lacks my cynicism. I cut him off in the middle of a speech about Shara and the *Stardance* that must have used up four ghostwriters.

"The answer is 'no.'"

He looked as though he had never heard the expression before. "—I—"

"Listen, Toke old boy, I read the papers. You and Skyfac Inc. and Lunindustries Inc. want to become our patrons. You're inviting us to move right in and start dancing, offering to underwrite the whole bloody venture. And none of this has anything to do with the fact that antitrust legislation was filed against you this week, right?"

"Mister Armstead, I'm merely expressing my gratitude that you and Shara Drummond chose to bring your high art to Skyfac in the first place, and my fervent hope that you and her sister will continue to feel free to make use of—"

"Where I come from we use that stuff for methane power." I took a lingering drag while he sputtered. "You know damn well how Shara came to Skyfac, and you sit in the chair of the man who killed her. He killed her by making her spend so many of her offstage hours in low or no gee, because that was the only way he could get it up. You ought to be bright enough to know that the day Norrey or I or any member of our company dances a step on Skyfac property, a red man with horns, a tail, and a pitchfork is going to come up to you and admit that it just froze over." The joint was beginning to hit me. "As far as I'm concerned, Christmas came this year on the day that Carrington went out for a walk and forgot to come back, and I will be gone to hell before I'll live under his roof again, or make money for his heirs and assigns. Do we understand each other?" Norrey was holding my hand tightly, and when I glanced over she was grinning at me.

Tokugawa sighed and gave up. "McGillicuddy, give them the contract."

Pokerfaced, Tom produced a stiff folded parchment and passed it to us. I scanned it, and my eyebrows rose. "Tom," I said blandly, "is this honest?"

He never even glanced at his boss. "Yep."

"Not even a percentage of the gross? Oh my." I looked at Tokugawa. "A free lunch. It must be my good looks." I tore the contract in half.

"Mister Armstead," he began hotly, and I was glad that Norrey interrupted him this time. I was getting to like it too much.

"Mr. Tokugawa, if you'll stop trying to convince us that you're a patron of the arts, I think we can get along. We'll let you donate some technical advice and assistance, and we'll let you sell us materials and air and water at cost. We'll even give back some of the skilled labor we hire away from you when we're done with them. Not you, Tom—

we want you to be our full-time business manager, if you're willing."

He didn't hesitate a second, and his grin was beautiful. "Ms. Drummond, I accept."

"Norrey. Furthermore," she went on to Tokugawa, "we'll make a point of telling everybody we know how nice you've been, any time the subject comes up. But we are going to own and operate our own studio, and it may suit us to put it on the far side of Terra, and we will be *independents*. Not Skyfac's in-house dance troupe: independents. Eventually we hope to see Skyfac itself settle into the role of the benevolent old rich uncle who lives up the road. But we don't expect to need you for longer than you need us, so there will be no contract. Have we a meeting of the minds?"

I nearly applauded out loud. I'm pretty sure he'd never had a personal executive secretary hired right out from under his nose before. His grandfather might have committed seppuku; he in his phony kimono must have been seething. But Norrey had played things just right, grudgingly offering him equals-status if he cared to claim it—and he *needed* us.

Perhaps you don't understand just how badly he needed us. Skyfac was the first new multinational in years, and it had immediately begun hurting the others where they lived. Not only could it undersell any industry requiring vacuum, strain-free environment, controlled radiation, or wide-range temperature or energy density gradients—and quite a few profitable industries do—but it could also sell things that simply could not be made on Earth, even expensively. Things like *perfect* bearings, *perfect* lenses, strange new crystals—none of which will form in a gravity well. All the raw materials came from space, unlimited free solar energy powered the factories, and delivery was cheap (a delivery module doesn't have to be a spaceship; all it has to do is fall correctly).

It wasn't long before the various nationals and multinationals who had not been invited into the original Skyfac consortium began to feel the pinch. The week before, antitrust actions had been filed in the US, USSR, China, France, and Canada, and protests had been lodged in the United Nations, the first steps in what would turn out to be the legal battle of the century. Skyfac's single most precious asset was its monopoly of space—Tokugawa was running scared enough to need any good press he could get.

And the week before *that,* the tape of the *Stardance* had been released. The first shock wave was still running around the world; we were the best press Tokugawa was ever likely to get.

"You'll cooperate with our PR people?" was all he asked.

"As long as you don't try to quote me as 'heartbroken' by Carrington's death," I said agreeably. I really had to hand it to him: he almost smiled then.

"How about 'saddened'?" he suggested delicately.

We settled on "shocked."

We left Tom in our cabin with four full briefcases of paperwork to sort out, and went to see Harry Stein.

We found him where I expected to, in a secluded corner of the metals shop, behind a desk with stacks of pamphlets, journals and papers that would have been improbable in a full gee. He and a Tensor lamp were hunched over an incredibly ancient typewriter. One massive roll fed clean paper into it, another took up the copy. I noted with approval that the manuscript's radius was two or three centimeters thicker than when last I'd seen it. "Say hey, Harry. Finishing up chapter one?"

He looked up, blinked. "Hey, Charlie. Good to see you." For him it was an emotional greeting. "You must be her sister."

Norrey nodded gravely. "Hi, Harry. I'm glad to meet you. I hear those candles in *Liberation* were your idea."

Harry shrugged. "She was okay."

"Yes," Norrey agreed. Unconsciously, instinctively, she was taking on his economical word usage—as Shara had before her.

"I," I said, "will drink to that proposition."

Harry eyed the thermos on my belt, and raised an eyebrow in query.

"Not booze," I assured him, unclipping it. "On the wagon. Jamaican Blue Mountain coffee, fresh from Japan. Real cream. Brought it for you." Damn it, I was doing it too.

Harry actually smiled. He produced three mugs from a nearby coffeemaker unit (personally adapted for low gee), and held them while I poured. The aroma diffused easily in low gee; it was exquisite. "To Shara Drummond," Harry said, and we drank together. Then we shared a minute of warm silence.

Harry was a fifty-year-old ex-fullback who had kept himself in shape. He was so massive and formidably packed that you could have known him a long time without ever suspecting his intelligence, let alone his genius—unless you had happened to watch him work. He spoke mostly with his hands. He hated writing, but put in two methodical hours a day on The Book. By the time I asked him why, he trusted me enough to answer. "Somebody's gotta write a book on space construction," he said. Certainly no one could have been better qualified. Harry literally made the first weld on Skyfac, and had bossed virtually all construction since. There was another guy who had as much experience, once, but he died (his "suit sold out," as the spacemen say: lost its integrity). Harry's writing was astonishingly lucid for such a phlegmatic man (perhaps because he did it with his fingers), and I knew even then that The Book was going to make him rich. It didn't worry me; Harry will never get rich enough to retire.

"Got a job for you, Harry, if you want it."

He shook his head. "I'm happy here."

"It's a space job."

He damned near smiled again. "I'm unhappy here."

"All right, I'll tell you about it. My guess is a year of design work, three or four years of heavy construction, and then a kind of permanent maintenance job keeping the whole thing running for us."

"What?" he asked economically.

"I want an orbiting dance studio."

He held up a hand the size of a baseball glove, cutting me off. He took a minicorder out of his shirt, set the mike for "ambient" and put it on the desk between us. "What do you want it to *do*?"

Five and a half hours later all three of us were hoarse, and an hour after that Harry handed us a set of sketches. I looked them over with Norrey, we approved his budget, and he told us a year. We all shook hands.

Ten months later I took title.

We spent the next three weeks in and around Skyfac property, while I introduced Norrey and Raoul to life without up and down. Space overawed them both at first. Norrey, like her sister before her, was profoundly moved by the personal confrontation with infinity, spiritually traumatized by the awesome perspective that the Big Deep brings to human values. And unlike her sister before her, she lacked that mysteriously total self-confidence, that secure ego-strength that had helped Shara to adjust so quickly. Few humans have ever been as sure of themselves as Shara was. Raoul, too, was only slightly less affected.

We all get it at first, we who venture out into space. From the earliest days, the most unimaginative and stolid jocks NASA could assemble for astronauts frequently came back down spiritually and emotionally staggered, and some adapted and some didn't. The ten percent of Skyfac personnel who spend much time EVA, who have any way of knowing they're not in Waukegan besides the low gee, often have to be replaced, and no worker is depended on until his or her second tour. Norrey and Raoul both came through it—they were able to expand their personal universe to encompass that much external universe, and came out of the experience (as Shara and I had) with a new and lasting inner calm.

The spiritual confrontation, however, was only the first step. The major victory was much subtler. It was more than just spiritual malaise that washed out seven out of ten exterior construction workers in their first tour: It was also physiological—or was it psychological?—distress.

Free fall itself they both took to nearly at once. Norrey was much quicker than Raoul to adapt—as a dancer, she knew more about her reflexes, and he was more prone to forget himself and blunder into impossible situations, which he endured with dogged good humor. But both were proficient at "jaunting," propelling oneself through an enclosed space, by the time we were ready to return to Earth. (I myself was pleasantly astonished at how fast unused dance skills came back to me.)

The real miracle was their equally rapid acclimation to sustained EVA, to extended periods outdoors in free space. Given enough time, nearly anyone can acquire new reflexes. But startlingly few can learn to live without a local vertical.

I was so ignorant at that time that I hadn't the slightest *idea* what an incredible stroke of good fortune it was that both Norrey and Raoul could. No wonder the gods smile so seldom—we so often fail to notice. Not until the next year did I realize how narrowly my whole venture—my whole life—had escaped disaster. When it finally dawned on me, I had the shakes for days.

That kind of luck held for the next year.

* * *

The first year was spent in getting the ball rolling. Endless millions of aggravations and petty details—have you ever tried to order dancing shoes for *hands*? With velcro palms? So few of the things we needed could be ordered from the Johnny Brown catalog, or put together out of stock space-hardware. Incredible amounts of imaginary dollars flowed through my and Norrey's right hands, and but for Tom McGillicuddy the thing simply would not have been possible. He took care of incorporating both the Shara Drummond School of New Modern Dance and the performing company, Stardancers, Inc., and became business manager of the former and agent for the latter. A highly intelligent and thoroughly honorable man, he had entered Carrington's service with his eyes—and his ears—wide open. When we waved him like a wand, magic resulted. How many honest men understand high finance?

The second indispensable wizard was, of course, Harry. And bear in mind that during five of those ten months, Harry was on mandatory dirtside leave, readapting his body and bossing the job by extreme long distance phone (God, I hated having phones installed—but the phone company's rates were fractionally cheaper than buying our own orbit-to-Earth video equipment, and of course it tied the Studio into the global net). Unlike the majority of Skyfac personnel, who rotate dirtside every fourteen months, construction men (those who make it) spend so much time in total weightlessness that six months is the recommended maximum. I figured us Stardancers for the same shift, and Doc Panzella agreed. But the first month and the last four were under Harry's direct supervision, and he actually turned it in under budget—doubly impressive considering that much of what he was doing had never been done before. He would have beat his original deadline; it wasn't his fault that we had to move it up on him.

Best of all, Harry turned out (as I'd hoped) to be one of those rare bosses who would rather be working with his hands than bossing. When the job was done he took a month off to collate the first ten inches of copy on his takeup reel into The First Book, sold it for a record-breaking advance and Santa Claus royalties, and then hired back on with us as set-builder, prop man, stage manager, all-around maintenance man, and resident mechanic. Tokugawa's boys had made astonishingly little fuss when we hired Harry away from them. They simply did not know what they were missing—until it was *months* too late to do anything about it.

We were able to raid Skyfac so effectively only because it was what it was: a giant, heartless multinational that saw people as interchangeable components. Carrington probably knew better—but the backers he had gotten together and convinced to underwrite his dream knew even less about space than I had as a video man in Toronto. I'm certain they thought of it, most of them, as merely an extemely foreign investment.

I needed all the help I could get. I needed that entire year—and more!—to overhaul and retune an instrument that had not been used in a quarter of a century: my dancer's body. With Norrey's support, I managed, but it wasn't easy.

In retrospect, all of the above strokes of luck were utterly necessary for the Shara Drummond School of New Modern Dance to have become a reality in the first place. After so many interlocking miracles, I guess I should have been expecting a run of bad cards. But it sure didn't *look* like one when it came.

For we truly did have dancers coming out of our ears when we finally opened up shop. I had expected to need good PR to stimulate a demand for the expensive commodity, for although we absorbed the bulk of student expenses (we *had* to—how many could afford the hundred-dollar-a-kilo elevator fee alone?) we kept it expensive enough to weed out the casually curious—with a secret scholarship program for deserving needy.

Even at those prices, I had to step lively to avoid being trampled in the stampede.

The cumulative effect of Shara's three tapes on the dance consciousness of the world had been profound and revolutionary. They came at a time when Modern dance as a whole was in the midst of an almost decade-long stasis, a period in which everyone seemed to be doing variations of the already-done, in which dozens of choreographers had beat their brains out trying to create the next New Wave breakthrough, and produced mostly gibberish. Shara's three tapes, spaced as she had intuitively sensed they must be, had succeeded in capturing the imagination of an immense number of dancers and dance lovers the world over—as well as millions of people who had never given dance a thought before.

Dancers began to understand that free fall meant free dance, free from a lifetime in thrall to gravity. Norrey and I, in our naivete, had failed to be secretive enough about our plans. The day after we signed the lease on our dirtside studio in Toronto, students began literally arriving at our door in carloads and refusing to leave—much before we were ready for them. We hadn't even figured out how to audition a zero-gee dancer on Earth yet. (Ultimately it proved quite simple: Dancers who survived an elimination process based on conventional dance skills were put on a plane, taken up to angels thirty, dumped out, and filmed on the way down. It's not the *same* as free fall—but it's close enough to weed out gross unsuitables.)

We were sleeping 'em like torpedomen at the dirtside school, feeding them in shifts, and I began having panicky second thoughts about calling up to Harry and putting off our deadline so he could triple the Studio's living quarters. But Norrey convinced me to be ruthlessly selective and take *ONLY* the most promising ten—out of hundreds—into orbit.

Thank God—we damned near lost three of those pigeons in two separate incidents, and we conclusively washed out nine. That run of bad cards I mentioned earlier.

Most often it came down to a failure to adapt, an inability to evolve the consciousness beyond dependence on up and down (the one factor skydiving *can't* simulate: a skydiver *knows* which way is down). It doesn't help to tell yourself that north of your head is "up" and south of your feet is "down"—from that perspective the whole universe is in endless motion (you're hardly ever motionless in free fall), a perception most brains simply reject. Such a dancer would persistently "lose his point," his imaginary horizon, and become hopelessly disoriented. Side effects included mild to extreme terror, dizziness, nausea, erratic pulse and blood pressure, the grand-daddy of all headaches and involuntary bowel movement.

(Which last is uncomfortable and embarrassing. P-suit plumbing makes country outhouses look good. Men have the classic "relief tube," of course, but for women and for defecation in either sex we rely on a strategic deployment of specially treated . . . oh, hell, we wear a diaper and try to hold it until we get indoors. End of first inevitable digression.)

Even in inside work, in the Goldfish Bowl or Raoul's collapsible trampoline sphere, such dancers could not learn to overcome their perceptual distress. Having spent their whole professional lives battling gravity with every move they made, they found that they were lost without their old antagonist—or at least without the linear, right-angled perceptual set that is provided: we found that some of them could actually learn to acclimate to weightlessness inside a cube or rectangle, as long as they were allowed to think of one wall as the "ceiling" and its opposite as the "floor."

And in the one or two cases where their vision was adequate to the new environment, their bodies, their instruments, were not. The new reflexes just failed to jell.

They simply were not meant, any of them, to live in space. In most cases they left friends—but they all left.

All but one.

Linda Parsons was the tenth student, the one that didn't wash out, and finding her was good fortune enough to make up for the run of bad cards.

She was smaller than Norrey, almost as taciturn as Harry (but for different reasons), much calmer than Raoul, and more open-hearted and giving than I will be if I live to be a thousand. In the villainous overcrowding of that first free-fall semester, amid flaring tempers and sullen rages, she was the *only* universally loved person—I honestly doubt whether we could have survived without her (I remember with some dismay that I seriously contemplated spacing a pimply young student whose only crime was a habit of saying, "There you go" at every single pause in the conversation. *There he goes,* I kept thinking to myself, *there he goes. . .*).

Some women can turn a room into an emotional maelstrom, simply by entering it, and this quality is called "provocative." So far as I know, our language has no word for the opposite of provocative, but that is what Linda was. She had a talent for getting people high together, without drugs, a knack for resolving irreconcilable differences, a way of brightening the room she was in.

She had been raised on a farm by a spiritual community in Nova Scotia, and that probably accounted for her empathy, responsibility, and intuitive understanding of group-energy dynamics. But I think the single over-riding quality that made her magic work was inborn:

she genuinely loved people. It could not have been learned behavior; it was just too clearly intrinsic in her.

I don't mean that she was a Pollyanna, nauseatingly cheerful and syrupy. She could be blistering if she caught you trying to call irresponsibility something else. She insisted that a high truth level be maintained in her presence, and she would not allow you the luxury of a hidden grudge, what she called "holding a stash on someone." If she caught you with such psychic dirty laundry, she would haul it right out in public and force you to clean it up. "Tact?" she said to me once. "I always understood that to mean a mutual agreement to be full of shit."

These attributes are typical of a commune child, and usually get them heartily disliked in so-called polite society—founded, as it is, on irresponsibility, untruth, and selfishness. But again, something innate in Linda made them work for her. She could call you a jerk to your face without triggering reflex anger; she could tell you publicly that you were lying without calling you a liar. She plainly knew how to hate the sin and forgive the sinner; and I admire that, for it is a knack I never had. There was never any mistaking or denying the genuine caring in her voice, even when it was puncturing one of your favorite bubbles of rationalization.

At least, that's what Norrey or I would have said. Tom, when he met her, had a different opinion.

"Look, Charlie, there's Tom."

I should have been fuming mad when I got out of Customs. I felt a little uneasy *not* being fuming mad. But after six months of extraterrestrial cabin fever, I was finding it curiously difficult to dislike *any* stranger—even a Customs man.

Besides, I was too *heavy* to be angry.

"So it is. Tom! Hey, Tom!"

"Oh my," Norrey said, "something's wrong."

Tom was fuming mad.

"Hell. What put the sand in his shorts? Hey, where're Linda and Raoul? Maybe there's a hassle?"

"No, they got through before we did. They must have taken a cab to the hotel already—"

Tom was upon us, eyes flashing. "So that's your paragon? Jesus

Christ! Fucking bleeding heart, I'll wring her scrawny neck. Of all the—"

"Whoa! Who? Linda? What?"

"Oh Christ, later—here they come." What looked like a vigilante committee was converging on us, bearing torches. "Now look," Tom said hurriedly through his teeth, smiling as though he'd just been guaranteed an apartment in Paradise, "give these bloodsuckers your best I mean your best shot, and *maybe* I can scavenge something from this stinking mess." And he was striding toward them, opening his arms and smiling. As he went I heard him mutter something under his breath that began with "Ms. Parsons," contained enough additional sibilants to foil the shotgun-mikes, and moved his lips not at all.

Norrey and I exchanged a glance. "Pohl's Law," she said, and I nodded (Pohl's Law, Raoul once told us, says that nothing is so good that somebody somewhere won't hate it, and vice versa). And then the pack was upon us.

"This way Mister when does your next tape come over here please tell our viewers what it's really believe that this this new artform is a valid passport or did you look this way Ms. Drummond is it true that you haven't been able to smile for the cameraman for the *Stardance*, weren't you going to look this way to please continue or are readers would simply love to no but didn't you miss Drummond pardon me Miz Drummond do you think you're as good as your sister Sharon in the profits in their own country are without honor to welcome you back to Earth *this* way please," said the mob, over the sound of clicking, whirring, snapping, and whining machinery and through the blinding glare of what looked like an explosion at the galactic core seen from close up. And I smiled and nodded and said urbanely witty things and answered the rudest questions with good humor and by the time we could get a cab I *was* fuming mad. Raoul and Linda had indeed gone ahead, and Tom had found our luggage; we left at high speed.

"Bleeding Christ, Tom," I said as the cab pulled away, "next time schedule a press conference for the next day, will you?"

"God damn it," he blazed, "you can have this job back any time you want it!"

His volume startled even the cabbie. Norrey grabbed his hands and forced him to look at her.

"Tom," she said gently, "we're your friends. We don't want to yell at you; we don't want you to yell at us. Okay?"

He took an extra deep breath, held it, let it out in one great sigh and nodded. "Okay."

"Now I know that reporters can be hard to deal with. I understand that, Tom. But I'm tired and hungry and my feet hurt like hell and my body's convinced it weighs three hundred and thirteen kilos and next time could we maybe just lie to them a little?"

He paused before replying, and his voice came out calm. "Norrey, I am really not an idiot. All that madness to the contrary, I *did* schedule a press conference for tomorrow, and I *did* tell everybody to have a heart and leave you alone today. Those jerks back there were the ones who ignored me, the sons of—"

"Wait a minute," I interrupted. "Then why the hell did we give *them* a command performance?"

"Do you think I wanted to?" Tom growled. "What the hell am I going to say tomorrow to the honorable ones who got scooped? But I had no *choice*, Charlie. That dizzy bitch left me no choice. I had to give those crumbs *some*thing, or they'd have run what they had already."

"Tom, what on earth are you talking about?"

"Linda Parsons, that's what I'm talking about, your new wonder discovery. Christ, Norrey, the way you went on about her over the phone, I was expecting . . . I don't know, anyway a professional."

"You two, uh, didn't hit it off?" I suggested.

Tom snorted. "First she calls me a tight-ass. Practically the first words out of her mouth. Then she says I'm ignorant, and I'm not treating her right. Treating her right, for Christ's sake. Then she chewes me out for having reporters there—Charlie, I'll take that from you and Norrey, I *should've* had those jerks thrown out, but I don't have to take that crap from a rookie. So I start to explain about the reporters, and *then* she says I'm being defensive. Christ on the pogie, if there's anything I hate it's somebody that comes on aggressive and then says you're being defensive, smiling and looking you right in the eye and trying to rub my fucking *neck*!"

I figured he'd let off enough steam by now, and I was losing count of the grains of salt. "So Norrey and I made nice for the newsies because they taped you two squabbling in public?"

"No!"

We got the story out of him eventually. It was the old Linda magic at work again, and I can offer you no more typical example. Somehow a seventeen-year-old girl had threaded her way through the hundreds of people in the spaceport terminal straight to Linda and collapsed in her arms, sobbing that she was tripping and losing control and would Linda please make it all *stop*? It was at that point that the mob of reporters had spotted Linda as a Stardancer and closed in. Even considering that she weighed six times normal, had just been poked full of holes by Medical and insulted by Immigration, and was striking large sparks off of Tom, I'm inclined to doubt that Linda lost her temper; I think she abandoned it. Whatever, she apparently scorched a large hole through that pack of ghouls, bundled the poor girl into it and got her a cab. While they were getting in, some clown stuck a camera in the girl's face and Linda decked him.

"Hell, Tom, I might have done the same thing myself," I said when I got it straight.

"God's teeth, Charlie!" he began; then with a superhuman effort he got control of his voice (at least). "Look. Listen. This is not some four-bit kids' game we are playing here. Megabucks pass through my fingers, Charlie, megabucks! You are not a bum any more, you don't have the privileges of a bum. Do you—"

"Tom," Norrey said, shocked.

"—have any *idea* how fickle the public has become in the last twenty years? Maybe I've got to tell you how much public opinion has to do with the *existence* of that orbiting junkheap you just left? Or maybe you're going to tell me that those tapes in your suitcase are as good as the *Stardance*, that you've got something so hot you can beat up reporters and get away with it. Oh *Jesus*, what a mess!"

He had me there. All the choreography plans we had brought into orbit with us had been based on the assumption that we would have between eight and twelve dancers. We had thought we were being pessimistic. We had to junk everything and start from scratch. The resulting tapes relied heavily on solos—our weakest area at that point—and while I was confident that I could do a lot with editing, well. . . .

"It's okay, Tom. Those bums got something their editors'll like better than a five-foot lady making gorillas look like gorillas—they worry a little about public opinion, too."

"And what do I tell Westbrook tomorrow? And Mortie and Barbara Frum and UPI and AP and—"

"Tom," Norrey interrupted gently, "it'll be all right."

"All right? How it is all right? Tell me how it's all right."

I saw where she was going. "Hell, yeah. I never thought of that, hon, of *course*. That pack o'jackals drove it clean out of my mind. Serves 'em right." I began to chuckle. "Serves 'em bloody right."

"If you don't mind, darling."

"Huh? Oh. No . . . no, I don't mind." I grinned. "It's been long enough coming. Let's do it up."

"Will somebody *please* tell me what the hell is—"

"Tom," I said expansively, "don't worry about a thing. I'll tell your scooped friends the same thing I told my father at the age of thirteen, when he caught me in the cellar with the mailman's daughter."

"What the hell is that?" he snapped, beginning to grin in spite of himself and unsure why.

I put an arm around Norrey. "It's okay, Pa. We're gettin' married tomorrow.'"

He stared at us blankly for several seconds, the grin fading, and then it returned full force.

"Well I'll be dipped in shit," he cried. "Congratulations! That's terrific, Charlie, Norrey, oh congratulations you two—it's about time." He tried to hug us both, but at that moment the cabbie had to dodge a psychopath and Tom was flung backwards, arms outstretched. "That's tremendous, that's . . . you know, I think that'll do it—I think it'll work." He had the grace to blush. "I mean, the hell with the reporters, I just—I mean—"

"You may always," Norrey said gravely, "leave these little things to us."

The desk phoned me when Linda checked in, as I had asked them to. I grunted, hung the phone up on thin air, stepped out of bed and into a hotel wastebasket, cannoned into the bedside table destroying table and accompanying lamp, and ended up prone on the floor with my chin sunk deep into the pile rug and my nose a couple of centimeters from a glowing clockface that said it was 4:42. In the morning. At the moment that I came completely awake, the clock expired and its glow went out.

Now it was *pitch* dark.

Incredibly, Norery still had not awakened. I got up, dressed in the dark, and left, leaving the wreckage for the morning. Fortunately the good leg had sustained most of the damage; I could walk, albeit with a kind of double limp.

"Linda? It's me, Charlie."

She opened up at once. "Charlie, I'm sorry—"

"Skip it. You done good. How's the girl?" I stepped in.

She closed the door behind me and made a face. "Not terrific. But her people are with her now. I think she's going to be okay."

"That's good. I remember the first time a trip went sour on me."

She nodded. "You know it's going to stop in eight hours, but that doesn't help; your time rate's gone eternal."

"Yeah. Look, about Tom—"

She made another face. "Boy, Charlie, what a jerk."

"You two, uh, didn't hit it off?"

"I just tried to tell him that he was being too uptight, and he came on like he couldn't imagine what I was talking about. So I told him he wasn't as ignorant as he gave himself credit for, and asked him to treat me like a friend instead of a stranger—from all you told me about him, that seemed right. 'Okay,' he says, so I ask him as a friend to try and keep those reporters off of us for a day or so and he blows right up at me. He was so defensive, Charlie."

"Look, Linda," I began, "there was this screwup that—"

"Honestly, Charlie, I tried to calm him down, I tried to show him I wasn't *blaming* him. I—I was rubbing his neck and shoulders, trying to loosen him up, and he, he pushed me away. I mean, really, Charlie, you and Norrey said he was so nice and what a creep."

"Linda, I'm sorry you didn't get along. Tom *is* a nice guy, it's just—"

"I think he wanted me to just tell Sandra to get lost, just let Security take her away and—"

I gave up. "I'll see you in the mor . . . in the afternoon, Linda. Get some sleep; there's a press conference in the Something-or-other Room at two."

"Sure. I'm sorry, it must be late, huh?"

I met Raoul in the corridor—the desk had called him right after me, but he woke up slower. I told him that Linda and patient were doing as well as could be expected, and he was relieved. "Cripes, Charlie, her and Tom, you shoulda seen 'em. Cats and dogs, I never would have believed it."

"Yeah, well, sometimes your best friends just can't stand each other."

"Yeah, life's funny that way."

On that profundity I went back to bed. Norrey was still out cold when I entered, but as I climbed under the covers and snuggled up against her back she snorted like a horse and said, "Awright?"

"All right," I whispered, "but I think we're going to have to keep those two separated for a while."

She rolled over, opened one eye and found me with it. "Darl'n," she mumbled, smiling with that side of her mouth, "there's hope for you yet."

And then she rolled over and went back to sleep, leaving me smug and fatuous and wondering what the hell she was talking about.

III

Those first-semester tapes sold like hell anyway, and the critics were more than kind, for the most part. Also, we rereleased *Mass Is A Verb* with Raoul's soundtrack at that time, and finished our first fiscal year well in the black.

By the second year our Studio was taking shape.

We settled on a highly elongated orbit. At perigee the Studio came as close as 3200 kilometers to Earth (not very close—Skylab was up less than 450 klicks), and at apogee it swung way out to about 80,000 klicks. The point of this was to keep Earth from hogging half the sky in every tape; at apogee Terra was about fist-sized (subtending a little more than 9° of arc), and we spent most of our time far away from it (Kepler's Second Law: the closer a satellite to its primary, the faster it swings around). Since we made a complete orbit almost twice a day, that gave two possible taping periods of almost eight hours apiece in every twenty-four hours. We simply adjusted our "inner clocks," our biological cycle, so that one of these two periods came between "nine" and "five" subjective. (If we fudged a shot, we had to come back and reshoot some multiple of eleven hours later to get a background Earth of the proper apparent size.)

As to the Studio complex itself:

The largest single structure, of course, is the Fish-bowl, an enormous sphere for inside work, without p-suits. It is effectively transparent when correctly lit, but can be fitted with opaque foil surfaces in case you don't *want* the whole universe for a backdrop. Six very small and very good camera mounts are built into it at various places, and it is fitted to accept plastic panels which convert it into a cube within a sphere, although we only used them a few times and probably won't again.

Next largest is the informal structure we came to call Fibber McGee's Closet. The Closet itself is only a long "stationary" pole studded with stanchions and line-dispensing reels, but it is always covered with junk, tethered to it for safekeeping. Props, pieces of sets, camera units and spare parts, lighting paraphernalia, control consoles and auxiliary systems, canisters and cans and boxes and slabs and bundles and clusters and loops and coils and assorted disorderly packages of whatever anyone thought it might be handy to have for free fall dance and the taping thereof, all cling to Fibber McGee's Closet like interplanetary barnacles. The size and shape of the ungainly mass change with use, and the individual components shift lazily back and forth like schizophrenic seaweed at all times.

We had to do it that way, for it is not at all convenient to reenter and exit the living quarters frequently.

Imagine a sledgehammer. A big old roustabout's stake pounder, with a large, barrel-shaped head. Imagine a much smaller head, coke-can size, at the butt end of the handle. That's my house. That's where I live with my wife when I'm at home in space, in a three-and-a-half room walkdown with bath. Try to balance that sledgehammer horizontally across one finger. You'll want to lay that finger right up near the *other* end, just short of the much massier hammerhead. That's the point around which my house pivots, and the countermass pivots, in chasing concentric circles, to provide a net effect of one-sixth gee at home. The countermass includes life-support equipment and supplies, power supply, medical telemetry, home computer and phone hardware, and some damn big gyros. The "hammer handle" is quite long: it takes a shaft of about 135 meters to give one-sixth gee at a rotation rate of one minute. That slow a rate makes the Coriolis differential minimal, as imperceptible as it is on a torus the size of Skyfac's Ring One but without a torus's vast cubic and inherently inefficient layout (Skyfac axiom: anywhere you want to go will turn out to be all the way round the bend; as, in short order, will you).

Since only a Tokugawa can afford the energies required to start and stop spinning masses in space on a whim, there are only two ways to leave the house. The axis of spin aims toward Fibber McGee's Closet and Town Hall (about which more later); one can merely go out the "down" airlock ("the back door") and let go at the proper time. If you're not an experienced enough spacehand, or if you're going somewhere on a tangent to the axis of rotation, you go out the "up" lock or front door, climb up the runged hammer handle to the no-weight point and step off, then jet to where you want to go. You *always* come home by the front door; that's why it's a walkdown. The plumbing is simplicity itself, and habitual attention must be paid to keep the Closet and Hall from being peppered with freeze-dried dung.

(No, we don't save it to grow food on, or any such ecological wizardry. A closed system the size of ours would be too small to be efficient. Oh, we reclaim most of the moisture, but we give the rest to space, and buy our food and air and water from Luna like everybody else. In a pinch we could haul 'em up from Terra.)

We went through all those hoops, obviously, to provide a sixth-gee home environment. After you've been in space for long enough, you find zero gee much more comfortable and convenient. Any gravity at all seems like an arbitrary bias, a censorship of motion—like a pulp writer being required to write only happy endings, or a musician being restricted to a single meter.

But we spent as much time at home as we could manage. Any gravity at all will slow your body's mindless attempt to adapt irrevocably to zero gee, and a sixth-gee is a reasonable compromise. Since it is local normal for both Lunar surface and Skyfac, the physiological parameters are standard knowledge. The more time spent at home, the longer we could stay up—and our schedule was fixed. None of us wanted to be marooned in space. That's how we thought of it in those days.

If we slipped, if physicals showed one of us adapting too rapidly, we could compensate to some degree. You go out the back door, climb into the exercise yoke dangling from the power winch, and strap yourself in. It looks a little like one of those Jolly Jumpers for infants, or a modified bosun's chair. You ease off the brake, and the yoke begins to "descend," on a line with the hammer handle since there's no atmospheric friction to drag you to one side. You lower away, effectively increasing the length of your hammer handle and thus your gee force. When you're "down" far enough, say at a half gee (about 400 meters of line), you set the brake and exercise on the yoke, which is designed to provide a whole-body workout. You can even, if you want, use the built-in bicycle pedals to pedal yourself back up the line, with a built-in "parking brake" effect so that if it gets too much for you and you lose a stroke, you don't break your legs and go sliding down to the end of your tether. From low-enough gee zones you can even hand-over-hand your way up, with safety line firmly snubbed—but below half-gee level you do not unstrap from the yoke for *any* reason. Imagine hanging by your hands at, say, one gravity over all infinity, wearing a snug plastic bag with three hours' air.

We all got pretty conscientious about . . . er . . . watching our weight.

The big temptation was Town Hall, a sphere slightly smaller than the Goldfish Bowl. It was essentially our communal living room, the place where we could all hang out together and chew the fat in person. Play cards, teach each other songs, argue choreography, quarrel choreography (two different things), play 3-D handball, or just appreciate the luxury of free fall without a p-suit or a job to do. If a couple happened to find themselves alone in Town Hall, and were so inclined, they could switch off half the external navigation lights—signifying "Do Not Disturb"—and make love.

(One-sixth gee sex is nice, too—but zero gee is *different*. Nobody's on top. It's a wholehearted cooperative effort or it just doesn't happen [I can't imagine a free-fall rape]. You get to use *both* hands, instead of just the one you're not lying on. And while a good half of the Kama Sutra goes right out the airlock, there are compensations. I have never cared for simultaneous oral sex, the classic "69," because of the discomfort and distraction. Free fall makes it not only convenient, but logical, inevitable. End of second inevitable digression.)

For one reason and another, then, it was tempting to hang out overlong at Town Hall—and so many standard daily chores *must* be done there that the temptation had to be sharply curbed. Extensive physiological readouts on all of us were sent twice daily to Doc Panzella's medical computer aboard Skyfac: as with air, food, and water, I was prepared to deal elsewhere if Skyfac ever lost its smile, but while I could have them I wanted Panzella's brains. He was to space medicine what Harry was to space construction, and he kept us firmly in line, blistering us by radio when we goofed, handing out exercise sessions on the Jolly Jumper like a tough priest assigning novenas for penance.

We originally intended to build five sledge hammers, for a maximum comfortable population of fifteen. But we had rushed Harry, that first year; when the first group of students got off the elevator, it was a miracle that as many as three units were operational. We had to dismiss Harry's crew early with thanks and a bonus: we needed the cubic they were using. Ten students, Norrey, Raoul, Harry, and me totals fourteen bodies. Three units totals nine rooms. It was a hell of a courtship . . . but Norrey and I came out of it *married*; the ceremony was only a formality.

By the second season we had completed one more three-room home, and we took up only seven new students, and everybody had a door they could close and crouch behind when they needed to, and all seven of them washed out. The fifth hammer never got built.

It was that run of bad cards I mentioned earlier, extending itself through our second season.

Look, I was just beginning to become a Name in dance, and rather young for it, when the burglar's bullet smashed my hip joint. It's been a long time, but I remember myself as having been pretty damn good. I'll never be that good again, even with the use of my leg back. A few of the people we washed out were better dancers than I *used* to be—in dirtside terms. I had believed that a really good dancer almost automatically had the necessary ingredients to learn to think spherically.

The first season's dismal results had shown me my error, and so for the second semester we used different criteria. We tried to select for free-thinking minds, unconventional minds, minds unchained by preconception and consistency. Raoul described them as "science-fiction-reader types." The results were ghastly. In the first place, it turns out that people who can question even their most basic assumptions intellectually can not necessarily do so physically—they could imagine what needed doing, but couldn't do it. Worse, the free-thinkers could not cooperate with other free-thinkers, could not work with *anyone*'s preconception consistently. What we wanted was a choreographer's commune, and what we got was the classic commune where no one wanted to do the dishes. One chap would have made a terrific solo artist—when I let him go, I recommended to Sony that they finance him to a Studio of his own—but we couldn't work with him.

And two of the damned idiots killed themselves through thoughtlessness.

They were all *well* coached in free-fall survival, endlessly drilled in the basic rules of space life. We used a double-buddy system with every student who went EVA until they had demonstrated competence, and we took every precaution I could or can think of. But Inge Sjoberg could not be bothered to spend a whole hour a day inspecting and maintaining her p-suit. She managed to miss all six classic signs of incipient coolant failure, and one sunrise she boiled. And nothing could induce Alexi Nikolski to cut off his huge mane of brown hair. Against all advice he insisted on tying it back in a kind of doubled-up pony tail, "as he had always done." The arrangement depended on a *single hairband.* Sure as hell it failed in the middle of a class, and quite naturally he gasped. We were minutes away from pressure; he would surely have drowned in his own hair. But as Harry and I were towing him to Town Hall he unzipped his p-suit to deal with the problem.

Both times we were forced to store the bodies in the Closet for a gruesomely long time, while next-of-kin debated whether to have the remains shipped to the nearest spaceport or go through the legal complication of arranging for burial in space. Macabre humor saved our sanity (Raoul took to calling it Travis McGee's Closet), but it soured the season.

And it wasn't much more fun to say good-bye to the last of the live ones. On the day that Yeng and DuBois left, I nearly bottomed out. I saw them off personally, and the "coitus with a condom" imagery of shaking hands with p-suits on was just too ironically appropriate. The whole semester, like the first, had been coitus with a condom—hard work, no product—and I returned to Town Hall in the blackest depression I had known since . . . since Shara died. By association, my leg hurt; I wanted to bark at someone. But as I came in through the airlock Norrey, Harry and Linda were watching Raoul make magic.

He was not aware of them, of anything external, and Norrey held up a warning hand without meeting my eyes. I put my temper on hold and my back against the wall beside the airlock; the velcro pad between my shoulder-blades held me securely. (The whole sphere is carpeted in "female" velcro; pads of "male" are sewn into our slippers—which also have "thumbs"—our seats, thighs, backs, and the backs of our gloves. Velcro is the cheapest furniture there is.)

Raoul was making magic with common household ingredients. His most esoteric tool was what he referred to as his "hyperdermic needle." It looked like a doctor's hypo with elephantiasis: the chamber and plunger were oversized, but the spike itself was standard size. In his hands it was a magic wand.

Tethered to his skinny waist were all the rest of the ingredients: five drinking bulbs, each holding a different colored liquid. At once I identified a source of subconscious unease, and relaxed: I had been missing the vibration of the air conditioner, missing the draft. Twin radial tethers held Raoul at the center of the sphere, in the slight crouch typical of free fall, and he *wanted* still air—even though it severely limited his working time. (Shortly, exhaled carbon dioxide would form a sphere around his head; he would spin gently around his tethers and the sphere would become a donut; by then he must be finished. Or move. I would have to be careful myself to keep moving, spiderlike, as would the others.)

He speared one of the bulbs with his syringe, drew off a measured amount. Apple juice, by the color of it, admixed with water. He emptied the syringe gently, thin knuckly fingers working with great delicacy, forming a translucent golden ball that hung motionless before him, perfectly spherical. He pulled the syringe free, and the ball . . . shimmered . . . in spherically symmetrical waves that took a long time to ebb.

He filled his syringe with air, jabbed it into the heart of the ball and squeezed. The bulb filled with a measured amount of air, expanding into a nearly transparent golden bubble, around which iridescent patterns chased each other in lazy swirls. It was about a meter in diameter. Again Raoul disengaged the syringe.

Filling it in turn from bulbs of grape juice, tomato juice and unset lime jello, he filled the interior of the golden bubble with spherical beads of purple, red, and green, pumping them into bubbles as he formed them. They shone, glistened, jostling but declining to absorb each other. Presently the golden bubble was filled with Christmas-tree balls in various sizes from grape to grapefruit, shimmering, borrowing colors from each other. Marangoni Flow—gradients in surface tension—made them spin and tumble around each other like struggling kittens. Occasional bubbles were pure water, and these were rainbow scintillations that the eye ached to fragment and follow individually.

Raoul was drifting for air now, holding the macrobubble in tow with the palm of his hand, to which the whole thing adhered happily. If he were to strike it sharply now, I knew, the whole cluster would *snap* at once into a single, large bubble around the surface of which streaks of colors would run like tears (again, by Marangoni Flow). I thought that was his intention.

The master lighting panel was velcro'd to his chest. He dialed for six tight spots, focusing them on the bubble-jewel with sure fingers. Other lights dimmed, winked out. The room was spangled with colors and with color, as the facets of the manmade jewel flung light in all directions. With a seemingly careless wave of his hand, Raoul set the scintillating globe spinning, and Town Hall swam in its eerie rainbow fire.

Drifting before the thing, Raoul set his Musicmaster for external speaker mode, velcro'd it to his thighs, and began to play.

Long, sustained warm tones first. The globe thrilled to them, responding to their vibrations, expressing the music visually. Then liquid trills in a higher register, with pseudowoodwind chords sustained by memory-loop beneath. The globe seemed to ripple, to pulse with energy. A simple melody emerged, mutated, returned, mutated again. The globe spangled in perfect counterpoint. The tone of the melody changed as it played, from brass to violin to organ to frankly electronic and back again, and the globe reflected each change with exquisite subtlety. A bass line appeared. Horns. I kicked myself free of the wall, both to escape my own exhalations and to get a different perspective on the jewel. The others were doing likewise, drifting gently, trying to become organic with Raoul's art. Spontaneously we danced, tossed by the music like the glistening jewel, by the riot of color it flung around the spherical room. An orchestra was strapped to Raoul's thighs now, and it made us free-fall puppets.

Improv only; not up to concert standard. Simple group exercises, luxuriating in the sheer physical *comfort* of free fall and sharing that awareness. Singing around the campfire, if you will, trying to out unfamiliar harmonies on each other's favorite songs. Only Harry abstained, drifting somehow "to one side" with the odd, incongruous grace of a polar bear in the water. He became thereby a kind of second focus of the dance, became the camera eye toward which Raoul aimed his creation, and we ours. (Raoul and Harry had become the fastest of friends, the chatterbox and the sphinx. They admired each other's hands.) Harry floated placidly, absorbing our joy and radiating it back.

Raoul tugged gently on a line, and a large expandable wire loop came to him. He adjusted it to just slightly larger than the bubblejewel, captured that in the loop and expanded the loop rapidly at once. Those who have only seen it masked by gravity have no idea how powerful a force surface tension is. The bubblejewel became a concave lens about three meters in diameter, within which multicolored convex lenses bubbled, each literally perfect. He oriented it toward Harry, added three low-power lasers from the sides, and set the lens spinning like the Wheel of Kali. And we danced.

After a while the knock-knock light went on beside the airlock. That should have startled me—we don't get much company—but I paid no mind, lost in zero-gee dance and in Raoul's genius, and a little in my own in hiring him. The lock cycled and opened to admit Tom McGillicuddy—which should have startled the hell out of me. I had no idea he was thinking of coming up to visit, and since he hadn't been on the scheduled elevator I'd just put Yeng and DuBois on, he must have taken a *very* expensive special charter to get here. Which implied disaster.

But I was in a warm fog, lost in the dance, perhaps a little hypnotized by the sparkling of Raoul's grape-juice, tomato-juice and lime-jello kaleidoscope. I may not even have nodded hello to Tom, and I know I was not even remotely surprised by what he did, then.

He joined us.

With no hesitation, casting away the velcro slippers he'd brought from the airlock's dressing chamber, he stepped off into thick air and joined us within the sphere, using Raoul's guy wires to position himself so that our triangle pattern became a square. And then he danced with us, picking up our patterns and the rhythm of the music.

He did a creditable job. He was in damned good shape for someone who'd been doing all our paperwork—but infinitely more important (for terrestrial physical fitness is so *useless* in space), he was clearly functioning without a local vertical, and enjoying it.

Now I *was* startled, to my bones, but I kept pokerfaced and continued dancing, trying not to let Tom catch me watching. Across the sphere Norrey did likewise—and Linda, above, seemed genuinely oblivious.

Startled? I was flabbergasted. The single factor that had washed out sixteen students out of seventeen was the same thing that washed out Skyfac construction men, the same thing that had troubled eight of the nine Skylab crewmen back when the first experiments with zero-gee life had been made: inability to live without a local vertical.

If you bring a goldfish into orbit (the Skylab crew did), it will flounder helplessly in its globe of water. Show the fish an *apparent* point of reference, place a flat surface against its water-sphere (which will then form a perfect hemisphere thereon quite naturally), and the fish will decide that the plane surface is a stream bed, aligning its body perpendicularly. Remove the plate, or add a second plate (no local vertical or too many), and the goldfish will soon die, mortally confused. Skylab was purposely built to have three *different* local verticals in its three major modules, and eight out of nine crewmen faithfully and chronically adjusted to a module's local vertical as they entered it, without conscious thought. Traveling all the way through all three in one jaunt gave them headaches; they hated the docking adapter which was designed to have no local vertical at all. It is physically impossible to get dizzy in zero gee, but they said they *felt* dizzy any time they were prevented from coming into focus with a defined "floor" and "walls."

All of them except one—described as "one of the most intelligent of the astronauts, as well as one of the most perverse." He took to the docking adapter—to life without up and down—like a duck to water. He was the only one of nine who made the psychological breakthrough. *Now* I knew how lucky I had been that Norrey and Raoul had both turned out to be Stardancer material. And how few others ever could be.

But Tom was unquestionably one of them. One of us. His technique was raw as hell, he thought his hands were shovels and his spine was all wrong, but he was trainable. And he had that rare, indefinable *something* that it takes to maintain equilibrium in an environment that forbids equilibration. He was at home in space.

I should have remembered. He had been ever since I'd known

him. It seemed to me in that moment that I perceived all at once the totality of my bloody blind stupidity—but I was wrong.

The impromptu jam session wound down eventually; Raoul's music frivolously segued into the closing bars of *Thus Spake Zarathustra*, and as that last chord sustained, he stabbed a rigid hand through his lens, shattering it into a million rainbow drops that dispersed with the eerie grace of an expanding universe.

"Hoover that up," I said automatically, breaking the spell, and Harry hastened to kick on the air scavenger before Town Hall became sticky with fruit juice and jello. Everyone sighed with it, and Raoul the magician was once again a rabbity little guy with a comic-opera hypo and a hula hoop. And a big wide smile. The tribute of sighs was followed by a tribute of silence; the warm glow was a while in fading. *I'll be damned,* I thought, *I haven't made memories this good in twenty years.* Then I put my mind back in gear.

"Conference," I said briefly, and jaunted to Raoul. Harry, Norrey, Linda and Tom met me there, and we grabbed hands and feet at random to form a human snowflake in the center of the sphere. This left our faces every-which-way to each other, of course, but we ignored it, the way a veteran DJ ignores the spinning of a record label he's reading. Even Tom paid no visible mind to it. We got right down to business.

"Well, Tom," Norrey said first, "what's the emergency?"

"Is Skyfac bailing out?" Raoul asked.

"Why didn't you call first?" I added. Only Linda and Harry were silent.

"Whoa," Tom said. "No emergency. None at all, everybody relax. Businesswise everything continues to work like a ridiculously overdesigned watch."

"Then why spring for the chartered elevator? Or were you stowing away in the regular that just left?"

"No, I had a charter, all right—but it was a taxi. I've been in free fall as long as you have. Over at Skyfac."

"Over at—" I thought things through, with difficulty. "And you went to the trouble of having your calls and mail relayed so we wouldn't catch on."

"That's right. I've spent the last three months working out of our branch office aboard Skyfac." That branch office was a postal address somewhere in the lower left quadrant of Tokugawa's new executive secretary's desk.

"Uh huh," I said. "*Why?*"

He looked at Linda, whose left ankle he happened to be holding, and chose his words. "Remember that first week after we met, Linda?" She nodded. "I don't think I've been so exasperated before in my whole life. I thought you were the jackass of the world. That night I blew up at you in Le Maintenant, that last time that we argued religion—remember? I walked out of there that night and took a copter straight to Nova Scotia to that damned commune you grew up in. Landed in the middle of the garden at three in the morning, woke half of 'em up. I raved and swore at them for over an hour, *demanding* to know how in the hell they could have raised you to be such a misguided idiot. When I was done they blinked and scratched and yawned and then the big one with the really improbable beard said, 'Well, if there's that much juice between you, we would recommend that you probably ought to start courting,' and gave me a sleeping bag."

The snowflake broke up as Linda kicked free, and we all grabbed whatever was handiest or drifted. Tom reversed his attitude with practiced ease so that he tracked Linda, continued to speak directly to her.

"I stayed there for a week or so," he went on steadily, "and then I went to New York and signed up for dance classes. I studied dance when I was a kid, as part of karate discipline; it came back, and I worked hard. But I wasn't sure it had anything to do with zero-gee dance—so I sneaked up to Skyfac without telling any of you, and I've been working like hell over there ever since, in a factory sphere I rented with my own money."

"Who's minding the store?" I asked mildly.

"The best trained seals money can buy," he said softly. "Our affairs haven't suffered. But I have. I hadn't intended to tell you *any* of this for another year or so. But I was in Panzella's office when the Termination of Monitoring notices came in on Yeng and DuBois. I knew you were hurting for bodies. I'm self-taught and clumsy as a pig on ice and on Earth it'd take me another five years to become a fourth-rate dancer, but I think I can do the kind of stuff you're doing here."

He wriggled to face me and Norrey. "I'd like to study under you. I'll pay my own tuition. I'd like to work with you people, besides just on paper, and be part of your company. I think I can make a Stardancer." He turned back to Linda. "And I'd like to start courting you, by your customs."

Then it was that the totality of my stupidity truly did become apparent to me. I was speechless. It was Norrey who said, "We accept," on behalf of the company, at the same instant that Linda said the same thing for herself. And the snowflake reformed, much smaller in diameter.

Our company was formed.

As to the nature of our dance itself, there is not much to be said that the tapes themselves don't already say. We borrowed a lot of vocabulary from New Pilobolus and the Contact Improv movement (which had been among the last spasms of inventiveness before that decade-long stasis in dance I mentioned earlier), but we had to radically adapt almost everything we borrowed. Although the Contact Improv people say they're into "free fall," this is a semantic confusion: *they* mean "falling freely;" *we* mean "free of falling." But a lot of their discoveries *do* work, at least in some fashion, in zero gee—and we used what worked.

Linda's own dance background included four years with the New Pilobolus company: if you don't know them, or the legendary Pilobolus company they sprang from, they're sort of Contact Improv without the improv—carefully choreographed stuff. But they too are into "using each other as the set"—dancing on, over, and around one another, cooperating in changing *each other*'s vectors. Dancing acrobats, if you will. We ourselves tried to achieve a balanced blend of both choreographed and spontaneous dance in the stuff we taped.

Linda was able to teach us a lot about mutually inter-reacting masses, hyperfulcrums, and the like—and a lot more about the *attitude* they require. To truly interact with another dancer, to spontaneously create shapes together, you must attempt to attune yourself to them empathically. You must know them—how they dance and how they're feeling at the moment—to be able to sense what their next move will be, or how they will likely react to yours. When it works, it's the most exhilarating feeling I've ever known.

It's *much* harder with more than one partner, but the exhilaration increases exponentially.

Because free fall requires mutual cooperation, mutual awareness on a spherical level, our dance became an essentially spiritual exercise.

And so, with a company of adequate size and an increasing grasp of what zero-gee dance was really about, we began our second and last season of taping.

IV

I fell through starry space, balanced like an inbound comet on a tail of fluorescent gas, concentrating on keeping my spine straight and my knees and ankles locked. It helped me forget how nervous I was.

"Five," Raoul chanted steadily, "four, three, two, now," and a ring of his bright orange "flame" flared soundlessly all around me. I threaded it like a needle.

"Beautiful," Norrey whispered in my ear, from her vantage point a kilometer away. At once I lifted my arms straight over my head and bit down hard on a contact. As I passed through the ring of orange "flame," my "tail" turned a rich, deep purple, expanding lazily and symmetrically behind me. Within the purple wake, tiny novae sparkled and died at irregular intervals: Raoul magic. Just before the dye canisters on my calves emptied, I fired my belly thruster and let it warp me "upward" in an ever-increasing curve while I counted seconds.

"Light it up, Harry," I said sharply. "I can't see you." The red lights winked into being *above* my imaginary horizon and I relaxed, cutting the ventral thrust in plenty of time. I was not heading precisely for the camera, but the necessary corrections were minor and would not visibly spoil the curve. Orienting myself by a method I can only call informed writhing, I cut main drive and selected my point.

On Earth you can turn forever without getting dizzy if you select a point and keep your eyes locked on it, whipping your head around at the last possible second for each rotation. In space the technique is unnecessary: once out of a gravity well, your semicirculars fill up and your whole balance system shuts down; you *can't* get dizzy. But old habit dies hard. Once I had my point star I tumbled, and when I had counted ten rotations the camera was close enough to see and coming up fast. At once I came out of my spin, oriented, and braked *sharply*—maybe three gees—with all thrusters. I had cut it fine: I came to rest relative to the camera barely fifty meters away. I cut all power instantly, went from the natural contraction of high acceleration to full release, giving it everything I had left, held it for a five-count and whispered, "Cut!"

The red lights winked out, and Norrey, Raoul, Tom, and Linda cheered softly (nobody does anything loudly in a p-suit).

"Okay, Harry, let's see the playback."

"Coming up, boss."

There was a pause while he rewound, and then a large square section of distant space lit up around the edges. The stars within it rearranged themselves and took on motion. My image came into frame, went through the maneuver I had just finished. I was pleased. I had hit the ring of orange "flame" dead center and triggered the purple smoke at just the right instant. The peelout curve was a little ragged, but it would do. The sudden growth of my oncoming image was so startling that I actually flinched—which is pretty silly. The deceleration was nearly as breathtaking to watch as it had been to do, the pullout was fine, and the final triumphant extension was frankly terrific.

"That's a take," I said contentedly. "Which way's the bar?"

"Just up the street," Raoul answered. "I'm buying."

"Always a pleasure to meet a patron of the arts. How much did you say your name was?"

Harry's massive construction-man's spacesuit, festooned with tools, appeared from behind and "beneath" the camera. "Hey," he said, "not yet. Gotta at least run through the second scene."

"Oh hell," I protested. "My air's low, my belly's empty, and I'm swimming around in this overgrown galosh."

"Deadline's coming," was all Harry said.

I wanted to shower so bad I could taste it. Dancers are all different; the only thing we *all* have in common is that we all sweat—and in a p-suit there's nowhere for it to go. "My thrusters're shot," I said weakly.

"You don't need 'em much for Scene Two," Norrey reminded me. "Monkey Bars, remember? Brute muscle stuff." She paused. "And we are pushing deadline, Charlie."

Dammit, a voice on stereo earphones seems to come from the same place that the voice of your conscience does.

"They're right, Charlie," Raoul said. "I spoke too soon. Come on, the night is young."

I stared around me at an immense sphere of starry emptiness, Earth a beachball to my left and the Sun a brilliant softball beyond it. "Night don't *come* any older than this," I grumbled, and gave in. "Okay, I guess you're right. Harry, you and Raoul strike that set and get the next one in place, okay? The rest of you warm up in place. Get sweaty."

Raoul and Harry, as practiced and efficient as a pair of old beat cops, took the Family Car out to vacuum up the vacuum. I sat on nothing and brooded about the damned deadline. It *was* getting time to go dirtside again, which meant it was time to get this segment rehearsed and shot, but I didn't have to like it. No artist likes time pressure, even those who can't produce without it. So I brooded.

The show must go on. The show must always go on, and if you are one of those millions who have always wondered exactly why, I will tell you. The tickets have already been sold.

But it's uniquely hard (as well as foolish) to brood in space. You hang suspended within the Big Deep, infinity in all directions, an emptiness so immense that although you know that you're falling through it at high speed, you make no slightest visible progress. Space is God's Throne Room, and so vasty a hall is it that no human problem has significance within it for long.

Have you ever lived by the sea? If so, you know how difficult it is to retain a griping mood while contemplating the ocean. Space is like that, only more so.

Much more so.

By the time the Monkey Bars were assembled, I was nearly in a dancing mood again. The Bars were a kind of three-dimensional gymnast's jungle, a huge partial icosahedron composed of transparent tubes inside which neon fluoresced green and red. It enclosed an area of about 14,000 cubic meters, within which were scattered a great many tiny liquid droplets that hung like motionless dust motes, gleaming in laserlight. Apple juice.

When Raoul and Harry had first shown me the model for the Monkey Bars, I had been struck by the aesthetic beauty of the structure.

By now, after endless simulations and individual rehearsals, I saw it only as a complex collection of fulcrums and pivots for Tom, Linda, Norrey and me to dance on, an array of vector-changers designed for maximal movement with minimal thruster use. Scene Two relied almost entirely on muscle power, a paradox considering the technology implicit in its creation. We would pivot with all four limbs on the Bars and on each other, borrowing some moves from the vocabulary of trapeze acrobatics and some from our own growing experience with free-fall lovemaking, constantly forming and dissolving strange geometries that were new even to dance. (We were using choreography rather than improv techniques: the Bars and their concept were too big for the Goldfish Bowl, and you can't afford mistakes in free space.)

Though I had taught individual dancers their parts and rehearsed some of the trickier clinches with the group, this would be our first full run-through together. I found I was anxious to assure myself that it would actually work. All the computer simulation in the world is no substitute for actually doing it; things that look lovely in compsim can dislocate shoulders in practice.

I was about to call places when Norrey left her position and jetted my way. Of course there's only one possible reason for that, so I turned off my radio too and waited. She decelerated neatly, came to rest beside me, and touched her hood to mine.

"Charlie, I didn't mean to crowd you. We can come back in eleven hours and—"

"No, that's okay, hon," I assured her. "You're right: 'Deadline don't care.' I just hope the choreography's right."

"It's just the first run-through. And the simulations were great."

"That's not what I mean. Hell, I know it's *correct*. By this point I can think spherically just fine. I just don't know if it's *any good*."

"How do you mean?"

"It's exactly the kind of choreography Shara would have loathed. Rigid, precisely timed, like a set of tracks."

She locked a leg around my waist to arrest a slight drift and looked thoughtful. "She'd have loathed it for herself," she said finally, "but I think she'd really have enjoyed watching us do it. It's a *good* piece, Charlie—and you know how the critics love anything abstract."

"Yeah, you're right—again," I said, and put on my best Cheerful Charlie grin. It's not fair to have a bummer at curtain time; it brings the other dancers down. "In fact, you may have just given me a better title for this whole mess: *Synapstract.*"

There was relief in her answering grin. "If it's got to be a pun, I like *ImMerced* better."

"Yeah, it does have a kind of Cunningham flavor to it. Bet the old boy takes the next elevator up after he sees it." I squeezed her arm through the p-suit, added "Thanks, hon," cut in my radio again. "All right, boys and girls, *—let's shoot this turkey.* Watch out for legbreakers and widowmakers. Harry, those cameras locked in?"

"Program running," he announced. "Blow a gasket." It's the Stardancer's equivalent of "Break a leg."

Norrey scooted back into position, I corrected my own, the lights came up hellbright on cameras 2 and 4, and we took our stage, while on all sides of us an enormous universe went about its business.

You can't fake cheerfulness well enough to fool a wife like Norrey without there being something real to it; and, like I said, it's hard to brood in space. It really was exhilarating to hurl my body around within the red and green Bars, interacting with the energy of the other dancers I happened to love, concentrating on split-second timing and perfect body placement. But an artist is capable of self-criticism even in the midst of the most involving performance. It's the same perpetual self-scrutiny that makes so many of us so hard to get along with for any length of time—and that makes us artists in the first place. The last words Shara Drummond ever said to me were, "Do it right."

And even in the whirling midst of a piece that demanded all my attention, there was still room for a little whispering voice that said that this was only the best I had been able to do and still meet my deadline.

I tried to comfort myself with the notion that every artist who ever worked feels exactly the same way, about nearly every piece they ever do—and it didn't help me any more than it ever does any of us. And so I made the one small error of placement, and tried to correct with thrusters in too much of a hurry and triggered the wrong one and smacked backward hard into Tom. His back was to me as well, and our air tanks *clanged* and one of mine blew. A horse kicked me between the shoulder blades and the Bars came up fast and caught me across the thighs, tumbling me end over end. I was more than twenty meters from the set, heading for forever, before I had time to black out.

Happening to smack into the Bars off center was a break. It put me into an acrobat's tumble, which centrifuged air into my hood and boots, and blood to my head and feet, bringing me out of blackout quicker. Even so, precious seconds ticked by while I groggily deduced my problem, picked my point and began to spin correctly. With the perspective that gave me I oriented myself, still groggy, figured out intuitively which thrusters would kill the spin, and used them.

That done, it was easy to locate the Bars, a bright cubist's Christmas tree growing perceptibly smaller as I watched. It was between me and the blue beachball I'd been born on. At least life would not be corny enough to award me Shara's death. But Bryce Carrington's didn't appeal to me much more.

My thighs ached like hell, the right one especially, but my spine hadn't begun to hurt yet—I hadn't yet worked out that it ought to. There were voices in my headphones, urgent ones, but I was still too fuzzy to make any sense out of what they were saying. Later I could spare time to retune my ears; right now figures were clicking away in my mind and the answers kept getting worse. There's much more pressure in an air tank than in a thruster. On the other hand, I had ten aimable thrusters with which to cancel the velocity imparted by that one diffused burst. On the third hand, I had started this with badly depleted thrusters. . . .

Even as I concluded that I was dead I was doing what I could to save my life: one by one I lined up my thrusters on the far side of my center of mass and fired them to exhaustion. Left foot, fore and aft. Right foot, likewise. Belly thruster. My back began to moan, then cry, then shriek with agony; not the localized knifing I'd expected but a general ache. I couldn't decide if that was a good sign or bad. Back thruster, clamping my teeth against a whimper. Left hand, fore and aft—

—*Save a little.* I reserved my right hand pair for last minute maneuvers, and looked to see if I'd done any good.

The Monkey Bars were still shrinking, fairly rapidly.

I was almost fully conscious now, feeling that my brains were just catching up with me. The voices in my headphones began to make sense at last. The first one that I identified, of course, was Norrey's—but she wasn't saying anything, only crying and swearing.

"Hey, honey," I said as calmly as I could, and she cut off instantly. So did the others. Then—"Hang on, darling. *I'm coming!*"

"That's right, boss," Harry agreed. "I've been tracking you with the radar gun since you left, and the computer's doing the piloting."

"She'll get you," Raoul cried. "The machine says 'yes.' With available fuel, it can get her to you and then back here, Charlie, it says 'yes.'"

Sure enough, just to the side of the Bars I could see the Family Car, nose-on to me. It was not shrinking as fast as the Bars were—but it did appear to be shrinking. That had been a hell of a clout that can of air fetched me.

"Boss," Harry said urgently, *"is your suit honest?"*

"Yeah, sure, the force of the blast was outwards, didn't even damage the other can." My back throbbed just thinking about it, and yes, damn it, the Car's visible disk was definitely shrinking, not a whole lot but certainly *not* growing, and at that moment of moments I recalled that the warranty on that computer's software had expired three days ago.

Say something heroic before you moan.

"Well, that's settled," I said cheerfully. "Remind me to sue the bas—hey! *How's Tom?*"

"We got it patched," Harry said briefly. "He's out, but telemetry says he's alive and okay."

No wonder Linda was silent. She was praying.

"Is there a doctor in the house?" I asked rhetorically.

"I called Skyfac. Panzella's on his way. We're proceeding home on thrusters to get Tom indoors now."

"Go, all three of you. Nothing you can do out here. Raoul, take care of Linda."

"Yah."

Silence fell, except of course for the by-now unheard constants of breathing and rustling cloth. Norrey began to cry again, briefly, but controlled it. The disc that was her and the Car was growing now, I had to stare and measure with my thumb but yes, it was growing.

"Attaway, Norrey, you're gaining on me," I said, trying to keep it light.

"That I am," she agreed, and when the *rate* of the Car's growth had just reached a visibly perceptible crawl, the corona of her drive flame winked out. "What the—?"

Visualize the geometry. I leave the Monkey Bars at a hell of a clip. Maybe a full thirty seconds elapse before Norrey is in the saddle and blasting. Ideally the computer has her blast to a velocity higher than mine, hold it, then turnover and begin decelerating so that she will begin to return toward the Bars *just as our courses intersect.* A bit tricky to work out in your head, but no problem for a ballistic computer half as good as ours.

The kicker was fuel.

Norrey *had* to cut thrust precisely halfway through projected total fuel consumption. She had used up half the content of her fuel tanks; the computer saw that at these rates of travel rendezvous could be accomplished eventually; it cut thrust with a computer's equivalent of a smile of triumph. I did primitive mental arithmetic, based on guesswork and with enormous margins for errors, and went pale and cold inside my plastic bag.

The second kicker was air.

"Harry," I rapped, "run that projection through again for me, but include the following air supply data—"

"Oh Jesus God," he said, stunned, and then repeated back the figures I gave him. "Hold on."

"Charlie," Norrey began worriedly. "Oh my God, Charlie!"

"Wait, baby. Wait. Maybe it's okay."

Harry's voice was final. "No good, boss. You'll be out of air when she gets there. She'll be damn low when she gets back."

"Then turn around and start back now, hon," I said as gently as I could.

"Hell no," she cried.

"Why risk your neck, darling? *I'm already buried*—buried in space. Come on now—"

"No."

I tried brutality. "You want my corpse that bad?"

"Yes."

"Why, to have it hanging around the Closet?"

"No. To ride with."

"Huh?"

"Harry, plot me a course that'll get me to him before his air runs out. Forget the round trip: Give me a minimum-time rendezvous."

"No!" I thundered.

"Norrey," Harry said earnestly, "there's *nothing else to come get you with.* There's not a ship in the sky. You blast any more and you'll never even get started back here, and you'll never even stop leaving. You've got more air than him, but both your air combined wouldn't last one of you 'til help could arrive, even if we could keep tracking you that long." It was the longest speech I'd ever heard Harry make.

"I'm damned if I want to be a widow," she blazed, and cut in acceleration on manual override.

She was dead as me, now.

"Goddammit," Harry and I roared together, and then, "Help her, Harry!" I screamed and "I am!" he screamed back and an endless time later he said sadly, "Okay, Norrey, let go. The new course is locked in." She was still dead, had been from the moment she overrode the computer. But at least now we'd go together.

"All right, then," she said, still angry but mollified. "Twenty-five *years* I wanted to be your wife, Armstead. I will be *damned* if I'll be your widow."

"Harry," I said, knowing it was hopeless but refusing to accept, "refigure, assuming that we leave the Car when it runs out of juice and use all of Norrey's suit thrusters together. Hers aren't as low as mine were."

It must have been damned awkward for Harry, using two fingers to keep himself headed for home at max thrust, holding the big computer terminal and pushing keys with the rest. It must have been even more awkward for Raoul and Linda, towing the unconscious Tom between them, watching their patch job leak.

"Forget it, boss," Harry said almost at once. "There's two of you."

"Well then," I said desperately, "can we trade off breathing air for thrust?"

He must have been just as desperate; he actually worked the problem. "Sure. You could start returning, get back here in less than a day. But it'd take *all* your air to do it. You're dead, boss."

I nodded, a silly habit I'd thought I'd outgrown. "That's what I thought. Thanks, Harry. Good luck with Tom."

Norrey said not a word. Presently the computer shut down her drive again, having done its level best to get her to me quickly with the fuel available. The glow around the Car (now plainly growing) winked out, and still she was silent. We were all silent. There was either nothing to say or too much, no in-between. Presently Harry reported docking at home. He gave Norrey her turnover data, gave her back manual control, and then he and the others went off the air.

Two people breathing makes hardly any noise at all.

She was a long long time coming, long enough for the pain in my back to diminish to the merely incredible. When she was near enough to see, it took all my discipline to keep from using the last of my jump-juice to try and match up with her. Not that I had anything to save it for. But matching in free space is like high-speed highway merging—one of you had better maintain a constant velocity, two variables are too many. Norrey did a textbook job, coming to a dead stop relative to me at the extreme edge of lifeline range.

The precision was wasted. But you don't stop trying to live just because a computer says you can't.

At the same split second that she stopped decelerating she fired the lifeline. The weight at the end tapped me gently on the chest: *very* impressive shooting, even with the magnet to help. I embraced it fiercely, and it took me several seconds of concentrated effort to let go and clip it to my belt. I hadn't realized how lonely and scared I was.

As soon as she was sure I was secure, she cut the drag and let the Car reel me in.

"Who says you can never get a cab when you need one?" I said, but my teeth were chattering and it spoiled the effect.

She grinned anyhow, and helped me into the rear saddle. "Where to, Mac?"

All of a sudden I couldn't think of anything funny to say. If the Car's fuselage hadn't been reinforced, I'd have crushed it between my knees. "Wherever you're going," I said simply, and she spun around in her saddle and gave it the gun.

It takes a really sensitive hand to pilot a tractor like the Family Car accurately, especially with a load on. It's quite difficult to keep the target bubble centered, and the controls are mushy—you have to sort of outguess her or you'll end up oscillating and throw your gyro. A dancer is, of course, better at seat-of-the-pants mass balancing than any but the most experienced of Space Command pilots, and Norrey was the best of the six of us. At that she outdid herself.

She even outdid the computer. Which is not too astonishing—there's always more gas than it says on the gauge—and of course it wasn't nearly enough to matter. We were still dead. But after a time the distant red and green spheroid that was the Bars stopped shrinking; instruments confirmed it. After a longer time I was able to convince myself that it was actually growing some. It was, naturally, at that moment that the vibration between my thighs ceased.

All the time we'd been accelerating I'd been boiling over with the need to talk, and had kept my mouth shut for fear of distracting Norrey's attention. Now we had done all we could do. Now we had nothing left to do in our lives but talk, and I was wordless again. It was Norrey who broke the silence, her tone just precisely right.

"Uh, you're not going to believe this . . . but we're out of gas."

"The hell you say. Let me out of this car; I'm not that kind of boy." *Thank you, hon.*

"Aw, take it easy. It's downhill from here. I'll just put her in neutral and we'll coast home."

"Hey listen," I said, "when you navigate by the seat of your pants like that, is that what they call a bum steer?"

"Oh Charlie, I don't want to die."

"Well, then don't."

"I wasn't *finished* yet."

"Norrey!" I grabbed her shoulder from behind. Fortunately I used my left hand, triggering only empty thrusters.

There was a silence.

"I'm sorry," she said at last, still facing away from me. "I made my choice. These last minutes with you are worth what I paid for them. That just slipped out." She snorted at herself. "Wasting air."

"I can't think of anything I'd rather spend air on than talking with you. That you can do in p-suits, I mean. I don't want to die either—but if I've got to go, I'm glad I've got your company. Isn't that selfish?"

"Nope. I'm glad you're here too, Charlie."

"Hell, I *called* this meeting. If I wasn't here, nobody would be." I broke off then, and scowled. "That's the part that bothers me the most, I think. I used to try and guess, sometimes, what it would be that would finally kill me. Sure enough, I was right: my own damn stupidity. Spacing out. Taking my finger off the number. Oh dammit, Norrey—"

"Charlie, it was an accident."

"I spaced out. I wasn't paying attention. I was thinking about the god damned deadline, and I blew it." (I was very close to something, then; something bigger than my death.)

"Charlie, that's cheating. At least half of that guilt you're hogging belongs to the crook that inspected that air tank at the factory. Not to mention the flaming idiot who forgot to gas the Car this morning."

It's a rotating duty. "Who was that idiot?" I asked, before I could think better of it.

"Same idiot who took off without grabbing extra air. Me."

That produced an uncomfortable silence. Which started me trying to think of something meaningful or useful to say. Or do. Let's see, I had less than an eighth of a can of air. Norrey maybe a can and a quarter: she hadn't used up as much in exercise. (Space Command armor, like the NASA Standard suits before them, hold about six hours' air. A Stardancer's p-suit is good for only half as much—but they're prettier. And we *always* have plenty of air bottles—strapped to every camera we use.) I reached forward and unshipped her full tank, passed it silently over her shoulder. She took it, as silently, and got the first-aid kit out of the glove compartment. She took a Y-joint from it, made sure both male ends were sealed, and snapped it onto the air bottle. She got extension hoses from the kit and mated them to the ends of the Y. She clipped the whole assembly to the flank of the Car until we needed it, an air soda with two straws. Then she reversed herself in the saddle, awkwardly, until she was facing me.

"I love you, Charlie."

"I love you, Norrey."

Don't ever let anybody tell you that hugging in p-suits is a waste of time. Hugging is *never* a waste of time. It hurt my back a lot, but I paid no attention.

The headphones crackled with another carrier wave: Raoul calling from Tom and Linda's place. "Norrey? Charlie? Tom's okay. The doctor's on his way, Charlie, but he's not going to get here in time to do you any good. I called the Space Command, there's no scheduled traffic *near* here, there's just nothing in the neighborhood, Charlie, just nothing at all what the hell are we going to *do*?" Harry must have been very busy with Tom, or he'd have grabbed the mike by now.

"Here's what you're going to do, buddy," I said calmly, spacing my words to slow him down. "Push the 'record' button. Okay? Now put the speakers on so Harry and Linda can witness. Ready? Okay. 'I, Charles Armstead, being of sound mind and body—'"

"Charlie!"

"Don't spoil the tape, buddy. I haven't got time for too many retakes, and I've got better things to do. 'I, Charles Armstead—'"

It didn't take very long. I left everything to the Company—and I made Fat Humphrey a full partner. Le Maintenant had closed the month before, strangled by bureaucracy. Then it was Norrey's turn, and she echoed me almost verbatim.

What was there to do then? We said our good-byes to Raoul, to Linda, and to Harry, making it as short as possible. Then we switched off our radios. Sitting backwards in the saddle was uncomfortable for Norrey; she turned around again and I hugged her from behind like a motorcycle passenger. Our hoods touched. What we said then is really none of your damned business.

An hour went by, the fullest hour I had ever known. All infinity stretched around us. Both of us being ignorant of astronomy, we had given names of our own to the constellations on our honeymoon. The Banjo. The Leering Gerbil. Orion's Truss. The Big Pot Pipe and the Little Hash Pipe. One triplet near the Milky Way quite naturally became the Three Musketeers. Like that. We renamed them all, now, re-evoking that honeymoon. We talked of our lost plans and hopes. In turns, we freaked out and comforted each other, and then we both freaked out together and both comforted each other. We told each other those last few secrets even happily-marrieds hold out. Twice, we agreed to take off our p-suits and get it over with. Twice, we changed our minds. We talked about the children we didn't have, and how lucky it was for them that we didn't have them. We sucked sugar water from our hood nipples. We talked about God, about death, about how uncomfortable we were and how absurd it was to die uncomfortable—about how absurd it was to die at all.

"It was the deadline pressure killed us," I said finally, "stupid damned deadline pressure. In a big hurry. Why? So we wouldn't get marooned in space by our metabolisms. What was so wrong about that?" (I was very close, now.) "What were we so scared of? What has Earth got, that we were risking our necks to keep?"

"People," Norrey answered seriously. "Places. There aren't many of either up here."

"Yeah, places. New York. Toronto. Cesspools."

"Not fair. Prince Edward Island."

"Yeah, and how much time did we get to spend there? And how long before *it's* a bloody city?"

"*People*, Charlie. Good people."

"Seven billion of 'em, squatting on the same disintegrating anthill."

"Charlie, look out there." She pointed to the Earth. "Do you see an 'oasis hanging in space'? Does that look crowded to you?"

She had me there. From space, one's overwhelming impression of our home planet is of one vast, godforsaken wilderness. Desert is by far the most common sight, and only occasionally does a twinkle or a miniature mosaic give evidence of human works. Man may have polluted hell out of his atmosphere—seen edge-on at sunset it looks no thicker than the skin of an apple—but he has as yet made next to no visible mark on the face of his planet.

"No. But it is, and you know it. My leg hurts all the time. There's never a moment of real silence. It stinks. It's filthy and germ-ridden and riddled with evil and steeped in contagious insanity and hip-deep in despair. I don't know what the hell I ever wanted to go back there for."

"Charlie!" I only realized how high my volume had become when I discovered how loud she had to be to out-shout me. I broke off, furious with myself. *Again you want to freak out? The last time wasn't bad enough?*

I'm sorry, I answered myself, *I've never died before. I understand it's been done worse.* "I'm sorry, hon," I said aloud. "I guess I just haven't cared much for Earth since Le Maintenant closed." It started out to be a wisecrack, but it didn't come out funny.

"Charlie," she said, her voice strange.

You see? There she goes now, and we're off and running again. "Yeah?"

"Why are the Monkey Bars blinking on and off?"

At once I rechecked the air bottle, then the Y-joint, hoses, and joins. No, she was getting air. I looked then, and sure as hell the Monkey Bars were blinking on and off in the far distance, a

Christmas-tree bulb on a flasher circuit. I checked the air again, carefully, to make sure we weren't both hallucinating, and returned to our spoon embrace.

"Funny," I said, "I can't think of a circuit malf that'd behave that way."

"Something must have struck the sunpower screen and set it spinning."

"I guess. But what?"

"The hell with it, Charlie. Maybe it's Raoul trying to signal us."

"If it is, to hell with him indeed. There's nothing more I want to say, and I'm damned if there's anything I want to hear. Leave the damn phone off the hook. Where were we?"

"Deciding Earth sucks."

"It certainly does—hard. Why does *anybody* live there, Norrey? Oh, the hell with that too."

"Yeah. It can't be such a bad place. We met there."

"That's true." I hugged her a little tighter. "I guess we're lucky people. We each found our Other Half. And before we died, too. How many are that lucky?"

"Tom and Linda, I think. Diane and Howard in Toronto. I can't think of anybody else I know of, for sure."

"Me either. There used to be more happy marriages around when I was a kid." The Bars began blinking twice as fast. A second improbable meteor? Or a chunk of the panel breaking loose, putting the rest in a tighter spin? It was an annoying distraction; I moved until I couldn't see it. "I guess I never realized just how incredibly lucky we are. A life with you in it is a square deal."

"Oh, Charlie," she cried, moving in my arms. Despite the awkwardness she worked around in her saddle to hug me again. My p-suit dug into my neck, the earphone on that side notched my ear, and her strong dancer's arms raised hell with my throbbing back, but I made no complaint. Until her grip suddenly convulsed even tighter.

"Charlie!"

"Nnngh."

She relaxed her clutch some, but held on. "What the hell is that?"

I caught my breath. "What the hell is what?" I twisted in my seat to look. *"What the hell is that?"* We both lost our seats on the Car and drifted to the ends of our hoses, stunned limp.

It was practically on top of us, within a hundred meters, so impossibly enormous and foreshortened that it took us seconds to recognize, identify it as a ship. My first thought was that a whale had come to visit.

Champion, said the bold red letters across the prow. And beneath, *United Nations Space Command.*

I glanced back at Norrey, then checked the air line one more time. "'No scheduled traffic,'" I said hollowly, and switched on my radio.

The voice was incredibly loud, but the static was so much louder that I knew it was off-mike, talking to someone in the same room. I remember every syllable.

"—pid fucking idiots are too God damned dumb to turn on their radios, sir. Somebody's gonna have to tap 'em on the shoulder."

Further off-mike, a familiar voice began to laugh like hell, and after a moment the radioman joined in. Norrey and I listened to the laughter, speechless. A part of me considered laughing too, but decided I might never stop.

"Jesus Christ," I said finally. "How far does a man have to go to have a little privacy with his wife?"

Startled silence, and then the mike was seized and the familiar voice roared, "You son of a bitch!"

"But seeing you've come all this way, Major Cox," Norrey said magnificently, "we'll come in for a beer."

"You dumb son of a bitch," Harry's voice came from afar. "You dumb son of a bitch." The Monkey Bars had stopped winking. We had the message.

"After you, my love," I said, unshipping the air tank, and as I reached the airlock my last thruster died. Bill Cox met us at the airlock with three beers, and mine was *delicious*.

The two sips I got before the fun started.

Like Phillip Nolan, I had renounced something out loud—and had been heard.

V

I took those two sips right away, and made them last. Officers and crew were frankly gaping at Norrey and me. At first I naturally assumed they were awed by anyone dumb enough to turn off their radios in an emergency. Well, I hadn't thought of being dead as an emergency. But on the second sip I noticed a certain subtle classification of gaping. With one or two exceptions, all the female crew were gaping at me and all the male crew were gaping at Norrey. I had not exactly forgotten what we were wearing under our p-suits; there was almost nothing to forget. We were "decently" covered by sanitary arrangements, but just barely, and what is commonplace on a home video screen on Earth is not so in the ready room of a warship.

Bill, of course, was too much of a gentleman to notice. Or maybe he realized there was not one practical thing to do about the situation except ignore it. "So reports of your demise were exaggerated, eh?"

"On the contrary," I said, wiping my chin with my glove. "They omitted our resurrection. Which by me is the most important part. Thanks, Bill."

He grinned, and said a strange thing very quickly. "Don't ask any of the obvious questions." As he said it, his eyes flickered slightly. On Earth or under acceleration they would have flicked from side to side. In free fall, a new reflex controls, and he happened to be oriented out of phase to my local vertical: his pupils described twin circles, perhaps a centimeter in diameter, and returned to us. The message was plain. The answers to my obvious next questions were classified information. Wait.

Hmmm.

I squeezed Norrey's hand hard—unnecessarily, of course—and groped for a harmless response.

"We're at your disposal," is what I came up with.

He flinched. Then in a split second he decided that I didn't mean whatever he'd thought I meant, and his grin returned. "You'll want a shower and some food. Follow me to my quarters."

"For a shower," Norrey said, "I will follow you through hell." We kicked off.

There was my second chance to gawk like a tourist at the innards of a genuine warship—and again I was too busy to pay any attention. Did Bill really expect his crew to believe that he had just happened to pick us up hitchhiking? Whenever no one was visibly within earshot, I tried to pump him—but in Space Command warships the air pressure is so low that sounds travel poorly. He outflew my questions—and how much expression does a man wear on the soles of his feet?

At last we reached his quarters and swung inside. He backed up to a wall and hung facing us in the totally relaxed "spaceman's crouch," and tossed us a couple of odd widgets. I examined mine: it looked like a wristwatch with a miniature hair dryer attached. Then he tossed us a pair of cigarettes and I got it. Mass priorities in a military craft differ from those of essentially luxury operations like ours or Skyfac's: the *Champion*'s air system was primitive, not only low-pressure but inefficient. The widgets were combination air-cleaner/ashtrays. I slipped mine over my wrist and lit up.

"Major William Cox," I said formally, "Norrey Armstead. Vice versa."

It is of course impossible to bow when your shoulders are velcro'd to the wall, but Bill managed to signify. Norrey gave him what we call the free-fall curtsy, a movement we worked out idly one day on the theory that we might someday give curtain calls to a live audience. It's indescribable but spectacular, as frankly sexual as a curtsy and as graceful.

Bill blinked, but recovered. "I am honored, Ms. Armstead. I've seen all the tapes you've released, and—well, this will be easy to misunderstand, but you're her sister."

Norrey smiled. "Thank you, Major—"

"Bill."

"—Bill. That's high praise. Charlie's told me a lot about you."

"Likewise, one drunken night when we met dirtside. Afterwards."

I remembered the night—weeks before I had consciously realized that I was in love with Norrey—but not the conversation. My subconscious tells me only what it thinks I ought to know.

"Now you must both forgive me," he went on, and I noticed for the first time that he was in a hurry. "I'd like nothing better than to chat, but I can't. Please get out of your p-suits, quickly."

"Even more than a shower, I'd like some answers, Bill," I said. "What the hell brings you out our way, just in the nicotine like that? I don't believe in miracles, not that kind anyway. And why the hush?"

"Yes," Norrey chimed in, "and why didn't your own Ground Control know you were in the area?"

Cox held up both hands. "Whoa. The answer to your questions run about twenty minutes minimum. In—" he glanced at his watch, "less than three we accelerate at two gravities. That's why I want you out of those suits—my bed *will* accommodate air tank fittings, but you'd be uncomfortable as hell."

"What? Bill, what the hell are you talking about? Accelerate where? Home is a couple o' dozen klicks that-away."

"Your friends will be picked up by the same shuttle that is fetching Dr. Panzella," Cox said. "They'll join us at Skyfac in a matter of hours. But you two can't wait."

"For *what*?" I hollered.

Bill arm-wrestled me with his eyes, and lost. "Damn it," he said, then paused. "I have specific orders not to tell you a thing." He glanced at his chronometer. "And I really do have to get back to the Worry Hole. Look, if you'll trust me and pay attention, I can give you the whole twenty minutes in two sentences, all right?"

"I—yeah. Okay."

"The aliens have been sighted again, in the close vicinity of Saturn. They're just sitting there. Think it through."

He left at once, but before he cleared the doorway I was halfway out of my p-suit, and Norrey was reaching for the straps on the right half of the Captain's couch.

And we were both beginning to be terrified. Again.

Think it through, Bill had said.

The aliens had come boldly knocking on our door once, and been met by a shotgun blast named Shara. They were learning country manners; this time they had stopped at the fence gate, shouted "hello the house," and waited prudently. (Saturn was just about our fence gate, too—as I recalled, a manned expedition to Saturn was being planned at that time, for the usual obscure scientific reasons.) Clearly, they wanted to parley.

Okay, then: if you were the Secretary General, who would *you* send to parley? The Space Commando? Prominent politicians? Noted scientists? A convention of used copter salesmen? You'd most likely send your most seasoned and flexible career diplomats, of course, as many as could go.

But would you omit the only artists in human space who have demonstrated a working knowledge of pidgin Alien?

I was drafted—at my age.

But that was only the first step in the logic chain. The reason that Saturn probe story had made enough of a media splash to attract even my attention was that it was a kind of kamikaze mission for the crew. Whose place we were assuming.

Think it through. Whatever they planned to send us to Saturn on, it was sure to take a *long* time. Six years was the figure I vaguely recalled hearing mentioned. And any transit over that kind of distance would have to be spent almost entirely in free fall. You could rotate the craft to provide gravity at either end—but one gee's worth of rotation of a space that small would create so much Coriolis differential that anyone who didn't want to puke or pass out would have to stay lying down for six years. Or hang like bolas from exercise lines on either end—not much more practical.

If we didn't dodge the draft, we would never walk Earth again. We would be free-fall exiles, marooned in space. Our reward for serving as mouthpieces between a bunch of diplomats and the things that had killed Shara.

Assuming that we survived the experience at all.

At any other time, the implications would have been too staggering for my brain to let itself comprehend; my mind would have run round in frightened circles. Unless I could talk my way out of this with whoever was waiting for us at Skyfac (why Skyfac?), Norrey and I had taken our last walk, seen our last beach, gone to our last concert. We would never again breathe uncanned air, eat with a fork, get rained on, or eat fresh food. We were dead to the world (S.I.C. TRANSIT:

gloria mundi, whispered a phantom memory that had been funny enough the first time). And yet I faced it squarely, calmly.

Not more than an hour ago I had renounced all those things.

And resigned myself to the loss of a lot of more important things, that it looked like I was now going to be able to keep. Breathing. Eating. Sleeping. Thinking. Making love. Hurting. Scratching. Bowel movements. Bitching. Why, the list was endless—and I had all those things back, at least six years' worth! Hell, I told myself, there were damned few city dwellers any better off—few of *them* ever got walks, beaches, concerts, uncanned air or fresh food. What with airlocks and nostril filters, city folk might as well be in orbit for all the outdoors they could enjoy—and how many of them could feel confident of six more years? I couldn't begin to envision the trip to Saturn, let alone what lay at the end of it—but I knew that space held no muckers, no muggers, no mad strangers or crazed drivers, no tenement fires or fuel shortages or race riots or blackouts or gang wars or reactor meltdowns—

How does Norrey feel about it?

It had taken me a couple of minutes to get this far, and as I turned my head to see Norrey's face the acceleration warning sounded. She turned hers, too; our noses were scant centimeters apart, and I could see that she too had thought it through. But I couldn't read her reaction.

"I guess I don't mind much going," I said.

"I *want* to go," she said fervently.

I blinked. "Phillip Nolan was the Man Without A Country," I said, "and he didn't care for it. *We'll* be the Couple Without A Planet."

"I don't care, Charlie." Second warning sounded.

"You seemed to care back there on the Car, when I was bum-rapping Earth."

"You don't understand. Those fuckers killed my sister. I want to learn their language so I can cuss them out."

It didn't sound like a bad idea.

But thinking about it was. Two gees caught us both with our heads sideways, smacking our cheeks into the couch and wrenching our necks. An eternity later, turn-over gave us just enough time to pop them back into place, and then deceleration came for another eternity.

* * *

There were "minor" maneuvering accelerations, and the "acceleration over" sounded. We unstrapped, both borrowed robes from Bill's locker, and began trading neckrubs. By and by Bill returned. He glanced at the bruises we were raising on opposite sides of our faces and snorted. "Lovebirds. All right, all ashore. Powwow time." He produced off-duty fatigues in both our sizes, and a brush and comb.

"With who?" I asked, dressing hastily.

"The Security-General of the United Nations," he said simply.

"Jesus Christ."

"If he was available," Bill agreed.

"How about Tom?" Norrey asked. "Is he all right?"

"I spoke with Panzella," Bill answered. "McGillicuddy is all right. He'll look like strawberry yoghurt for a while, but no significant damage—"

"Thank God."

"—Panzella's bringing him here with the others, ETA—" he checked his chronometer pointedly "—five hours away."

"*All* of us?" I exclaimed. "How big is the bloody ship?" I slipped on the shoes.

"All I know is my orders," Bill said, turning to go. "I'm to see that the six of you are delivered to Skyfac, soonest. And, I trust you'll remember, to keep my damn mouth shut." *Why Skyfac?* I wondered again.

"Suppose the others don't volunteer?" Norrey asked.

Bill turned back, honestly dumbfounded. "Eh?"

"Well, they don't have the personal motivations Charlie and I have."

"They have their duty."

"But they're *civilians.*"

He was still confused. "Aren't they humans?"

She gave up. "Lead us to the Secretary-General."

None of us realized at the time that Bill had asked a good question.

Tokugawa was in Tokyo. It was just as well; there was no room for him in his office. Seven civilians, six military officers. Three of the latter were Space Command, the other three national military; all thirteen were of high rank. It would have been obvious had they been naked. All of them were quiet, reserved; none of them spoke an unnecessary word. But there was enough authority in that room to sober a drunken lumberjack.

And it was agitated authority, nervous authority, faced not with an issue but a genuine crisis, all too aware that it was making history. Those who didn't look truculent looked extremely grave. A jester facing an audience of lords in this mood would have taken poison.

And then I saw that all of the military men and one of the civilians were trying heroically to watch everyone in the room at once without being conspicuous, and I put my fists on my hips and laughed.

The man in Carrington's—excuse me, in Tokugawa's chair looked genuinely startled. Not offended, not even annoyed—just surprised.

There's no point in describing the appearance or recounting the accomplishments of Siegbert Wertheimer. As of this writing he is still the Secretary-General of the United Nations, and his media photos, like his record, speak for themselves. I will add only that he was (inevitably) shorter than I had expected, and heavier. And one other, entirely subjective and apolitical impression: In those first seconds of appraisal I decided that his famous massive dignity, so beloved by political cartoonists, was intrinsic rather than acquired. It was the cause of his impressive track record, I was certain, and not the result of it. He did not *seem* like a humorless man—he was simply astounded that someone had *found* some humor in this mess. He looked unutterably weary.

"Why is it that you laugh, sir?" he asked mildly, with that faintest trace of accent.

I shook my head, still grinning uncontrollably. "I'm not sure I can make you see it, Mr. Secretary-General." Something about the set of his mouth made me decide to try. "From my point of view, I've just walked into a Hitchcock movie."

He considered it, momentarily imagining what it must be like to be an ordinary human thrust into the company of agitated lions, and grinned himself. "Then at least we shall try to make the dialogue fresh," he said. A good deal of his weariness seemed to be low-gee malaise, the discomfort of fluids rising to the upper body, the feeling of fullness in the head and the vertigo. But only his body noticed it. "Let us proceed. I am impressed by your record, Mr.—" He glanced down, and the paper he needed was not there. The American civilian had it, and the Russian general was looking over his shoulder. Before I could prompt him, he closed his eyes, jogged his memory, and continued, "—Armstead. I own three copies of the *Stardance*, and the first two are worn out. I have recently viewed your own recordings, and interviewed several of your former students. I have a job that needs doing, and I think you and your troupe are precisely the people for that job."

I didn't want to get Bill in trouble, so I hung a dumb look on my face and waited.

"The alien creatures you encountered with Shara Drummond have been seen again. They appear to be in a parking orbit around the planet Saturn. They have been there for approximately three weeks. They show no sign of any intention to move, nearer to or farther from us. Radio signals have been sent, but they have elicited no response. Will you kindly tell me when I come to information that is new to you?"

I knew I was caught, but I kept trying. In low gee, you *chase* spilled milk—and often catch it. "*New* to me? Christ, all of it's—"

He smiled again. "Mr. Armstead, there is a saying in the UN. We say, 'There are no secrets in space.'"

It is true that between all humans who choose to live in space, there is a unique and stronger bond than any of them and anyone who spends all his life on Earth. For all its immensity, space has always had a better grapevine than a small town. But I hadn't expected the Secretary-General to know that.

Norrey spoke while I was still reevaluating. "We know that we're going to Saturn, Mr. Secretary-General. We don't know how, or what will happen when we get there."

"Or for that matter," I added, "why this conference is taking place in Skyfac cubic."

"But we understand the personal implications of a space trip that long, as you must have known we would, and we know that we have to go."

"As I hoped you would," he finished, respectfully. "I will not sully your bravery with words. Shall I answer your questions, then?"

"One moment," I interjected. "I understand that you want our entire troupe. Won't Norrey and I do? We're the best dancers—why multiply your payload?"

"Payload mass is not a major consideration," Wertheimer said. "Your colleagues will be given their free choice—but if I can have them, I want them."

"Why?"

"There will be four diplomats. I want four interpreters. Mr. Stein's experience and proven expertise are invaluable—he is, from his record, unique. Mr. Brindle can help us learn the aliens' response to visual cues designed by computers which have seen the *Stardance* tapes—the same sort of augmentation he provides for you now. A sort of expanded vocabulary. He will also provide a peaceful excuse for us to judge the aliens' reaction to laser beams."

His answer raised several strong objections in my mind, but I decided to reserve them for later. "Go on."

"As to your other questions. We are guests of Skyfac Incorporated because of a series of coincidences that almost impels me to mysticism. A certain ballistic transfer is required in order to get a mission to Saturn at all expediently. This transfer, called Friesen's Transfer, is best begun from a 2:1 resonance orbit. Skyfac has such an orbit. It is a convenient outfitting base unequalled in space. And by chancc *Siegfried*, the Saturn probe which was just nearing completion, is in a precessing ellipse orbit which brought it within the close vicinity of Skyfac at the right time. An incredible coincidence. On a par with the coincidence that the launch window for Saturn opened concurrent with the aliens' appearance there.

"I do not believe in good fortune of that magnitude. I suspect personally that this is some kind of intelligence and aptitudes test—but I have no evidence beyond what I have told you. My speculations are as worthless as anyone's—we must have more information."

"How long does that launch window remain open?" I asked.

Wertheimer's watch was as Swiss as he, exquisite and expensive but so old fashioned that he had to look at it. "Perhaps twenty hours."

Oof. Now for the painful one. "How long is the round trip?"

"Assuming zero time in negotiation, three years. Approximately one year out and two back."

I was pleasurably startled at first: three years instead of twelve to be cooped up in a canful of diplomats. But then I began to grasp the acceleration implied—in an untested ship built by a government on low-bid contracts. And it was still more than enough time for us all to adapt permanently to zero gee. Still, they obviously had something special and extraordinary up their sleeves.

I grinned again. "Are you going?"

A lesser man would have said, "I regret that I cannot," or something equally self-absolutory—and might have been completely honest at that. Secretary-Generals don't go chasing off to Saturn, even if they want to.

But all he said was, "No," and I was ashamed that I had asked the question.

"As to the question of compensation," he went on quietly, "there is of course none adequate to the sacrifice you are making. Nevertheless, should you, upon your return, elect to continue performing, all your operating costs will be covered in perpetuity by the United Nations. Should you be disinclined to continue your careers, you will be guaranteed unlimited lifetime transport to and from, and luxury accommodations at, any place within United Nations jurisdiction."

We were being given a paid-up lifetime plane ticket to anywhere in human space. If we survived to collect it.

"This is in no sense to be considered a payment; any attempt at payment would be laughable and grotesque. But you have chosen to serve; your species is grateful. Is this satisfactory to you?"

I thought about it, turned to Norrey. We exchanged a few paragraphs by facial telegraph. "We accept the blank check," she said. "We don't promise to cash it."

He nodded. "Perhaps the only sensible answer. All right, let us—"

"Sir," I said urgently, "I have something I have to say first."

"Yes?" He did me the honor of displaying patience.

"Norrey and I are willing to go, for our own reasons. I can't speak for the others. But I *must* tell you that I have no great confidence that *any* of us can do this job for you. I will try my best—but frankly I expect to fail."

The Chinese general's eyes locked onto me. "Why?" he snapped.

I continued to look at Wertheimer. "You assume that because we are Stardancers, we can interpret for you. I cannot guarantee that. I venture to say that I know the *Stardance* tapes, even the classified ones, better than any person here. I shot them. I've monkeyed with speed and image-field until I knew every frame by name and I will be damned if I understand their language. Oh, I get flashes, insights, but . . .

"Shara understood them—crudely, tentatively, and with great effort. I'm not half the choreographer she was, nor half the dancer. None of us is. No one I've ever seen is. She told me herself that what communication took place was more telepathy than choreography. I have no idea whether any of us can establish such a telepathic rapport through dance. I wasn't *there*; I was in this oversized donut, four bulkheads away from here, filming the show." I was getting agitated, all the pressure finding release. "I'm sorry, General," I said to the Chinese, "but this is not something you can order done."

Wertheimer was not fazed. "Have you used computers?"

"No," I admitted. "I always meant to when I got time."

"You did not think we would fail to do so? No more than you, do we have an alien/human dictionary—but we know much. You can choreograph by computer?"

"Sure."

"Your ship's computer memories should offer you a year's worth of study on the trip out. They will provide you with at least enough 'vocabulary' to begin the process of acquiring more, and they will provide extensive if hypothetical suggestions for doing so. The research has been done. You and your troupe may be the only humans alive capable of assessing the data and putting them to use. I have seen your performance tapes, and I believe you can do it if anyone can. You are all unique people, at least in your work. You think as well as a human . . . but not *like* a human."

It was the most extraordinary thing anyone had ever said to me; it stunned me more than anything else that was said that day.

"All of you, apparently," he went on. "Perhaps you will meet with failure. In that case you are the best imaginable teachers and guides for the diplomat team, of whom only one has even minimal experience with free-fall conditions. They will need people who are at home in space to help them, whatever happens."

He took out a cigarette, and the American civilian turned up the air for him unobstrusively. He lit it with a match, himself. It smoked an odd color: it was tobacco.

"I am confident that all of you will do your best. All of your company who choose to go. I hope that will be all of you. But we cannot wait until the arrival of your friends, Mr. Armstead; there are enormous constraints on us all. If you are to be introduced to the diplomatic mission before take-off, it must be now."

Wuh oh. Red alert. You're inspecting your housemates for the next two years—just before signing the lease. Pay attention: Harry and the others'll be interested.

I took Norrey's hand; she squeezed mine hard.

And to think I could have been an alcoholic, anonymous video man in New Brunswick.

"Go ahead, sir," I said firmly.

"You're shitting me," Raoul exclaimed.

"Honest to God," I assured him.

"It sounds like a Milton Berle joke," he insisted.

"You're too young to remember Milton Berle," Norrey said. She was lying down on the near bunk, nodding off in spite of herself.

"So don't I have a tape library?"

"I agree with you," I said, "but the fact remains. Our diplomatic team consists of a Spaniard, a Russian, a Chinaman, and a Jew."

"My god," Tom said from his reclining position on the other bed, where he had been since he arrived. He did indeed look like strawberry yoghurt, lightly stirred, and he complained of intermittent eye and ear pain. But he was shot full of don't-hurt and keep-going, and his hands were full of Linda's; his voice was strong and clear. "It even makes sense."

"Sure," I agreed. "If he's not going to send one delegate from each member nation, Wertheimer's only option is to keep it down to The Big Three. It's the only restriction most everybody can live with. It's *got* to be a multi-national team; that business about mankind uniting in the face of the alien menace is the bunk."

"Headed by the proverbial Man Above Reproach," Linda pointed out.

"Wertheimer himself would have been perfect," Raoul put in.

"Sure," I agreed drily, "but he had some pressing obligations elsewhere."

"Ezequiel DeLaTorre will do just fine," Tom said thoughtfully.

I nodded. "Even I've heard of him. Okay, I've told you all we know. Comments? Questions?"

"I want to know about this one-year trip-home business," Tom spoke up. "As far as I know, that's impossible."

"Me too," I agreed. "We've been in space a long time. I don't know if they can understand how *little* prolonged acceleration we can take at this point. What about it, Harry? Raoul? Can the deed be done?"

"I don't think so," Harry said.

"Why not? Can you explain?"

Guest privileges aboard Skyfac include computer access. Harry jaunted to the terminal, punched up a reference display.

The screen said:

$$t_3 - t_1 = \sqrt{2p^3/u}\left[\tan\frac{f_1}{2} + \frac{1}{3}\tan^3\frac{f_2}{2} - \tan\frac{f_1}{2} - \frac{1}{3}\tan^3\frac{3f_1}{2}\right]$$

"That's the simplest expression for a transfer time from planet to planet," he said.

"Jesus."

"And it's too simple for your problem."

"Uh—they said something about a freezing transfer."

"Got it," Raoul said. "Friesen's Transfer, on the tip of my mind. Sure, it'd work."

"How?" everyone said at once.

"I used to study all the papers on space colonization when I was a kid," Raoul bubbled. "Even when it was obvious that L-5 wasn't going to get off the ground, I never gave up hope—it seemed like the only way I might ever get to space. Lawrence Friesen presented a paper at Princeton once . . . sure, I remember, '80 or a little earlier. Wait a minute." He hopped rabbitlike to the terminal, used its calculator function.

Harry was working his own belt-buckle calculator. "How're you gonna get a characteristic velocity of 28 klicks a second?" he asked skeptically.

"Nuclear pulse job?" Tom suggested.

That was what I had been afraid of. I've read that there are people who seriously propose propelling themselves into deep space by goosing themselves with hydrogen bombs—but you'll never get me up in one of them things.

"Hell no," Raoul said—thank goodness. "You don't need that kind of thrust with a Friesen. Watch." He set the terminal for engineering display and began sketching the idea. "You wanna start from an orbit like this."

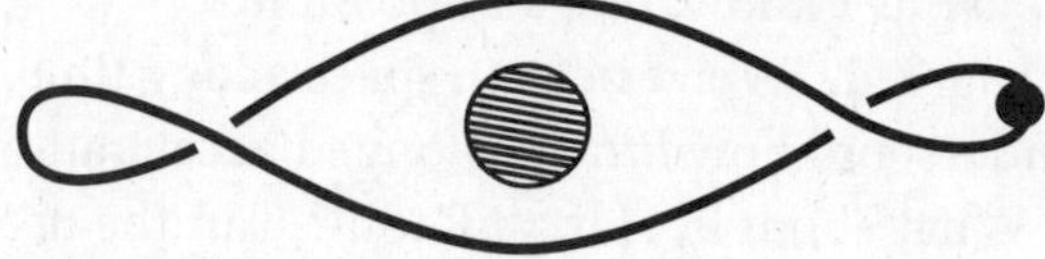

"A 2:1 resonance orbit?" I asked.

"That's right," he affirmed.

"Like Skyfac?" I asked.

"Yeah, sure, that'd—hey! Hey, yeah—we're just where we want to be. Gee, what a funny coincidence, huh?"

Harry, I could see, was beginning to smell the same rat Wertheimer had. Maybe Tom was, too; all that yoghurt got in the way. "So then?" I prompted.

Raoul cleared the screen and calculated some more. "Well, you'd want to make your ship lose, let's see, a little less than a kilometer per second. That's—well, nearly two minutes acceleration at one gravity. Hmmmm. Or a tenth-gee, say, about a seventeen-minute burn. Nothing.

"That starts us falling toward Earth. What we want to do then is slingshot around it. So we apply an extra . . . 5.44 klicksecs at just the right time. About nine minutes at one gravity, but they won't use one gravity because you need it *fast*. Might be, lemme see, 4.6 minutes at two gees, or it might be 2.3 at four."

"Oh, fine," I said cheerfully. "Only a couple of minutes at four gees. Our faces'll migrate around the back of our heads, and we'll be the only animals in the system with frontbones. Go on."

"So you get this," Raoul said, keying the drafting display again:

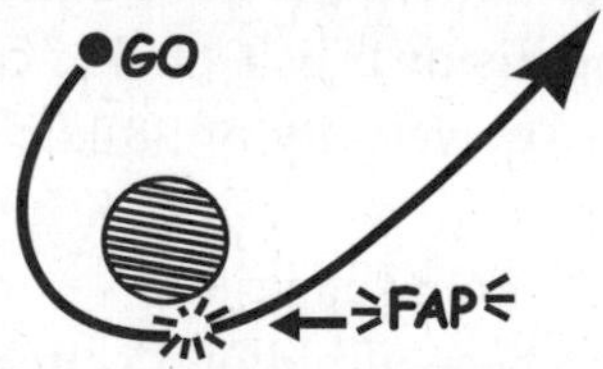

"And that gives us a year of free fall, in which to practice our choreography, throw up, listen to our bones rot, kill the diplomats and eat them, discuss Heinlein's effect on Proust, and bone up on Conversational Alien. Then we're at Saturn. Gee, that's another lucky break, the launch window for a one-year Freisen being open—"

"Yeah," Harry interrupted, looking up from his calculator, "that gets you to Saturn in a year—at twelve klicksecs relative. That's more'n escape velocity for Earth."

"We let the ship get captured by Titan," Raoul said triumphantly.

"Oh," Harry said. "Oh. Dump eight or nine klicksecs—"

"Sure," Raoul went on, punching keys. "Easy. A tenth gee for two-and-a-half hours. Or make it easy on ourselves, a hundredth of a gee for a little more than a day. Uh, twenty-five and a half hours. A hundredth gee isn't enough to make pee trickle down your leg, even if you're free-fall adapted."

I had actually managed to follow most of the salient points—computer display is a wondrous aid for the ignorant. "Okay then," I said sharply, in my "pay attention, here comes your blocking" voice, focusing everyone's attention by long habit. "Okay. This thing can be done. We've been talking it over ever since two hours before your shuttle docked here. I've told you what they want of us, and why they want all of us. My inclination is to tell you to have your answers ready along about next fall. But the bus is leaving soon. That launch window business you mentioned, Raoul." Harry's eyes flashed suspiciously, and yes, Tom too had picked up on the improbability of such luck. "So," I went on doggedly, "I have to ask for your final answers within the hour. I know that's preposterous, but there's no choice." I sighed. "I advise you to use the hour."

"Damn it, Charlie," Tom said in real anger, "is this a family or isn't it?"

"I—"

"What kind of shit is that?" Raoul agreed. "A man shouldn't insult his friends."

Linda and Harry also looked offended.

"Listen, you idiots," I said, giving it my very best shot, "*this is forever.* You'll never ski again, never swim, never walk around under even Lunar gravity. You'll never take a shit without technological assistance again."

"Where on Earth can you take a shit without technological assistance today?" Linda asked.

"Come on," I barked, "don't give me satire, *think about it.* Do I have to get personal? Harry—Raoul—how many women you figure you're going to date in space? How many would leave behind a whole world to stay with you? Seriously, now. Linda—Tom—do you know of any evidence at all to suggest that childbirth is *possible* in free fall? Do you want to bet two lives someday? Or had you planned to opt for sterilization? Now the four of you stop talking like comic book heroes and *listen to me,* God dammit." I discovered to my transient surprise that I genuinely was blazing mad; my tension was perfectly happy to find release as anger. I realized, for the first time, that a little histrionics can be a dangerous thing. "We have no way of knowing whether we can communicate with the goddam fireflies. On a gamble with odds that long, stakes this high, two lives is enough to risk. *We don't need you guys anyway,*" I shouted, and then I caught myself.

"No," I went on finally, "that's a lie. I won't try to claim that. But we can *do* it without you if it can be done at all. Norrey and I have personal reasons for going—but what do *you* people want to throw away a planet for?"

There was a glutinous silence. I had done my best; Norrey had nothing to add. I watched four blank, expressionless faces and waited.

At last Linda stirred. "We'll solve zero-gee childbirth," she said with serene confidence, and added, "when we have to," a second later.

Tom had forgotten his discomfort. He looked long at Linda, smiling with puffy lips amid his burst capillaries, and said to her, "I was raised in New York. I've known cities all my life. I never realized how much tension was involved in city life until I stayed at your family's home for a week. And I never realized how much I hated that tension until I noticed how much I was getting to dread having to go dirtside again. You only realize how stiff your neck and shoulders were when someone rubs them out for you." He touched her cheek with blood-purple fingernails. "It will be a long time before we have to put a lock on our airlock. Sure, we'll have a child someday—and we won't have to teach it how to adapt to a jungle."

She smiled, and took his purple fingers in her own. "We won't have to teach it how to walk."

"In zero gee," Raoul said meditatively, "I'm taller." I thought he meant the few centimeters that every spine stretches in free fall, but then he said, "In zero gee *nobody* is short."

By golly, he was right. "Eye-level" is a meaningless term in space;

consequently so is height.

But his voice was speculative; he had not committed himself yet.

Harry sucked beer from a bulb, belched, and studied the ceiling. "On my mind. For a long time. This adapting stuff. I could work all year insteada half. See a job through for once. Was thinking of doing it anyway." He looked at Raoul. "Don't figure I'll miss the ladies any."

Raoul met his eyes squarely. "Me either," he said, and this time his voice held commitment.

Light dawned in the cerebral caverns, and my jaw hung down. "Jesus Christ in a p-suit!"

"It's just a blind spot, Charlie," Linda said compassionately.

She was right. It has nothing to do with wisdom or maturity or how observant I am. It's just a personal quirk, a blind spot: I never will learn to notice love when it's under my nose.

"Norrey," I said accusingly. "You know I'm an idiot, why didn't you *tell* me? Norrey?"

She was sound asleep.

And all four of them were laughing like hell at me, and after a second I had to laugh too. Any man who does not know himself a fool is a damned fool; any man who tries to hide it is a double-damned fool, for he is alone. Together, we laughed, diminishing my foolishness to a shared thing, and Norrey stirred and half-smiled in her sleep.

"All right," I said when I could get my breath, "someone for all and all for someone. I won't try to fight the weather. I love you all, and will be glad of your company. Tom, you stretch out and get some sleep yourself; Raoul, get the light; the four of us'll go get briefed and come back for you and Norrey, Tom; we'll pack your comic books and your other tunic. You still mass around seventy-two, right?" I bent and kissed Norrey's forehead. "Let's *roll* it."

STARSEEDER

I

It was a week after that day that we next found an opportunity to all talk together—and we spent the first hour and a half of our opportunity in relative silence. A week locked in a steel can with many strangers had turned out to be even less fun than a comparable period with as many students. Most of these strangers were our employers, the other two were our Space Command keepers, none of them were our subordinates and nearly all of them were temperamentally unsuited to live with artists. All things considered, we handled the close quarters and tension much better than we had in the early days of the Studio—which surprised me.

But as soon as we could, we all went out for a stroll together. And discovered that we had *much* more important things to do than compare notes, first.

Distance shrank the mighty *Siegfried*, but refused to turn it into a Space Commando model; it retained its massive dignity even when viewed from truly Olympian perspective. I felt an uncharacteristic rush of pride at belonging to the species that had built it and hurled it at the sky. It lightened my mood like a shot of oxygen. I tugged at the three kilometers of line that connected me to the great ship, enjoyed the vast snakelike ripples I caused, let their influence put me in a slow roll like an infinite swan dive.

Space turned around me.

Tom and Linda came into view. I didn't call out to them—their breathing told me that they were in deep meditative trance, and my eyes told me how they had got there. You take that oldest and most enduring of children's toys, the Slinky. You weld thin flat plates on either end, and bring the accordionlike result out into free space.

You place the plates together, so that the Slinky describes a circle. Then you let go. Watch the result for long enough, and you will go into deep trance. The Worm Ourobouros endlessly copulating with himself. They would hear me if I called them by name; they would hear nothing else.

Raoul came into frame next, seen side-on to me. With deadly, matter-of-fact accuracy, he and Harry were hurling that other most durable of toys—a Frisbee (neon-rimmed for visibility)—back and forth across a couple of kilometers of emptiness. This too was more a meditational exercise than anything else; there is next to no skill involved. A flying saucer, it turns out, really *is* the most dynamically stable shape for a spacecraft. (Take a missile shaped like the old science fiction spaceships, fins and all, and throw it any way you want, with "Kentucky rifle" spin or without: sooner or later it will tumble. A sphere is okay—but unless it was formed in free fall, it's imperfect: it'll wobble, worse and worse as it goes.) They were practiced partners; their thruster use was minimal.

Norrey was skipping rope with a bight of her lifeline. Naturally she was rotating in the opposite direction. It was incredibly beautiful to watch, and I canceled my rotation to enjoy it. Perhaps, I thought lazily, we could work that into a dance someday. Dynamic balance, yin and yang, as simple and as complex as a hydrogen atom.

"Don't atoms dance, Charlie?"

I stiffened, then grinned at myself and relaxed. *You can't haunt me, Shara,* I told the hallucinatory voice. *You and I are at peace. Without me you could never have done the thing you did; without you I might never have been whole again. Rest in peace.*

I watched Norrey some more, in a curiously detached state of mind. Considered objectively, my wife was nowhere near as stunningly beautiful as her dead sister had been. Just strikingly beautiful. And never once in the decades of our bizarre relationship had I ever felt for Norrey the kind of helpless consuming passion I had felt for Shara every minute of the few years I knew her. Thank God. I remembered that passion, that mindless worship that sees a scuff on an apartment floor and says *There she placed her foot*, that sees a battered camera and says *With that I taped her.* The sleepless nights and the rivers of scotch and the insulted hookers and the terrible awakenings; through it all the continuous yearning that nothing will abate and only the presence of the loved one will assuage. My passion for Shara had died, vanished forever, almost at the same moment that she did. Norrey had been right, two years ago in Le Maintenant: you only conceive a passion like that for someone you think you can't have. And the very worst thing that can happen to you is to be wrong.

Shara had been very kind to me.

The love I now shared with Norrey was much quieter, much gentler on the nervous system. Why, I'd managed to overlook it for years. But it was a richer kind of love in the end.

Look, I used this metaphor before I ever *dreamed* of coming to space, and it's still good. Picture us all as being in free fall, all of us that are alive. Literally falling freely, at one gee, down a tube so unimaginably long that its ultimate bottom cannot be seen. The vast tube is studded with occasional obstacles—and the law of averages says that at some finite future time you will smash into one: you will die. There are literally billions of us in this tube, all falling, all sure to hit some day; we carom off each other all the time, whirling more or less at random in and out of lives and groups of lives. Most of us construct belief structures which deny either the falling or the obstacles and place them underneath our feet like skateboards. A good rider can stay on for a lifetime.

Occasionally you reach out and take a stranger's hand and fall together for a while. It's not so bad, then. Sometimes if you're really desperate with fear, you clutch someone like a drowning man clinging to an anchor, or you strive hopelessly to reach someone in a different trajectory, someone you can't possibly reach, just to be doing something to make you forget that your death is rushing up toward you.

That was the kind of need I had for Shara. I had learned better, from her and from space, and finally from my Last Ride with Norrey a week ago. I had reconciled myself to falling. Norrey and I now fell through life together with great serenity, enjoying the view with a truly binocular vision.

"Has it occurred to any of you," I asked lazily, "that living in space has just about matured us to the point of early childhood?"

Norrey giggled and stopped skipping. "What do you mean, love?"

Raoul laughed. "It's obvious. Look at us. A Slinky, a Frisbee, and a jump rope. The thrusting apex of modern culture, kids in the biggest playground God ever made."

"On tethers," Norrey said, "like country kids, to keep us out of the garden."

"Feels good to me," Harry put in.

Linda was coming out of meditation; her voice was slow, soft. "Charlie is right. We have matured enough to become childlike."

"That's closer to what I meant," I said approvingly. "Play is play, whether it's a tennis racquet or a rattle. I'm not talking about the kinds of toys we choose, so much. It's more like. . . ." I paused to think, and they waited. "Listen, it seems to me that I have felt like an old old man since I was about, what, nine years old. This past few years has been the adolescence I never had, and now I'm happy as a child again."

Linda began to sing:

Can't remember when I've ever been so happy
Happier than I can say
I used to feel older than my own grandpappy
But I'm getting younger every day

"It's an old Nova Scotia song," she finished quietly.

"Teach it to me," Raoul said.

"Later. I want to pursue this thought."

So did I—but just then my alarm watch went off. I fumbled the stud home through the p-suit, and it subsided. "Sorry, gang. Halfway through our air. Let's get together for the group exercises. Form up on Linda and we'll try the Pulsing Snowflake."

"Shit—work again?" "Phoeey—we've got a year to get into shape," "Wait'll I catch this sonumbitch, boss," and "Let's get it over with," were the entirely natural-sounding responses to the code phrase. We closed ranks and diddled with our radios.

"There we go," I said as I closed. "Right, and Harry, you cross over and take Tom's . . . that's right. Wait, *look out*! Oh Christ!" I screamed.

"No!" Harry shouted.

"Ohmigod," Raoul bubbled, "Ohmigod his suit's ripped *his suit's ripped.* Somebody *do* something, ohmigod—"

"May Day," I roared. "*Siegfried* from Stardancers, May Day, God damn it. We've got a blown suit, I don't think I can fix it, *answer me*, will you?"

Silence, except for Harry's horrible gurgling.

"*Siegfried*, for the love of God, come *in*. One of your precious interpreters is dying out here!"

Silence.

Raoul swore and raged, Linda said calming things to him, Norrey prayed softly.

Silence.

"I guess that damper circuit works, Harry," I said approvingly at last. "We've got privacy. By the way, that gurgling was horrible."

"When did I have a chance to rehearse?"

"You got that heavy-breathing tape going?"

"In circuit," Harry agreed. "Heavy breathing and cadence counts, no repeats. Hour and a half's worth."

"So if anyone's listening, they're just, eh, getting into our pants," Raoul said almost inevitably.

"*O*-kay," I said, "let's talk family talk. We've each spent some time with our assigned partners. What's the consensus?"

Some more silence.

"Well, has anybody got presentiments of doom? Choice gossip? Tom? You follow politics, you knew most of these people by reputation anyway. Tell us all about that first, and then we can compare personal impressions."

"All right, let's see—is there anything to be said about DeLaTorre? If he is not a man of honor and compassion, no one is. Even his critics admire him, and a good half of them are willing to admit it. I'll be honest: I'm not as certain of *Wertheimer*'s integrity as I am of DeLaTorre's. Except of course that he *picked* DeLaTorre to head this posse, which raises him a notch. Anybody feel different? Charlie, he's your puppetmaster, what do you say?"

"A heartfelt ditto. I'd turn my back on him in the airlock. Go on."

"Ludmilla Dmirov has a similar reputation for moral toughness, unpusharoundable. She was the first diplomatic official ever to turn down a state-owned *dacha* in Sovmin. Those of you who don't know *nomenklatura*, the patronage system in Moscow, a *dacha* is sort of a country cabin for high-ranking officials, and turning one down is like a freshman senator refusing to vacation or junket, or a rookie cop turning down the usuals. Unthinkable . . . and dangerous." He paused. "But I can't be as certain that's it's integrity with her. It may just be orneriness. And compassionate she is *not*."

Norrey was assigned to Dmirov; she spoke up. "I'm not sure I agree, Tom. Oh, she plays chess like a machine, and she sure knows how to be impenetrable—and maybe she *doesn't* know enough about when and how to turn it off. But she showed me all her son's baby pictures, and she told me that the *Stardance* made her cry. 'Weep from the chest,' she said. I think the compassion's in there."

"Okay," Tom said. "I'll take your word. And she *was* one of the ones who pushed hard for a UN Space Command. Without her there just might not *be* a UN anymore, and space might have become the next Alsace-Lorraine. I'm willing to believe her heart's in the right place." He paused again. "Uh, with all due respect, I don't think I'd be prepared to turn my back on her in the airlock yet. But my mind's open.

"Now, Li," he went on, "was also a prime mover in the formation of the Space Command—but I'll lay odds that it was a chess-player's move for him. I think he took a cold extrapolative look at the future and decided that if the world *did* blow itself up over the issue of space, it would seriously restrict his political career. He is reputed to be one sharp horse trader and one cold son of a bitch, and they say the road to Hell is paved with the skins of his enemies. He owns a piece of Skyfac Inc. I wouldn't turn my back on him on live network TV, and Linda, I hope you won't either."

"That is certainly the image he has cultivated," she agreed. "But I must add a few things. He is impeccably polite. He is a philosopher of incredible perception and subtlety. And he is rock steady. Hunger, lack of sleep, danger—none of these will affect his performance or his judgment in any measurable way. Yet I find his mind to be open, to change and to changes. I believe he might well be a real *statesman*." She broke off, took a deep breath, and finished, "But I don't think I trust him either. Yet."

"Yeah," Tom said. "Is he a statesman for mankind or for the People's Republic? Okay, that leaves my own man. Whatever else you can say about the others, they're probably all statespersons. Sheldon Silverman is a politician. He's held just about every elective office except President and Vice President. He could have been the latter any time he was silly enough to want to; only some incredibly subtle errors cost him the former. I think he bought or bribed his way onto this trip somchow, as his last chance to earn a whole page in the history books. I think he sees *himself* as the leader of the team, by virtue of being an American. I despise him. He costs Wertheimer the notch that DeLaTorre earned him, as far as I'm concerned." He shut up suddenly.

"I think you may be holding his past against him," Linda said.

"Damn right," he agreed.

"Well—he's old. Some old people change, quite radically. Zero gee has been working on him; wait and see. We should bring him out here sometime."

"My love, your fairness is showing."

"Damn right," she said, forcing a grin from him. "It sort of has to."

"Huh?"

"He gives me the *creeps*."

"Oh. I see. I think."

"Harry, Raoul," I said, "you've been hanging out with the Space Commandos."

Raoul took it, of course. "Cox we all know or know about. I'd let him hold the last air bottle while I took a leak. His second-in-command is an old-time NASA science officer type."

"Jock," Harry put in.

Raoul chuckled. "You know, she is. Susan Pha Song was a Viet Nam War baby, raised in Nam by her aunt after her father split and her mother got napalmed. Hasn't got much use for America. Physicist. Military through and through; if they told her to she'd nuke Viet Nam and drop rose petals on Washington. She disapproves of music and dance. And me and Harry."

"She'll follow orders," Harry asserted.

"Yeah. For sure. She's a chicken colonel as of last week, and in the event Commander Cox drops dead, the chain of command goes to her, then Dmirov, presumably. She's got pilot training, she's a space freak."

"If it comes to that extreme," I said, "I for one am going free lance."

"Chen Ten Li has a gun," Linda said suddenly.

"*What?*" Five voices at once.

"What kind?" from Harry.

"Oh, I don't know. A small handgun, squarish looking. Not much barrel."

"How did you get a look at it?" I asked.

"Jack-in-the-box effect. Took him by surprise, and he recovered late."

The jack-in-the-box effect is one of the classic surprises of free fall, predictable but unexpected, and it gets virtually every new fish. Any container, cabinet or drawer you open will spew its contents at you—unless you have thought to velcro them all in place. The practical joke possibilities are nearly inexhaustible. But I smelled a rat. "How about that, Tom?"

"Eh?"

"If Chen Ten Li has been one of the major forces behind intelligent use of space, wouldn't he know about jack-in-the-box?"

Tom's voice was thoughtful. "*Huh*. Not necessarily. Li is one of those paradoxes, like Isaac Asimov refusing to fly. For all his understanding of the issues of space, this is the first time he's been further off-planet than a jetliner goes. He's a groundlubber at heart."

"Still," I objected, "jack-in-the-box is standard tourist anecdote. He's only need to have spoken with one returned spacegoer, for any length of time."

"I don't know about the rest of you," Raoul said, "but there was a lot about zero gee that I knew about intellectually, that I still tripped over when I got there. Besides, what motive could Li have for letting Linda see a gun?"

"That's what bothers me," I admitted. "I can think of two or three reasons offhand—and they all imply either great clumsiness or great cunning. I don't know which I'd prefer. Well . . . anyone else see any heat?"

"I haven't seen a thing," Norrey said judiciously, "but I wouldn't be surprised if Ludmilla has a weapon of some kind."

"Anybody else?"

Nobody responded. But each of the diplomats had fetched a sizable mass of uninspected luggage.

"Okay. So the upshot is, we're stuck in a subway with three rival gangleaders, two cops and a nice old man. This is one of the few times I've ever been grateful that the eyes of the world are upon us."

"Much more than the eyes of the world," Linda corrected soberly.

"It'll be okay," Raoul said. "Remember: a diplomat's whole function is to maintain hostilities short of armed conflict. They'll all pull together at the showdown. Most of 'em may be chauvinists—but underneath I think they're all *human* chauvinists, too."

"That's what I mean," Linda said. "Their interests and ours may not coincide."

Startled silence, then, "What do you mean, darling? We're not human?" from Tom.

"Are we?"

I began to understand what she was driving at, and I felt my mind accelerate to meet her thought.

What does it mean to be human? Considering that the overwhelming mass of the evidence has been taken from observation of humans under one gravity, pinned against a planet? By others in the same predicament?

"Certainly," Tom said. "Humans are humans whether they float or fall."

"Are you sure?" Linda asked softly. "We are different from our fellows, different in basic ways. I don't mean just that we can never go back and live with them. I mean spiritually, psychologically. Our thought patterns change, the longer we stay in space—our brains are adapting just like our bodies."

I told them what Wertheimer had said to me the week before—that we choreographed as well as humans but not like humans.

"That's John Campbell's classic definition of 'alien,'" Raoul said excitedly.

"Our souls are adapting, too," Linda went on. "Each of us spends every working day gazing on the naked face of God, a sight that groundhogs can only simulate with vaulting cathedrals and massive mosques. We have more perspective on reality than a holy man on the peak of the highest mountain on Earth. There are no atheists in space—and *our* gods make the hairy thunderers and bearded paranoids of Earth look silly. Hell, you can't even make out Olympus from the Studio—much less from here." The distant Earth and Moon were already smaller than we were used to.

"There's no denying that space is a profoundly moving place,"

Tom maintained, "but I don't see that it makes us other than human. I *feel* human."

"How did Cro-Magnon know he was different from Neanderthal?" Raoul asked. "Until he could assess discrepancies, how would he know?"

"The swan thought he was an ugly duckling," Norrey said.

"But his *genes* were swan," Tom insisted.

"Cro-Magnon's genes started out Neanderthal," I said. "Have you ever examined yours? Would you know a really subtle mutation if you saw one?"

"Don't tell me you're buying into this silliness, Charlie?" Tom asked irritably. "Do you feel inhuman?"

I felt detached, listening with interest to the words that came out of my mouth. "I feel other than human. I feel like more than a new man. I'm a new thing. Before I followed Shara into space, my life was a twisted joke, with too many punchlines. Now I am alive. I love and can be loved. I didn't leave Earth behind. I put space ahead."

"Aw, phooey," Tom said. "Half of that's your leg—and I know what the other half is because it happened to me, at Linda's family's place. It's the city-mouse-in-the-country effect. You find a new, less stressful environment, get some insights, and start making better, more satisfying decisions. Your life straightens out. So something must be magic about the place. Nuts."

"The Mountain *is* magic," Linda said gently. "Why is magic a dirty word for you?" At that stage of their relationship, it suited Tom and Linda to maintain a running pseudodisagreement on matters spiritual. Occasionally they realized what was obvious to the rest of us: that they almost never actually disagreed with each other on anything but semantics.

"Tom," I said insistently. "This is *different*. I've *been* to the country. I'm telling you that I'm not an improved version of the man I was—I'm something altogether different now. I'm the man I could never have been on Earth, had lost all hope of being. I—I believe in things that I haven't believed in since I was a kid. Sure I've had some good breaks, and sure, opening up to Norrey has made my life more than I ever thought it could be. But my whole makeup has changed, and no amount of lucky breaks will do that. Hell, I used to be a drunk."

"Drunks smarten up every day," Tom said.

"Sure—if they can find the strength to maintain cold turkey for the rest of their lives. I take a drink when I feel like it. I just hardly ever feel like it. I stopped *needing* booze, just like that. How common is that? I smoke less these days, and treat it less frivolously when I do."

"So space grew you up in spite of yourself?"

"At first. Later I had to pitch in and work like hell—but it started without my knowledge or consent."

"When did it begin?" Norrey and Linda asked together.

I had to think. "When I began to learn how to see spherically. When I finally learned to cut loose of up and down."

Linda spoke. "A reasonably wise man once said that anything that disorients you is good. Is instructive."

"I know that wise man," Tom sneered. "Leary. Brain-damage case if I ever heard of one."

"Does that make him incapable of having ever been wise?"

"Look," I said, "we are all unique. We've all come through a highly difficult selection process, and I don't suppose the first Cro-Magnon *felt* any different. But the overwhelming evidence suggests that our talent is not a normal human attribute."

"Normal people can live in space," Norrey objected. "Space Command crews. Construction gangs."

"If they've got an artificial local vertical," Harry said. "Take 'em outdoors, you gotta give em straight lines and right angles or they start going buggy. Most of 'em. S'why we get rich."

"That's true," Tom admitted. "At Skyfac a good outside man was worth his mass in copper, even if he was a mediocre worker. Never understood it."

"Because you are one," Linda said.

"One *what*?" he said, exasperated.

"A Space Man," I said spacing it so the capitals were apparent. "Whatever comes after *Homo hablis* and *Homo sapiens.* You're space-going Man. I don't think the Romans had the concept, so *Homo novis* is probably the best you can do in Latin. New Man. The next thing."

Tom snorted. "*Homo excastra* is more like it."

"No, Tom," I said forcefully, "You're wrong. We're *not* outcasts. We may be literally 'outside the camp,' 'outside the fortress'—but the connotation of 'exile' is all wrong. Or are you regretting the choice you made?"

He was a long time answering. "No. No, space is where I want to live, all right. I don't feel exiled—I think of the whole solar system as 'human territory.' But I feel like I've let my citizenship in its largest nation lapse."

"Tom," I said solemnly, "I assure you that that is the diametric opposite of a loss."

"Well, the world does look pretty rotten these days, I'll grant you that. There isn't a *lot* of it I'll miss."

"You miss my point."

"So explain."

"I talked about this with Doc Panzella some, before we left. What is the normal lifespan for a Space Man?"

He started to speak twice, stopped trying.

"Right. There's no way to frame a guess—it's a completely new ball game. We're the first. I asked Panzella and he told me to come back when two or three of us had died. We may all die within a month, because fatigue products refuse to collect in our feet or our corns migrate to our brains or something. But Panzella's guess is that free fall is going to add at *least* forty years to our lifespans. I asked him how sure he was and he offered to bet cash."

Everyone started talking at once, which doesn't work on radio. The consensus was, "Say *what*?" The last to shut up and drop out was Tom. "—possibly *know* a thing like that, yet?" he finished, embarrassed.

"Exactly," I said. "We won't *know* 'til it's too late. But it's *reasonable*. Your heart has less work to do, arterial deposits seem to diminish—"

"So it won't be heart trouble that gets us," Tom stipulated, "assuming that lowering the work load drastically turns out to be good for a heart. But that's one organ out of many."

"Think it through, Tom. Space is a sterile environment. With reasonable care it always will be. Your immune system becomes almost as superfluous as your semicircular canals—and do you have any idea how much energy fighting off thousands of wandering infections drains from your life system? That might have been used for maintenance and repair? Or don't you notice your energy level drop when you go dirtside?"

"Well sure," he said, "but that's just . . ."

"—the gravity, you were gonna say? See what I mean? We're healthier, physically and mentally, than we *ever* were on Earth. When did you ever have a cold in space? For that matter, when was the last time you got deeply depressed, morose? How come we hardly ever, any of us, have dog days, black depressions and sulks and the like? Hell, the *word* depression is tied to gravity. You *can't* depress something in space, you can only move it. And the very word gravity has come to be a synonym for humorlessness. If there's two things that'll kill you early it's depression and a lack of a sense of humor."

In a vivid rush came the memory of what it had felt like to live with a defective leg under one gravity. Depression, and an atrophying sense of humor. It seemed so long ago, so very far away. Had I ever really been that despairing?

"Anyway," I went on, "Panzella says that people who spend a lot of time in free fall—and even the people in Luna who stay in one-sixth gee, those exiled miners—show a lower incidence of heart and lung trouble, naturally. But he also says they show a much lower incidence of cancers of all kinds than the statistical norm."

"Even with the higher radiation levels?" Tom asked skeptically. Whenever there's a solar flare, we all see green polliwogs for a while, as the extra radiation impacts our eyeballs—and it doesn't make any difference whether we're indoors or out.

"Yep," I assured him. "Coming out from under the atmosphere blanket was the main health hazard we all gambled on in living in space—but it seems to've paid off. It *seemed* there should have been a *higher* risk of cancer, but it just doesn't seem to be turning out that way. Go ask why. And the lower lung trouble is obvious—we breath real air, better filtered than the Prime Minister's, dust free and zero pollen count. Hell, if you had all the money on Earth, you couldn't have a healthier environment tailor-made. How about old Mrs. Murphy on Skyfac? What is she, sixty-five?"

"Sixty-six," Raoul said. "And free-fall handball champ. She whipped my ass, three games running."

"It's almost as though we were *designed* to live in space," Linda said wonderingly.

"All right," Tom cried in exasperation. "All right, I give up. I'm sold. We're all going to live to be a hundred and twenty. Assuming that the aliens don't decide we're delicious. But I still say that this 'new species' nonsense is muddy thinking, delusions of grandeur. For one thing, there's no guarantee we'll breed true—or, as Charlie pointed out, at all. But more important, *Homo novis* is a 'species' without a natural habitat! *We're not self-sustaining,* friends! We're utterly dependent on *Homo sapiens,* unless and until we learn how to make our own air, water, food, metals, plastics, tools, cameras—"

"What are you so pissed off about?" Harry asked.

"I'm not pissed off!" Tom yelled.

We all broke up, then, and Tom was honest enough to join us after a while.

"All right," he said. "I am angry. I'm honestly not sure why. Linda, do you have any handles on it?"

"Well," she said thoughtfully, "'anger' and 'fear' are damned close to synonyms. . . ."

Tom started.

Raoul spoke up, his voice strained. "If it will help any, I will be glad to confess that our pending appointment with these super-fireflies has me, for one, scared shitless. And *I* haven't met 'em personally like you and Charlie, Tom. I mean, this little caper could cost us a lot more than just Earth."

That was such an odd sentence that we just let it sit there a while.

"I know what you mean," Norrey said slowly. "Our job is to establish telepathic rapport with what seems to be a group-mind. I'm almost . . . almost afraid I might succeed."

"Afraid you might get lost, darling?" I said. "Forget it—I wouldn't let go of you long enough. I didn't wait twenty years to be a widower." She squeezed my hand.

"That's the point," Linda said. "The worst we're facing is death, in one form or another. And we always *have* been under sentence of death, all of us, for being human. That's the ticket price for this show. Norrey, you and Charlie looked death right in the eye a week ago. Sure as hell you will again some day. It might turn out to be a year from now, at Saturn: so what?"

"That's the trouble," Tom said, shaking his head. "Fear doesn't go away just because it's illogical."

"No," Linda agreed, "but there *are* methods for dealing with it—

and repressing it until it comes out as anger is *not* one of them. Now that we're down to the root, though, I can teach you techniques of self-discipline that'll at least help a lot."

"Teach me too," Raoul said, almost inaudibly.

Harry reached out and took his hand. "We'll learn together," he said.

"We'll all learn together," I said. Maybe we are other than human, but we're not *that* different. But I would like to say that you are about the bravest folks I know, all of you. If anybody—wups! There goes the alarm again. Let's get some real dancing done, so we come home sweaty. We'll do this again in a couple of days. Harry, take that heavy-breathing tape out of circuit and we'll boost our signal strength together at three, two, one, *mark*."

I repeat the above conversation in its entirety partly because it is one of the few events in this chronicle of which I possess a complete audio recording. But also partly because it contains most of the significant information you need to know about that one-year trip to Saturn. There is no point in describing the interior of *Siegfried*, or the day-to-day schedules or the month-by-month objectives or the interpersonal frictions that filled up one of the most busy, boring years of my life.

As is common and perhaps inevitable on expeditions of this kind, crew, diplomats, and dancers formed three reasonably tight cliques outside working hours, and maintained an uneasy peace during them. Each group had its own interests and amusements—the diplomats, for instance, spent much of their free time (and a substantial percentage of their working time) fencing, politely and otherwise. DeLaTorre's patience soon earned the respect of every person aboard. Read any decent book on life in a submarine, then throw in free fall, and you've got that year. Raoul's music helped keep us all sane, though; he became the only other universally respected passenger.

The six of us somehow never discussed the "new species" line of thought again together, although I know Norrey and I kicked it around hood-to-hood a few times, and Linda and I spoke of it occasionally. And of course we never mentioned it at *all* anywhere aboard *Siegfried*—spaceships are *supposed* to be thoroughly bugged. The notion that we six dancers were somehow other-than-human was not one that even DeLaTorre would have cared for—and he was about the only one who treated us as anything but hired hands, "mere interpreters" (Silverman's expression). Dmirov and Li knew better, I believe, but they couldn't help it; as experienced diplomats they were not conditioned to accept interpreters as social equals. Silverman thought dance was that stuff they did on variety shows, and why *couldn't* we translate the concept of Manifest Destiny into a dance?

I will say one thing about that year. The man I had been when I first came to space could not have survived it. He would have blown out his brains, or drunk himself to death.

Instead I went out for lots of walks. And made lots of love with Norrey. With music on, for privacy.

Other than that the only event of note was when Linda announced that she was pregnant, about two months out of Saturn. We were committed to solving zero-gee childbirth without an obstetrician. Or, for that matter, a GP.

Things got livelier as we neared Saturn.

II

We had not succeeded in persuading any of the diplomats to join us in EVA of any kind. Three refused for the predictable reason. EVA is measurably more dangerous than staying safely indoors (as I had been forcibly reminded on the day I had gotten into this), and duty forbade them from taking *any* avoidable risk on their way to what was literally the biggest and most important conference in history. We dancers were considered more expendable, but pressure was put on us to avoid having all four dancers outboard at the same time. I stuck to my guns, maintaining that a group dance must be planned, choreographed, and rehearsed *ensemble*—that what Stardancers, Inc. *was,* was a creative collective. Besides, the more buddies you have, the safer you are.

The fourth diplomat, Silverman, had been specifically ordered not to expose himself to space. So early on he asked us to take him out for a walk. Sort of a "they can't tell a fearless SOB like me not to take risks" thing: the order impugned his masculinity. He changed his mind when p-suit plumbing was explained to him, and never brought the subject up again.

But a few weeks before we were to begin deceleration, Linda came to my room and said, "Chen Ten Li wants to come out for a walk with us."

I winced, and did my Silverman imitation. "It would kill you, first to sit me down and say, 'I have bad news for you'? Like that you tell me?"

"Like that *he* told *me.*"

What would DeLaTorre think? Or Bill? Or the others? Or old Wertheimer, who had told me with his eyes that he believed I could be trusted not to fuck up? And as important, why did Chen now want to earn his wings? Not for scenery—he had first-class video, the best Terra could provide, which is *good*. Not for jackass reasons like Silverman.

"What does he *want*, Linda? To see a rehearsal live? To drift and meditate? What?"

"Ask him."

I had never seen the inside of Chen's room before. He was playing 3-D chess with the computer. I can barely follow the game, but it was clear that he was losing badly—which surprised me.

"Dr. Chen, I understand you want to come outside with us."

He was dressed in tastefully lavish pajamas, which he had expertly taken in for free fall and velcro'd (Dmirov and DeLaTorre had been forced to ask Raoul for help, and Silverman's clothes looked as though he had backed into a sewing machine). He inclined his shaven head, and replied gravely, "As soon as possible." His voice was like an old cornet, a little feathery.

"That puts me in a difficult position, sir," I said as gravely. "You are under orders not to endanger yourself. DeLaTorre and all the others know it. And if I did bring you outside, and you had a suit malf, or even a nausea attack, the people's Republic of China would ask me some pointed questions. Followed by the Dominion of Canada and the United Nations, not to mention your aged mother."

He smiled politely, with lots of wrinkles. "Is that outcome probable?"

"Do you know Murphy's Law, Dr. Chen? And its corollary?"

His smile widened. "I wish to risk it. You are experienced at introducing neophytes to space."

"I lost two out of seventeen students!"

"How many did you lose in their first three hours, Mr. Armstead? Could I not remain in the Die, wearing a pressure suit for redundancy?"

The Die wasn't cast; it was spot-welded. It was essentially an alloy-framed cube of transparent plastic, outfitted for minimal life support, first aid, and self-locomotion through free space. The crew and all the diplomats except Chen called it the Field Support Module. This disgusted Harry, who had designed and built it. The idea was that one of us Stardancers might blow a gasket in midconference, or want to sit out a piece, or conserve air, or for some other reason need a pressurized cubic with a 360° view. It was currently braced tight against the hull of the big shuttlecraft we called the Limousine, mounted for use, but it could easily be unshipped. And Chen's pressure suit was regulation Space Command armor, as good as or better than even our customized Japanese-made suits. Certainly stronger; better air supply. . . .

"Doctor, I have to know *why*."

His smile began to slo-o-owly fade, and when I hadn't blanched or retracted by half past, he let it remain there. About a quarter to frowning. "I concede your right to ask the question. I am not certain I can satisfy you at this time." He reflected, and I waited. "I am not accustomed to using an interpreter. I have facility with languages. But there is at least one language I will never acquire. I was once informed that no one could learn to think in Navajo who was not raised a Navajo. Consequently I went to great lengths to accomplish this, and I failed. I can make myself understood to a Navajo, haltingly. I cannot ever learn to think in that language—it is founded on basically different assumptions about reality that my mind cannot enfold.

"I have studied your dance, the 'language' you will speak for us shortly. I have discussed it with Ms. Parsons at great length, exhausted the ship's computer on the subject. I cannot learn to think in that language.

"I wish to try one more time. I theorize that confrontation with naked space, in person, may assist me." He paused, and grinned again. "Ingesting buds of peyote assisted me somewhat in my efforts with Navajo—as my tutor had promised me. I must expose myself to *your* assumptions about reality. I hope they taste better."

It was by far the longest speech I had gotten out of the epigrammatic Chen since the day we met. I looked at him with new respect, and some astonishment. And a growing pleasure: here was a friend I had almost missed making. *My God, suppose old Chen is* Homo novis?

"Dr. Chen," I said, when I could get my breath, "let's go see Commander Cox."

Chen listened with total absorption to eighteen hours' worth of instruction, most of which he already knew, and asked infrequent but highly insightful questions. I'm willing to bet that before the instruction he could have disassembled any subsystem in his suit in the dark. By the end I'd have bet he could *build* 'em in the dark, starting with free-floating components. I have been exposed to a rather high number of extraordinary minds, and he impressed me.

But I *still* wasn't sure I trusted him.

We held the party to three, on the less-to-go-wrong theory—in space, trouble seldom comes in ones. I was the obvious Scoutmaster; I had logged more EVA hours than anyone aboard except Harry. And Linda had been Chen's Alien 101 instructress for the past year; she came along to maintain classroom continuity. And to dance for him, while I played Mother Hen. And, I think, because she was his friend.

The first hour passed without incident, all three of us in the Die, me at the con. We put a few klicks between us and *Siegfried*, trailing a suspenders-*and*-belt safety line, and came to rest, as always, in the exact center of infinity. Chen was reverentially silent rather than isolated. He was, I believed, capable of encompassing that much wonder—it was almost as though he had always known the universe was that big. Still he was speechless for a long time.

So were Linda and I, for that matter. Even at this distance Saturn looked unbelievably beautiful, beyond the power of words to contain. That planet must unquestionably be the damndest tourist attraction in the Solar System, and I had never seen anything so immensely moving in my life.

But we had seen it before in recent days—the whole ship's complement had been glued to the video tanks. We recovered, and Linda told Chen some last thoughts about the way we danced, and then she sealed her hood and went out the airlock to show him some solo work. By prearrangement we were all to remain silent for this period, and Bill too maintained radio silence on our channel. Chen watched with great fascination for three quarters of Linda's first hour. Then he sighed, glanced at me oddly, and kicked himself across the Die to the control panel.

I started to cry out—but what he reached for was only the Die's radio. He switched it off. Then he removed his helmet in one practiced-seeming move, disconnecting his suit's radio. I had my own hood off to save air, and grabbed for it when I saw him kill the radio, but he held a finger to his lips and said, "I would speak with you under the rose." His voice was high and faint in the low pressure.

I considered the matter. Assuming the wildest paranoid fantasy,

Linda was mobile and could see anything that happened in the transparent cube. "Sure," I called.

"I sense your unease, and understand and respect it. I am going to put my hand in my right pouch and remove an object. It is harmless." He did so, producing one of those microcorders that looks like a fancy button. "I wish there to be truth between us," he added. Was it low pressure stridency alone that gave his voice that edge?

I groped for an appropriate response. Beyond him, Linda was whirling gracefully through space, sublimely pregnant, oblivious. "Sure," I said again.

He thumbnailed the playback niche. Linda's recorded voice said something that I couldn't hear, and I shook my head. He rewound to the same cue and underhanded it gently toward me.

"That's what I mean," Linda's voice repeated. "Their interests and ours may not coincide."

The tape record I spoke of a while ago.

My brain instantly went on computer time, became a hyperefficient thinking machine, ran a thousand consecutive analysis programs in a matter of microseconds, and self-destructed. *Hand in the cookie jar. Halfway down the Mountain and the brakes are gone. I'd have sworn I closed that airlock.* The microcorder hit me in the cheek; instinctively I caught it on the rebound and shut it off as Tom was asking Linda, "Aren't we human?"

And *that* echoed in the Die for a while.

"Only an imbecile would find it difficult to bug an unguarded pressure suit," Chen said tonelessly.

"Yeah," I croaked, and cleared my throat. "Yeah, that was stupid. Who else—?" I broke off and slapped my forehead. "*No.* I don't want to ask any stupid questions. Well, what do *you* think, Chen Ten Li? *Are* we *Homo novis*? Or just gifted acrobats? I'm God damned if I know."

He jaunted cleanly back to me, like an arrow in slow-motion flight. Cats jaunt like that. "*Homo caelestis,* perhaps," he said calmly, and his landing was clean. "Or possibly *Homo ala anima.*"

"Allah who? Oh—'winged soul.' Huh. Okay. I'll buy that. Let me try a whammy on *you*, Doc. I'll bet a cookie that you're a `winged soul' yourself. Potentially, at least."

His reaction astonished me. I had expected a sudden poker face. Instead naked grief splashed his face, stark loss and hopeless yearning, etched by Saturnlight. I never saw such wide-open emotion on his face before or since; it may be that no one but his aged mother and his dead wife ever had. It shocked me to my socks, and it would have shocked him too if he had been remotely aware of it.

"No, Mist' Armstead," he said bleakly, staring at Saturn over my shoulder. His accent slipped for the first and last time, and absurdly reminded me of Fat Humphrey. "No, I am not one of you. Nor can time or my will make it so. I *know* this. I am reconciled to this." As he got this far, his face began relaxing into its customary impassivity, all unconsciously. I marveled at the discipline of his subconscious mind, and interrupted him.

"*I* don't know that you're right. It seems to me that any man who can play three-D chess is a prime candidate for *Homo* whateverthehell."

"Because you are ignorant of three-D chess," he said, "and of your own nature. Men play three-D chess on Earth. It was designed under one gravity, for a vertical player, and its classic patterns are linear. I have tried to play in free fall, with a set that is not fixed in that relationship to me, and I cannot. I can consistently beat the Martin-Daniels Program at flat chess" (world class) "but in free-fall three-D Mr. Brindle could easily defeat me, if I were unvain enough to play him. I can coordinate myself well enough aboard the *Siegfried* or in this most linear of vehicles. But I can never learn to live for any length of time without what you call a 'local vertical.'"

"It comes on slow," I began.

"Five months ago," Li interrupted, "the night light failed in my room. I woke instantly. It took me twenty minutes to locate the light switches. During that entire time I wept with fear and misery, and lost control of my sphincters. The memory offended me, so I spent several weeks devising tests and exercises. I must have a local vertical to live. I am a normal human."

I was silent a long time. Linda had noticed our conversation; I signaled her to keep on dancing and she nodded. After I had thought things through I said, "Do you believe that our interests will fail to coincide with yours?"

He smiled, all diplomat again, and chuckled. "Are you familiar with Murphy's Law, Mr. Armstead?"

I grinned back. "Yeah, but is it *probable*?"

"I don't believe so," he answered seriously. "But I believe that

Dmirov would believe so. Possibly Ezequiel. Possibly Commander Cox. Certainly Silverman."

"And we must assume that any of them might also have bugged a suit."

"Tell me: Do you agree that if this conference generates any information of great strategic value, Silverman will attempt to establish sole possession of it?"

Chatting with Chen was like juggling chainsaws. I sighed. We were being honest. "Yeah—if he got a chance to pull it off, sure. But that'd take some doing."

"One person with the right program tapes could bring *Siegfried* close enough to Terra for retrieval," he said, and I noticed that he didn't say "one man."

"Why are you telling me this?"

"I am presently jamming any possible bugs in this vehicle. I believe Silverman will attempt this thing. I smell it. If he does, I will kill him at once. You and your people react quickly in free fall; I want you to understand my motives."

"And they are?"

"Preservation of civilization on Terra. The continued existence of the human race."

I decided to try throwing *him* a hot one. "Will you shoot him with that automatic?"

He registered faint distaste. "I cycled that out the airlock two weeks after departure," he said. "An absurd weapon in free fall, as I should have realized. No, I shall probably break his back."

Don't give this guy strong serves: his return is murder.

"Where will you stand in that event, Mr. Armstead?"

"Eh?"

"Silverman is a fellow Caucasian, a fellow North American. You share a cultural matrix. Is that a stronger bond than your bond with *Homo caelestis*?"

"Eh?" I said again.

"Your new species will not survive long if the blue Earth is blown apart," Chen said harshly, "which is what that madman Silverman would have. I don't know *how* your mind works, Mr. Armstead: *what will you do*?"

"I respect your right to ask the question," I said slowly. "I will do what seems right to me at the time. I have no other answer."

He searched my face and nodded. "I would like to go outside now."

"Jesus Christ," I exploded, and he cut me off.

"Yes, I know—I just said I couldn't function in free space, and now I want to try." He gestured with his helmet. "Mr Armstead, I anticipate that I may die soon. Once before that time I must hang alone in eternity, subject to no acceleration, without right angles for frames, in free space. I have dreamed of space for most of my life, and feared to enter it. Now I *must.* As nearly as I can say it in your language, I must confront my God."

I wanted to say yes. "Do you know how much that can resemble sensory deprivation?" I argued. "How'd you like to lose your ego in a space suit? Or even just your lunch?"

"I have lost my ego before. Someday I will forever. I do not get nauseous." He began putting his helmet on.

"No, dammit, watch out for the nipple. Here, let me do it."

After five minutes he switched his radio back on and said, shakily. "I'm coming in now." After that he didn't say anything until we were unbuttoning in *Siegfried*'s shuttlecraft bay. Then he said, very softly, "It is I who am *Homo excastra.* And the others," and those were the last words he said to me until the first day of Second Contact.

What I replied was, "You are always welcome in my home, Doctor," but he made no reply.

Deceleration brought a horde of minor disasters. If you move into a small apartment (and never leave it) by the end of a year your belongings will have tended to *spread out* considerably. Zero gee amplifies the tendency. Storing *everything* for acceleration would have been impossible even if all we'd had to contend with was the twenty-five hours of a hundredth gee. But even the straightest, laser-sighted pipeline has some kinks in it, and our course was one of the longest pipelines ever laid by Man (over a billion klicks). Titan's gravity well was a mighty small target at the end of it, that we had to hit just precisely right. Before Skyfac provided minimicrochip computer crystals the trick would not have been possible, and we had had small corrections en route. But the moon swam up fast, and we took a couple of one-gee burns that, though mercifully short, made me strongly doubt that we could survive even a two-year return trip.

They also scattered wreckage, mostly trivial, all over the ship: Fibber McGee's closet, indoors. The worst of it, though, appeared to be a ruptured water line to the midships shower bags, and the air conditioning handled it.

Even being forewarned of an earthquake doesn't help much.

On the other hand, cleanup was next to no problem at all—again, thanks to zero gee. All we had to do was wait, and sooner or later virtually all of the debris collected on the air conditioning grilles of its own accord, just like always. Free-fall housekeeping mostly involves replacing worn-out velcro and grille screens.

(We use sleeping webs and cocoons when we sleep, even though *everything* in a free-fall domicile is *well* padded. It's not as restful—but without any restraints, you keep waking up when you bump in to the air grille. One idiot student had wanted to nap in Town Hall, which has no sleeping gear, so he turned off the air conditioning. Fortunately someone came in before he could suffocate in the carbon dioxide sphere of his own exhalations. I paid for an unscheduled elevator and had him dirtside twenty hours later.)

And so nearly everyone found time to hang themselves in front of a video monitor and eyeball Titan.

From the *extensive* briefing we all studied, this abstract:

Titan is the sixth of Saturn's moons, and quite the largest. I had been expecting something vaguely Luna-sized—but the damned thing has a diameter of almost 5,800 klicks, roughly that of the planet Mercury, or about four tenths that of Earth! At that incredible size its mass is only about .002 that of Earth's. Its orbital inclination is negligible, less than a degree—that is, it orbits almost precisely around the equator of Saturn (as does the Ring), at a mean distance of just over ten planetary diameters. It is tidally locked, so that it always presents the same face to its primary, like Luna, and it takes only about sixteen days to circle Saturn—a speedy moon indeed for its size. (But then Saturn itself has a ten-and-a-quarter-hour day.)

From the time that it had been close enough to eyeball it had looked reddish, and now it looked like Mars on fire, girdled with vast clouds like thunderheads of blood. Through them lunarlike mountains and valleys glowed a slightly cooler red, as though lit by a gobo with a red gel—which, essentially, they were. The overall effect was of hellfire and damnation.

That preternatural red color was one of the principal reasons why Cox and Song went into emergency overdrive the moment we were locked into orbit. The world scientific community had gone in to apoplexy when its expensive Saturn probe had been hijacked by the military, for a diplomatic mission, and into double apoplexy when they understood that the scientific complement of the voyage would consist of a single Space Command physicist and an engineer. So Bill and Col. Song spent the twenty-four hours we remained in that orbit working like fishermen when the tide makes, taking the absolute minimum of measurements and recordings that would satisfy *Siegfried*'s original planners. Led by Susan Pha Song, they worked from taped instructions and under the waspish direction of embittered scientists on Terra (with a transmission lag of an hour and a quarter, which improved no one's temper), and they did a good, dogged job. It is a little difficult to imagine the kind of mind that would find chatting with extrasolar plasmoids *less* exciting than studying Saturn's sixth moon, but there are some—and the startling thing is, they're not entirely crazy.

It's that red color. Titan should look sort of blue-greenish. Yet even from Earth it is clearly red. Why? Well, the thing that had professors in a flutter was that Titan's atmosphere (mostly methane) and temperature characteristics made it about the last place in the Solar System where theory grudgingly admitted the possibility of "life as we know it." Experiments with a Titan-normal chamber produced Miller's "primal flash" chemical reactions, a good sign, and the unspoken but dearly beloved theory was that maybe the red cloud-cover was organic matter of some kind—or even conceivably whatever kind of pollution a methane-breather would produce. I couldn't follow even Raoul's popularization of the by-play, and I was only peripherally interested, but I gathered that by the end of twenty-four hours, a pessimist would have said "no" and an optimist "maybe." Raoul mentioned a lot of ambiguous data, stuff that seemed self-contradictory—which didn't surprise me in light of how prematurely *Siegfried* had been rushed into commission.

I divided my own attention between Titan and Saturn, which the scientists wouldn't be interested in until after the conference, when they could get a closer look. From where we were it took up about a 6 or 7° piece of sky (for reference, Luna seen from Earth subtends an angle of about half a degree; Earth seen from Luna is about 2°wide. Your fist at arm's length is about 10°), and the Ring, edge on to us, added another couple of planetary diameters or almost 14°. Call it a total package of 20°, two fists' width. Not cosmic; at home, at the Studio, I've seen Mother Terra take up more than half the sky at perigee. But when Earth *did* take up 20°, we were about 22,000 klicks from its surface. Saturn was 1.2 *million* klicks away.

It's a hellacious big planet—the biggest in the System if you don't call Jupiter a planet (I don't call it at all. It might answer). Its diameter is a little over 116,000 klicks, roughly nine Earths, and it masses a whopping ninety-five Earths. This makes its surface gee of 1.15 Earth normal seem absurdly low—but it must be borne in mind that Saturn is only .69 as dense as a comparable sphere of water (while Earth has more than five times the density of water.) Even that low a gee field was more than enough to kill a *Homo caelestis or* a *Homo excastra,* were we silly enough to land on Saturn. And the escape velocity is more than three times that for Earth (a weak gravity well—but a *big* one).

It doesn't exactly *have* a surface, though, as I understand it. Oh, there's probably rock down there somewhere. But long before you got down that far, you'd come to rest, floating on methane, which is what Saturn (and its "atmosphere") mostly is.

Its mighty Ring appears to be a moon that didn't make it, uncountable trillions of orbiting rocks from sand-to boulder-size, covered with water ice.

Together they present an indescribably beautiful appearance. Saturn is a kind of dreamy ocher yellow with wide bands of dark, almost chocolate brown, and it is quite bright as planets go. The Ring, being dirty ice, incorporates literally every color in the visible spectrum, sparkling and shifting as the independent orbits of its component parts change relation. The overall impression is of an immense agate or tiger-eye circled by the shattered remnants of a mighty rainbow. Smaller, literal rainbows come and go randomly within the orbiting mass, like lights seen through wet glasses.

It was a sight I never tired of, will never forget as long as I live, and it alone was worth the trip from Earth and the loss of my heritage. I couldn't decide whether it was more beautiful at the height of our orbit, when we were above the Ring, or at the other end when we were edge-on; both had their points. Raoul spent virtually every minute of his free time glued to the bulkhead across from his video screen, his Musicmaster on his lap, its headphones over his ears, fingers seeking and questioning among its keys. He would not let us put the speakers on—but he gave Harry the auxiliary 'phones. I have subsequently heard the symphony he derived from that working tape, and I would have traded Earth for *that.*

The aliens, of course, were the utter and total center of Bill Cox's attention. Their high-energy emissions nearly overloaded his instruments, though they were too far away to be seen. About a million klicks, give or take a few hundred thousand, waiting with apparent patience at the approximate forward Trojan point for Saturn-Titan. The actual locating of that point was extremely complicated by the presence of eight other moons, and I'm told that no Trojan point would be stable in the long term—even if the O'Neill Colony movement ever gets going at L-5, it'll never spread to Saturn. But what it came down to was that the aliens were waiting about 60° "down the line" of titan's orbit, at a sensible place for a conference. Which made it even more probable that that was their intention.

So *our* next move was to go say howdy. *Siegfried* and all: the Trojan point was a good four light-seconds away, and the lag was not acceptable to any of us.

We dancers also had business of our own to occupy us while Bill and Col. Song were slaving, of course. We didn't spend *all* our time rubbernecking.

The Limousine had been fully supplied and outfitted, field- and board-tested down to the last circuit, and secured long since, in transit. So naturally the first thing we did was to check the supplies and fittings and board-test down to the last circuit again. If we should buy the emptiest of farms, the next expedition would be two or three years in arriving at the very least—and maybe by then the aliens' Trojan stability would have decayed enough to irritate them and they'd have gone home.

Besides, I wanted personal words with them.

And *that* was the root of the *last* thing we did before blasting for their location, which was to hold the last several hours of a year-long quarrel with the diplomats over choreography.

I finally jaunted right out on them, prepared to float in my room and let *them* dance. I hadn't lost my temper; only my will to argue. DeLaTorre waited a polite interval and then buzzed at my door.

"Come in."

The free-fall haircut spoiled his appearance; he should have had hair like Mark Twain. He had had to shave his beard too—there's no room for one in a helmet—and hating shaving he did it badly; but it actually improved his looks, almost enough to compensate for the big fuzzy skull. His warm brown eyes showed unspeakable fatigue, their lids raisinlike with wrinkles. He stuck himself to the wall, moving with the exaggerated care of the bone-tired, so that he was aligned with the local vertical built into it by its terrestrial designers (when Harry builds his first billion-dollar spaceship, he'll be more imaginative).

DeLaTorre would, at his age, never make a Space Man. Out of respect, I assumed the same orientation. What little anger I had had was gone; my determination remained.

"Charles, an accommodation must be reached."

"Ezequiel, don't tell me you're as blind as the rest of them."

"They only feel that the *first* movement might more properly be respectful, rather than stern; solemn rather than emotional. Once we have established communication, opened relations with these beings in mutual dignity, then would be the time to state our grievances. The third or fourth movement, perhaps."

"Dammit, it doesn't *feel* right that way."

"Charles, forgive me, but—surely you will admit that your emotional judgment might be clouded in this matter?"

I sighed. "Ezequiel, look me in the eye. I have not been in love with Shara Drummond since shortly before she died. I have examined my soul and the dance that came out of it, and I feel no urge for personal vengeance, no thirst for retribution."

"No, your dance is not vengeful," he agreed.

"But I *do* have a grievance—not as a bereaved lover but as a bereaved human being. I want those aliens to know what they cost my race when they wrought the death of Shara Drummond, when they forced her hand and made her into *Homo caelestis* before there was any place or any way for one to live—" I broke off, realizing that I had blundered, but DeLaTorre did not even blink.

"Was she not already *Homo caelestis*, or *ala anima*, when they arrived, Charles?" he asked as blandly as if he was supposed to know those terms. "Would she not have died on her return to Earth in any case, by that point?"

I recognized and accepted the sudden rise in our truth level, distracted by his question. "Perhaps, Ezequiel. Her body must have been on the borderline of permanent adaptation. I have lain awake many nights, thinking about this, talking it over with my wife. I keep thinking: Had Shara visualized what her *Stardance* would do financially, she might have endured a brief wait at Skyfac, might have survived to be a more worthy leader for our Studio. I keep thinking: Had she thought things through, she might not have chosen to burn her wings, so high above her lost planet. I keep thinking: Had she known, she might have lived."

I sucked rotten coffee from a bulb and made a face. "But all the fighting spirit had been sucked out of her, drained into the *Stardance* and hurled at those red fireflies with the last of her strength. All of her life, right up to Carrington, had been slowly draining the will to live out of her, and threw all that she had left at those things, because that was what it took to scare them back to interstellar space, to frighten them so bad that their nearest subsequent approach was a billion klicks away. There was no will to live left after that, not enough to sustain her.

"I want to convey to those creatures the value of the entity their careless footstep crushed, the enormity of her people's loss. If grief or remorse are in their emotional repertoire, I want to see some. Most of all, I think, I want to forgive them. And so I have to state my complaint *first*. I believe that their reaction will tell us quicker than anything else whether we can *ever* learn to communicate and peacefully coexist with them.

"They *respect* dance, Ezequiel, and they cost us the greatest artist of our time. A race that could open with any other statement is one I don't much want to represent. That'd be Montezuma's Mistake all over again. Norrey and the others agree with me: this is a deal-breaker."

He was silent a long time. The last thing a diplomat will concede is that compromise is impossible. But at last he said, "I follow your thought, Charles. And I admit that it leads me to the same conclusions." He sighed. "You are right. I will make the others accept this." He pushed free and jaunted to me, taking both my shoulders in his wrinkled, mottled hands. "Thank you for explaining to me. Come, let us prepare to go and state our grievance."

He was closeted with the other three for a little over twenty minutes, and emerged with an extremely grudging accord. He was indeed the best man Wertheimer could have chosen. Half an hour later we were on our way.

III

It took the better part of a day to coax *Siegfried* from Titan orbit to the Trojan point, without employing accelerations that would kill us all. Titan is a mighty moon, harder to break free of than Luna. Fortunately we didn't want to break free of it—quite. We essentially widened the circle of our orbit until it intersected the Trojan point—decelerating like hell all the way so that we'd be at rest relative to it when we got there. It had to be at least partly by-guess-and-by-God, because any transit in Saturn's system is a ten-body problem (don't even *think* about the Ring), and Bill was an equal partner with the computer in that astrogating job. He did a world-class job, as I had known he would, wasting no fuel and, more important, no passengers. The worst we had to endure was about fifteen seconds at about .6 gee, mere agony.

Any properly oriented wall will do for an acceleration couch—since everything in a true spaceship is well padded (billion-dollar spaceprobe designers aren't *that* unimaginative.) I don't know about all the others, but Norrey and I and anybody sensible customarily underwent acceleration naked. If you've got to lie flat on your back under gravity, you don't want wrinkly clothes and bulky velcro pads between you and the padding. When we drifted free of the wall and the "acceleration over" horn sounded, we dressed in the same p-suits we had worn on our Last Ride together, a year before. Of the five models of custom-made suits we use, they are the closest to total nudity, resembling abbreviated topless bathing suits with a collared hood. The transparent sections are formfitted and scarcely noticeable; the "trunks" are not for taboo but for sanitary reasons; and the hood-and-collar section is mostly to conceal the unaesthetic amount of hardware that must be built into a p-suit hood. The thrusters are ornate wrist and ankle jewelry; their controls golfing gloves. The group had decided unanimously that we would use these suits for our performance. Perhaps by the overt image of naked humans in space we were unconsciously trying to assert our humanity, to deny the concept of ourselves as *other than human* by displaying the evidence to the contrary. See? Navel. See? Nipples. See? Toes.

"The trouble with these suits, my love," I said as I sealed my own, "is that the sight of you in yours always threatens to dislodge my catheter tube."

She grinned and made an unnecessary adjustment of her left breast. "Steady, boy. Keep your mind on business."

"Especially now that the bloody *weight* is gone. How did you women put up with it for centuries? Having some great clod *lay* on you like that?"

"Stoically," she said, and jaunted for the phone. She diddled its controls, and said, "Linda—how's the baby?"

Linda and Tom appeared on the screen, in the midst of helping each other suit up. "Fine," Linda called happily. "Nary a quiver."

Tom grinned at the phone and said, "What's to worry? She still fits into her p-suit, for crying out loud."

His composure impressed and deeply pleased me. When we left Skyfac I would have predicted that at this pre-curtain moment, with a pregnant wife to worry about, Tom would be agitated enough to chew pieces off his shoulder blades. But free space, as I have said, is a tranquilizing environment—and more important, he had allowed Linda to teach him much. Not just the dance, and the breathing and meditational exercises for relaxation—we had all learned these things. Not even the extensive spiritual instruction she had given that ex-businessman (which had begun with loud arguments, and calmed down when he finally got it through his head that she had no creed to attack, no brand label to discredit), though that helped of course.

Mostly it was her love and her loving that had finally unsnarled all the knots in Tom's troubled soul. Her love was so transparently genuine, and heartfelt that it forced him to take it at face value, forced him therefore to love himself a little more—which is all anyone really needs to relax. Opening up to another frees you at least temporarily of all that armor you've been lugging, and your disposition invariably improves. Sometimes you decide to scrap the armor altogether.

Norrey and I shared all of this in a smile and a glance, and then she said, "That's great, you two. See you at the Garage," and cleared the screen.

She drifted round in space, her lovely breasts majestic in free fall, till she was facing me. "Tom and Linda will be good partners for us," she said, and was silent.

We hung at opposite ends of the room for a few seconds, lost in each other's eyes, and then we kicked off at the same instant and met, hard, at the center of the room. Our embrace was four-limbed and fierce, a spasmodic attempt to break through the boundaries of flesh and bone and plastic and touch hearts.

"I'm not scared," she said in my ear. "I ought to be scared, but I'm not. Not at all. But *oh*, I'd be scared if I were going into this without you!"

I tried to reply and could not, so I hugged tighter.

And then we left to meet the others.

Living in *Siegfried* had been rather like living below-decks in a luxury liner. The shuttlecraft was more like a bus, or a plane. Rows of seats with barely enough room to maneuver above them, a *big* airlock aft, a smaller one in the forward wall, windows on either side, engines in the rear. But from the outside it would have appeared that the bus or plane had rammed a stupendous bubble. The bow of the craft was a transparent sphere about twenty meters in diameter, the observation globe from which the team of diplomats would observe our performance. There was extremely little hardware to spoil the view. The computer itself was in *Siegfried* and the actual terminal was small; the five video monitors were little bigger, and the Limousine's own guidance systems were controlled by another lobe of the same computer. There would be no bad seats.

There had, inevitably, been scores of last-minute messages from Earth, but not even the diplomats had paid any attention to them. Nor was there much conversation on the trip. Everyone's mind was on the coming encounter, and our Master Plan, insofar as we could be said to have one, had been finalized long since.

We had spent a year studying computer analyses of *both* sides of the *Stardance,* and we believed we had gotten enough out of them to prechoreograph an opening statement in four movements.

About an hour's worth of dance, sort of a Mandarin's Greeting. By the end of that time we would either have established telepathic rapport or not. If so we would turn the phone over to the diplomats. They would pass their consensus through DeLaTorre, and we would communicate their words to the aliens as best we could. If, for some reason, consensus could not be reached, then we would dance that too. If we could *not* establish rapport, we would watch the aliens' reply to our opening statement and we and the computer would try to agree on a translation. The diplomats would then frame their reply, the computer would feed us choreographic notation, and we'd try it that way. If we got no results by the end of nine hours—two air changes—we'd call it a day, take the Limo back home to *Siegfried* and try again tomorrow. If we got good or promising results, we had enough air cans to stay out for a week—and the Die was stocked with food, water and a stripped-down toilet.

Mostly we all expected to play it by ear. Our ignorance was so total that anything would be a breakthrough, and we all knew it.

There was only one video screen in the passenger compartment, and Cox's face filled it throughout the short journey. He kept us posted on the aliens' status, which was static. At last deceleration ended, and we sank briefly to our seats as the Limousine turned end over end to present the bubble to the aliens, and then we were just finally *there*, at the crossroads. The diplomats unstrapped and went forward to the bubble's airlock; the Stardancers went aft to the big one. The one that had the EXIT light over it.

We hung there together a moment, by unspoken consent, and looked around at each other. No one had a moving, *Casablanca*-ending speech to deliver, no wise-cracks or last sentiments to exchange. The last year had forged us into a *family*; we were already beginning to be mutually telepathic after a fashion. We were beyond words. We were ready.

What we did, actually, we smiled big idiotic smiles and joined hands in a snowflake around the airlock.

Then Harry and Raoul let go on either end, kissed each other, seated their hoods, and entered the airlock to go build our set. There was room for four in the airlock; Tom and Linda squeezed in with them. They would deploy the Die and wait for us.

As the door slid closed behind them, Norrey and I shared our own final kiss.

"No words," I said, and she nodded slightly.

"Mr. Armstead?" from behind me.

"Yes, Dr. Chen?"

He was half in his airlock, alone. Without facial or vocal expression he said, "Blow a gasket."

I smiled. "Thank you, sir."

And we entered the lock.

There is a kind of familiarity beyond déjá vu, a recall greater than total. It comes on like scales falling from your eyes. Say you haven't taken LSD in a long while, but you sincerely believe that you remember what the experience was like. Then you drop again, and as it comes on you simply say, "Ah yes—reality," and smile indulgently at your foolish shadow memories. Or (if you're too young to remember acid), you discover real true love, at the moment you are making love with your partner and realize that all of your life together is a single, continuous, ongoing act of lovemaking, in the course of which you happen to occasionally disengage bodies altogether for hours at a time. It is not something to which you *return*—it is something you suddenly find that you have never really left.

I felt it now as I saw the aliens again.

Red fireflies. Like glowing coals without the coals inside, whirling in something less substantial than a bubble, more immense than *Siegfried*. Ceaselessly whirling, in ceaselessly shifting patterns that drew the eye like the dance of the cobra.

All at once it seemed to me that the whole of my life was the moments I had spent in the presence of these beings—that the intervals between those moments, even the endless hours studying the tapes of the aliens and trying to understand them, had been unreal shadows already fading from my memory. I had always known the aliens. I would always know them, and they me. We went back about a billion years together. Like coming home from school to Mom and Dad, who are unchanging and eternal. *Hey*, I wanted to tell them, *I've stopped believing I'm a cripple,* as a kid might proudly announce he's passed a difficult Chem test. . . .

I shook my head savagely, and snapped out of it. Looking away helped. Everything about the setting said that something more than confused dreams had occurred since our last meeting. Just past the aliens mighty Saturn shone yellow and brown, ringed with coruscating fire. The Sun behind my back provided only one percent of the illumination it shone on Terra—but the difference was not discernible: the terrestrial eye habitually filters out 99% of available light. (It suddenly struck me, the coincidence that this meeting place the aliens had chosen happened to be precisely as far away from the Sun as a human eye could go and still see properly.)

We were "above" the Ring. It defied description.

To my "right," Titan was smaller than Luna (under a third of a degree), but clearly visible, nearly three-quarters full from our perspective. Where the terminator faced Saturn the dull red color softened to the hue of a blood-orange, from the reflected Saturnlight. The great moon still looked smoky, like a baleful eye on our proceedings.

And all around me my teammates were floating, staring, hypnotized.

Only Tom was showing signs of self-possession. Like me, he was renewing an old acquaintance; reaffirming strong memories takes less time than making new ones.

We knew them better, this time, even those who were facing them for the first time. At that last confrontation, only Shara had seemed able to understand them to any degree—no matter how hard I had watched them, then, understanding had eluded me. Now my mind was free of terror, my eyes unblinded by need, my heart at peace. I felt as Shara had felt, saw what she had seen, and agreed with her tentative evaluations.

"There's a flavor of arrogance to them—conviction of superiority. Their dance is a challenging, a dare."

". . . biologists studying the antics of a strange, new species . . . ."

"They want Earth."

". . . in orbits as carefully choreographed as those of electrons. . . ."

"Believe me, they can dodge or withstand anything you or Earth can throw at them. I know."

Cox's voice broke through our reverie. "*Siegfried* to Stardancers. They're the same ones, all right: the signatures match to 3 nines."

We had planned for the possibility that these might have been a *different* group of aliens—say, policemen looking for the others, or possibly even the second batch of suckers to buy a Sol-System Tour on the strength of the brochure. Even low probabilities had been prepared for. As Bill spoke, he, the diplomats and the computer flushed several sheafs of contingency scenarios from their memory banks and confirmed Plan A in their minds.

But *all* of us Stardancers had known already, on sight.

"Roger, *Siegfried*," I acknowledged. "I'm terrible on names, but I never forget a face. 'That's the man, officer.'"

"Initiate your program."

"All right, let's get set up. Harry, Raoul, deploy the set and monitor. Tom and Linda, deploy the Die—about twenty klicks thataway, okay? Norrey, give me a hand with camera placement, we'll all meet at the Die in twenty minutes. Go."

The set was minimal, mostly positional grid markers. Raoul had not taken long to decide that attempting flashy effects in the close vicinity of the Ring would be vain folly. His bank of tracking lasers was low-power, meant only as gobos to color-light us dancers vividly for the camera—and to see how the aliens would react to the presence of lasers, which was their real purpose. I thought it was a damned-fool stupid idea—like Pope Leo picking his teeth with a stiletto as he comes to dicker with Attila—and the whole company, Raoul included, agreed wholeheartedly. We all wanted to stick to conventional lights.

But if you're going to win arguments with diplomats of that stature you've got to make some concessions.

The grid markers were color organs slaved to Raoul's Musicmaster through a system Harry designed. If the aliens responded noticeably to color cues, Raoul would attempt to use his instrument to make visual music, augmenting our communication by making the spectrum dance with us. Just as the sonic range of the Musicmaster exceeded the audible on both ends, the spectral range of the color organs exceeded the visible. If the aliens' language included these subtleties, we would have rich converse indeed. Even the ship's computer might have to stretch itself.

The Musicmaster's audio output would be in circuit with our radios, well below conversational level. We wanted to enhance the possibility of a kind of mutual telepathic resonance, and we were conditioned to Raoul's music that way.

Norrey and I set up five cameras in an open cone facing the aliens, for a proscenium-stage effect, as opposed to the six-camera globe we customarily used at home for 360° coverage. Neither of us felt like traveling around "behind" the aliens to plant the last camera there. This would be the only dance we had ever done that would be shot from every angle *except* the one toward which it was aimed, recorded only "from backstage," as it were.

To tell you the truth, it didn't make that much difference. Artistically it wasn't much of a dance. I wouldn't have released it commercially. The reason's obvious, really: it was never intended for humans.

That had been the real root of our struggle with the diplomats over the last year. They were committed to the belief that what would be understood best by the aliens was precise adherence to a series of computer-generated *movements*. We Stardancers unanimously believed that what the aliens had responded to in Shara had been *not* a series of movements but *art*. The artistic mind behind the movements, the amount of heart and soul that went into them—the very thing an over-rigid choreography destroys in space. If we accepted the diplomats' belief-structure, we were only computer display models. If they had accepted our belief-structure, Dmirov and Silverman at least would have been forced to admit themselves forever deaf to alien speech—and Chen would never have been able to justify siding with us to his superiors.

The result was, of course, compromise that satisfied no one, with provisions to dump whichever scheme didn't seem to be working, *if* consensus could be reached. That was another reason I had had to gamble our lives and our race's fortune on the damned lasers in order to win control of the first movement. The balance would be biased slightly our way: Our very first "utterances" would be—something more than could be expressed mathematically and ballistically.

But even if we had had a totally free hand, our dance would surely have puzzled the hell out of anyone but another *Homo caelestis*. Or a computer.

I think Shara would have loved it.

At last all the pieces were in place, the stage was set, and we formed a snowflake around the Die.

"Watch your breathing, Charlie," Norrey warned.

"Right you are, my love." My lungs were taking orders from my hindbrain; it seemed to want me agitated. But *I* didn't. I began forcing measure on my breaths, and soon we were all breathing in unison, in, hold, out, hold, striving to push the interval past five seconds. My agitation began to melt like summer wages, my peripheral vision expanded spherically, and I felt my family as though a literal charge of electricity passed from hand to p-suited hand, completing a circuit that *tuned* us to one another. We became like magnets joined around a monopole, aligned to an imaginary point at the center of our circle. It was an encouraging analogy—however you disperse such magnets in free fall, eventually they will come together again at the pole. We were family; we were one. Not just our shared membership in a hypothetical new genus: we knew each other backstage, a relationship like no other on Earth or off it.

"Mr. Armstead," Silverman growled, "I'm sure you'll be glad to know that for once the world actually *is* waiting for you. Can we get on with the show?"

I just smiled. We all smiled. Bill started to say something, so I cut him off. "Certainly, Mr. Ambassador. At once." We dissolved the snowflake, and I jetted to the Die's external Master Board. "Program locked and . . . *running*, lights *up*, cameras *hot*, hold four three two *curtain*!"

Like a single being, we took our stage.

Feet first, hands high and blasting, we plunged down on the firefly swarm.

Raoul's stage marks pulsed gently with the color analog of the incredible piece he called *Shara's Blues*. Its opening bars are entirely in deep bass register; they translated as all the shades of blue there are, a visual pun. Somehow the incredible splendor of color about us—Saturn, Ring, aliens, Titan, lasers, camera lights, Die, Limousine like a soft red flashlight, and two other moons I didn't know—all only seemed to emphasize the intolerable blackness of the empty space that framed it, the immensity of the sea of black ink through which we all swam, planets and people alike. The literally cosmic perspective it provided was welcome, calming. *What are man or firefly that Thou shouldst be mindful of them?*

It was not detachment. Quite the opposite: I had never before felt so alive. For the first time in years I was aware of my p-suit clinging to my skin, aware of the breathing in my earphones, aware of the smell of my own body and of canned air, aware of the catheter and telemetry contacts and the faint sound of my hair rustling against the inside of my hood. I was perceiving totally, functioning at full capacity, exhilarated and a little scared. I was completely happy.

The music swelled suddenly. The far-flung grid pulsed with color.

We poured on full thrust, all four of us in a tight formation, so that we seemed to fall upon the alien swarm from a great height. They grew beneath our feet with breath-taking rapidity, but we were more than three klicks away when I gave the standby command. We stiffened our bodies, oriented and triggered heel thrusters together on command, opening out like a Blue Angels flower into four great loops. We let them close into circles, one of us spiraling about each of the "compass points" of the alien sphere, bracketing it with bodies. After three full circles we broke out in unison and met at the same point where we had split apart, slowing as we arrived and making a four-way acrobat's catch. Hard jetting brought us to a halt; we whirled in space and faced the aliens; pinwheeled apart into a square fifty meters on a side and waited.

Here I am again, fireflies, I thought. *I have hated you for a long time. I would be done with hating you, however that may be.*

Lasers turned us red, blue, yellow and aching green, and Raoul had abandoned known music for new; his spiderlike fingers wove patterns undreamed an hour before, stitching space with color and our ears with sound. Melancholy his melody, minor its wrestling two chords, with a throbbing undercurrent of dysharmonic bass like a migraine about to happen. It was as though he were pouring pain into a vessel whose cubic capacity might be inadequate.

With that for frame and all space for backdrop, we danced. The mechanical structure of that dance, the "steps" and their interrelation, are forever unknowable to you, and I won't try to describe them. It began slowly, tentatively; as Shara had, we began by defining terms. And so we ourselves gave the choreography less than half our attention.

Perhaps a third. A part of our minds was busy framing computer themes in artistic terms, but an equally large part was straining for any signs of feedback from the aliens, reaching out with eyes ears skin mind for any kind of response, sensitizing to any conceivable touch. And with as large a part of our minds, we felt for each other, strove to connect our awareness across meters of black vacuum, to see as the aliens saw, through many eyes at once.

And something began to happen. . . .

It began slowly, subtly, in imperceptible stages. After a year of study, I simply found myself understanding, and accepting the understanding without surprise or wonder. At first I thought the aliens had slowed their speed—but then I noted, again without wonder, that my pulse and everyone's respiration had slowed an equal amount. I was on accelerated time, extracting the maximum of information from each second of life, *be*ing with the whole of my being. Experimentally I accelerated my time sense another increment, saw the aliens' frenzy slow to a speed that anyone could encompass. I was aware that I could make time stop altogether, but I didn't want to yet. I studied them at infinite leisure, and understanding grew. It was clear now that there was a tangible if invisible energy that held them in their tight mutual orbits, as electromagnetism holds electrons in their paths. But this energy boiled furiously at their will, and they surfed its currents like wood chips that magically never collided. They created a never-ending roller coaster before themselves. Slowly, slowly I began to realize that their energy was *more than* analogous to the energy that bound me to my family. What they were surfing on was their mutual awareness of each other, and of the Universe around them.

My own awareness of my family jumped a quantum level. I heard Norrey breathing, could see out her eyes, felt Tom's sprained calf tug at me, felt Linda's baby stir in my womb, watched us all and swore under Harry's breath with him, raced down Raoul's arm to his fingers and back into my own ears. I was a six-brained Snowflake, existing simultaneously in space and time and thought and music and dance and color and something I could not yet name, and all of these things strove toward harmony.

At no point was there any sensation of leaving or losing my *self*, my unique individual identity. It was right there in my body and brain where I had left it, could not be elsewhere, existed as before. It was as though a part of it had always existed independent of brain and body, as though my brain had always known this level but had been unable to *record* the information. Had we six been this close all along, all unawares, like six lonely blind men in the same volume of space? In a way I had always yearned to without knowing it, I touched my selves, and loved them.

We understood entirely that we were being shown this level by the aliens, that they had led us patiently up invisible psychic stairs to this new plane. If any energy detectable by Man had passed between them and us, Bill Cox would have been heating up his laser cannon and screaming for a report, but he was still on conference circuit with the diplomats, letting us dance without distraction.

But communication took place, on levels that even physical instruments could perceive. At first the aliens only echoed portions of our dance, to indicate an emotional or informational connotation they understood, and when they did so we *knew* without question that they had fully grasped whatever nuance we were trying to express. After a time they began more complex responses, began subtly altering the patterns they returned to us, offering variations on a theme, then counterstatements, alternate suggestions. Each time they did so we came to know them better, to grasp the rudiments of their "language" and hence their nature. They agreed with our concept of sphericity, politely disagreed with our concept of mortality, strongly agreed with the notions of pain and joy. When we knew enough "words" to construct a "sentence," we did so.

We came these billion miles to shame you, and are ashamed.

The response was at once compassionate and merry. *NONSENSE,* they might have said, *HOW WERE YOU TO KNOW?*

Surely it was obvious that you were wiser than we.

NO, ONLY THAT WE KNEW MORE. IN POINT OF FACT, WE WERE CULPABLY CLUMSY AND OVEREAGER.

Overeager? we echoed interrogatively.

OUR NEED WAS GREAT. All fifty-four aliens suddenly plummeted toward the center of their sphere at varying rates, incredibly failing to collide there even once, saying as plain as day, *ONLY RANDOM CHANCE PREVENTED UTTER RUIN.*

The nature of the utter ruin eluded us, and we "said" as much. *Our dead sister told us you needed to spawn, on a world like ours. Is this your wish: to come and live with humans?*

Their response was the equivalent of cosmic laughter. It resolved finally into a single unmistakable "sentence":

ON THE CONTRARY.

Our dance dissolved into confusion for a moment, then recovered.

We do not understand.

The aliens hesitated. Something like solicitude emanated from them, something like compassion.

WE CAN—WE MUST—EXPLAIN. BUT UNDERSTANDING WILL BE VERY STRESSFUL. COMPOSE YOURSELVES.

The component of our self that was Linda poured out a flood of maternal warmth, an envelope of calm; she had always been the best of us at prayer. Raoul now played only an *om*-like A-flat that was a warm, golden color. Tom's driving will, Harry's eternal strength, Norrey's quiet acceptance, my own unfailing sense of humor, Linda's infinite caring and Raoul's dogged persistence all heterodyned to produce a kind of peace I had never known, a serene calm based on a sensation of completeness. All fear was gone, all doubt. This was meant to be.

This was meant to be, we danced. *Let it be.*

The echo was instantaneous, with a flavor of pleased, almost paternal approval.

NOW!

Their next sending was a relatively short dance, a relatively simple dance. We understood it at once, although it was utterly novel to us, grasped its fullest implications in a single frozen instant. The dance compressed every nanosecond of more than two billion years into a single concept, a single telepathic gestalt.

And that concept was really only the aliens' name.

Terror smashed the Snowflake into six discrete shards. I was alone in my skull in empty space, with a thin film of plastic between me and my death, naked and terribly afraid. I clutched wildly for nonexistent support. Before me, much too close before me, the aliens buzzed like bees. As I watched, they began to gather at the center, forming first a pinhole, then a knothole and then a porthole in the wall of Hell, a single shimmering red coal that raved with furious energy. Its brilliance dwarfed even the Sun; my hood began to polarize automatically.

The barely visible balloon that contained the molten nucleus began to weep red smoke, which spiraled gracefully out to form a kind of Ring. I knew it at once, what it was and what it was for, and I threw back my head and screamed, triggering all thrusters in blind escape reflex.

Five screams echoed mine.

I fainted.

IV

I was lying on my back with my knees raised, and I was much too heavy—almost twenty kilos. My ribs were struggling to inflate my chest. I had had a bad dream. . . .

The voices came from above like an old tube amp warming up, intermittent and distorted at first, resolving at last into a kind of clarity. They were near, but they had the trebleless, faraway characteristic of low pressure—and they too were finding the pseudogravity a strain.

"For the last time, tovarisch: *speak to us.* Why are your colleagues all catatonic? How do you continue to function? *What in Lenin's Name happened out there?*"

"Let him be, Ludmilla. He cannot hear you."

"I will have an answer!"

"Will you have him shot? If so, by whom? The man is a hero. If you continue to harass him, I will make full note of it, in our group report and in my own. *Let him be.*" Chen Ten Li's voice was quite composed, exquisitely detached until that last blazing command. It startled me into opening my eyes, which I had been avoiding since I first became aware of the voices.

We were in the Limousine. All ten of us, four Space Command suits and six brightly colored Stardancers, a quorum of bowling pins strapped by twos into a vertical alley. Norrey and I were in the last or bottom row. We were obviously returning to *Siegfried* at full burn, making a good quarter gee. I turned my head at once to Norrey beside me. She seemed to be sleeping peacefully; the stars through the window behind her told me that we had already passed turnover and were decelerating.

I had been out a long time.

Somehow everything had gotten sorted out in my sleep. By definition, I guess: my subconscious had kept me under until I was ready to cope and no longer. A part of my mind boiled in turmoil, but I could encompass that part now and hold it in perspective. The majority of my mind was calm. Nearly all questions were answered now, and the fear dwindled to something that could be borne. I knew for certain that Norrey was all right, that all of us would be all right in time. Not direct knowledge; the telepathic bond was broken. But I knew my family. Our lives were irrevocably changed; into what, we knew not yet—but we would find out together.

At least two more crises would come in rapid succession now, and we would share these fortunes.

Immediate needs first.

"Harry," I called out, "you did a good job. Let go now."

He turned his big crewcut head and looked down past his headrest at me from two rows up. He smiled beatifically. "I almost lost his music box," he said confidentially. "It got away from me when the weight came on." At once he rolled his head up and was asleep, snoring deeply.

I smiled indulgently at myself. I should have expected it, should have known that it would be Harry, great-shouldered great-hearted Harry who would be the strongest of us all, Harry the construction engineer who would prove to have infinite load-bearing capacity. His shoulders had been equal to his heart's need, and his breaking strain was still unknown. He would waken in an hour or so like a giant refreshed.

The diplomats had been yelping at me since I spoke to Harry; now I put my attention on them. "One at a time, please."

By God, not one of the four would yield. Knowing it was foolish they all kept talking at once. They simply couldn't help themselves.

"SHUT UP!" Bill's voice blasted from the phone speaker, overriding the cacophony. They shut up and turned to look at his image. "Charlie," he went on urgently, searching my face in his own screen, "*are you still human*?"

I knew what he was asking. Had the aliens somehow taken me over telepathically? Was I still my own master, or did an aggressive hive-mind live in my skull, working my switches and pulleys? We had discussed the possibility earnestly on the trip out, and I knew that if my answer didn't convince him he would blast us out of space without hesitation. The least of his firepower would vaporize the Limousine instantly.

I grinned. "Only for the last two or three years, Bill. Before that I was semipure bastard."

Later he would be relieved; he was *busy*. "Do I burn them?"

"*Negative.* Hold your fire! Bill, hear me good: If you shot them, and they ever found out about it, they might just take offense. I know you've got a Planet Cracker; forget it: *from here they can turn out the Sun.*"

He went pale, and the diplomats held shocked silence, turning with effort to gape at me. "We're nearly home," I went on firmly. "Conference in the exercise room as soon as we're all recovered, call it a couple of hours from now. All hands. We'll answer all your questions then—but until then you'll just have to wait. We've had a hell of a shock; we need time to recover." Norrey was beginning to stir beside me, and Linda was looking about clear-eyed; Tom was shaking his head with great care from side to side. "Now I've got my wife and a pregnant lady to worry about. Get us home and get us to our rooms and we'll see you in two hours."

Bill didn't like it a little bit, but he cleared the screen and got us home. The diplomats, even Dmirov and Silverman, were silent, a little in awe of us.

By the time we were docked everyone had recovered except Harry and Raoul, who slumbered on together. We towed them to their room, washed them gently, strapped them into their hammock so they wouldn't drift against the air grille and drown in carbon dioxide, and dimmed the lights. They held each other automatically in their sleep, breathing to the same rhythm. We left Raoul's Musicmaster by the door, in case he might ever want it for something, and swam out.

Then the four of us went back to our respective rooms, showered, and made love for two hours.

The exercise room was the only one in *Siegfried* with enough cubic to contain the entire ship's complement comfortably. We could all have squeezed into the dining room; we often did for dinner. But it was cramped, and I did not want close quarters. The exercise room was a cube perhaps thirty meters on a side. One wall was studded with various rigs and harnesses for whole-body workout in free fall. Retaining racks on another held duckpins, Frisbees, hula hoops, and handballs. Two opposing walls were trampolines. It offered elbow room, visibility, and marvelous maneuverability.

And it was the only room in the ship arranged with no particular local vertical.

The diplomats, of course, arbitrarily selected one, taping velcro strips to the bare handball wall so that the opposed trampolines were their "ceiling" and "floor." We Stardancers aligned ourselves against the far wall, among the exercise rigs, holding on to them with a hand or foot rather than velcroing ourselves to the wall between them. Bill and Col. Song took the wall to our left.

"Let's begin," I said as soon as we had all settled ourselves.

"First, Mr. Armstrong," Silverman said aggrievedly, "I would like to protest the high-handed manner in which you have withheld information from this body to suit your convenience."

"Sheldon," DeLaTorre began wearily.

"No sir," Silverman cut him off, "I vigorously protest. Are we children, to be kept twiddling our thumbs for two hours? Are all the people of Earth insignificant, that they should wait in suspense for three and a quarter hours while these—*artists* have an orgy?"

"Sounds like you've been twiddling volume controls," Tom said cheerily. "You know, Silverman, I knew you were listening the whole time. I didn't mind. I knew how much it must be bugging you."

His face turned bright red, unusual in free fall; his feet must be just as red.

"No," Linda said judiciously, "I rather think he was monitoring Raoul and Harry's room."

He went paler than he had started and his pupils contracted with hatred. Bullseye.

"All right, can it," Bill rapped. "You too, Mr. Ambassador. Snipe on your own time—as you say, all Terra is waiting."

"Yes, Sheldon," DeLaTorre said forcefully. "Let Mr. Armstead speak."

He nodded, white-lipped. "So speak."

I relaxed my grip on an exercise bike and spread my arms. "First tell me what happened from your perspective. What did you see and hear?"

Chen took it, his features masklike, almost waxen. "You began your dance. The music became progressively stranger. Your dance began to deviate radically from the computer pattern, and you were apparently answered with other patterns of which the computer could make nothing. The speed of your movements increased drastically with time, to a rate I would not have believed if I had not witnessed it with my unaided eyes. The music increased in tempo accordingly. There were muffled grunts, exclamations, nothing intelligible. The aliens united to form a single entity in the center of their envelope, which began to emit quantities of what we are told is organic matter. You all screamed.

"We tried to raise you without success. Mr. Stein would not answer our calls, but he retrieved all five of you with extreme efficiency, lashed you together, and towed you all back to the shuttlecraft in one trip."

I pictured the load that five of us, massing over three hundred kilos, must have been when the thrust came on, and acquired new respect for Harry's arms and shoulders. Brute muscle was usually so superfluous in space—but another man's muscles might have parted under that terrible strain.

"As soon as the airlock had cycled he brought you all inboard, strapped you in place, and said the single word 'Go.' Then he very carefully stowed Mr. Brindle's musical instrument and—just sat down and stared at nothing. We were abandoning the task of communicating with him when you awoke."

"Okay," I said. "Let me cover the high spots. First, as you must have guessed, we achieved rapport with the aliens."

"And are they a threat to us?" Dmirov interrupted. "Did they harm you?"

"No. And no."

"But you screamed, like ones sure to die. And Shara Drummond clearly stated before she died—"

"That the aliens were aggressive and arrogant, that they wanted Earth for a spawning ground, I know," I agreed. "Translation error, subtle and in retrospect almost inevitable. Shara had only been in space a few months; she said herself she was getting about one concept in three."

"What is the correct translation?" Chen asked.

"Earth *is* their spawning ground," I said. "So is Titan. So are a lot of places, outside this system."

"What do you mean?" Silverman barked.

"The aliens' last sending was what kicked us over the deep end. It was stunningly simple, really, considering how much it explained. You could render it as a single word. All they really did was tell us their collective name."

Dmirov scowled. "And that is?"

"Starseeder."

Stunned silence at first. I think Chen was the first to begin to grasp it, and maybe Bill was nearly as fast.

"That's their name," I went on, "their occupation, the thing they do to be fulfilled. They farm stars. Their lifetime spans billions of years, and they spend them much as we do, trying to reproduce a good part of the time. They seed stars with organic life. They seeded *this* solar system, a long time ago.

"They are our race's creator, and its remotest ancestor."

"Ridiculous," Silverman burst out. "They're nothing like us, *in no way* are they like us."

"In how many ways are you like an amoeba?" I asked. "Or a paramecium or a plant or a fish or an amphibian or any of your evolutionary forebears? The aliens are at least one or two and possibly three evolutionary stages beyond us. The wonder is that they can make themselves understood to us at all. I believe the next level beyond them has no physical existence in space or time."

Silverman shut up. DeLaTorre and Song crossed themselves. Chen's eyes were very wide.

"Picture the planet Earth as a single, stupendous womb," I went on quietly, "fecund and perpetually pregnant. Ideally designed to host a maximum of organic life, commanded by a kind of super-DNA to constantly grow and shuffle progressively more complex life forms into literally billions of different combinations, in search of one complex enough to survive outside the womb, curious enough to try.

"I nearly had a brother once. He was born dead. He was three weeks past term by then; he had stayed in the womb past his birthing time, by God knows what subtle biological error. His waste products exceeded the ability of the placenta to absorb and carry them away; the placenta began to die, to decay around him, polluted by his wastes. His life support eroded away and he died. He very nearly killed my mother.

"Picture your race as a gestalt, a single organism with a subtle flaw in its genetic coding. An overstrong cell wall, so that at the moment when it is complex enough that it ought to have a united planetary consciousness, each separate cell continues to function most often as an individual. The thick cell wall impedes information exchange, allows the organism to form only the most rudimentary approximation of a central nervous system, a network that transmits only aches and pains and shared nightmares. The news and entertainment media.

"The organism is not hopelessly deformed. It trembles on the verge of birthing, yearns to live even as it feels itself dying. It may yet succeed. On the verge of extinction, Man gropes for the stars, and now less than a century after the first man left the surface of Earth in powered flight, we gather here in the orbit of Saturn to decide whether our race's destiny should now be extended or cut short.

"Our womb is nearly filled with our poisonous by-products. The question before us is: Are we or are we not going to outgrow our neurotic dependence on planets—before it destroys us?"

"What is this crap," Silverman snarled, "some more of your *Homo caelestis* horseshit? Is that your next evolutionary step? McGillicuddy was right, it's a goddam evolutionary *dead end*! You couldn't be self-supporting in fifty years from a standing start, the speed you recruit. If the Earth and Moon blew up tomorrow, God forbid, you would be dead within two or three years at the outside. You're parasites on your evolutionary inferiors, Armstead, exiled parasites at that. You can't live in your new environment without cell walls of steel and slashproof plastic, essential artifacts that are manufactured *only back there in the womb.*"

"I was wrong," Tom said softly. "We're not an evolutionary dead end. I couldn't see the whole picture."

"*What did you miss*?" Silverman screamed.

"We have to change the analogy now," Linda spoke up. "It starts to break down." Her warm contralto was measured and soothing; I saw Silverman begin to relax as the magic worked on him. "Think of us now not as sextuplets, or even as a kind of six-personed fetus. Think of the Earth not as a uterus but as an ovary—and the six of us a single ovum. Together we carry *half* of the genes for a new kind of being.

"The most awesome and miraculous moment of all creation is the instant of syngamy, the instant at which two things come together to form so infinitely much more than the sum or even the product of their parts: the moment of conception. That is the crossroads, with phylogeny behind and ontogeny ahead, and that is the crossroads at which we are poised now."

"What is the sperm cell for your ovum?" Chen asked. "The alien swarm, I presume?"

"Oh, no," Norrey said. "They're something more like the yin/yang, male/female overmind that produces the syngamy, in response to needs of its own. Change the analogy again: Think of them as the bees they so resemble, the pollinators of a gigantic monoclinous flower we call the Solar System. It is a true hermaphrodite, containing both pistil and stamen within itself. Call Earth the pistil, if you will, and we Stardancers are its combined ovule and stigma."

"And the stamen?" Chen insisted. "The pollen?"

"The stamen is Titan," Norrey said simply. "That red organic matter the aliens' balloon gave off was some of its pollen."

Another stunned silence.

"Can you explain its nature to us?" DeLaTorre asked at last. "I confess my incomprehension."

Raoul spoke now, tugging his glasses out from the bridge of his nose and letting the elastic pull them back. "The stuff is essentially a kind of superplant itself. The aliens have been growing it in Titan's upper atmosphere for millennia, staining the planetoid red. Upon contact with a human body, a kind of mutual interaction takes place that can't be described. Energy from another . . . from another plane infuses both sides. Syngamy takes place, and perfect metabolism begins."

"*Perfect* metabolism?" DeLaTorre echoed uncertainly.

"The substance is a perfect symbiotic complement to the human organism."

"But—but . . . but *how*?"

"You wear it like a second skin, and you live naked in space," he said flatly. "It enters the body at mouth and nostrils, spreads a million microtendrils throughout the system, emerges to rejoin itself at the anus. It covers you inside and out, becomes a part of you, in total metabolic balance."

Chen Ten Li looked poleaxed. "A *perfect* symbiote . . ." he breathed.

"Right down to the trace elements," Raoul agreed. "Planned that way a billion years ago. It is our Other Half."

"How is it done?" he whispered.

"Just enter a cloud of the stuff and open your hood. The escaping air is their chemical cue: they home in, swim upstream and spawn. From the moment they first contact bare flesh until the point of total absorption and adsorption, complete synthesis, is maybe three seconds. About a second and a half in, you cease being human, forever." He shivered. "Do you understand why we screamed?"

"No," Silverman cried. "No, I do *not.* None of this makes sense! So the red crap is a living spacesuit, a biologically tailored what you said, you give it carbon dioxide it gives you oxygen, you give it shit it gives you strawberry jam. Very lovely; you've just eliminated all your overhead except for fuel and leisure aids. Very nice fellows, these aliens. How does it make you inhuman? Does the crap take over your mind or what?"

"It has no 'mind' of its own," Raoul told him. "Oh, it's remarkably sophisticated for a plant, with awareness above the vegetable. There are some remarkably complex tropisms, but you couldn't call it sentient. It sort of sets up partnership with the medulla, and rarely gets even as preconscious as a reflex. It just performs its function, in accordance with its biological programming."

"What would make you inhuman then?"

My voice sounded funny, even to me. "You don't understand," I said. "You don't *know.* We would never die, Silverman. We would never again hunger or thirst, never need a place to dispose of our wastes. We would never again fear heat or cold, never fear vacuum, Silverman; we would never fear anything again. We would acquire instant and complete control of our autonomic nervous systems, gain access to the sensorium keyboard of the hypothalamus itself. We would attain symphysis, telepathic communion, become a single mind in six immortal bodies, endlessly dreaming and never asleep. Individually and together we would become no more like a human than a human is like a chimpanzee. I don't mind telling you that all six of us used our diapers out there. I'm still a little scared."

"But you are ready. . . ." Chen said softly.

"Not yet," Linda said for all of us. "But we will be soon. That much we know."

"This telepathy business," Silverman said tentatively. "This 'single mind' stuff—is that for sure?"

"Oh, it's not dependent on the aliens," Linda assured him. "They showed us how to find that plane—but the capacity was always there, in every human that ever lived. Every holy man that ever got enlightened came down off the mountain saying, 'We're all one'—and every damn time the people decided it must be a metaphor. The symbiote will help us *some*, but—"

"How does it help?" Silverman interrupted.

"Well, the distraction factor, mostly. I mean, most people have flashes of telepathic ability, but there are so many *distractions*. It's worse for a planetdweller, of course, but even in the Studio we got hungry, we got thirsty and horny and bored and tired and sore and angry and afraid. 'Being in our heads,' we called it. The animal part of us impeding the progress of the angel. The symbiote frees you from all animal needs—you can experience them, at whim, but never again are you subject to their arbitrary command. The symbiote does act as a kind of mild amplifier of the telepathic 'wave band,' but it helps much more by improving the 'signal-to-noise ratio' at the point of origin."

"What I mean," Silverman said, "if God forbid *I* were to let this fungus infest me, *I* would become at least mildly telepathic? As well as immortal and beyond having to go to the bathroom?"

"No sir," she said politely but firmly. "If you were *already* mildly telepathic before you entered symbiotic partnership, you would become significantly more so. If, at that time, you happened to be in the field of a fully functioning telepath, you would become exponentially more so."

"But if I took, say, the average man in the street and put him in a symbiote suit—"

"—you'd get an average immortal who never needed to go to the bathroom and was more empathic than he used to be," I finished.

"Empathy is sort of telepathy's kid brother," Linda said.

"More like its larval stage," I corrected.

"But two average guys in symbiote suits wouldn't necessarily be able to read each other's minds?"

"Not unless they worked long and hard at learning how that's done," I told him, "which they would almost certainly do. It's *lonely* in space."

He fell silent, and there was a pause while the rest of them sorted out their opinions and emotions. It took a while.

I had things to sort out myself. I was still possessed of that same internal *certainty* that I had felt since I woke up in the Limousine, feeling that almost prescient sense of inevitability, but the cusp was approaching quickly now. *What if you should die, at this moment of moments*? whispered an animal voice from the back of my skull.

As I had at the moment I confronted the aliens, I felt totally alive.

"Mr. Armstead," DeLaTorre said, shaking his head and frowning mightily, "it seems to me that you are saying that all human want is coming to an end?"

"Oh no," I said hastily. "I'm very sorry if we accidentally implied that. The symbiote cannot live in a terrestrial environment. Anything like that kind of gravity and atmosphere would kill it. No, the symbiote will not bring Heaven to Earth. *Nothing* can. Mohammed must go to the mountain—and many will refuse."

"Perhaps," Chen suggested delicately, "terrestrial scientists might be able to genetically modify the aliens' gift?"

"No," Harry said flatly. "There is no *way* you can give symphonies and sunsets to a fetus that insists on staying in the womb. That cloud of symbiote over Titan is every person's birthright—but first they gotta earn it, by consenting to be born."

"And to do that," Raoul agreed, "they have to cut loose of Earth forever."

"There is an appealing symmetry to the concept," Chen said thoughtfully.

"Hell, yes," Raoul said. "We should have expected something like it. The whole business of adaptation to free fall being possible but irreversible . . . look, at the moment of your birth, a very heavy miracle happened, in a single instant. One minute you were essentially a fish, with a fish's two-valved circulatory system, parasitic on the womb. Then, all at once, a switch slammed shut. Zippo-bang, you were a mammal, just like that. Four-valved heart, self-contained—*you made a major, irreversible physiological leap, into a new plane of evolution.* It was accompanied by pain, trauma, and a flood of data from senses you hadn't known you possessed. Nearly at once a whole bunch of infinitely more advanced beings in the same predicament began trying to teach you how to communicate. 'Appealing'? The fucking symmetry is overwhelming! *Now* do you begin to understand why we screamed? We're in the very midst of the same process—and all babies scream."

"I don't understand," Dmirov complained. "You would be able to live naked in space—but how could you *go* anywhere?"

"Light pressure?" Chen suggested.

"The symbiote can deploy itself as a light sail," I agreed, "but there are other forces we will use to carry us where we want to go."

"Gravity gradients?"

"No. Nothing you could detect or measure."

"Preposterous," Dmirov snorted.

"How did the aliens get here?" I asked gently, and she reddened.

"The thing that makes it so difficult for me to credit your story," Chen said, "is the improbablity factor. So much of your coming here was random chance."

"Dr. Chen," I cut him off, "are you familiar with the proverb that says there is a destiny which shapes our ends, rough-hew them how we will?"

"But any of a thousand things might have conspired to prevent any of this from occurring."

"Fifty-four things conspired to make it all occur. Superthings. Or did you think that the aliens just happened to appear in this system at the time that Shara Drummond began working at Skyfac? That they just happened to jump to Saturn when she returned to Skyfac to dance? That they just happened to appear outside Skyfac at the moment that Shara was about to return to Earth forever, a failure? Or that this whole trip to Saturn just happened to be feasible in the first place? Me, I wonder what they were doing out Neptune way, that first time they appeared." I considered it. "I'll have to go see."

"You don't understand," Chen said urgently, and then controlled himself. "It is not generally known, but six years ago our planet was nearly destroyed by nuclear holocaust. Chance and good fortune saved us—there were no aliens in our skies then."

Harry spoke up. "Know what a pregnant rabbit does if conditions aren't favorable for birth? Reabsorbs the fetuses into the womb. Just reverses the process, recycles the ingredients and tries again when conditions are better."

"I don't follow."

"Have you ever heard of Atlantis?"

Chen's face went the color of meerschaum, and everyone else gaped or gasped.

"It comes in cycles," I said, "like labor pains building to a peak. They come as close together as four or five thousand years—the Pyramids were built that far back—and as far apart as twenty thousand."

"Sometimes they get pretty rough," Harry added. "There used to be a planet between Mars and Jupiter."

"Bojemoi," Dmirov breathed. "The Asteroid Belt. . . ."

"And Venus is handy in case *we* screw up altogether," I agreed, "reducing atmosphere all ready to go, just seed with algae and wait. *God,* they must be patient."

Another extensive stunned silence. They believed now, all of them, or were beginning to. Therefore they had to rearrange literally everything they had ever known, recast all of existence in the light of this new information and try to determine just who, in relation to this confusion, they themselves might be. They were advanced in years for this kind of uprooting, their beliefs and opinions deeply ingrained by time; that they were able to accept the information and think at all said clearly that every one of them possessed a strong and flexible mind. Wertheimer had chosen well; none of them cracked, rejected the truth and went catatonic as we had. Of course, they were not out in free space, thinking seriously of removing their p-suits. But then, they had pressures *we* lacked: they represented a planet.

"Your intention, then," Silverman said slowly, "is to do this thing?"

Six voice chorused, "Yes."

"At once," I added.

"Are you are sure that all you have told us is true, that the aliens have told no lies, held out nothing?" Ever so casually he had been separating himself from the other diplomats.

"We're certain," I said, tensing my thighs again.

"But where will you go?" DeLaTorre cried. "What will you *do*?"

"What all newborns do. We'll examine our nursery. The Solar System."

Silverman kicked off suddenly, jaunting to the empty fourth wall. "I'm very sorry," he said mournfully. "You'll do nothing of the kind."

There was a small Beretta in his hand.

V

There was a calculator in his other hand. At least, it looked like one. All at once I knew better, and feared it more than the gun.

"This," he said, confirming my guess, "is a short-range transmitter. If anyone approaches me suddenly, I will use it to trigger radio-controlled explosives, which I placed during the trip here. They will cripple the ship's computer."

"Sheldon," DeLaTorre cried, "are you mad? The computer oversees *life support*."

"I would rather not use this," Silverman said calmly. "But I am utterly determined that the information we have heard will be the exclusive possession of the United States of America—or of no one."

I watched diplomats and soldiers carefully for signs of suicidal bravery, and relaxed slightly. None of them was the kind of fool who jumps a gunman; their common expression was intense disgust. Disgust at Silverman's treachery, and disgust at themselves for not having expected it. I looked most closely at Chen Ten Li, who *had* expected it and had promised to kill Silverman with his hands—but he was totally relaxed, a gentle, mocking smile beginning at the corners of his lips. Interesting.

"Mr. Silverman," Susan Pha Song said, "you have not thought this thing through."

"Colonel," he said ironically, "I have had the better part of a year in which to do little else."

"Nevertheless, you have overlooked something," she insisted.

"Pray enlighten me."

"If we were all to rush you now," she said evenly, "you might shoot perhaps two or three of us before you were overwhelmed. If we do not, you will certainly kill us all. Or had you planned to hold a gun on us for two years?"

"If you rush me," Silverman promised, "I will kill the computer, and you will all die anyway."

"So either we die and you return to Earth with your secret, or we die and you do not." She put a hand on the wall on either side of her.

"Wrong," Silverman said hurriedly. "I do not intend to kill you all. I don't have to. I will leave you all in this room. My pressure suit just so happens to be in the next room—I will put it on and instruct the computer to evacuate all the compartments adjacent to this one. I will of course have disabled your own terminal here. Air pressure and the safety interlocks will prevent you from opening a door to vacuum: a foolproof prison. And so long as I detect no attempts to escape on the phone, I will continue to permit food, air and water systems to operate in here. I have the necessary program tapes to bring us back to Earth, where you will all be treated as prisoners of war under international conventions."

"What war?"

"The one that just started and ended. Have you heard? America won."

"Sheldon, Sheldon," DeLaTorre insisted, "what can you hope to accomplish by this insane expedient?"

"Are you kidding?" Silverman snorted. "The biggest component of capital investment in space exploitation is life support. This moon full of fungus is a free ticket to the whole Solar System—with immortality thrown in! And the United States is going to have it, that I promise you." He turned to Li and Dmirov and said, with utter sincerity, the most incredible sentence I have ever heard in my life: "I am not going to allow you to export your godless way of life to the stars."

Chen actually laughed out loud, and I joined him.

"One of those Canuck socialists, eh, Armstead?" Silverman snarled.

"That's the thing that bugs you the most, isn't it, Silverman?" I grinned. "A *Homo caelestis* in symbiosis has no wants, no needs: *there's nothing you can sell him.* And he submerges himself in a group: a natural Commie. Men without self-interest scare you silly, don't they?"

"Pseudophilosophical bullshit," Silverman barked. "I'm taking possession of the most stupendous military intelligence of the century."

"Oh my God," Raoul drawled disgustedly, "Hi Yo Silverman, the John Wayne of the Spaceways. You're actually visualizing soldiers in symbiote suits, aren't you? The Space Infantry."

"I like the idea," Silverman admitted. "It seems to me that a naked man with a symbiote would evade most detection devices. No metals, low albedo—and if it's a perfect symbiosis there'd be no waste heat. What a saboteur! No support or supplies required . . . by God, we could *use infantry to interdict Titan.*"

"Silverman," I said gently, "you're an imbecile. Assume for a moment that you can bludgeon GI Joe into letting what you call a fungus crawl up his nose and down his throat. Fine. You now have an *extremely* mobile infantryman. He has no wants or needs whatsoever, he knows that he will be immortal if he can avoid getting killed, and his empathic faculty is at a maximum. *What's going to keep him from deserting?* Loyalty to a country he'll never see again? Relatives in Hoboken, who live in a gravity field that'd kill him?"

"Laser beams if necessary," he began.

"Remember how fast we were dancing there before the end? Go ask the computer whether we could have danced around a laser beam—even a computer-operated one. You said yourself we'd be bloody hard to track."

"Your military secret is worthless, Silverman," Tom said.

"Better minds than mine will work out the practical details," he insisted. "I know a military edge when I see one. Commander Cox," he said suddenly, "you are an American. Are you with me?"

"There are three other Americans aboard," Cox answered obliquely. Tom, Harry, and Raoul stiffened.

"Yeah. One's got a pregnant Canadian wife, two are perverts, and all three are under the influence of those alien creatures. Are you with me?"

Bill seemed to be thinking hard. "Yeah. You're right. I hate to admit it, but only the United States can be trusted with this much power."

Silverman was studying him intently. "No," he decided, "no, Commander, I'm afraid I don't believe you. Your oath of allegiance is to the United Nations. If you had said no, or answered ambiguously, in a few days I might have believed a yes. But you are lying." He shook his head regretfully. "All right, ladies and gentlemen, here is how we shall proceed. No one will make a move until I say so. Then, one at a time, on command, you will all jump to that wall there with the dancers, farthest from the forward door. I will then back out this door, and—"

"Mr. Silverman," Chen interrupted gently, "there is something everyone in this room should know first."

"So speak."

"The installations that you made at Conduits 364-B and 1117-A, *and* at the central core, were removed and thrown out the airlock some twenty minutes after you completed them. You are a clumsy fool, Silverman, and an utterly predictable one. Your transmitter is useless."

"You're lying," Silverman snarled, and Chen didn't bother to answer. His mocking smile was answer enough.

Right there Silverman proved himself a chump. If he'd had the quickness to bluff, to claim *other* installations Chen didn't know about, he might even then have salvaged something. I'm sure he never thought of it.

Bill and Colonel Song made their decisions at the same instant and sprang.

Silverman pressed a button on the transmitter, and the lights and air conditioning *didn't* go out. Crying with rage, he stuck up his silly gun and fired.

Ian Fleming to the contrary, the small Beretta is a miserable weapon, best suited to use across a desk. But the Law of Chaos worked with Silverman: The slug he aimed at Bill neatly nicked open Colonel Song's jugular, ricocheted off the wall behind her—the wall opposite Silverman—and smacked into Bill from behind, tumbling him and adding acceleration.

Silverman was not a complete idiot—he had expected greater recoil in free fall and braced for it. But he wasn't expecting his own slug to bring Bill to him quicker—before he could re-aim, Bill smacked into him. Still he retained his grip on the pistol, and everyone in the room jumped for cover.

But by that time I was across the room. I slapped switches, and the lights and air conditioning *did* go out.

* * *

It was simple, then. We had only to wait.

Silverman began to scream first, followed by Dmirov and DeLaTorre. Most humans go a little crazy in total darkness, and free fall makes it *much* worse. Without a local vertical, as Chen Ten Li had learned when his bedroom lights failed, you are *lost*. The distress is primeval and quite hard to override.

Silverman hadn't learned enough about free fall—or else he hadn't heard the air conditioning quit. He was the only one in the room still velcro'd to a wall, and he was too terrified to move. After a time his screams diminished, became gasps, then one last scream and silence. I waited just a moment to be sure—Song was certainly dead already, but Bill's condition was unknown—then jaunted back to the switches and cut in lights and air again. Silverman was stuck like a fly to the wall, dying of oxygen lack in a room full of air, an invisible bubble of his own exhalations around his head. The gun drifted a half meter from his outstretched hand.

I pointed, and Harry collected it. "Secure him before he wakes up," I said, and jaunted to Bill. Linda and Raoul were already with him, examining the wound. Across the room Susan Pha Song drifted limply, and her throat had stopped pumping blood. I had lived with that lady for over a year, and I did not know her at all; and while that had been at least half her idea, I was ashamed. As I watched, eight or ten red softballs met at the air grille and vanished with a wet sucking sound.

"How is he?"

"I don't think it's critical," Linda reported. "Grazed a rib and exited. Cracked it, maybe."

"I have medical training," Dmirov, of all people, said. "I have never practiced in free fall—but I have treated bullet wounds before."

Linda took him to the first aid compartment over by the duckpins and Frisbees. Bill trailed a string of red beads that drifted in a lazy arc toward the grille. Dmirov followed Linda, shaking with rage or reaction or both.

Harry and Tom had efficiently trussed Silverman with weighted jump ropes. It appeared superfluous—a man his age takes anoxia hard; he was sleeping soundly. Chen was hovering near the computer terminal, programming something, and Norrey and DeLaTorre were preparing to tow Song's body to the dispensary, where grim forethought had placed supplies of embalming fluid.

But when they reached the door, it would not open for them. Norrey checked the indicator, which showed pressure on the other side, frowned, hit the manual override and frowned again when it failed to work.

"I am deeply sorry, Ms. Armstead," Chen said with sincere regret. "I have instructed the computer to seal off this room. No one may leave." From behind the terminal he produced a portable laser. "This is a recoilless weapon, and can kill you all in a single sweep. If anyone threatens me, I will use it at once."

"Why should anyone threaten you, Li?" I asked softly.

"I have come all this way to negotiate a treaty with aliens. I have not yet done so." He looked me right in the eye.

DeLaTorre looked startled. "Madre de Dios, the aliens—what are they doing while we fight among ourselves?"

"That is not what I mean, Ezequiel," Chen said. "I believe that Mr. Armstead lied when Commander Cox asked him if he was still human. We have yet to negotiate terms of mutual coexistence between his new species and our own. Both lay claim to the same territory."

"*How?*" Raoul asked. "We have no interest in common."

"We both propose to eventually populate what is known as human space."

"But you're welcome to any of it that's of any conceivable human value," Tom insisted. "Planets are no use to us, the asteroids are no use to us—all we need is cubic and sunshine. You're not begrudging us *cubic*, are you? Even *our* scale isn't that big."

"If ever Cro-Magnon and Neanderthal lived in peace in the same valley, it took an extraordinary social contract to enforce it," he insisted. "Precisely because you will need nothing that we need, you will be difficult to live with. As I speak I realize that you will be *impossible* to live with. Looking down godlike on our frantic scurrying, amused by our terrible urgency—how I hate you already! Your very existence makes nearly every living human a failure; and only those with a peculiar acrobat's knack for functioning spherically—and the resources to get to Titan!—can hope to strive for success. If you are not an evolutionary dead end, then most of the human race *is*.

No, Stardancers: I do not believe we could ever share the same volume of space with you."

He had been programming the computer as he spoke, by touch, never taking his full attention from us.

"The world we left behind us was poised on a knife edge. It has been a truism for a long time that if we did not blow ourselves up by the year 2010, the world would be past the crisis point, and an age of plenty would follow. But at the time that we left Earth, the chances of surviving that long were slim, I think you will all agree.

"Our planet is wound to the bursting point with need," he said sadly. "Nothing could push it more certainly over the edge than the erosion of planetary morale which your existence would precipitate—than the knowledge that there *are* gods, who have no more heed for Man than Man has for the billions and trillions of sperm and eggs that failed to become gametes. That salvation and eternal life are only for a few."

Ezequiel was glowering thoughtfully, and so was Dmirov, who had just finished bandaging Bill. I began to reply, but Chen cut me off.

"Please, Charles. I recognize that you must act to preserve your species. Surely you can understand that I must protect my own?"

In that moment he was the most dangerous man I had ever known, and the most noble. With love and deep respect I inclined my head. "Li," I said, "I concede and admire your logic. But you are in error."

"Perhaps," he agreed. "But I am certain."

"Your intentions?" I knew already; I wanted to hear him state them.

He gestured to the computer terminal. "This vessel was equipped with the finest computer made. Made in Peking. I have set up a program prepared for me before we left, by its designers. A tapeworm program. When I touch the "Execute" key, it will begin to disembowel the computer's memory banks, requiring only fifteen minutes to complete a total core dump."

"You would kill us all, like Silverman?" DeLaTorre demanded.

"Not like Silverman!" Chen blazed, reddening with anger. At once he recovered, and half-smiled. "More efficiently, at the very least. And *for different reasons*. He wished this news communicated only to his own country. I wish it communicated to no one. I propose to disable this ship's deep-space communications lasers, empty its memory banks, and leave it derelict. Then I shall kill you all, quickly and mercifully. The bomb you call the Planet Cracker has its own guidance system; I can open the bomb-bay doors manually. I do not believe I will bring my pressure suit." His voice was terrifying calm. "Perhaps the next Earth ship will find the aliens still here, four or five years hence. But Saturn will have eight moons and two Rings."

Linda was shaking her head. "So wrong, Li, so wrong, you're a Confucian Legalist looking at the Tao—"

"I'm part of a terrified womb," Chen said firmly, "and it is my judgment that birth now would kill the mother. I have decided that the womb must reabsorb the fetus of *Homo caelestis.* Perhaps at the peak of the *next* cycle the human race will be mature enough to survive parturition—it is not now. *My* responsibility must be to the womb—for it is all the world I know or can know."

It had begun at the instant that I asked him his intentions, knowing them already.

It had happened before, briefly and too late, at the moment of showdown with Silverman. It had faded again unnoticed by the humans in the room. There had been nothing visible to notice: our only action had been to darken the room. We had been afraid then—and a person had died.

But this threat was not to our freedom but to our existence as a species. For the second time in fifteen minutes, my family entered rapport.

Time spiraled down like an unwound Victrola. Six viewpoints melded into one. More than six camera angles: the 360° visual integration was merely useful. Six *viewpoints* combined, six lifetimes' worth of perceptions, opinions, skills, and insights impinged upon each other and coalesced like droplets of mercury into a single entity. Since the part of us that was Linda knew Li best, we used her eyes and ears to monitor his words and his energy in realtime, while beneath and around them, we contemplated how best to bring tranquility to our cousin. At his only pause for breath, we used Linda's words to try and divert his energies, but were unsurprised to fail. He was too blind with pain. By the time the monitor fragment of her awareness reported that his finger was tensing to reach for the "Execute" key, the whole of us was more than ready with our plan.

All six of us contributed choreography to that dance, and polished it mentally until it filled our dancers' souls with joy. The first priority was the tapeworm program; the second was the laser. It was Tom the martial-arts expert who knew precisely where and how to strike so as to cause Chen's muscles to spasm involuntarily. It was Raoul the visual-effects specialist who knew where Chen's optical "blind spot" was, and knew that Norrey would be in it at the critical instant. Norrey *knew* the position of the racked Frisbees behind her because Harry and I could see them peripherally from where we were. And it was Linda who supplied me with the only words that might have captured Chen's attention in that moment, fixing his gaze on me and his blind spot on Norrey.

"And what of your grandchildren, Chen Ten Li?"

His tortured eyes focused on me and widened. Norrey reached behind her with both arms, and surrendered control of them. Harry, who was our best shot, used her right arm to throw the Frisbee that yanked Chen's right hand away from the terminal in uncontrollable pain reflex. Raoul, who was left-handed, used her left arm to throw the Frisbee that ruined the laser and smashed it out of the crook of Chen's left arm. Both missiles arrived before he knew they had been launched; even as they struck, Tom had kicked Song's corpse between Linda and the line of fire in case of a miss, and Norrey had grabbed two more Frisbees on the same chance. And I was already halfway to Chen myself: I was intuitively sure that he knew one of the ways to suicide barehanded.

It was over in less than a second of realtime. To the eyes of DeLaTorre and Dmirov we must have seemed to . . . *flicker* and then reappear in new relative positions, like a frightened school of fish. Chen was crying out in pain and rage and shame, and I was holding him in a four-limbed hammerlock, conspicuously not hurting him. Harry was waiting for the ricocheting Frisbees, retrieving them lazily; Raoul was by the computer, wiping Chen's program.

The dance was finished. And correctly this time: no blood had been spilled. We knew with a guiltless regret that if we had yielded to rapport more freely the first time, Song would not be dead and Bill wounded. We had been afraid, then, yielded only tentatively and too late. Now the last trace of fear was gone; our hearts were sure. We were ready to be responsible.

"Dr. Chen," I said formally, "do I have your parole?"

He stiffened in my grip, and then relaxed totally. "Yes," he said, his voice gone empty. I released him, and was stunned by how *old* he looked. His calendar age was fifty-six.

"Sir," I said urgently, trying to hold him with my eyes, "your fears are groundless. Your pain is needless. *Listen to me:* you are *not* a useless by-product of *Homo caelestis.* You are not a failed gamete. You are one of the people who personally held our planet Earth together, with your bare hands, until it could birth the next stage. Does that rob your life of meaning, diminish your dignity? You are one of the few living statesmen who can help ease Earth through the coming transition—do you lack the self-confidence, or the courage? You helped open up space, and you have grandchildren—didn't you mean for them to have the stars? Would you deny them now? Will you listen to what *we* think will happen? Can happen? Must happen?"

Chen shook his head like a twitching cat, absently massaging his right arm. "I will listen."

"In the first place, stop tripping over analogies and metaphors. You're not a failed gamete, or anything of the kind, *unless you choose to be.* The whole human race can be *Homo caelestis* if it wants to. Many of 'em won't, but the choice is theirs. And yours."

"But the vast majority of us cannot perceive spherically," Chen shouted.

I smiled. "Doctor, when one of my failed students left for Earth he said to me, 'I couldn't learn to see the way you do if I tried for a hundred years.'"

"Exactly. I have been in free space, and I agree."

"Suppose you had *two* hundred years?"

"Eh?"

"Suppose you entered symbiosis, right now. You'd have to have a tailored environment of right angles to stay sane, at first. But *you'd be immortal.* With absolutely nothing better to do, could you not unlearn your gravitic bias in time?"

"There's more," Linda said. "Children born in free space will think spherically from infancy. They won't have to unlearn a lifetime of essentially false, purely local information about how reality works. Li, in free fall you are not too old to sire more children. You can learn with them, telepathically—and inherit the stars together!"

"All mankind," I went on, "all that wants to, can begin preparing at once, by moving to Trojan-point O'Neill Colonies and entering symbiosis. The colonization of space can begin with this generation."

"But how is such a migration to be financed?" he cried.

"Li, Li," Linda said, as one explaining to a child, "the human race is *rich*, as of now. The total resources of the System are now available to all, for free. Why haven't L-5 colonies gotten off the ground, or the asteroid mining that would support them? Silverman said it ten minutes ago: The biggest single component of expense has always been life support, and elaborate attempts to prevent the crew from adapting to free fall by simulating gravity. If all you need is a set of right angles that will last for a few centuries, you can build cities out of aluminum foil, haul enormous quantities of symbiote from Titan to Terra."

"Imagine a telepathic construction gang," Harry said, "who never have to eat or rest."

"Imagine an explosion of art and music," Raoul said, "raining down on Earth from the heavens, drawing every heart that ever yearned for the stars."

"Imagine an Earth," Tom said, "filled with only those who want to be there."

"And imagine your children-to-be," Norrey said. "The first children in all history to be raised free of the bitter intergenerational resentments that arise from a child's utter dependence on his parents. In space, children and parents will relate at eyelevel, in every sense. Perhaps they need not be natural enemies after all."

"But you are not human!" Chen Ten Li cried. "Why should you give us all this time and energy? What is Man, that you should be mindful of him?"

"Li," Linda said compassionately, "were we not born of man and woman? Does not the child remember the womb, and yearn for it all his life? Do you not honor your mother, although you may never be part of her again? We would preserve and cherish the Earth, our womb, that it may remain alive and fruitful and bear multiple births to its capacity."

"That is our only defense," I said quietly, "against the immense loneliness of being even *Homo caelestis* in empty space. Six minds isn't enough—when we have six billion united in undisturbed thought, then, perhaps, we will learn some things. All mankind is our genetic heritage."

"Besides," Raoul added cheerfully, "what's a few centuries of our time? *We're in no hurry.*"

"Li," I went on, "to be human is to stand between ape and angel. To be angel, as are my family and I, is to float between man and the gods, *partaking fully of both.* Without gravity or a local vertical there can be no false concept of the 'high' and the 'low': how could we act other than ethically? Immortal, needing nothing, how could we be evil?"

"As a species," Tom picked up, "we naturally will deal only through the United Nations. Dr. Chen, believe me: we've studied this on something faster than computer-time. There is no way for our plans to be subverted, for the symbiote to be hijacked. All the evil men and women on Earth will not stop us, and the days of evil are numbered."

"But," I finished, "we need the help and cooperation of you and every man like you, on the globe or off it. Are you up to it, Chen Ten Li?"

He drifted freely, in the partial crouch of complete relaxation, his face slack with thought and his eyes rolled up into his head. At long last his pupils reappeared, and life returned to his features. He met my eyes, and a gentle slight smile tugged at his mouth.

"You remind me greatly," he said, "of a *man* I once knew, named Charles Armstead."

"Dr. Chen," I said, feeling tension drain away, "Li my friend, I *am* that man. I am also something else, and you have rightly deduced that I am maintaining my six discrete conversational *personas* only as a courtesy to you, in the same way that I adapt my bodies to your local vertical. It demonstrates clearly that telepathic communion does not involve what you would call ego loss." Shifting *persona* as I spoke, so that each of us uttered a single word, I/we said:

"I'm"

"more"

"than"

"human"

"not"

"less."

"Very well," Li said, shaking his head. "Together we will bring the millennium to our weary planet."

"I am with you," DeLaTorre said simply.

"I too," Dmirov said.

"Let's get Bill and Col. Song's body to sickbay," six voices said.

And an hour later we six departed for the Starseeders' location. We didn't bother with the shuttlecraft, this time. Our suit thrusters held enough for a one-way trip . . .

SNYGAMY

I

Saturn burned ocher and brown against an aching blackness so vast it was barely interrupted by the cold light of a billion billion suns.

We danced as we jetted through that blackness, almost without thinking about it. We were leaving human life behind, and we danced our leaving of it. Essentially each of us created our own *Stardance*, and the great empty cosmic hall rang with Raoul's last symphony. Each dance was individual and self-complete; each happened to mesh with the other three and with the music, in a kind of second-level statement; and although all of these were conceived without any perceived constraints of time or distance, Harry's overawareness saw to it that all five works of art happened to end, together, before the aliens. It was always Harry who made us meet our deadlines.

None of this was taped. Unlike Shara's *Stardance*, this was not meant to be witnessed. It was meant to be shared, to be danced.

But it was witnessed. The Starseeders (aliens they were *not*) writhed in something analogous to applause as we hung before them, gasping for breath, savoring the feel of the last sweat we would ever know.

We were no longer afraid of them.

YOU HAVE MADE YOUR CHOICE?

Yes.

IT WILL BE A FINE BIRTHING.

Raoul hurled his Musicmaster into deep space. *Let it begin without delay.*

AT ONCE:

There was an excitement in their dance, now, an elemental energy that somehow seemed to contain an element of humor, of suppressed mirth. They began a pattern that we had never seen before, yet seemed to know in some cellular fashion, a pattern that alternated between the simple and the complex, without ever resolving. The Harry part of our mind called it "the naming of pi," and all of us raptly watched it unfold. It was the most hypnotic pattern ever dreamed, the dance of creation itself; the most essential expression of the Tao, and the stars themselves seemed to pay attention.

As we stared, transfixed, the semivisible sphere around the Starseeders began for the second time to weep bloody tears.

They coalesced into a thin crimson ring about the immense sphere, then contracted into six orbiting bubbles.

Without hesitation we each jetted to a bubble and plunged inside. Once we were in, we skinned out of our p-suits and flung them at the walls of our bubbles, which passed them out into space. Raoul added his glasses. Then the bubbles contracted around and into and through us.

Things happened on a thousand different levels, then, to all six of me; but it is Charlie Armstead who is telling you this. I felt something cool slide down my throat and up my nostrils, suppressed gag reflex with free-fall training, thought briefly of Chen Ten Li and the ancient Chinese legends of the edible gold that brings immortality—felt suddenly and forever a total awareness, knowledge, and control of my entire body and brain. In a frozen instant of timelessness I scanned my life's accumulation of memories, savored them, transmitted them in a single sending to my family, and savored theirs. Simultaneously I was employing eyes that now registered a wider spectrum to see the universe in greater depth, and simultaneously I was playing the keys of my own internal sensorium, tasting crisp bacon and Norrey's breast and the sweet taste of courage, smelling woodsmoke and Norrey's loins and the sweet smell of caring, hearing Raoul's music and Norrey's voice and the sweet sound of silence. Almost absentmindedly I healed the damage to my hip, felt complete function return as if it had never been gone.

As to happenings on a group level, there is not much I can tell you that will mean anything. We made love, again almost absentmindedly, and we all felt together the yearnings toward life in Linda's belly, felt the symbiote that shielded her body make the same perception and begin preparing its own mitosis. Quite consciously and deliberately, Norrey and I conceived a child of our own. These things were only incidentals, but what can I tell you of the essentials? On one major level we shared each other's every memory and forgave each other the shameful parts and rejoiced in all the proud parts. On another major level we began what would become an ongoing lifespan symposium on the meaning of beauty. On another we began planning the last details of the migration of Man into space.

A significant part of us was pure-plant consciousness, a six-petaled flower basking mindlessly in the sunlight.

We were less than a kilometer from the Starseeders, and we had forgotten their very existence.

We were startled into full awareness of our surroundings as the Starseeders once again collapsed into a single molten ball of intolerable brilliance—and vanished without a good-bye or a final sending.

They will be back, perhaps in a mere few centuries of realtime, to see whether anybody feels ready to become a firefly.

In stunned surprise we hovered, and, our attention now focused on the external universe, saw what we had missed.

A crimson-winged angel was approaching us from the direction of Saturn's great Ring. On twin spans of thin red lightsail, an impossible figure came nearer.

Hello, Norrey, Charlie, the familiar voice said in our skulls. *Hi Tom, Harry. Linda and Raoul, I don't know you yet, but you love my loved ones—hello.*

Shara! screamed six voiceless brains.

Sometimes fireflies pick up a hitchhiker.

But how—?

I was more like an incubator baby, actually, but they got me to Titan alive. That was my suit and tanks you saw burning up. They were desperate and overeager, just as they said. But you didn't really think they were clumsy enough to waste me, did you? I've been waiting in the Ring for you to make your decision. I didn't want to influence its outcome.

The Snowflake that was me groped for "words."

You have made a good marriage, she said, *you six.*

Marry us! We cried.

I thought you'd never *ask.*

And my sister swarmed into me and we are one.

That is essentially the whole of this story.

I—the Charlie Armstead component of "I"—began this work long ago, as an article for magazine and computer-fax sale. So much nonsense had been talked and written about Shara that I was angry, and determined to set the record straight. In that incarnation, this manuscript ended with Shara's death.

But when I was done, I no longer needed to publish the article. I found that I had written it only to clarify things in my own mind. I withheld it, and hung on to the manuscript with the vague idea of someday using it as a seed for my eventual memoirs (in the same spirit in which Harry had begun his Book: because someone had to and who else was there?). From time to time, over the next three years, I added to it with that purpose in mind, "novelizing" rather than "diarizing" to spare the trouble of altering the manuscript later. I spent a lot of the year of *Siegfried's* outward flight in writing and revising the total, bringing the history up to the point where Chen Ten Li took his first space walk, a few weeks out of Saturn.

All of the subsequent material has been written in a single half-day "sitting," here at the Die's computer terminal. I have been limited only by the physical speed at which the terminal's heat-sensitive "keys" can disengage. As I write, other parts of me drift through eternity. We make love. We worship. We sing. We dance. Endlessly we are each other, yet are ourselves. I know it does not seem that this could be: that is why I have chosen to tell my story by completing Charlie's memoirs (while Shara, approving, reads over my shoulder from a hundred klicks away). I want you to know that Charles Armstead has not been dissolved or diluted into something alien. In no sense have I died. I never will. It would be more accurate to say that I am Charlie Armstead to the seventh power. At long last I have managed to destroy the phone company, and great is my glee. I still choreograph dances with Norrey and Shara and the others, still swap abominable multilevel puns with Raoul (right now he's singing an old '40s love song, "I May Never Come Back to Earth Again"), still taste in my mind (where I always did) the smell of fine coffee, the bite of strong drink, the flavor of good grass. The distance between me and you is only time and changes. Once I was a bitter, twisted cripple, poisoning the air around me; now I know no evil because I know no fear.

I have spent the minuscule fraction of energy to complete this manuscript because Bill Cox is preparing to blast for Terra (he'll be back) and it must go now if ever.

This news will not fit into any diplomat's laser message, nor will even those extraordinary men and women be able to express it as I can.

I am Charlie Armstead, and my message to you is: The stars can be even yours.

STARSEED

Acknowledgments

We'd like to thank master roboticist Guy Immega for technical assistance in matters scientific, and Zoketsu Norman Fischer for technical assistance in matters of Zen. (Any mistakes, however, are ours, not theirs.) We also thank Dr. Oliver Robinow, Anya Coveney-Hughes, Herb Varley, David Myers, Evelyn Beheshti, Don H. DeBrandt, Greg McKinnon, Lynn Katey, all the members of Jeanne's women's group, and of course our patient and long-suffering agent, Eleanor Wood of the Spectrum Agency, for various kinds of aid and comfort without which we might never have finished this book. And we thank our editors, Susan Allison and Peter Heck.

In addition to the sources cited in the Acknowledgments of our original *Stardance* novel, we drew upon *Zen Mind, Beginner's Mind* by Shunryu Suzuki, *Everyday Zen* by Charlotte Joko Beck, *Walkabout Woman* by Michaela Roessner, *How Do You Go to the Bathroom in Space?* by William R. Pogue, *Carrying the Fire* by Michael Collins, and *Zen to Go* by Jon Winokur, in completing this book. Further assistance was derived from Kenya AA and Kona Fancy coffee, Old Bushmills whiskey, and the music of Johnny Winter (who was playing guitar 20 meters away while Jeanne wrote the Prologue), Ray Charles, Frank Zappa, Harry Connick, Jr., Benjamin Jonah Wolfe, Davey Graham, Michael Hedges, "Spider" John Koerner, and Mr. Amos Garrett, as well as Co-Op Radio and all the other jazz and blues FM stations received in Vancouver.

—*Vancouver, B.C*
4 August 1990

Prologue

When Buddha transmitted our practice to Maha Kashyapa he just picked up a flower with a smile. Only Maha Kashyapa understood what he meant. No one else there understood.

We do not know if this is a historical event or not—*but it means something* . . .

—Shunryu Suzuki-roshi
ZEN MIND, BEGINNER'S MIND
(italics added)

I always danced.

Like all babies I was born kicking; I just never stopped. All during my childhood it was that way. In the 1980s Gambier Island had a permanent population of about sixty, which no more than doubled in the summer—but it sure had a lot of theatres, with proscenium stages. The garden, the livingroom, a certain clearing in the woods near Aunt Anya's place . . . I danced in them all, and most of all in my room with the door closed. Sometimes there was thunderous applause; sometimes I danced for no one but myself; sometimes for intimate friends who vanished at a knock on the door. I remember clearly the moment I first understood that dancing was what I was going to do with my life.

Near sunset in late summer, 1985. Dinner and chores finished. My feet tickled. I told Dad where I was going, avoided Mom, and slipped out through the shed without banging the door. It was a kilometer and a half to the government wharf. The afternoon had been warm and wet—wet enough, I thought, to keep most of our neighbors indoors, and most boats at anchor. As I came over the last crest of the road and started down to the wharf, I saw I was right: I had the place to myself.

I began to run down the hill, kicking off my shoes and tossing my jacket to the side of the road. At the far end of the wharf I slowed and carefully descended the swaying gangway to the big dock-float down at water level. I turned halfway down and scanned the shoreline one more time to be sure. No one in sight. I circled around the boathouse at the foot of the gangway. The boathouse cut off sight of the land; there was nothing but me and the sea and the islands in the distance, grey-green mountains rising from the water. The water was highlit with sparkles of colour from the sun setting behind me over the forest. A warm mist came and went, invisibly. Even dry clothes are a nuisance when you dance. My clothes went under the rowboat that lay turtle-backed against the boathouse. The float's surface was rough enough for safe footing when wet, but soft enough for bare feet.

I turned my back to the land and faced the sea. There *are* bigger theatres, but not on Earth. My parents were unreconstructed hippies, quasi-Buddhist; for their sake I bowed to the sea . . . then waved to it for my own: the sober, dignified wave a serious artist gives her expectant public when she is eleven years old. A passing gull gave my cue. Ladies and gentlemen, Rain McLeod! The music swelled. . .

I've become too sophisticated to remember the steps I improvised. They must have been some mutant amalgamation of what I thought ballet was, and all the Other Kinds of dance I'd felt in my body but had no names for then. Nomenclature doesn't matter to an eleven-year-old. I danced, and what was in my heart came out my limbs and torso. I've wished since that I could still dance like that, but I've lost the necessary ignorance. I do remember that I was very happy. Complete.

Someone in the back row coughed—

Zalophus Californianus. A sea lion. Distinguished from harbor seals, even at that distance, by the distinct ears. Passing Gambier on his way back home from a day of raiding. Fishermen hate sea lions, call them pirates of the sea. They'll take one bite from each fish in your net, spoiling the whole catch . . . then leave with the best one, waving it at you mockingly as they go. I always secretly liked them. They *always* danced: so it seemed to me. Drama and tragedy in the water; slapstick comedy when they were on land. He was perhaps fifty meters due east of the dock, treading water and staring at me. He coughed again, sounding very much like Grandfather.

I didn't let him interrupt me. I worked a friendly hello wave into what I was doing, and kept on dancing. I noticed him out of the corner of my eye from time to time, watching me in apparent puzzlement, but he was no more distraction than a cloud or gull would have been—

—until there were two of him.

For a moment I "treaded water" myself, planting my feet so I faced them and dancing only with torso and arms. They were identical, grey and wet, a few meters apart, their eyes and slick heads glistening with reflected sunset. The new one gave a cough of its own, softer and higher. Grandfather and Grandmother Meade. They watched me with no discernible expression at all, giving me their complete attention, perfect bobbing Buddhas.

So I danced for them.

Well, at them. I made no attempt to "translate" what I was feeling into Sea Lion dance, to mimic the body-language I'd seen them use, so they could understand better. Even at eleven I was arrogant enough to be more interested in teaching them *my* dance language, telling them who *I* was. When you're that young, expressing yourself is better than being understood. So I continued to dance in Human, and for the whole cycloramic world of sea and sunset—but began subtly aiming it at the sea lions, as though they were the two important critics in a packed theatre, or my actual grandparents come to see my solo debut.

What luck, to have spent my childhood so far from Vancouver's ballet classes that no one had yet told me how I was supposed to move. I was still able to move the way I needed to, to invent anything my heart required. It felt good, that's all this highly trained forty-six-year-old can remember. For a time machine and video gear, you can have anything I own.

The sea lions were twenty meters closer, and there were four of them now.

They were treading water in ragged formation, close enough for me to see whiskers. By logical extension of my original whimsy, the new arrivals were the paternal grandparents I'd never met, the McLeods. Ghosts in the audience. It gave an added layer of meaning to what I was doing, as much awareness of mortality and eternity as an eleven-year-old is capable of. I danced on.

The first breezes of evening found the sweat under my hair and on my chest and chilled them. I increased my energy output to compensate. I was grinning, spinning.

Seven sea lions. Twenty meters away, faces absolutely blank, staring.

Everything came together—sea, sky, purple clouds of sunset, sea lions—to generate that special magic always sought and so seldom found. I lost myself; the dance began dancing me. It burst out of me like laughter or tears, without thought or effort. My legs were strong, wind infinite, ideas came, every experiment worked and suggested the next. There's a special state of being, the backwards of a trance, where you transcend yourself and become a part of everything—where you seem to stand still, while the world dances around and through you. Many dancers never experience it. I'd been to that level a few times before, for fleeting moments. This time I knew I could stay as long as I wanted.

Time stopped; I went on.

Even an eleven-year-old body has limits; every dance has a natural, logical end. Eventually, with warm contentment and mild regret, I left Nirvana and returned to the world of illusion again. I was still, upright, arms upthrust toward the clouds, reaching for the unseen stars.

The float was ringed by more than a dozen sea lions, the farthest within five meters of me. I looked round at them all, half-expecting them to clap and bark like cartoon seals. They stared at me. Bobbing in silent syncopation, seeming to be thinking about what they'd just seen. My first applause . . .

I bowed, deeply.

And then waved, grandly.

Darkness was falling fast. Sweat dripped from me, my soles tingled, and many muscles announced their intention to wake up stiff tomorrow. I was perfectly happy.

This, I thought, *is what I'm supposed to do.* My Thing, as Mom was always calling it: what I would do with my life. I understood now what I had always sensed, that Mom was going to hate it (though I didn't yet understand why) . . . but that didn't matter anymore.

Maybe that's when you become an adult. When your parents' opinions no longer control.

I kept silent when I returned home that night. But the next day I called Grandmother in Vancouver, and told her that she had won the tug of war with my mother. I moved into her huge house on the mainland, and let her enroll me in ballet class, and in normal school, like other kids. Within weeks I had been teased so much over the name "Rain M'Cloud" (which had never struck anyone on Gambier Island as odd) that I changed it to Morgan. It seemed to me a much more dignified name for a ballerina.

It was a long time before I saw Gambier Island again.

I always danced. But from the day of the sea lions, dancing was just about all I did, all I was. For thirty-two years. Until the day came when my body simply would not do it anymore. The day in April of 2017 when Doctor Thompson and Doctor Immega told me that even more surgery would not help, that I could never dance again. My lower back and knees were spent.

I tried the dancer's classic escape hatches for a few years. Choreography. Teaching. When they didn't work for me, I tried living without dance. I even tried relationships again. Nothing worked.

Including me. There were lots of trained, experienced professionals looking for work, as technological progress made more and more occupational specialties obsolete. There were few job openings for a forty-six-year-old who couldn't even type. Even the traditional unskilled-labour jobs were increasingly being done by robots. Sure, I could go back to school, and in only a few years of drudgery acquire a new profession—ideally, one which would not be obsolete by the time I graduated. But what for? Nothing interested me.

The salt of the earth had lost its savor.

I went back to Gambier Island. By now it was becoming a suburb of Vancouver; even in winter there were stores and cars and paved roads and burglaries. There was talk of a condominium complex. I sat for six months in the cabin where I had been born, waiting for some great answer to come from out of the sky. I visited my parents' graves frequently. Sat zazen in the woods. Split cords of wood. Read the first twenty pages of a dozen books. Walked the parts of the Island that were still wild, by day and night. Nature accepted my presence amiably enough, but offered no answers. Nothing.

I went down to the wharf and consulted the sea lions, as I had many times. They had nothing to say. They just looked at me, as if waiting for me to begin dancing.

After enough days of that, "nothing" started to look good to me. I filled out the Euthanasia application I had brought with me, putting down "earliest possible" for Date and leaving the space for Reason blank. I'd have a response within a week or two; by the end of the month, unless I changed my mind, my problems would be over.

In my bones, I was a dancer. And I couldn't dance anymore.

Not anywhere on Earth . . .

That very night I was lying in the hammock behind the house, watching the stars, when my eye was caught by a large bright one. It moved relative to the other stars, so it was a satellite. It moved roughly north to south, and was quite large: it had to be Top Step. Funny I'd never thought of it before. The House the Stardance Built, as the media called it. Transplanted asteroid, parting gift of alien gods—the place where they made angels out of people. Hollow stone cigar, phallic womb in High Orbit. Gateway to immortality, to the stars, to freedom from every kind of human fear or need there was . . . and all it cost was everything you had, forever.

Dancers say, you go where the work is. Suddenly, at age forty-six, I had nowhere to go but up.

I

What shall it harm a man
If he loseth the whole world,
Yet gaineth his soul?

—Linda Parsons
14th Epistle to the Corinthians
And Anyone Else Who Might Be Listening;
transmission received 8 May 2005

Hundreds of thoughts ran through my head as the Valkyrie song of the engines began to rise in pitch. But most of them seemed to be variations on a single theme, and the name of the theme was this: Farewell—Forever—to Weight.

So many different *kinds* of weight!

Physical weight, of course. I had been hauling around more than fifty kilos of muscle and bone for the better part of four decades—and like all dancers, cursing every gram, even after I switched from ballet to modern. (That's 110 pounds, if you're an American.) Any normal person would have considered me bone-thin . . . but the ghost of Balanchine, damn his eyes, has haunted dancers for over half a century.

Soon I would have no weight, for the first time in my life, and for the rest of it—only my mass would remain to convince me I existed. A purist, they had told us at Suit Camp, will insist that there is no such thing as zero gravity, anywhere in the universe . . . only degrees of gravity, from micro to macro. But where I was going—any second now—I would experience microgravity too faint to be perceived without subtle instruments, so it would be zero as far as I was concerned.

It should have been a dancer's finest moment. To leap so high that you never come down again . . . wasn't that what all of us wanted? Why did I feel such a powerful impulse to bolt for the nearest exit while I still could?

Weight had always been my shame, and my secret friend, and my necessary enemy—the thing I became beautiful in the act of defying. In a sense, to an extent, weight had defined me.

In the end it had beaten me. I could try to kid myself that I was outmaneuvering it . . . but what I was doing was escaping it, leaving the field of battle in defeat, conceding victory.

But the physical weight was probably least in my thoughts as I sat there in my comfortable seat, on my way to a place where the concept of a comfortable seat had no meaning.

Do you have any idea how many kinds of weight each human carries? Even the most fortunate of us?

The weight of two million years of history and more . . .

Until this century, all the humans that had ever lived walked the earth, worked to stay erect, strove to eat and drink and to get food and drink for their children, sought shelter from the elements, yearned to acquire wealth, struggled to be understood. Everyone's every ancestor needed to eliminate their wastes and feared their deaths. Every one of us lived and died alone, locked in a bone cell, plagued by need and fear and hunger and thirst and loneliness and the certainty of pain and death. That long a heritage of sorrow is a weight, whose awful magnitude you can only begin to sense with the prospect of its ending.

And in a time measurable in months, all that weight was going to leave me, (if) when I entered Symbiosis. Allegedly forever, or some significant fraction thereof. I would never again need food or drink or shelter, never again be alone or afraid.

On the other hand, I could never again return to Earth. And some people maintained that I would no longer be a human being . . .

Now tell me: isn't that a kind of dying?

Not to mention the small but unforgettable possibility that joining a telepathic community might burn out my brain—no, more accurately and more horribly: burn out my *mind.*

Then there was the weight of my own personal emotional and spiritual baggage. Perhaps that should have been as nothing beside the weight of two million years, but it didn't feel that way. I was forty-six and my lifework was irrevocably finished, and I was the only person in all the world to whom that mattered. Why not go become a god? Or at least some kind of weird red angel . . .

Somewhere in there, among all my tumbling thoughts, was a little joke about the extremes some women will go to in order to lose weight, but no matter how many times that joke went through my head—and it was easily dozens—it refused to be funny, even once.

The Completist's Diet: you give up *everything*. That was another.

There were quite a few jokes in that cascade of last-minute thoughts, but none of them was funny, and I knew that none of my seventy-one fellow passengers wanted to hear them. There *was* a compulsive joker aboard, at the back of the cabin and to my right, loudly telling jokes, but no one was paying the slightest bit of attention to him. He didn't seem to mind. Even he didn't laugh at any of his witticisms.

The engine song which was the score for my thoughts reached a crescendo, and the joker shut up in mid-punchline. I vaguely recognized his voice; he'd been in my Section at Suit Camp; he was an American and his name was something Irish.

Just my luck. The wave of food poisoning that had run through Camp just days before graduation, cutting our Section down by over 30 percent, had spared this clown—and knocked out my roommate Phyllis, with whom I'd intended to keep on rooming at Top Step, and every other person I'd met whom I could imagine living with. Now I would probably end up paired off at random with some stranger who had the same problem. I hoped we'd be compatible. I'm not good at compatible.

I glanced around for the hundredth time for the nonexistent window . . . and my inner ear informed me that we were in motion.

Goodbye, world . . .

I felt a twinge of panic. *Not yet! I'm not ready* . . .

When I was a girl, travel to space *always* involved a rocket launch, with its familiar trappings of acceleration couches and countdowns and crushing gee forces on blastoff. I'd been vaguely aware of modern developments, but they hadn't really percolated through yet. So subconsciously I was expecting the irony of having my liberation from so many kinds of weight preceded by a whopping if temporary overdose of weight.

As usual, life served me up a subtler irony. The technology had improved. My last moments on Earth were spent sitting upright in something which differed from a commercial airliner mostly in its lack of windows and its considerably smaller dimensions—and the takeoff, when it came, yielded no more sense of acceleration than you get taking a methanol car from zero to sixty when you're first thinking of switching from fossil fuel.

I felt the spaceplane's wheels leave the ground, understood that my last connection with my mother planet was severed. Forever, unless I changed my mind in the next few months.

I fought down my growing sense of panic, flailing at it with big clumsy bladders full of logic. What had Earth ever done for me, that was worth sorrowing over its loss? What place on it was still fit for human habitation, and for how long? What did it have to offer, compared to greatly extended lifespan and freedom from every kind of suffering I knew—and *the chance that I might dance again?*

Like all babies leaving the womb, I felt the overwhelming impulse to burst into tears. Being mature enough to be self-conscious, I strove to suppress the urge. Apparently so did my fellow passengers; the engine song crescendoed without any harmonies from us. It began to diminish slightly as we passed the speed of sound and outran all but the vibrations that conduction carried through the hullplates.

It was then that my panic blossomed into full-grown terror.

It caught me by surprise. I had thought I'd already mastered this kind of fear, by preparing for it and educating it to death. All at once my gut did not care how confident I was of modern technology. It dimly understood that it was being taken to a place where any trivial mistake or malfunction could interrupt its all-important job, the production of feces and urine, and it reacted like a labor union, by convulsing with rage and threatening to shut down the whole system, right now. Other sister unions—heart, lungs, adrenals, sweat glands, autonomic nervous system—threatened to join the walkout, in the name of solidarity but on a wildcat basis. And management—my brain—had nothing to say except what management always says: I'm sorry, it's too late now, we're committed; let's pull together and try to salvage the situation.

Salvage the situation? said my body. *You're kidding. Remember Gambier Island in the winter, before you went to live in town with*

Grandmother? How silly it seemed to live someplace where all the heat could spill out through leaks, and if you couldn't make more fast enough you'd die? You're taking us to someplace where the air *can leak out.* And *the heat. Any time some piece of machinery goes wrong. The definition of machine is, a thing that goes wrong the moment you start to depend on it. Get us out of this,* now!

To both this line of reasoning, and the specific sanctions my body threatened if it were thwarted, I could only reply like a long-suffering mother, *You should have thought of that before you left the house.* I could not even get the poor thing to a toilet for another hour, and I didn't care *how* good everybody said p-suit plumbing was these days. Like management every-when, I had to dig in and try to tough out the strike, even if it meant sending goon-squads to hold the sphincters by force.

I tried Zen breath control; I had none. I tried the mantra they'd given me at Suit Camp; it was only a meaningless series of syllables, and they kept speeding up in my head rather than slowing down. I tried all of what I call my Wings Things—the little rituals you perform in the wings to suppress stage fright, just before taking your stage—and none of them worked.

I was ignoring my two seatmates because I didn't know them and was too wound up to deal with small talk, and we hadn't been allowed carry-on luggage even as small as a book, and they don't put windows on spacecraft. That left only one source of diversion. I leaned forward and turned on the TV.

Because it looked just like a conventional airliner's flat-screen seatback TV, I was expecting the usual "choice" of six banal 2-D channels. There were only two—and I did not want the video feed from the bridge that mimicked a window; I switched it off hastily. But the other channel was carrying the one program—out of all the millions the human race has produced—that I would have wished for. I suppose I should have been expecting it.

The Stardance, of course.

That piece has always been a kind of personal visual mantra for me. For millions, yes, but especially for me. It turned my whole life upside down, once, triggered both my divorce and my switch from ballet to modern dance when I first saw it at twenty-two. It made me realize that my marriage was dead and that something had to be done about that, and it forced me to rethink dance and dancing completely. It consoled me at the end of a dozen ruined love affairs, got me through a thousand bad nights. I had seen it on flatscreen and in simulated holo, with and without Brindle's score; I'd once wasted three months trying to translate the entire piece into a modified Labanotation. I knew every frame, every step, every gesture.

It was midway through the prologue, when no one knows the Stardance is about to happen, and Armstead is just trying to study, with his four cameras, the aliens who've appeared without warning nearby in High Earth Orbit. Seen from different angles: a barely visible bubble containing half a hundred swarming red fireflies, glowing like hot coals, dancing like bees in a hive, like electrons in orbit around some nonexistent nucleus. Brindle's music is still soft and hypnotic, Glass-like; it will be a few more five-counts before Shara enters.

I glanced unobtrusively around. Most of the passengers I could see were looking at their own TVs, and several were swaying slightly in unison, like tall grass in a gentle breeze. The Stardance was important to all of us. We were following it into space.

Shara Drummond's p-suited image forms and grows larger on the screen. The music swells. The camera gives that involuntary jump as Armstead, horrorstruck, recognizes her. She was just on her way back to Earth on doctor's orders when the Fireflies arrived: any more exposure to zero gravity and her body will lose—forever—its ability to tolerate Earth-normal gravity. No one knows better than Armstead that his love is now a dead woman breathing. She has chosen to sacrifice herself, because of her Great Understanding (that the aliens communicate by dance) and her Great Misunderstanding (that they are hostile).

As always, the dialogue between her and the nearby Space Command battleship is edited down to her refusal to get out of the line of fire until she has tried to talk to the dancing Fireflies; the hour she spends in silent contemplation of them, trying to deduce their language of motion, is shrunk down to thirty seconds that always seem to take an hour to go by—

—and then it changed. At the point where she says, "Charlie . . . this is a take," and he says, "Break a leg, kid," and she begins to dance, the tape departed from the classic release version as edited by Armstead.

Charlie Armstead had four cameras in space that day, bracketing Shara and the aliens. But in cutting the Stardance, later, he used footage only from the three that were on Shara's side. This makes sense: from the other camera's vantage, the Fireflies are in the way. But the result is that the Stardance is seen only from a human perspective: we are either behind, or below Shara, watching as she (apparently) dances the aliens right out of the Solar System.

The version we were being shown now was from the fourth camera. I'd seen it before; years ago I had once gone to the trouble and expense of studying the raw, unedited footage from all four cameras. But I'd paid least attention to the fourth. Its footage was edited out for good artistic reasons: some of the best movements of the dance are obscured. The swarming aliens in the foreground spoil the view, glowing like embers, leaving ghost trails in their wake.

But in this context, it had a powerful impact. We saw Shara, for once, from the aliens' point of view.

She looked much smaller, more fragile. She was no longer the greatest choreographer of her century creating her masterpiece. She was a little dog telling a big dog to get the hell out of her yard, *now*. You could almost sense the Fireflies' amusement and admiration. And pride: Shara was the end result of something they had set in motion many millions of years before, when they seeded Earth with life.

I saw things I had missed on my last viewing. From all three other POVs Shara's helmet is opaque with reflected glare. From this one you could see into it, see her face . . . and now I saw that what I had taken on my previous viewing for a proud, snarling, triumphant grin was in fact a rictus of terror. For the first time it really came home to me that this woman was dancing through a fear that should have petrified her.

I felt a powerful surge of empathy, and my own fear began to ease a little. As I watched Shara's magnificent Stardance from this new perspective, my breathing began to slow; my heartbeat, which usually raced as the Stardance climaxed, slowed too.

Peace came to me. It was the calm, the empty mind, that I had sat zazen for countless hours to achieve for minutes. My kinesthetic awareness faded; for once I was not acutely conscious of the relative position of each muscle; my body seemed to become lighter, to melt away . . .

Suddenly I smiled. It wasn't an illusion: my body *was* growing lighter! We were already entering Low Earth Orbit.

It didn't diminish the feeling of tranquillity; it enhanced it. Space was going to be a good place to go. I no longer cared how strange and dangerous this voyage was. I was where I was supposed to be.

Onscreen, the Stardance reached its brilliant coda. The Fireflies vanish, leaving only Shara, and far behind her the twinkling carousel of the factory complex where she invented zero gravity dance, where Armstead is watching her on his monitors.

She poises in space for a long time, getting her breath, then turns to the nearest camera and puffs out the famous line, "We may be puny, Charlie . . . but by Jesus we're *tough.*" The music overrides their audio then, but we know he is begging her to come back inboard, and she is refusing. It's not just that she is permanently adapted to free fall now and can never return to Earth; nor that the only place she could live indefinitely in space belongs to a man she despises with her whole heart.

She is *done now.* She has accomplished everything she was born to do. Or so she believes.

She waves at the camera, all four thrusters go off, and she arcs down toward Earth, visible in frame now for the first time. Brindle's score swells for the last time, we follow her down toward the killing atmosphere—

—and again it changed. I'd never seen this footage before. It must have been shot by some distant Space Command satellite peace-camera, hastily tracking her as she fell through Low Orbit. The image was of inferior quality, had the grainy look of maximum enlargement and the jerkiness you get when a machine is doing the tracking. But it provided a closer look at those last moments than Armstead's cameras had from back up in a higher, slower orbit.

And so we saw now what everyone had missed then, what the world was not to know about for over three more years. Whoever examined that tape for the Space Command at the time must have just refused to believe either his eyes or his equipment, but there was no mistaking it. Shara Drummond simply disappeared. When her p-suit tumbled and burned in the upper atmosphere, it was limp, empty.

The next time any human would see her, years later, she would be a crimson-winged immortal orbiting one of the moons of Saturn, no more in need of a pressure suit than a Firefly. The first human ever to enter Symbiosis. The first and greatest Stardancer.

I felt awed and humble. As the credits rolled I reached out to shut off the set so I could savor the sensation—and knew at once that we were all the way into zero gravity. My arm did not fall when I told it it could; my center of mass pivoted loosely around my seatbelt.

The main engines had fallen silent, unnoticed, while I'd watched. We were more than halfway through our journey, officially in space. Now there would be a period of free fall before we began matching orbits with Top Step. I realized that my face felt flushed, and that my sinuses were filling up, just as I'd been told to expect. I was pleased to feel no stirrings of the dreaded dropsickness. Apparently the drugs they'd given us worked, for me at least.

Part of me wanted to unstrap and play, couldn't wait to explore this new environment, begin learning whether or not I could really dance in it. I hadn't danced in so long!

I saw other passengers experimenting with their limbs, grinning at each other. Why should it be surprising that in zero gee, one is lighthearted? No one seemed bothered by dropsickness. I turned and grinned at each of the seatmates I'd been ignoring.

To my left, in what would have been the window seat if spaceplanes had windows, was a black girl whose answering grin was spectacular; she had the whitest, most perfect teeth I'd ever seen. Zero gee made her already round cheeks cherubic. She was not a North American black but something more exotic; her hair was both wavy and curly, and her skin was the color of bitter chocolate. She looked startlingly young, no more than twenty-five, when I had understood the cutoff age was thirty; but for the instant our gazes met we communicated perfectly across cultural and generational distance.

The aisle seat to my right was occupied by a Chinese man in his late thirties. He was clean-shaven, and like everyone else's aboard, his hair was short. His face was impassive, and I couldn't tell whether his eyes were smiling or not. (In zero gee, *everyone* looks sort of Chinese: the puffy features caused by upward migration of body fluids mimic epicanthic folds at the eyes. If you *start out* Chinese, your eyes end up looking like paper-cuts.) But something in those eyes responded to me, I felt; we communicated too. A little more than I wanted to; I looked away abruptly. Wave of dizziness. Not a good idea to move your head quickly in free fall.

There was a soft overall murmuring in the passenger cabin, audible even over the engine sound: the sum of everyone's grunts and sighs and exclamations. It was a sound of optimism, of hope, of pleased surprise. I think in another minute someone would have ignored instructions and unstrapped himself . . . and then we all would have, no matter what the flight attendants said.

But then there was a sound like a gunshot or the crack of a bat, and a banshee was among us, and I felt a draft—

In that year, 2020, the Space Command's traffic satellites were (as predicted since the 1980s) tracking over 20,000 known manmade objects larger than ten centimeters in diameter in the Low Earth Orbit band. Naturally no flight plan was accepted that could intersect any of them. But there were (also as predicted) countless *hundreds* of thousands, perhaps millions, of objects *smaller* then ten centimeters whizzing around in Low Orbit: too many to keep track of even if sensors had been able to see them. Screws, bolts, nuts, fittings, miscellaneous jettisoned trash, fragments of destroyed or damaged spacecraft, bits of dead spacemen burst by vacuum and freeze-dried by space, the assorted drifting trash of sixty years of spaceflight. Some of these little bits of cosmic shrapnel had relative velocities of more than fifteen kilometers a second. That's 5400 kilometers an hour—or a little more than 3200 miles per hour. At that speed, a beer-can ring is a deadly missile.

The chances of a collision depended on whose figures you accepted. The most optimistic estimate at that point in history was one chance in twenty; the most pessimistic, one in four. But even the pessimists conceded that the probability of a *life-threatening* collision was much lower than that.

Our number came up, that's all.

Whatever it was hulled us forward and from the left, just aft of the bulkhead that separated the passenger cabin from the cockpit.

Two months of training kicked in: nearly all of us got our p-suit hoods over our heads and sealed in a matter of seconds. The banshee wail was cut off, and the roar of air overridden by a softer hissing behind my head. Within moments I could feel my suit expanding. I could see now why they'd been so tight about carry-on items; even with the strict security, the air was filled with a skirling vortex of smuggled items: tissues, gum wrappers, a rabbit's foot, a pen and postcard dancing in lockstep, all converging on the source of the pressure leak. Small lighted panels in each seatback began blinking urgently in unison, as though the whole plane had acquired a visible pulse, doubtless telling us to fasten our seatbelts and return our seatbacks to the upright position. In my earphones grew the white noise of dozens of passengers talking at once in assorted languages and dialects. I tried to switch to Emergency channel . . . but for some reason this suit was not like the ones I had trained in: it had no channel selector switch.

I was not especially afraid. The warm glow of the Stardance was still on me, and we had rehearsed this dozens of times. There was nothing to worry about. Any second now, automatic machinery would begin dispensing globules of blue sticky stuff. The globs would be sucked onto the hole in the hull, and burst there. When enough of them had burst, the hole would be patched.

The hurricane went on, and there were no globs of blue sticky. I spotted one of the nozzles that should have been emitting them.

Okay, failsafes fail; that was why we had live flight attendants. Now they would converge on the leak with a pressure patch, and—

—where were the attendants?

I strained to see over the seats in front of me. Seconds ticked by and I could see no one moving. Finally I had to see what was going on: I unstrapped myself and tried to stand.

But my reflexes were obsolete. I rose with alarming speed, got my hands up too slowly, smacked my skull against the overhead hard enough to cross my eyes, ricocheted downward, hit the seat, bounced back upward, cracked my head again, and clutched desperately at the arms of my seat as I plumped back into it; the girl on my left grabbed my arm firmly to steady me. The seat to my right was empty; at the apex of my flight I had seen my other seatmate, the young Chinese, soaring forward down the aisle, graceful as a slow-motion acrobat.

I had also spotted the chief attendant, strapped into the front row aisle seat he had taken after giving us the standard preflight ritual. He was leaning to his left, arms waving lazily, like a dreaming conductor. His p-suit was slowly turning red from the hood down, and from the left side of the hood a fluid red rope issued. It rippled like a water snake, and ran with all the other airborne objects toward the hole in the hull, breaking up into red spheroids just before being sucked out into space. By great bad fortune the chief attendant's head had been in the path of whatever had hulled us . . .

Moving carefully, I managed to wedge myself into an equilibrium between the back of my seat and the overhead, and looked aft. I saw at once what was keeping the other attendant: Murphy's Law. She was struggling with her jammed seatbelt, weeping and shouting something I couldn't hear.

I looked forward again in time to see the young Chinese land feet first like a cat against the forward bulkhead, absorb the impact with his thighs so that he did not bounce from it, and instantly position all four limbs correctly to brace himself against the draft. Suddenly some other, powerful force pulled on him briefly, trying to yank him sideways and up, but he sensed it and corrected for it at at once. (The same force acted on me and the others; I could not figure out how to correct, and settled for clutching the seatback and overhead as tightly as I could until it passed.) A part of me wondered if he gave lessons. He had obviously been in free fall before.

But not in this vessel! The pressure patches could have been in any of four separate locker-sections—a total of more than two dozen small compartments, identified only by numbers.

I could see him pleading for silence, but no one could hear him above the general roar. I could see him gesturing for silence, but almost no one else could. The aft attendant could tell him which locker, but he could not hear her. He looked at me pleadingly.

I spun back to her, and wondered for a moment if she had gone mad with frustration: she had torn her hood back over her head and was waving furiously. Then I got it and pulled my own hood off. The babble of the earphones went away, and I could hear her shouting.

Just barely. The air was getting thin in here. But it was also coming my way: I could just make out a high distant Donald Duck voice, squawking the same word over and over again.

I should have been terrified that the word made absolutely no sense to me, but I did not seem to have time. Once I was sure I'd heard it right, I whirled and dutifully began braying it as loud as I could toward the Chinese.

"Before," I screamed, *"Before, before, before, before—"*

It felt good to scream: pressure change was trying to explode my lungs, and emptying them that way probably saved them serious damage. He already had his own hood off, he was quick; no, he was better than quick, because he instantly solved the puzzle that had baffled me; he yanked his hood back over his head, oriented himself and kicked off, and within seconds he was pulling the most beautiful pressure patch I'd ever seen out of Compartment B-4.

By then I was so dizzy from spinning my head back and forth I felt as though my eyeballs were about to pop out of their sockets—as indeed they probably were—and I had to pull my hood back on and let my seatmate haul me back down into my seat . . . where I spent some minutes concentrating on not soiling my p-suit. The internal suit pressure rose quickly, but at least as much of it came from my intestines as from my airtanks, and it got ripe enough in there to steam up my hood and make my eyes water for a few moments.

I became aware that my seatmate was shaking my shoulder gently. I opened my eyes, and some of the dizziness went away.

She was pointing to her ears, then to her belt control panel, and shaking her head. I nodded, and fumbled until I found the shutoff switch for my suit radio. The babbling sound of dozens of frightened passengers went away. I noticed for the first time that all the blinking seatback signs were saying, not "FASTEN YOUR SEATBELTS," but "MAINTAIN RADIO SILENCE."

She touched her hood to mine. "Are ya right?" she called.

"Occasionally," I said lightheadedly, but I got it. Several weeks in Australia, even in the multilingual environments of Suit Camp, will give you a working familiarity with Aussie slang. She was an Aborigine. Now that I thought about it, I had noticed her once or twice in Camp, had wondered vaguely why, in the midst of one of the largest remaining Aboriginal reserves in Australia, she seemed to be the only Abo who was actually taking Suit Camp training. All the others I'd seen had been outside the Camp, in town and at the Cairns airport.

"You took an awful bloody chance," she said.

"It seemed like a good idea at the time," I called back.

"Too right! You saved us all, I reckon—you and the Chinese bloke. Fast as a scalded cat he was, eh? Hold on, here he comes."

The Chinese rejoined us. He was moving more slowly now that the emergency was past. The delicate grace with which he docked himself back in his chair, without a wasted motion or a bounce, pleased my dancer's eyes. I resolved to ask him at the first opportunity to tutor me in "jaunting," the spacer's term for moving about in zero gee.

He joined his hood to ours. "Thank you," he said to me.

As our eyes met I felt the old familiar tingle in the pit of the stomach that I had not felt in ages.

And suppressed it. I thanked him right back—but without putting any topspin on it. *I'm too old to climb these stairs again,* I told myself, *even in zero gee . . .*

"I thank you both," the Aborigine girl said. "Best put our ears on, but. I think they're getting it sorted out."

The seatbacks were now flashing, "MONITOR YOUR RADIO." We separated, and I switched my radio back on in time to hear the surviving attendant say, "—xt person that makes a sound, I am personally going to drag aft and cycle through the airlock, is that *fucking well understood*?"

She sounded sincere; the only sound in response was dozens of people breathing at different rates.

"Passenger in seat 1-E: is Mr. Henderson dead?"

"Uh . . . no. I've got my hand over the leak and the . . . the entry wound. His chest is still—"

"Jesus! Wait . . . uh . . . ten more seconds for cabin pressure to come back up and then get his hood off. Gently! Passenger 1-F, there's a first-aid kit in Compartment D-7 in front of you; get a pressure bandage and give it to 1-E; then try to get a pulse rate. Is anyone here a doctor or a paramedic?"

Breathing sounds. Someone grunting softly. A cough.

"Damn. Passenger in 6-B, answer yes or no, do you require medical assistance?"

Breathing sounds.

"Dammit, the woman who passed the word!—do you need help?"

Whoops—she meant me! I started to reply . . . and my body picked that moment to finish restoring equilibrium, with prolonged and noisy eructations at both ends of my alimentary canal.

". . . no-o-o . . ." I finished, and everyone, myself included, began to howl with tension-breaking laughter—

—everyone except the attendant. "SILENCE!" she roared, loud enough to make my earphones distort, and the laughter fell apart. "It is past time you started acting like spacers. A real spacer is dying while you giggle. We all nearly died because none of you could read a flashing sign six inches from your face! You in 1-E—" That passenger was muttering *sotto voce* to someone who was helping him remove the injured attendant's hood. "—switch off your radios and chatter hood to hood if you must. Does anyone else need medical aid? No? Then listen up! I want all of you to keep your hoods on—even after you're certain the pressure has come back up. I'm going to switch to command channel now and report. You won't be able to hear it. I'll fill you all in the moment I am good and God damned ready . . . but not if I hear *one word* on this channel when I come back on. And if you switch off your radio, for Christ's sake *watch your seatback signs this time.*"

The moment she switched frequencies, several people began chattering. But they were loudly shushed; finally even the most determined—the loudmouth who'd been making jokes before takeoff—had been persuaded to shut up. The attendant's anger had sobered, humbled us. Despite weeks of training, we had screwed up, in our first crisis. Now we had to sit in silence like chastened children while the grown-ups straightened things out.

I switched my own mike off, and huddled with my seatmates until our three hoods were touching. There was an awkward silence. We all grinned at each other nervously.

"What happens now?" I said finally. "Losing all that air must have pushed us off course, right? Spoiled our vector, or whatever?"

"So we miss our bus," the Aborigine girl said. "Question is, how many go-rounds does it take to match up with it again—and how much air have we got to drink while we wait?"

"I think we'll be all right," the Chinese said. "The pilot maneuvered to correct, and I think she did a good job." His voice was a pleasant tenor. His English was utterly unaccented, newscaster's English.

"How do you reckon?" she asked.

"She didn't blast too quickly, and she didn't blast too slowly. And it was one short blast. I think she's good. We might make the original rendezvous, or something close to it."

His confidence was very reassuring. I thought again about asking him to teach me how to jaunt. And decided against it. There would be plenty of qualified instructors around . . . and I was here to simplify my life, not complicate it again.

The attendant came swimming down the aisle past us as he spoke. We sat up to watch. She checked the pressure patch first, popping a little round membrane of blue sticky between her fingers and watching to see if any of its droplets migrated toward the patch. Only when she was satisfied did she turn and check on Mr. Henderson, holding a brief hood-to-hood conference with the passenger who was taking care of him. Then she drifted aimlessly in a half crouch, talking to the pilot on the channel we couldn't hear. Finally she nodded and did something to her belt. The seat-back signs began flashing "MONITOR YOUR RADIO" again. I switched mine on.

"Make sure your neighbor has his ears on," she said. "Is everybody listening? Okay, here's the word. Captain de Brandt is going to attempt to salvage our original rendezvous window. In about fifteen minutes the main engines will fire. You can expect about a half gee for about two minutes. There may be additional maneuvering after that, so remain strapped in and braced until I tell you otherwise. Expect acceleration warning in twelve minutes; until then I want you to take your hoods off to save your suit air. But be ready to seal up fast!"

"When will Channel One be coming back on TV?" someone asked. "I want to watch the docking." It was the compulsive joker, aft.

"We can't spare the bytes."

"Huh? That's not—"

"Shut up." She switched back to command frequency.

I took off my hood. The cabin pressure was lower now than it had been before the blowout. Which was good: all the foul air gushed out of my suit as I unsealed it. I was briefly embarrassed, but in low pressure no one can smell anything very well; it passed without comment, as it were.

I wondered how much air I had left, if I should need it. These were cheap tourist p-suits we were wearing, with just enough air to survive a disaster like we'd just had, in four small cylinders fitted along our upper arms and shins. (In proper p-suits with full-size tanks at our backs, we'd have needed awfully complicated seats.)

There was a subdued murmur of conversation. Suddenly the

attendant's strident voice overrode it; she must have pulled off her hood. "You! Nine-D, sit down and buckle up!"

"What the hell for? You said we've got twelve minutes—"

"Sit down!"

It was the joker again. "See here," he said, "we're not soldiers and we're not convicts. I've been looking forward to free fall for a long time, and I have a right to enjoy it. You have no authority—"

"Don't tell me: you're an American, right? This vessel is in a state of emergency; I have authority to break your spine! Sit or be restrained."

"Come, come, the emergency is passed, you said so yourself. Stop being hysterical and lighten up a little." He drifted experimentally out into the aisle. "We have a perfect right to *Jesus*!"

She had pushed off much too hard, I thought, with the full force of terrestrial muscles. She came up the aisle not in graceful slow motion, as my seatmate had earlier, but like a stone fired from a sling. Even I knew not to jump that hard in zero gee: you bash your head. But as she came she was tucking, rolling—

—she flashed past me quickly, but it's just about impossible to move too fast for a dancer to follow: I spun my head and tracked her. She ended her trajectory heels foremost, *smacked* those heels against the seats on either side of him, took all the kinetic energy of her hurtling body on her thighs, and came to a dead stop with her nose an inch from his, drifting just perceptibly to her left.

Try it yourself sometime: drop from a third-story window, and land in a sitting position without a grunt of impact, without a bruise.

I may had been the only one present equipped to fully appreciate what a feat she had just accomplished—but it made the loudmouthed American cross his eyes and shut up.

"You have the right to remain silent," she told him, loud enough to be heard all over the vessel; he flinched. "If you give up that right, I will break your arm. You have no right to counsel until such time as we match orbits with or land upon UN soil—which we don't plan to do." I don't think he was hearing her. He was busy with the tricky mechanics of getting back into his seat. "Does anyone else have any questions? No? You—strap him in there."

She kicked off backwards, repeated her feat by flipping in midair and braking herself against the first row of seats, came to rest with her back against the forward bulkhead, and glared around at us. Suddenly her expression softened.

"Look, people," she called, her voice harsh in the low air pressure, "I know how you feel. I remember my first time in free fall. But you'll have plenty of time to enjoy it later. Right now I want you strapped in. We're in a new orbit, one we didn't pick: there's no telling when the Captain may have to dodge some new piece of junk." She sighed. "I know you're not military personnel. But in space you take orders from anyone who has more experience than you, and ask questions later. A lot later. I've logged over six thousand hours in space, half of them in this very can, and I *will* space the next jerk who gives me any shit."

"Fair go," my Aborigine seatmate called. "We're with you!"

There was a rumble of agreement in which I joined.

"Look, Miss—" she added.

"Yes?"

"You asked for a doctor before. I ain't no whitefella doctor. My people reckon me a healer, but. Can I come see the bloke?"

The attendant started to answer, frowned and hesitated.

"I won't hurt him any."

"All right, come ahead. But be careful! Come *slow*. And headfirst—don't try to flip on the way, you're too green."

She unstrapped and clambered over me with some difficulty, clutching comically in all directions. A few people tittered. The Chinese steadied her and helped. Presently she was floating in the aisle like someone swimming in a dream . . . except that her swimming motions accomplished nothing. She looked over her shoulder to the Chinese. "Give us a hand then, will you, mate?"

He hesitated momentarily . . . then put his hand where he had to and gave her a gentle, measured push.

If a male dancer had done that in the studio, in a lift, I'd have thought nothing of it. But he wasn't a dancer, and this wasn't a studio. That's how I explained my sudden blush to myself.

"Ta," she called as she slowly sailed away. This time the titters were louder.

No, maybe I would not ask him for lessons in free fall movement.

He turned to me. "Excuse me," he said politely.

"No, no," I said, "I understand. If you'd pushed on her feet, she'd

In a matter of seconds the acceleration went away, and we drifted freely again. We all waited a few moments for a bang or bump to signal docking. Nothing happened.

As the three of us started to say embarrassment-melting things to each other, thrust returned again—in precisely the opposite direction. I suppose it made sense: first you turn the wheel, and then you straighten the wheel. But even Robert was caught by surprise. This time we were hanging upside down and sideways from our seats, Kirra and I with wrists locked like arm wrestlers and *Robert's* head in *my* lap. It felt dismayingly good there. Even through a cheap p-suit. Again the thrust went away.

"I wonder how long it'll be before we—" Kirra began, when an acceleration warning finally sounded, a mournful hooting noise. The attendant had time to call out, "All right, I want everybody to—" Then the big one hit.

Well, maybe a half gee, or a little more. But half a gee is a lot more than none, and it came on fast, and in an unexpected and disturbing direction. The pilot was blasting directly forward, along our axis, as though backing violently away from danger. The whole vessel shuddered. We all fell forward toward the seatbacks in front of us—"below" us now—and held a pushup together for perhaps thirty or forty seconds. There were loud complaints above the blast noise.

The acceleration faded slowly down to nothing again. There were two or three seconds of silence . . . and then there was a series of authoritative but gentle thumps on the hull, fore and aft, as though men with padded hammers were surreptitiously checking the welds. The seatbacks began flashing *PLEASE REMAIN SEATED.*

"We're here," Robert said. "A very nice docking. A little abrupt, but clean." I thought he was being ironic but wasn't sure.

"Keep your seatbelts buckled," the attendant called. "We'll disembark after Doctor Kolchar has cleared Mr. Henderson to be moved."

"That's it?" Kirra said.

I knew what she'd meant. On TV the docking of spacecraft is always seen from a convenient adjacent camera that gives the metal mating dance a stately Olympian perspective, an elephantine grace. A trip to space—especially one's first and last—should begin with trumpets, and end with the Blue Danube. This had been like riding a Greyhound bus through an endless tunnel . . . blowing a tire . . .

riding on the rim for a while . . . and then running out of gas in the middle of the tunnel.

"That's it," Robert agreed. "Even if they'd had the video feed running, it wouldn't have looked like much up until the very end. To really appreciate a docking you've got to speak radar. But we're here, all right."

"We truly have reached the Top Step," I said wonderingly.

"That we have," Robert said. "Here comes the doctor." The red light was on over the airlock up front.

The hatch opened explosively, with a popping sound, and the airlock spat out a white-haired man in Bermuda shorts and a loud yellow Hawaiian shirt. His body orientation, fluttering hair and clothes, and the pack affixed somehow to his midsection made him look like a skydiver. The attendant caught him, began to warn him that this pressure was not secure, but he shushed her and began examining Mr. Henderson with various items taken from his belly pack. After a time I heard him say, "Okay, Shannon, let's move him. You help me with him. We're going to do it nice and slow."

"You!" the attendant called up the aisle. "The Chinese spacer in Row Six: you're in command." Robert blinked. "Come forward and take over, now. Breathing and digestion are permitted; limited thinking will be tolerated; everything else is forbidden, savvy?"

"Yes, Ma'am," he called forward.

Our eyes met briefly as he was unbuckling. For the first time I was able to see past that impassive expression, guess his thoughts. He was embarrassed, flattered . . . disappointed? At what?

"To be continued in our next," he murmured, and vaulted away.

At the interruption of our conversation?

"I hope so," I heard myself call after him.

Come to think of it, he still hadn't said whether or not he'd give me lessons in jaunting.

Oh God. What was I doing? What good could possibly come of this? Even for me, this was rotten timing.

"You want to mind that top step, they say," Kirra said softly, and when I turned to look at her she was grinning.

2

Two moves equals one fire.
—Mark Twain

We didn't have long to wait. Less than a minute after the doctor and attendant left, the lock cycled open again and someone emerged. The newcomer got our instant attention.

"Afternoon, folks," she said. "Welcome to Top Step. I'm a Guide, and my name is Chris."

No one said a word.

"Oh, excuse me." She courteously turned herself rightside up with respect to us.

It didn't help much. Even upside down in that confined space, her face had been far enough from the floor to be seen from the last row. And even rightside up she was startling.

Chris's p-suit had no legs, and neither did Chris.

I know I tried hard not to gape. I'm pretty sure I failed. One person actually gasped audibly. Chris ignored it and continued cheerfully, "I usually make a little speech at this point, but we want to get you out of suspect pressure as quickly as possible, so you've got a temporary reprieve. You are now about to do something you probably thought was impossible: leave a plane intelligently. By rows, remaining seated until it's your turn, and then leaving *at once.* You have no carryons or coats to fumble with, no reason to block the aisle—and good reason not to.

"See, if we cycle you through the airlocks a few at a time it'd take over an hour. But to keep the lock open at both ends and march you all out we have to equalize pressure between this can and Top Step—and there's no telling if or how long that patch there will take pressure. So we're going to do this with suits sealed, and we are not going to dawdle. I know you're all free fall virgins; don't worry, we'll set up a bucket brigade and you'll be fine. One thing: if there's a blowout as you're passing through the lock, *get out of the doorway.* It doesn't matter which direction you pick, just don't be in the way. Okay? All right, Ev!"

That last was apparently directed to the Captain in the cockpit ahead. My ears began to hurt suddenly. The pressure was rising back toward Earth-normal. Like everybody, I swallowed hard, and watched that pressure patch as I sealed my hood.

"Okay, this side first. No chatter. First person to slow up the line gets assigned to the Reclamation Module for the next two months." A light over the lock blinked and the door opened. "First row: move!"

Getting up the aisle to the front was easy. Once there were no seat-backs to navigate with, it got trickier. But Chris fielded me like a shortstop and lobbed me to Robert at second, who pivoted and threw me to someone at first for the double play. That must have ended the inning; others tossed me around the infield to celebrate for a while.

I ended up turning slowly end over end in a large pale blue rectangular-box room. Several yellow ropes were strung across it from one biggest-wall to the opposite one. I caught a rope as I sailed past it.

Because I seemed to be drifting light as a feather, I badly underestimated how hard it would be to stop drifting. If that rope hadn't had some give to it, I might have pulled my arms out of their sockets. I had no weight, but I still had all my mass. I found the experience fascinating and mildly dismaying: in that first intentional vector change I made in space, I knew that some of the zero-gee dance moves I'd envisioned weren't going to work.

But I was too busy to think about kinesthetics just then. The room was half-full of my shipmates, with more coming at a steady pace. I saw that all of us were treating the biggest-walls as "floor" and "ceiling," and lining ourselves up parallel to the ropes between them—but there seemed to be considerable silent disagreement as to which way was up. Visual cues were all ambiguous. It was a comical sight.

Finally one side preponderated and the others gradually switched around to that "local vertical." I was one of the latter group, and as I reached the decision that I was upside down, I realized for the first time that I felt faintly nauseous. The feeling increased as I flipped myself over, diminished a little as the room seemed to snap back into proper perspective again.

The last of us came tumbling in, followed by the last member of the bucket brigade. The latter sealed the hatch, oriented himself upside down to us, let go of the hatch, and floated before it, hands thrust up into his pockets. He looked at us, and we craned our heads at him. A few of us cartwheeled round to his personal vertical again, and before long everyone had done so, with varying degrees of grace.

He seemed to be in his fifties. He wore a p-suit, opaque and deep purple. Compared to the clunky suits we wore, his looked like a second skin. His complexion was coal black, the kind that doesn't even gleam much under bright light. He was lean and fit, going bald and making no attempt to hide it, frowning and smiling at the same time. He looked relaxed and competent, avuncular. He reminded me a little of Murray, the business manager of one of the companies I'd worked with almost a decade before. Murray did the work of four men, yet *always* seemed perfectly relaxed, even during the week before a performance.

"You folks don't seem to know which way is up, do you?" he said pleasantly.

There were a very few polite giggles, and one groan.

He did something, and was suddenly upside down to us again. He was stable in the new position and had not touched anything. I didn't quite catch the move at the time—and still can't describe it; I'd have to show you—but I was fascinated. I wanted to ask him to do it again.

This time we all let him stay upside down.

"All right. My name is Phillipe Mgabi. I am your Chief Administrator for Student Affairs. On behalf of the Starseed Foundation, I'd like to welcome you all to Top Step, and wish you a fruitful stay. I'm sorry you had such an eventful journey here, and I assure you all that Top Step is considerably less vulnerable than your shuttle was. You're as safe as any terrestrial can be in space, now."

No one said thanks.

"I must remind you that you are no longer on United Nations soil, in even a figurative sense. Top Step is an autonomic pressure, like Skyfac or The Ark, recognized by the UN but not eligible for membership, and wholly owned by the Starseed Foundation. At the moment, you are technically Landed Immigrants, although we prefer the term Postulants."

It was weirdly disorienting to be addressed by an upside down person. It was almost impossible to decipher his facial expressions.

"You were given the constitution and laws of Top Step back at Suit Camp, and you'll find them in the memory banks—along with maps, schedules, master directory, and for that matter the entire Global Net. You have unrestricted and unmetered access, Net-inclusive, free of charge for as long as you're resident here."

There were murmurs. Unmetered access to the Net? For everybody?

This whole operation struck me as being run like a dance company financed by task-specific grants. In some areas they were as cheap as a cut-rate holiday (Suit Camp had featured outdoor privies, just like the ones I'd used as a little girl on Gambier Island) . . . but when they spent, they spent like sailors on leave. It seemed schizophrenic.

"The point is that you are responsible. You are presumed to know your obligations and privileges as a Postulant. The Agreements you have made are all in plain language, and you are bound by them. They allow you a great deal of slack . . . but where they bind, there is no give at all. I recommend that you study them if you haven't already."

Out of the corner of my eye I saw the loudmouthed joker start to say something, then change his mind.

"I hope all of you paid attention at Suit Camp. I said you were as safe as any terrestrial in space. That compares favorably with, say, New York . . . but not by much, and space bites in different places and unexpected ways. As you learned on your way up here." Ouch. "To survive long enough to enter Symbiosis, you must all acquire and maintain a state of alert mindfulness—and there are few second chances. Space is not fair. Space is not merciful. I see you all nodding, and I know that at least three of you will be dead before your term is up. That is the smallest number of Postulants we have lost from a single class. I would like it very much if your class turns out to be the first exception to that rule."

Mgabi cocked his head, listening to something we couldn't hear. "And now I'm going to hand you over to your Orientation Coordinator. Any and all problems, questions, requests or complaints you may have during your stay in Top Step will go to her; I'm afraid I will not be seeing you on any regular basis myself. Dorothy?"

The hatch opened and admitted a red-haired woman in her seventies, frail and thin, dressed in Kelly green p-suit. One look at her face and I knew I was in good hands. She looked competent, compassionate and wise. She aligned herself to us rather than Mgabi.

"Hello, children," she said. "I'm Dorothy Gerstenfeld. I'm going to be your mother for the next two months. Daddy here—" She indicated Mgabi. "—will be away at the office most of the time, so I'll be the one who tucks you in and makes you do your chores and so on. I've got a squad of Guides to help me. My door is always unlocked and my phone is always on.

"Now I know you've all got a thousand questions—I know at least a few of you urgently want a refresher course in zero-gee plumbing!—but I've got a little set speech, and I find if I start with the questions I never get to it. So here goes:

"I've used the maternal metaphor for a reason . . . just as Doctor Mgabi entered this room upside down to you for a reason. He was trying to show you by plain example that you have come to a place where up and down have meaning only within your own skull. I am trying to suggest to you that for the next two months you are no longer adults, whatever your calendar age."

Mgabi drifted nearby in a gentle crouch. It was hard to read his inverted face, and he must have heard this dozens of times, but it seemed to me he paid careful attention, though he was looking at us. He reminded me of an old black and white film I saw once of Miles Davis listening to Charlie Parker take a solo.

"It is said," she continued, "that space makes you childlike again. Charles Armstead himself noted that in the historic Titan Transmission. Free fall makes you want to play, to be a child again. Look at you all, trying to be still, wanting to hop around. Well you should . . . and shall! Look at me: I'm considerably over thirty, and I've been six-wall-squash champion in this pressure for over five years now.

"Now, what are the three things a child hates the most? Aside from bedtime, I mean. Going to school, doing chores, and going to church, am I right?" People chuckled, including me. "Well, you've all just spent several weeks in school. It probably even felt like summer school, since all the Suit Camps are in tropical locations. And now that school's out, you're going to have to spend some time doing chores and being in church." There were scattered mock-groans. "Not only that, you're going to have to remember, every single time without fail, to wear your rubbers when you go out!" That got giggles.

"Don't worry," she went on, "before long you'll be going out a lot, all you want—and there'll be plenty of time for play. But church—or temple or zendo or synagogue or whatever word you use for 'place where one prays'—is sort of what Top Step is all about, what it's for. It's just a kind of church it's okay to play in, that's all. It has only one sacrament, and only you know—if you do—what it will take to become ready to receive it. We know many ways to help you.

"If you use your time here wisely, then soon church will be done, and school will be out forever, and you will become more ideally childlike than you ever were as a child.

"I hope every one of you makes it."

A facile and pious cliché, surely—but when she said it, I believed it. Your mother doesn't lie. This one didn't, at least.

"Remember: if you have any *practical* difficulties, I'm the one you want to consult; don't bother Administrator Mgabi or his staff without routing through me first. But few of your problems are going to turn out to be practical—and some of your practical problems will kill you before you have a chance to complain. When you do need help, it's more likely to be spiritual help. You'll find that Top Step has more *spiritual* advisers than any other kind. We have representatives of most of the major denominations inboard—you'll find a directory in your computer—but please don't feel compelled to stick with whatever faith you were raised in or presently practice. You'll find that personal rapport is a lot more important than brand name. All right, enough speeches—"

People with full bladders sighed, anticipating relief—but there was an interruption from the loudmouth. He wanted to report Shannon, our flight attendant for what he called outrageous authoritarianism and psychological instability. "The woman is dangerous," he said. "I actually thought for a moment she was going to strike me! I want her relieved of duty and punished."

The rest of us made a collective growling sound. He ignored us.

"We'll discuss this in my office," Dorothy said, "as soon as I've—"

"Dammit, I want satisfaction, now."

Dorothy looked sad. "Eric," she said, "did you read your contracts with us?" It struck me, that she knew his name.

He didn't seem to notice. "I ran 'em past my legal software, sure. But she had no right—"

"She had every right. I saw all that happened, from my office. If Shannon had chosen to kill you, I would have been sad—but I would not have been cross with her."

He snorted. "She'd have had a busy time trying!"

Dorothy looked even sadder. "No, she wouldn't. Eric, *can't* we discuss this later, in my office?"

"I'm afraid not, ma'am. If the setup here actually requires me to take orders from every hired hand, let's get it straight right now so I can return to Earth at once."

Now she mastered her sorrow; her face smoothed over. "Very well. I'll take you back to your shuttle now. It will be departing almost immediately." She kicked off gently and jaunted toward him.

At once he was waffling. "Wait a minute! You can't just throw me out without a hearing, after all the time I've invested—and you certainly can't make me go back in *that* crate, it's defective. And these p-suits are substandard, I want a real one, with a proper radio, and—"

She approached slowly, empty hands outstretched in a gesture of peace, maternal concern on her face. She killed most of her momentum on the empty rope just in front of his, setting it shivering, covered the last few meters very slowly, reached for his rope—

—and her hands slipped past it, touched Eric behind each ear with delicate precision. His eyes rolled up and he let go of the rope, slowly began to pivot around her hands. He snored gently.

Towing Eric, Dorothy jaunted slowly back to her original place by the hatch; it opened as she got there, and she aimed Eric out through it to someone out in the corridor. Then she turned to us.

All the sadness was gone from her face, now, replaced by resolution. She looked as strong, as powerful, as my own grandmother. "I'm sorry you've all had such an inauspicious trip so far." Small smile. "It can only get better from here. Now: Eric raised a good point. The p-suits you're all wearing *are* inadequate. They're tourist suits, designed only for emergency use by passengers in transit. They'll be going back to Earth on the shuttle, so please remove them now. You'll be just a little while." We all began removing our suits. "From here you'll go through Decontam, where there'll be washrooms for those who need one—

and, I'm afraid, for those who don't think you do—and then you'll be guided to your rooms. You've got three hours before dinner; I recommend you spend them either at your terminals, learning your way around Top Step, or resting. They'll be plenty of time for physical exploring, believe me."

Again there was a bucket-brigade. We were warned not to attempt any maneuvers of our own along the way, but I intended to cheat just a little . . . until the line was held up by the first couple of jerks to do so, and people with full bladders began to get surly. Sure, I knew more about kinesthetics than the two jerks. That gave me the opportunity to make an even bigger jerk out of myself. I decided to be patient.

There was plenty of time. We wouldn't be allowed to go EVA for another four weeks, and we wouldn't be allowed to enter Symbiosis until we'd had at least four weeks of EVA practice . . . and we were entitled to hang around Top Step making up our minds for another four weeks after *that,* if we chose, before we had to either take the Symbiote, or go back to Earth and start making payments on the air, food and water we had used. I'd have lots of time to play with zero gee.

Having toured a lot of strange places with various dance companies, I'd been through several sorts of stringent international decontamination rituals before, and thought I was prepared for anything. You don't want to know about Top Step Decontam, and I don't want to discuss it. Let's just say they were thorough. Top Step is a controlled environment, and they want it as sterile as possible.

When I got out the other end, naked, dry, and bright red, I found myself drifting in a boardroom-sized cubic with five other naked females. Kirra was among them, and I recognized Glenn Christie, an acquaintance from Suit Camp. At the far end of the space were what looked like several dozen drifting footballs, tethered together. Kirra threw me a grin. "Am I still black?" she called softly.

"On this side," I agreed.

She giggled, and . . . wriggled, somehow, so that she spun end over end gracefully, like a ballerina pirouetting but in three dimensions.

"Couple of pink places," I said, "but I think you had them when you started. How did you *do* that?" It hadn't looked at all like the maneuver Mgabi had used.

"Little pinker now, maybe. I dunno how I did it. You try it."

When I try out a new move, I'm alone in the studio. I was saved by the bell. An amplified voice came from nowhere in particular. (I tried to locate the speaker grille, but it seemed to be hidden.) It was female, a warm friendly contralto. After what we'd just been through, it shouldn't have mattered much if she'd been a male with a leer in his voice . . . but I found myself liking her somehow, whoever she was. She sounded sort of like the best friend I never really had. "Welcome, all of you, to community pressure. One of the containers you see on the inboard side of the chamber will have your name on it. Please put on the contents and check them for fit: let me know if you have any problems." We all thanked her.

It occurred to me briefly to wonder why she wasn't present in the room. Surely we were as thoroughly decontaminated as we were ever going to be. But the tone of her voice said that whatever the reason was, it was unimportant, not anything scary, so I put it out of my mind.

Getting to the football-shaped containers got comical; we were like kids in some Disneyland ride, giggling and trying to help each other and getting tangled up and giggling some more. By the time I located the box with my name on it, we all had aching sides. The unseen woman did not chastise us for our antics; she seemed to understand that we were ready for some laughter.

The football opened along one seam. Inside it was a wad of something. As I stared at it in puzzlement, it swelled like bread-dough, like a backpacker's raincoat opening up.

"It's a p-suit!" Kirra said delightedly, shaking out hers.

Sure enough, we had all been issued our real p-suits. Expensive, state of the art, personally customized and form-fitting ones, as opposed to the cheap standardized movie-costumes we'd all worn aboard the Shuttle.

We'd practiced this in Suit Camp. Timing myself, I slid the bottom half on like greased pantyhose, pulled the rest up behind me and around my torso, put my arms in the sleeves, sealed the seam, and pulled the transparent hood down over my head. Elapsed time, twelve seconds. I thought that was pretty good. It went on easier than a body-stocking: while it was snug, the interior had been treated somehow to reduce friction. I didn't test the radio or any of the other gear, though I should have. Instead I pulled the hood back, and grinned at Kirra and Glenn and the other women. They grinned back.

Our suits were custom tailored to our bodies, and fit like hugs. They were also, we discovered, customized for colour. They came out of the egg transparent, so we could inspect them for fit and flaws, and except for the barely visible tracery of microtubules that carried coolant and such around them, they looked like an extra layer of skin. But when we located the "polarization enabler controls" they'd taught us about in Suit Camp, and opaqued our suits, each of us was, from toes to collarbone, a different—and well chosen—colour. My own suit turned a light shade of burgundy that suited my complexion and hair colour, and Kirra's suit became a cobalt blue very close to the highlights that normal lighting raised on her dark black skin.

I liked the colours a lot. To me they were among the first signs that artists had had a part in the creative planning of this outfit.

"Any problems?" our unseen friend asked. "No? Then exit the chamber through the green-marked hatch in Wall Four. You'll be directed from there."

I looked around for the green-marked hatch. Where the hell was Wall Four? No walls were marked that I could see—at least not with numbers. One of them, to our right (we were all instinctively aligned to the same local vertical, without knowing how we'd selected it) was painted with a large broad red arrow, pointing in the direction we had come from, but that was little help. My companions were looking confused, too, but the unseen woman didn't cue us.

It took so long to find the hatch that in a few seconds I guessed where it must be. Sure enough, it was "up," over our heads. People hardly ever look up, for some reason. (Which seems to suggest that we haven't evolved significantly since before we came down out of the trees, yes?) I nudged Kirra and pointed. She unsealed the hatch and went through. I followed on her heels, and we found ourselves at the bottom of a huge well-lit padded cavern.

I should have been expecting it; I'd seen pictures. But you just don't expect to step from someplace as clean and sterile and right-angled and high-tech and profoundly artificial as a Decontam module into the Carlsbad Caverns. I nearly lost my grip and fell up into it.

It was about the size of a concert hall and roughly spherical—but the accent was on rough. Rough curves and joins, the rough fractal topography of natural rock, overlaid with some rough surface covering that looked like cheap kitchen sponge stained dark grey. Tunnels departed from the cavern in all directions; their gaping, irregularly sized and shaped mouths were spaced asymmetrically around the chamber. Each tunnel had one or more pairs of slender elastic bungee cords strung criss-cross across its mouth, obviously used to either fling oneself into the tunnel, or catch oneself on the way out; the larger the tunnel, the more cords.

This spheric pressure was half natural and half artificial. It had happened, as much as it had been built. It was a sculpted and padded cave. Perhaps a dozen people (none of them in p-suits; one was naked) were drifting slowly across the vast chamber in different directions. No two of them were using the same local vertical, and none of them used ours. It was like something out of Escher.

No, it *was* something out of Escher.

I remembered to move aside so others could use the hatch. There were lots of handgrips nearby; I worked myself sideways like a crab and "lay on my back" a few inches "above" the bulkhead I'd just come through. As Glenn and the other three women emerged into the cave behind us, they too grabbed handholds, stabilized themselves, and stared.

After a long few moments of silence, Glenn cleared her throat. "Which way to the egress, do you suppose?"

The unseen woman spoke again. "Can all of you see the tunnel that's blinking green over there, Inboard and One-ish?"

Again I failed to spot any speakers, and realized this time that there were none; her voice was simply homing in on my ears somehow. The last two terms she'd used were meaningless to me, but there was no mistaking the tunnel she meant. Soft green lights around its mouth had suddenly started to flash on and off. "We see it."

"That's where you're headed for, now."

"All the bloody way up there?" Kirra squeaked.

"Push off gently, Kirra," our companion said soothingly. I hadn't realized she knew our names. She must have a terrific memory. "Be prepared to take a long time getting there. You'll find that in jaunting long distances, aim is much more important than strength. And you're not in a hurry. Why don't you go first?"

"Well . . . I guess I—bloody hell!"

Kirra had absently let go of her handhold at some point, instinctively trusting to gravity to keep her in place. But there was none. In the twenty seconds or so we'd been here, she'd drifted far enough away from the floor (as I called that wall in my mind, since it had been under my feet when I started) to be unable to touch it again. Her attempts only put her into a tumble from which she couldn't figure out how to emerge. "Oh my," she groaned as she spun. "I think I'm gonna be a puke pinwheel in a minute . . ."

I tried to reach her, but I couldn't quite do it without letting go with my other hand myself. And the gap between us was slowly widening.

"Make a chain," our friend said, and one of the women I didn't know, who was nearest to me, reached and got one of my ankles in a one-handed deathgrip. I let go of my handhold, lunged, and got an equally firm grip on one of Kirra's ankles as it went by. Her mass tried to tug me sideways as I stabilized her spin, and partially succeeded. The woman holding me reeled us both in, a little too hard: Kirra and I *thumped* firmly together into what I thought of as the floor, and clutched it and each other.

Perhaps we shouldn't have used up our giggles earlier; we could have used some now.

"I'm right," Kirra said. "Ta, love . . . I feel a right idjit."

"It happens to everyone here, sooner or later," our unseen friend told her. "Proper etiquette is to lend assistance if needed and otherwise ignore it. Are you ready to jaunt now, Kirra?"

She was game. "Reckon so. Where's that blinkin' tunnel? Pun unintended." She spun round to face the cavern and got her feet under her. "Oh, there it is. See you on the other side, mates—"

She kicked off, gently, and began to rise into the air.

Now we giggled. We couldn't help it. Her lazy ascension looked *exactly* like a bad special effect. We heard her laughing too, with a child's delight. She mugged for us as she went, folded her arms and legs into tailor seat, opened out into a swan dive, then tucked and rolled and came out of it making exaggerated swimming motions—in our direction. Any embarrassment she might have felt a moment ago was gone. "I *dreamed* of this," she sang, her voice high and dreamy, "so many years ago, it's like a memory—"

I set my feet, let go of the wallbehindme/floorbeneathme bulkhead, took a deep breath, and jaunted after her.

If you've done it you know what I mean, and if you haven't I can't convey it. All I can say is, mortgage your condo, take the Thomas Cook Getaway Special, and jaunt in free fall once before you die. That way you'll know your way around Paradise when you get there.

We were all giggling like schoolgirls as we jaunted up through the vast chamber, drawing amused looks from the old hands. "I like it, Morgan," Kirra called down to me.

"Me, too," I called back. I was mildly disappointed that this big cave had no perceptible echo. But I suppose the fun of one would have worn off the first time you smacked your head on bare rock, or tried to make yourself understood to someone on the other side of the chamber.

Kirra had followed instructions, jaunted very gently and therefore slowly. My own jaunt had been a little more impulsive: I was gradually overtaking her. "Look out above—here I come!"

She glanced down, rotated on her axis, and opened her arms for me so that I slid up into a hug—one of the oddest, most pleasant experiences of my life! We grinned with delight and embraced.

Looking past her fanny I noticed four p-suited males emerging from a hatch near the one we'd just left. Robert wasn't among them. Well, what did I care?

At about the mid-point Kirra and I began to think about the other end of the journey, and plan our landing. As we did so, it suddenly dawned on us both that we were not floating *up*—we were upside down, falling. It was as if the whole cave had flipped end over end in an instant. We clutched each other even tighter . . . and then relaxed, trying to laugh at ourselves. But there was a queasy feeling in my stomach that hadn't been there before. This "thinking spherically" business they kept talking about at Suit Camp was going to take some work. And time . . .

I could see, now, why some people just can't ever get it. For the first time, I seriously wondered whether—dancer or no dancer—I might be one of them. I had automatically assumed that spherical perception would be a snap for any modern dancer, since we do our moving much farther from the vertical axis than ballet dancers . . .

but when I thought about it, weren't even modern dancers *more* tied into gravity and perpendicularity than ordinary people? A civilian tries to not fall down; a modern dancer tries to move all over the place in odd and interesting ways, and not fall down: therefore she pays more attention, more of the time, to not falling down—pays more heed to gravity. Maybe I had *more* to unlearn than my companions . . .

But I thrust aside the thought, determined to keep enjoying this magic jaunt, and got Kirra to show me that reversing-your-vertical trick. It turned out to be something like trying to exaggerate a swan dive, if that helps you. I ordered my stomach to settle down. *Fine,* it said, *Define "down."* I told it "down" was toward my feet, and that seemed to help a little.

When I'd kicked off to follow Kirra, she'd been a near target, so I'd aimed well enough to jaunt right into her embrace. But the target she'd been aimed at was much farther away, and docking with me had probably further disturbed her course. We landed close to the tunnel mouth we wanted, but not very. About ten seconds later Glenn threaded it like a needle, spinning around the bungee cord like a high-bar gymnast, and those of us who could applauded. The others did no better than Kirra and I. We all met at the tunnel mouth.

"Not bad at all," our woman friend said. "And Glenn, that was excellent."

I understood that she was monitoring us from some remote location—but it seemed odd that she was still giving us her attention. Surely there were other women coming out of Decontam after us. Yes, there was one now: I could see her "up" there, emerging upside down from the hatch we'd left, gaping up at us . . .

The penny dropped.

Now how did one phrase this? "Uh . . . excuse me?"

"Yes, Morgan?" she said.

". . . are you organic?"

There was a smile in her voice now. "Elegantly put, dear. No, as you've guessed, I'm an AI program in Top Step's master computer."

"And a bloody clever one you are," Kirra said delightedly. "I never sussed. What's your name, love?"

"I'm generally known as Teena. If you think of a name you like better, tell me and I'll answer to that with you. At the moment I have one hundred and sixty-seven names. But if you want to refer to me, to another person, call me Teena."

I'd been crabwalking my way to the tunnel mouth with the others, but suddenly I paused. "Uh . . . Teena?" I began, pitching my voice too low for the others to hear. ". . . do you—I mean, is there any way to—"

"May I try to guess your questions, Morgan?" she murmured in my ear. "Yes, I will be monitoring you every minute you're in or near Top Step, while you're feeding the felcher or making love or just trying to be alone. No, there is no way to switch me off. But there's only a very limited sense in which I can even metaphorically be said to be *thinking about* what I perceive. In a very real sense, there is no me, save when I am invoked. My short-term memory is much less than a second, I don't save anything that is not relevant to health, safety or your direct commands, and even that can be accessed by only eight people in Top Step—to all of whom you gave that specific right when you sighed your contract. So please don't think of me as a Peeping Teena, all right?"

"I'll try," I said, resuming my journey to the tunnel mouth. "It's just that . . . well, I've heard AIs before—but you're so good I'd swear you're sentient." Glenn heard that last and said, "Me too."

"Artificial sentience may be possible," Teena said, "but it won't be silicon-based."

One of the women I didn't know said something in Japanese.

"Why not?" Glenn translated.

"The map is not the territory," Teena said—and apparently the Japanese woman heard the answer in her own language. What a marvelous tool Teena was!

Glenn seemed disposed to argue, but Teena went on, "It's time we got you six to your quarters. Follow me—"

A group of little green LED lights along the tunnel wall began twinkling at us, then moved slowly away into the tunnel like Tinkerbell.

One at a time, we put our soles against the bungee cord and jaunted after them.

The tunnel itself was laser-straight, though its walls were roughly sculpted. There were numbered hatches let into the padded rock at odd intervals, and other, smaller tunnels intersected at odd intervals and angles. The main corridor was about eight or ten meters in cross section, with rungs spiraling along its length so that you could never be far from one. These came in handy as we progressed; we were to learn that a perfect tunnel-threading jaunt is almost impossible, even for free fall veterans. Old hands boast of their low CPH, or Contact-Per-Hectometer rate. (If you're a diehard American, a hectometer, a hundred meters, is the rest of humanity's name for about a hundred yards.) We soon began to pick up the trick of slinging ourselves along with minimal waste effort. No matter how fast or slow we progressed, the blinking lights that we followed stayed exactly five meters ahead of the foremost one of us, like one of those follow-from-in-front tails you see cops or spies do in the movies.

We overtook and passed a group of especially clumsy males. They were following pixies of a different colour, so there was minimal confusion between our two groups.

"Who you roomin' with, Morgan?" Kirra asked as we jaunted together.

"I don't know. The woman I planned to room with came down with the Foul Bowel three days ago—bad enough to get flown off to hospital. I guess I get pot luck."

"S'truth!" Kirra exclaimed. "Mine got right to the airlock this morning and decided what she really wanted to do was go back to her husband. Hey, you don't reckon. . . ? I mean, they sat us next to each other on the Shuttle, do you suppose that means— Hey Teena—"

"Yes, Kirra?" Teena said.

"Who's my bunkie gonna be?"

"You and Morgan will be rooming together. That is why you were seated adjacent on the Shuttle."

"That's great!" Kirra said.

I was oddly touched by the genuine enthusiasm in her voice; it had been a long time since anyone had been especially eager for my company. I found that I was pleased myself; Kirra was as likeable as a puppy. "Thanks," I told her. "I think so too."

She grinned. "I ought to warn you . . . I sing. All the time, I mean. Puts some people off."

"Are you any good?"

"Yah. But I don't sing anything you know."

"I'll risk it. I dance, myself."

"So I hear; like to see it. That's settled, then. Thanks, Teena!"

It occurred to me that Teena hadn't answered Kirra's question until Kirra asked it. She'd heard us discussing it, presumably, but had not volunteered the information until asked. She'd told the truth, earlier: unless we called on her, she "paid attention" only to things like pulse, respiration, and location coordinates. (If everyone in Top Step ever called her at the same moment, would her system hang? Or did she have the RAM to handle it?) I found that reassurance comforting.

A woman who knew everything, needed nothing and was only there when you wanted her. I was willing to bet a man had written Teena. She was what my ex-husband had been looking for all his life.

Shortly Teena said, "We'll be pausing at that nexus ahead: the one that's blinking now. Prepare to cancel your velocity."

The "nexus" was an intersection of several side tunnels, important enough to have bungee cords strung across the middle of the main tunnel to allow changes of vector. We all managed to grab one.

"We split up here," Teena said. "Soon Li, Yumiko, your quarters are this way—" Tinkerbell skittered off down one tunnel, then returned to hover at its entrance. "—Glenn, Nicole, Morgan and Kirra, yours are this way." Another tunnel developed green fairies.

We did each say leave-taking politenesses appropriate to our culture, but even Yumiko didn't linger over it. We were all too eager to see our new home, our personal cave-within-a-cave. Have you ever approached a new dwelling for the first time . . . *after* the lease has been signed? Remember how your pulse raced as you got near the door? The schizoid cheap/lavish style of Top Step might just pinch here.

Our wing was P7; Teena pointed out the wing bathroom and kitchenette as we jaunted past them, stopped Kirra and me at a door marked P7-23. I'm not even sure I said goodbye to Glenn as she continued on past our door toward her own room and roommate. Teena had Kirra and me show the door-lock our thumbprints, whereupon it opened for us.

Home, sweet spherical home . . .

3

When the 10,000 things are viewed in their oneness,
we return to the origin and remain where
we have always been.
—Sen T'san

Our new home didn't look *too* weird to us because we'd seen pictures in Suit Camp. Still it was exotic; flat pictures don't do justice to a spherical living space. We drifted around in it for a while, staring at everything, trying out the various facilities, lights and sound and video and climate control, teaching them all to recognize our voices and so on, but the room somehow kept refusing to become real for me. It was just too strange.

There was no "upper bunk" to fight over; one half of the room was as good as the other. The hemisphere I arbitrarily chose had, as a small concession to the ancient human patterns of thought I was here to unlearn, a local vertical, a defined up and down—the Velcro desk lined up with the computer monitor and so on—but Kirra's half had a different one, at a skewed angle to mine. Neither had any particular relationship to the axis of the corridor outside. Looking from my side of the room to Kirra's made me slightly dizzy. My eyes wanted to ignore anything that disagreed with their personal notion of up and down. Such things did not play by the rules, were impolite, beneath notice.

Kirra and I each adapted to our own local orientation for a moment, blinked at the items and documents attached to our desks, the monitor screens that read *WELCOME TO TOP STEP*, and so on. Then we turned back to look at each other. Being out-of-phase was unsatisfactory; without discussion or thought we both adapted to a compromise orientation halfway between our two differing ones. We snapped into phase with an almost audible click.

And we broke up.

We could not stop laughing. There was more than a bit of hysteria in it, on both sides. It was different by an order of magnitude from the giggling we had done earlier while scrambling for our new p-suits. Since breakfast I had been literally blown off the face of the Earth, nearly killed in orbit, told that I was a forty-six-year-old child, sexually—aroused? well, intrigued—for the first time in forever, molested most intimately and impersonally by Decontam devices, dumped into a weird Caveworld where falling off a log was not *possible,* guided through a bunch of absurdly Freudian tunnels by a woman who wasn't there . . . and now I was "home," in a place where my bed was a holster, and I could look up and see the soles of my roommate's feet. I can't speak for Kirra, but it wasn't until about halfway through that laugh that I realized just how lonely and scared and disoriented I was—which only made me laugh harder.

We laughed until the tears came, and then roared, because tears in free fall are so absurd, from both inside and outside. Kirra's eyes exuded little elongated saline worms, that waved and broke up into tiny crystal balls. I seemed to see her through a fish-eye lens that kept changing its focal length. Every time our laughter began to slow down, one of us would gasp out something like, "*Long* day," or, "Do you *believe* this?" and we'd dissolve again, as though something terribly funny had been said.

Our convulsions set us caroming gently around the room, and eventually we collided glancingly and climbed up each other into a hug. We squeezed each other's laughter into submission.

"Thanks, love," Kirra said finally. "I needed that bellybuster."

"Me too!" We sort of did a pushup on each other: pushed apart until we held each other by the biceps at arms' length. "Whoever decided you and I would be compatible roommates was either very good at their job or very lucky. I couldn't have laughed like that alone, or with somebody like Glenn."

We kept hold of each other's upper arms in order to maintain eye contact, to match our personal verticals. But nothing is still in free fall unless anchored. To keep our lower bodies from drifting, we had instinctively invented a way of bracing our shins against each other with ankles interlocked. I became aware of it now, and admired it. Could there *be* such a thing as an instinctive response to zero gravity?

Or was it just that bodies are a lot more adaptable than brains?

"All right," Kirra said, "let's get down to it. Who are you, Morgan? Why are *you* here?"

I was more amused than offended by her forthrightness. "You sure don't beat around the bush, do you?"

"Hell, I was born in the bush."

I pinched her.

"But I'll go first if you want," she continued.

"No, that's okay," I said. " 'Why am I here?' is easy. I'm . . . I was a dancer. I was pretty famous, but more important I was pretty good, but most important I was married to it, it's all I ever did, and I can't do it anymore. I don't mean I can't get hired. I mean I can't dance anymore. Not on Earth, anyway. Not for a long time now. I looked around and found out there's nothing else on Earth I care about. And my problems are lower back and knees, and zero gee is supposed to be great for both."

"I can see that," Kirra agreed.

"It's more than just the reduced stress. It's the calcium loss. There's this doctor thinks it will actually help."

Human bones lose calcium rapidly in zero gravity—one of many reasons why people who stay in space too long are stuck there for life. The bones become too frail to return to terrestrial gravity. Many of my fellow Postulants would be taking calcium supplements, just in case they decided to change their minds and return to Earth. But it happened that overcalcification was a factor in both my back trouble and my knee problems.

"So space is a place where one out of the three doctors says *maybe* I could dance again. For one chance in three of dancing again, I would skin myself with a can opener. If I have to put up with great longevity and freedom from all human suffering and telepathic union with a bunch of saints and geniuses to get that chance . . . well, I can live with that, I guess." I grinned. "That sounds weird, huh?"

"Not to me. Well, what do you think? Can you dance here?"

"Well . . . I won't know until I've had time alone to experiment. I won't really know until I wake up the next morning. And I won't be sure for at least a week or two. But it feels good, Kirra. I don't know, it really does. I think it's going to work, maybe. Oh shit, I'm excited!"

She squeezed my arms and showed me every one of those perfect teeth. "That's great, love. I'm glad for you. Good luck, eh?"

The trite words sounded real in her mouth. "Thanks, hon. Okay, your turn now. What brings you to Top Step?"

"Well . . . do you know anything about Aborigines, Morgan?" she asked. "The Dreamtime? The Songlines?"

I admitted I did not.

"This is gonna take a while . . . you sure you want to hear it?"

"Of course."

"Back before the world got started was the Dreamtime, my people reckon. All the Ancestors dreamed themselves alive, then, created themselves out of clay, created themselves as people and all the kinds of animals and birds and insects there are. And the first thing they did was go walkabout, singin'—makin' the world by singin' it into existence. Sing up a river here, sing a mountain there. Wherever they went, they left a Songline behind 'em, and the Song made the world around there, see? So there's Songlines criss-crossin' the world, and everyplace is on or near a Songline, with a Song of its own that makes it what it is. That's why we go Walkabout—to follow the Songlines and sing the Songs and keep recreating the world so's it doesn't melt away. Get it?"

"I think so. All Aboriginals believe this?"

"Most of us that's left. Our Dreaming ain't like whitefella religions. Our Songs were maps, trade routes, alliances, history: they held the whole country together, kept hundreds of tribes and clans living together in peace for generations. Even the whitefella couldn't completely change that. Those of us they didn't kill outright had trouble keepin' our faith, but. Some of us went to the towns, tried on European ideas. Railroads were cuttin' across Songlines. Our beliefs didn't seem to account for the world we saw anymore, so we had to change 'em a bit. But we never got the Dreamtime out of our bones and teeth. Tribes that did . . . well, they're gone, see?

"So the last few generations, a mob of us left the reserves, left the cities and towns. We've gone back to the bush, gone back to bein' nomads, followin' the Songlines. There's not many of us left, see. We want to touch where we came from before we go from the world.

"If we're gonna try to keep our beliefs alive, we got to make 'em account for the world we see. And space is part of that world now.

We've got to weave it into our world-picture somehow. Some o' the old stories speak of Sky-Heroes, spirit Ancestors departed into the sky. If that's so, they left Songlines, and Aborigines can follow them to space. That's my job: to try and find the Songlines of the Sky-Heroes."

I was fascinated. The bravery, the audacity of trying to make an ancient pagan religion fit the modern world was breathtaking. "Why you?"

"It's my Dreaming." She saw that I did not understand, and tried again: "Like you with dancin'. It's what I was born for. My mob, the Yirlandji, we're reckoned the best singers. And I'm the best o' the lot." There was neither boasting nor false modesty in her voice.

"Sing me something."

"I can sing you a *tabi,*" she said. "A personal song. But you'll have to back off: I gotta slap me legs."

We let each other go, and drifted about a decimeter apart. She closed her eyes in thought for perhaps ten seconds, filling her lungs the whole time. Then she brought her thighs up and slapped them in slow rhythm as she sang:

Mutjingga, kale neki
Mingara, wija narani moroko
Bodalla, Kaylan ungu le win
Naguguri mina Kurria
Jinkana kandari pirndiri
Yirlandji, turlu palbarregu

Her voice was indeed eerily beautiful. It had the rich tone of an old acoustic saxophone, but it was not at all like a jazz singer's voice. It had the precision and the perfect vibrato of a MIDI-controlled synthesizer, but it was natural as riversong, human as a baby's cry, a million years older than the bone flute. It was warm, and alive, and magical.

The song she sang was made of nine tones that repeated, but with each repetition they changed so much in interval and intonation and delivery as to seem completely different phrases. Considering that I didn't understand a word, I found it oddly, powerfully, astonishingly moving; whatever she was saying, it was coming directly from her heart to my ears. As I listened, I was radically reevaluating my new roommate. This cute little puppy I'd been mentally patronizing was someone special, deserving of respect. She was at least as good at her art as I had ever been at mine.

When her song was over I said nothing for ten seconds or more. Her eyes fluttered open and found mine, and still I was silent. There was no need to flatter her. She knew how good she was, and knew that I knew it now.

Then I was speaking quickly: "Teena! Did you hear Kirra's song just now? I mean, do you still have it in memory?"

"Yes, Morgan."

"Would you save it for me, please? And download it to my personal memory?"

"Name this file," Teena requested.

"'Kirra, Opus One.'"

"Saved." And that's why I can give you the words now—though I can't vouch for the spelling.

"Do you mind, Kirra? If I keep a copy of that—just for myself?"

"Shit no, mate. I sang it to you, di'n I?" she looked thoughtful. "Hoy, Teena, would you put a copy in *my* spare brain as well? Label it 'Bodalla,' and put it in a folder named 'Tabi.'"

"Done."

She returned her attention to me. "I was singin' about—"

I interrupted her softly. "—about saying goodbye to Earth, about coming to space, something about it being scary, but such a wonderful thing to do that you just have to do it. Yes?"

She just nodded. Maybe people always understood her when she sang. I wouldn't be surprised.

I've since asked Teena for a translation of "Bodalla." She offered three, a literal transposition and two colloquial versions. The one I like goes:

All-Mother, creator of us all
Great spirit who controls the clouds, now I have come to the sky
Farewell to the place-where-the-child-is-flung-into-the-air
I journey now to see the Crocodile who lives in the

Milky Way
So I can send back a rope ladder
to the Yirlandji, and to all the tribes

"But that's just a tabi," Kirra said. "Just a personal song of my own, like. That's not why I got sent here. See, what I'm special good at is feelin' the Songlines. Been that way since I was a little girl. Whenever my mob'd move to a new place, I always knew the Song of it before anybody taught me. Yarra, the . . . well, a woman that taught me, this priestess, like . . . she used to blindfold me and drive me to strange country, some place I'd never been. And when I'd been there a while, sometimes an hour, sometimes overnight, I could sing her the Song of that place, and I always got it right. I got famous for it. Tribes that had forgotten parts of their own Songs, or had pieces cut out of 'em by whitefella doin's, would send for me to come help 'em. So when the Men and Women of Power figured out this job here needed doing, there never was any question whose job it was."

"And you don't mind?" I asked. It was sounding to me a little as though she'd been drafted, and was too patriotic to complain.

"Mind?" she said. "Morgan, most of us do pretty good if we can get through life without screwin' anybody else up too bad. How many get even a chance to do somethin' *important,* for a whole people? I wouldn't miss it for the world. Oh Christ, I made a pun. That's just what I'm doin': not missin' it for the world."

"Where in Australia are you from?"

"Not far from Suit Camp," she said.

"You're saying double goodbyes today, then," I said without thinking.

I felt like kicking myself, but I had to explain now. "A few months ago I said goodbye to Vancouver—to my home—in my heart. All of us here left home before we came to Suit Camp. Today all we're leaving is Earth. You're leaving home and Earth at the same time."

Implausibly, her grin broadened. "You're not wrong." Somehow at this aperture, the grin made her look even younger, no more than twenty. "This's the first time I been out of Oz in me life, and it feels dead strange. Probably be just as strange to go to Canada, but. Oz, Earth, all one to me. Hey, what do you say we get out of these suits and see if our new clothes fit?"

Each of us had been issued several sets of jumpsuits, in assorted colors. It wasn't especially surprising that they fit perfectly: after all, they'd been cut from the same set of careful measurements used to make our formfitting p-suits. We also got gloves and booties and belts, all made of material that did not feel sticky to the touch, but was sticky when placed against wall-material. Traction providers. Teena explained that although social nudity was acceptable here, it was customary for Postulants, First-Monthers like us, to wear jumpsuits if they wore anything; second-month Novices usually lived in their p-suits, for as long as it took them to make up their minds to Symbiosis. We admired ourselves in the mirror for a while, then I slid into my sleepsack and began learning how to adjust it for comfort, while Kirra got Teena to display three-dimensional maps.

"Teena," I said while Kirra was distracted, "where is Robert Chen billeted?" Absurdly, I tried to pitch my voice too low for Kirra to hear, without making it obvious to Teena that I was doing so. I have no idea whether Teena caught it, or if so whether it conveyed any meaning to her. How subtle was her "understanding" of humans?

All I know is that Kirra didn't seem to hear her reply, "P7-29."

Just down the corridor! "Thanks."

"You're welcome."

Okay, it's dopey to thank an electric-eye for opening the door for you. I wasn't thinking clearly; I was too busy kicking myself for asking the question. And for being elated by the answer. What did I care where he slept? I was *not* going to get that involved.

Certainly not for days yet.

When Kirra and I got bored with exploring our new home, we discovered we were hungry. We headed for the cafeteria, following some of Teena's pixies. And found ourselves outside in the corridor, at the end of a long line of hungry people, most hanging on to handrails provided for the purpose. Standing On Line is not much enhanced by zero gravity. Your feet hurt less, but there are more annoying ways for your neighbors to fidget. The line, like all lines, did not appear to be moving.

Kirra nudged me. From up ahead, someone was waving to us. Robert.

"You think we should join him?" she asked.

I hesitated. "Maybe he's just saying hello."

"Up to you," she said, and waved back.

He waved again. It was definitely an invitation for us both to join him.

My blood sugar decided for me. I think.

Cutting ahead on line in zero gee without actually putting my foot in anyone's face was tricky. In fact, I didn't manage it. Kirra and I were both cordially hated by the time we reached Robert. He ignored it and made room for us. "Morgan McLeod, Kirra—I'd like you to meet my roommate, Ben Buckley, from Sherman Oaks, California."

Ben was one of the strangest looking—and strangest—men I'd ever met. A big boney redhead with a conversational style reminiscent of a happy machine gun, he wore a permanent smile and huge sunglasses with very peculiar lenses. They stuck out for several centimeters on either side of his face, and flared. The temple shafts of the glasses were wide, and had small knobs and microswitches along their length. When we asked, he told us he had designed and made them himself . . . and his motivation just floored me.

Their purpose was to bring him 360° vision.

"Ever since I was a kid I loved messing with perception," he told us, his words tumbling all over one another. "Distortions, gestalt-shifts, changing paradigms, I couldn't get enough. New ways of seeing, hearing, grokking. My folks were die-hard hippies, I caught it from them."

"Mine, too," I said, and he gave me an incandescent smile.

"Then you know those funny faceted yellow specs they used to have, gave you bee's eyes? Most people keep them on for about ten seconds; a really spaced-out doper might leave 'em on for the duration of an acid trip, but I used to wear 'em for days, 'til my parents got nervous. And my dad had this colour organ, turned music into light patterns, and I spent time with that sucker until I could not only name the tune with the speakers disconnected, I could harmonize, and enjoy it." I'm putting periods at the ends of his sentences so you can follow them, but he never really paused longer than a comma's worth. "Learning to read spinning record labels, eyeglasses with inverting lenses, I loved all that stuff. When I was fourteen, I built a pair of headphones that played ambient sound to me backwards, a word at a time, so fast that once I learned to understand it the lip-synch lag was just barely noticeable. That's the kind of stuff that's fun to me. Then one day a year ago I thought, hey, what do I need a blind side for? so I built these glasses." Robert was looking very interested. "They're dual mode. I can get about 300° on straight optical—glasses like that were available back in the Nineties, although they didn't sell well—or I can kick on the fiber-optics in the earpieces and get full surround. I like to switch back and forth for fun. I like to put the front hemisphere into one eye, and the back half into the other—and switch *them* back and forth—but I can get something like full stereo parallax in both eyes at once with a heads-up-display like fighter pilots use."

Kirra managed to get in a word in edgewise. "Could I look through 'em, Ben?"

He smiled. "Sure. But if you're a normal person, it'd take you about three months to learn to interpret the data. It'd look like a funhouse mirror."

"Oh. Turn round, okay?"

"Sure," he said again, and did so.

"Now: what am I doing?"

"Being somewhat rude," he reported accurately. "And that fingernail needs trimming."

Robert looked thoughtful . . . and tossed a pen at Ben's back. Ben reached around behind himself and caught it . . . then tumbled awkwardly from the effect of moving his arm. "See what I mean?" he said, stabilizing himself. "It has survival advantage: you can't sneak up on me. But I just enjoy it, you know?"

Kirra was getting excited. "I'll bet you're the only one in the class that really likes this zero-gee stuff, aren't you? It's what you enjoy best: bein' confused. Gosh, that must be a great thing to enjoy!"

He stared. "I like you," he said suddenly.

"Sure," she said.

They smiled at each other.

"Kirra's right," Robert said. "This 'thinking spherically' business that the rest of us are having so much trouble with must be the kind of thing you've been dreaming of all your life. Why did it take you so long to come to space?"

"I think I know," Kirra said.

Ben looked at her expectantly.

"You didn't want to use it up too quick," she said.

He smiled and nodded. "I held off as long as I could stand it," he agreed. His smile broadened. "God, it's great, too. Do you *believe* they gave us unlimited Net access?"

It was not sparks flying, not a mutual sexual awareness. It was a new friendship taking root. It was nice to watch. Yet as I watched them I felt vaguely melancholy. I wished I had a friend of the opposite sex. Robert and I might just be friends some day . . . but if so I could tell we were going to have to go through being lovers first, and I just didn't know if I had the energy.

A lover of mine used to have a quote on his bedroom wall, from some old novel: *It's amazing how much mature wisdom resembles being too tired.*

My melancholy lasted right up until Kirra said, "Hey, the bloody queue's movin'!" Starving dancers are too busy for melancholy . . . the only reason their suicide rate isn't higher than it already is.

The cafeteria took some getting used to. But there was plenty of assistance; without any apparent formal structure to it, Second-Monthers (identifiable because they wore p-suits rather than our First-Monther's jumpsuits, but lacked the Spacer's Earring of EVA-qualified Third-Monthers) seemed to take it on themselves to be helpful to newcomers. They were extraordinarily patient about it, I thought. We must have been more nuisance than a flock of flying puppies. Maybe we were vastly entertaining.

Tables lined with docking rails jutted out from five of the six walls. The inner sides of the rails were lined with Velcro, like our belts, so you could back yourself up to one end and be held in reasonable proximity to your food; there was a thin footrail on which to brace your feet—both "above" and "below" the table. *Both* sides of the tables were used. It provided an odd and interesting solution to the problem of sharing a table with strangers; you adopted the opposite vertical to theirs, and your conversation never clashed. On the other hand, especially clumsy footwork in docking at table could kick your neighbor's dinner clear across the room. And you came to really appreciate the fact that in free fall, feet don't smell.

Eventually we got down to the real business of a meal: talking.

You hesitate to ask a new chum, so why did you come to Top

Step? The answer may be that they're running away from some defeat on Earth. You're especially hesitant if you're there because you're running from some defeat on Earth yourself.

I didn't exactly question Robert over dinner, and he didn't exactly volunteer autobiography, but information transfer occurred by some mysterious kind of osmosis. In between the distractions of learning to eat in zero gravity, I learned that he had a fifteen-year-old son, who lived with his mother; she and Robert had divorced eight years before. I also found out how he had acquired his "spacer's legs." He was an architect; apparently he had already established himself as a successful traditional architect in San Francisco . . . when suddenly the new field of space architecture had opened up. The technical challenge had excited him; he had followed the challenge into orbit, found he had the knack for it, and prospered.

I'm not sure whether this next part is something he implied or I inferred, but the progression seemed logical. He found that he liked space—the more time he spent there, the more he liked it. In time he came to resent being forced to return to Earth regularly just to keep his body acclimated to gravity. The obvious question *Why not just stay in space, like a Stardancer?* had led naturally to *Why not* become *a Stardancer?* At this point in the history of human enterprise in space, a free-lance spacer's life is usually one of total insecurity . . . and a Stardancer's life is one of great and lasting security. And so, wanting to stay in space without having to scramble every moment to buy air, Robert found himself here on Top Step.

It seemed a rather shallow reason to come all this way. To abandon a whole planet and the whole human race, just to save on overhead while he pursued his art . . .

On the other hand, who was I to judge? He wasn't fleeing defeat, like me. Maybe architecture was as exciting an art as dance; maybe for him it was making elements dance. Maybe space was just an environment he liked.

Maybe there were no shallow reasons to become a Stardancer.

Maybe it didn't matter what your reasons were.

As all this was going through my mind, Robert went on: "But there's a little more to it than that. Another part of it is that when I started spending time in space, I found myself watching Earth a lot, thinking about what a mess it's in, how close it is to blowing itself up.

I read somewhere once, Earth is just too fragile a basket for the human race to keep all its eggs in. We've got to get more established in space, soon.

"I know you can say Stardancers aren't part of the human race anymore, but I don't buy that. They all came from human eggs and sperm, and they've done more for Earth than the rest of the race put together. They fixed the hole in the ozone layer, they put the brakes on the greenhouse effect, they built the mirror farms and set up the Asteroid Pipeline, they mad the Safe Lab so we can experiment with nanotechnology without being afraid the wrong little replicator will get loose and turn the world into grey goo—they can afford to be altruistic, because they don't *need* anything but each other. I think without the Starseed Foundation, there'd have been an all-out nuclear war years ago.

"So I guess I decided it was time I put some back in. From all I can learn, there aren't many architects in the Starmind, so I think I can be of help. I want to design and build things a little more useful to mankind than another damn factory or dormitory or luxury hotel."

"And the eternal life without want part doesn't hurt, does it?" Ben said, grinning, and Robert smiled back. It was the first real smile of his I'd seen. I tend to trust people or not trust them on the basis of their smiles; I decided I trusted Robert.

But I wished he'd smile more often.

4

How is it possible that mystics 3,000 years ago have plagiarized what we scientists are doing today?
—Karl Pribram

I could write a whole chapter about my first free fall cafeteria meal, my first free fall sleep, my first free fall pee . . . but you can get that sort of thing from any traveler's account. The next event of significance, the morning after our arrival at Top Step, was my first class with Reb Hawkins-roshi.

The course was titled "Beginner's Mind"—a clue to me that I would like it, since my mother's battered old copy of Shunryu Suzuki-roshi's *Zen Mind, Beginner's Mind* had been my own introduction to Buddhism. There are as many different flavors of Buddhism—even just of Zen!—as there are flavors of Christianity, and some of them give me hives . . . but if this Hawkins's path was even tangent to Suzuki's, I felt confident I could walk it without too much discomfort.

You couldn't really have called me a Buddhist. I had no teacher, didn't even really sit zazen on any regular basis. I'd never so much as been on a retreat, let alone done a five-day *sesshin.* My mother taught me how to sit, and a little of the philosophy behind it, was all. By that point in my life I mostly used Zen as a sort of nonprescription tranquilizer.

Robert, on the other hand, approached it with skepticism. He was not, I'd learned the night before, a Buddhist—it's silly, I know, but for some reason I kept expecting every Asian I meet to be a Buddhist—but he had mentioned in passing that if he *were* going to be one, he'd follow the Rinzai school of Zen. (A rather harsh and overintellectual bunch, for my taste.) Pretty personal conversation for two strangers, I know; somehow we hadn't gotten around to less intimate things, like how we liked to have sex. Nonetheless, I was proud of myself: I hadn't physically touched him even once.

Well, okay: once. But I *hadn't* kissed him goodnight before returning to my place! (Kirra kissed Ben . . .)

And I didn't look for him in the cafeteria crowd during breakfast—and didn't kiss him good morning when we met accidentally in the corridor on the way to class. I was too irritated: I'd had to stall around for over three minutes to bring about that accidental encounter, and I was mildly annoyed that he hadn't looked me up during breakfast. God, lust makes you infantile!

But he was adequately pleased to encounter me, so I let him take my arm and show me a couple of jaunting tricks I'd already figured out on the way to breakfast—with the net result that we were nearly late for class, and I arrived in exactly the wrong frame of mind: distracted. So a nice thing happened.

As the door of the classroom silently irised shut behind us, my pulse began to race. What could be more disorienting than being inside your headful of racing thoughts, toying with the tingles of distant horniness—and suddenly finding yourself face to face with a holy man?

He was in his fifties, shaven-headed and clean-shaven, slender and quite handsome, and utterly centered and composed. He was not dressed as a Zen abbot, he wore white shorts and singlet, but his face, body language and manner all quietly proclaimed his office. I think I experienced every nuance of embarrassment there is.

He met my eyes, and his face glowed briefly with the infectious Suzuki-roshi grin that told me he was a saint, and he murmured the single word, "Later," in a way that told me I was forgiven for being late and I had not given offense and we were going to be good friends as soon as we both had time; meanwhile, lighten up.

All of this in an instant; then his eyes swept past me to Robert, they exchanged an equally information-packed glance which I could not read, and he returned his attention to the group as a whole.

If I hadn't arrived for class in an inappropriate mental state, it might have taken me minutes to realize how special Reb was.

Most of the spiritual teachers I've known had a tendency to sit silently for a minute or two after the arrival of the last pupils, as if to convey the impression that their meditation was so profound it took them a moment to shift gears. But Reb was a genuinely mindful man: he was aware Robert and I were the last ones coming, and the moment we had ourselves securely anchored to one of the ubiquitous bungee cords, he bowed to the group—somehow without disturbing his position in space—and began to speak.

"Hello," he said in a husky baritone. "My name is Reb Hawkins, and I'll be your student for the next eight to twelve weeks."

Inevitably someone spoke up, a New Yorker by her accent. "'Student'? I thought you were supposed to be the teacher."

"I am supposed, by many, to be a teacher," he agreed pleasantly. "Sometimes they are correct. But I am *aways* a student."

"Aah," said the New Yorker, in the tones of one who has spotted the hook in a commercial.

Reb didn't seem to notice. "I *am* going to try to teach all of you . . . specifically, how to enter Titanian Symbiosis without suffering unnecessary pain. Along the way, I will teach you any other lessons I can that you request of me, and from time to time I will offer to teach you other things I think you need to know . . . but in this latter category you are always privileged to overrule me."

"If that's true," the New Yorker said, "I'm actually impressed."

I was becoming irritated with the heckling—but Reb was not. "In free fall," he said, "raising one's hand for attention does not work well. Would you help me select some other gesture we all can use, Jo?"

Jo, the New Yorker, was so surprised by the question that she thought about it. "How 'bout this?"

Is there a proper name for the four-fingered vee she made? My parents were Star Trek fans, so I think of it as the Spock Hello.

He smiled. "Excellent! Unambiguous . . . and just difficult enough to perform that one has a moment to reconsider how necessary it really is to pre-empt the group's attention. Thank you, Jo." He demonstrated it for those who could not see Jo. "Is there anyone who can't make this gesture?"

Several of us found it awkward, but no one found it impossible. I was less interested in my manual dexterity than in his social dexterity. Hecklers heckle because they need everyone in the room to know how clever they are. He had given her a chance to make that point, reproved her so gently that she probably never noticed, and I knew he would have no further trouble from her that day. By persuading her not to be his enemy, he had defeated her. I smiled . . . and saw him notice me doing so. He did not smile back—but I seemed to see an impish twinkle for a moment in his eye.

I like spiritual teachers with an impish twinkle. In fact, I don't think I like any other kind.

"If any of you happen to be Buddhist, I am an Abbot in the Soto sect. I trace my dharma lineage through Shunryu Suzuki, and will be happy to do *dokusan* with any who wish it in the evenings, after dinner."

I don't know how to convey the significance of Reb's dharma lineage to a non-Soto-Buddhist. Perhaps the rough equivalent might be a Christian monk who had been ordained by one of the Twelve Apostles. Shunryu Suzuki-roshi was one of the greatest Japanese Zen masters to come to America, way back in the middle of the twentieth century—founder of the San Francisco Zen Center and the famous Tassajara monastery near Carmel.

"But this is not a class in Zen," he went on, "and you need not have any interest in Buddha or his Eightfold Path. What we're going to attempt to do in this class is to discuss spirituality without mentioning religion. The former can often be discussed by reasonable people without anger; the latter almost never can."

Glenn made the Spock Hello; he returned it, to mean she had the floor. "What *is* 'spirituality without religion,' sir?"

"Please call me 'Reb,' Glenn. It is the thing people had, before they invented religion, which caused them to gape at sunsets, to sing while alone, or to smile at other people's babies. And other things which defy rational explanation, but are basic to humanity."

"I'm not sure what you mean," she said.

"By happy coincidence, practically the next thing in the syllabus is an example of what I mean," he said. "We're going to take a short field trip in just a few minutes, to see something spiritual. Can you wait, Glenn?"

"Of course, Reb."

"Good. Now: one of the main things we need to do is to begin dismantling the *patterns* in which you think. Some of you may think that you've never given much thought to spirituality—but in fact you've thought too much about it, in patterns and terms that were only locally useful. Space adds dimensions unavailable to any terrestrial. It's time you started getting used to the fact that you live in space now. So I'd like you all to unship all those bungee cords, and pass them to me."

I began to see what he was driving at. The cords, to which we were all loosely clinging, imposed a strictly arbitrary local vertical, the same one Reb had been using since I'd entered. But as we followed his instruction, "up" and "down" went away. . . and he began (without any visible muscular effort) to tumble slowly and gracefully in space. His face was always toward us, but seldom "upright," and as some of us unconsciously tried to match his spin—and failed—there was suddenly no consensus as to which way was up. We had to stop trying to decide. Soon we were all every which way, save that we all at least tried to face Reb. I found it oddly unsettling to pay attention to someone who was spinning like a Ferris wheel—which was his point.

I noticed something else. He had positioned himself roughly at the center of the wall behind him—and the majority of us, myself included, had unconsciously oriented ourselves, not only "vertical" with respect to him . . . but "below" him as well. He was the teacher, so most of us wanted to "look up to him." Several of the exceptions looked like people who'd pointedly if subconsciously fought that impulse. (Robert was one of them.) Now the "upper" portion of the room was starting to fill up, as we redistributed ourselves more . . . well, more equally. Which again, I guess, was his point.

"That's more like it," he said approvingly as he stowed the bungee cords in a locker. "When you've been in free fall a while longer, you'll find the sight of a roomful of people aligned like magnets amusing—because in this environment it is."

An uneasy chuckle passed around the room.

"It's possible," he went on, continuing to rotate, "for a normal terrestrial to enter Symbiosis without permanent psychic damage; it has happened. But *any* spacer will find it enormously easier. Now for that field trip."

He reached behind himself without looking, caught the hatch handle on the first try, pivoted on it while activating it, and lobbed himself out of the room. His other hand beckoned us to follow.

We left the room smoothly and graciously, with no jostling for position or unnecessary speech. This man was having an effect on us.

We proceeded as a group down winding, roughly contoured

corridors of Top Step. The image that came to my mind, unbidden, was of a horde of corpuscles swimming single file through some sinuous blood vessel. Whoever it belonged to needed to cut down on her cholesterol.

I glanced back past my feet, saw that Robert had managed to take up position immediately behind me. He smiled at me. My mental image of our group changed, from corpuscles to spermatozoa. I looked firmly forward again and tried to keep my attention on spirituality—and on not jaunting my skull into the foot of Kirra in front of me.

In a few minutes we had reached our destination. To enter, we had to go through an airlock, big enough for ten people at once—but it was open at both ends: there was pressure beyond it. I wondered what the airlock was for, then. As I passed through it I heard a succession of gasps from those exiting before me; despite this foreknowledge, as I cleared the inner hatch, I gasped too. It was not the largest cubic in Top Step—not even the largest I'd seen so far; you could have fit maybe three of it in that big cavern where I'd met Teena the talking computer—but its largest wall was transparent, and on the other side of it was infinity.

We were at Top Step's very skin, gazing at naked space, at vacuum and stars. At the place where all of us hoped to live, one day soon . . .

From this close up, it did not look like terribly attractive real estate. Completely unfurnished. Drafty. No amenities. Ambiguous property lines, unclear title. *Big.* Scary . . .

How weird, that I was getting my first naked-eye view of space after more than twenty-four hours in space. Those stars were bright, sharp, merciless, horribly far away. It was hard to get my breath.

I wished Earth were in frame; it would have been less scary. This cubic seemed to be on the far side of Top Step. I wondered if there were a similar cubic on the other side, for folks who liked to look at the Old Home. Or did all of Top Step turn its collective back to Terra?

The last of us entered the room behind me and found a space to float in. We all gaped out the huge window together in silence.

Something drifted slowly into view, about ten meters beyond the window. A sculpture of a man, made of cherry Jell-O, waving a baton . . .

A Stardancer!

A real, live, breathing Stardancer. (No, unbreathing, of course . . . Stardancers must have some internal process analogous to breathing, but they do not need to work their lungs.) A *Homo caelestis*, a former human being in Titanian Symbiosis: covered, within and without, by the Symbiote, the crimson life-form that grows in the atmosphere of Saturn's moon Titan and is the perfect complement to the human metabolism. A native inhabitant of interplanetary space.

Except for the four-centimeter-thick coating of red Symbiote, he was naked. He would never need clothes again. Or, for that matter, air or food or water or a bathroom or shelter. Just sunshine and occasional trace elements. He was at home in space.

Of *course* we'd seen Stardancers before; we'd all come here to *become* Stardancers. We'd seen them hundreds of times . . . on film, on video, on holo. But none of us had ever actually been this close to one before. Stardancer and Symbiote mate for life, and the Symbiote cannot survive normal terrestrial atmosphere, pressure, moisture or gravity. Stardancers sometimes lived on Luna for short periods, and it was said that one had once survived on Mars for a matter of days . . . but no Stardancer would ever walk the Earth.

The Symbiote obscured details like eyes and expression, but it was clear that, back when he'd been a human being, he'd been a big, powerful man, heavily muscled . . . and very well hung, I couldn't help but notice. He was cartwheeling in slow motion as he came into view, but when he reached the center of the vast window, he made a brief, complex gesture with his magic wand and came to a halt relative to us. From my perspective he was upside down; I tried to ignore it.

With a small thrill, I recognized him, even under all that red Jell-O. I'd seen his picture often enough, his and all the other members of The Six. He was Harry Stein!

The Harry Stein—designer/engineer of the first free fall dance studio—less than five meters away from me. Others began to recognize him too: a susurrant murmur of, "SteinHarrySteinthat'sHarry Stein," went round the room.

Reb spoke at normal volume, startling us all. "Hello, Harry."

What happened then startled me even more. I suppose I should have been expecting it: I knew that Teena could project audio directly to my ear, like an invisible earphone—and a voice on *two* earphones sounds like it's coming from inside your head. Nonetheless I twitched involuntarily when Harry Stein's voice said, "Hi, Reb. Hi, everybody. My name is Harry," right in my skull.

What made it even stranger was that I happened to have been looking at his face when he spoke, and even under that faintly shimmering symbiote I was sure his lips had not moved. His suit radio was linked directly to the speech-center of his brain: the speech impulses were intercepted on their way to his useless vocal cords and sent directly. I'd studied all this in Space Camp, but it was something else again to experience it directly.

"Hi, Harry," several voices chorused raggedly.

"Can't stay long," he said. "Got a big job in progress over to spinward. Just wanted to say hi. And so did I." With that last sentence, there was an odd, inexpressible change in his voice. Not in pitch or tone or timbre—it was still Harry Stein's voice—but it was not him speaking it. "Hello, everybody, this is Charlie Armstead speaking now." Armstead himself! "I'm sorry I can't be there to meet you all personally—as a matter of fact, I'm a few light-hours away as you hear this—but Harry's letting me use his brain to greet you. I *will* be meeting you all when you graduate, of course—but so will the rest of the gang, all of us at once, and I couldn't resist jumping the gun. Neither could I— Hi, everyone, Norrey Armstead, here." Jesus! "I'm out here with Charlie, I guess you're all a little confused right about now . . . but don't let it worry you, okay? Just take your time and listen to what Reb tells you, and everything will be fine. Now I'll hand you over to Raoul Brindle for a minute. Oh, before I go, I want to say a quick hello to Morgan McLeod—"

I gulped and must have turned almost as red as Harry Stein.

"—I've been a fan of yours for years. I loved your work with Monnaie Dance Group in Brussels, especially your solo in the premiere of Morris's *Dance for Changing Parts.* I hope we can work together some day."

"Thank you," I said automatically—but my voice came out a squeak. People were staring. Robert, Kirra and Ben were smiling.

"Here's Raoul, now. Howdy, gang! I'm on my way home from Titan with the Harvest Crew, riding herd on about a zillion tons of fresh Symbiote—but I wanted to pass on a personal greeting of my own, to Jacques LeClaire and to Kirra from Queensland; hi, guys! I hope you'll both make some music for me one day; I've heard tapes of your work, and I'd love to jam with both of you when I get back. Or maybe you'll graduate before then and come meet me halfway. I'll hand you back to Harry now. So long . . ."

I don't think an Aboriginal can blush; Kirra must have been expressing her own embarrassment with body language. Fluently. And it was easy to pick out Jacques LeClaire in the crowd, too.

"Well, like I said," Harry went on, sounding like himself now—and don't ask me to explain that. "Work to do. Deadline's coming. I hope you'll all be in my family soon. See you later." He waved his thruster-baton negligently, and began drifting out of our field of view.

Not a word was spoken until he was gone. Then someone tried for irony. "What, Shara Drummond was too busy to say hello?" Some of us giggled.

"Yes," Harry's voice said, and the giggle trailed off. "Oh," the joker said, chastened.

There was another long silence. Then Kirra said softly, "Spirituality without religion—"

There was a subdued murmur of agreement.

"Lemme see if I've got this straight, Reb," she said. "If I needed to talk to one of that mob—"

"Just call them on the phone, like you would anyone else in space," Reb agreed. "If you really need an *instantaneous* response, you can ask for a telepathic relay through some other Stardancer whose brain happens to be near Top Step—but bear in mind that you will almost certainly be distracting their attention from something else. Don't do so frivolously. But if you don't mind waiting for both ends of the conversation to crawl at lightspeed, by radio, you can chat any time with any Stardancer who'll answer, anytime. Yes, Kirra."

"What was that Raoul said about a harvest crew?"

"When Armstead and The Six originally came back from Titan after entering Symbiosis, they brought an enormous quantity of the Symbiote back with them, using the *Siegfried* to tow it. But that was about thirty years ago, and Top Step has graduated a lot of Stardancers since then. It's becoming necessary to restock . . . so an expedition was sent out three or four years ago to mine more from Titan's upper atmosphere. They're on their way back right now, with gigatonnes of fresh Symbiote. Some of you in this class will be partaking of it. Yes, Jo?"

Jo was using her Teacher-May-I gesture, I noticed. "Is there, like, a directory of their phone numbers, or what?"

"You just say, 'Teena, phone . . .' and the name of the Stardancer you want, just like calling anyone else in Top Step. If there are no Stardancers nearby with attention to spare to relay for you, she'll tell you, and ask if you want her to contact your party directly, by radio. Glenn, what's bothering you?"

Glenn did have a frown. "This business of telepathy being instantaneous. It just doesn't seem natural."

"Where you come from, it is not especially natural, occurs rarely and often requires decades of training and practice. Where you are going, it is far more natural than that discarded old habit, breathing."

"But everything else in the universe is limited to lightspeed. Why should telepathy be different?"

"Why should you ask that question?" Reb asked.

Glenn fell silent . . . but her frown deepened.

A thin professorial-looking man gestured for attention. "Yes, Vijay?" Reb said.

"I think I understand Glenn's dilemma. To be confronted with empirical proof that there is more to reality than the physical universe . . . how is one supposed to deal with that? It's—"

"—terrifying, yes. There might be a God lurking around out there, armed with thunderbolts, demanding insane proofs of love, inventing Purgatories and Hells. There are techniques for helping with that fear. You were taught some back at Suit Camp. Sitting correctly. Breathing correctly. I'll teach others to you, and they'll help a lot. But the only way to really beat that fear—or the other, perfectly reasonable fear many of you have, that you'll lose your ego when you join the Starmind—is to keep on confronting it. If you retreat from it, suppress it, try to put it out of your mind, you make it harder for yourself." He was looking at Glenn as he said that sentence, and she slowly nodded. Reb smiled. "All right, now we're going to learn the first technique of Kûkan Zen. Namely, how to sit zazen . . . in zero gee."

"I thought you said, 'without religion,'" Glenn complained.

He looked surprised. "But Zen isn't a religion—not in the usual sense, at least."

"It isn't? I thought it was a sect of Buddhism. Buddhism's a religion. It's got monks and temples and doctrines and all of that."

Reb nodded. "But it has no dogmas, no articles of faith, no God. It has nothing to do with telling other people how they ought to behave. There has never been a Buddhist holy war . . . except intellectual war between differing schools of thought. You can be a Catholic Buddhist, a Muslim Buddhist, an atheist Buddhist. So although it may be religious, in the sense that it's about what's deepest in us, it's not *a* religion."

"What is it, then?"

"It is simply an agreement to sit, and look into our actual nature."

The very first chapter of Suzuki-roshi's *Zen Mind, Beginner's Mind* concerns correct sitting posture: that should be a clue to how important he considered it.

On Earth the classic full lotus position is something a Soto Zen Buddhist may take or leave alone, as his joints and ligaments allow. But in Kûkan Zen (I learned later that Reb coined the term: *kûkan* is Japanese for "space"), the lotus posture becomes both more important and less difficult. It is fundamental in "sitting" kûkanzen, the space equivalent of sitting zazen.

In the absence of weight, if you *don't* tuck your feet securely under the opposite knees, any "sitting" posture you assume will require considerable muscular effort, impossible to maintain for any length of time. When you relax, you end up in the Free Fall Crouch, the body's natural rest position, halfway between sitting and standing.

What's wrong with that? you may ask. Well, the idea is that Sitting, in the Zen sense, is something you do with full and powerful awareness. It requires some effort to do properly. Sitting zazen on Earth is not like sitting in a chair or standing or lying down or squatting or anything else humans do as a matter of course. It is a special posture you assume for the purpose of meditation, and after enough self-conditioning, just assuming that posture will make you begin to enter a meditative state.

And terrestrial zazen posture involves total relaxation *in the midst of total attention.* If relaxation alone were the goal, you would meditate lying down. The attempt to maintain a specific, defined posture (spine straight, chin down, hands just so) involves just enough effort and attention to make you see that you are, in a way, accomplishing something although you're merely sitting. It's one of those paradoxes—like using your mind to become so mindful you can achieve no-mind—that lie at the heart of Zen.

Reb felt it necessary to maintain that paradox, even in an environment where it's more difficult to maintain anything but Free Fall Crouch. Full lotus position is stressful for most beginners, in gravity—but it becomes quite tolerable in zero gee. Even for someone a lot less limber than I am: over the next few days I saw senior citizens who hadn't touched their toes in decades spend time in lotus. The worst part is getting unfolded again.

Similarly, Reb was forced to modify hand arrangement. Suzuki's "cosmic mudra"—left hand on top of right, middle joints of middle fingers aligned, thumb tips touching—tends to come apart without gravity's help. Reb interlaced the fingers to compensate.

And of course the *zafu* (round pillow), and the slanted wooden meditation bench used by other Eastern religions, are useless in space. In their place Kûkan Zen uses one of the most ubiquitous items of space hardware, as humble and commonplace as a pillow on Earth: the Velcro belt.

If you simply drift freely while meditating, you will naturally drift in the direction of airflow, and sooner or later end up bumping against the air-outgo grille. Distracting. But if you temporarily shut down the room's airflow to maintain your position, in a short time your exhalations will generate a sphere of carbon dioxide around your head and suppress your breathing reflex. Even more distracting.

So you leave the airflow running . . . and stick the back of your Velcro belt to the nearest convenient wall. People can tell you're meditating, rather than just hanging around, because your legs are tucked up in lotus and your hands are clasped.

When two or more people are sitting kûkanzen together, it's customary to all use the same wall, all face the same way, for the same reason that on Earth Suzuki's disciples sit facing the wall rather than the group. Humans are so gregarious it's hard for them to be in each other's visual field without paying attention to each other.

That's Kûkan Zen. Simple elegance, elegant simplicity.

The *second* chapter of Suzuki's book deals with breathing. We didn't get to that until the following day. Hawkins-roshi would put special emphasis on breathing (even for a Zen teacher), since once we graduated, we wouldn't be doing it anymore. . . .

At the close of our first lesson in Kûkan Zen 101, Reb said, "One thing before I let you all go. Does everyone understand why I brought you *here* to meet Harry Stein?"

Perhaps we did, but no one spoke.

"One of the reasons I brought you to this Solarium, when I could just as easily have had video piped into the classroom, is that here in this room you were as close to Harry as you could possibly get—you'd be little closer EVA, since a p-suit is a layer too—*and it made a difference.* You've all seen high-quality video and holo of Stardancers, dozens of hours of it in Suit Camp alone. . . but God, that was *the* Harry Stein himself, one of the original Six, right *there,* inches away, and it made a difference, didn't it?" There were nods and murmurs of agreement. Everyone in the room knew it made a difference. "Just what that difference *was* is one of those things—like the phenomenon of 'contact high'—that defy explanation unless you admit the existence of the thing I've labeled 'spirituality.' And your personal religion, whatever it may be, had nothing to do with it, did it?"

We left in a very quiet, thoughtful mood.

There was a food fight at lunch. A zero-gee food fight is amazing. Almost everybody misses, because they can't help aiming too high. Robert, having "space legs," did well—but his roommate Ben did almost as well, despite his klutziness. You couldn't sneak up on him. . . .

Glenn, I noticed, was infuriated at both the food fight, and how badly she lost. I could tell, just from her expression, that she believed handling oneself in free fall was something best conquered by intellect—and therefore, she ought to be one of the best at it. I'd seen the expression before, on the faces of beginner dance students who were also intellectuals. They see people they consider their inferiors picking up the essentials of movement quicker than they can, and it forces them to admit there are kinds of intelligence that do not live in the forebrain.

I didn't do very well in the food fight myself. I found that just as infuriating as Glenn did. But I covered it better.

* * *

Glenn's and my problem was addressed almost immediately. The schedule called for spending our afternoons in Jaunting class, learning how to move in zero gee.

Our instructor was Sulke Drager, a powerfully built woman whose primary job, I later learned, was rock-rat: one of the hardboiled types who blasted new tunnels and cubics into Top Step when needed. In between, she worked in the Garden and taught Jaunting, and worked two more jobs in other space habitats. She was not here for Symbiosis, like us; she was a spacer. A permanent transient, citizen of the biggest small town in human history. I think she privately thought we were all crazy.

I thought *she* was crazy. She had chosen a life with all the disadvantages of a Stardancer, and none of the advantages, it seemed to me. She could never go back to Earth; her body was long since permanently adapted to free fall. But she was not a telepathic immortal as we hoped to be. Just a human a long way from home, hustling for air money, hoping to bank enough to buy her retirement air. Talk about wage slaves! Sulke was as dependent as a goldfish.

Most of us were disappointed when she confirmed that it would be a good month before we got any EVA time. For about the first fifteen minutes, we were disappointed. That's how long it took us to convince ourselves that we weren't ready to go outdoors yet, Suit Camp or no Suit Camp. Theory is not practice.

(One thing I had never anticipated, for instance, in all the hours I'd spent trying to imagine movement in this environment: sweat that trickled *up*. Or refused to trickle at all, and just sort of pooled up in the small of your back until you flung or toweled it off. What a *weird* sensation!)

We were given wrist and ankle thruster-bracelets, but Sulke only allowed us to use them to correct mistakes: the first step was to learn to be as proficient as possible without external aids.

As I had been during the food fight—hell, since I'd arrived in space—I was dismayed to learn how clumsy I was in this environment. Like Glenn, I had assumed I had a secret weapon that would allow me to outstrip all the others. Instead, it seemed I had more to *unlearn* than most: inappropriate habits of movement were more deeply ingrained in me.

This infuriated me. So much that I probably worked twice as hard as anyone else in the class, using all the discipline and concentration I'd learned in thirty years of professional dance.

"No, no McLeod," Sulke said. "Stop trying to swim in air, you look like a drunken octopus." She jaunted to me and stopped my tumble, without putting herself into one. "Use your spine, not your limbs!"

It was a particularly galling admonition: in transitioning from ballet to modern dance, I had spent countless hours learning to use my spine. In one gee. "I thought I *was*." Someone giggled.

"Watch Chen, there, see how he does it? Chen, pitch forward half a rev, and yaw half." Robert performed the maneuver requested: in effect he stood on his head, spinning on his long axis so he was still facing her when he was done. His legs barely flexed, and his arms left his sides only at the end of the maneuver. "See what he did with his spine?"

"Yes, but I didn't understand it," I admitted.

"Put your hands on him, here, and here." She indicated her abdomen and the small of her back.

I refused myself permission to blush. I used my thrusters to jaunt to him, and was relieved to do a near-perfect job, canceling all my velocity just as I reached him, without tumbling myself again. He was upside down with reference to me; I couldn't read his expression. I put my hands where I'd been told.

"Keep a light contact as he begins, then pull your hands away," Sulke directed. "Reverse the maneuver, Chen."

So I didn't get my hands quite far enough out of the way, quite fast enough. As he spun backwards, his groin brushed down across the palm I'd had on his belly. Now I was blushing. When he finished—a little awkwardly this time—he wore that inscrutable-Asian face of his. But he was blushing a little too. The giggles from the rest of the class didn't help. "You're jumping ahead," Sulke called. "We don't get to mating for days, yet."

In free fall maneuvering, mating simply means interacting with another body. We'd all heard dozens of puns on the terms before we'd left Suit Camp, but this feeble one put the class in stitches. I thought wistfully about putting a few of them in traction. Then I did a quarter-yaw, to face Sulke, and copied Robert's maneuver, very nearly perfectly. The giggling became applause.

"Much better," Sulke said. "It must be a question of motivation. Buckley, you try it."

Robert and I exchanged a meaningful glance . . . and as I was trying to decide just what meaning to put into my half, something cracked me across the skull. It was one of Ben's elbows. Without cafeteria tables to hold on to and brace himself against, his enhanced visual perception was little help to him: he would be one of the klutziest in our class—that day, anyway. "Sorry, Morgan!"

I welcomed the distraction. "Forget it."

"Uh . . . could I . . . I mean, would you mind . . . ?"

For the next five or ten minutes, an orgy of belly-and-back-touching spread outwards from Robert and me, until everyone had mastered the forward half-pitch. (At least one other male was as careless with his hands as I had been with Robert. I pretended not to notice.) Then Sulke turned our collective attention to the roll and yaw techniques, which took up the rest of the class period.

After class there were a couple of free hours before dinner. I had Teena guide me back to Solarium One, where we'd seen Harry Stein—where Norrey Armstead had addressed me by my name!—and sat kûkanzen for a timeless time, seeking some clarity, some balance. There were about a half dozen of us there, all doing the same thing. I don't know about the others; I left as confused and scattered as I'd arrived.

I sat by myself at dinner. A lot of us did, I think.

When I got back to my room Kirra was not there. I spent an hour or so at my desk, browsing through data banks, learning basic things about Top Step's layout. It is a huge, complex place, but interactive holographic maps help a lot in understanding it. I only had to bother Teena once. The important thing to remember from a navigational standpoint is that the arrow will always be painted on the wall farthest from Earth, and will point "outboard," toward the main docking area through which everyone enters Top Step. Eventually I sighed and collapsed the display back to the simple overview map I'd started with.

There was no sense putting it off any longer. I'd already stalled for almost a full day. I was as ready as I was ever going to be.

I described my requirements to Teena, and she found me a gym not presently in use, where I could try to dance.

* * *

The space Teena directed me to was terrific—spacious, well padded, fully equipped, complete with top of the line sound and video gear. I could lock it from inside for up to an hour at a time. I locked it, selected music that did not dictate tempo, and—at last!—began trying my first dance "steps" in space.

The session was a disaster.

I spent a longer, slower time than usual warming up, and was careful not to overextend myself. But it was a fiasco. After an hour and a half of hard sweaty effort I had not put together five consecutive seconds I would want to show anyone. Not one single sequence I'd invented in my mind worked the way it was supposed to; not one combination I'd memorized from videos of Stardancers worked the way I'd thought it would. I was less graceful than a novice skater. Part of the problem was that the moves I'd envisioned always *stopped* when I was done with them . . . whereas every motion in free fall keeps going until something stops it. Every once in a while I accidentally created a moment of beauty . . . then could not reproduce it a second later. It was as though someone had randomly rewired a computer keyboard so there was no way to predict the effect of hitting any given key. And I kept poking my face through drifting mists of sweat globules that I'd spun off earlier, a truly disgusting experience.

I had not expected this to be easy. Well, okay, maybe I had. As I watched the video replay of my flounderings on the monitor, I was not sure it was possible.

It *had* to be possible. There was nothing back on Earth for me to return to. Shara Drummond had done this. Her sister Norrey had done it. Crippled defeated old Charlie Armstead had managed it. I had seen countless tapes of Stardancers who had had no dance training before coming to space, making shapes of almost unbearable beauty. Dammit, I was a good dancer, a great dancer.

Back on Earth, yeah, said the video monitor, *when you were younger . . .*

Finally I'd had all I could take for now. "That's it. Teena, wipe all tapes of this session."

"Yes, Morgan. There is a message for you, left after you told me to see that you were not disturbed. Will you accept it now?"

I sighed. "Why not?" Nothing happened, of course. I sighed again.

"I mean, 'Yes, Teena, I'll take it now.'"

The monitor filled with Robert's face, wearing the vague smile everyone wears when leaving a phone message. "Hello, Morgan. You asked me if I'd tutor you in jaunting. I have time free this evening. Call me if you're still interested."

I thought about it while I got my breathing under control and toweled up sweat. I'd begun this evening confused and scattered. With diligent effort I had brought myself to miserable and depressed. It was time to cut my losses. "Record this message, Teena—" The screen turned into a mirror. "—Jesus, audio only!" It opaqued again. "Take one: 'Hello, Robert, this is Morgan. Thank you for your offer. Perhaps another time.' Cut. Too stiff. Take two: 'Hi, Robert, Morgan here. Maybe another night, okay? I just washed my spine and I can't do a thing with it.' Oh my God. . . take three: 'Robert, this is Morgan. Look, I don't know if it's a good idea if we—I don't think I—" I stopped and took a deep breath. "Teena, just send take one, to 'cut', okay? Then refuse all calls until I tell you otherwise."

"Yes, Morgan."

I used the gym's shower bag—God, I'll never get used to water that *slithers,* it's even weirder than sweat that won't trickle—and went back to my room. Halfway back, as an experiment, I had Teena stop guiding me, and tried to find my own way. I barked my shins a couple of times misjudging turns, I had to double back once, and my Contact-Per-Hectometer rate was humiliating . . . but I found my own damn home without help.

As the door irised open, song spilled out. Kirra was home. She was halfway into her sleepsack, her "swag," as she called it, and the lights were out in her hemisphere. My own lights were on low standby. She stopped singing to greet me. "Oh, don't stop," I protested, closing the door behind me.

"I haven't," she said. "You just can't hear it anymore. What you been up to, lovey?"

"Wasting time," I answered evasively. "Sing so I can hear, Kirra, really. If I fall asleep listening to music, I dream dances. At least I used to. I could use the inspiration."

So she went back to it. In this song her voice had about the range, pitch and tone of an alto recorder, if you know that sound. (I don't know why they were called that: they had no recording capacity at all.) It was soothing, hypnotic, resonated in my belly somewhere like a cat's purr.

I stripped and stuffed myself into my own sleepsack, told my room lights to slow-fade. *Today I talked with Charlie Armstead and Norrey Armstead,* I told myself. Kirra's warm sweet voice rose and fell in ways as unfamiliar to me as the words themselves. Just as I was drifting off to sleep I understood that they were unfamiliar to her too. She was singing about space, about zero gee. If there is no up or down, what's a melody to do? Her soothing voice washed away all turbulent emotion, set me adrift from my drifting body.

In my dreams there were sea lions. Highlit crimson by sunset, the colour of Stardancers. Floating all around me, all oriented to my personal vertical, treading air. Waiting patiently. For the first time, I wished I spoke Sea Lion.

5

I humbly say to those who study the mystery,
Don't waste time.

—Sekito Kisen
Sandokai Sutra
(translated by Thomas Cleary)

Kirra and I both woke up with stiff necks. We hadn't learned yet that if you don't secure your head while you sleep in zero gee, you nod all night long, in time with your breathing. A terrestrial equivalent might be watching a tennis match for eight hours while lying on your side. We gave each other neck rubs before we got dressed. Kirra gave a first-rate neck rub. It's a rare skill, and blessed in a roommate. It was the first time I'd had friendly hands on me, and the first warm flesh I'd touched with my fingers, in I couldn't remember how many months.

I didn't see Robert at breakfast the next morning, and was just as glad. I wasn't sure what to say to him, how to act with him, how I felt about him. So far he had made no moves that were not ambiguous, that could not be read as simple friendliness. How would I respond if he did? Dammit, I didn't need this distraction now. I would tell him so . . . if the son of a bitch would only give me a clear opportunity!

When I realized I had spent all of breakfast thinking about not thinking about him, it occurred to me that it might be simplest to just get it over with. Have a quick intense affair, end it cleanly, and get on with preparing for Symbiosis.

Right. When had I ever had a quick intense affair that ended cleanly? Symbiosis would be hard enough without going out of my way to risk ego damage just beforehand.

He was in class when I got there, on the far side of the room. I took a vacant space near the door. In what would become a daily ritual, we all sat kûkanzen together for a half an hour; then we pushed off the wall and expanded to fill the room again. There were no bungee cords today; we were all in constant slight motion, forced into frequent touching, into learning the knack of stabilizing each other without setting up chain reactions of disturbance. It was interesting. When you're part of an unsecured group in free fall, you're *part of a group.* Like a driver watching cars far ahead for possible danger, you find yourself keeping track of movements three or four people away from you, because any motion anyone else makes will sooner or later affect you. You can't withdraw inward and ignore your fellows—because if you do, sooner or later you get an elbow in the eye.

Reb spoke that day of Leavetaking. It was his word for our primary task during our first month of Postulancy. Taking our leave, emotionally and psychologically, of all earthly things, of the kin and kindred we were leaving behind. "In effect you must do what a dying person does . . . with the advantages that you are not in pain or drugged or immobilized. You can take your leave with a clear mind and a clear heart. Most important, you have no need to be afraid. In your case, you *know* that the kind of dying you do will not mean the end of you, and your universe. In a sense, you'll get to have your afterlife now, while you're around to enjoy it." There were a few chuckles. "But I apologize, sincerely and humbly, if to any of you that sounds like blasphemy. I do not mean to imply that Symbiosis is the same as the afterlife or rebirth that terrestrial religions speak of. It is not. But it carries nearly the same price tag. You have to abandon everything to get there.

"You're a little like terminal patients with three months to live. You have one month to grieve, and one month to prepare, and then one month to decide. Don't waste a minute of it, is my advice. Life on earth is something to lose. Get your mourning done, so you can put it aside. Because life in space is something to look forward to."

Someone asked how you mourn your past.

"One of the best methods," Reb said, "is something of a cliché. Let your whole life pass before your eyes. Only you don't have to cram it into one final instant. Take a month. Remember. Re-member: become a member again. Remember your life, as much of it as you can; write your memoirs in your mind, or type them out or dictate them to Teena if it helps you. Every time you remember a good part, say goodbye to it. Every time you remember a bad part, say goodbye to that as well. If you come to a part that hurts to remember, sit kûkanzen with it until it doesn't hurt anymore. If you have a place you just can't get past, come to me for further help."

The rest of class was devoted to a long lecture/demonstration on how to breathe correctly—"You ought to get it right once before you give it up for good," he told us—but I won't record it here. Read Shunryu Suzuki-roshi if you're really interested, or Reb's book *Running Jumping Standing Still.* Before breaking for the day, Reb announced that anyone interested in formal kûkanzen sitting, with traditional Soto Buddhist forms, was welcome to come to his zendo any evening after dinner. He was also available for *dokusan,* private interviews. It seemed to me that his eyes brushed mine while he said this. After class I approached him and, when I had his attention, told him that I intended to join his evening meditation group, but that I had a private project of my own to complete first. He smiled and nodded. "You need to know if you can dance," he agreed. "Good luck." He gave his attention to the next person who wanted it.

I tottered off to lunch, more than a little surprised. Yes, he'd known every one of us by name on the first day. But to know so much about me as an individual implied either remarkable research for a teacher . . . or insight approaching telepathy.

On my way to lunch I missed a transition and spent a humiliating few minutes drifting free in the center of a corridor intersection until a Second-Monther came along and bailed me out. It caused me to work through a logic chain. If I was ever going to learn to remaster my body in this weird environment, and dance again, I was going to need all the help I could get. But help from Robert came with ambiguous strings attached. Therefore I needed someone else. A Second-Monther, like the one who'd just helped me? I'd seen a few of them so far, they were billeted in a different section of Top Step, and the ones I'd passed in the corridors had all worn an air of quizzical distraction and seemed in a hurry. (I still hadn't seen any Third-Monthers, but Kirra had; she said he'd looked "awful holy or awful high, or maybe both," in a sort of daze.) Still, there had been helpful Second-Monthers at meals; maybe I'd ask one of them for tutoring and see what they said.

But as I entered the cafeteria I changed my mind. Sulke Drager was eating by herself; I took my food over to her table and asked if I could join her. After a few conversational politenesses, I asked her if she'd be willing to tutor me after hours.

She laughed in my face. "How much are you offering per hour?"

Since Suit Camp, I'd gotten out of the habit of thinking about money. It was part of what I was leaving behind. But what money I owned was still mine until I entered Symbiosis and thereby donated it all to the Starseed Foundation. There wasn't much, mostly the carefully measured trickle of Grandmother's trust fund, but what did I need it for? Symbiosis or Euthanasia were my choices, and neither required capital. "How about two hundred dollars an hour? Uh, Canadian dollars."

She grimaced. "What do I know from dollars? How much is that in air-days or calories? Or even Deutschmarks? Never mind, you don't know and I don't care. Whatever it is, it isn't enough."

"Why not?"

She stopped eating and faced me. "I just got here from six hard sweaty hours in a p-suit over at the Mirror Farm. After I finish trying to teach you clowns here, I go put in another six hours as a glorified lab clerk over at the NanoTech Safe Lab—only six hours turns into eight because of what they put you through every time you enter and leave that place. Like what you got at Decontam, but worse. Then I can catch the shuttle home to Hooverville and catch a few hours of sleep. All this buys me just enough air and food to keep going. I haven't got an hour to spare. And if I did, the last thing in the System I'd spend it on is more of teaching one of you freebreathers how to swim."

"Sorry I asked."

"Look, you're a dancer, right? Do you enjoy teaching first position and pliés to beginners?"

I certainly couldn't argue with that. We finished our meals without further conversation.

I watched her during that afternoon's class. She worked hard and well with us, but she did it with a barely submerged air of resentment. I thought of her term for us. Freebreather. Analogous, no doubt, to freeloader. We did not sweat for the air we breathed. It was given to us by the Starseed Foundation. We loafed and probed our souls while Sulke scrambled to survive. She and the other hundreds of zero-gee-adapted spacers must all dislike us.

I noticed something else as I floundered with the others, trying instinctively and uselessly to swim in air. Robert's roommate Ben had become terrific at this . . . literally overnight. Yesterday he'd been as clumsy as the rest of us—and today he was as graceful and controlled in his movements as Robert. He learned new moves and tactics as fast as Sulke could show them to him; he even showed her one she didn't know. I don't think I could describe it; it seemed to involve having eyes in the back of your head.

Sulke called both Ben and me aside after class. Kirra and Robert both drifted a polite distance away to wait for us. "You still go a lot to learn—but you got damn good damn fast," she told him. "How?"

The trouble with asking Ben a question is, he's liable to answer. "Well, you know that psych experiment where they tape inverting lenses over your eyes, and for a while you're blind and then on the second day suddenly you can see again? Your brain tears down the whole visual system and rebuilds it upside down in two days; well I've been doing that kind of stuff for fun for almost thirty years, rewiring my brain for new paradigms; two days is what it usually takes me, I'm right on schedule. It's amazing what you can do with your own brain when you start messing around with the circuitry—do you know about the time The Great Woz rebuilt his own memory after an accident? He said he thought his brain from the zero to the one state. Sometimes I think I know what he means—"

Sulke got a word in edgewise. "Whatever. McLeod here needs some tutoring evenings. Why don't you help her out?"

He smiled at me sheepishly. "Gee, Morgan, I'd love to help you, but I'm kind of busy myself just now. I've got this little project I just started this morning; I'm working with Teena on memorizing Top Step; I want to get to the place where I can close my eyes and point to anyplace in the rock and get it right. And I want to spend more time with Kirra too. Uh, could I get back to you in two days?" While I was trying to cope with the enormity of his assumption that he could master the three-dimensional geography of this huge place in another two days, and wondering whether I could stand to study jaunting with this happy madman, he got a brainstorm. "No, you know what you should do? Robert! Hey, *Robert*—c'mere. You should ask Robert to help you, hey, that's a great idea, he's good at this stuff too, hey Robert, Morgan needs somebody to teach her jaunting and I'm booked: why don't you help her?"

Robert and I looked at each other. We both wanted to kick Ben, and neither wanted to show it. "I've offered," he said expressionlessly.

Sulke was studying us. "Well," she said, "I have to jet." She kicked away and left.

"Well, there you go, then," Ben said, hugely pleased with himself.

"Ben, love," Kirra said, "let's you and me go get some tucker and let them talk it over, eh?" You can't kick somebody in the shin surreptitiously in zero gee: you bounce away.

"Huh? Oh, sure. See you at supper, folks." He and Kirra left us alone.

I wanted to join them. But I suddenly realized I couldn't. I had carelessly let go of my handhold to let Sulke by, then failed to regain it in time. We'd all handed in our thruster units at the close of class. I was adrift; unless Robert helped me, it'd be at least a couple of minutes before I drifted near another wall. Damn!

He kept his position near the hatch and watched me. When the silence had stretched out for oh, half of forever, he said, "So what time tonight is good for you?"

'Robert," I said slowly, "we have to talk."

"Yes."

I was spinning very slowly; soon I'd be facing away from him. I knew the maneuver to correct for that. But if I screwed it up I'd put myself into a tumble from which he'd more or less have to rescue me. "Look . . . can we skip past a lot of bullshit?"

"Yes."

"What exactly do you want from me? I've been around, I know you're interested. But interested in what? I've got too much on my mind for high school guessing games: I'm busy. You want a quick roll in the hay, you want to go steady, you want my autograph, you want to have my baby, *what?*"

There are probably a thousand wrong answers to that question. The only right one I can think of is the one he came up with. "I want to get to know you better."

I sighed and studied his strange, beautiful face. I wanted to get to know him better. And I needed the distraction like a hole in the head.

I was having to crane my neck now to keep eye contact. So I tried to reverse my spin, and of course I bungled it and went into a slow tumble. They say you're not supposed to get dizzy in free fall, because your semicircular canals fill up completely and your sense of balance shuts down. But I'd only been in space a few days; the room whirled, I lost all reference points, I got dizzy.

"Stiffen up," Robert called, his voice coming closer. "Don't try to help me." I tensed all my limbs. He took me by the wrists, we pivoted around each other like trapeze artists and headed for the far wall together. He changed his grip and did something and we were in a loose embrace, feet toward our destination. "Ready? Landing . . . now." We let our legs soak up most of our momentum, ended up headed back toward the hatch, but moving slowly. We were touching at hands and knees. His eyes were a meter from mine.

"Look," I said, "the timing is lousy."

"Yeah," he agreed.

"See, I came here to dance. That's all, I came here to dance. Anything else comes second. I can't dance anymore on Earth. If I can't dance here either, I don't know if I'm going through with Symbiosis. And I don't know if I can dance here or not. I thought I could, but I can't even seem to learn the equivalent of crawling on all fours. Maybe I'm one of the ones who just can't get it. I can't give you any kind of an answer until I know. Does that make any sense?"

He thought about it as we reached the midpoint of the room and he led us through our turnover. "It makes me want to teach you everything I can, as fast as possible. What time is good tonight?"

"Did you hear what I—"

"We Chinese are a notoriously patient people."

I sighed in exasperation.

"Let me help you, as a friend. No obligations. I've admired your work for a long time; allow me this honour."

What the hell can you say to something like that? That evening we spent two hours working out together in "my" gym.

And it was a fiasco.

Early on we identified my major problem: an unconscious, instinctive tendency to select one of the possible local verticals and stubbornly declare it the "correct" one in my mind, so that I became disoriented when out of phase with it. It is the most common problem of a neophyte in free fall. Ten million years of evolution insist on knowing which way "down" is, just in case this weightlessness business should suddenly fail. Even a false answer is preferable to no answer.

Identifying the problem didn't help solve it at all. Robert was indeed patient, but I must have tried his patience. Finally I thanked him, politely kicked him out, and spent another couple of hours alone, trying to dance.

It wasn't a *total* disaster. But damn close. In the last ten minutes I managed to put together one eight-second sequence that didn't stink. The first time I did it was dumb luck, an accident with serendipitous results. But I was able to reproduce it again . . . and again. About three times out of five. If I didn't crash into something while I was trying. In playback, it looked good from five of the six camera angles.

But I could not connect that eight seconds up with *anything*. The third time I had to stop to towel away sweat from the middle of my back I said the hell with it, got in and out of the shower bag, and went back to my room. Kirra was out. I climbed into my sleepsack, dimmed the lights, and studied holograms of some of my favorite Stardancer dance pieces, trying to understand how they made what they did look so effortless. I even went back as far as the oldest zero-gee dance there is, Shara Drummond's *Liberation.* She'd only been dancing in space for three weeks when Armstead recorded it. Until now, I'd never fully appreciated just how good it was.

After a while Kirra came in, humming softly to herself. "Hello, lovey. How'd it go?"

I collapsed the holo. "How'd it go with you? Ben show you any good moves?" She'd gone to his place to learn 3-D chess.

She came and docked with my sleepsack. Her grin was about to split her face. "Benjamin showed me his very best moves," she said in a dreamy singsong voice.

My eyes widened. "You're kidding!"

She shook her head, beaming. We squealed together and burst into giggles. "Tell me everything!" I demanded.

"Well, you know, I'd always wondered," she said, settling into a hug, "what'd it be like? I mean, what'd keep you squished together if not the weight?"

I'd always wondered too. "Right. So?"

"So it turns out it's as natural as breathin'. You hug with four arms is all, and then you . . . well, you dance. Nowhere near as hard as the stuff we do in class." She closed her eyes in reminiscence. "It was lots gentler than it is on Earth. And nicer. He didn't need to hold himself up, so he could keep on usin' his hands all the way through." She squealed and opened her eyes again. "Oh, it was awful nice!

Benjamin says we'll get even better with time."

I nodded. "Wait'll you see how good he is in two days' time," I said, and made her laugh from deep inside.

She was my friend; I shared her joy. But a part of me was envious. I tried hard to hide it, to make the right noises as she chattered happily on, and thought I succeeded.

Maybe she smelled it. "So how'd you make out with your dancing, love?" she asked finally.

I found myself pouring out my frustrations to her. "And I can't even *start* to figure out where I stand with him until I know whether or not I can dance in free fall," I finished, "and I can't even guess how long it's going to be before I know."

She looked thoughtful. "Tell me something."

"Sure."

"How's your back feel?"

"Why, not too—oh!"

"How 'bout those knees, then?"

My back did not hurt. My knees did not hurt.

"You worked out more in the last two days than you did in the last year, tell me I'm wrong," she said. "Have your legs buckled? Got crook back?"

No and no, by God. I was tired and ached in a dozen places, but they were no worse than one should expect when getting back into shape after a long layoff.

"You can do this. Matter of time, that's all."

I was thunderstruck. She was absolutely right. *My instrument was working again.* Hell, I had managed to transition from ballet to modern dance once: I could learn this. There was nothing stopping me! Nothing but time and courage. The sense of relief was overwhelming. I felt a surge of elation, and at the same time a delicious tiredness. Moments before I'd been suffering from fatigue; now I was just sleepy.

"Kirra, you're an angel," I cried, and hugged her harder, and kissed her. Then we smiled at each other, and she jaunted to her own bed and dimmed the lights. She undressed quickly and slid into the sack. "Night, lovey," she called softly.

"G'night, Kirra," I murmured. "I'm happy for you. Ben's sweet."

My last thought was *I'm going to sleep sounder tonight than I have in years,* and then almost at once I was deep under—

* * *

—and then I was wide awake, saying, "What the hell was that?" aloud, and Kirra said it too and we both listened and heard nothing but silence, total silence, and at last I thought *Silence? In a space dwelling?*

The air circulation system in Top Step is whisper quiet—but boy, do you miss that whisper when it stops!

Then a robot was speaking with Teena's voice, loudly, in my left ear.

In only the one ear, and very slowly, unmistakably Teena's voice but without any inflections of tone or pitch: she must have been talking to or with nearly every resident of Top Step at once, time-sharing like mad, no bytes to spare for vocal personality or stereo effect. "Attention! Attention! There has been a major system malfunction. There is no immediate cause for alarm, repeat, no cause for alarm. The circulation system is temporarily down. It is being repaired. All personnel are advised to remain in constant motion until further notice. Do not let yourself remain motionless for more than a few moments. If you can reach p-suit or other personal pressure, please do so, calmly." Not wanting to drain her resources any further, we asked no questions.

A moment later, her voice was superseded by that of Dorothy Gerstenfeld. She explained the nature of the problem, assured us it would be fixed long before it became serious, entreated us all not worry, and sounded so serene and confident herself that I did stop worrying. Her explanation was too technical for me to follow, but her tone of voice said I should be reassured by it, so I was.

The circulation system was only down for half an hour. Nothing to be afraid of: Top Step was immense and a lot of it was pressurized; there was more than enough air on hand to last us all much longer than half an hour in a pinch. The worst of it was nuisance: when the air stops flowing in a space habitat, you *must not* be motionless. If you are, exhaled CO_2 forms an invisible sphere around your head and slowly smothers you. There are many jobs aboard Top Step for which constant head motion is contraindicated, tracking a large-mass docking, for instance; such people had to find someone to fan their heads, or stop work for the duration. And everyone else had to keep moving. You can't imagine how annoying that can be until it's forced upon you. Not that being in motion takes any hard work, in zero gee—it's just that your natural tendency and subconscious desire is to *stop* moving as much as possible, to stimulate the terrestrial environment you remember as natural, and overcoming that impulse gets wearing very quickly. Especially if you were tired to begin with.

But it was over soon enough. Kirra and I experimented with fanning each other's faces, and told each other campfire stories, and at last we heard the soft sound of the pumps coming back up to speed. Because I was alert for it, I became consciously aware for the first time of the movement of air on my skin as soon as it resumed.

"The emergency is over," Teena said, still in robot mode. "Repeat, the emergency is over. There have been zero casualties. Resume normal operations. Thank you."

"Thank you all for not panicking," Dorothy's voice added. "We have everything under control now. Resume your duties. Those of you on sleep shift, try to get back to sleep; you've a long day ahead."

I had surprisingly little difficulty feeling sleepy again, and Kirra was snoring—musically—before I was. As I was fading out again I had a thought. "Teena?" I whispered.

"Yes, Morgan?" Her reply was also whispered, but I could tell this was the old, fully human-sounding Teena again, so it was all right to bother her now.

"What caused the circulation system to go down?"

She almost seemed to hesitate. Silly, of course; computers don't hesitate. "A component was improperly installed through carelessness. It has been replaced."

"Oh. Glad it wasn't anything serious. A meteor or something. That reminds me: how is Mr. Henderson, the Chief Steward on my flight up here?"

"I'm sorry to say he died about four hours ago, without regaining consciousness."

"Oh." No one had needed to fan his head while the air was down.

"Good night. Morgan."

"G'night."

My last drifting thought was something about how lucky I'd been lately. Two life-threatening emergencies in forty-eight hours, and I'd lived through them both.

There weren't any more for *weeks.*

6

Tom Seaver: What time is it, Yogi?
Yogi Berra: You mean now?

A company manager I toured Nova Scotia with once summed up that province as follows: "Too many churches; not enough bars." I'm afraid the same could be said of Top Step.

That overgrown cigar had churches and temples of almost every possible kind in its granite guts, over three dozen, including three different *zendos;* if I had wanted to do nothing but kûkanzen "sitting" or Rinzai chanting with my free time, I could have. But I'd never been all that committed as a Buddhist—I'd never been fully committed to *anything* except the dance—and somehow it felt wrong to spend all of my last three months as a human being pursuing no-thought. I intended to do a *lot* of thinking, before I stepped outdoors and jaunted into a big glob of red goo and opened up my p-suit. I still wasn't absolutely sure I was going to go through with this.

I tended to spend my free time in one of four places: Solarium Three, Le Puis, my room, and the gym I came to think of as my studio.

Sol Three was a popular hangout for just about everyone in my class, and for some from the two classes ahead of us and some of the staff as well. Not Sol One, where I'd met Harry Stein and three others of The Six: this Solarium was, as its number indicates, all the way round the other side of Top Step. An accidental pun, for that's the side facing Earth: Sol Three overlooking Sol III. It was more commonly and informally known as the Café du Ciel—a reference I understood the first time I saw its spectacular view.

Have you ever been to New Orleans, to the old French Quarter? Do you know the Café du Monde? You sit outdoors and sip chicoried café au lait, and eat fresh hot beignets smothered with so much powdered sugar you mustn't inhale while biting, and you watch the world go by. Look one way, and there's the Mississippi, Old Man River himself, just rolling along. Look another and you're seeing Jackson Square, another and you're looking at the French Market. Street buskers play alto sax, or vibes, or clarinet, very well. They say if you sit in the Café du Monde long enough, sooner or later you'll see everyone you know pass by.

The same is said of the Café du Ciel—and it's literal truth.

It tended to have a lot of people in it, and it tended to be rather quiet, although there was no rule about noise. There were no buskers there. There were no beignets available either—powdered sugar isn't practical in free fall—but you could bring a bulb of coffee from the cafeteria. What made the Solarium reminiscent of the Café du Monde was the view.

The scenery was so majestic it was like being in some great cathedral. When the Fireflies originally whisked Top Step from the asteroid belt into High Earth Orbit as their final parting gift to humanity, they picked a polar orbit concentric to the day/night terminator, to keep the big stone cigar in perpetual sunlight. So the Earth we saw from Solarium Three was always half in sunlight and half in darkness, an immense yin-yang symbol. Our orbit was high enough that you could just see the entire globe at once. The slow grandeur of the dance it did I cannot describe, spinning end-on when we were passing over one of the Poles, then seeming to lurch crazily sideways as our orbit flung us toward the Equator and the opposite Pole. A whole planet endlessly executing the same arabesque turn. If you haven't got graphic software that'll simulate it, get an old-fashioned globe and see it for yourself, it's the grandest roller coaster I know, endlessly absorbing. We all felt its pull: there in the big window was everything we were about to say goodbye to.

Second-month Postulants generally seemed to graduate into being attracted more by Solariums One and Four, which faced raw empty space: everything they were about to say hello to. I visited those cubics a few times; they had even more of that cathedral-hush feel. Too much for me, then.

(Only dedicated tanners spent much time in Sol Two—the only true solarium, the one which always faced the Sun—and for them I suppose it must have been Paradise. You could put a spin on yourself, go to sleep, and toast evenly on all sides without effort. But I never got the habit; skin cancer aside, a dancer with a tan is a dancer who's out of work.)

But sometimes looking at Earth made you want to make noise and have a little fun. So if I wasn't in Sol Three I could usually be found in Le Puis, our only tavern, where things were livelier.

To serve its several purposes, a tavern should have both places where one can be seen, and places where one cannot be seen. The designer of Le Puis had accomplished this splendidly. Being there was a little like being inside a stupendous honeycomb made of dozens of transparent globes, with a large spherical clearing at the center, in which danced two or three dozen small table-spheres, fuzzy with Velcro. The tables kept perfect station with each other; you could not move one more than a few inches before it maneuvered to correct, with little semivisible squirts of steering gas. (Odorless, I'm happy to report.) The pattern the tables made in space was not a simple grid, more of a starburst effect. You could hang around one of the tables (literally) until you met someone you liked, then adjourn for more private conversation to one of the dozens of surrounding sphericles—a word exactly analogous to "cubicle." By simply pulling the lips of the door closed, you soundproofed your sphericle. If you found that you wanted to get *really* private, the walls could be opaqued. It reminded me a little of the private chambers you sometimes find in really first-rate Japanese restaurants, with rice-paper-and-bamboo walls, soft cushions, and a door that sometimes slides open to admit attentive servers, fragrant food, and the chuckle of a nearby fountain.

I was with Kirra on my first visit to Le Puis; I guess it was our third or fourth day in Top Step. As we emerged from the igloo-tunnel that led from the main corridor into the heart of the honeycomb, we were approached by the largest and happiest human being I've ever seen, before or since.

"Crikey," Kirra said, watching him draw near. "Is that—?"

"God, I think it is," I said. "I should have guessed when I heard the name of this place."

"Hello, ladies," the apparition boomed as he came to a halt beside us. He wore an expression of barely contained glee. When he smiled, his cheeks looked like grapefruits. "Welcome to my joint. I got a nice little table for you. If you'll follow me . . ." He spun and jaunted gracefully away.

I've met a lot of celebrities in my time, but I felt a touch of awe. It was Fat Humphrey Pappadopolous, who used to own Le Maintenant, the Toronto restaurant in which Stardancers Incorporated was founded at the turn of the century. He was every bit as colorful and extraordinary as Charlie Armstead made him sound in the famous Titan Transmission of 1999.

Armstead says Humphrey was very fat when he was a groundhog. But I don't think he could have been as big then as he was the day I met him. I don't think you can be that fat in a one-gee field. In free fall, he was as graceful as any ballerina, and moved with stately elegance, like an extremely well-bred zeppelin.

He docked at a table with a good view of the room—even his bulk could not displace the table much—and we docked there too. "Let's see," he said to me, "you look to me like a nice dry white wine, maybe a Carrington 2004. And for you," he said to Kirra, "I got some Thomas Cooper, fresh from Oz. Peanuts and a little sharp cheese and some of those little oyster cracker things, right?" He drifted away, beaming.

He was one of those special people who so obviously love life, so much, that you feel like a jerk for not enjoying it as much as they are. And so you cheer up to about half their level, which is twice as cheerful as you were. And for the next little while, you notice that everyone you talk to seems to be smiling at you.

But how had he known Kirra was from Australia?

"Funny," I said, "he didn't *look* red. But that was exactly what I would have ordered, if he'd given me a chance. If I'd known he had a vintage that good in stock."

"Me too," she agreed. "Armstead didn't lie about that bloke. He reads minds, all right. Without Symbiosis."

"Natural talent, I guess."

The airflow in this space was breezier than usual, with the temperature upped just a notch to compensate. I understood why when someone a few tables away lit up a pipe of marijuana. The smell was familiar, pleasant. I hadn't smoked in years myself, but it reminded me of good times past. Childhood on Gambier Island. The dorms at SFU, and the party on Legalization Day. Motel rooms after performances on the road. Perhaps it was time I took it up again. No, not until *after* I had mastered zero gee well enough to dance. If then.

Fat Humphrey returned with our drinks in free-fall drinking bulbs, docked on the next table while passing them to us. Kirra's was three times the size of mine. I'm not much of a drinker; it seemed she was. "How do you do that, Mr. Pappadopolous?" I asked. "Know what we want and how much?"

"Call me Fat. How do you know how much to breathe?"

I gave up. "This is my friend Kirra. I'm Morgan McLeod."

"Hello, Kirra." He held out his hand, and when she tried to shake it he took hers and kissed it. She dimpled. The same thing happened to me. "You wouldn't be the Morgan McLeod that danced *Indices of Refraction* with Morris, would you?"

I admitted it.

"Goddamn. It's a pleasure to have you in my joint. You ever see her dance, Kirra?"

"No," she said.

"Then you one lucky person; you got a treat in store. Get Teena to dig some of her tapes and holos out of the Net for you."

"I will," she agreed.

I had never achieved the level of fame of a Baryshnikov or a Drummond, did not often get recognized by someone who was not in the dance world. It was dawning on me that Top Step was a nest of dance lovers.

"You wouldn't be Kirra from Queensland, wouldja?" he went on. "The singer?" Kirra dimpled and admitted it.

A nest of arts lovers.

"Both of you please be sure you sign my visitors' book on the way out. Look, I gotta tell this to ev'body comes here the first time: be careful with these." He produced from somewhere on his person a pair of small mesh bags, and tossed them to us. Peanuts and oyster crackers. A wedge of sharp cheese followed after them. "It ain't so bad if a little piece o' cheese gets away from you . . . but them peanuts and crackers got salt on 'em. Somebody gets one o' them in the eye, and maybe the bouncer has to go to work. And if you didn't guess from lookin' at me, I'm the bouncer." He shook with mirth at his own joke. We both promised we'd be careful. "Oh, Kirra, one more t'ing. You drinkin' that beer, an' you feel like you wanna burp, s'cuse me, but don't."

"Why not, Fat?"

"You back on Earth, your stomach got food on the bottom an' air on top, so you burp, no problem. But up here, the air an' the food is all mixed together, you see what I mean?"

She frowned. "Thanks, mate. Hey, how about the other direction?"

"No problem there. Lotsa people spend all their time up here fartin' around." He shuddered with mirth again. "I'll come back later and talk, okay? Meanwhile you both have a good time." He drifted majestically away.

We looked at each other and giggled together. Then we looked down at our drinks and snacks. Twice as many peanuts as oyster crackers. Kirra generally ate twice as much as I did at cafeteria meals. Fat Humphrey magic again.

"Something else, i'nt he?" Kirra said.

"He sure is. All right, out with it: tell me everything about Ben."

Her face glowed. "Oh, Morgan, i'nt he smashing? I don't usually fall for a bloke this quick—but oh my, he lights me up. He's so excited about everything, you know? The least little thing is special to him, and so it makes everything special for you to be around him. You know comin' here to space wasn't exactly my idea, I told you that: it just sort of landed on me plate and I took a bite—but Benjamin! He wants it so much, looks forward to it so much, I'm startin' to get kind of excited about it meself. He explains to me all about how marvelous it's gonna be, and I can understand it better. I was just thinkin' of all this as an extra long Walkabout—but he makes it sound like more fun than Christmas." She took a long swig of ale.

"He is fun to be around," I agreed. "He's sort of the backwards of my ex-husband. He had a way of making a good time dull."

She lowered her voice. "And he's a champion lover! He does a bit o' what Fat just did, knows what you want about a second before you know it yourself."

"Definitely the backwards of my ex."

"If I hadn't had to clear out so Robert could get some sleep, I might be there still. Hey, how are you and Robert gettin' along, then?"

"What the hell is that stuff floating in your beer?"

"What, this? It's yeast. Thomas Cooper leaves it in, for flavor. Kinda interestin' the way it swirls about like that: the zero gee saves you having' to shake up the bottle to get it off the bottom. Seriously, though, what about you and Robert? I had this lovely idea how handy it'd be if you two hit it off like Ben and me. We could swap roomies and—"

"Whoa!" I said. "Take your time." Change the subject again? No, deal with it. "I don't know how I feel about Robert . . . but I do know I'm not in any hurry. The most important thing on my mind right now is learning how to dance all over again, and that's all I want to think about until I get it done or it kills me. Robert will have to wait." *Now* change the subject. "I wonder how Fat Humphrey manages to decant wine properly in free fall? This is delicious."

Kirra started to answer, then took a sip of beer instead. "Look, Morgan, answer me this. Are we roommates, or are we friends?"

"Friends," I answered without hesitation. "I hope."

"Then listen'a me. There some blokes you can hold at arm's length and after a while they go away. But I know you, and I've seen you with Robert. He's got a hook in you . . . just a little one, maybe, but a hook. And you got one in him. You try keepin' him at arm's length forever, your arms're gonna start gettin' shorter. He ain't gonna go away. You want to get on with your dancin', it might be less distraction to just go ahead an' get it over with, see where it goes an' get it integrated. Might help to have somethin' to dance *about,* eh?"

I don't remember exactly what mumbled evasion I made. Just then a welcome distraction presented itself: the floorshow began.

Well, not exactly a floorshow. A single performer, a busker, doing an act I would have thought impossible in zero gee: juggling.

Free fall juggling is done barefoot. You do not make the balls or clubs or whatever go in a circle, because they won't. Instead you make them go in a rectangle. Hand to hand to foot to foot to hand. This particular juggler used orange balls of some resilient material, the size of real oranges. It seemed he was known and liked here; people broke off conversations to watch him and clap along. He had twinkling eyes and a goatee. Except for a G-string, he was barefoot to the eyebrows. He began in a slow motion that would simply not have been possible on Earth, then got faster and faster until the balls began to blur into an orange rectangle in the air before him. He started with four, but keep adding more from a pouch at his waist. I thought I counted as high as sixteen. Then suddenly he changed the pattern, so that they crossed over and back in front of him in an X-pattern, and then went back to a rectangle again. There was applause. He brought his feet up and hands down until the rectangle was a square, then a horizontal rectangle, and returned to the basic position. More applause. Suddenly he had one hand high over his head and the rectangle was a triangle. With the suddenly free left hand he took a joint from his pocket and struck it alight, took a deep puff. Loud applause. He seemed to pay no attention at all to the balls. He took another puff, tossed the joint to the nearest patron, and resumed work with all four limbs. The balls began to ever so gradually slow down, until they were individually distinguishable, and continued to slow. Within a minute he was back in the slow motion he'd started with—yes, there were sixteen balls—and still they kept decelerating. Without warning he flipped over, upside down to his original orientation, without disturbing the stately progress of the balls. Thunderous applause. Suddenly all the balls exploded outward from him, in a spherical distribution. I half-ducked, not one came near me, or anyone else. All sixteen bounced off something harmless and returned to him in almost-unison; he caught them all in his pouch and folded at the waist in a free fall bow. The house came down.

"Teena," I asked, "how do I tip that juggler five dollars?"

"It's done, Morgan," Teena said in my ears. "I've debited your account. His name is Christopher Micah."

He began a new routine involving what seemed to be razor-sharp knives. I didn't see how he could deal with knives with his feet—and didn't get to find out that day, because just then there was a small disturbance behind me. Kirra and I turned to look. Micah kept on working, properly ignoring the distraction.

Fat Humphrey was drifting just outside one of the opaqued bubble booths, talking softly to someone inside, who was answering him in too loud a voice. It seemed to be the second-oldest argument in history: the customer wanted more booze and Fat was cutting her off, politely and firmly. I started to turn back to catch Micah's knife act, when all at once I recognized the voice. It was Sulke.

Everyone else had returned their attention to the show. Kirra and I exchanged a glance and quietly slipped over to see if we could be of help, taking our drinks and munchies with us.

We were. Fat was handicapped somewhat by being an old friend of hers, but because Kirra and I were her students we were able to cheerfully bully her into quieting down. We swarmed into her booth with her, winked at Fat, and sealed the door to keep the noise inside.

"S'not fair, gahdammit," she complained. "I'm not even *near* drunk enough."

Kirra sent a peanut toward her in slow motion. "Catch that."

She missed in three grabs, then tried to catch it in her mouth and muffed that too. It went up her nose, and she blasted it clear with a loud snort. "I didn't say I wasn't drunk. Said I wasn't drunk *enough.*"

"For what?" I asked soothingly.

"To fall asleep, gahdammit. This is my one day off a week, the day I catch up on all the sleep I missed, an' if I fuck up and miss any I'll never get caught up."

"How come you gotta be drunker'n this to fall asleep?" Kirra asked.

"Because I'm scared." She heard the words come out and frowned. "No, I'm not, gahdammit, I'm pissed off is what I am! I'm not scared of anything. But I'm mad as hell."

"About what?"

She sneered. "Hmmph! How would you know? You groundhogs. You freebreathers. Never paid for an hour's air in your life, either of you. Where'd you come from, McLeod, North America somewhere, right? Worst come to worst, you could always go on welfare. Kirr', you could always jungle up and live off the land. There's *no fuckin' land to live off up here.*"

"Rough," Kirra agreed.

"You don't know the half of it! Nineteen friggin' outfits in space I can work for, and eighteen of 'em suck wind. The only place that doesn't treat you like shit is this one . . . and now crazy bastards are shootin' at it."

"Shooting at it!" I exclaimed. "What do you mean?"

"Aw fer chrissake, you really think the air plant went down last night by accident? You have any idea how many different systems have to fail in cascade before that can happen? You probably think it was space junk put a hole in your Elevator on the way up here, huh?"

I was shocked. "What makes you think it wasn't?"

"You were there. Did you see the object that hulled you?"

"Well, no. I think it ended up in the Steward's head."

She shook her head. "There was nothin' in Henderson's head but burned meat. It was a laser. They're keepin' it quiet, but a frenna mine saw the hull."

"But who the hell would want to hurt Top Step?"

She stared. "You serious? Religious fanatics, wanna pull down the false angels and their wicked cosmic orgy. Shiites, Catholics, Fundamentalists, take your pick. Then you got the Chinese, since old Chen Ten Li got tossed out on his ear. Then there's the other eighteen sonofabitch outfits I tol' you 'bout, and their parent corporations dirtside. Top Step could outcompete any one of them at what they do, and the only reason it doesn't is because the Starseed Foundation chooses not to. How could they not all hate this place?"

I thought of the epidemic of food poisoning that had run through Suit Camp just before takeoff. "Jesus."

She was frowning hugely. "Gahdammit. Not supposed to talk about this shit with you people. Prob'ly get shit for it. Bad for morale. Might get scared an' go home, kilobucks down'a tube. Forget I said anything, okay?"

"Sure," Kirra said soothingly.

"Thanks," Sulke said. "You're okay, for a freebreather." She reached out and snatched Kirra's beer, finished it in a single squeeze.

I placed my own drink unobtrusively behind me, and hoped it would stay there. "Sulke, tell me something. If being a free-lance spacer is really so bad—and I believe you—then why not opt out? Take that last step and become a Stardancer like us? Then you could tell Skyfac and Lunindustries and all the rest to go take a hike."

She boiled over. "You outa your gahdamn mind? You people are all assholes. Worse than assholes, you're *cowards:* solving your problems by runnin' away from them. You won't catch me doin' that shit. Maybe I can't ever go home again, but at least I'm human! I've hung around Stardancers a long time, and by Jesus they ain't human, and I can't *understand* how in hell a human bein' could deliberately stop being a human bein'. I'll teach you fools how to swim, but I got nothing but contempt for ya. Nobody gets inside Sulke Drager's head but Sulke Drager, an' don' you forget it, see?"

Like all true spacers, she was a rugged individualist. She was certainly paying a high price to be one in space.

"Do you have to go EVA to get home, Sulke?"

"Crash here on my day off," she said, eyes beginning to cross. "And even if I did, I can navigate safely in free space when I'm *dree* times trunker than this. That's why it's not fair that fat bastard cut me off."

"Well, since he did," Kirra said reasonably, "what do we want to stay around here and class up his place for him, then?"

"Damn right," I agreed. "Sleep's too precious to miss on his account. Let's quit this program."

Sulke allowed herself to be taken home. Teena guided the three of us to the dormitory where employees crashed. It was basically a cube full of sleepsacks, with minimal amenities and few entertainment facilities. If Top Step was the best of nineteen employers in space, the others had to be pretty bad.

By the time we got back to Le Puis, Micah had finished for the night. But the tenor sax player who'd replaced him was very good, had a big full Ben Webster sound, so we stayed and drank and tipped him, and this time remembered to sign Fat Humphrey's guest book—in tipsy scrawls—before we left. As we were doing so, he came up beside us. "You handled Sulke real nice," he said, "and I like her. You two didn't spend no money in here tonight, you understand?" We thanked him.

Then Kirra went to keep her rendezvous with her bug-eyed lover, and I went off to my gym to work.

To my surprise, the wine helped. This time I managed to set sixteen beats I could stand to watch on replay, and repeat them more or less at will. I was going to beat this! It was even harder than transitioning from ballet to modern had been, and I was no longer in my twenties . . . but I was going to do it.

It helped me forget the uneasiness that Sulke's talk of sabotage had put in the back of my mind. I was pretty sure she was wrong, anyway.

Kirra was still out when I got back to our room. I sat kûkanzen for about an hour, watched dance holos for a while in bed, then put on a sleep mask and earphones that played soft music so she wouldn't wake me when she came in.

Nevertheless I woke an hour or so later. There are no bedsprings to creak in zero gee, and they were probably making an honest effort to be quiet, but Kirra was after all a singer.

I thumbed the sleep mask up onto my forehead.

I can't claim I was a voyeurism virgin. Dancers generally lead a lively life, and once or twice in my checkered past I had watched live humans go at it—often enough, it had seemed to me. It's the oldest dance there is, of course, but as a spectator art it palls quickly, once the excitement of taboo-breaking is past.

But I never watched anyone *make love,* which is different, even to a mere witness.

Let alone in zero gee, which changes things.

They were beautiful together, moving in slow joyous unison, singing a soft, wordless song in improvised harmony, flexing together inside their sleepsack like a single beating heart.

A host of emotions ran through my mind. Annoyance that they were being so impolite, followed by the thought that in a few months I would be "in the same room with" *thousands* of love-making people, that soon none of us would ever again make love in private, that dealing with this disturbing situation was the best possible rehearsal I could have for what was to come, that if I couldn't deal with two friends making love three meters away, I'd never be able to deal with forty-odd thousand strangers making love inside my skull . . .

. . . and I couldn't get around the fact that watching them was turning me distinctly on. I had to deal with that, and with the fact that I was staring as much at Kirra as at Ben, and with jealousy of Kirra, and with the way my own growing arousal wanted me to get up and go find Robert and fuck his brains out, and with how another part of me that I didn't understand wouldn't let me do that, and it was hard to think about any of this stuff when I was getting horny enough to bark, and finally my hand crept down to my clitoris and began to move in slow circles, and as they increased in speed I realized with shock that Ben, unlike most men, had not taken his glasses off to copulate—

—his 360° vision glasses!

I froze in embarrassment for a long moment . . . and then I told myself he was too busy to pay attention to what was going on behind his back—no, I told myself the hell with it—and finished what I had started.

Eventually so did they. And then I think all three of us fell asleep. I know I did, feeling more relaxed than I had since I'd left Earth.

The next day the three of us discussed it over breakfast—Kirra brought it up, asking if they'd awakened me—and after some talk we agreed to be the kind of friends who can be that intimate among one another. It was something new for me, and a bit of a stretch: I'd never allowed anyone to observe me in ecstasy before except the one who was causing it. But in the days that followed I came to find it quite pleasant and natural to read a book, or watch TV, while Kirra and Ben made love a few meters away . . . and more than once the sight inspired me to pleasure myself. Kirra and Ben were delighted with this state of affairs, as it gave them a convenient place to make love whenever they wished—it seemed Robert was more inhibited, and so it was less comfortable for them in Ben's room.

I think it's different for men, harder to watch and not participate, harder to let yourself be watched. For some of them masturbating seems to represent a kind of defeat in their minds. Sad.

Those first few days in Top Step pretty much set the pattern for the next four weeks . . . to the extent that there was a pattern. Meals and classes loosely defined the day, but we had great slabs of unstructured free time after both morning and afternoon class, and our evenings, to spend as we wished—piefaced in Le Puis if that was what we chose.

One thing we all did was swap life stories. There'd been no time to do so back at Suit Camp, where every spare minute was spent studying or undergoing tests. I can't recall how many times I told my own story until everyone had heard it. One common theme that ran through the stories I heard in return was technological obsolescence. Just as the automobile had once ruined the buggy whip trade, the recent enormous strides in nanotechnology (made with much help from the Starseed Foundation) had made a lot of formerly lucrative occupations superfluous. Suddenly a lot of white-collar workers found themselves facing the same dilemma as a dancer or an athlete in her forties: should I start life over from square one, or opt out of the game altogether? Quite a few of them chose Symbiosis.

Another common topic of conversation was politics, but—and I know you'll find this hard to believe, for I did—political discussions somehow never once degenerated into arguments. Even in the first weeks, we were starting to find all political differences of Earthbound humans less and less relevant to anything in our own lives—and the tendency increased with time.

I'd expected to work harder than this. I said as much to Reb one day during class, sometime during the first week. "I guess I just pictured us all spending most of our time . . . working."

"At what, Morgan?"

"I don't know, studying concrete stuff we'll need when we're

Stardancers. Solar system navigation, ballistics, solar sailing, astronomy, uh, zero-gee engineering and industry, nanotechnology, picotechnology—things like that." There was a murmur of agreement from the others in the class.

"You may study any of those, if you wish," he said. "Some of you are doing so, on your own initiative. But it's not necessary. Studying *data,* memorizing facts, is not necessary. You won't need those facts until you become a Stardancer and join the Starmind . . . and then you'll *have* them. That's the beauty of telepathy."

He was right, of course. The instant I entered Symbiosis, I'd be part of the group consciousness Reb called the Starmind. I'd have total access to the combined memories of all living Stardancers, something over forty thousand minds. Anything they knew, I would know, when and if I needed to know it.

As they would know everything I knew . . .

You can be told about something like that a thousand times, and remind yourself a million . . . and still you just can't get your mind around it, somehow.

"What you need to study," Reb continued, "is not facts . . . but attitude, a flexible mindset, so that encompassing that much scope doesn't destroy you. That's why meditation is the best work you can do."

"What exactly do you mean by 'destroy'?" a woman named Nicole asked. I thought: *what a dumb question.*

Reb brightened. "A good question."

"I think so," Nicole agreed. "I know the *odds* of failure—I passed the exam like everybody. One percent of those who enter Symbiosis suffer what they called 'catastrophic mental trauma.' But I don't know what that *means.* I mean, they explained it to me back dirtside—but I need somebody to explain the explanation. Can somebody's mind really . . . well, collapse, from having forty thousand other minds suddenly crash in on it?"

There was nervous laughter.

Reb did not smile. "Sometimes," he said.

The laughter died.

"Those forty thousand minds do *not* all come crashing in at once . . . but the significance of their existence does. Some minds find that intolerable."

"What happens to them?" Nicole asked.

"What happens when a star implodes?" Reb replied.

"Depends on how massive it is," someone said.

Reb nodded. "It is much the same with a panicked ego. Whether it can survive telepathic union depends on how massive it is."

"How do you mean?"

"Think of a mind which has never loved," Reb said. "It *knows* that it is the center of the Universe, the only thing that is truly real, that matters. Then its body swallows some mysterious red gunk, and WHACK! Suddenly it knows better. The walls of its skull drop away; for the first time ever, it is naked. Observed . . . no, more; *touched* . . . in its most intimate chinks and crannies by forty thousand strangers. Mind sees Starmind, and knows its own true smallness. By all accounts it is a terrifying realization."

This was exactly what I had been trying to imagine for weeks. Could I live with that much truth? Did I have the courage to be that naked? To let that big audience come swarming over the stage?

"Now sometimes an ego is so entrenched in itself that it *refuses* to yield the floor, *will not* love nor be loved. It rejects what it perceives—incorrectly—as a threat to its identity. Mad with fear, it seeks escape, and there is nowhere to go but inward. It implodes like a collapsing star, literally an ego deflating. Most often it shrinks down to a small hard dense core, like a neuron star. Invisible. Invulnerable. It must hurt terribly. Such catatonics can sometimes be saved, healed. With time. With skill. Many wise and compassionate minds work nonstop to do so; so far they have a discouraging success rate."

He had our total attention.

"But once in a long while, an imploding star is so massive, it collapses past the point where it can exist. It leaves our Universe, becomes a black hole. Similarly, if an ego is massive enough, it may react to telepathic union by collapsing past the point where it can sustain itself. It suicides rather than surrender. It simply . . . goes away. The flame blows out. You could say it dies. What is left is a very long-lived humanoid with the mind of a plant or a starfish. These few are placed in stable orbits, and they are. . ." He paused. "Uh, 'cherished' is closer than 'mourned,' I think. By the rest of the Starmind."

"What's the ratio of deaths to comas?" Nicole asked.

"About one to a hundred. Roughly the same as the overall ratio of failures to successes."

You could hear gears grinding as she tried to work out the arithmetic. Several seconds passed. "So out of every thousand people who eat red—"

"Out of every *ten* thousand who attempt Symbiosis, ninety-nine will go into stasis, and one will die," he told her. "Approximately. In fact there have been eight deaths, and five hundred and eighty-seven catatonics, of whom fifty-three have been healed so far . . . and an additional six have died."

There was a glutinous silence in the room.

Not that many of us, or even any of us, were surprised. Nicole may have been the only person in the room to whom these figures were news. I certainly knew them; it seemed to me that anyone who had come this far without knowing them was an idiot. But they were sobering statistics just the same.

And, it was just dawning on me for the first time that the Starmind, as Reb called it, the telepathic community I was proposing to join, did not discriminate against people I considered idiots. I was dismayed by how dismayed that made me. Me, an intellectual snob? Apparently.

"Look on the bright side," Reb said. "You are five hundred times *more* likely to die *during training,* before you ever get to Symbiosis. Die completely, soul *and* body, in some EVA accident. And you're two hundred times more likely to suffer serious mental breakdown and be sent dirtside."

Now, there were some grim figures. Out of every hypothetical standard class of one hundred, an average of five died before ever attempting Symbiosis . . . and two went seriously nuts from brooding about it. I'd read about one class, back in the early days of Top Step, where nearly half had died, most of them in a single ghastly accident.

Then there was the drop-out rate to be considered. An average of twelve in every class changed their minds and went home—often at the last minute. Another five balked: when three months were up, they decided not to decide. The Foundation would let you hang around Top Step as long as you wanted . . . *if* you were willing to work for your air, *and* had a job skill they needed at the time. After eleven more months—if you were still alive—your body was permanently, irrevocably adapted to zero gee: you had to either sign on with the Foundation permanently—if they would have you—or else become part of the permanent-transient population of spacers, like Sulke. Or, of course, get off the dime and eat Symbiote.

"But if you survive long enough to attempt Symbiosis," Reb went on, "your chances of success are much higher than those of, say a pregnant woman to birth successfully. The kind of mind that will collapse when exposed to telepathy tends not to come here to Top Step at all. Either it never applies, or we filter it out in the preselection stage, or it drops out during Suit Camp."

"So why go through two or three months of preparation?" Nicole asked. "I read that some people have become Stardancers without it."

"Because experience has shown it eases the transition," Reb said patiently. "At best, Symbiosis is painful . . . one Stardancer likened it to a turtle having its shell ripped away . . . but those who have had the training agree it helps enormously. If you can learn to live without the false distinctions of 'up' and 'down,' you probably can learn to live with the equally false distinctions between 'me' and 'not-me.' "

"So why so much free time, why aren't we working all the time?" Nicole wanted to know.

"Oh, for Christ's sake, Nicole!" Glenn blurted. By this time I was so annoyed with Nicole's broken-record questioning myself that I grunted in agreement.

Reb looked at me. "You cannot think Nicole's question is foolish, Morgan. You asked it yourself a minute ago."

You blush easier in free fall, and more spectacularly.

"But it is foolish, nonetheless," he went on gently. "You *are* working all the time, Nicole. Everyone is, everyone everywhere. You can't help but keep working. Didn't you know that?"

She looked confused.

"Nicole, I could have uncommon intuition and insight, and spend every minute of the next two months in your company, and *still* I would not know a tenth as much as you do about what you need to learn now, and what is the best way for you to learn it. Even Fat Humphrey's kind of 'telepathy' doesn't go that deep. That's why we try to make sure you'll have lots of so-called 'free' time here, to work on it without being distracted. There isn't a lot of time left before you will have to make a big decision, and we don't want your schooling to get in the way of your education."

"But what are we supposed to *do* with all this free time?"

"You will know," Reb told her. "You will know."

7

When the ordinary man attains knowledge
He is a sage;
When the sage attains understanding
He is an ordinary man.
—Zen koan

I certainly knew what to do with *my* time. Each night Robert tutored me for an hour, then I spent the rest of the evening dancing in private until I couldn't move anymore. I hadn't worked so hard in years. But my back and knees continued to hold up, thanks to free fall . . . and as the days turned into weeks, I began to get somewhere. By the end of the second week I could do a fair imitation of *Liberation,* and I could quote sections of *Mass Is a Verb*. More important, I was making some progress on a new piece of my own. Choreography had never been my strong suit—but there was something about zero gee that made it come easier. I still wasn't ready to show anything to an audience, but I was content to be making progress, however slow it might be. I had thought, for an endless time, that I was finished as a dancer. It was like a miracle, like being reborn, to get another chance; there was no hurry. I luxuriated in each painful minute.

Ben and Kirra knew what to do with their time too—and I don't just mean making love. Ben did *not* fully acquire all the fundamentals of jaunting in two days—much less the fine points—but he did become the star pupil in our shift, and under his tutelage Kirra too became something of prodigy. They progressed just as fast in morning class, learning less tangible skills like spherical thinking, spatial orientation and conscious control of their own metabolisms and mental states. By the third week Reb admitted that they were good enough to start EVA instruction right away . . . but the system wasn't set up to allow it, and they stayed behind with the rest of us dummies, serving as assistant instructors in Sulke's class. (And, at Reb's insistence, getting paid for doing so. They both donated their unwanted salaries to the Distressed Spacer's Fund, which made Sulke happy.)

Robert was almost as adept when he arrived as Ben became, but seemed disinterested in teaching the group. He spent most of his free time, according to Ben, designing free fall structures on his computer terminal in his room. I rarely saw him in Le Puis. Occasionally I ran across him in Sol Three. He was always by himself. We would chat quietly, then part. Part of me had hoped that he'd take me off the hook by becoming involved with some other woman. I certainly wouldn't have blamed him if he had; most of our fellow students seemed to be pairing up. He continued to tutor me every night, without pressing me for further intimacy. We remained aware of each other, slowly building a charge.

It had been a long time since a man had courted me with that kind of mixture of determination and patience. I liked it.

According to Teena, our class had one of the most painless, trouble-free Postulancies in the history of Top Step. Only three of us dropped out and went back to Earth during the first two weeks (all three for the most common of reasons: persistent inability to tolerate a nonlinear environment, to live without up and down). None of us got so crazy that we had to be sent home. None of us died, or sustained serious injuries. There were no incidents of violence, even on the level of a fistfight. Six of us got married—all at once, to each other. (Ben and Kirra were that kind of committed, but never bothered with any formal ceremony or celebration.) All of us formed friendships, which expanded in informal affinity groups, which somehow did not become exclusionary cliques. Dorothy Gerstenfeld logged an all-time record minimum of complaints and emergencies. As Reb said one day, smiling his Buddha smile, "Good fellowship seems to be metastasizing." People who wanted them gravitated to temple or zendo or shrink or encounter group or whatever it took to ease their pain or enhance their mindfulness, and Le Puis became the first bar I'd ever seen that rarely seemed to have anything but happy drunks.

All this was in sorry contrast to the planet we orbited. From the great window in Sol Three, Earth *looked* peaceful, serene. But we all followed Earthside news, and knew just what an anthill in turmoil it really was. That was the month that China and Argentina were making war noises, and none of the other major players could figure out which side to back. For one three-day period we honestly thought they might start setting off Big Ones down there at any moment. Who really knew whether the UN-SDI net would actually work? One afternoon when I was meditating in Sol Three I mistook a sudden flare of reflected sunlight off Mar Chiquita, a huge Argentinian lake, for a nuke signature—just for an instant, but it was a scary instant.

I was surprised to find that political upheaval on Earth did not carry over to Top Step. We had several ethnic Chinese besides Robert in our class, and close to a hundred inboard altogether, as well as an equal number of Hispanophones and four actual Argentinians. (One of the three Suit Camps was located in Ecuador.) If there was ever so much as a harsh word exchanged among any of them, I didn't hear about it—and any space habitat has a grapevine that verges on telepathy.

I did some reading, guided by Teena, and learned that from the very beginnings of space exploration, spacers have always tended to feel themselves literally above the petty political squabbles of the groundhogs below. Immigrants to a new country can continue to cling to their ethnic or national or religious identity for a generation or two, but immigrants to space quite often seem to leave theirs on the launchpad. And Stardancer-candidates have even less reason to get agitated about the doings of nations than most spacers. In a matter of weeks, we'd all be surrendering our passports.

As for myself, I'd never felt especially patriotic about being a Candadian. But then, that was a notorious characteristic of most Canadians. The only thing we were proud of was not being Americans.

We all followed Earth news . . . but even as the drama below us began to get dangerously interesting, it became less and less relevant to us. We spent less and less time watching Earth in Sol Three. We retained concern for the suffering of human beings—but for humans *as a species:* the labels and abstractions they used to separate themselves seemed more and more absurd.

We weren't spacers yet. But we were no longer Terrans.

* * *

By the end of the third week, Reb and Sulke between them had brought us former groundhogs to the point where we could not only stand to be in the dark in zero gee, but could navigate reliably in darkness.

Do you have any idea how incredibly far that was?

One of the first humans ever to *live* in space, a member of the Skylab crew, woke one night to find that the light in his sleeping compartment had failed. That compartment compared with a coffin for roominess. He knew exactly where the switch for the emergency backup lighting was located. It took him nearly half an hour to find it, half an hour on the trembling verge of fullblown panic. And he was a hypertrained jock. The first time Reb doused the lights, for not more than a minute, the classroom rang with screams, and about a third of us ended up having to go change our clothes. In the total absence of either visual or kinesthetic cues, your hindbrain decides that the sensation of falling is literal truth, and you just come unstuck. All the rational thought in the world doesn't help. You clutch the first wall or structure or person you encounter like a panicking drowner, and hang on for dear life, heart hammering. Five of us dropped out that night.

But methodical disciplines of breath-control and muscle-control and self-hypnosis do help, and practice helps most of all. Once you get past the terror part, the disorientation diminishes quickly. We played orientation and navigation games. For instance: three of you crawl along the walls of the classroom in the dark, humming to each other, until your ears tell you that you're all roughly equidistant in the spherical room; then you jaunt for where you think the center of the room is, and try to meet your mates there . . . ideally without cracking your skull or putting someone's eye out. It was fun, once we all started getting good at it.

And it took us that last step toward being comfortable without even an imaginary local vertical. We lost our tendency to line up with whomever we were talking to or working with, and started living three-dimensionally without having to make a mental effort.

And that started to affect us all in subtle psychological ways, broadening us, opening us up, undoing other sorts of equally rigid preconceptions about the universe. Up/down may be the first dichotomy a baby perceives (even before self/notself), the beginning of duality, or either/or, yes/no logic. Hierarchy depends on the words "high" and "low" having meaning. Floating free of gravity is just as exhilarating in space as it is in dreams, and constant exhilaration can help solve a lot of human problems. The therapeutic value of skydiving has long been known, and we never had to snap out of the reverie and pull our ripcords.

One by one, we became more pleasant people to be with than we had been back on terra firma. Glenn, for instance, lost a great deal of her dogmatism, became more flexible, started making friendships with people she had considered airheads back in Suit Camp. Eventually she even lost the frown that had seemed her natural expression.

Yes, it was our time of Leavetaking, of saying goodbye to our earthly lives, and yes, some of it was spent in solemn meditation in Solarium or zendo or chapel or temple. But the solemnity was balanced by an equal and opposite quantum of gaiety.

Dorothy Gerstenfeld had been right, back on that first day: zero gee tended to make us childlike again in significant ways. We were doing some of the same sort of metaprogramming that a small child does—redoing it, really, with different assumptions—and do you remember how much *fun* it was being a small child?

We had the kind of late-night bull sessions I hadn't had with anyone since college, full of flat-out laughter and deep-down tears, like kids around an eternal campfire with all the grownups gone to bed.

There are so many games you can play in zero gee. Acrobatics; spherical handball, billiards, and tennis; monkey bars; tag . . . the list is endless. Even a moderately good frisbee thrower becomes a prodigy. You'd be astonished how many solid hours of entertainment you can get from a simple glass of water, coaxing it into loops and ropes and bubbles and lenses with the help of surface tension. A man named Jim Bullard devised a marvelous game involving a hollow ball within which a small quantity of mercury floated free, causing it to wobble unpredictably in flight; in gravity it would have just been a nuisance, but in zero gee it was an almost-alive antagonist. I used my Canadian background to invent one of my own: 3-D curling. The idea was to scale pucks so gently that air resistance caused them to come to rest in an imaginary sphere in the center of the room, while knocking away your opponent's pucks. Your teammate tried to help by altering the puck's trajectory inflight with a small compressed-air pen—with strictly limited air which had to last him the whole round. As in curling, it took forever to find out how good your shot was . . . and you all had to keep moving while you waited, since the room's air-circulation had to be shut off. Robert and I teamed up at it and soon were beating all corners. Ben invented a three-dimensional version of baseball—but it was so complicated that he never managed to teach it to enough people to get a game going. With assistance from Teena, Kirra actually managed to locate a piece of genuine wood somewhere inboard (at a guess, I'd say there isn't enough real wood in all of space to build a decent barn; even the legendary Shimizu Hotel uses a superb fake), and borrowed tools to work it from one of the construction gangs who daily burrowed ever deeper into the rock heart of Top Step. When she was done, she got permission from Chief Administrator Mgabi, and took her creation down to the Great Hall. A small crowd went along to watch. She tested the breeze, locked her feet under a handrail to steady herself, and threw the thing with considerable care and skill. That boomerang was still circling the Hall when she reached out and caught it three hours later. I wanted her to let it keep going, but she and I and the volunteers at the major tunnel mouths who kept passing pedestrians from jaunting out into the thing's flight path all had to get to class.

One of the best games of all could be played solo in your room without working up a sweat: browsing through the Net. We all had Total Access, like the most respected and funded scholars in the Solar System, and could research to exhaustion any subject that interested us, initiate datasearches on a whim which would have bankrupted us back on Earth, download music and literature and visual art to our heart's content. Ben in particular was heavily addicted to Netwalking, and it was a common occurrence for Kirra to have to drag him away from his terminal to go eat . . . whereupon he would begin babbling to her about what he'd just been doing or reading. Glenn too binged heavily, as did several others. As for myself, all I really used my access for was to watch hour after hour of Stardancer works, especially the ones that Shara Drummond and the Armsteads performed in. They were unquestionably the best dancers in space, and not just because they had been the first. By that point in history, all Stardancer dances were officially choreographed by the Starmind as a whole, in concert . . . and that must have been to a large extent true. But from time to time I was sure I recognized phrases or concepts that were pure Shara or pure Charlie/Norrey, even in works in which they didn't physically appear.

On the last day of week three, Kirra sprang a surprise on us. Reb called her up beside him in class that morning, and told us that she had something special to share with all of us. Most of us knew by then about her background and reason for being here; for the benefit of those who didn't know all the details, she briefly sketched out the history of the Dreamtime, and the Songlines, and the importance of Song in the Aboriginal universe.

"My people want to start movin' out into space," she finished up, "and so my job is to start sussin' out the Songs for all this territory, so's we can come make Walkabout here without bein' afraid it'll all up and turn imaginary on us."

"How're you doing?" someone asked.

"Well, that's what I'm doin' here in front of you. It's been a lot slower goin' than I expected . . . I got the Song o' Top Step now, but. An' I want to sing it for all you bastards." (By now we had all learned that to an Australian, "bastard" held no negative connotations, meaning simply "person," usually but not always male. Similarly, "tart" merely meant "female person.")

A surprised and delighted murmur went through the room: most of us knew how much her responsibility weighed on her. I was thrilled.

"I just finished it this mornin' before brekkie, even Ben an' me roomie haven't heard it yet. You all been here as long as I have, you ought to hear it. This ain't just a tabi, a personal song, this is a proper *corroboree* Song, an' it calls for an audience. Anyway I wanted you all to hear it, an' Reb said it was all right with him if I did it here."

There were universal sounds of approval and encouragement.

"All right, then: here goes."

She took her boomerang from her pocket, slapped it rhythmically against her other palm for ten counts, and began to sing.

I cannot supply a translation of the words, and will not reproduce them as she sang them, because they were in Padhu-Padhu, a secret ritual language known only to Aboriginals, so secret (she explained to me later) that its very existence was unsuspected by Caucasian scholars until the late twentieth century.

And it doesn't matter, because there were very few words in what she sang. Very little of her song's information content was verbal. It was the melody itself that was important.

How can I describe that melody to you? I doubt that there is anything in your experience to compare it to. In fact, I doubt that there would have been much in another Aboriginal's experience to compare it to; I'd heard a number of their Songs from Kirra and this was unlike them in ways I'm not equipped to explain even if you were equipped to understand me. It did not behave like any other melody I'd ever heard, yet somehow without thereby becoming unpleasing to the ear.

It began at the very bottom of her alto register, and arced up in a smooth steady climb that suggested the shuttle flight from Earth. It opened out into a repeated five-tone motif whose majesty and regularity seemed to represent Top Step in its great slow orbit. Then the song changed, became busier. It behaved much like a jaunting Postulant, actually, gliding lazily, then putting itself into tumbles, then straightening out, bouncing off imaginary walls, coming to a halt and then kicking off again. Like a jaunter's progress, her melody never really stopped, for she had mastered the didgeridu player's trick of breathing in and out at the same time so that she never had to pause for breath. I closed my eyes as I listened, and the twists and turns her voice took evoked specific places in Top Step powerfully for me. The Great Hall, Solarium Three, a merry little flurry that was unmistakably Le Puis, a slow solemn ululation that was Harry Stein at the window of Solarium One. Somewhere in the middle was a frankly sensual movement that expressed zero gravity lovemaking, explicitly and movingly. Ben's humour was in it, and Kirra's mischievousness, and the richness of their love for each other. At the end, the five-tone theme returned, first with little trills of embellishment and then at last in its pure form, slower and slower until she drew out its last note into a drone, and fell silent.

I don't know how long we all drifted, silent, motionless, like so many sea lions. Reb was the first to shake off stasis and put his hands together, then Ben joined and then me and then the whole room exploded in applause and cheers that lasted for a long time. One of the loudest was Jacques LeClaire, the other musician in the room. She accepted our applause without smiling, as her due—or so I thought.

"It's called "Taruru,'" she said when the noise had died down. "That means a lot o' things, really. 'Last glow of evening,' and 'dying embers,' and 'peace o' mind,' kinda rolled into one."

"Teena," Reb said, "save the Song Kirra just sang to her personal files as 'Taruru.'"

"Yes, Reb."

"Kirra," Reb went on, "I think you should send that recording, as is, to your tribe."

"You think? I can do it again any time, just like that: that's the point of a Songline Song."

"I understand. But send that copy. Please. I would be honoured." Ben and I and others made sounds of vigorous agreement. Jacques called, "*Oui!* That is a take."

She nodded. "Right, then. Teena, transmit `Taruru' to my Earthside number, would you?"

"It's done. Receipt has . . . just been acknowledged by your phone."

"What time is it in Queensland now?"

"Five-fourteen PM."

"Bonzer. Yarra can play it for the Yirlandji Elders tonight after supper. Teena, everybody here can have a copy if they want."

There were more cheers. Kirra was well liked.

"You'll void your copyright," Glenn warned.

Kirra blinked at her. "What copyright? I didn't *make up* the bloody thing, mate, I just sang it. It's the Song of this place, see? It was here before I got here. You can't copyright the wind."

Now I understood why she'd heard our applause without smiling. She'd assumed we were applauding the Song, not here performance.

"One suggestion," Reb said.

"Yes, Reb?"

"Transmit a copy to Raoul Brindle."

There was a murmur. Brindle had been the most famous living composer for over thirty years. *"Oui,"* Jacques called again, and several others echoed him. *"Da!" "Si!" "Hai!"*

Kirra looked thoughtful. "Be a bloody expensive phonecall, but.

He an' the Harvest Crew aren't more than halfway back from Titan, it'd have to go by laser."

"If it did," Reb said, "Top Step would pay the cost; Raoul has left specific orders that he wants to hear anything you want to send him. But a laser is not necessary. Since you are willing to release the Song to the public domain, just phone any nearby Stardancer and sing it. Raoul will hear it instantly."

"Why, sure! I'll never get used to this telepathy business. Hey, Teena, send that Song to the nearest Stardancer that ain't busy, addressed to Raoul Brindle, would ya?"

"Transmission in progress," Teena said. "Routing through Harry Stein, in realtime. Transmission ends in a little over five minutes."

There was one more round of applause, and then Kirra joined the rest of us and Reb began regular class. But five minutes later, Reb paused in the middle of a sentence.

"Excuse me, friends. Teena has just informed me that there is a phonecall for Kirra from Raoul Brindle. Kirra?"

"Open line, Teena."

Raoul Brindle said, "Hello, Kirra."

"G'day, mate," she said, as though living legends phoned her up all the time.

"I don't want to interrupt your class. I just wanted to say that your Song has been heard by all members of the Starmind presently in circuit, from the orbit of Venus to that of Uranus. Our response condenses down to: *hurry, sister*. We await your Graduation. I'd be honoured if you'd sail on out here and meet me once you're Symbiotic. Oh, and there's a waiting list of one hundred and eighty-seven Stardancers who'd like to have a child with you if you're willing. Uh, I'm one of 'em."

Kirra blinked. "Well, if I'm gonna live forever I suppose I got to do somethin' with my time. I'm willin' to discuss it with the lot of you bastards—but the line forms behind me Benjamin here. I think he's got dibs on the first half dozen or so."

"No hurry," Raoul agreed. "I would like to score your Song for didgeridu, mirrimba and walbarra, if you don't mind."

"Oh please!" she said. "And send it me, will you? I hated havin' to leave me instruments behind. Have you really got 'em all out there with you?"

"In my head," he said. "Once you're Symbiotic, you'll find that's all you really need. But I can reprogram my simulator to make a recording you can hear now."

"That'd be smashin'. About this comin' out there to meet you, though . . . what's the point? I mean, I'll be just as near to you if my body's right here, won't I?"

"Even for telepaths, touch has special meaning," he said. "In one sense you're right . . . but I'd like to shake your hand sooner, rather than later. It shouldn't take you more than a few weeks."

"It would make a lovely honeymoon trip, love," Ben said. Under her influence he had lately been developing the ability to speak short sentences, and then stop. It was some of the strongest evidence I'd seen yet that Top Step could radically alter character.

She smiled suddenly. "Right, then. We'll do it—singin' all the way!"

The room rocked with cheers.

I could not completely suppress a twinge of envy. I wished I were coming along in my art as fast as she was in hers. But I was terribly happy for her.

The next day was Sunday. (I did mention that we used a six-day work week in Top Step, didn't I?) I spent the whole morning working out with Robert, the whole afternoon rehearsing in my studio, and the whole evening drinking Irish coffee in Le Puis with Robert and Kirra and Ben. Fat Humphrey had solved the zero-gee Irish coffee problem with a custom drinking bulb: a large chamber for coffee and booze, and a smaller one full of whipped cream; you sucked the former through the latter. Micah juggled, and Jacques LeClaire put on a lovely impromptu performance on the house synth. To everyone's surprise, Glenn jumped in and sang two numbers, very well, in a pure, controlled alto. She was roundly cheered, and blushed deeply. Then Kirra had to sing the Song of Top Step for those who hadn't heard it. The applause was deafening. So many drinks were credited to her account that she never paid for another dram the whole time she was inboard. It was a memorable night.

Robert kissed me goodnight at my door, not pushing it. I sort of wished he had. But not enough to push it myself.

* * *

Monday we all came to class excited—some eager, some anxious. Today a new stage in our training began. We were all dressed in our p-suits, airtanks and all, and we certainly were a colourful bunch. As we entered the room, Reb gave each of us a quick, warm handclasp and a private smile. His p-suit was forest green. The room looked different: all Velcro had been stripped from the chamber; its spherical wall was smooth and shiny.

"As you know," he said when we were assembled, "today we begin a week of EVA simulation. We've discussed and prepared for it. Some of you may experience disorientation, fear, perhaps even panic. This is normal and nothing to be self-conscious about. If you feel it's becoming too much, say so and I'll turn the walls off at once. It may help to take a visual fix, now, on those nearest you."

I mapped myself in relation to Robert and Reb.

"Close your hoods, now."

We did so, and there was a soft sighing as my suit air kicked in. It was the only sound: these p-suits had radios that filtered out breathing sounds automatically, and there was no chatter.

"Remember," Reb's voice said in my ear then, "please do not use your thrusters until I tell you to. Try to remain still. This is going to be startling enough without having a train wreck. Are you all ready? Teena, begin simulation."

Top Step went away!

Suddenly we were all floating in raw, empty space. It didn't matter that we were all expecting it: the transition was as shocking as a roller-coaster plunge. A flurry of involuntary motion went through the room, and my earphones buzzed with the sum of dozens of grunts, gasps, and assorted exclamations—including my own "Dear Christ!" I swallowed hard and clung to my fix on Robert and Reb. If they were all right, I was too.

"Remember your breathing!" Reb called.

Oh yes. Inhale, *slowly,* hold it for the same interval, exhale *completely,* hold, *feel* the breath, follow it, become it . . . three weeks of training kicked in and I began to calm down, to try and appreciate the incredible sight.

The illusion provided by the spherical holo wall of the classroom was terribly effective. Seeing space through the window of a Solarium is much different than actually being out *in* it, surrounded on all sides by infinity. Intellectually I knew it was an illusion, but it took my breath away just the same.

Earth was off to my left, turning lazily, Luna above my head, and the Sun was at my back. Top Step did not exist in this simulation, nor the Nanotech Safe Lab nor any of the other factories and modules that surrounded Top Step. All around me was eternal cold dark, and the ancient coals of a billion billion suns. For the first time in my life I began to get an emotional grasp of just how *far away* they were. In TV scifi the stars are just down the street. It suddenly came home to me just how preposterous was the notion that Man or Stardancer would ever reach them. Me, the whole human race, the whole Starmind: we were all brief, inconsequential flickers in this endless blackness—

The holo was so good that even the shadows were right. That is, the side of anyone that faced the Sun was brightly lit . . . and the other side seemed not to exist at all, unless it occulted some sunlit object behind it. In space there is no atmosphere to diffuse light and mitigate shadows. Of course there, in the room, there actually *was* air—we were breathing p-suit air only to maintain the simulation—but the holo corrected for that and fooled our eyes.

I had thought I was used to being in free fall. But I had never had this far to fall. In Top Step the longest you could possibly jaunt in a straight line before docking with something was about a hundred meters, in the Great Hall. But if someone were to give me a mischievous shove now, I would fall *for eternity* . . . or so my eyes tried to tell me, and my stomach believed them implicitly. I had no umbilical tether to catch me; in this simulation there was nothing closer than Terra to tether *to*.

Inhale, hold, exhale . . .

From Earth all you can see of the Milky Way is a streak in the sky like a washed-out rainbow. I could see the whole stupendous galactic lens edge on, bisecting the Universe. The starfield was so magnificent that for the first time in my life I understood how even some educated people could believe it ruled their destinies.

Reb said nothing further, let us soak in it. Someone was swearing, softly and steadily and devoutly, a female voice. Someone else was weeping, a male. Kirra was humming under her breath, quite unconsciously I think. All at once someone giggled, and then Jacques did too, and then others, and the very idea of giggling in space was so brave and silly that I had to laugh myself, and I think we might have gotten a group belly-laugh going if Nicole hadn't picked just then to scream. That first split second of it before the radio's automatic level control damped her volume went through my ears like a hot knife; involuntarily I started and went into a tumble. So did almost everyone else, and a train wreck began—

"Cut!" Reb told Teena calmly, and the illusion vanished at once.

We were back in our familiar classroom. The transition was just as wrenching as it had been in the other direction; we seemed to have been instantaneously teleported into the heart of Top Step. We floundered about like new chums, and gaped at each other. Reb flashed to Nicole's side and held her until she stopped screaming and began to cry softly against his chest. He summoned her roommate with his eyes, and had Nicole conducted from the room, sobbing feebly.

I found that Robert was by my side, and that I was glad he was there, and indeed was clutching tightly to his strong arm. Somehow he mentally integrated up our separate masses and vectors and used his wrist and ankle thrusters to bring us to a dead stop together, in a spot where no one else was on a collision course.

"Wow!" he said hoarsely.

"It still gets to you?" I asked.

"What do you mean, 'still'? I've been in space many times, yes—but that was my first time EVA. In simulation that good, I mean."

It surprised me a little, I'd sort of assumed a space architect would have to go outdoors to check on details of a job in progress. But it warmed me toward Robert to find him as moved and shaken as I was by the experience.

He was kind and sensitive and patient and attentive, and very attractive, and he wanted me. What was I waiting for? I couldn't explain it, even to myself. I just knew I wasn't ready.

"Are you ready?" Reb called, making me jump involuntarily. "All right, let's get back to the simulation."

Class went on.

Nicole showed up at lunch, looking wan and pale. But she wasn't at supper that night. She never came to classes again, and within two days she was back Earthside.

I visited her and said goodbye before she left. It was awkward.

We had EVA simulation in Sulke's class too for the rest of that week—only her simulations included holographic "objects" we had to match vectors with, and for the last two days she installed a real set of monkey bars which we learned to use like zero-gee monkeys. (Part of our training consisted of watching holos of real monkeys bred in free fall. God, they're fast! They make lousy pets, though: so far only cats and some dogs have ever learned to use a zero-gee litterbox reliably.)

Three more people had dropped out by the end of the week. Their egos were simply not strong enough to handle being dwarfed into insignificance by the sheer size of the Universe.

I asked Reb about that in class one day. "It just seems paradoxical. You need a strong ego to endure raw space—and we're all here to lose our egos in the Starmind."

"You are not here to lose your ego," he corrected firmly. "You're here to lose your irrational fear of *other* egos."

"Irrational?" Glenn said.

"On Earth it is perfectly rational," Reb agreed. "On Earth, there are finite resources, and so underneath everything is competition for food and breeding rights. All humans have occasional flashes of higher consciousness, in which they see that cooperation is preferable to competition—but as long as the game *is* zero sum, competition is the rational choice for the long run every time. Read Hofstadter's *Metamagical Themas,* the chapter on the Prisoner's Dilemma game.

"But what the Symbiote has done is to change the rules, utterly. A human in Symbiosis has nothing to compete *for*. Cooperation becomes more than rational and pleasant: it's inevitable."

"How long does it take to unlearn a lifetime's habit of competition?" Glenn asked.

"An average of about three-tenths of a second," Reb said. "It's what your heart has always yearned for: to stop fighting and love your neighbor. Once you become telepathic you *know,* in your bones, without question, that it's safe to do that now."

Robert spoke up—unusually; he seldom drew attention to himself in Reb's class. "Isn't competition good for a species? What pressure is there on Stardancers to evolve? Or have they evolved as far as they can already?"

"Oh, no," Reb said. "Charlie Armstead said once, 'We are infants, and we hunger for maturity.' Animals improve through natural selection only—the fit survive. Humans improve through natural selection, and because they want to. We did not *evolve* the science of medicine, we *built* it, painfully, over thousands of years, to preserve those natural selection would have culled. Stardancers improve because they want to, only. Their brave hope is that intelligence may just be able to do as well at evolution as random chance."

Robert nodded. "I think I see. It took *millions* of years for chance to produce human sentience . . . and then it took that sentience *thousands* of years to produce civilization. Telepathic sentience, that didn't have to fight for its living, might do comparable things in a lifetime."

I signaled for the floor. "I have trouble imagining how a telepathic society evolves."

Reb smiled. "So does the Starmind. Does it comfort you to know that our current knowledge suggests you'll have at least two hundred years to think about it?"

I grinned back. "It helps."

Robert signaled for attention again. "Reb, I've heard that a couple of Stardancers have died."

"Accidental deaths, yes. A total of four, actually."

"Well . . . how can a Stardancer die? I mean, each one's consciousness is spread through more than forty-thousand different minds. So for a Stardancer, isn't death really no more than having your childhood home burn down? Your *self* persists, doesn't it, even if it can't ever go home again?"

Reb looked sad. "I'm afraid not. It isn't consciousness that diffuses through the Starmind, but the products of consciousness: thoughts and feelings. Consciousness itself is rooted in the brain, and when a brain is destroyed, that consciousness ends. Telepathy does not transcend death—the Starmind knows no more about what lies beyond death than any human does."

Robert frowned. "But all the thoughts that brain ever had, remain on record, in the Starmind—and you've told us the Starmind's memory is perfect. Wouldn't it be possible, given every single thought a person's mind ever had, to reconstruct it, and maintain it by time-sharing among forty-some thousand other brains?"

"It has been tried. Twice. It is the consensus of the Starmind that it never will be tried again."

"Why not?"

"What results is something like a very good artificial intelligence package. It has a personality, mannerisms, quirks . . . but no *core.* It doesn't produce *new* thoughts, or feel new feelings. Both such constructs asked to be terminated, and were."

"Oh."

"On the other hand, no Stardancer has yet died of so-called natural causes, and individuals as old as a hundred and ten are as active and vigorous as you are. So I wouldn't lose any sleep over it."

"I won't," Robert agreed. "I just wondered."

That Sunday there was a small celebration in the Café du Ciel, acknowledging our transition from Postulant to Novice. Phillipe Mgabi attended, the first time most of us had seen him since our arrival, but it was mostly Dorothy's show. There were no speeches, scant ceremony. Mostly it was tea and conversation and good feelings. Some of us came forward and told of things we had thought or felt since our arrival, difficulties we had overcome. A new marriage was announced, and cheered. To my surprise, no gripes were aired. I think that had a lot to do with Phillipe Mgabi having been too busy to show his face for the past four weeks. I'd never seen such a smoothly running, well-organized *anything* before, and I knew how much hard work that kind of organization requires.

Under the influence of all this good fellowship, Robert and I reached a new plateau in our relationship, to wit, publicly holding hands and necking. Nothing more serious than friendly cuddling; I think each of us was waiting for the other to make the first move. Well, I don't really know what he was waiting for.

Come to think of it, I don't know what I was waiting for either.

And then came the day we'd anticipated for so long. I think it's safe to say we all woke up with a kids-on-Christmas-morning feeling. Today we would be allowed to leave the house!

Everyone showed up for breakfast, for once, and almost nothing was eaten. The buzz of conversation had its pitch and speed controls advanced one notch apiece past normal. A lot of teeth were showing. Then in the middle of the meal there was a subtle change. The feeling went from kids on Christmas morning to teenagers on the morning of the Chem Final. The laughter came more often, and more shrilly. A restless room in zero gravity is really restless; people bob around like corks in a high sea rather than undulating like seaweed. Smiles became fixed. A bulb of coffee got loose and people flinched away from it.

Kirra began to hum.

Under her breath at first, with a low buzzing tone to it. By the time I was aware of it, I found that I was humming along with her, and recognized the tune we were humming. The Song of Top Step. Ben joined softly in an octave below us. Kirra started to gently tap out the rhythm on the table. Someone two tables over picked up the melody, and that gave all of us the courage to increase our volume. Soon people were chiming in all over the cafeteria, even people from classes before or after ours. Not all of us knew the Song well enough to sing it, but most of us knew at least parts of it, and could join in for those. Those who couldn't carry a tune kept the rhythm with utensils. Those few who didn't know the Song at all stopped talking to listen. Even the spacers on the cafeteria staff stopped what they were doing.

We went through it three times together. The third was the best; by then almost everyone had it down. It was the kind of tune that's easy to learn quickly; even to ears raised on different musical convenience, it was *hummable*. Kirra held the final note, then let her voice tumble slowly down to the bottom of her range and die out. There was no applause. There was not a sound. Not a cough. Still bodies.

"Let's do it, then," Kirra said, and the stasis was ended. We went off to school together calmly, joyfully, quietly, as one.

8

Assuming Ascension, Assumption, Assent
All of our nonsense is finally non-sent—
With honorable mention for whatever we meant
You are my content, and I am content.
—Teodor Vysotsky

Reb and Sulke were both waiting for us in Solarium Two. (For the rest of this week they would be teaching us together, twice a day; after that they'd teach separately again.) Although they knew us all by name and by sight, they marked us off on an actual checklist as we came through the open airlock chamber, and sealed both hatches carefully when we were all mustered. Reb was especially saintly, radiating calm and compassion, and Sulke was especially sour, nervous as a cat.

"If you haven't checked your air, do so now," she called. "We've got fresh tanks if you need them." We were all in our p-suits, and I would have bet all of us had been smart enough to check our air supply. I certainly had—six times. But little Yumiko had to come forward, shamefaced, to accept a pair of tanks and a withering glare from Sulke. "Check your thruster charges too. You're not gonna get much use out of them today, but start the habit of keeping them topped up." Three people had to disgrace themselves this time, coming forward to have their wristlets or anklets recharged. Ben was one of them.

"You've heard it a million times," Sulke told us in parade-ground voice. "I'll tell you one more time. Space does not forgive. If you take your mind off it for five seconds, it will kill you."

She took a breath to say more, and Reb gently cut her off. "Be mindful, as we have learned together, and all will be well."

She exhaled, and nodded slowly. "That's right. Okay, earthworms—" She caught herself again. "Sorry, I can't call you that anymore, you've graduated." She grinned. "Okay, *space*worms, attach your umbilicals. Make damn sure they're hooked tight."

The term was outdated: they weren't real umbilicals like the pioneers used, carrying air from the mothership; they were only simple tethers. But they did fasten at the navel so that imagery was apt. Each of us found a ring to anchor ours to on the wall behind us. I checked carefully to make sure the snaplock had latched snugly shut. The umbilical was about the same diameter as spaghetti, guaranteed unbreakable, and was a phosphorescent white so it would not be lost in the darkness.

"Radios on Channel Four," Sulke said. "Seal your hood and hold on to your anchor. Is there anyone whose hood is not sealed? Okay, here we go."

There was a dysharmonic whining sound as high-volume pumps went into operation, draining the air from the Solarium. As the air left, the noise diminished. The cubic was large, it took awhile. We spent the time staring out the vast window.

Two was the only true solarium, the one that always faced the Sun. Its window worked like modern sunglasses: you could stare directly at the Sun, without everything else out there turning dark as well. The p-suit hood added another layer of polarization. The Sun looked like an old 60-watt bulb head-on, but by its light you could see Top Step's own mirror farm a few miles away, a miniature model of the three immense ones that circle the globe, beaming down gigawatts for the groundhogs to squabble over. It looked like God's chandelier. I could also just make out two distant Stardancers, their Symbiotes spun out into crimson discs, a little One-ish of the mirror farm. (That's the side away from Earth in Top Step parlance.) They looked like they were just basking in the sun, rippling slightly like jellyfish, but for all I knew they could have been directing construction out in the Asteroid Belt. Who knows what a Stardancer is thinking? All other Stardancers, that's who, and nobody else. There were no p-suited Third-Monthers visible at the moment, though there were surely some out there, too far to see or in other quadrants of space.

The sound of the pumps was gone now. The outside world is miked in a p-suit, but the mike only functions in atmosphere. There was no longer any air to support sound outside our suits, so we heard none.

"Hard vacuum," Sulke announced in my ear. "Maintain radio silence unless you have an emergency. And don't have an emergency. Here we go."

A crack appeared at the bottom of the great window. In eerie utter silence, it slid upward until it was gone. A great gaping hole opened out on empty space. Radio silence or no, there was a soft susurrant murmur. For a moment my mind tried to tell me that the Sun and empty space were *below* me, that the huge opening was a bomb bay and I was about to fall out. But I suppressed the fear easily. Reb had trained me well.

"All right," Sulke said, "starting over at this end, *one at a time,* move out when I tell you. Don't move until the person before you has reached the end of their leash, I don't want any tangles today. Try to fan out, so we end up making a big shaving brush. Rostropovitch, you're first."

Reb arranged himself like a skydiver, feet toward us, and gave a short blast on his ankle thrusters. "Follow me, Dmitri," he said softly, and jaunted slowly out into emptiness. Dmitri followed him, and then Yumiko, and the exodus began. When my turn came I was ready. A one-second blast, and I was in motion. As I passed through the open window there was a sensation as if I had pierced some invisible membrane . . . and then I was in free space, tether unreeling slightly behind me, concentrating on my aim.

The umbilical placed enough drag on me that I had to blast again halfway out. I did it for a hair too long, and reached the end of my rope with a jerk that put me into a slow-motion tumble. I stabilized it easily, and could have come to a stop—Sulke had trained me well, too—but I didn't. Like someone standing on a mountaintop and turning in circles, I rotated slowly. Now that I was no longer busy, I let myself take it all in.

And like my mates, I was dumbstruck.

It's like the psychedelic experience. It cannot be described, and only a fool will try. I know that even my clearest memories of the event are pale shadows.

In free space you seem to see better, in more detail than usual. Everything has an uncanny "realer than real" look, because there is no air to scatter the light that reaches your eyes. You see about 20 percent more stars than can be seen on the clearest night on Earth, just a little brighter and clearer than even the best simulation, and none of them twinkle. Venus, Mars and Jupiter are all visible, and visibly different from the other celestial objects.

For the first time I gained some real sense of the size of Top Step. It looked like a mountain that had decided to fly, a mountain the size of Mount Baker back where I came from. (Already I had stopped thinking, "back *home.*") Even though at that point in history something over a quarter of it had been tunneled out and put to assorted uses, the only externally prominent sign of human occupancy was the mammoth docking complex at the tip—and it had the relative dimensions of the hole in the tip of a fat cigar.

And at the same time all of Top Step was less than a dust mote. So vast is space that mighty Earth itself, off Three-ish, was a pebble, and the Sun was a coal floating in an eternal sea of ink. That made me some kind of subatomic particle. A pun awful enough to be worthy of Ben came to me: it had been too long since I'd been lepton. That made me think of Robert, and I recalled vaguely that the force that keeps leptons together is called the Weak Force. I was rummaging through my forebrain, looking for wordgames to anchor me to reality, cerebral pacifiers.

I looked around for Robert, spotted his turquoise p-suit coming into my field of vision perhaps twenty meters away—why, we were practically rubbing elbows. As in the classroom simulation holo, half of him was in darkness . . . but here in real space, there was enough backscatter of light from Top Step to make his dark side just barely visible. Other students floated beyond him; I picked out Kirra and Ben, holding hands. Jaunting as a couple is trickier than jaunting solo, but they had learned the knack.

Reb and Sulke let us all just be there in silence for a measureless time.

A forest of faint white umbilicals, like particle tracks from a cyclotron, led back to the Solarium we'd come from. Its huge window now seemed a pore in the skin of Top Step. All around us, stars burned without twinkling, infinitely far away. I became acutely aware of my breath whistling in and out, of the movement of my chest and belly as I breathed, of my pulse chugging in my ears, of the food making its way along my digestive tract and the sensation of air flowing across my skin. I felt a powerful spontaneous urge to try a dance step I'd been working on, something like an arabesque crossed with an Immelman roll. I squelched the urge firmly. Right place, wrong time.

I seemed to be at the center of the Universe, turning lazily end over end. My breathing slowed. Time stopped.

"I'm sorry, Reb," Yoji Kuramatso said sadly.

"It's all right, Yoji-san," Reb said at once. *"Daijôbu-da!"* he jetted toward Yoji, flipped over halfway there and decelerated, came to a stop beside him.

"I really thought I could handle it," Yoji said, his voice trembling slightly.

"*Simpai suru-na,* Yoji-san," Reb said soothingly. "Switch to Channel Six now."

They both switched their radios to a more private channel, and Reb began conducting Yoji back to Top Step, letting their umbilicals reel them slowly in rather than trying to use thrusters.

There was a murmur of embarrassment and sympathy. Yoji was liked.

"He did that great," Sulke said. "If you're going to panic, that's the way to do it. Quietly. Slowly. Is anyone else having trouble?"

No one spoke.

"Okay, we'll marinate until Reb gets back, and then we'll get to work."

Robert was passing through my visual field again. I didn't want to break radio silence, so I waited until he was facing my way and made a tentative come-here gesture. He worked himself into the right attitude, pointed his hands down at his feet and gave a short blast on both wrist thrusters. He glided toward me in ultraslow motion, stretching his hands out toward me as he came. I oriented myself to him. When he arrived, we locked hands like trapeze acrobats, only pressing instead of pulling, and I gave an identical blast in the opposite direction with my ankle-thrusters to kill his velocity. Maybe it was because we got it right that Sulke didn't chew us out for maneuvering without permission . . . or she may have had other reasons.

We drifted, facing each other, holding hands. The sun was at my back, so there was too much glare from his hood for me to see his face clearly. He must have seen mine well in the reflected light.

By mutual consent we moved to a new position, side to side, each with an arm around the other, facing infinity together. Part of me wanted to switch off my radio and talk with him hood-to-hood. But Sulke would have skinned me . . . and there really were no words, anyway.

If you are going to fall through endless darkness for timeless time, it is nice to have someone's arm around you.

After a while, Reb returned and we started doing simple maneuvers. Even classwork didn't break the mood, pop the bubble of our dreamlike state of awe and wonder. I don't mean we were in a trance—at all times we remained mindful, of our tethers and our thruster placement and our air supply—but at the same time we experienced something like rapture, a three-dimensional awareness. I had been in a similar mental/physical state before, often . . . but only onstage. I wondered which of the others had anything in their experience to liken this to.

I was going to like this. This had been a good idea. Way to go, Morgan.

We stayed out there until lunch time—and still it was over much too soon.

I demolished twice as much food as usual at lunch; I'd have eaten more but they ran out. Most of the group was keyed up, happy, darting around like hummingbirds and chattering like magpies. Robert and I did not chatter. We touched hands, and legs, and ate together in silence, totally aware of each other.

That afternoon's class was with Reb only, in the cubic where he'd always held morning classes during the first month. For the first time, he allowed the gathering to devolve into a gabfest, encouraging us all to speak of what we had felt and thought that morning, to tell each other what it had meant to us. I was surprised at the diversity of things different people likened the experience to. Taking LSD, being in combat, falling in love, *kensho,* orgasm, electroshock, dying, being born, giving birth, writing when the Muse is flowing, doing math, an Irish coffee drunk . . . the variations were endless. For Robert it was the instant when a new design leaped into his head and began explaining itself.

One thing surprised me even more. Three of us reported that

there was nothing in their previous lives to compare space to. They were the most profoundly affected of all of us, all three close to tears. This had been their first taste of transcendence. It seemed hard to believe, and terribly sad, to have lived so long without wonder.

Glenn confessed that she had several times come near giving up like Yoji and going back indoors. "I can take it as long as I'm perfectly still," she said. "I just tell myself I'm watching an Imax movie. But the minute I start to move the least little bit, and it all starts spinning around me, I just lose it. I lose my place. I lose my self. I can handle it okay indoors, even in the simulations, but out there is *different* . . ."

"But you didn't panic," Reb said.

"I came damned close!"

"So did I," Yumiko said softly.

"*Da.* Me too," Dmitri chimed in.

She stared at them. "You did?"

They nodded.

"Experienced spacers have been known to panic," Reb said. "Glenn, don't worry. You may simply not be ready yet to have a revelation of the scale you were given this morning. That is not a failure. You don't have to go back out tomorrow if you decide you're not ready. You may need to spend more time in meditation first. I'll be glad to spend private time with you if you like. Don't force yourself to continue if you feel it is harmful to you. Charlotte Joko Beck once said, 'A premature enlightenment experience is not necessarily good.' Looked at from a certain angle, enlightenment is a kind of annihilation—a radical self-emptying. There is time, plenty of time."

"All right," she said, "I'll sleep on it and let you know."

"You can do it, love," Kirra called out. "I know you can!"

"Goddam right," Ben seconded, and there were noises of agreement from others.

Glenn smiled, embarrassed but pleased. "Thanks."

Reb dismissed class early, suggesting we all meditate privately when we felt ready.

Robert and I paused in the corridor outside the classroom, off to one side. As other Novices jaunted past us, we stared deep into each other's eyes, communicating wordlessly.

It seemed that almost everything I'd seen outside was there to be seen in those almond hazel eyes. Perhaps more—for space was indifferent to me, and utterly cold. Effortlessly I reached a decision which had eluded me for a month.

"A lot of things came clear out there today," I said. My voice was rusty.

"Yes." So was his.

"Teena, is my studio free for the afternoon?"

"Yes, Morgan."

I reached out and took Robert's left hand with my right. "Come with me."

He nodded, and we kicked off together.

Once inside the studio I dimmed the lights slightly, to about the level of dusk on Earth. I told Teena to hold all calls, and to see that we had privacy. I gently maneuvered Robert to a handhold near the camera I'd been calling Camera One and using for main POV.

"Stay here," I told him.

He nodded.

It took an effort to look away. I spun and jaunted to the far side of the room. I paused there. I unsealed my p-suit and took it off, making no attempt to strip erotically, simply skinning out of my clothes like an eleven-year-old on a shielded wharf. I worked the thrusters from the suit and slid them over my bare wrists and ankles, seated the controls against my palms. I closed my eyes, and cleared my mind . . .

. . . and danced.

I had been working on a piece, but did not dance that. Nor did I quote existing works of others, although I was capable of it now. I had no choreographic plan; for the first time in over thirty-five years I simply let the dance come boiling out of me.

One of the reasons I had failed as a choreographer on Earth was that I had let them teach me too much, absorbed too many rules and conventions of dance to ever again be truly spontaneous. But here I was a child again. Once again I could create.

And what came boiling up out of me first was much the same as what had come boiling out of the eleven-year-old Rain McLeod. I can't describe the dance to you: it was improvised, and the cameras were not rolling. But I can tell you what I was saying with it, when I began.

I was saying the same thing I had said with that first dance, back on Gambier Island. The same thing Shara Drummond had been saying in the Stardance.

Here I am, Universe! I'm here; look at me. I exist. I matter.

I was talking back to endless empty blackness spattered with shards of ancient starlight, to a universe cold and burning down forever, to all the awful immensity I had seen that morning.

At first I danced only with my muscles, maintaining my position in space while I spun and turned around my center, making shapes and changing them, stretching and contracting, hurling my spine about with the force of my limbs. Then I began to use my thrusters, first to alter attitude, and then to move me around the room. I borrowed some vocabulary from ice-skating, and adapted it to three-dimensionality, swooping in widening curves that came ever closer to the wall of the spherical gym, decorating them with axel-spins.

Robert watched, as expressionless as a sea lion, bobbing slowly in the air currents I was creating.

I made him the focal point of my dance, danced not just to him, but of him. As I did my dance began to change. I danced Robert, as I saw him. I danced quiet competence, and ready courage, and strength and self-reliance and patience and mystery and grace.

There you are! You're there: I see you. You exist. You matter.

He understood. I saw him understand.

My dance changed again. I began to dance not of the awesome immensity of space, but of the exhilaration of being alive in it; to speak not of eternity but of now. I had proclaimed myself to the Universe; now I offered myself to him.

Here we are! We're here: look at us. "We" exists. We will matter.

He watched, so utterly relaxed that his head began to nod slowly with his breathing, as though he were asleep with his head unsecured. Or was he nodding agreement?

Finally I was done. I had said everything that was in my arms and legs and spine, everything in my heart. I floated facing him across the room, arms outstretched, waiting.

He sighed deeply, and let go of his handhold. Eyes locked with mine, he removed his p-suit, and released it to drift. And then he came to me, and then he came into me, and soon he came in me.

* * *

We made love for hours, slow dreamy love in which orgasms were merely the punctuation in a long and unfolding statement. Zero gee changes everything about the oldest dance. Together we learned and invented, made shapes and figures impossible under gravity. Both of us kept the use of our hands; neither of us was on top. The room spun around us. We cried together, and giggled together, and planed sweat from each other's backs with our hands. We told each other stories of our failed marriages and past lovers. Even with the freedom of three dimensions, we were unable to find any embrace in which we did not fit together as naturally as spoons. We drifted in each other's arms between rounds of lovemaking, bumping occasionally into the wall, but never hard enough to cause us to separate.

By the time we remembered the existence of the so-called real world, it was too late to get supper at the cafeteria. Well, we might just have made it . . . but we had to shower first, and that turned into more lovemaking. But the grill at Le Puis is always open, so we headed there, arm in arm, aglow, kissing as we jaunted. People we passed smiled.

We stopped along the way to leave our p-suits in our rooms. We discussed dressing, but could not come up with any reasons for doing so, so we didn't bother. (I don't recall whether I've mentioned it before, but it should be obvious that Top Step had no nudity taboo. People who are uncomfortable with social nudity are not good candidates for Symbiosis.)

Fat Humphrey greeted us with a grin incredibly even bigger than usual, and a roar of delight. "So you finally got off the dime, eh? I t'ought I was gonna hafta be the one to tell you two you were in love. Hey, this makes me happy! Let's see, you gonna want a booth—right this way!"

He led us to a booth off in what would have been a corner if Le Puis had corners—far from any other patrons, I mean. We did not bother stating requests, indeed didn't even think about it. We gazed deep into each other's eyes in silent communication until Fat returned with food and drink. He opaqued the booth, and sealed it behind him as he left. I was mildly surprised by the amount of food, but Fat didn't make mistakes. Sure enough, when I next noticed, it was all gone. I don't remember what it was . . . but the drink was champagne.

As we were squeezing the last sips into each other's mouths, Fat scratched discreetly at the closure of our booth. Robert unsealed it; Fat passed in a pipe, then departed again, beaming. It turned out to contain just enough hashish for two tokes apiece. Robert took all four, and passed them to me in kisses; I drank intoxication from his mouth. We caressed each other, slowly, dreamily, not so much lustfully as affectionately. Music, selected by Fat Humphrey, began to play softly in the background. I hadn't heard it before then, but it fit the moment perfectly: Vysotsky's "Afterglow." I'm terrible with song lyrics, but one verse I retain verbatim:

Incandescent invention, and blessed event
Tumescent distention, tumultuous descent
Our bone of convention at last being spent
I am your contents, and I am content

Finally, I said, "Put that thing away so we can leave here without making a spectacle of ourselves."

"Oh, sure," he said. "Reb's taught me how to control my metabolism: I'll just wish it away."

"Right," I agreed, and struck the most erotic pose I could.

Fifteen seconds later he conceded defeat by tickling me.

"Why leave?" he said. "It's private in here."

"True. But we'd jiggle it so much we might as well do it out in plain sight—and people are trying to eat. Besides, I want more room than this."

"Good thinking." He eased away from me and glanced down. "Well, if we wait for this to go away, we'll be here come Graduation. Let's brazen it out."

So we did. If anyone noticed, they kept it to themselves. Fat Humphrey waved as we left, clearly overjoyed at our happiness.

We ran into Glenn along the way, headed in the same direction we were. She didn't notice Robert's condition. She had left Le Puis just before us, and was a little squiffed. We said hello, and then regretted it, for she wanted to talk.

No, worse. If she'd just wanted to talk, we could have politely brushed her off when we reached our door. But she *needed* to talk.

She was still trying to come to terms with all she'd seen outside that morning.

She had always been polite, taciturn, reticent to intrude on anyone's privacy with personal conversation; if she needed to unload now I felt an obligation to help. So when we reached my place I queried Robert with my eyes, got the answer I'd hoped for, and invited Glenn in.

"You know what it was?" she told us. "I was doing just fine for the first while, I really was. And then I started thinking of the only other times I'd ever felt . . . I don't know, felt that close to God. Once when I birthed my daughter . . . and just about every time I ever walked in a forest. I started thinking that I could birth kids again for the next couple of centuries, if I go through with this—but that if I go through with this, I'll never go for a walk in the woods again. And I started to panic."

"Reb says once you're Symbiotic, you can reexperience any moment of your life, so vividly it's like living it again," I said. "Or anybody else's life who's in the Starmind."

"I know," she said. "But it won't be the same as being there. Even if it's close enough to fool me, it won't be the same."

"How real do you need reality to be?" Robert asked reasonably. "If it passes the Turing Test—if you can't tell it from a real experience—then what's the difference?"

"I *don't know,*" she said, "but there's a difference. Look, you've walked in woods, haven't you?"

"Not in years," he admitted. "Woods are kind of hard to come by where I lived."

"But you know what I mean. When you walk in the woods, there are so many things going on at once, nobody could notice and remember them all. Leaves fluttering, birds chirping, wind in the branches, a hundred different smells of things growing and rotting—I could list things there are to notice in the woods for the next two hours and there'd still be a thousand things I left out, things I don't even consciously notice. So how am I going to remember them all clearly enough to recreate them in my mind? It just doesn't seem possible."

Robert frowned. "I don't know how to answer you."

I had an inspiration. "I know somebody who does. Teena—who's the nearest Stardancer who's got time to talk?"

"Greetings, Morgan McLeod," a feminine voice said. "I am Jinsei Kagami. May I do you a service?"

I was taken a little aback. I hadn't expected such snappy service; I'd been planning on time for second thoughts. It was like praying . . . and getting an answer! I was a little awed to find myself talking to a real live Stardancer.

Well, I told myself, *if you didn't want the djinn, you shouldn't have rubbed the lamp. At least don't waste her time . . .*

"My friends Glenn Christie and Robert Chen are here with me. Glenn would like to talk to you, if you're not too busy."

"There is time. Greetings, Glenn and Robert."

Robert said hello and made a low *gassho* bow to empty air. Glenn said, "Hello, Jinsei; Glenn here. I'm sorry to bother you."

Voices can smile. I know because hers did. "You do not, cousin. How may I help you?"

"Well, I . . ." Glenn frowned and gathered her thoughts. "I guess I'm having trouble believing that I won't miss Earth after Symbiosis. I've been trying to say goodbye to it since I got here—and today I went EVA for the first time, and all I could think of was the places on Earth that I have loved. Jinsei-*sama,* don't you ever miss . . . your old home?"

"Do you ever miss your mother's womb?" Jinsei asked.

Glenn blinked, and did not reply.

"Of course you do," Jinsei went on, "especially when you are very tired. And a fine sweet pain it is. I did too, when I was human. But I do not miss my mother's womb anymore. I can *be* there, whenever I want. I have access to *all* my memories, back to the moment my brain formed in the fifth month of my gestation. You cannot remember the events of one second ago as vividly as I remember every instant I have lived—I and all my brother and sister Stardancers. I can be anywhere any of us has ever been, do anything any of us has ever done. For the memories of fetal life alone, I would trade a dozen Earths."

Somehow even after meeting Harry Stein I had subconsciously expected that a Stardancer in conversation would be sort of dreamy and . . . well, spacey, like someone massively stoned. She sounded as alert and mindful as Reb.

"'Every instant . . .' Even the painful ones?" Glenn asked.

"Oh, yes."

"Don't they hurt?"

"Oh, yes. Beautifully."

Glenn looked confused.

"I think what you are asking," Jinsei said gently, "is whether a Stardancer ever regrets Symbiosis."

"Uh . . . yes. Yes, that's just what I'm asking."

"No, Glenn. Not one. Not so far."

That extraordinary assertion hung there in the air for a moment. A life without regret? No, these Stardancers were not human.

Glenn was frowning. "What about the catatonics?" she asked.

"They're not Stardancers," Robert pointed out.

"They have not enough awareness to regret," Jinsei said. "When they are healed, they no longer regret . . . or perhaps it is the other way around. And the fraction who die renounce regret forever, along with all other possible experiences."

There was a short silence. Finally Glenn nodded slowly. "I think I see. Thank you, Jinsei. You have comforted me."

"I am glad, Glenn."

"Jinsei-*san*?" Robert said.

"Yes, Robert?"

"Can a Stardancer lie?"

I thought the question rude, opened my mouth to say so . . . and found that I wanted to hear the answer. It was a question that had never occurred to me before.

Jinsei found it amusing. "Can you think of any answer I could make that would be meaningful?"

Robert blinked in surprise, and then chuckled ruefully. "No, I guess not. I don't even now why I asked that. I know the answer, or I wouldn't be here."

"Thank you," she said, and he looked relieved. "Forgive me: I find that I am needed; is there anything else I can do for you three?"

We said no and thanked her, and she was gone.

Glenn jaunted near and offered a hug. I accepted without hesitation. Her p-suit was cool on my bare flesh, but not unpleasantly so. "Thank you, Morgan, very much. I'd never have had the nerve to do that."

"Glad to. It seemed like it was called for. Are you okay now?"

"Yes, I think I am. I need to sit kûkanzen some more, but I think I'll be able to go back out there tomorrow—thanks to you and Robert. Good night."

To my mild surprise, she hugged Robert too. "Thank you for lending me some of your courage," she said, and left.

Robert and I looked at each other and smiled.

"Where were we?" I said.

"About to make some memories so good that we'll relive them every day for the next two hundred years," he said.

We certainly did our best. After a while reality turned all warm and runny, and when I was tracking again I noticed idly that Kirra and Ben were in the room now too. But there was no need to restart my brain: they were busy, just like we were. I don't think Robert even noticed. Good concentration, that man.

Yumiko died the next day.

For the second day in a row, she failed to check her air supply—and this time Sulke did not remind us before opening the Solarium window. An hour later Yumiko failed to respond to a direction. It's hard to see how one could run out of air without noticing something is wrong . . . but if Yumiko ever did realize she had a problem, she was too polite to bring it up. They say lifeguards in Japan have to be terribly alert, because drowners there can be too self-effacing to disturb everyone's *wa* by calling for help. When she was missed, it was too late.

(Reb flashed to her side, diagnosed her problem, threw her empty tanks into deep space and replaced them with his own, headed for home on what air he had in his suit, squeezing her chest energetically enough to crack ribs as he went—to no avail. When they got her out of the suit she was irretrievably brain dead.)

Sulke would not cancel the rest of the class, and insisted on taking us all out again in the afternoon. She was so clearly controlling anger that I knew she must be feeling horrid guilt—and she did not deserve it, in my opinion: there comes a time when the teacher must stop wiping the students' noses. She had *told* us yesterday, *space does not forgive*. But she could not forgive herself, either.

Reb conducted the funeral service that night. Little Yumiko had been a follower of *Ryobu Shinto,* or Two-aspect Shinto, an attempt to reconcile Shinto with Buddhism which had recently been revived in Japan after more than a thousand years of dormancy; apparently they used the Buddhist funeral rites. There were prayers offered in all the other holy places in Top Step as well; sadly, those pages were well thumbed in all the hymnals.

Robert and I attended none of these observances. We held one of our own, in my room, saying goodbye to Yumiko and consoling ourselves in the only real way there is, the oldest one of all. I'm pretty sure Kirra and Ben were doing the same thing down the hall . . . and doubtless others were too. Sudden death seems to call for the ultimate affirmation of life. Sharing it brought Robert and me closer together; all smallest reservations gone, I gave my heart to him, opened to him as though he were my Symbiote, and he flowed into me.

As I was trying to fall asleep, I kept thinking that I had barely known Yumiko. Sure, she had been shy—but if I had made the effort, gotten to know her, she could have lived forever as real as real in my brain once I became Symbiotic. I hoped her roommate Soon Li had made the effort.

9

This is merely a series of events. Their only correlation is that they all occurred within the same time-frame.

—Boeing official,
after eleven passengers were sucked out of an airliner,
Boeing's eighth public relations disaster within a year

The next morning's EVA was also eventful. Nobody died, but the near miss was spectacular.

We had progressed in proficiency to the point where Sulke would have half a dozen of us at a time unsnap our umbilicals and practice thruster use without constraint—six being the most she and Reb were confident of being able to supervise at one time. Learning precise thruster control was *not* easy, and several times Reb and Sulke had to rescue someone who'd blundered into something they couldn't figure out how to undo. Sulke tended to hair-trigger reflexes; she was determined not to lose any more students. But Reb's gentle good humor counterbalanced her and kept it being fun.

Raise your hands as if in surrender, palms forward. Your thrusters are now pointing in the same direction you're facing. Put your arms down at your sides with your thumbs against your thighs, and the thrust is in the opposite direction. By torquing your forearms you can aim in almost any direction or combination of directions. Your ankle-thrusters, however, face in only one direction, "down," and have only the one axis of motion. From those postulates all the equations of free-space jaunting are derived—and they're complicated and often counterintuitive.

It took, believe me, a lot of courage to let go of that umbilical and hang alone and unsupported in space. I managed to do it, and to get through my short stint without disgracing myself or alarming Sulke, but my heart was pounding when I reconnected myself to my tether. Ben and Kirra were in the next group, and I watched with interest, knowing that they would do this well.

They did it beautifully, well enough to draw spontaneous applause. (Clapping your hands in a p-suit is a waste of energy. You applaud by making approving sounds. *Softly,* as dozens of people are sharing the same radio circuit.) What they did was more calisthenics than dance, but the consummate grace and skill with which they did it made it dance. Ben especially had pin-point control, using the tiniest bursts of gas to start himself moving and stop himself again when he was where he wanted to be. When they had run through the sequence of exercises, he and Kirra improvised a phrase similar to a square dance do-see-do, jetting toward each other and pivoting in slow motion around each other's crooked elbow. As they separated again, Ben suddenly went into a violent high-speed spin, spraying yellow gas like a Catherine Wheel. It was lovely, and we started to applaud . . . and then suddenly it was ugly, asymmetrical and uncontrolled. The applause died away and we could clearly hear him say, "Oh, shit."

"*What's wrong?*" Kirra cried, beating Sulke to it by a hair.

"Both left thrusters jammed full open." I could see now that he was beating his right fist into his left palm, trying to free up the jammed controls, but it wasn't working. He gave it up and flailed wildly for a moment, moving through space like a leaf in a storm.

"Here I come!" Kirra cried.

"No!" Sulke roared.

"No—stay clear!" Ben agreed. "I'm rogue, it's too dangerous. Besides, I think maybe I . . ." Suddenly he came out of his tumble and his attitude stabilized. His left wrist was cocked over his head, balancing the ankle thrust; he was vectoring slowly away from us, but at least he was no longer a pinwheel. "There."

Kirra had reached him by then, having ignored both warnings. "What should I do, love?" she asked him, decelerating to match his vector, doing it perfectly.

"Dock with me upside down." She did, locking her arms behind his knees, being careful not to kick him in the face. "Can you find the snap-release for that ankle-thruster?"

"Right."

"Okay, on the count of three, hit it—and be sure you're not in the way of it when it lets go! One, two, *three*!" He disengaged his fuming wrist thruster at the same instant she released the other one. She and Ben wobbled briefly as the two renegade thrusters blasted off for opposite ends of the galaxy; then they used their remaining six thrusters to recover. By then Sulke had arrived, swearing prodigiously in low German. The three of them jaunted back to us together hand in hand, and Sulke snapped their tethers back on herself.

It was over too quickly for me to have time to be terrified for them—no more than twenty seconds from start to finish.

Sulke finished cursing and paused for breath. "You two—" she began, and took another breath. Reb started to say something, but she overrode him. "—are EVA rated. As far as I'm concerned, you can graduate yourselves whenever you're ready."

Ben and Kirra looked at each other. "There's still a lot you can teach us," Kirra said.

"Maybe so," Sulke said, "and I'll be happy to if you want—but you've both got what it takes to survive EVA. Hell, I couldn't have recovered that fast."

"That's just my trick specs," Ben said. "It's easier getting out of a spin if you can see everything at once: you don't have those long gaps when no useful information is coming in."

"That makes sense. But Kirra was just as quick."

"I had a secret weapon too," Kirra said. "I'm in love with the bastard."

We all broke up. Tension release.

"What the hell went wrong, exactly?" Sulke asked. "Did the palm-switches physically freeze closed?"

"No," Ben said. "The controls worked fine . . . they just stopped controlling anything. If I had to guess—and I do, the damn things are halfway to Luna by now—I'd say a passing cosmic ray fried the chip."

"Possible," Sulke agreed reluctantly. "Or it could have been a passing piece of space junk, the odds are about the same. Damn bad luck. The rest of you spaceworms take heed. *Anything* can happen out here. Stay on your toes. Okay, next group—"

Ben and Kirra were even merrier than usual at lunch. But I noticed that they slipped away early, and got to afternoon class late.

"My best advice to you all," Reb said about five minutes after they arrived, flushed and smiling, "would be to make love as much as you conveniently can during the next three weeks."

The whole room *rippled.* There was a murmur made of giggles and gasps and exclamations and one clear, "I heard *that,*" which provoked more giggles.

"I'm completely serious," Reb said. "I can think of no better rehearsal for telepathy than making love. If you're a strict monosexual, now would be an excellent time to try to conquer your prejudice. *There are no sexual taboos in Top Step, because there are none in the Starmind.* You are preparing to enter a telepathic community, and in a telepathic community, you are naked to *everyone.* Sexual taboos won't work there. Even more important, they're unnecessary there—humans need taboos precisely because humans are not telepathic."

The room was now in maximum turmoil, as physical touching took on sudden significance. "But what about disease?" someone called.

"If you weren't healthy when you got to Suit Camp, you are now," Reb said. "Confirmed at Decontam and guaranteed."

"What about pregnancy?"

"All methods of contraception are available at the Infirmary. But you have no reason to fear pregnancy. Where you are going, there is no possibility of any child ever wanting for anything, no such thing as an unhappy childhood or a bad parent. All children are raised by everyone."

That took some thinking about. Finally someone said, "Are you . . . are you trying to say that all Stardancers spend their time screwing? That this Starmind is some kind of ongoing orgy?"

"In a physical sense, no. Stardancers only physically join when conception is desired. But in a mental and spiritual sense, your description is close to the truth. Telepathic communion cannot be described in words, nor understood until it is experienced—but it is generally agreed that lovemaking is one of the closest analogies in human experience. The most essential parts of lovemaking—liberation from the self, joining with others, being loved and touched and needed and cherished, gaining perspective on the universe by sharing viewpoint—are all a constant part of every Stardancer's life. Regardless of whether he or she chooses to ejaculate or lubricate at any given moment. Leon, you have a question?"

"What's zero-gee childbirth like?" asked the man addressed. "Gravity can be kind of handy there."

"Not for the first nine months," Glenn called out, and was applauded.

Reb smiled. "In Symbiosis, childbirth is easy and painless. The symbiote assists the process, and so does the child itself."

Wow! In spite of myself, an idea came to me. I made the finger gesture for attention, and Reb recognized me with a nod. "Reb? How old is too old to birth in Symbiosis?"

"We don't know yet. No woman has ever reached menopause while in Symbiosis. Those women who've entered Symbiosis after menopause resumed ovulating, and Stardancers as old as ninety-two have conceived and birthed successfully. Ask again in fifty years and we may have an answer for you."

The class went on for quite some time, and a lot of people said a lot of things, but I don't remember much after that. I spent the rest of class trying to grapple with the fact that a door I had thought closed forever was opening up again, that all of a sudden it wasn't too late anymore to change my mind and have children. The thought was too enormous to grasp. I had known about this, intellectually, before I had ever left Earth—but somehow I had never let the implications sink in before.

Probably because I had not known anyone whose children I wanted to have . . . until now.

"Robert," I said that night in afterglow, "how do you feel about you and me having a child?"

He blinked. "Are we?"

"Not yet. I've still got my implant. But I could have it taken out at the Infirmary in five minutes, and be pregnant in ten. What do you think?"

He had sense enough not to hesitate. "I think I would love to make a baby with you. But I also think it would be prudent to wait until after Graduation."

"Huh. Maybe you're right."

"Are you absolutely a hundred percent sure you're going to go through with Symbiosis? I'm not. And I wouldn't want a decision either way to be forced on either one of us. If we both do Symbiosis, fine. If we both go back to Earth, fine. But wouldn't it be awful if we started a child, and then—"

"I guess." It would be least awful, perhaps, if I stayed in space and Robert went home: a husband/father must be much less essential in a telepathic family than in human society. But Robert had already had to walk away from one child in his life, and still felt grief over it.

And there was another horrid possibility. What if we conceived together—and then one of us was killed in training? It could happen. I didn't think I could have survived what had happened to Ben that morning, for instance.

"Another month or so, maybe less, and we'll know. Okay?"

"You're right." I was disappointed . . . but only a little. Morning sickness in a p-suit could be a serious disaster. There was plenty of time.

Without any actual discussion, Kirra started spending most of her time at Ben's place, leaving our room for Robert and me. They gave the two of us a week to focus on each other and our new love without distraction. Then one day they came by and invited us to join them for drinks at Le Puis, and the four of us reformed and reintegrated our friendship again. Soon it stopped making any difference which room we used, or whether it was already occupied when we got there. Robert was a little more reticent than I about making love with Ben and Kirra present, at first, but he got over it. I could sense that one day, whether before or after Graduation, we four were all going to make love with each other. But there didn't seem to be any hurry for that, either, and for the present I was just a little too greedy of Robert.

Even falling in love couldn't distract me completely from dance. After our first few days together, I resumed working for a few hours every evening. Sometimes Robert watched and helped; sometimes he stayed back in the room and designed support structures for asteroid mining colonies, or wrote letters to his son in Minneapolis. I slowly began to evolve a piece of choreography, which I took to calling *Do the Next Thing.*

Kirra too made progress in her art. In the middle of the week, while we were all outside in class, she sang her second song for us, the Song of Polar Orbit. I had to get my p-suit radio overhauled that night—the applause overloaded it—and so did others. Raoul Brindle phoned more congratulations and repeated his invitation to Kirra. Within a few days, Teena reported that the recording had been downloaded by over eighty percent of the spacer community, and that audience response was one hundred percent positive. Kirra told me privately that she was tickled to death; she had never before received so much approval from non-Aboriginals and whitefellas for her singing. And according to her Earthside mentor Yarra, the Yirlandji people were equally pleased. Ben, for his part, was fiercely proud of her.

On Sunday afternoon the four of us took a field trip together, to watch a Third-Monther enter Symbiosis. I cleared it with Reb; he had no objection. "As long as Ben and Kirra and Robert are along, you can't get into too much trouble. They're pretty much spacers already. But you be sure to stay close to them," he cautioned with a smile. I smiled back and agreed that we could probably manage that.

We left, not via the Solarium, but by a smaller personnel airlock closer to the docking end of Top Step. It was about big enough to hold three comfortably, but we left in pairs, as couples, holding hands.

The Symbiote mass floated in a slightly higher orbit than Top Step, because Top Step routinely exhausted gases that, over a long period of time, could have damaged or killed it. I can't explain the maneuvering we had to do to get there without using graphics prefaced by a boring lecture on orbital ballistics; just take my word for it that, counterintuitive as it might seem, to reach something ahead of you and in a higher orbit, you *decelerate*. Never mind: with Ben astrogating, we got there. It took a long lazy time, since we didn't have a whole lot of thruster pressure to waste on a hurried trip.

My parents used to have an antique lava lamp, which they loved to leave on for hours at a time. The Symbiote mass looked remarkably like a single globule of its contents: a liquid blob of softly glowing red stuff, that flexed and flowed like an amoeba. Years ago there had been so much of it that you could see it with the naked eye from Top Step. So many Stardancers had graduated since then that the remaining mass was not much bigger than an oil tanker. (That was why the Harvest Crew was fetching more from Titan.) But it was hard to tell size by eye, without other nearby objects of known size to give perspective—a common problem in space.

As we got nearer, we picked out such objects: half a dozen Stardancers, their solar sails retracted. We came to a stop relative to the Symbiote mass, and saw perhaps a dozen p-suited humans approaching it from a slightly different angle than us. One of them had to be Bronwyn Small, the prospective graduate, and the rest her friends come to wish her well. By prior agreement, we maintained radio silence on the channel they were using, so as not to intrude. We had secured Bronwyn's permission to be present, through Teena, but there can be few moments in anyone's life as personal as Symbiosis.

The p-suited figures made rendezvous with the six Stardancers. We approached, but stopped about a kilometer or so distant.

I guess I had been expecting some sort of ceremony, the speech-making with which humans customarily mark important events. There was none. Bronwyn said short goodbyes to her friends, hugged each of them, and then turned toward the nearest of the Stardancers and said, "I'm ready."

"Yes, you are," the Stardancer agreed, and I recognized the voice: it was Jinsei Kagami. She did nothing that I could see—but all at once the Symbiote extended a pseudopod that separated from the main mass, exactly the way the blob in a lava lamp will calve little globular chunks of itself. The shimmering crimson fragment homed in on Bronwyn somehow, stopped next to her, and expanded into a bubble about four meters in radius, becoming translucent, almost transparent.

Without another word, Bronwyn jaunted straight into the bubble and entered it bodily. Within it, she could be seen to unseal her p-suit and remove it. She removed its communications gear, hung it around her neck, and then pushed the suit gently against the wall of the bubble that contained her. The Symbiote allowed the suit to emerge, sealed again behind it, and at once began to contract.

We were too far away to see clearly, but I knew that the red stuff was enfolding her and entering her at every orifice, meeting itself within her, becoming part of her.

She cried out, a wordless shout of unbearable astonishment that made the cosmos ring, and then was silent. She seemed to shudder and stiffen, back arched, arms and legs trembling as if she were having a seizure. She began turning slowly end over end.

There was silence for perhaps a full minute.

Then Jinsei said to Bronwyn's friends, "You may leave whenever you choose. Your friend will not be aware of her immediate surroundings again for at least another day . . . and it might be as much as one more day before you will be able to converse with her. She has a great deal to integrate."

"Is she all right?" one of them asked, sounding dubious.

"'All right' is inadequate," Jinsei said, with that smile in her voice. "'Ecstatic' is literally correct—and even that does not do it justice. Yes, she has achieved successful Symbiosis."

Bronwyn's friends expressed joy and relief at the news, and left as a group, talking quietly amongst themselves.

Ben gestured for our attention and pointed at his ear. We four all switched to a channel on which we could chatter privately.

"Not much of a show," he said.

"I dunno," Kirra said dreamily. "I thought it was lovely."

"Me too," I said. "I could almost feel it happening to her. That moment of merging."

"So did I," Ben said. "I don't know, I guess I expected there to be more to it."

"More what?"

"Ceremony. Speeches. Hollywood special effects. Fanfares of trumpets. Moving last words."

"You men and your speechmaking," I said. "All those things ought to happen too every time a sperm meets an egg . . . but they don't."

"And I thought those *were* moving last words," Kirra said. "She said, 'I'm ready.' Can't get much more movin' than that."

"You're pretty quiet, darling," I said to Robert. "What did you think?"

He was slow in answering. "I think I feel a little like Bronwyn: it's going to take me at least a week to integrate everything well enough to talk about it."

"Too right," Kirra agreed. "I've had enough o' words for a while. But I *could* use a little nonverbal communication. Come on, Benjamin, let's go on home an' root until sparrowfart."

(If you ever spend time in Oz, don't speak of rooting for your favorite team; "root" is their slang term for "fuck." Whether this is a corruption of "rut," or an indication that Aussies are fond of oral sex, I couldn't say. And "sparrowfart" is slang for "dawn.")

"That sounds like exactly what I'd like to do right now," he said.

"Me too," I agreed. "'Ecstatic,' she said. I could use some of that. How about you, darling?"

"'I'm ready,'" he quoted simply.

The trip back to Top Step was as long as the trip out, but there was no further conversation along the way. When we got there we found that four could fit into that airlock at once if they didn't mind squeezing. The route back to our quarters was one we had taken only once before, on the day of our arrival at Top Step—save that we bypassed Decontam. As we jaunted across the Great Hall, I felt again many of the same confused and confusing feelings I'd experienced on that first day, and hugged Robert tightly. He squeezed back.

Without any discussion, we all headed for my and Kirra's room, and entered together. Pausing only to store our p-suits and dim the lights, we went to bed.

Actually, the euphemism is misleading: we didn't use our sleep-sacks. I did not want to be confined, needed to feel as free as a Stardancer, and it seemed Kirra did as well.

For over an hour I was almost completely unaware of Ben and Kirra, or anything else but Robert. We caromed off walls or furniture from time to time, but barely noticed that either. Then at some point the two drifting couples bumped into each other in the middle of the room, at a perpendicular so that we formed a cross. The small of my back was against Kirra's; our sweat mingled. I sensed her flexing her legs and tightening her shoulders, and knew kinesthetically what she was going to do and matched it without thinking: we spun and flowed and traded places. Ben blinked and smiled and kissed me, and I kissed him back. The dance went on. Ben was sweet, bonier and hairier than Robert but just as tenderly attentive. Perhaps half an hour later, we all met again at the center of the universe and made a beast with four backs; awhile later I was back in Robert's arms, and slept there until Teena told us it was time for dinner.

We ate together without awkwardness, talking little but making each other smile often. After the meal, Ben kissed me, Robert kissed Kirra, and Robert and I went off to my studio together, while Kirra and Ben headed for Le Puis. They were asleep in Kirra's sleepsack when we got back: we slid into mine and were asleep almost at once.

Glenn was murdered the next day.

We had all been weaned from our umbilicals by that point, and were spending that class touring the exterior of Top Step. Most of the interesting stuff was down by the docking area. We were able to watch the docking of a Lunar robot freighter, carrying precious water from the ice mines. We should not have been able to: that freighter was not scheduled to arrive for another four hours, or Sulke would not have had us down there. Vessels are almost always punctual in space—the moment the initial acceleration shuts down, ETA can be predicted to the second. But while this can was on its way, the Lunar traffic control computer apparently detected a small pressure leak from the hold, and applied additional acceleration and deceleration to minimize transit time. Sulke was angry when the word came over the ops channel.

Oh, we were safe enough: we were at least half a kilometer from the docks. Sulke's gripe was that the event constituted an unplanned distraction from our curriculum—but we were all so eager to watch the docking that, after consultation with Reb, she reluctantly conceded that it would be instructive, and suspended lessons until it was over. I was pleased, since events had prevented me from watching my own docking five weeks earlier.

Long before we could see the freighter itself, we saw the tongue of fire it stuck out at us as it decelerated. Then the torch shut off, and we could see a spherical-looking object the size of a pea held at arm's length. It grew slowly to baseball size, then soccer ball, and by then it was recognizable as a cylinder seen end-on. It grew still larger, and began to visibly move relative to the stars behind it as it approached Top Step. Now it could be seen to be as large as the Symbiote mass I'd seen the day before, tiny in comparison to Top Step but huge in comparison with a human. From one side a thin plume of steam came spraying out of the hull to boil and fume in vacuum; on the opposite side you could just make out the less visible trail of the maneuvering jet that was balancing the pressure leak, keeping it from deforming the freighter's course to one side.

The ship was coming in about twice as fast as normal. But that's not very fast; dockings are usually glacial. Sulke had run out of educational things to point out long before the ship had approached close enough for final maneuvers. Since our first day EVA she'd generally kept us too busy to stargaze or chatter, but now we had time to rubberneck at the cosmos and ask questions.

"What's that, Sulke?" Soon Li asked, pointing to a far distant object in a higher orbit than our own.

Sulke followed her pointing arm. "Oh. That's Mir."

"Oh." Silence. Then: "I think someone ought to . . . I don't know, tear it down or blow it up or something."

"Would you want *your* grave disturbed?" Dmitri asked.

More silence.

"What are those people doing?" Dmitri wanted to know.

We looked where he was pointing, at the docking area itself. At first I saw nothing: those docks are *huge,* designed to accommodate earth-to-orbit vehicles, orbit-to-orbit barges or taxis, and Lunar shuttles like the one we were watching—as many as two of each at one time. But then I saw the two p-suited figures Dmitri meant, just emerging from a personnel lock between the two biggest docking collars.

"Those are wranglers," Sulke said. "As soon as that bucket docks, they'll hook up power feeds and refueling hoses and so on. If there's a nesting problem, they've got enough thruster mass to do some shoehorning too."

"What's wrong with that star?" Glenn asked, pointing in the direction of the slowly approaching freighters. She happened to be closest of us to it.

"Which one?" Sulke replied.

"That big one, a little Three-ish of the ship."

I spotted the one she meant. Indeed, there were three things odd about it. It was just slightly bigger than a star ought to be, and it was the only one in the Universe that was twinkling, the way stars appear to on Earth, and it had a little round black dot right smack in the center of it. That certainly was odd. It grew perceptibly as I watched; could it be a supernova? What luck, to happen to see one with the naked eye . . .

"Jesus Christ!" Sulke cried out. "Reb—"

"I see it," he said calmly. "Everyone, listen carefully: I want you to follow me at maximum acceleration, right now." He spun and blasted directly away from the docking freighter, all four thrusters flaring.

We wasted precious seconds reacting, and Sulke roared, *"Run for your fucking lives!"* That did it: we all took to our heels, slowly but with growing speed. I cannoned into someone and nearly tumbled, but managed to save myself and continue; so did the other.

"Operations—Mayday, Mayday!" Reb was saying. "Incoming ASAT, ETA five seconds. Wranglers—" He broke off. There was nothing to be said to the wranglers.

The antique antisatellite hunter-killer slammed into the freighter at that instant. There was no sound or concussion, of course. I caught reflected glare from the flash off Top Step in my peripheral vision, and tried to crane my neck around to look behind me, but I couldn't do it and stay on course, so I gave up. I'm almost sorry about that; it must have been something to see.

The water-ship was torn apart by the blast, transformed instantly into an expanding sphere of incandescent plasma, shrapnel and boiling water. It killed Ronald Frayn and Sirikit Pibulsonggram, the two wranglers, instantly. A half-second later it killed a Third-Monther named Arthur Von Brandenstein who had been meditating around the other side of Top Step, and had come to watch the docking like us, but had approached closer than Sulke would let us.

And a second later it caught up to our hindmost straggler, Glenn.

I'll remember the sound of her death until my dying day, because there was so little to it. It was a sound that would mean nothing to a groundhog, meant nothing to me then, and that every spacer dreads to hear: a short high whistle, with an undertone of crashing surf, lasting for no more than a second and ending with a curious croaking. It is the sound of a p-suit losing its integrity, and its inhabitant's final exhalation blowing past the radio microphone.

Later examination of tapes showed that the first thing to hit her was a hunk of shrapnel with sharp edges; it took both legs off above the knees, and that might well have sufficed to kill her, emptying her suit of air instantly. But you can live longer in a vacuum than most groundhogs would suspect, and it is just barely possible that we might have been able to get her inboard alive. But a split second later a mass of superheated steam struck her around the head and shoulders. P-suits were never designed to take that kind of punishment: the hood and most of the shoulders simply vanished, and the steam washed across her bare face—just as she was trying desperately to inhale air that was no longer there. When Sulke had us decelerate and regroup, she kept on going, spinning like a top. A couple of people started off after her, but Sulke called them back.

No one else died, but there were more than a dozen minor injuries. The most seriously injured was Soon Li, who lost two fingers from her left hand; she would have died, but while she was gawking at her fountaining glove, Sulke slapped sealant over it and dragged her to the nearest airlock. She suffered some tissue damage from exposure to vacuum, but not enough to cost her the rest of the hand. Antonio Gonella managed to crash into Top Step in his panicked flight, acquiring a spectacular bruise on his shoulder and a mild concussion. Two people collided more decisively than I had, and broke unimportant bones.

But the casualty that meant the most to *me* was Robert.

10

Once is happenstance;
twice is coincidence;
three times is enemy action.
—Ian Fleming

A small piece of shrapnel, the size and shape of a stylus, was blown right through his left foot from bottom to top. It was a clean wound, and his p-suit was able to self-seal around the two pinhole punctures. If he cried out, it was drowned out by the white noise of dozens of others shouting at once, and when Sulke called for casualty reports, he kept silent. I didn't know he'd been hurt until we were approaching the airlock, several minutes after the explosion, and I saw that the left foot of his p-suit had turned red. My first crazy thought was that some Symbiote had gotten into his p-suit somehow; when I realized it was blood I came damned near to fainting.

Cameras caught the entire incident—there are always cameras rolling around the docks—and replay established conclusively that Robert was following me, keeping me in his blast shadow, when he was hit. Or else that shrapnel might have hit me.

The explosion had shocked me, and Glenn's ghastly death had stunned me, but learning of Robert's comparatively minor injury just about unhinged me. I think if Reb had not been present I would have thrown a screaming fit . . . but his simple presence, rather than anything he said, kept me from losing control. He got us all inside, kept us organized and quiet, did triage on the wounded and had them all prioritized by the time the medics arrived. Sulke was the last one in, but when she did emerge from the airlock she paused only long enough to inventory us all by eye, and then went sailing off to goddammit get some answers.

Robert was pale, and his jaw trembled slightly, but he seemed otherwise okay. The sight of his torn foot, oozing balls of blood, made me feel dizzy, but I forced myself to hold it between my palms to cut off the bleeding. It felt icy cold, and I remembered that was a classic sign of shock. But his breathing was neither shallow nor rapid, and his eyes were not dull. He seemed lucid, responded reassuringly to questioning; I relaxed a little.

The medical team was headed by Doctor Kolchar, the doctor I'd seen briefly during my first minutes at Top Step. He was a dark-skinned Hindu with the white hair, moustache and glowering eyebrows of Mark Twain, dressed as I remembered him in loud Hawaiian shirt and Bermuda shorts. He handed off Nicole to Doctor Thomas, the resident specialist in vacuum exposure, and came over to look at Robert. He checked pulse, blood pressure and pupils before turning his attention to the damaged foot.

"You're a lucky young man," he said at last. "You couldn't have picked a better place to drill a hole through a human foot. No arterial or major muscle damage, the small bone destroyed isn't crucial, most of what you lost was meat and cartilage. Even for a terrestrial this would not be a serious injury. Do you want nerve block?"

"Yes," Robert said quietly but emphatically. Doctor Kolchar touched an instrument to Robert's ankle, accepted its advice on placement, and thumbed the injector. Robert's face relaxed at once; he took a great deep breath and let it out in a sigh. "Thank you, Doctor."

"Don't mention it. That block is good for twelve hours; when it wears off, come see me for another. Don't bother to set your watch, you'll know when it's time. Meanwhile, drink plenty of fluids—and try to stay off your feet as much as possible." He started to jaunt away to his next patient.

I was in no mood for bad jokes. "Wait a minute! Are you *crazy*? You haven't even dressed his foot. What about infection?"

He decelerated to a stop and turned back to me. "Madam, whatever punctured his foot was the size and shape of a pen. There's nothing like that in a cargo hold, and that's the only place I can imagine a bug harmful to humans living on a spacecraft. And you know, or should know, that Top Step is a sterile environment. His bleeding has stopped, and there was a little coagulant in what I gave him. If it makes you happy to dress his foot, here." He tossed me a roll of bandage. "But I'm a little busy just now." He turned his back again and moved away. I looked down at the bandage and opened my mouth to start yelling.

"It's all right, Morgan," Robert said. "Believe me, I won't bang it into anything." He smiled weakly in an attempt to cheer me up.

My rage vanished. "Oh, darling, I'm so sorry. Are you all right?"

"Nerve block is a wonderful thing. That hurt like fury!"

I pulled his head against my chest and hugged him fiercely. "Oh, Robert, my God—poor Glenn! What a horrible thing."

He stiffened in my arms. "Yes. Horrible."

A thought struck me. "Her body! Somebody's got to go and retrieve it! Teena, is anyone retrieving Glenn's body?"

"No, Morgan." Her voice was in robot mode; she must have been conducting many conversations at once.

"But someone has to!" Why? "Uh, her family might want her remains sent home. They can still track her, can't they?"

"Her suit transponder is still active," Teena said. "But in her contract with the Foundation she specified the 'cremation in atmosphere' option for disposition in the event of her death."

"Oh. Wait a minute—her last vector was a deceleration with respect to Top Step. She was slowing down in orbit—so she'll go into a *higher* orbit, right? I did the same thing myself yesterday. The atmosphere won't get her, she'll just . . . go on forever . . ." Oh God, without her legs, boiled and burst and dessicated! Much better to burn cleanly from air friction in the upper atmosphere, and fall as ashes to Earth—

"Your conclusion is erroneous, Morgan," Teena said. "She is presently in a higher orbit, yes—but she does not have the mass to sustain it, as Top Step does. In a short time her orbit will decay, and she will have her final wish."

"Oh." I felt inexpressible sadness. "Robert, let's go home. You need rest. And I don't care what the doctor says, I'm going to bandage your foot."

"I'm not going anywhere until I get some answers," he said grimly. "I want to know who shot at us!"

Somehow I had not given that question a conscious thought—but as he said the words I felt a surge of anger. No, more than anger—bloodlust. "Look, there's Dorothy. Let's ask her, maybe she'll know something."

Dorothy Gerstenfeld had arrived just after the medics, and now she was the center of a buzzing swarm of people. She wore the impervious expression Mother wears when the children are throwing a tantrum, and spoke in firm but soothing tones. We jaunted in that direction, with me making sure no one jostled Robert's foot.

"—no hard information," she was saying. "We simply must wait until the investigation is complete. An announcement will be—"

"How do we know there aren't more missiles on the way right now?" Dmitri called out, and the crowd-buzz became more fearful than angry. I felt my stomach lurch; it had not occurred to me that we might still be in danger.

"At the moment we do not," she said. "But a UN Space Command cruiser is warping this way right now, and will be here in minutes. It has much more sophisticated detectors than we do. But if our assailants were planning any further attacks, I can't see why they would wait and give us time to regroup."

"How come our own anticollision gear didn't pick up that missile?" Jo demanded.

"Because it's designed to cope with meteors and debris, not high-speed ASATs at full acceleration," Dorothy said.

"Why the hell not?" Jo said shrilly. "You mean to tell me this place is a sitting duck?"

"Any civilian space habitat is a sitting duck," she said patiently. "Not one of them is defended against military attack."

"That's what the United Nations is for," Ben said.

Robert chimed in. "An effective defensive system for this rock would cost millions, maybe billions. It's not too hard to swat rocks and garbage—but if you want to stop ASATs *and* lasers, *and* particle beams, *and*—"

"I don't care *how* much it costs," Jo said angrily. "It's fucking crazy to have something this big and expensive undefended."

"Robert's right," Ben said. "There's just no way to do it effectively. What I don't understand is why we even have a system as good as we do. I mean, why did the Foundation burrow into Top Step from the front end instead of the back? If the docks were around behind, in shadow, there'd be a lot fewer collisions to defend against."

I recognized what Ben was trying to do by presenting an intriguing digression. Unfortunately someone knew the answer.

"They figure it's more important to keep the Nanotech Safe Lab back there."

"You mean the Foundation thinks microscopic robots are more important than people?" Jo squawked.

"Jo, you know that's not fair," Dorothy said. "Nanoreplicators are important precisely because they could conceivably threaten people—all the people in the biosphere, not just the handful in this pressure."

"The hell with that," Jo said. "'We're naked here . . . and you've got a responsibility to us." A handful of others buzzed agreement.

"Teena," Dorothy said calmly, "have the UN vessels arrived yet?" We could not hear the reply, but Dorothy relaxed visibly and said, "Repeat generally."

Teena's robot voice said, "*S.C. Champion* and *S.C. Defender* have matched our orbit and report `situation stable.'"

There was a murmur of general relief.

"Teena," Dmitri called suddenly, "who fired that missile at us?"

"I do not know," Teena said.

There was a bark of laughter behind me. "Nicely done."

I spun and saw that Sulke had returned. She was smiling, but she looked angry enough to chew rock.

"What Teena means," she said to all of us, "is that she doesn't know the name of the individual who pushed the button."

"Sulke—" Dorothy began, with a hint of steel in her voice.

"You can't sit on it," Sulke said. "It's already on the Net, for Christ's sake. And they're entitled to know."

Dorothy took a deep breath and let it out with a sigh. "Go ahead."

Sulke's smile was gone now. "Credit for the attack has been formally claimed by the terrorist group known as the Gabriel Jihad."

Another incoming missile could not have caused more shock and consternation. "The fucking Caliphate!" Jo cried.

Dorothy's voice cut through the noise of the crowd. "The Umayyad Caliphate does not officially support the Gabriel Jihad."

"Oh, no," Jo shouted back. "The best police state since Stalin just can't seem to stamp out those nasty renegades somehow!"

"The Caliphate has publicly disassociated itself from the attack and denounced the Jihad," Dorothy insisted. "They maintain that the terrorists stole control of one of their hunter-killer satellites and launched one of its missiles."

"Yeah, sure! What is it, fifteen minutes since the fucking thing went off? That's plenty of time for a government to react to a total surprise!" That provoked a collective growl of anger. "The goddam Shiites have always hated Stardancers, everybody knows that."

"The Jihad are claiming that they've destroyed us," Sulke said. "The exact words were, 'the phallus of the Great Satan has been ruined.' They think they finished us."

"What, by blowing up a water-ship?" Ben said.

"Bojemoi," Dmitri burst out. "They did not know the ship would be there—it was not supposed to be for hours. They were trying to destroy the docking complex!"

"Jesus!" Robert exclaimed. "If the docks were destroyed, we . . . my God, we'd have to evacuate Top Step! We'd have to—there'd be no way to reprovision."

There was a stunned silence as we absorbed his words.

"There is nothing further we can accomplish here," Dorothy said. "Please return to your rooms and try to calm yourselves. We are safe for the present—and Administrator Mgabi and the Foundation Board of Directors are pursuing every possible avenue to ensure that nothing like this ever happens again."

"What avenues?" Jo said. "Diplomacy? Fuck that! My friend Glenn is dead, they hard-boiled her head—I say we all go see Mgabi and—"

"Jo?" Reb interrupted.

"—demand that . . . what, Reb? I'm talking for Chrissake—"

"Dorothy said 'please.'"

Jo stared at him, and opened her mouth to say something, and stared some more. It was the closest thing to anger I'd ever heard in Reb's voice.

"She did," Ben agreed, iron in his own voice.

"That's right," Robert said. "I heard her clearly."

"Fair go, Joey," Kirra urged. "Mgabi needs us like a barbed wire canoe right now. Let the poor bastard do 'is bleedin' job, eh?"

Jo closed her mouth, looked around for support without finding any, and then shut her eyes tight and grimaced like a pouting child. "All right, God dammit," she said. "But I—"

"Thank you, Jo," Reb said. "Our sister Glenn was Episcopalian; funeral services will be held by Reverend Schiller in the chapel this evening at the usual time, and as usual there will be observances in all other holy places. I will be free from after lunch until then if any of you need to speak with me."

He spun and jaunted away, and the group dispersed.

I carried Robert back to our room like a package of priceless crystal, determined to bury my confusion and heartache in bandaging and nursing my wounded mate. Ben and Kirra discreetly left us alone and went on down the hall. And in less than five minutes, Robert and I were having our first and last quarrel.

I hate to try and recreate the dialogue of that argument. It was bad enough to live through once.

It came down to this: Robert wanted to go back to Earth. As soon as possible.

No, I must recall some of the words. Because what he said first was *not* "I think we ought to go back to Earth as soon as possible." It wasn't even, "I want to go back to Earth; what do you think?" Or even, "I plan to go back to Earth, how do you feel?"

What he said, as soon as the door sealed behind us, was, "Can I use your terminal? I want to book a seat on the next ship Earthbound. Shall I book one for you too?"

Any of the other three would have been shock enough. God knows I had already had shock enough that day. But the way he phrased it added a whole additional layer of subtext that was just too overwhelming to absorb. He was saying, I want to go back to Earth so badly that I do not care whether you want to or not. He was saying, I can want something so much that I don't care what you want. It took me days to get it through my head, to convince my brain—I *refused* to know it, for just as long as I was able—but an instant after he said that, the pit of my stomach knew that Robert did not love me.

My brain reverted to the intelligence level of a be-your-own-shrink program. "You want to book a seat on the next ship to Earth."

"If it's not already too late. But it should take the others awhile to work it out. Hours, maybe days. None of them is exactly a theoretical relativist. Glenn probably would have caught on fast."

"And you want to know if I want you to book a seat for me."

"Come on, Morgan, I *know* you're bright enough to figure it out."

"I'm bright enough to figure it out."

"Marsport Control to Morgan: come in. You know exactly what I mean. We have to get off this rock."

He was right—I did know what he meant. And he was wrong—because that was only half of what he meant, and the least important half. But that was the half I chose to pursue. "Leave Top Step? *Why?*" I said, already knowing the answer.

"Why? Because *they're shooting at us!* This pressure is not safe anymore."

Perhaps I should have taken a long time to absorb that too. It made me remember Phillipe Mgabi's words to us, our first day inboard: *You are as safe as any terrestrial can be in space, now.* It should have been a shock to realize how unsafe that really was, that even in vast Top Step I was terribly vulnerable. But I come from the generation that grew up being told that rain is poison and sex can kill. Part of me wasn't even surprised.

Argue it anyway. This argument is better than the next one will be.

"Just because some religious fanatics stole a missile?"

"Remember the mysterious something that hulled us on the way up here? You know that was a laser—hell, you and Kirra told *me.* And the failure in the circulation system that first week—do you have any idea how many failsafes there are on an air plant? That was only the fifth failure there's ever been, in fifty years of spaceflight! And now this. You know what they say: 'Three times is enemy action.'"

"But they're just a bunch of terrorists in burnooses, for Christ's sake—nobody can even prove they've got the Caliphate behind them."

He drifted close, stopped himself with a gentle touch at my breast. "Morgan, listen to me. If the People's Republic of China were to declare open war on the Starseed Foundation, I would not be unduly worried. But terrorists are *weak*—that's what makes them so terribly dangerous."

"They fired one lousy missile. If they could hack their way into a hunter-killer satellite, they could just as well have fired a dozen if they wanted to."

"What they did was scarier. They used precisely the minimum amount of force that would achieve their objective. That tells me they are *not* fanatics in burnooses. They've studied their Sun Tzu. One missile, all by itself, should have done the job. That it didn't is a miracle so unlikely I'm still shaking. If that water-ship hadn't sprung a leak at *just* the right time on its way here, we'd all be trying to figure out how to walk back to Earth right now. Without the docks, this place can't support life."

Oh God, he was right. I wanted badly to be hugged. He was close enough to hug. "Jesus Christ, Robert—they've been trying to kill us for two months, and the total body count is five. We ought to have time to finish out our course and Graduate."

"You just said yourself, they could send more missiles any time they want. There could be more on the way now."

"There are two goddam UNP heavy cruisers out there!"

"Right now, yeah. They may even stay awhile. But have you considered the fact that *the Starseed Foundation is not a member of the United Nations, and the Caliphate is?*"

"But—that's ridiculous!"

"Sure, there's a friendly relationship of long standing—the member nations all know perfectly well there wouldn't still *be* a UN if it weren't for the Stardancers, whether they'll admit it or not—even the Caliphate knows that, that's just what's driving them crazy. But you tell me: if it comes to it, is the UN going to go to war to defend a corporation from one of its member nations? When, as you pointed out, it can't even prove the Caliphate is involved? You wait and see: within two or three days, India will have lodged a protest over the diversion of UN resources to protect a Canadian corporation, and then Turkey will chime in, and finally China . . . and one day those two ships will quietly warp orbit."

"They wouldn't."

"They might have no choice. Suppose there were a plausible diversion somewhere else. Say, somebody bombed the Shimizu Hotel? At any given time there's upwards of seven trillion yen on the hoof jaunting around inside that pressure, some of the most influential humans there are. The Space Command *hasn't* got a lot of military strength in space to spare: most of their real muscle is the Star Wars net, and that's aimed one way, straight down. I don't know how soon the next ship leaves here for Earth, but I do know I'm going to be on it."

Whether I'm beside you or not.

"You're just going to run away?"

Think well before saying that to your man, even if it's true—

maybe especially if it's true; I might just as well have stuck a knife in his belly. Even his unexpressive face showed it. For an instant I remembered his torn foot, injured in trying to shield me, and almost said something to at least try to recall my words. But I was too angry.

He didn't let the pain reach his voice; it came out flat, firm, controlled. "You bet your life."

"You mean, just go home and waste all this? All this time, all this work, forget Symbiosis and run away?"

"It will not be wasted. We can always come back, sometime when it is safe again. Even if we never *do* come back, it hasn't been a waste: we've learned a lot and acquired a lot of very useful skills, and we found each other—" *You're a good three or four minutes late in mentioning that, buster.* "—but surely you see that all of that *will* be wasted if we die?"

"But—but we don't have to *quit*. We could . . . look, we could go to Reb and tell him we want to Graduate early! Right away. We could make him buy it—hell, you're spaceworthy already, and I know enough to survive long enough to reach the Symbiote mass, I've proved that, what more do I really need to know? Whatever it is, I'll *know* it as soon as I enter the Starmind! We could pull it off—"

He looked me square in the eye. "Are you ready to take Symbiote? Right now?"

I looked away. "Soon, I mean. A week, say."

He took my face in his hands and made me look back at him. "Morgan—I am not one hundred percent certain I want to go through with Symbiosis. It scares me silly. But I am one hundred percent sure I do not want to be pressured into it. If it's a choice between do it within a week and don't do it, make up your mind, the clock's ticking . . . I pass." He let go of me. "I don't know about you, but I could *use* another six months or so to think about it. And besides, I have no way to know we *have* a week."

"You think the UN will sell us out that fast?"

"No—but how would you like to go EVA tomorrow and find out you've got tanks full of pure nitrogen? The Jihad got to the circulation system: they could get to the tank-charging facilities. Or the Garden. There could be an unfortunate outbreak of botulism, or plague, or rogue replicators from the Safe Lab—all my instincts tell me to get out of here, fast. You mark my words: in twenty-four hours every scheduled seat Earthside will be booked, and they'll be screaming for special extra flights to handle the overflow. And a lot of people will be suddenly making plans to Graduate ahead of schedule, like you said. But I won't be one of them. I don't want to die. I don't want to risk dying, just at the very verge of life eternal. I'm going home, as fast as I can."

Damn him for being so intelligent! With anyone else I might have kept that first argument going for hours yet—but he had gone and won the fucking thing. What now? Refuse to concede that, and have us both repeat our lines with minor variations in word choice two or three more times?

No. God damn it. It was time to have the second argument . . .

"And you don't care if I come along or not?"

His mouth tightened and his nostrils flared. Again I had stung him. Good.

And again the son of a bitch controlled it and answered reasonably. "Of course I care, Morgan. You must know how much I care. But you're a free adult: I can't make your choice for you."

"The hell you can't! That's what you're trying to do!"

"I am not. I am trying very hard not to. Look, it's very simple, Morgan. There are two choices: Graduate too early, for the wrong reasons, under the gun, gamble with our lives and our sanity—or fall back and try again later. There's only one *sensible* choice. I hope with all my heart that you'll be sensible. But I can't *make* you be."

"You do, huh? Why do you hope that, Robert?"

He did not answer.

"Why do you hope that, Robert? Say the words. You've never said the words."

"Neither have you."

"Because I didn't think we needed to!"

"I didn't either!" he snapped back, letting anger show in his voice for the first time.

"Well, maybe we were wrong! *God damn you, I love you!*"

That silly statement hung in the air between us. As if any more irony were needed, the violence of our combined shouting had caused us to start drifting ever so slowly apart. I waved air with my cupped hands to try and cancel it, but he didn't follow suit, so I stopped.

He seemed to consider several responses. What he finally settled on was, "Do I correctly hear you say that if I loved you, I would be trying to tell you what to do with your life?"

"Of course not!"

"Don't you see that if you and I hadn't talked Glenn into staying here, she'd be alive now?"

That *hurt*. I counterattacked hastily. "And I don't mean anything more to you than Glenn did?"

"Morgan, for heaven's sake, be reasonable! I've spent thirty years trying to unlearn the idea that women are property, and if you want someone to go twentieth century and start giving you orders like a Muslim or a Fundamentalist . . . well, I'm afraid you'll have to get somebody else; it's just too late for me to start all over again. I don't want to be any grown-up's father."

Is there anything more infuriating than an argument-opponent with impeccable logic? The correct answer was: *I don't want you to give me orders—I want you to be so crazy in love with me that you can't cut your own marching orders until you know my plans*—but I just could not say that out loud . . . or even to myself.

"Damn you," I cried, "you leave my father out of this!"

Yes, there is something more infuriating than a logical opponent. A man who is impervious to illogic. He turned and found a hand-hold, pushed himself over to my terminal. He belted himself in so he could punch keys without ricocheting away, and looked back to me. "May I? I could just go through Teena, but I think you can guess why I'd rather not do that."

Days ago we had given each other the booting code to our personal terminal . . . as lovers will, and mere sexers will not. It's a step more intimate than swapping housekeys, much more intimate than sharing bodily fluids. Someone who can access your personal memory node can drain your financial accounts, read your mail, read your diary if you keep one, send messages in your name. Hands on your keyboard touch you more deeply than hands on your vagina. "Use your own terminal," I said.

"Certainly," he said calmly, and unstrapped again. "How many seats shall I reserve?"

"One!" I shouted.

"Morgan—" he began.

"Dammit, you don't want to be pressured to Graduate, but you're trying to pressure me into giving it up! Maybe forever—suppose *two* months from now they blow this place up, and the chance is gone for our lifetime?"

"Then we'll have a lifetime. That's the most they promise you when you get born. And we could have it together."

"But I could never *dance* again!"

"Then you have to decide whether it's me you want, or dance. If you stay here, and it happens just as you say . . . you and I will never see each other again."

"Not if you don't run out on me!"

At last I got to him. "I won't *be* running out on you if you do the smart thing and leave with me!" he said, raising his voice for the first time.

I had to press the advantage. "Go on, get out of here—you've got a plane to catch!"

He drew in breath . . . and let it out. And took another deep breath, and let that out, a little more slowly. "I'll reserve two seats. You can always cancel if you choose to."

I was still in my p-suit; I unsnapped an air bottle and threw it at him. Stupid: he was the only one of our class who had ever beaten Dorothy Gerstenfeld in 3-D handball. He side-stepped like a bull-fighter and the tank shattered the monitor screen above my terminal, rebounded with less than half of its original force but spinning crazily. I was spinning myself from having thrown it, and whacked my head on something. The tank *swack*ed into Kirra's sleepsack and was stopped by it. When I looked around, Robert was gone.

Good riddance, I thought, and doubled over and wept in great racking sobs. My eyes grew tendrils of silvery tears; I smashed them into globular fragments that danced and eddied in the air like little transparent Fireflies before breaking apart and whirling away.

God damn him to hell, turning it around like that and dumping it back on me! Now if we break up it'll be my choice, because I choose to cancel my seat home—and it's his fierce respect for my free woman-hood that keeps him from saying anything more than 'he hopes I'll be sensible.' He wouldn't say the fucking words, even after I did!

So close to having it all! Another lousy two or three weeks and I would have had dance and *Symbiosis* and *Robert. How* could *I have been so stupid, thinking they'd let me have it all?*

A part of my mind tried to argue. *You can still have Symbiosis. The whole Starmind, all these people, will enfold you and—*

—and love me, right? When nobody else ever has.

A thought forced its way into my head. Robert had gone down the hall to use his own terminal. Kirra and Ben were presumably there. They would see what he was typing. Or he'd shield the monitor, which would make them curious. At any moment Kirra might come jaunting in here, grimly determined to have me cry on her shoulder. I don't cry on anybody's shoulder. When I cry, I cry alone. I forced my sobs to subside. I could not achieve control of my breath, but I made the tears dry up. I jaunted to the vanity, got tissues, and honked and wiped and snuffled and wiped. I checked my face in the mirror, made myself wash it. "Teena, is my studio free?"

"Repeat, please, Morgan," Teena said in her mechanical voice.

I took a shuddering deep breath, got my voice under control, and repeated the question. Yes, she said, it was available. I told her I wanted it for the rest of the day, and she said that was acceptable. I told her I wanted it for the rest of month, and she said I would have to clear that with Dorothy Gerstenfeld or Phillipe Mgabi. I started to tell her I wanted it for the rest of my life . . . and thanked her and left for the studio. I actually got within fifty meters of it before collapsing into tears again. What triggered it was the sudden realization that I had not given a single thought to Glenn since I'd gotten back to my room. And now I was going to miss her funeral. The tears flew from my eyes like bullets. No one was around to see, and I sealed the hatch behind me before anyone came along.

If you're ever going to have a day like that, try to have it later in the day. It took me *hours* to cry myself to sleep.

In similar situations back on Earth I used to lie on the studio floor and cry, let the floor drink my tears as it so often drank my blood. Here there was no floor. I missed it bitterly.

11

A fallen blossom
Come back to its branch?
No, a butterfly!
—Moritake (1452-1549)

I got home a few hours before breakfast. Kirra was alone in the room, and woke as I came in. "Are you right, love?"

I knew that was Aussie for, *are you* all *right?,* but I couldn't help hearing the words as they sounded too. "Ask me again next year," I said to both questions. "You heard, huh?"

"We heard." She slipped out of her sleepsack. "Robert's found himself another room until the ship leaves."

"Where's Ben?"

"I told him I'd wait here for you alone 'til brekkie, then we were gonna hunt you down together."

By then she had reached me, and was hugging me. It helped a little, as much as anything could help. She did not say a single one of the clichés I'd been dreading, only held me. After a time she began singing softly, in Yirlandji, and that helped me a little too.

Awhile later she said, "Tucker?" and I said, "No. You go," and she nodded. "Bring you back somethin'?" she asked, and I said, "No." She left, and I slid into my sleepsack and went fetal.

She let me have the rest of the day, and then at around suppertime she showed up with what might just have been the only thing in human space that could have made me feel like eating. "You're not serious," I said when she took it out of its thermos bag and tossed it to me. "How could you possibly—"

"Sulke knows a bloke at the Shimizu."

"But it must have cost—"

"The bloke liked me Song o' Polar Orbit a lot; it's his shout."

Even in my misery it reached me. A full litre of fine Chilean chocolate chip ice cream. Back in Vancouver it would have been an expensive luxury; here it was a pearl without price. She had heard me speak longingly of it several times; she'd even remembered my favorite flavour. I had no idea what her favorite flavour was. "Pull up a spoon," I said, and we dug in together.

As we ate she filled me in on the news.

It was going just as Robert had predicted. Third-Monthers were Graduating en masse. Some of the rest of us, mostly Novices, had decided they were ready for early Graduation—from one to five weeks early!—and some, mostly Postulants, had suddenly remembered pressing business dirtside. Already there were no more seats available on the next regularly scheduled transport (two days hence), and the special charter that had been announced was filling up fast. Robert and I were not the only couple who had split up.

There were some students who took neither course. Some lacked the imagination to realize how comprehensive a disaster it would have been if that missile had destroyed the docks—and some were just the kind of people who insist on building their home on the slopes of Mount Vesuvius or in San Francisco. (Come to think of it, Robert was going home to San Francisco. What kind of logic was that?)

And of course there were the spacers on staff. Going dirtside was not an option for them. Those who could were trying to change jobs, or rather, eliminate Top Step from their job rotations. Those who could not were trying to get work deep inboard, on the theory that they'd be safer from attack. It was a shaky theory.

I was unsurprised to learn Kirra and Ben's choice.

"We're doin' it, love. Ben and me, this Sunday. I reckon you guessed we would."

"Good for you," I said. My eyes were stinging. "Pushing ahead the wedding. That makes me really happy."

"You want to join us?"

"Thanks for asking. But no. I'm not ready. Reb would never let me do it in this state. You two go on—I'll catch you up as soon as I can."

Privately I wondered if I meant that. I still was not utterly certain that I wanted to go through with Symbiosis. The idea of lowering all my defenses, forever, was seeming less and less attractive. Wouldn't it be just perfect if I finally decided to chicken out . . . *after* cutting my ties with Robert? If I played my cards right, I could come out of this with nothing at all.

The next couple of days were sheerest hell. I kept going over and over it in my mind. A thousand times I asked myself, why not just go back to Earth and Robert? So he didn't love me the way I loved him; he cared, and that could well become love in time. A thousand times I answered, because he had made it an ultimatum, and because he would not admit he had done so, and because I just couldn't risk losing dance forever, even for him.

And because he hadn't asked me to—just assumed I'd "be sensible."

A thousand times I concluded I had made the right decision. But I didn't call Teena and tell her to cancel the reservation Robert had made in my name.

He called me once, about twenty-four hours after the quarrel. I had instructed Teena not to put through any calls from him, so he recorded a long message. When she told me, I had her wipe it, unplayed. A mistake: I spent hours wondering what he had said.

Twice I forced myself to go to the cafeteria, using Teena to make sure he was not there at the time. The food tasted like hell. Once I let Ben and Kirra (almost literally) drag me to Le Puis. Even Fat Humphrey didn't cheer me up, nor the Hurricanes he prescribed for me. With Kirra right there listening, Ben made the politest pass I'd ever received; I almost smiled as I thanked him and turned him down.

That night Reb came to visit me in my room. He expressed sympathy, and offered to help in any way he could. He did not, as I'd half expected, try to persuade me to stop grieving. Instead he encouraged me to grieve, the faster to use it up. But I noticed something subtle about his word choice. He never said he was sorry Robert and I were breaking up. He only said he was sorry I was suffering over it.

A friend of my parents, back on Gambier Island, once responded to his wife's leaving him by taking their beloved dog back up into the woods and shooting him. I'd never understood how anyone could do something so simultaneously selfish and self-destructive until I found myself on the verge of making a pass at Reb. Hurt people do crazy things, that's all. I was luckier than my parents' friend had been: I caught myself in time, and Reb failed to notice, the nicest thing he could have done.

Later that night I started to record a message for Robert . . . then gave up and erased it unsent.

The next day the shuttle left for Earth.

I found myself in the corridor outside the Departure Lock, in an alcove where I could watch the queue forming. I avoided the gazes of those who lined up, and they avoided mine. Robert was one of the last to arrive, coming to a stop right outside my alcove. I saw him before he saw me. It had an almost physical impact. Then he saw me, and that was even worse. We looked at each other, treading air. He glanced at the others, then back to me.

He waved Earthward. "Come with me."

I waved starward. "Come with me."

He made no reply. After a time I left the alcove, grabbed a handhold and flung myself away into the bowels of the rock, not stopping until I reached hardhat territory. I joined a handful of gawkers and watched a new tunnel being cut. They struck ice, and that was good, because soon there were so many warm water droplets in the ambient air that a few tears more or less went unnoticed.

I cut classes that day, as I had the previous two, and spent some time in the studio in the afternoon, trying to dance. It was a fiasco. I sought out Reb's after-classes sitting group, and sat kûkanzen for a couple of hours, or tried to. It was my first time with the group. I had done a fair amount of sitting outside class, but never with the group. But that night I needed them to keep me anchored, to keep me from bursting into tears. Sitting, and the chanting after, helped, a little. Not enough.

I went to Le Puis, where Fat Humphrey allowed me to get drunk. He did so with skill and delicacy, so that I woke the next day without a hangover despite my best efforts.

But I was dumb enough to decide to go to morning class, and logy enough to sleepwalk through suit inspection, and so I came damned close to dying when a thruster I should have replaced went rogue on me at just the wrong moment. I was not able to recover as Ben had from a similar problem, and had to be rescued. By Ben, since Robert was no longer there to take care of it.

It straightened me up. I did not want to die—not even subconsciously,

I think. Or if I did, I wanted it to be at a time and place, and by a method, of my own choosing; not in some stupid accident, not over a man. I won't say I started to feel better . . . but I did start to take better care of myself again. That's a beginning.

Sulke didn't chew me out for my stupidity. She was the one I'd gotten drunk with the night before, the one who'd gotten me to bed, as I had once done for her.

I don't know, maybe it's easier to turn your back on Earth if there's someone down there you never want to see again. Perhaps it's easier to attain Zen no-thought if your thoughts are all painful ones anyway. I started to make real progress in my studies, both practical and spiritual.

When I arrived at Top Step, free fall had seemed an awkward, clumsy environment; the graceful Second- and Third-Monthers had seemed magical creatures. I didn't feel particularly magical now, but free fall seemed a natural way to live, and the new crop of Postulants seemed incredibly awkward and clumsy. My p-suit had once seemed exotic, romantic; now it was clothing. Sitting kûkanzen had once been unbearable boredom and discomfort; now it was natural and blissful. I told myself that I had learned a brutal lesson in nonattachment, which would actually help me in the transition to Symbiosis. All my bridges were burnt behind me. All I had left to lose were dance and my life itself. All I had to do was to go forward, or die trying.

One thing never changed. Space itself was always and forever a place of heart-stopping majesty and terrible beauty.

I even learned to stop resenting Kirra and Ben's happiness in time to preserve our friendship. I'm ashamed to admit how hard a learning that was. Other happy couples, triads and group marriages in Top Step somehow did not grate on me—but at first it seemed disloyal for my friends to be joyous when I was not. And Ben certainly had more than enough quirks for which one could work up a dislike. But Reb caught me at it, diagnosed my problem, and talked it over with me until I could be rational again. In my heart of hearts, I loved them both, and wished them well.

They both made an effort to bring me out myself, to invite me for drinks and include me in their games and discussions. We three had been friends like this before I'd become Robert's lover; now we were again, that was all.

Only one thing was really keeping me from symbiosis, now. I wanted to make one last dance before I went, to choreograph my farewell to human life while I was still human. I knew I would make other dances in concert with my Stardancer brothers and sisters, and perform in theirs, for centuries to come—but this last one would be mine alone, the last such there could ever be. In a way, it was almost good that Robert was gone, for now the dance could be all my own personal farewell, rather than ours.

I stopped calling the piece *Do the Next Thing.* Although those words are a pretty fair approximation of the meaning of life—they'll get you through when life itself has lost its meaning—they were a little too flip for the title of my last work as a human. Instead I began thinking of it simply as *Coda.*

There is a pun in there that perhaps only a choreographer would get. In music, a coda is the natural end of a movement, the passage that brings it to a formal close. In dance, it is the end of a *pas de deux.*

I worked on it for hours at a time, throwing out ideas like a Roman candle, ruthlessly pruning every one that wasn't just right, then trying them in different combinations and juxtapositions, like someone trying to solve a Rubik's Cube by intuition alone. I had the constant awareness that something might kill me at any minute, but I tried not to let it hurry me. Better to die with it incomplete than do a sloppy job of it.

It ate up a lot of time. Or kept the time from eating me up. One of those.

"When are we gonna see this bleedin' dance, then?" Kirra asked me that Friday. "Ben and me are gone day after tomorrow."

"I'm sorry, love," I told her. "It's just not ready to show yet."

"Why don't you do a bit of it just before we swallow the stuff? It don't have to be finished—just a little bit to send us off in style, like."

"Yeah," Ben chimed in. "We'd love to have you dance at our GraduWedding, Morgan."

"And I'd love to," I said, "but it just won't be ready in time. I'm sorry, I wish it could be."

"Ah, don't be stingy with it, Morgan," Kirra said. "I sung for you, ain't I? An' Benjy taught you free fall handball an' all. It's your shout."

I started to get irritated. Tact had never been the strong suit of either of them . . . but this was a little excessive. Suddenly I understood something. Underneath their excitement and anticipation, Kirra and Ben were both scared silly.

"I'll dance it at my own Graduation," I said, softer than I might have. "You can both see it then."

"We'll be halfway to Titan by then," she protested.

"So what? As long as one Stardancer is in the neighborhood, you'll have a front-row seat."

"Huh. Right enough, I guess."

"Have you two recorded your Last Words for your families, yet?"

They let me change the subject. But I kept thinking about their request, wishing I had something to give them for a wedding gift, and a little while later I had a very bright idea. I excused myself, went off and made a phone call. It worked even better than I had hoped. I had to work hard to conceal my excitement when I rejoined them.

We three slept together that night, for the last time. It was a memorable night; people who are scared silly make incredible lovers. We spent the next day together, visiting all their favorite places. Solariums One and Three, Le Puis, the Great Hall, the games rooms and all the places where we'd shared so much fun and laughter. After dinner I slipped away while they weren't looking and let them have their last evening to themselves. They didn't come back to the room, and I fell asleep with a smile on my face.

The next day was Sunday. I didn't see them until dinner time; according to Teena they never left Ben's room until then. We talked awhile, and they gave some attention to their last meal. Then the two of them instigated one last food fight. It was glorious. You could tell how close a person was to Graduation by how little food they wore when the fight was over. Ben and Kirra were the only ones who ended up completely unmarked—somewhat unfairly, as they had started it. Either of them could dodge anything they saw coming, and Ben had no blind spot, and had enough attention to spare to guard Kirra's back and warn her of sneak attacks. I only got hit a couple of times myself, each time from behind.

I showered and was done in time to catch them coming out of Reb's room. "Hey, you guys. Hello, Reb."

"Hi, Morgan," Kirra said. "Guess it's time to get it done, eh?"

"Yeah. Listen, I know this is kind of last-minute, but . . . would you mind a bit of dance at your Graduation after all?"

They both brightened. "That'd be great, love," Kirra said. "Gee, I'm glad you changed your mind."

"Yeah," Ben agreed. "I'm dying to see *Coda.*"

"Oh, it won't be *Coda,*" I said. "I came up with something special for the occasion. I think you'll like it. Are you coming, Reb?"

"I wouldn't miss it," he said. He took Kirra's arm and I took Ben's, and the four of us jaunted away like a chorus line on skates.

A fair-sized group was waiting at the airlock. Kirra and Ben had invited anyone who wanted to come, and they were well liked; all of our class that were still around were present, and even some people I didn't know. There were hugs and handshakes and goodbyes, and then everybody put their hoods on. It took awhile to cycle everybody through the lock. While we were waiting outside, Kirra asked me, "Don't you need to warm up or somethin', love?"

"Not this time," I said.

She made a sound of puzzlement, but let it go.

When everyone was assembled outside, we set off as a group, led by Reb. Newer chums who drifted out of formation did their best to recover without drawing attention to themselves. We ascended like a slightly tipsy celestial choir; Top Step slowly fell away below us, and when it had dwindled into a distant cigar, the Symbiote Mass was visible above us. "Above" in an absolute sense, relative to Earth: by that time we had flipped ourselves so that it seemed to be below our feet. "I don't see any Stardancers waitin' to meet us," Kirra said as we closed in on the red cloud.

"Don't worry," I said. "They'll be along."

"Bloody well better. *I* don't know how to make that big glob squeeze off a piece my size."

"Relax, Kirra," Reb said. "Be your breath."

"Right. No worries, mate."

Our formation became most ragged as we came to rest near the Mass, but Reb issued quiet instructions and got us all together again with minimal confusion. Kirra and Ben floated a little apart from the rest of us. Ben's p-suit was a pale yellow that suited him and his red hair as well as cobalt blue suited Kirra. Between the two of them and the glowing red Symbiote Mass beside them, they had the rainbow covered. There was a moment of silence.

"Well, here we are," Kirra said finally. "I'd like to thank you all for comin'—"

"—or however you're reacting." Ben interjected, and she aimed a mock blow at him that he dodged easily. We all chuckled, and some of the solemnity went out of the occasion.

"We got no speeches to make or anythin'," she went on. "But before we get down to it, our good friend Morgan McLeod is going to dance for us all." An approving murmur began.

"Me?" I said. "Oh, no!"

"What do you mean, 'no'? You promised."

"I asked if you'd mind a bit of dance. I didn't say I'd be dancing. Curtain!"

"I don't get you, love."

"Wait a second, spice," Ben said. "Here comes our stuff, I think." (Ben and Kirra called each other "spice," a term of endearment I find distinctly superior to "honey" or other sticky sweetness.)

She processed to face the way he seemed to be looking. "Where?"

"No, no, there," he said, and pointed behind him and to his right.

"You and your trick eyes," she said, and faced the way he was pointing. "Right you are, here it comes. Still don't see any Stardancers, though." A red blob was slowly growing larger in the distance.

"You're looking at six of them," I said, enjoying myself hugely.

"Where?"

"Twelve, actually, but they're squeezed into six bodies at the moment. Kirra and Benjamin Buckley, allow me to present Jinsei Kagami, Yuan Zhongshan, Consuela Paixao, Sven Bjornssen, Ludmilla Vorkuta, and Walerij Pietkow."

The red blob was much closer now. Music swelled out of nowhere, a soft warm A chord with little liquid trills chasing in and out of it. It couldn't seem to make up its mind whether it was major or minor.

"They are all trained dancers themselves, but they have all agreed to lend remote-control of their bodies to six of their more distant siblings, who will now dance in your honour. These are Shara Drummond, Sascha Yakovskaya, Norrey Armstead, Charles Armstead, Linda Parsons, and Tom McGillicuddy. Choreography is by all six, around a frame by Shara. Music prerecorded by Raoul Brindle; playback, set design and holographic recording by Harry Stein. The piece is called *Kiss the Sky.*"

By now the jumbled murmuring of our group was as loud as the soft music. Shara Drummond . . . and *all* of the original Six. . . *and* Yakovskaya, the first truly great dancer to join them in space, the man who had choreographed the *Propaedeutics* in his first week as a Stardancer. . . all dancing together, if only by proxy, for the first time in over a decade—with Brindle on synth! "Pull the other one," Kirra said. "I don't see a bloody soul. Just that great hunk of—oh!"

She and everyone fell silent. The approaching blob of Symbiote had suddenly flexed, and stretched in six directions at once to become a kind of six-pointed red snowflake, swirling gently as it approached, like a pinwheel in a gentle breeze, its axis of rotation pointed right at us.

It took a moment for the eye to get it into correct perspective: it was *not* just enough Symbiote for two people, but enough and more than enough for six, therefore somewhat farther from us than it had seemed to be. Six Stardancers had mingled their Symbiotes and were joined at the feet, held together by their linked hands, a hundred meters from us. The snowflake shifted and flowed, as the six dancers who comprised it changed their position in unison from one pattern to another by flexing elbows and knees, contracting and releasing.

The music acquired a slow, steady pulse in the bass. The pattern of the spinning snowflake changed with each beat, as if it were some great red heart clenching rhythmically. Percussion instruments and a Michael Hedges-like guitar began adding counterpoint accents to the rhythm. The total mass of Symbiote began to swell away from the dancers it contained, until it was a translucent crimson disc with six people at its heart, perhaps twenty meters in diameter. The disc swelled from the center and became a convex lens, nearly transparent; pink stars swam behind it, rippling. Lights came up. The lamps themselves were invisible to us, since they were tiny and dull black and pointing away from us, but we saw their blue and yellow reflections come up as highlights on the crimson lens, highlights that bled all the other colours there are at their edges.

The six children of the lens separated like a bud opening into a flower, fanned out in six directions and wedged themselves into the narrow parts of the lens wall. One of them doubled and jaunted back to the center of the lens, came to rest there . . . and began to move. Even at a hundred meters, even behind that carmine film of Symbiote, even wearing a different body, there was no mistaking her. The familiar motif that emerged in brass in the underlying music only confirmed it. Jinsei's body it may have been, but it was Shara Drummond, the greatest dancer of our time, who took the first solo.

She wore thrusters at wrists and ankles, but could not have used them inside that lens, I think. She danced only with body and muscles, moving three-dimensionally in place, with her unmistakable fluidity and precision of line. It reminded me of a piece I'd seen years ago by a colleague recovering from a leg injury called *Dancing in Place:* confining himself to one spot on stage, standing on one leg, he had explored more ways of dancing and looking at dance than most performers can do using an entire stage. Shara/Jensei did the same now, tumbling, arching, turning, while her center stayed anchored to the center of the lens. She could have been a butterfly gifted with limbs, or a leaf in flight, or a protozoan swimming in the primordial soup. The brass stopped hinting at Shara's Theme and made a new statement, underlined by strings. Soon, inevitably, she drifted far enough from the center of the lens to touch its inner surface, and used it to jaunt back to her original place at the periphery.

This time two figures moved to the center and met there. Linda Parsons and Tom McGillicuddy, the hippie and the businessman who had met in space, fallen in love, and become the fourth and fifth founding members of Stardancers Incorporated (after Charlie, Norrey and Raoul). McGillicuddy at least was easy for me to identify: he had always been the least trained of the original company; even after decades of practice, and even wearing a better-trained body than his own, there were minor limitations to his technique. But Linda compensated for them so perfectly after thirty-four years of dancing with him that I don't think anyone else noticed. They did a *pas de deux* at the heart of the lens, like mating hummingbirds, and now the brass and strings made different but complementary statements to accompany them.

When they returned to their places at the rim, three figures replaced them. Charlie and Norrey and Sascha, legendary partners and friends, did a trio piece loosely derived from their famous *Why*

Can't We?, as woodwinds brought in a third theme that fit the brass and string motifs like an interlocking puzzle; all three resolved into a major chord as the trio broke up and returned to the rim again.

Next a quartet of both Drummond sisters and Armstead and Yakovskaya, faster and more vigorous, interacting with the kind of precision and intuition that nontelepaths would have needed weeks of rehearsal to achieve; a great pipe organ added its voice to the music, which rose in tempo and resolved into a four-note diminished chord at the quartet's end.

Then everyone but Shara met at the center for a flashing quicksilver quintet, tumbling over one another like kittens in a basket; the music was all tumbling five-note ninth chords.

Finally all six danced together as a single organism, making strange, indescribable geometrical figures in three dimensions. As they danced, the lens filled out, became a sphere, which slowly contracted in on them, thickening and darkening as it came. Before long there was only a nearly opaque glowing red ball of Symbiote, flexing and shifting in time to the racing music. It quivered, trembled—

—then burst apart, becoming six separate Stardancers flying in different directions like a firework detonation. Their thrusters protruded through their individual coatings of Symbiote now, and they used them to put themselves into graceful wide loops, so that they returned to their starting point, missed colliding by inches, and then arced out again. Each had a different-coloured thruster exhaust; comet-tails of red, yellow, blue, orange, green, and purple attended them as they flew, leaving the afterimage of a multicoloured Christmas ribbon against the star-spangled blackness. The music swelled and soared with them as they danced, spilling trills in all directions to match their thruster spray. Eventually they all came together again in a tight formation like exhibition aircraft, and took turns passing each other back and forth from hand to hand.

There was joy in their dance, and hope, and endless energy, and manifest love for one another; from time to time one or another of them would laugh for sheer pleasure. I found that I was smiling unconsciously as I watched their dance unfold. I sneaked a look at Kirra and Ben; they were smiling too.

There was a short movement in which they were performing a kind of kinesthetic pun, moving mentally as well as physically, passing their *selves* from one host body to another. I don't know how many others caught it, but I clearly saw Shara Drummond's essence change bodies several times. Once or twice I spotted Yakovskaya or McGillicuddy transmigrating too. I think that for a time, the bodies' original owners were present and dancing as well.

Then Shara was stationary, spinning slowly around her vertical axis, apart from the other five as they continued to interact, watching how their dance changed in her absence; then in a reversed reprise of their solo-to-group progression. Tom dropped out, then Linda, then Charlie, then Norrey. Quintet, quartet, trio, pair, finally Yakovskaya was soloing within a pentagon of stationary spinning companions, and then he too stopped dancing and went into a spin. The music had decayed too, to a single voice, a cello, and the theme it was quoting was not Shara's signature motif this time, but Kirra's Song of Polar Orbit.

By some means I didn't and don't understand, all six of them began to move relative to one another, around their common center, as though they were jointly orbiting some invisible mini black hole. The orbits tightened inexorably, until they darted like the Firefly aliens themselves, like electrons dancing in mad attendance on some invisible nucleus. Hands met and joined just as the Song of Polar Orbit reached its coda; again they were a six-personed snowflake. Thrusters sprayed coloured fire and smoke, and they became a living, madly spinning Catherine Wheel.

The thrusters went dark, and they were a scarlet pinwheel.

Their Symbiotes merged, and they were a disc again.

A hole appeared in the center, making the disc look for all the world like an old-fashioned phonograph record (all right, I'm dating myself) spinning on a turntable, seen from above. My parents used to own an album like that, red and translucent, a novelty gimmick. The hole enlarged, so that the disc looked like a 45 RPM single; paradoxically its spin slowed rather than speeded up.

Suddenly the disc exuded some of its mass into the hole in the center, where a globe of red Symbiote grew like a pearl forming within an oyster. It moved away from the disc, coming toward us with infinite slowness. Toward Kirra and Ben. As it did so, the disc broke up into six Stardancers again, and they all braked violently to an instant stop, sudden total motionlessness. The music broke like a wave on a shore and faded to silence, the lights went out.

After several seconds of silence, there was wild applause.

Oh, I know I haven't conveyed it; dance can't be described. Look it up for yourself, it's on the Net. Not a major work by any means, but a moving and lyrical piece, just right for a wedding feast and Graduation. I was terribly pleased on Kirra and Ben's account.

They thanked me lavishly for the gift, and thanked all twelve of the dancers individually. "That was bloody marvelous," Kirra said. "Morgan, really, it was special!" She was grinning, but her p-suit hood was full of tear-tendrils.

"Just my version of chocolate chip ice cream from Chile," I said, grinning back at her. *Though it marks a much happier occasion than your gift did.* Dammit, I was leaking saline worms too.

"We're deeply honoured," Ben said. "Our GraduWedding has become part of dance history. Or almost. Get ready, spice, here it comes!"

Their blob of Symbiote was nearly upon them, a bead of God's blood.

"I'll sing at your Graduation, Morgan," Kirra promised me hastily. "Wait an' see if I don't! Goodbye—see you soon—cheerio, all! Let's go meet it, Benjy: one, two, three . . ."

They jaunted forward together, hit the Symbiote dead center, passed inside it. They stripped quickly, took the communications gear from their p-suits and hung it around their necks, pushed the suits clear of the Symbiote and joined hands. It contracted in upon them and around and through them, and they were two Stardancers, convulsing with their first shock of telepathic onslaught but still holding hands. Their combined shout of exaltation was picked up by their throat mikes and hurled to the stars.

Then they were silent and adrift, marinating in Symbiosis.

The dancers had already begun tiptoeing away on scarlet butterfly wings of lightsail. The show was over.

Reb took my arm, and we all headed back to Top Step.

They phoned me up five or six days later. They were well on their way out to meet the Harvest Crew returning with new Symbiote from Titan, about a day from rendezvous. It was an odd conversation. They both sounded as though they were very drunk or very stoned. Ben commented giddily that space now looked to him just like a newspaper. Black and white and red all over. They both assured me that Symbiosis was glorious, wonderful, not to be missed, but were quite unable to describe it in any more detail than that, at least in words. They did say they had two new senses, as expected, but could not describe or explain them any better than the instructors back at Suit Camp had. Kirra sang me part of a work in progress. *The Song of Symbiosis,* and made me promise to send a copy of it to Yarra and the Yirlandji people for her. It was terribly beautiful but very strange, haunting and confounding, hinting at things that even music can't carry. She said she was collaborating on a Song with Raoul (whom she would be physically meeting in only a few more hours), but did not sing any of it for me. I told them my dance was about two-thirds finished, and they both exhorted me to hurry up and complete it so I could come join them. I assured them I was going as fast as I could, especially since I no longer had any close friends inboard to take up my free time. Kirra, pausing to consult some mathematician I didn't know, worked out that they would in all likelihood be back with the fresh Symbiote just in time for my Graduation. We agreed to meet then, and I was very pleased to know they would be present for my own last breath.

I was hard at work on the piece the next day, had just solved a tricky and hard-to-describe esthetic problem in the third movement, when Teena said, "Morgan, Reb Hawkins needs to speak to you as soon as possible."

"Put him on," I said, brushing sweat from my back, and she did. I can't reproduce the dialogue and won't try. He told me the news, and I'm sure he did it as compassionately as it could have been done.

Shortly after Ben and Kirra had made rendezvous with the returning Harvest Crew, there had been an unexplained catastrophic explosion, cataclysmic enough to disrupt the entire mass of new Symbiote and kill the entire Crew. Raoul Brindle, Ben, Kirra, more than a dozen others, all were dead.

Black and white and red all over.

12

We die, and we do not die.
—Shunryu Suzuki-roshi,
ZEN MIND, BEGINNER'S MIND

The news rocked the Solar System, stunned humans and Stardancers alike.

Credit for the explosion was formally claimed, not by the Gabriel Jihad, but by a much older terrorist group, Jamaat al-Muslimeen. They too were rumored to have ties to the Umayyad Caliphate, though they were based in Trinidad rather than Medina, black Muslims rather than brown. It didn't seem to make much difference. There was so much outcry and mutual vituperation at the UN that they were forced to suspend all operations of the General Assembly for a week. That didn't seem to make much difference, either, at least not to those humans in space.

Just how the Jamaat had managed to pull off the bombing, they did not say. Of all the questions the incident raised, that one seemed to me to matter least of all.

But it seemed to fascinate Sulke. "It just couldn't possibly have been a missile," she insisted angrily.

We were drinking together in Le Puis, heavily, a few days after the tragedy; I was still in something like a protracted state of shock, and cared not at all for the question, but found myself arguing automatically. "Why not?"

"It's obvious. Peace missiles only aim down. ASATs only aim sideways, nothing shoots *away* from Earth except lasers and particle beams, and the biggest one there is would have to have been focused on the Symbiote for nearly an hour to burst it. But it was an instantaneous *blam.*"

"Anything with a power plant could be a big slow bomb."

"Self-propelling hardware in space is *very* carefully monitored, for pretty obvious reasons. There just isn't anything missing. And besides, if something had left its usual orbit and headed out of cislunar space, it would have been tracked by the Space Command. The screens prove no artifact ever approached the new Symbiote. The Chinese have got some scientific stuff vectoring around out in that general direction, but not within a hundred thousand klicks of the spot where the explosion took place, and they couldn't have fired off anything big enough to make that big a bang without being seen."

Janani Luwum, a huge First-Monther truckdriver from Uganda, was at the next table, near enough to eavesdrop, and wedged himself into the conversation. "I don't understand the ambiguity. Wasn't the new Symbiote itself being tracked?"

"Yes," Sulke agreed, "but not very closely or carefully. It wasn't *doing* anything interesting. They would have started paying more attention in a few days when deceleration began, but as things stand we have nothing better than automatic radar tracking at poor resolution."

"Then you don't *know* that there was no incoming missile: you only infer it."

"From goddam good evidence," she insisted. "Anything on a closing course would have triggered alarms. That aside, the Stardancers present would have noticed it coming, with that weird radar sense of theirs, and tapes of radio transmissions and reports from Stardancers who were in rapport at the time show no one was expecting trouble right up to the second it went off."

"Christ," Janani said, "I wonder what that must be like: being in telepathic rapport with someone while they're blown to pieces."

"I don't know," Sulke said with a shudder, "but I hear they have more than fifty new catatonics to try and heal."

"Those were not the first Stardancers ever to die," Janani's lover Henning Fragerhøi pointed out.

"No, there've been half a dozen accidental deaths since the first Symbiosis," Sulke said. "But never before have so many died, so suddenly, so savagely. No Stardancer was ever murdered before."

"But how can you be sure it was murder?" Janani said. "You just finished proving there was no shot fired."

"That's right—but there was nothing along with them that could possibly have blown up like that. Nothing but Stardancers and Symbiote."

"Well, then," I said, tired of all the chattering, "it didn't happen. That's a relief. Thanks, Sulke. Can we get back to some serious drinking, now? Hey, Fat! Oh shit, I mean 'Pål'. Hey, Pål, we need more balls over here." We were able to get shitfaced in Le Puis because Fat Humphrey was not on duty; it was said that he'd been locked in his own quarters, drinking himself into a coma, since the disaster had happened. He had loved Kirra almost as much as I had. And he had been a personal friend of Raoul—had been there the day Raoul joined the newly formed Stardancers Incorporated, twenty years before. His relief bartender Pål Bøgeberg didn't seem to much care if the customers got drunk enough to riot; he brought the balls of booze I ordered without protest.

"It fucking well happened, all right," Sulke said. "But there's only one fucking way in the System it could have happened."

"Spontaneous combustion," I said sourly, and sucked a great gulp of gin.

"Stalking horse," she said, and squeezed a stream of gin at her own mouth, catching it with the panache of a longtime free fall lush.

"I don't understand," said Henning, for whom English was a second language. " 'Stocking hose'?"

"Stalking horse. A living mine. One of those Stardancers was boobytrapped. And since they were all telepathic, it had to have been done without their knowledge. Just how it was done, I can't imagine. My best guess is some kind of very tiny dart carrying seed nanoreplicators. It penetrated somebody's Symbiote without them noticing, somehow, and then the sneaky little nanoreps used that body's own materials to construct a bomb. As soon as it was big enough, *blooey*!"

"More likely the Symbiote itself was injected somehow," Janani said. "Enough matter there for a really big bomb, without the risk its host would notice it growing. Stardancers monitor their own bodies pretty closely, control even the unconscious systems and so forth: you'd think they'd notice a tumor large enough to explode with so much force."

"Either could be true," Sulke said. "There was a helluva lot of Symbiote, but it's made up of the wrong chemicals to make a really powerful bomb easily, and you'd see discoloration as it formed. But I've read in spy thrillers that nanoreplicators could synthesize a very powerful explosive from the materials in an ordinary human body, without disturbing any essential function. It could be hidden in the one large part of the body a Stardancer never pays any attention to."

"Where's that?"

"The lungs. Plenty of room, and all the nerves to that area are switched off permanently at Symbiosis, to keep you from panicking when you stop breathing for good."

"Shut *up,* for Christ's sake," I cried, horrified by the mental picture of death coalescing around someone's living heart while they jaunted along oblivious.

"The only thing I don't get is why whoever it was didn't notice the injection. The seed would have to have mass enough to be perceptible, be at least as big as a pinhead—and Stardancers notice collisions with objects that big. They have to, they live in a world of micrometeorites."

"If the subject is not changed in the next sentence spoken, I am going to squirt the rest of this gin in your eye," I said, and held it up threateningly. Sulke was not an easy drunk to intimidate, but maybe there was something in my voice. Her next sentence was a *non sequitur* that started a different argument, about who was *really* behind the bombing. It wasn't a true change of subject, but I let it go.

I don't remember much of the rest of that night, and what I remember of the next day doesn't bear repeating. I spent most of it in my sleepsack, moaning, with an icepack at the back of my neck—or rather, shuttling back and forth between there and the john. After an endless time of misery I decided I needed to sweat the pain out of me, and went to my studio.

There I found that my thoughts danced and whirled more than my body ever could.

Sick of this goddam piece. Sick of everything I can think of. Not one close friend left anywhere in the Solar System. More than forty-three thousand new lovers waiting to marry me, but not one goddam friend. Reb'll be on my back any time now; I've cut classes for three days straight. Probably not the only one. Fuck it, there's nothing more they can teach me now that I need to know. Only thing holding me back is this goddam dance, and I wish I'd never started the frigging thing. Hadn't been so busy and distracted with it, self-involved, I might have put together a stronger thing with Robert. Jesus, my back hurts. Been hurting quite a bit lately; snuck up on me. Old injury trying to make a comeback. Repair it myself once I eat the Big Red Jell-O. Unless somebody injects me with a teeny little bomb factory. Or already has. No, I'd have noticed. Or would I? Apparently somebody *failed to notice it being done to them. How the hell could that be? How do you introduce something the size of a pinhead into someone's body without them noticing? Slip it in their soup? Awful chancey—might leave the wrong few drops in the container. Aerosol spray? No, the victim might choke on the thing. Damn, that knee's starting to twinge a bit too. Or am I imagining it? Oh, God damn it all. Everything, everything, everything falling apart at once. Friends gone, lover gone, never again the joyous invasion of my—*

I cried out.

"Are you all right, Morgan?" Teena asked with concern.

"Absolutely wonderful," I snarled.

She was sharp enough to detect pain in a human voice, but not subtle enough for sarcasm. "Sorry I disturbed you."

"Privacy, Teena. Switch off. Butt out!"

"Yes, Morgan," she said, and was gone, her monitors on me shut off until I called her again.

I tried to vomit, but there was nothing left in my system to expel. The new thought in my brain was so monstrous, so unthinkable, I wanted to spew it out of me like poison food, but I could find no way to do so even symbolically. I was suffused with horror. I curled up into a fetal ball, trembling violently.

—it can't be (it could be) it can't be (it could be) there must be some other way (name one) it can't be—

All at once I knew a way you could invade someone's body without them noticing. By concealing the invader in another, larger invasion they were joyfully accepting.

By fucking them.

Literally or figuratively, by sperm in one set of mucous membranes or by saliva in another at the other end, what difference did it make? The pinhead-sized object need not be hard or metallic like a real pinhead, might have been soft and malleable, easily mistaken for a morsel of food politely ignored in a passionate kiss—or unnoticed altogether amid ten ccs of ejaculate.

It made no sense for Ben to have infected Kirra, or the other way around: they had died together.

But Robert had made love with both of them.

(And left for Earth the very next day. Without inviting me to accompany him.)

And I was the only living person who knew that . . .

*—it can't be, he couldn't (he could) he wouldn't (how the hell do you know) why would he, why would he, WHY WOULD HE DO SUCH A THING? (he's Chinese, they hate Stardancers) He's Chinese-*American, *not from China (who says so, and so what) no, I just can't believe it (oh you can believe it, all right, you just don't know for sure) I don't* want *to believe it, I don't want to* know, *it isn't true (there's only one good way to find out) it can't be—*

In my blind drifting, I contacted the studio wall. And screamed.

Perhaps—no, certainly—I should have gone right to Reb with what I had figured out. Or to Dorothy Gerstenfeld, or Phillipe Mgabi . . . or all three. I had an urgent need to share my terrible hypothesis with *someone.* For all I knew, I was carrying a bomb inside *me.*

But I did not go to Reb, or anyone else. In fact, I stayed there in my studio, fetal and moaning, until I had recovered sufficiently that I thought I could keep the sick horror out of my face—at least well enough to fool shipboard acquaintances.

Part of it might have been reticence to share a sexual secret of my friends, whose permission I could no longer seek. But I don't think so. No sexual behaviour was scandalous in Top Step, and I did not think either Kirra or Ben would have considered it a secret.

No, what stopped me was simply that my theory was just that. A theory. I just could not make an accusation of such ghastly magnitude against a man I had loved, without the slightest shred of proof. The accusation alone would be so utterly damning—and how could a man possibly defend himself against such a charge if he were innocent? If I opened my mouth, and were wrong, and Robert were torn to pieces down on Earth by an angry mob of Stardancer-lovers . . .

But when I thought back, I realized that I could not recall any time Reb had expressed an opinion of Robert as a person—or of our relationship. And when we broke up, he'd said only that he was sorry I was sad. Had that hyperintuitive man sensed something about Robert that I had missed? I could not bring myself to ask him.

I had to know. For myself, for sure. And as soon as physically possible. No shilly-shallying around, like I'd been doing about Symbiosis; it was time to get off the dime and make a move, *now.* I might be carrying a second bomb, and who knew when it might go off?

It took me an hour or so to get my lines together and rehearse them until I could make them sound truthful. At first I wasn't sure I could do it. But I've always been a trouper. When I had it right, I called Reb and told him I was quitting.

He wanted to talk about it, of course, but I cut it as short as I could. In essence I claimed that Kirra's and Ben's deaths had soured space for me; it was no longer a place I wanted to go. There was enough truth in it for me to sound plausible, I guess: he bought it, reluctantly. He sounded sad, but made no real effort to argue, simply making sure my mind was made up.

Half an hour later Dorothy Gerstenfeld called and told me that I had a reserved seat on the next ship to Earth, leaving in a little under twenty-four hours. I thanked her and switched off. She didn't call back.

I spent the time wrestling with myself. What I hypothesized was grotesque, impossible. Logical, yes; theoretically and intuitively reasonable, yes, but simply not possible. Not my Robert! Inscrutable Oriental be damned, I just could not have known him so intimately and known him so little. Could I? What was the point of sabotaging my own Symbiosis, the only thing life had left to offer me, to chase down such a wild and ugly idea?

I had to, that was all.

As Robert himself had pointed out when he left, I could always come back again. I would see Robert, and question him closely, and look into his eyes as I did . . . and then I would apologize, and call Reb, and he would pull strings to let me come back up to Top Step and Graduate. One last quick visit to Earth, to lay two ghosts to rest, that was all.

I spent so much time convincing myself that I had to be mistaken that I gave no conscious thought at all to what I would do if it turned out that I was not mistaken.

* * *

I was surprised by how hard it was to leave my p-suit behind. I had been essentially living in it for nearly a month now, and it had become home. But it did not belong to me anymore. I rode to Earth wearing a cheap tourist suit just like the one I'd worn on the trip up, a hundred thousand years ago.

No one came to see me off. Not even Reb. I'd been half-expecting him, but was grateful to be spared the task of trying to maintain a lie before so intuitive a man. Four other students left on the same shuttle, for the same reason I had claimed, and there were a handful of other passengers, mostly staff members traveling to Earth on business.

The trip itself was utterly without incident, or at least none that forced itself into my attention. I could have had a simulated window-view on my seatback TV this time, but did not want one. Emotionally it was my trip up, run backwards. The closer I got to Earth the heavier I felt, in body and mind, the further my spirit sank, and I landed in a state of maximum confusion and upset, heart pounding wildly under the unaccustomed load.

To my great relief, the spaceplane did not land at the same spaceport from which I had left Earth. I didn't think I could have borne seeing Queensland again, Kirra's home, and thinking of her sweet smile blown into particles, expanding slowly to fill the universe. Instead we grounded outside Quito, Ecuador.

That was good in another way, too. Closer to San Francisco.

I felt like an elephant. Gone the dancer. My work had kept me in good shape, so I didn't have as much trouble bearing my returned weight as some others have. But I still felt like an elephant. A pregnant elephant, pregnant with a son (they take several months longer to bake than girl elephants, I've read) and in my last month. Most disturbing to my dancer's mind, my balance was no longer a matter of intuition. I had unlearned a lot of habits in two and a half months of zero gee. I had to keep reminding myself that it *mattered* whether I kept a perpendicular relationship to the wall called "floor" or not, and I tended to totter like an elderly drunken mammoth. Hair felt weird lying against the back of my neck and against my forehead. I kept letting go of things and then being startled when they raced away to one of the six walls. Everything had a cartoon, fun-house mirror look. The air smelled funny, and didn't move enough; unconsciously I tended to keep moving my head around so I couldn't smother in my exhalations. It seemed weird never to see anyone moving around below my feet or above my head, to be stuck to the surface of a planet, like a fly caught in the kind of flypaper my parents used to hang from the ceiling on Gambier Island when I was a child.

Customs was no problem, as I arrived with no possessions whatsoever, not so much as a pair of socks. Credit was only a thumbprint away. And getting outfitted with clothes and necessaries took only an hour in the spaceport Traveler's Shop; it would have been half that but I insisted on styles that would not be out of place in San Francisco and that took more time and more money.

But going through Immigration, first Ecuadorian (horrid) and then U.S. (three times as bad) took up the next day and a half; I finally emerged into the smoggy air of San Francisco with my nerves shot and my teeth aching from long clenching. I weighed a thousand kilos and felt a million years old and the air tasted like burnt flannel. I decided to get a hotel room and sleep for a week before taking further action. The driver of the cab I hailed was fascinated by an airplane passenger from Quito with no luggage of any kind. I ignored him.

When I checked in, I signed the register, and then tried to *push* the pen back to the clerk. It bounced high from the countertop, and he looked at me with a knowing air. "Just down, eh? We have waterbeds available for those guests who suffer from gravity fatigue." I thanked him and accepted the service. As the bellhop was showing me into my room he made a discreet suggestion concerning other services he could arrange for guests, and I laughed in his face. A full month ago I had sworn never again to have sex in a gravity field, and I was in no mood to change my mind. That dreaded old friend, lower back pain, was already back in full force, for the first time in months.

I didn't leave that waterbed for three days, and didn't leave my room for a week.

If you want to know what that week was like, go to hell.

That's a kind of pun, I guess. By going to hell, you could certainly simulate that week.

Because now it was time to confront that burning question: *what if it turns out you're right?*

This had bearing on both strategy and tactics.

Suppose Robert were innocent. In that case, there was no problem. I could call him up, arrange to meet somewhere, watch his eyes very carefully while I outlined my suspicions, learn that I was wrong, and apologize if I decided I wanted to bother. In any case, my biggest problem would be coming up with a good exit line; I could be back in Top Step in a matter of days.

But suppose he were guilty? I call him up . . . and a little while later there is an unfortunate incident, a failed Stardancer candidate commits suicide in her hotel room in San Francisco; very sad but no next of kin to push it. Or perhaps, if there really is a little nanotechnological horror hidden somewhere in my body, the whole hotel vanishes in a large mysterious explosion.

No, wait. Just because I called him wouldn't mean the jig was up. I might well have thought things over up in Top Step and decided to follow Robert back to Earth for love. A nuisance, if he really was a high-tech assassin who cared nothing for me, but not a serious one. In that case, meeting with me somewhere for a fast brushoff would be the simplest way to get me off his back. So he agrees to meet me in a restaurant, and *then* he finds out the jig is up . . . and maybe I suffer a sudden heart attack over lunch, fall face down into the salad.

Dammit, if he *was* a hatchetman, it was for a large and wealthy and well-organized conspiracy. Half-assed terrorist groups don't have access to nanotechnological weapons; if they did they wouldn't be half-assed terrorists. If Robert was guilty, he was hotter than the fire that killed Kirra. In that case he was probably not even at his nominal address in San Francisco, but hiding in Beijing or someplace even harder to crack. Just leaving a message on his answering machine might be enough to get me snuffed by Triad hitmen.

Of course, that kind of paranoia only made sense if I assumed he was guilty. But if I didn't at least partly believe he was guilty, what was I doing here, fighting for breath and cursing the glue of gravity?

I had never thought along these kinds of lines in my life, had never known anyone who did except characters in holothrillers and spy novels. I had to work my plans out slowly, laboriously, all the while wanting desperately to believe I was making a fool of myself.

And I kept coming to a jerk at the end of the thought-chain.

If Robert is guilty, and if you work out some clever and safe scheme to get close enough to prove that to yourself—

—then what will you do?

Kill him?

Was I capable of it?

Was I physically capable, first? The part of me that remembered his physical speed, grace and coordination raised a few questions as to how a laywoman suffering from gee fatigue went about killing a trained assassin in a public restaurant . . . but was willing to concede in theory that it might be done, with the element of surprise, if I didn't care about being arrested afterward, and if I struck the instant I was sure, without any hesitation at all.

That led to: was I psychologically and emotionally capable of murder? Of anyone, or of Robert? The part of me that liked to watch old Stallone movies wanted to think so. *Yo—lover or no lover, he killed my friends, he dies, end of story.* The part of me that had thought of him as my last forlorn chance at human love wanted to think so too. *He used me as a wartime convenience; no man does that to me and lives.* The part of me that was loyal to the Starmind wanted the deaths of so many Stardancers and the ruin of so much sacred Symbiote avenged. *His action was an act of war; a sneak attack must be repaid.*

But the part of me that thought of itself as an ethical person questioned my right to execute a sentence of death on another human being, however monstrous his crimes . . . and doubted I had the guts.

But what other option did I have? Denounce him to Stardancers Incorporated and the United Nations, betray him to Interpol, charge him before the High Court and the state courts of Queensland and California? With nothing but circumstantial evidence and lover's intuition to support the charges? I couldn't so much as nail him for breach of promise; the son of a bitch had never promised me anything.

Nagging additional minor thought: our brief four-way sexual liaison was not scandalous in Top Step, nor in many circles on Earth nowadays—but it might seem so to Kirra's or Ben's surviving kin.

That put those people in my mind. So the first thing I did upon leaving that grim hotel room was to make two short side trips. Well, one short, to Sherman Oaks . . . and the other rather longer, to north Queensland; I decided I had to face that land again after all.

Before I left, I put the best detective agency I could find onto tracing and locating Robert, with specific warning that he might just be clever enough to spot someone checking him out, and dangerous enough to kill them. It didn't faze them in the least. They didn't bother asking why, just told me when and where I could go for a report—so that it need not be sent to me at any address—and how much it would cost. I was spending life savings like water, but I didn't give a jaunting damn.

The visit to Ben's father was too sad to recount. The old man was utterly shattered by this latest in a series of crushing disappointments; Ben had been his last surviving blood kin, and now he was alone in the world. I knew all too well how he felt. I told him what a good man his son had been, and something of what Ben had meant to me, and what I could of his last few months of life. It seemed to comfort Mr. Buckley some, but not enough. We were both crying when I left.

With a last-minute attack of the cutes, I had introduced myself to him as Glenn Christie. I'd even gotten cash before leaving San Francisco so I wouldn't leave a digital credit trail, taken cabs so I wouldn't have to use my credit to rent a car.

I couldn't get to Australia that way, but I did take time to alter my appearance, by changing wardrobe, having my hair cut close to my skull and permed within an inch of its life, and darkening my complexion several shades. I paid cash for a standby seat, but had to give my right name; to compensate I made sure I was one of the last to board and sat in the wrong seat; on arrival I got in the wrong line at Customs & Immigration, with people from a different flight, and while I stood on line wedged my way into a voluble discussion in German despite knowing almost none of that language; mostly I nodded and listened alertly to whoever was speaking. Maybe it all helped; no one followed me from the airport. Or maybe I made a jerk of myself to no point—how could I tell?

Only by fucking up and being killed. I bought a minijeep from a used car lot in cash under a false name and headed north.

From Cairns International Airport to Yirlandji country is a long day's drive, about 800 kilometers as the crow flies—and stoned are any crows who ever flew like that. The road up the coast, looking out toward the Great Barrier Reef, is exquisitely beautiful, one of the greatest scenic drives left on Earth—and consequently winds and bucks like a snake caught in an accordion. Driving on the left side of the road for the first time in decades, I did well to average 60 kph. Even ignoring the scenery and banging straight along it would have been a thirteen-hour drive. But it was winter in Queensland, which means, just cool enough to stand it, and that beach constantly beckoning from the right got irresistibly inviting, even to a monomaniacal apprentice secret agent. The water had "cooled" to a temperature Canadian surf will never reach, maybe 26°C, which meant, the nice Beach Club lifeguard explained to me, that the box jellyfish (or sea-wasps, the deadliest things afloat) had all gone away for the season. It was the most glorious swim I'd ever had in my life, and the buoyancy of the water was so near to and yet far from zero gee that I wept salty tears into the sea, and gave serious thought to seeing if I could swim the forty or fifty kilometers out to the Reef. Finally I literally crawled ashore like some primordial ancestor, and baked for an hour before trying to walk again.

I stopped for directions in the Aboriginal Reserve north of Cooktown, and again the next day at the one north of Coen, where I left the main road and struck west toward the Gulf of Carpentaria. In mid-afternoon I met an Aboriginal at a gas station, Thomas Tjarndai, who agreed to guide me to Yirlandji country. I followed his ancient yammering motorbike through an hour of bad road, then followed him on foot through the bush for another hour, wondering darkly whether Yirlandji ever ate whitefella tourists. My back had been aching for days now. At least the knee was not acting up. When we reached the Yirlandji encampment, Thomas brought me to an elder named Billy Huroo, no more than five hundred years old and sharp as a Chinese pawnbroker. I gave him my right name in spite of myself, and told him a little of why I had come. In the distance, a child sang. To my shock I recognized a passage from the Song of Top Step. My eyes stung. At dusk Billy Huroo led me to the campfire of the witch woman Yarra and left me there.

She was ancient and thin, her skin like wrinkled black leather. Like Kirra's, her teeth were gleaming white. She wore only shorts and a knife. Her eyes made me think of Reb, decades older and female. She bade me welcome, gave me tea from a billy. I can't describe the taste, but it was very good. I told her my real name, started to tell her why I was there, and she cut me off. "You knew my *badundjari,*" she told me. "My beloved dream spirit. Kirra, the Singer, who makes Walkabout among the stars. You were her friend."

I nodded, and started to say that I was here to tell her of Kirra's last days. She cut me off again.

"You are here to ask me if you should kill her killer."

I dropped my jaw.

The fire crackled, the sparks flew upward. At last I sighed and said, "How can you know that?"

"From the way you sit. From your voice. I do not hear your words so much as the song of your voice. It is a song of blood rage."

"Yes." There was nothing else to say.

"You know who killed my *badundjari*?"

"I think so. I may know for sure in a day or two. If I am right . . . it was the blackest of betrayals." I explained as carefully as I could my suspicions.

"You believe he gave her a poison that became a bomb, this Symbiote to destroy. And he gave her this poison in the act of love?"

"I hope to know for sure in a day or two," I repeated, then blurted, "Oh, but *what will I do if it's true?*"

She grimaced at me, and slowly shook her head. "No one can tell you that. Not I. Not Emu, or Goanna Lizard, or Kangaroo, not a Rainbow Serpent nor a Sky-God nor any of the Ancestors who were here in the Dreamtime. Not even Menura, the lyrebird of the gullies, who was Kirra's totem. *You* must decide."

I closed my eyes and sighed again. A didgeridu was playing in the far distance, like a mournful dragon. "Yes. You're right."

"But tell me his full name and where he lives," she said. "When you have done whatever you decide to do . . . if he still lives . . . perhaps I will decide *I* need to do something about him."

"I'll tell you the moment I'm sure," I countered, knowing that I might be dead seconds after the moment I was sure. "If you have not heard from me within a week, then I was right and he has overcome me. In that case, and only then, call Top Step and ask Reb Hawkins who my lover was there. You can get access to a phone?"

She took one from a bag at her side. Of course. She'd probably first heard Kirra's space Songs on it. I recalled suddenly, with sharp pain, that I had never carried out my final promise to Kirra, to send her last song-fragments home to that very telephone. "You have my number?" she asked.

Yes I did. In my personal memory node in Teena, up in Top Step. I had not yet downloaded it, and didn't want to access it now for fear of leaving a trail to where I was on Earth. Yarra gave me the number again, and I memorized it rather than write it down. I gave her my personal security code, so that she could get at that last Song of Kirra's if I failed to live through what I was planning.

I slept beside her campfire that night. Nothing bit me.

13

Canst thou draw out Leviathan with an hook?
—Job, xli. 1

Forty-eight hours later I was back in my hotel room in San Francisco and my skin was its normal colour again. If anyone was following me, they were too good to be spotted. I was getting close to broke, but treated myself to the finest dinner the hotel could provide. I gave them fresh roasted coffee beans I had bought the day before from an unlikely madman named Gebhardt Kaiserlingck, who ran a wonderful screwball coffee plantation outside of Daintree, and insisted that the kitchen drip-brew them for me. I drank four cups with dessert and wanted more. It was the finest coffee I had ever tasted. A good omen, I felt.

The next morning I had three more cups with breakfast, and adjourned to the ladies' room. There I changed into male drag, using much the same makeup I had used for drag roles on stage in years past, and left without causing any apparent notice (well, it was San Francisco). I spent some time re-learning how to walk like a male, and knew I was remembering it correctly when a stewardess gave me the eye as I was passing through the lobby. An hour later I identified myself to a taco vendor as a client of the Bay City Detective Agency; he insisted on a thumbprint, did something with it under the counter, squinted at it and then at me, and passed me an envelope containing a report on one Chen, Robert. I read it on the city's last remaining cable car, holding it close so the passengers on either side could not have read it even with Ben's trick glasses.

The top sheet mostly recapitulated what little I already knew about Robert from the things he had told me; most of the new information was irrelevant, except that he had in fact been observed to be living at the address I had for him. For the first time since I'd left Top

Step I began to seriously wonder if the whole thing wasn't only a grotesque figment of my overheated imagination, a psychosis manufactured by my mind to distract me from a series of traumas.

But then there was the second page.

". . . first-order identity check seemed to establish that subject's stated identity and background were genuine; all expected records were in fact on file and no inconsistencies or alterations were noted. But since you had expressed doubt concerning subject's bona fides, further and more stringent inquiries were instituted, as per attached statement. Second-order ID check also proved out. Third-order check however revealed that subject's given ID is bogus.

"Subject's true name is Chen Po Chang. He is the bastard son of Chen Hsi-Feng, who is the son of the late Premier of the People's Republic, Chen Ten Li. His last official place of residence is Shanghai; he disappeared there four years ago in March of 2016, concurrent with his father's disappearance during the political upheaval which followed the death of Chen Ten Li. He is not presently wanted in any jurisdiction for any crime or malfeasance. Additional information may be accessed from any public database. Please inform us if you wish any of this information communicated to relevant authorities, or if you require any further action from us. See attachments."

The third sheet was an itemized statement that said I was a pauper. It didn't know how right it was.

I had the evidence I had sought, right there in my hands. Not proof that Robert had murdered Kirra and Ben—but enough to throw strong suspicion on him. With that as a start, further information might possibly be found by Interpol, maybe even enough to tie him to the nanotechnological bomb. The People's Republic had more nanotechnologists than any other nation. (Not too surprising. They had more *anythings* than most other nations.)

And so what?

Suppose I could tie him to the killing, with monofilament strands of evidence. Who had jurisdiction over raw space, outside the cislunar band?

Was it even against thc law—any nation's law or the UN's—to murder a Stardancer? The subject had never come up before. Nearly all motives for a murder were irrelevant in the case of Stardancers.

They had nothing to steal, no territory to conquer, made love only with other Stardancers, and were damn near impossible to find if they didn't want to be found. The one thing generally agreed was that they were not human beings in the legal sense.

If I blew Robert's cover skyhigh, spread it across human space via UPI or Reuters, all I'd accomplish might be merely to annoy him and his secret masters, perhaps cause them to alter slightly whatever their plans were. At most Robert himself might suffer a tragic accident, walk out into traffic, say, and then no one would ever know what those plans were.

I composed an in-the-event-of-my-death letter, and used the last of my credit to send it up to Top Step, to my own personal memory node where Interpol itself couldn't get at it, programmed to start announcing itself to Reb, Dorothy and Phillipe Mgabi if I didn't personally disable it within twenty-four hours.

Then I called Robert's home.

"Morgan, is that really you? I can't see you—where are you?"

I told him I was in a phone booth at the airport and the phone's eye had been vandalized. He sounded so genuinely glad to hear my voice, to learn that I was really on Earth and in his city, that I was happy he could not see my face. I put great effort into controlling my voice. He offered to buy me dinner, named a restaurant. I demurred, insisting that I wanted to dine in a place I remembered from an old tour, picking the name out of the Yellow Pages as I spoke. I did vaguely remember it; mostly it was a place he had not chosen and could not have staked out already. And it was large enough and public enough to make violence awkward.

On the way I used the last of my cash to buy a Gyro model dart gun from a wirehead in a back alley off Haight Street. He claimed that the rocket-darts were tipped with lethal nerve poison, and used a passing rat the size of a raccoon to prove that at least the first one was. There were four left in the gun. He backed away from me very carefully after we'd made the exchange.

I was stone broke now. Maybe I should let Robert pick up the check for dinner before I killed him. If I was going to. I still did not honestly know whether I could.

Or even for sure that I intended to.

* * *

I deliberately got to the restaurant almost half an hour early. As the maître d'hôtel greeted me, I realized for the first time that the gravity had stopped bothering me. Even my lower back no longer ached unless I put stress on it. A little under two weeks to recover from over two months in free fall. Remarkable. I was an earthling again.

But on sudden impulse I decided to simulate gee fatigue for Robert, as though I had just landed within the past few days. He might underestimate me if he thought I was weak and logy, and I needed any edge I could get. As the maître d' led me to my table I tried to walk as though I were strapped with heavy weights, and sank into my chair with a great sigh.

The body language part was no trouble for me; most dancers are half actor. It was actually an interesting technical challenge: instead of doing what dancers almost always did, making difficult movements look easy, I had to make easy ones look difficult. The tricky part was the intellectual details. When had the most recent shuttle landed, and at which of the three Stardancer spaceports? I could fake small talk about either Queensland or Ecuador, but I knew nothing at all of Uganda. What day of the week was this, and what was the date? Damn, this melodrama stuff was more complicated than it looked. It seemed to me that the most recent shuttle had grounded three days before, in Australia. Excellent. I had a fund of fresh trivia about that part of the world.

An adorable waiter took my order for Irish coffee with no Irish whiskey in it. "*I* get it," he said archly as he set it before me, "you want him to think you're drinking. Good luck, honey." I winked at him, and he giggled. I sipped coffee with exaggeratedly weary gestures and looked around the restaurant, trying to spot a stakeout. There was a high percentage of tables with two or more males and no females, but perhaps not abnormally high for this town. And there was no reason why a stakeout team could not include female agents. Everyone looked normal and authentic and undangerous. Normal urban dinner crowd, Pacific Rim version. Every one of them could have been in the pay of the People's Republic for all I knew. Half of them were Asian. The roof seemed to hover over me oppressively, a potentially destructive mass held away by four flimsy walls. A pianist with a shaky left hand was mangling "We Are in Love" in the far corner of the room. Waiters glided to and fro as smoothly as if they were jaunting. The lights had a tendency to strobe if I looked at them. I wanted Fat Humphrey to float up and tell me what I wanted to eat. I wanted Reb to come and tell me what to do.

Thinking of Reb, I straightened my spine, joined my hands in *mudra* on my lap, and began measuring my breath. It helped.

I spotted Robert before he saw me.

Suddenly I remembered my ex-husband telling me once that I could lie very well with my body, but not with my face. Well, a lot had happened since then.

Robert spoke with the maître d', who pointed me out, and looked my way. Our eyes met. I concentrated on my breathing. I kept my face impassive, tried to relax every facial muscle completely. *I am suffering from high-gee lethargy.* He crossed the room to my table, with the graceful loping walk of a jungle cat, as I had imagined he would. No limp: his injured foot was healed. He stopped beside me, took my right hand in both of his, bent over it and kissed it. His lips lingered just an instant. He released it, sat across from me.

His expression was neutral, his eyes open and seemingly guileless. His face was different than I remembered, longer and leaner, the eyes less squinty, the wrinkles slightly more pronounced. His head appeared smaller, the hair lying close to the skull instead of fanning out. This was how he looked under gravity. I decided it made him even more attractive.

"It's good to see you," he said.

I said, "I'm glad to see you too. You look different in a gravity field."

He nodded. "Yes. So do you. I like what you've done with your hair."

There now, just what I needed: a nice sample lie to calibrate my bullshit detector. I knew perfectly well that my hair looked awful. "Thank you for the gallantry," I said. "It was ungodly hot in Queensland. The hair was always wet, and it kept crawling down my neck, so I had them hack it all off. I think I'm going to end up regretting it."

"No, really, it suits you well."

Okay, now see if you can get him to make some true *statements for comparison, and we'll get this polygraph interrogation started.* "I just hit dirt a few days ago. I can't get used to this up and down nonsense. It seems so arbitrary, like making all music be in the same key. And I can't believe how much my feet hurt!"

He nodded. "My first couple of days dirtside I couldn't imagine how humans had ever put up with gravity. It was just barely tolerable back when we didn't know any better—but now, something's simply got to be done about it. You must be exhausted."

"Irish coffee helps," I said. "It's great for reconciling you to gravity: it's got up and down built into it. The booze calms you down and then the coffee wakes you up." *Small talk, small talk—*

"Small talk," he said.

I nodded. "What do you say—stick to small talk until we've eaten?"

He nodded back. "Sounds sensible." The waiter arrived, and Robert ordered Irish coffee, "like the lady." The waiter nodded gravely, turned away—then stopped outside Robert's field of vision, pointed at him, and gave me an exaggerated thumbs up. *Keep this one.* When he returned a few moments later with the coffee, he stopped behind Robert again, pointed at the coffee and fanned himself: *this* glass had whiskey in it, in good measure. I slipped him another wink when Robert wasn't looking. I hoped Robert was going to tip him well, since I couldn't. Robert ordered something to eat and I said I'd have the same and he twinkled away, delighted at his role in my little intrigue.

"So you just got into town? Where are you staying?"

I'd anticipated the question, and had decided there was no reason to lie. I told him the correct name of my hotel. It didn't seem to matter; I need never go back there again. He nodded and said it was a good place, and I agreed.

Whatever it was we had ordered arrived. As we ate we kept jousting with our eyes, making contact and then finding reasons to look away, busying ourselves with the food. I felt like I was drowning in quicksand. No, in slowsand. But there was no hurrying things. I didn't want him to have any busy little distractions available when I started asking pointed questions.

Which led to: *what* pointed questions? I had been thinking about this moment for something like two weeks now, and I still did not know how to play it. Should I go right for the jugular, tell him everything I knew and all I had guessed, and demand a response? Or keep what I knew to myself, give him to understand that I wanted to resume our relationship, and see what he said about that? That could lead in short order to a bedroom, and what would I do then?

Or should I indicate ambiguous feelings, which would allow me to prolong our contact without having to go to bed with him? The problem with that one was, it made it easy for him to get rid of me if he didn't want to be under close scrutiny. No, the smart thing to do was feign passion and try to get as far inside his guard as I could. Feigning passion is natural for a performer. I could always plead gee-fatigue when things got intense.

But as I watched him eat, watched his slender fingers move, I knew I just could not go through with it. Perhaps it was exactly what he had been doing to me, all those passionate days and nights back in Top Step. But I could not do it to him.

The plates were empty. The second round of Irish coffees arrived. Mine was again denatured. The waiter winked at me for a change.

Well, then? Charge right in or dance around it as long as possible? Cowardice and caution both said to stall. *Crazy to risk everything on one roll of the dice. Lots of misdirection first, then slip it in under his guard while he's trying to figure out how to get into your pants.*

"Chen Po Chang?" I said suddenly.

"Yes, Morgan?"

And there it was.

"It was on your tongue, wasn't it?" *That's it, baffle him with misdirection.*

"Yes."

"Which one got it? Ben, or Kirra?"

"Kirra."

I nodded. "I just wondered. You knew they'd both be meeting the Harvest Crew." Under the table, I slid my hand into my handbag. Just the one question left, now. "Why?"

He seemed to think about it, as if for the first time. He started to answer twice, and changed his mind each time. Finally he said, "For my species."

"For your species." I seemed to be having trouble with my voice. "And what species would that be? Insect, or reptile?"

"Homo sapiens," he said calmly. "It's us or them. Us or *Homo caelestis.* The universe isn't big enough for both of us."

"Why *not?* What could the two species possibly compete for?"

"Nothing at all. And everything. That's the point. Here below we scurry about like blind rats in a two-dimensional maze, hungry and thirsty and horny and terrified and alone, fighting like rats for food and power and breeding room and a chance to live before we die. And right over our heads, at the literal top of the hierarchy, there fly the angels, free of everything that plagues us, needing nothing, fearing nothing, looking down with fond amusement at our ape antics. Of course I hate them. Who would not?"

"For God's sake, this planet would have gone to pieces years ago if it weren't for—"

"And that too is the point. It would be bad enough if they kept themselves aloof, ignored us in our misery—but how can we not resent their monstrous charity? How long can the human race stand playing the role of the idiot nephew who must be cared for by his betters, the welfare client who has nothing conceivable to offer his benefactors in return? The racial psychic damage which that awareness causes is half the reason the world is so close to hysteria, so angry and self-destructive."

"So you want to exterminate the hand that feeds you."

"It may come to that," he agreed. "Sometimes I think that it might be enough to drive them from human space, to force them far above or below the ecliptic or out beyond Mars where we don't have to keep seeing them and interacting with them, take their damned Promised Land off somewhere where we don't have to look at it every day, right overhead, just out of reach."

"But it's *not* out of reach—"

"Oh shit, it is too! If all the Chinese in the world lined up at Suit Camps, how long would it take the last one to pass Top Step? Assuming a sufficient mass of Symbiote could be brought to orbit without pulling Luna out of its track."

"If the world wanted to, it could build more Suit Camps."

"And it doesn't. Most of us know in our guts that Stardancers are just plain inhuman. They're *alien.* They're like ants. They're a hive-mind. They're our enemy, and they'll be a damned hard one to beat."

"But why do they have to be *enemies*?"

"Morgan, *think,* won't you? Think about that hive-mind. That 'Starmind.' I know they breed like hamsters up there, but even after twenty years of it, well over half the minds that make up what they call the Starmind started out as human beings, on Earth, yes?"

"Exactly. They're our brothers and sisters, or at least our cousins."

"And how many million years old would you say is the human lust for power? For control? For dominance?"

"But there's none of that in the Starmind."

"Exactly. What can 'power' mean to a member of a telepathic commune? What is there to control? By what means can dominance be asserted? Mental machinery that has served men for countless generations is useless." He leaned forward and locked eyes with me. "But I ask you to consider this: that a telepathic group consciousness implies a group *subconscious* too. Submerged in that Starmind are the instincts of thousands of killer apes, the genetic heritage of the most successful predator ever evolved. Maybe competition and aggression aren't inherited, maybe they're not instinct but learned behaviour transmitted to each new generation—maybe the Stardancers born in space, who've never known want or fear or envy, are gentle creatures, without the Mark of Cain. But the majority of the Starmind comes from a long line of cutthroats. Human beings weren't built for Utopia, no matter what weird things may happen to their metabolisms. They know the only thing they could possibly need to fear, must fear, is us, is the rage and envy of the irrational human beings they have to share the Solar System with. They know a clash is inevitable one day, and they're doing their best to see that they'll win it. By creating a planet full of helpless welfare dependents. By showering us with gifts that lead us to a place where we need their gifts to survive. They've read their Sun Tzu. Don't you see, they're killing us with kindness!"

I closed my eyes briefly. I remembered one of my old dance-circle acquaintances, an intellectual snob, a sort of Alexander Woolcott/H.L. Mencken/Oscar Wilde wanna-be, saying, when he heard I was about to go to Top Step, "Stardancers? A society with no corruption, no hypocrisy, no neurosis and total respect for art—and worst of all, they're willing to let me join? How could I *not* despise them?" And I had laughed with the others, but privately thought he was a cripple, seeking approval of his deformity.

I felt a sense of unreality, a Through-the-Looking-Glass feeling. In my wildest fantasies of this moment, it had gone much like this, with

Robert calmly, rationally explaining why he had blown our friends to plasma. *Why is he telling me all this? Surely to God he does not expect that I will nod and say, Damn, you're right, I hadn't thought it through, Kirra and Ben just got in the line of fire, guess you can't make an interplanetary omelet without breaking some eggs, what can I do to help fight the menace of gods who have the nerve to be benevolent?*

I met his eyes again. "So you acted selflessly. For the good of humanity."

He didn't even shrug. "Of course not. Am I a Stardancer? I acted out of intelligent self-interest, like any sane human." He leaned forward, lowered his voice. "If our plans bear fruit, the *least* of the prizes to be won will be my father's return from exile to unchallenged power over China."

"So you put death in Kirra's sweet mouth." I slid the Gyrojet from the handbag. My thumb caressed the safety catch. Four darts. One for him, one for me, two surplus.

"Morgan, listen to me: for the first time in human history, total planetary domination is a genuine possibility—and it's only the first step in the forging of a System-wide empire. The tools are nearly at hand! How many lives, how many betrayals is that worth?"

His eyes were boring into mine. "I have a gun aimed at your belly, Chen Po Chang," I said softly. I hadn't meant to warn him.

"I know," he said just as quietly. "But you're not ready to use it yet."

"No. No, I'm not. First I want to know why you're telling me such weighty secrets. Do you think you can persuade me to join you?"

He hesitated before answering. "No. I wish I could. But you're a romantic. Because Stardancers look like angels, they must be angels. There's not enough greed in you for your own good." He looked bleak. "Oh, but I wish I could!"

"Why?" I said, a little too loudly. A woman at an adjacent table looked round; I lowered my voice again. "What the hell do you care? One day you'll be Emperor of the Galaxy and you can have the hottest concubines your precious race can produce. I'm a broken down forty-six-year-old has-been dancer you screwed for a few weeks once on assignment."

This was why I wasn't ready to shoot him yet. Or at least part of it. I needed to know what, if anything, I had been to him.

For the first time his iron control cracked. Pain showed in his eyes. He looked down at the table. "Screwing you was good cover. You were my target's roommate. Falling in love with you was stupid. So I was stupid." He finished his Irish coffee in a single gulp. "I was horrified at how hard it was to leave you. That terrorist bombing was the perfect excuse to cut out, just when I needed it . . . and it took me half an hour to make up my mind to take advantage of it. I knew there was no way I could take you with me—but it killed me to leave you behind. When I heard your voice on the phone, realized you were here on Earth again, there was a whole five or ten seconds there when I . . . when I . . ."

"When you got a hard on, wondering how I am in a gravity field. But now you know I know you for what you are, and how I feel about your cause. So I repeat: why are you admitting everything and telling me your secrets? You have a gun on me too, is that it?"

He shook his head. "I'm unarmed. And no one else will try to kill you. That much influence I have." He ran a hand nervously through his hair, brushing it back from his eyes, a gesture he'd never had in free fall. "I guess I'm telling you . . . because I have to. Because I wanted you to know."

"Pardon me," a kindly voice said.

A large heavily bearded stranger in a charcoal grey suit was standing at my side, hearty and jovial and avuncular. If they ever remade *Miracle on 34th Street* with an all-Asian cast, he'd be a finalist for the role of Kris Kringle. "I hope you'll forgive me for disturbing you . . . but are you Morgan McLeod, the dancer?"

I had danced in San Francisco hundreds of times, had actually achieved more fame here than in Vancouver, where I was "only a local." "Yes, but I'm afraid this isn't a good—"

"I won't disturb you. But please—would you?" He held out a scrap of paper and a pen. "Your work with Morris meant a lot to me."

The quickest way to get rid of him was to indulge him. I left the Gyrojet on my lap, concealed by the handbag, and signed the stupid autograph. As I handed it back, he took my hand, bent to kiss it—and just as he did so, he turned my hand over, so that instead of kissing the back of it, his full warm moist lips pressed my palm. I felt his tongue flicker momentarily between them. It was an odd, vaguely erotic thing for a man his age to do, with an escort sitting right there across from me. I retrieved my hand hastily. "Thank you very much; you're very kind. Please excuse us."

"Of course, Ms. McLeod. Thank you. I have always loved your work." He turned away.

I turned back to Robert. No, to Po Chang. "All right," I tried to say to him, "Now I know. Now what?"

It came out, "All eyes down the put go, legs. Blower?"

I blinked and tried again. "Didn't dog core stable imagine? Both pressure."

A zipper appeared under his Adam's apple. It peeled down to his diaphragm, splitting his sternum and spreading his ribs, exposing his pink wet chest cavity. A tiny Negro in a clown suit was clinging desperately to the top of his heart, fighting to stay aboard as it beat and surged beneath him. As I watched, fascinated, he managed to get to his feet and wedge himself into equilibrium between the lungs. He opened a door in the left lung and showed me something awful inside. I turned away in shame. The stranger was still standing there, but he stood ten meters tall now on rippling rainbow legs. His beard was made of worms. I knew he wanted to see me dance, but there wasn't enough room on the table and the damned local vertical kept changing and there weren't enough pens.

A little corner of my mind, way in the back, understood what was happening. I had forgotten that these people could kill with their kiss.

Chen Po Chang's voice came from the far side of the universe, metallic and atonal. "The first one was just chemical. Call it truth serum. But the second one was a nanobandit."

I reached for my lap, and it wasn't where I had left it. Everything I found seemed to bend in the wrong directions; some of it felt wet and some of it was sticky to my questing fingers.

"Absorbed through the palm," he was saying, "one heartbeat to the brain, another second to crack the blood-brain barrier, then it starts secreting."

I had to find my lap—that was where I had left my gum! Gum? That wasn't right. Gub? I couldn't read my own goddamn handwriting. Where the hell was my fucking p-suit? Mist was closing in from all sides—

I beat at the mist, fought for control of my mind. I knew what I had to do. It was necessary to yell as loud and as clearly as possible, "Help me! I have been drugged and they're going to take me out of here and kill me." My old friend the waiter would then come and slap them both to death. My body was made of taffy, but I summoned all my will, directed all my desperate energy to making my mouth and tongue firm enough to function, obedient to my command.

"Productive marbles. Didn't to bite wonder-log with it, the palaces. Curt! Curt!"

The waiter was back. There were four of him. "I'm very sorry, sir," they all said slyly. "She had quite a few of those Irish coffees before you arrived. Maybe you'd better take her home. Can I call you a cab?"

"No, thank you," Kris Kringle said. "We have a car outside. We'll get her home."

"Both of you? My." Four eyebrows arched.

"Gunders," I said, smiling to show I was in mortal danger. "S'ab."

"She's been under a lot of stress lately," Robert/Po Chang said. His chest was closed up again now, but his face was melting. Never a dull moment with Chen Po Chang. It ran down his chest and formed an oily pool on the table. I tilted my head to see my reflection in it, and suddenly the local gravity changed. The spaceplane was taking evasive action. "Down" was *that* way. No, *that* way! No—

Lap dissolve.

Horrid dreams, that went on forever. My body was made of putty, which I twisted into the ugliest shapes I could devise. I butchered an infant, grew an enormous steel penis and raped a child, skinned and ate a living cat, burned a city, strangled a bird, poisoned a planet, masturbated with someone's severed hand, stepped on a galaxy out of sheer malice, gutted God, gathered everything anywhere that had ever been good or beautiful and defecated on it. My laughter killed flowers, my gaze boiled steel, my touch made the Sun grow cold. I tortured my parents to death, brought them back to life and killed them again, and again, and again. I danced on Grandmother's face with razor feet for days on end. Throughout all this, horrid little things with leathery wings at the edges of my peripheral vision watched and chittered and cheered me on. A snail kept oozing past, leaving a greasy trail, offering arch aphorisms in a language I could almost understand. My old shrink Alma appeared once, in a hockey uniform, and told me that my trouble was I kept everyone at arm's length; I needed to open up and let someone love me. I vomited acid on her until she went away, and then cried carbonated tears.

Peace came at last, when the last star in the Universe burned out and the blessed darkness fell all around, like warm black snow in summer.

14

In pride, in reasoning pride, our error lies;
All quit their sphere, and rush into the skies.
Pride still is aiming at the blessed abodes,
Men would be Angels, Angels would be Gods . . .
—Pope, *Essay on Man*

A switch was thrown and I was awake. My mind was clear, and my body was its normal shape and consistency. There was an insistent ringing in my ears, but otherwise reality seemed real again. The leather-winged things were gone. I was very glad of that.

I was sitting in a chair. I was naked. My bearded Chinese uncle was looking at me from half a meter away, clinical curiosity on his face. "Can you hear me all right?" he asked.

Lie. "Yes," I said. *Okay, you can't lie. More of that truth drug shit. Keep trying. Meanwhile, can you move?*

"The neuroscrambler should have largely dismantled itself by now. How do you feel?"

Yes, but without precision. So don't try any more now. "As if I were in free fall. Or wrapped in cotton." It was true. I felt light as a feather. I seemed to be sitting in a chair, involuntarily I gripped it to keep from drifting away.

"Do you have any questions?"

"Yes."

"You may ask them."

"Is there a bomb in me?"

"No. A single detonation was both necessary and sufficient."

"Why am I still alive?"

"I must know exactly what you know, and what you have done about it. You've already told me of the letter you left for your teacher, and I know your security code. But before I send an erasure command after the letter, I want to know exactly what it says."

I started to recite the letter verbatim; after a few sentences he cut me off. "This will take forever. I have it: ask me any questions you still have about our activities. The gaps in your knowledge will define what you know. And you will have the comfort of dying with no unanswered questions, a rare blessing. It is safe enough: I know you are not wired in any way. What would you like to know?"

I tried prioritizing my questions, but couldn't make them hold still. All over my body and brain, switches were hanging open, wires were cut. My mental thumb was mashed down on the panic button, but somewhere between there and my adrenal glands a line was down. In fact, the whole limbic system seemed to be down; my emotions were nothing more than opinions, with no power to command my body. My heart wasn't even pounding particularly hard. I picked a question at random, sent a yapping dog to cut it out of the herd, and stampeded it toward Uncle Santa.

"Are you Chen Hsi-Feng?"

Why do they say, the corners of his mouth turned up? They don't, you know; they just get farther apart and grow parentheses. "Ah, excellent: you are not certain. Yes, I am Chen Hsi-Feng."

"Where are we?" Now there was a stupid, irrelevant question. What the hell difference could it make? *Pick a better one next time.*

"In one of my homes. Near Carmel, if it matters to you."

I had been in Carmel once, on my way somewhere else. Down the coast from San Francisco. Upper-class stronghold; high fences and killer dogs; Clint Eastwood had once been Sheriff there or something. Estates big enough and private enough to hold a massacre without disturbing the neighbors.

"How come you do your own hatchetwork? If I were you, I'd be about eight layers of subordinates away, playing golf in some public place."

He shook his head. "Your grasp of tactics is thirty years out of date. Multilayer insulation was indeed useful in conspiracy or fraud for centuries: before a fallible lazy human investigator could work his way to the top of the chain he was likely to give up or be reassigned or retire or die. But then they started buying computers, and interconnecting them. Now every layer of intermediaries is merely another weak point, another thread the enemy may stumble across, and pull on to unravel the entire knot in a twinkling. I have many such chains of influence, whose sole purpose is to be found and keep investigators happy and harmlessly employed. Really important work I assign to the only person I know will not betray me. What else puzzles you?"

"Your ultimate aim. Do you plan to keep on blowing up Stardancers until they get annoyed and go away?"

"I plan to annihilate them, root and branch."

"But that's silly." Hunt down and kill more than forty thousand individuals in free space, who had low albedo, no waste heat, and nothing bigger than fillings in their teeth to show up on radar? Fat chance. With those huge variable light-sails attached to insignificant mass, they were more maneuverable than any vessel in space could ever be. What he proposed was not merely impossibly expensive, but impossible. "How could you hope to succeed?"

"By raising up an army against them," he said blandly. "And for that I need a technological edge, an unbeatable one. I need the Symbiote, tamed."

In my present state, I was incapable of shock. I was only mildly confused. I tightened my grip on the edges of my chair, so that I would not float away. " 'Tamed'?"

"You did not know. Good." He sat back and lit up a joint. No, a cigarette. My ex-husband had been a diehard smoker too. "By coincidence, it was a resident of Carmel, Sheldon Silverman, who first proposed the concept of a Symbiotic army—less than ten minutes after the existence and nature of the Symbiote was first revealed. It's in the Titan Transmission. But Charles Armstead pointed out the flaw in the idea. An immortal, telepathic soldier will mutiny the moment he joins the Starmind. He cannot be coerced anymore. I have tried placing spies in the Starmind; all ceased working at the instant of their Symbiosis. Fortunately I had anticipated this; none of them carried knowledge especially dangerous to me.

"But just suppose one could genetically modify the Symbiote, to produce a strain which does *not* convey telepathy, and has a limited life-span without regular reinfection."

He had not phrased it as a question, so I could not answer. I did as I was told, just supposed. The drug kept me physically calm, relaxed and at ease—but inside my head a tiny part of me was screaming, beating at the walls of my skull.

The toughest part of having an army is keeping it fed and supplied and in motion. If you had a Symbiotic army, all you'd have to do was issue them lasers and turn them loose. So long as they needed regular fresh doses of false Symbiote to keep breathing vacuum, they would follow orders.

"It would be useful," he went on, "to further modify the altered Symbiote so that it could survive terrestrial conditions. But I am told that is fundamentally impossible. No matter: who controls space controls the planet, in the final analysis. And the only military force in space that cannot be defended against is naked human beings who never hunger and thirst, an infantry who cannot be seen until it is too late. Do you see a flaw in the plan?"

"How can you genetically modify Symbiote? You can't get a *sample*, without giving yourself away."

Again his mouth grew tiny parentheses. "I have done so. That is precisely why your friends died."

The Symbiote Mass! Its mass and vector to several decimal places had been public information. Place an explosive of known force near it, trigger it by radio at a predetermined instant, apply a little chaos theory, and when the mass blows to smithereens . . . you'll know the projected new vector of the largest smithereens. There's no way anyone else can track shards of organic matter in open space—but you can happen to have a ship in the right place to intercept some.

I lacked the capacity to be horrified. I appraised the idea dispassionately, like the emotionless Vulcan Jerald in *Star Trek: the Third Generation* on 3V. The scheme was brilliant, without flaw that I could see. Not only did he have sample Symbiote for his geneticists to experiment on, no one even suspected that. His biggest problem would be making sure no human accidentally touched any of the Symbiote while working with it—but that's why they make remote-operated waldos; it was nowhere near as complex a problem as coping with dangerous nanoreplicators.

I'd been asked if I saw any flaws in the plan. "Stardancers would still have tactical advantage in combat. Instant, perfect communications."

He shrugged. "Telepathy is not *that* much more effective than good radio, at close quarters. I will match my generalship against any component of the Starmind. And they are utterly unarmed."

"There are a lot of them."

"Do you have any idea how many men I can put in space in a hurry, if I do not mind heavy losses in transit? At most, the Stardancer population is one ten thousandth of that of the People's Republic. The outcome is foreordained." He blew a puff of smoke toward the ceiling. "Well, what do you think?"

"I think you are the biggest monster I ever heard of."

He nodded. "Thank you," he said.

A phone chimed beside him. He answered at once. "Yes?"

Maybe the drug enhanced my hearing. I could make out Robert's voice. "Is she all right?"

Chen Hsi-Feng frowned slightly. "Did I not promise?"

"Let me speak to her."

"No."

"Then I'm coming in. I have to see her once more, before you take her mind."

His frown deepened . . . then disappeared. "Of course. Come."

He put down the phone, and took an object from an inner pocket. My own Gyrojet, it looked like, or one like it. "There is time for one last question," he said distractedly.

I nodded. "You're not going to let me live, are you? You lied to him."

"Yes. I dare not simply wipe your memory. Organic memory differs from electronic in that any erasure can be undone, with enough time and effort. A pity: it will cost me a son."

So I was going to die. And so was Robert, or Po Chang, or whoever he was today. Interesting. Regrettable. At least I would be forever safe from the things with the leather wings. Or perhaps not; perhaps they came from the land beyond life. No matter. An old traditional blues song went through my head.

One more mile,
Just one more mile to go.
It's been a long distance journey:
I won't have to cry no more.

"Sit there and be silent," he commanded me. He swiveled his chair away, faced the door with his back to me. The door opened and Robert came in. Not Chen Po Chang—my Robert Chen. The door closed behind him, and locked. He registered that at the same instant he saw the gun. His face did not change, but his shoulders hunched the least little bit, then relaxed again. "I have been stupid," he said.

His father nodded. "When you called *her* a romantic in the restaurant, I nearly laughed aloud. Do you remember what I told you on your thirteenth birthday?"

". . . 'Love is to be avoided, for it causes you to believe not what is so, but what you must believe.' You were right. You must kill her . . . and so you must kill me. Pray proceed."

No!

"I know you do not share my religious views," Chen Hsi-Feng said. "But I will summon a priest of any denomination you wish."

Robert grimaced. "No, thank you."

"You are sure? There is no hurry, and this much I can do for you. Of course, whoever shrives you must die also—I never understood why a good priest should fear death."

Robert shook his head without speaking.

"Is there anything else you want to do first?"

Robert thought about it. "Cut your throat," he suggested.

"So sorry," his father said, and lifted the gun.

I had spent the last seconds, scurrying about inside my skull, recruiting every neuron I could. Now I threw everything I had into a massive last-ditch internal effort, trying desperately to throw off my chemical chains and regain control of my body. The counterrevolution was a qualified disaster. I could not invest the motor centers—or even, equally important to me, regain access to my emotional glandular system—but I managed to briefly retake the speech center. "He . . . is . . . your . . . son," I said in a slurring drawl.

I succeeded in surprising him. He stiffened slightly, and rolled his chair to one side so that he could watch me without taking his gaze off Robert. Then he answered. "He is my illegitimate son. True, he is worth two of my heirs. But that is exactly why I have not been able to afford him since the moment he stopped being ruled by self-interest. I can no longer predict his actions. Last words, Po Chang?"

"Fuck you," Robert said.

His father shot him in the face. The dart worked exactly as the demonstrator slug had worked on the rat. Robert stiffened momentarily, then began to tremble, then fell down and shivered himself to death. Blood ran from his eyes, ears, nose and mouth, then stopped. From the *huff* of the shot to the end of his death rattle took no more than five or ten seconds. I wished I could scream.

Chen Hsi-Feng spun his chair to me. "Last words?" he said again.

Even without emotions, and with nothing objective left to live for, I was not ready to die. "I would like to . . . I guess the word is, pray."

"Do you require a cleric of some kind? I'm afraid I will not go to as much trouble for you as I was prepared to for my son."

I shook my head. "I just want to sit zazen for a few minutes."

He nodded at once. "Ah—Zen! An excellent faith. You may have five minutes. Who knows? Perhaps you will attain enlightenment this time." He composed himself to wait.

I tried to get down from my chair and sit on the floor. But the persistent delusional feeling of being in low gravity threw me off; I fell to the floor with a crash. Distantly I heard the unmistakable sound of a bone cracking—every dancer's nightmare horror sound—but it didn't seem important at all. I didn't even bother identifying which bone it was. I established that I could still force my legs into lotus, with the ease of two months of training. I tried to straighten my spine, but could not get a strong fix on local vertical. "Antidote," I said. "Partial at least."

He shook his head. "No. It is not a drug that hinders you, but a team of nanoreplicators. They will completely disassemble themselves when your temperature falls below 20 Celsius, but until then nothing can counteract them. Do the best you can. You have five minutes."

All that is important is to sit, I had heard Reb say once. *And to breathe.* Last chance for both.

I closed my eyes and became my breath.

Time stopped, and so, for once, did I.

The state Buddhists call "enlightenment," or *satori,* is so elusive, so full of contradiction and paradox, that many outsiders throw up their hands and declare it a chimera, a verbal construct with no referent. You seek to attain thought that is no-thought, feeling that is no-feeling, being that is non-being, and the cosmic catch-22 is that if you try, you cannot succeed. You must free yourself of all attachments, including even your attachment to freeing yourself. This state seems, verbally at least, to be *so* synonymous with, so identical to, death, that some scholars go so far as to say that everyone becomes enlightened sooner or later in his or her own turn, and there is no problem in the universe. The literature is filled with cases of Buddhists who claimed to have found enlightenment in the moment that they looked certain death in the face. Uyesugi Kenshin once said, "Those who cling to life, die, and those who defy death live." Taisen Deshimaru said, "Human beings are afraid of dying. They are always running after something: money, honour, pleasure. But if you had to die now, what would you want?" And Reb Hawkins had once told Glenn and the rest of us in class, "Looked at from a certain angle, enlightenment is a kind of annihilation—a radical self-emptying."

Perhaps it was nearness to death, then. Perhaps the microscopic nanoreplicators in my brain actually helped, by switching off emotions, making it impossible for me to feel thalamic disturbance, insulating me from physical aches and restlessness and even boredom. Perhaps it was the brutal fact of my despair—which is *not* an emotion, but a point of view. Freedom's just another word for nothing left to lose.

Whatever the reason, all at once I attained *satori.*

I was one with all sentient beings, and there was nothing that was not sentient in all the universe, not even space, not even chance. Everything that was, was simply quantum probability wavefronts collapsing into phenomena, dancing a teleological dance that was choreographed and improvised at the same time. "I" still existed, but I coexisted with and was identical to everyone/everything else.

I had been here before, for brief instants in my life, up until I gave my life to cynicism in my twenties—and then again, for a scattered few seconds, in Top Step, during a long period of kûkanzen. One of the things that had subconsciously held me back from entering Symbiosis, I now saw, had been a desire to experience it again for *more* than seconds, one last time the "natural" way, before I gave up and ate it prepackaged. A kind of spiritual pride.

It happened now, since I no longer yearned for it. Once again I was little Rain M'Cloud dancing on a floating dock, and was bobbing sea lions, and was the dance that connected us, all at the same time. And then I was not even that.

Sentient beings are numberless, says the Great Vow. I became one with that numberless number. And being one, we perceived ourself, with great clarity.

First, the things called no-thing. Vacuum, space, time, gravity, entropy, the void.

Next, the things called nonliving matter. Rock. Water. Gases. Plasma. Endless reshuffled combinations of hydrogen and the various ashes of its fusion.

Next, the things called living. The film of life that crawled and swam and flew and ran through and ultimately sank back into the surface of the Earth. I was all the viruses that swam in the soup of the world, all the grasses that grew, insects and reptiles and birds and fish and mammals, all striving to make ever-better copies of themselves. I seemed to be a part of all that lived, without being distinct from that which did not.

Then the things called sentient. I could *see* sentience as if it were a fire burning in the darkness. A tapestry of cool fires that was the dolphins and the orcas. Every dull selfish glow that was the consciousness of a cat. Every hot coal of fear and self-loathing that was a human being. I could pick out every Buddhist among them, tell the adepts from the students. There were all the Christians, and there the Muslims, those were the superstitious atheists and those all the lonely agnostics. I knew everyone on Earth who was happy, and everyone who was in agony. High overhead, and scattered about the Solar System from the orbit of Mercury to the fringes of the Oort Cloud, I saw/felt/was every Stardancer and all Stardancers, the Starmind—for the first time I began to understand it, what it was and what it was trying to become, I knew that it was a Starseed, and that if/when it finally bore fruit, there would be joy among the stars, and on Earth.

And further out I sensed things that were as far beyond sentient as I was beyond an idiot. The Fireflies, who had grown all of this from Earthseed, and others greater even than them, beyond all describing or human understanding. Of all, they were furthest removed from my experience, and thus most interesting. I could know them, there was time, there was no-time—

But just as my awareness left Earth to expand and encompass

them, began to pass through High Orbit . . . there was a change.

I became conscious of a level I had missed. It lay roughly halfway between human being and Stardancer, partaking of both. There were only a few of that nature, a tiny fraction of the sons and daughters of Eve—but a fraction that had stayed nearly constant for the last two million years. They were scattered here and there at apparent random, like salt particles in a bland soup, and they were all connected and interconnected by strands of something that has no name. Call them enlightened ones. Call them holy people. Call them the good and wise, or whatever you like. They had no collective name, only collective awareness. All their awareness was collective: none of them suffered from the delusion that they were anything more than neurons in a larger brain, cells in a body, atoms in a molecule. They were intimately connected with the Starmind, though separate from it.

In the same instant I became aware of their antithesis. Call them the destroyers. The truly evil, if you will. The ones who fear everything, and so seek to destroy everything they can reach. It did not surprise me that there were fewer of them by far. Their interconnections were fewer and much feebler. Each fought all the others, even when cooperation would further their aims. They were essentially stupid at their core, but so corrosively destructive in their childish rage that if they'd had numerical parity with their opposites, the human race would have ended long since.

Back in the reality I had left, frozen in the amber of now, one of them sat a few meters from me, waiting politely to kill me.

Ideas are like viruses. They transmit copies of themselves from host mind to host mind, changing themselves slightly in the process, and the ideas which are unfit soon perish, and the ones that survive grow strong. They compete for resources. Christianity competes with Islam for space in the brains of mankind; the idea of capitalism competes with the idea of Marxism, while theocratic monarchy nips at both their heels. The idea of freedom battles with the idea of responsibility, and so on.

On the highest level, the idea of Life competes with the idea of Death. Hope versus cynicism. Yes versus no. Joy versus despair. Enlightenment versus delusion. Conception versus suicide. This happens in all people . . . but some take sides.

I could see the human avatars of both sides, now. Call them the white magicians and the black, those who loved greatly and those who hated hugely, in awful stasis, terrible balance, like irresistible thrusters straining to move implacable mass. The black haters were far outnumbered, but they would not yield.

And they said nothing, put out nothing but a steady scream of rage and terror. While the others spoke, sang, reached out, reasoned, soothed. I could see them all, hear them all, almost touch them all.

One of them spoke to me from high over my head.

Morgan.

Yes, Reb, I said, with my mind only.

Another sang, from a different direction. **Friend of my *badund-jari*—**

Yes, Yarra.

Miz McLeod, said the widowed Harry Stein in a third location.

Harry.

Rain, said a fourth, from impossibly far away.

Hello, Shara.

I was connected to their kind by four strands, now. I could see the strands, like spacer's umbilicals, feel energy pulse along them in both directions.

Reb spoke for all. **Cusp approaches. Action is needful.**

I'm glad you know. Can you help me?

We shall.

What must I do?

Go within, deep within, and you will know.

I went within.

Deep within my own body, my own skull, my own bones. The knowledge of how to do so came from hundreds of minds, funneled through the four to whom I was connected. I went back past consciousness to preconsciousness. I was a fetus, swimming a warm saline sea, with a two-valved heart like a fish, parasitic on the mother-thing. I invested my limbs, kicked, dreamed. I was born, acquired a four-valved heart and eyes to match my ears, began my long battle with gravity. I was a growing youth, then a dying adult, and my awareness went further inward. I was a cell, absorbing nutrient and preparing to divide. I was a strand of DNA, scheming patiently to take over every speck of matter in the universe, measuring time in epochs.

Suddenly I was a corpuscle, racing through my own bloodstream like a cruise missile, singing at the top of my voice. I shrank down to an atom and roamed through tissue and bone and fluid. In moments I understood my whole body, better than any doctor ever could. I had the autonomic control of a yogi, a Zen master, a firewalker. Absentmindedly I destroyed the bacteria in my teeth, cured an incipient cold, strengthened my bad back and trick knee, began the repair of a lifetime of damage to my heart, lungs and other vital systems. I happened across the swarm of nanoreplicators deep in the vitals of my brain, huge slow clumsy things that moved at speeds measurable in great long picoseconds. I slipped inside one, studied its programming, and told it to become a factory for converting nanoreplicators like itself into norepinephrine, finishing with itself. Then I slipped out and down the medulla to the top of the spinal cord, checked all the skills I had spent a lifetime storing there, upgraded and enhanced them to their optimax. I located the bone I had cracked falling down, in my right ankle, saw that it would take at least half an hour to mend it, worked its limitation into my choreography, and ignored it thereafter. I devoted a huge portion of my body's emergency reserve energy to enhancing my strength and coordination.

I polished the choreography for an endless time, perhaps as much as a second, with a thousand minds looking over my figurative shoulder and doublechecking me, making suggestions for improvement. My four pipelines, Shara Drummond, Yarra, Harry Stein and Reb Hawkins took a personal interest, and there were a number of other dancers out there in the Starmind who had ideas to offer, in particular an Iranian Muslim named Ali Beheshti who had been a dervish before he accepted Symbiosis, and a former break-dancer from Harlem named Jumping Bean.

There was one last question to be decided. Was it necessary that Chen Hsi-Feng die? Opinion was divided, consensus oscillated.

Fat Humphrey spoke from near at hand. **Forget necessary or unnecessary. You know what he wants to drink. Serve him.**

The debate was ended.

I was out of full lotus and on my feet before he knew I was moving. The broken ankle made a horrid sound and hurt like blue fury, but I was expecting that, ignored it. I had not danced in a one-gee field for years, had not danced at all in weeks, but it didn't matter at all, I was now at least briefly capable of anything that any human could do, factory rebuilt from the inside out, in a controlled adrenaline frenzy. I became a dervish, spinning and whirling and leaping.

In my normal state of performance mania I am capable of moving faster than the eye can follow for brief periods. Now I was inspired, exalted. My feet had not kissed the stage in so long! I flashed to and fro before him, must have seemed to have multiple arms and legs, like the goddess Kali. I had no clothes to hinder me; my bare feet gripped the hardwood floor beautifully.

Instinctively he thrust his feet away from him so that he and his chair flew backwards away from me. He brought up his gun and gaped at me, thunderstruck.

I danced for him.

It was a true dance, a thing of art, a statement in movement. I knew he could sense that, even though he could not slow down his time-sense enough to grasp the statement. He stared, fascinated as a rabbit by a cobra, for nearly ten seconds.

But he was no rabbit. He realized what my dance implied, and exactly when I had known he would, he shook off his shock and awe and pulled the trigger.

The first of the three remaining rocket-darts came floating toward me as slowly as a docking freighter in free fall. I could see the dot of wetness at its tip.

I made it part of the dance, teasing it as a matador teases a bull, eluded it with ludicrous ease.

The harsh flat sound of laser-rifle fire came from outside the room. Someone in the distance screamed. There was a *chuff* sound just outside the door. He sprang from the chair to a point where he could see both me and the door, the gun waving back and forth. I was waiting for that: I went into a spin, standing in one spot and whirling like a top, tempting him. Just after he passed out of my field of vision for the eighth time, he fired; the needle was halfway to me by the time I could see it. I had all the time in the world. It was heading for my heart; the easiest thing to do would have been to simply squat and let it pass overhead. Instead I *jumped,* impossibly high, and it passed under my feet. When I landed I broke out of the spin and resumed my dance, completing the second movement in two or three seconds.

I reprised the final phrase, then did it again, and again, giving him a predictable pattern to extrapolate.

He had one rocket left, and just then something outside struck the door heavily. But he must have decided that whatever lay outside that door, it could only be human. Clearly I was not. Without any real hope—what could he know of real hope?—he sobbed and fired his last round at me.

The instant he did so his fight was over, one way or another. I could see him grasp that, and devote his last second to trying to comprehend the meaning of my dance.

I ran *toward* the dart, reached it halfway to him, before it had had a chance to build up to full speed, snatched it out of the air, let the force of it put me into a turn and then fling me at him again, and closed on him before he could lift a hand to defend himself.

And with an overhand looping right, I rammed his death dart down his throat.

As I was yanking my hand clear, he bit off the tip of my index finger in death-spasm. My ankle gave way beneath me at last and we went down together, side by side, facing in opposite directions. He kicked me sharply in the ribs, and died.

The door shattered. A man sprang into the room and landed in a crouch, beautifully. He wore black shirt and trousers, and was barefoot. His face and skull were clean-shaven. His expression was serene. There was a fresh laser burn through one of his outflung hands, but it didn't appear to bother him. He took in the scene in a glance and straightened up from his combat stance. Then he made deep *gassho.*

"I am Tenshin Norman Hunter," he said, with the mild voice of a teacher. "I am the Abbot of Tassajara, a Zen monastery in the mountains east of here."

I sat up, cupping my injured hand. I had already stopped the bleeding and sterilized the wound, was already beginning to regrow the missing fingertip, but it still hurt, and I could indulge things like that now. "I've heard of it," I said. "And I felt you coming. I am Rain M'Cloud, of Top Step. Thank you for coming."

"Reb called, when you were captured in San Francisco," he said. "I answered. It takes some time to come up over the mountain."

Thank you, Reb, for watching over me.

You're welcome, Rain.

I glanced at Robert's body. Whatever else he had done, he had died for love of me. I bade him goodbye, and looked away, forever. "Are there any hostiles left out there?"

The abbot shook his head. "All the guards sleep. The gas grenades we used are good for at least an hour. Three other monks are here: Katherine, and Yama, and Dôjô Sensei, who is badly wounded."

I got to my knees. "*Anmari-kuyokuyo-suru-na, kare-ga kitto umaku-yaru-sa,*" I rattled off.

He looked slightly discomfited. "I'm sorry, I don't really speak Japanese."

I smiled at him. "I don't either. Never mind, I just said 'don't worry, he'll make it.'"

"I think so. But it would be good to leave here quickly."

I managed to get my good leg under me and stand. The adrenalin was wearing off, and while I was cushioning it as much as I could, a crash was somewhere on my horizon. I had just used up about three days' worth of energy in less than a minute. "Let's go."

Tenshin Hunter had a large and rugged four-wheel drive ATV waiting. As soon as I was strapped into a seat, I relaxed a block in my brain, and human emotions returned to me for the first time since I'd blacked out in the restaurant. They didn't overwhelm me, didn't bring me back from my state of *satori.* I knew they were illusory, impermanent, transient. But I experienced them to the fullest. I had been storing up a backlog for a long ghastly time.

I cried and cried for the whole two hours it took us to crawl up over a mountain and crawl down to Tassajara, rocking with sobs, bawling like a child, while Katherine held my head to her shoulder and stroked my hair. I cried for Robert, and for Kirra and Ben, and Glenn, and Yumiko, and poor angry Sulke; for Grandmother and my parents; for my ex-husband David and the Chief Steward of my first shuttle flight to orbit; and for Morgan McLeod, who had suffered so bitterly for all her stubborn attachments.

When we finally reached Tassajara in the cool dark of evening, I was done with crying, done with a lifetime of suppressed crying. I never cried again, and I don't think I ever will.

Five days later I was in Top Step again, and eight hours after that—just long enough to conceive a child with Reb—I entered Symbiosis fully. Twelve hours ago, I came out of the Rapture of First Awakening. I have taken the time to tell this story, impressing it directly into the memory of Teena at the highest baud rate she can accept, because it is the consensus of the Starmind that the world must know what happened, and what nearly happened, and I am in the best position to tell it.

Now I am done, and now I will spread my blood-red wings and sail the photon currents beyond the orbit of Pluto, where something truly wonderful is happening. There I will physically touch, for the first time, Shara and Norrey Drummond and Charlie Armstead and Linda Parsons and Tom McGillicuddy, and a thousand more of my brothers and sisters. We will dance together.

We will always dance.

I am Rain M'Cloud, and my message to you is: the stars are at hand.

STARMIND

PART ONE

I

Provincetown, Massachusetts
1 December 2064

Rhea Paixao was considered odd even by other writers. But some things are universal. Like most of her colleagues, Rhea got some of her best writing done in the bathroom.

And this was her favorite bathroom. She stopped in the doorway and examined it before entering. She had known it since earliest childhood, and the passage of time and changing fashions had altered it very little.

True, it now contained a modern toilet and bath; there was such a thing as carrying quaintness too far. But the wall opposite her was simply that, a wall, not programmable in any way: it displayed nothing, could not even become a mirror. An actual silvered-glass mirror hung on the wall, over the sink, its image speckled and distorted by surface impurities. Between mirror and sink, offset to the left, was a widget that had once been used to hold toothbrushes and a plastic cup of germ culture. Farther to the left was an antique cast-iron radiator, unused in decades. The sink itself had mechanical taps, two of them, completely uncalibrated; one had to adjust the flow-rate and temperature by hand with each use. There was a depression behind the rim meant to hold a decomposing lump of phosphate soap. And slung beneath the sink was an antique seldom seen anymore in 2064: a spring-loaded roller intended to hold a roll of toilet paper. (There was no roll there now, of course—but there had been for years after people stopped using the horrid stuff. Nana Fish had insisted on it. Even after she had broken down and accepted modern plumbing,

Nana had insisted on keeping a roll of the Stone Age tissue handy, "just in case." She went back to the days when machinery used to fail all the time.) Every time Rhea saw that roller, she wanted to giggle.

The room was, in fact, almost a microcosm of the town around it. From its earliest days, Provincetown had always conceded as little as possible to the passing of years, changing only with the greatest reluctance and even then pretending not to. That had been the town's—most of Cape Cod's—stock in trade for centuries now . . . and a good living there was in it, too. Even in these days, when "progress" was no longer quite as dirty a word as it had once been, there were still people who would pay handsomely for the illusion of an allegedly simpler time. P-Town, as the natives called it, was tailor-made for the role.

She stepped into the bathroom and let the door close behind her. No terminal in here, no phone, rotten ventilation—it was possible to make the mirror steam up—and nothing in the room accepted voice commands. In here, all three avatars of the house's AI were blind, deaf, mute and impotent. The wind outside was clearly audible through the walls. Rhea loved this bathroom more than even she suspected. She had plotted out at least three books here, and worked on a thousand poems, songs, articles and stories. At age fifteen, she had renounced Catholicism forever in this very room . . . sitting on that same oaken toilet seat over there!

Just like that, a perfectly good story idea popped into her head—

She gave it a lidded glance, not wanting to seem too interested, and sauntered to the toilet. It followed her, and her pulse quickened. Studiously ignoring the idea, she urinated, let the commode cleanse and dry her, and went to the sink. Again it was at her shoulder. She used her dental mouthwash, making a rude production of it, and spat noisily into the porcelain sink. The idea did not take offense.

She continued to ignore it, studied herself in the mirror. Still a couple of years to go before her fortieth birthday. Black hair, black eyes that others called "flashing," coffee-with-cream complexion. Exotic high-cheeked Portuguese features that always reminded Rhea of old 2-D pictures of Nana Fish as a girl, back in the twentieth century, an impression reinforced by the old-fashioned nightgown and robe she wore now. She ran water and splashed some on her face, rubbing especially at her eyes and cheeks and lips as though her makeup could be washed off, a childhood habit so trivial it wasn't worth unlearning. Colly was asleep, and Rand was not expecting her back in the bedroom any time soon so far as she knew; there was time to dally at least briefly with the idea. She studied it out of the corner of her eye: a short-story idea probably, really no more than a situation—but one she knew she could do something good with.

For Rhea's kind of writer, plot and theme and even character were always secondary, mere craftsmanship, constructed as needed to flesh out the story. For her, the heart of a story, the first flash that impelled and enabled her to dream up all the rest, was always that special suffering called "antinomy." "Conflict between two propositions which seem equally urgent and necessary," as a professor of hers had once defined it. The juncture between a rock and some hard place. The place right out at the very tip of the sharpest point on the horns of a dilemma. Give someone an impossible choice, and *then* you had a story. Once the Muse revealed to you a deliciously impossible choice, you could begin deciding what sort of person would squirm most revealingly when confronted with it, and from that you could infer your theme, which gave you your plot.

This idea, for instance . . .

It had been born in that brief flash of recollection she'd had as she first walked into the bathroom, of the long-ago night when fifteen-year-old Rhea had made up her mind in the privacy of this very room that she *wasn't* scared, dammit, Catholicism was *bullshit,* there *was* no God. As the adult Rhea had remembered that night, and thought of the Catholic Church for the first time in years, she'd been reminded of an artistically beautiful tragedy she knew about and had never exploited dramatically before.

Donny—Mr. Hansen—and Patty. She could no longer recall Patty's last name. Mr. Hansen had been Rhea's Sunday School teacher, twenty-three and gorgeous and devout in his faith, and every girl in the class had had a crush on him, but they all knew it was hopeless. Donny Handsome (as they called him, giggling, among themselves) was blatantly and terminally in love with Patty, who was also twenty-three, and just as gorgeous and devout, and just as clearly daffy about him. Together they were so beautiful—their love was so beautiful to see—that the girls in Mr. Hansen's class actually forgave her for existing.

Then, a single week before they were to be married, Patty had announced that God had called her to be a nun.

Teenage Rhea had been transfixed by Mr. Hansen's dilemma. He was a good Catholic to the soles of his feet. According to the rules he lived by, *he was not even allowed to be sad.* Not only could he not argue with Patty, try to change her mind . . . he was not allowed to *want* to. It was his spiritual duty to rejoice for his beloved, and the special grace she had been granted. He had, in the metaphorical terms of his church, been jilted for Christ, and was expected to smile as he gave away the bride.

That had been the beginning of the end of Rhea's faith: seeing Donny Handsome stumble around P-Town like a zombie, smiling aimlessly. She had refused to believe that the universe and butterflies could have been made by so sadistic a God. Now, why hadn't she ever thought to convert such a splendidly awful antinomy into a story before?

Her craft-mind went to work on the idea now. Just put it down, as it had happened? No, it was always best to change it in the telling, she found: the way it changed told you what was most important to keep. Besides, that made it art and not journalism. Did she need the Catholicism angle, for instance? Or could she change it to some other, equally inflexible faith? With celibate clergy . . . hmmmm, weren't a lot of those left anymore these days. Weren't a lot of Catholics left, for that matter. Maybe it didn't even need to have religion in it at all. But if not, what else had that same implacable weight?

She tried an old trick. Refine it all down to a single sentence: the sentence that the suffering protagonist screams (even if only inside) at the moment that the point enters the belly. Then throw out everything that doesn't lead inexorably to that scream. Okay, what was Donny Handsome's scream?

My beloved, how can you want to go where I cannot follow?

In the instant of that crystallization, Rhea knew what the story was really about . . . and knew that she could not write it. No matter how she disguised it dramatically. Not yet. And maybe never.

She told the story idea to get lost. Until she knew what its ending was.

She went to the window—missing the sudden chill that used to come from December windows when she was a little girl—and pulled aside the ancient curtain to look out at the night. And was rewarded. In the distance, above the shadowy housetops of P-Town, the silhouette of the Pilgrim Monument showed clearly against the night sky, an eighty-five-meter tower of grey granite—and poised beside it, midway up its length, seeming to be only meters from its crenulated stone windows, was a brilliant crescent moon. The juxtaposition was weirdly beautiful, quintessential Provincetown magic. Rhea became conscious of her breath. It swept her mind clear—of the captive story idea and her ongoing concerns and the day's cares and her self. She watched without thought for a timeless time, long enough for the moon to climb perceptibly higher up the Monument.

She became aware of herself then, and let the curtain fall closed. She felt a sudden close connection with the child she had once been in this room, in this house, in this town. More than that, deeper than that—a connection with the family that had raised her here, and with their forebears, fishermen and fishermen's wives, back seven or eight generations to old Frank Henrique Paixao, who had gone over the side of a Portuguese whaler in a two-man dory off Newfoundland one cold day in 1904. He and his partner Louis Tomas had successfully gotten themselves lost in the fog, miraculously survived to reach Glace Bay in Cape Breton, landed there without formalities or paperwork, and somehow made their way overland across the border and down the coast to Massachusetts, eventually fetching up in P-Town. The cod fishing there was as good as they had heard. After five years or so, both men had sent for their families back in Portugal, and settled down to founding dynasties in the New World—just as the Pilgrim Monument was being raised.

Rhea felt that Frank's wife Marion must have seen the Monument and moon looking just like this more than once, and could not help listening for the echo of her ancestor's thoughts. She heard only the sighing of night winds outside.

She sighed in accompaniment, went to the mirror and ran a brush through her hair. She was ready to join Rand in bed. A month he'd been home already, and she was just getting used to having him around again. Every home should have a husband. She shut off the light with a wall switch and left the bathroom, walked down the short hallway to the bedroom. In her mind's eye she was still seeing the slow dance of Monument and moon in the crisp cold starlight as she opened the bedroom door and stepped into New Mexico desert at high noon.

Rhea was so startled she closed the door by backing into it. The sudden sense of *distance,* of vast expanse, was as staggering as the sudden brightness. The horizon was unimaginably far away; she saw a distant dark smudge, bleeding purple from beneath onto the ground below, and realized it was a thunderstorm large enough to drench a county. Between her and the horizon were endless miles of painted desert, broken occasionally by foothills and jagged rock outcroppings; close at hand were scrub hills and cacti and a dry wash. Right before her was an oasis, a natural watering hole. Beside it was an old-fashioned wooden bedframe with a curved solid oak headboard and a thick mattress. On the bed reclined one of Rhea's favorite holostars, dressed only in black silk briefs. He was nearly two meters tall, as dark as her, and glistening with perspiration or oil. He was holding out a canteen toward her, smiling invitingly.

She discovered she was thirsty. Hot in this desert. She stepped forward and accepted the canteen. The hand that offered it was warm. He was real, then. Icy cold water, sweet and pure. He looked even better up close. She handed back the canteen. He moved over to make room. She let the robe fall from her shoulders and drop to the sand. His eyes went up and down her slowly, as she took off the nightgown and dropped that too. She stepped out of her slippers; the sand felt strangely furry. She spun around once, taking in the vast silent desert that receded into infinity in all directions, and leaped into the bed. That started it bouncing, and it did not stop for some time.

She nearly drifted into sleep afterward, the desert sun warm on her back and buttocks and legs. But an inner voice caused her to rouse herself and nudge her celebrity companion. Might as well get it over with. "That was really wonderful, darling," she said sleepily. "All of it. But really—purple rain?"

His famous features melted and ran, becoming the familiar face of her husband. His hair lightened to red and his complexion to fair. "No, honest—I've seen it, outside of Santa Fe. Near the pueblos. Just that color. I've wanted to show it to you." Rand reached out a lazy arm, did something complicated to nothing at all in mid-air, and the desert sun diminished sharply in brightness without leaving the center of the sky. The effect was of a partial eclipse: twilight with the shadows in the wrong places. Power of suggestion made the temperature seem to drop, or perhaps he had dialed that, too; they slid under the covers together.

"I'm glad you did," she said, snuggling. "It's lovely." She looked around at the dusky desert, noting small excellences of detail. An eagle to the east, gliding majestically. Intricate cactus flowers, no two quite alike. Ripples on the surface of the water in the oasis, seeming to be wind-driven. Microfilaments of lightning, convincingly random, flickering in that distant purple rain. "This is the best one yet. Is the music this far along too?"

He shook his head. "Just some ideas, so far. But having the basic visual will help."

"I'm sure it will. It was a beautiful gift, really. The set *and* the sex. Thank you."

He grinned. "You're welcome. I'm glad you liked it."

"*Very* much. So . . . what's the catch?"

"Catch?" he asked innocently.

The reason she knew there was a catch was because it was not possible for her husband to conceal something important from her, not while making love. But she could not let him know that, so she made up a logic-chain. "It's not our anniversary. It's not my birthday. I don't keep score, but I don't *think* I've been unusually nice to you lately. You're not having an affair; you haven't had *time.* It was a wonderful present and I thank you for it, and"—she grinned and poked him in the ribs—"what is it going to cost me?"

He opened his mouth as if to say something, changed his mind, and reached out into the empty air beside the bed again, typing new commands onto his invisible keyboard. The desert went away. So did everything, except the bed and themselves. All at once they were in space, surrounded by blackness and blazing stars, tumbling slowly end over end. High Orbit: the Earth swam into their field of view, huge and blue and frosted with clouds. The illusion was so powerful that Rhea felt herself clutching at the bed to keep from drifting away from it, even though she knew better. All at once the rotating universe burst into song. Rand's fourth symphony, of course, as familiar to her as her name. He muted the sound with a gesture after a few bars, left the visual running.

It was her heart plummeting; that was what made the illusion of free-fall seem so real. "But—but you're not going up again for another eight months—"

"Things have changed, love," he said. "I mean, really changed. Sit down."

"Sit down? I'm *lying* down, what the hell do you mean?"

"You know what I mean."

She lay back. "Okay, I'm 'sitting down.' Go on."

"My brother called. While I was down at the shore a while ago."

"Oh? How is Jay? Cancel that, I don't give a damn how he is: what did he say?"

"Pribhara bombed. Big-time. She hates space, the customers hate her—even the company hates her new work. But most important of all, she says she just can't adapt. She's a born perpendicular. So she's thrown in the towel . . . a few seconds before they would have yanked it out of her hand."

Rhea was confused. She knew there was a booby-trap in this somewhere, but couldn't find one big enough to justify all this buildup yet. "So that's good news, right? Now there are only three of you competing—"

"It goes beyond that," he said, looking uncomfortable. He dithered with his invisible controls until their shared rotation in space slowed and stopped. The starry universe stabilized around them.

She took a deep breath. "Tell me."

"The competition is over," he said. "I won."

"What?" she cried in dismay. "*You* won?"

It was only that: a misplaced emphasis. Had she said, "You *won*?" there might not have been a quarrel at all. That night, at least.

Rand had been one of four competitors for a plum position: Co-Artistic Director and Resident Shaper/Composer at the legendary Shimizu Hotel, the first hotel in High Earth Orbit and still by far the grandest. The creator and first holder of that position had held it with great distinction for fifty years—then a year ago, both he and his heir apparent had been killed in the same freak blowout while vacationing off Luna. Replacing an artist of Willem Ngani's stature overnight had been a daunting task: the management of the hotel had narrowed the field to four candidates, and then found itself unable to reach a final decision. It had elected instead to postpone the question for a three-year trial period. The first year of that period was nearly over: each of the four candidates in turn had gone to space for a three-month residency at the Shimizu. Rand had drawn the third shift, and had only returned from his own highly successful season a month earlier; the fourth and final composer, Chandra Pribhara, was supposed to be just now entering the second month of her own first residency.

But Pribhara had turned out to be a "perpendicular"—one of those rare unfortunates who simply cannot adapt to space, who cannot make the mental readjustment that allows a human being to retain her sanity in a sustained zero-gravity environment. She had abruptly canceled her contract after only a single month in free-fall, accepting the huge penalties and creative disgrace, and returned to Earth early.

This left the Shimizu's management with a quick decision to make. A hotel must have entertainment. The show must go on. The Resident Choreographer—Rand's half-brother Jay Sasaki—needed a Shaper to collaborate with. *Someone* had to replace Pribhara, fast. They might have simply advanced the rotation schedule, summoned Wolfgar Mazurski back to orbit two months earlier than he was expecting, and continued from there on a three-shift rotation while they pondered their final decision. But Mazurski had other commitments, and so did Choy Mu Sandra, the other contender.

Which left Rhea's husband.

But Rand was only just back from orbit. Returning to space for another three-month shift this soon would raise his total free-fall time to six months in one calendar year: very likely enough time for his body to begin adapting—completely and permanently—to zero gravity. It would take fourteen months for the transition to be finished . . . but deleterious metabolic changes often began much sooner. If they asked him to replace Pribhara now, the competition was over: they would have to give him the permanent position to forestall a costly lawsuit.

The Shimizu management had little choice. And Rand's first season *had* been the most well-received of the four so far. So they had sent word, through his half brother, Jay. The job was his if he wanted it—along with a scandalous salary, outrageous perks, immense cachet and luxury accommodations in-house for himself and his wife and daughter. For life—which was how long they would need them.

Rhea hated the very thought of moving.

And if she *were* going to move, space was the very last place she'd pick. The only one-way ticket there was. Fourteen months or more in space, and you had to stay there forever. You couldn't even *hope* to go back home again someday. . . .

Worse, Rand knew all this. Or at least, he should have known. A decade ago, he had solemnly promised Rhea—as a condition of marriage—that he would never ask her to move away from her beloved P-Town, from her home and family and roots.

When he had first mentioned the possibility of this job, she had been shocked and hurt. But she had not reminded him of his promise . . . partly because she loved her husband and knew how badly he wanted the job, and mostly because she *knew* in her heart that there was no way Rand would ever actually be offered it. That had been clear to her from the start. For one thing, his blood relationship with Jay would work against him—allowing disgruntled losers to cry nepotism. For another, he was the most talented of the four—traditionally a handicap. To nail it down, he was by far the least political—traditionally the kiss of death.

Ironically, it was that which had clinched the deal. Mazurski and Choy *each* had a powerful and influential clique of friends, skilled at vicious infighting: they canceled each other out. Rand was the only choice everybody could (barely) live with. And so it was the very same aspect of her husband's character which had in fact won him the job that caused Rhea to say to him now so injudiciously, "*You* won?"

The ensuing quarrel was so satisfactory a diversion that it was a full hour before they got around to the actual argument they had been avoiding for over a year now.

"God dammit, Rhea, just tell me: what's so awful about space?"

"What's so fucking good about it?"

"Are you kidding? Sterile environment, pure air, pure water, perfect weather all day every day, no crime, no dirt, longer lifespan—and weightlessness! You don't *know,* honey, you haven't been there long enough to get a feeling for it; everything is so easy and convenient and restful in space. Nothing is too heavy to lift, nobody's a weakling, your back never hurts. And the freedom! Freedom from the boredom and tyranny of up and down, freedom to live in three dimensions for a change! To use *all* of a room instead of just the bottom half—to see things from different angles all the time—to let go of something and not be afraid gravity's going to smash it against the wall by your feet. Put that all together, throw in a better class of neighbors and the best view God ever made, and it doesn't sound half bad to me."

"It sounds horrible to me! The same weather, *every day?* The first thing you said: 'a sterile environment,' that's exactly what it sounds like. Living in a little sterile tin can surrounded by cold vacuum, breathing canned air and peeing into a vacuum cleaner. What about Colly? Where's an eight-year-old going to find playmates in space? Think about never again going out for a walk, never getting rained on or snowed on or going to watch the sun rise—"

"—the sun rises fourteen times a day at the Shimizu—"

"—it's not the same and you know it—"

"—no, it's not the same, it's better—"

"—bullshit—"

"—how the hell would you know? You were up there for three whole days! I'm telling you, I've been there for three months and it's better—"

"*—maybe it is, but it's* different, *God dammit—*"

He flinched at her vehemence. After a few seconds of silence, he slapped at his control panel, and set the universe spinning around them again. "What's so bad about different?"

She reached irritably past him and felt for the keyboard, found it and quit the holo program abruptly. Blink: they were in their quaint comfortable moonlit bedroom in their magnificent old home in picturesque P-Town. "What's so bad about what we have?" she cried, gesturing around her at hardwood floor and lace curtains and quilted comforter and scrimshaw and Frank Paixao's barometer and fading photographs of Nana Fish and Nana Spaghetti on the walls.

He looked round, at the familiar trappings of their marriage, of their shared life. When he spoke, his voice was softer. "It's good. You know I love it here too. But it's not all there is."

"It is for me!" she said. *Oh my beloved, how can you want to go where I cannot follow?*

He closed his eyes and took a deep breath, and played his hole card. "It isn't for me."

She clutched his shoulder and played her own. "You promised, Rand! Back when you first asked me to marry you, you promised . . ."

There was nothing he could say to that, because it was true. She had him dead to rights. The argument was effectively over, now. She had won . . .

. . . and cost her beloved husband the professional and personal opportunity of a lifetime, the crowning achievement of his career. . . .

He nodded, and rolled over on his right side, back to her. "When you're right, you're right," he said very quietly, and mimed preparing to sleep. But his shoulder blades were eloquent.

She savored her triumph for as long as she could stand it, staring at the ceiling. Then, keeping her voice as neutral as possible, she said, "Anyway . . . how would we deal with Colly's education?"

His shoulder blades shut up in midsentence.

"Well—" he said finally, and rolled over to face her.

2

Rand Porter had been waiting for that question, of course. Their eight-year-old would get a *better* education if he took the job; Rhea had known that when she asked the question. On his new salary, they could afford to enroll Colly in any school on or off Earth, with full bandwidth and as much individual attention as she wanted. Hell, they could afford to have teachers physically brought up to her if they wanted, in corporation shuttles. And Rhea could have Unlimited Net Access herself too.

And all these things, he added, would be merely perks—over and above a salary so immense that they could easily have afforded to pay for them. Full Medical would be another such perk. Rhea's literary reputation could only benefit from all the publicity that would accrue. Rand stressed all these points, without ever quite saying aloud a point that mattered to him almost as much as the honor or the creative challenge or the prestige or the money *per se*.

If he took this job, he would be earning more money than Rhea, and would be more famous than her. For the first time in their relationship.

He *couldn't* mention that aloud. They had agreed back at the start that they would never mention it; that was how little it meant to them; therefore he couldn't bring it up now.

"Worse comes to worst, why couldn't we compromise?" he suggested desperately. "Have one of those commuter marriages? I'd take the job, and you could come up for three months out of every six. Lots of people do that, when only one half of the team wants to be a spacer."

"Sure," she said. "That worked out just great for your brother, didn't it?" Jay had maintained such a relationship with a dancer in one of his two rotating companies for over five years—then about six months ago, Ethan had sent him a Dear-Jay/resignation fax from Fire Island. The scabs were just beginning to turn into scar tissue.

"We're more committed than Jay and Ethan were," Rand protested. But privately he was not sure that was true—and the stats on groundhog/spacer marriages *were* discouraging.

When they were exhausted enough, they agreed to sleep on it.

At five in the morning he slipped from the bed without waking her and went down the hall to his Pit. Strains of melody were chasing each other in his head, but when he booted up his synth, he could not isolate any of the strands in his headphones. Sounded aloud, they were an inseparable jangle of discord—like his feelings.

So he went to the kitchen, and found he was not hungry. He went to the bathroom and discovered he didn't have to pee. He put the headphones back on and learned that he didn't want to hear anything in his collection. He went up to Colly's room and found that she didn't need to be covered. As he bent to kiss her, he startled himself by dropping a tear on the pillow next to her strawberry blonde hair. He went quickly back downstairs to the living room and wept, as silently as he could. When he was done, he dried his eyes and blew his nose.

What *did* he need?

That was easy. He needed someone to tell him he wasn't a selfish bastard.

He had promised her. Worse, he had thought about it first. He had not specifically envisioned this situation, no—but he had made his promise without reservations. *No matter what, love—*

But this offer was beyond any dreams he'd had a decade ago. How could he have known? The carrot was irresistible. . . .

Or was it? What was so irresistible? The money would be great—but while they had been middle-class for their whole marriage, they had never been poor, never missed a meal. There were other jobs. Indeed, this was about the only job he could possibly take that would require them to move from P-Town, that he couldn't basically phone in. It was certainly the only job that would have required *permanent* exile. What was so great about the damn job?

Two things. It was the most prestigious job in his field, one of the most prestigious there was. And it would make him the principal breadwinner in his family, for the first time.

Not very proud reasons to break a solemn promise to your wife . . .

No, dammit, there was more to it than that. The job was the richest creative opportunity he had ever had. His three-month stint just past had been the hardest work he'd ever done . . . and had drawn some of his very best music and shaping out of him. Collaborating with his half-brother Jay had been exhilarating; although Jay was thirteen years older than Rand's thirty-five, their minds had meshed.

I see: your wife will be a little sadder, but your chops will improve . . .

It wasn't just that. Part of what had made his work better in the Shimizu had been the heart-stopping grandeur of space itself, the bliss of zero gee. Space was as magical as Provincetown, in a different way; maybe more so—surely Rhea would see and respond to that, just as he had.

You hope . . .

Anyway, what was so great about P-Town? Okay, it was beautiful; sure, it was timeless; granted, it was magical. This chair he was rocking in, for instance: beautiful and timeless and magical. But it made noises like rifle fire, and leaned ever so slightly out of true, and wasn't especially comfortable without the pillows that always slipped out of adjustment. So what if it had belonged to Rhea's great-grandmother? So what if it had been the chair in which the infant Rhea had been breast-fed . . . and Colly too?

The answer was all around him—hanging from every wall, perched on nearly every flat surface. Pictures of eight generations of Paixaos, as far back as imaging technology allowed, ranging from faded black and white daguerrotypes of Cap'n Frank and Marion to paused holoblocks of Rhea, Colly and himself. Hundreds of Paixaos and their kin, in dozens of settings . . . and every single image had Provincetown somewhere in the background. Beautiful. Timeless. Magical . . .

On the mantle, amid the more recent Paixaos, was a holo of Rand's parents, Agnes and Tom, taken just before their divorce. The background was Newark, New Jersey.

There was no point to this: he already knew he wanted the job badly enough to take it; whether he *should* want it that badly or not seemed irrelevant. Nonetheless he flogged himself, as his penance, endlessly replaying the argument until it became a loop that annihilated time.

I want to be great. Is that so terrible?

Just as he felt that his brain might explode, thirty-five kilos of eight-year-old reality landed on his lap like a tonne of bricks, shouting, "Boo!" and his heart nearly exploded instead. Daylight and his daughter had crept up on him.

"I scared you, Daddy!" she reported with glee. "I did, didn't I?"

For an instant he was tempted to use Colly as a new club to beat himself—*how can you ask a child to go pioneering?*—but he shifted gears instead, grabbed her in his arms and stood up. "That you did, baby," he said, clutching her close. "That you did."

"Did you catch it, Daddy?"

"Huh?"

"Whatever made you stay up all night. Did you get it?"

"Oh. Uh . . . not yet, sweetheart. I got a look at it, but it got away."

"Don't matter about it," she advised him. "You'll get it next time."

Her optimism—and the boundless, unquestioning faith that underlay it—floored him. *I can't be a bastard,* he thought. *I'd never have fooled her.* He hugged her even closer, making her squeal. "That I will," he agreed. "Right now, let's you and me get us some grub."

"I cook," she said quickly. Her faith in him had practical limits. That was why he could trust it.

"Deal," he agreed.

And she did cook a better breakfast than he could have—albeit somewhat more messily. Rhea came in while she was doing it, and stood in the doorway in her bathrobe watching and trying not to smile. Colly refused to let either of them help, or even coach. By the time they were all sitting down eating together, it seemed to have been decided that today was a happy day. Rhea's eyes were unguarded when they met his. The Issue was still there between them, but it was on hold for the moment.

After the meal, it was Rhea who said, "Colly, sit back down. You can be a little late for playgroup today. Your father and I need to talk about something with you."

"Aw, Mom—do you have to? Sarah's gonna bring her cat in today, and she swears it has thumbs!"

"Yes, honey, it's important."

"Four of 'em! Oh, okay, go ahead." She sat back and adjusted her nervous system to fidget mode.

Rhea handed the ball to him. "Rand?"

He cleared his throat. "Colly . . . have you ever thought about . . . living somewhere else?"

"You mean I'm going to grandma's house again? How long this time?"

"No, honey, that's not what I meant. I mean . . . all three of us moving away from here, to a new home."

"And not coming back?"

"That's right. Not ever."

The notion did not seem to shock Colly. "Where?" she asked practically.

"Well, remember that time we went to visit Uncle Jay?"

She got excited. "Go to space, you mean? And stay there? In that cool hotel? Oh, wow!"

"You really liked it that much?" Rhea asked, surprised.

"Da! Si! Ja! Oui!" Colly said. *"I'm not little in space!"*

Both parents were startled into laughter.

"It's true," she insisted. "I can reach everything there, and look grown-ups in the eye, and I'm as strong as anybody and not clumsy like everybody else. Besides, it's *fun!* When do we go?"

Even Rand was taken aback by support this enthusiastic. "But baby . . . you know if we stay in free-fall for long, we have to stay forever?"

"Sure."

"Well . . . won't you miss your friends?"

She thought about it. "I could still call them up, right? We could holo-play. And they could come visit me realies, sometimes. And I'd make lots of new friends. I'm good at that."

Rand squelched a grin. "Well . . . yes, you are. But won't you miss . . . this house, and P-Town . . . and everything?"

"And the beach?" Rhea prompted. "And the ocean?"

Colly looked around her. "I guess. But if I do, you can just make it for me, Daddy. Anyway, you can't play six-wall here. I tried."

He didn't have to look at his wife to know that she was looking faintly stricken. Her only potential ally had defected. He wanted to put an arm around her, but was not sure whether that would make it worse.

Colly had gone from fidget to bounce mode. "Can I go tell everybody now, Daddy? How soon are we going, Mommy? I gotta go get dressed! Oooh, Kelly's gonna be *so* jealous—"

"Hold your horses, young lady. Nothing's been decided yet. Your mother and I are still discussing the idea—"

Colly wasn't listening. Her eyes had gone wide. "Wait a minute—this means you got the job, didn't you, Daddy? You get to work with Uncle Jay now! They picked you! Oh, I knew they would! I *told* you they would!"

Rhea winced.

"We are going, we are! Can I go tell Kelly now? And Sigrid? And Bobby?"

The choices were let her go or strap her down. "Maybe you better get dressed first," Rhea said.

Colly looked down at her rumpled pajamas, and giggled. "Oh, okay, if you insist," she said, and ran for the stairs. She was naked before she reached the top.

Rand and Rhea looked at each other. Each waited for the other to speak, with voice or expression.

"We have to laugh," he said finally.

"Oh yeah? Why?"

"Because if we strangle each other, who's going to take Colly to playgroup?"

And so they laughed.

"Come on, somebody," Colly called from upstairs. "Get dressed! I'm almost ready already!"

They laughed harder, and then got up together and sprinted up the stairs, shouting, "Yes, ma'am! Right away, Your Highness!"

"I still don't see why you have to *live* there," Rhea said thirty minutes later. They had dropped Colly off at playgroup in the West End, and now were sitting in the car at the edge of the sea at Herring Cove, half watching a group of eight or ten Trancers in sleek thermal clothing dancing on the shore, spinning and jumping in the December breeze, falling and recovering but always springing back up at once. They made Rand think, as always, of birds trying to batter their way through an invisible ceiling. Provincetown had been a magnet for Trancers since the strange fad had begun and spread around the planet with the speed of a catchphrase. P-Town had always been a Mecca for all kinds of odd behavior.

"It's stupid," Rhea went on. "It's just stupid elitist thinking. There's no sensible reason why you can't phone it in, like any other job. They only *have* the best holo gear in human space."

"That's what the Shimizu is all about," Rand said patiently. "That's what they're buying. The most conspicuous consumption there is. Nothing canned, nothing piped-in—"

"I know, I know—the celebrity artists are all on-site for the customers to press flesh with, and half the robot-work is done by human beings, just to prove they can afford to waste money. Snob logic."

"You can't make art for a place without going there," he said. "Holo isn't enough. I can't explain why, but it isn't. I always go to the site if there is one, at least at first. You know all this."

"So you've *been* there for three months! Isn't that enough?"

It was a fair question. He tried to find the words to answer it. All he could come up with was, "Space is different."

"Different how?"

"Look: you were there."

"For three days."

"Long enough to get a taste. Now, tell me: can you remember what it was like?"

She started to answer, then stopped. "No," she said finally. "I can remember what I told people about it. I can remember what I wrote about it. But no, you're right. I can't remember what it was like. Not really. I have a lingering feeling about it—"

"If you had to write a poem about it, right now, could you? Or a story set there?"

Her shoulders slumped. "I'd have to go back. For longer than a few days. And either write it there, or right after I got back down."

"That's why Ngani bullied the Board into putting in writing a provision that his successors would have to live in-house. And that's why Jay bullied them into honoring the agreement when Ngani died."

This was all old ground. They had had this conversation over a year ago, when he had first become a candidate for the position. He saw her momentarily as a trapped animal, doubling back on its tracks in search of a way out overlooked earlier, and felt a pang of guilt.

She gestured at the ocean and half a world of clouds, at the crazy Trancers moving in harmony—then turned and gestured in the other direction, at P-Town. "And all of this, we're supposed to give up, forever, so that Willem Ngani's artistic vision isn't violated?"

The question was so unfair that he returned fire with some irritation. "Only if we want me to have the job."

She left the car and walked a short way along the beach, past the gyrating dancers. By the time she returned, he had cooled down and she looked chilly despite her thermally smart clothing. The Trancers too had finally run out of manic energy, and were dispersing, looking blissed-out.

"How about this?" Rand said, as the car heater switched on to normalize the temperature in the vehicle. "We give it a couple of months. I'll complete Pribhara's season. Then if you absolutely hate it, I'll quit."

"You couldn't break your contract!"

"Hell, Pribhara did. I'll reserve the right. If they want me bad enough, they'll negotiate. It's perfectly reasonable—considering they're wrecking my whole schedule on no notice at all. By rights they ought to be paying me a whopping bonus. If they don't like it, let 'em give Mazursky and Choy socks full of dung, and let *them* fight it out."

She thought about it. "Huh. Two more months wouldn't be long enough to change you into a spacer. And it's long enough for me to form an opinion . . ."

"I promise if you want to come back, there won't be an argument."

The device didn't fool either of them; he could see that in her eyes. But it brought the situation a little closer to tolerable. It would buy some time.

"How soon would we have to leave?"

"I'll call Jay."

3

Yawara
Queensland, Australia
2 December 2064

At about that moment, not too far from the opposite point on the planet's surface, an old—no, ancient—woman switched off her ancient compact disc player, brushed the headphones out of her hair with a palsied hand, and decided it was time for sleep. Or at least for bed. Slowly and carefully she got up from her rocking chair, then used it to steady herself while she removed the denim shorts which were her only clothing. She walked with halting steps through the darkness to her bed, but when she reached it, she dropped easily and comfortably into a squat beside it. Reaching beneath it, she drew out her chamber pot and removed the lid. When she maneuvered it beneath her, its weight and a small sloshing sound reminded her that she had forgotten to empty it that morning. As she was about to put it to its accustomed use, she suddenly stopped, clamping her sphincter and flaring her nostrils. Her head turned from side to side, twice. Then she looked down between her legs, bent her head lower and sniffed. She took the chamber pot from beneath her and brought it to her nose and sniffed again.

She *knew,* then, but nonetheless she reached up and got matches from the bed table. In the sudden flaring light, her eyes confirmed what her nose had told her. Her chamber pot contained wine.

It delighted her. It had been a long time since anything had surprised her. This was a good one. She thought about it, savoring the puzzle. No one had approached her home closer than a hundred yards all day. She had not left it for a moment. She had *not* emptied the utensil after using it that morning, she was sure of that. She might be old—no, ancient—but her memory was still sharp as the long edge of a war boomerang. There was no logical explanation . . . so she went inside herself, to her special place.

And at once, contradictory things happened on her face. Her eyes brightened, and bitter tears spurted from them, and years—no, decades—melted from her visage, and her mouth smiled while her brows knotted in a fierce frown. She glanced across the room at her CD player, and ran a hand across her head to confirm that she had taken its headphones off. "*Badunjari . . . ?*" she whispered, and cocked her head as if listening.

Whatever she heard caused her to smile even wider and weep even harder—but the frown relaxed. She sat back on her heels and began to rock slowly from side to side. After a time, she lifted the chamber pot to her lips and drank from it. The wine was excellent, delicious and immediately powerful. She took a deeper draught.

"Really?" she said in Yirlandji. "What is?"

If there was an answer, no microphone could have recorded it.

Her tears ceased; the smile remained, and became the mischievous grin of a little girl. "Okay," she agreed, and drank again. "I will wait and see."

She had not been this happy in forty-four years. Magic, real Dreamtime magic, was loose in the world again. . . .

PART TWO

4

The Shimizu Hotel, High Orbit
2 December 2064

Jay Sasaki was in the studio when his AI spoke up. "Phone, Jay: your brother, Rand, flatscreen only." It waited patiently while he finished a movement phrase for the camera and toweled off sweat.

"Thanks, Diaghilev," he said then. "Monochrome head-shot, minimum audio, accept." It was the cheapest possible earth-to-orbit call, small black-and-white image and rotten sound, probably relayed on a satellite circuit so old its expiry date began with "19." Rand would have been offended if Jay had tried to reverse the charges—and it was not yet settled whether his kid half-brother could afford to make fullscreen color calls to High Earth Orbit on his own dollar. Jay spoke before the AI finished producing an image, to let Rand know the circuit was completed. "Well, how did she take it?"

"She's right here," Rand said. "Ask her yourself." He swiveled the carphone so that Rhea came into frame. She was smiling wryly.

"'Oops,' he said gracefully," Jay said. "Hi, Rhea. Well, how did you take it?"

"Rectally," she said sourly.

The joke cued him—first, that Rand would indeed be coming back up to work in the Barn . . . and second, that it would not be a good idea to sound too delighted just yet. Was Rhea coming up with him right away? Was Colly? "You'll really like it up here, I promise you," he said experimentally.

"I'd better."

Good. Rand would arrive still married. "And Colly will love it. Space was made for kids."

"It must be," she said. "You like it." But she was smiling.

He relaxed, trying not to let the extent of his relief show. The worst that could happen now was that his half-brother's wife would make Rand's life miserable to the end of his days. *But he'll be able to work with me again!* It would take a lot of the sting out of Ethan not being around anymore. . . .

"We're going to give it a trial period," Rand said. He swiveled the phone again so that he was back in frame. "Two months, so Rhea and Colly can check it out before they commit themselves."

Jay managed to hold his poker face. Fortunately, in zero gravity one's face does not pale as blood pressure drops. If Rhea left in two months, Rand would go with her. With the example of Jay's own disaster with Ethan before him, Rand would not risk losing her in a long-distance marriage. Kate was going to have a blowout when she heard this. "That'll be hard to sell to the Board. They want this settled. Face, you know."

"I've got face too," Rand said. "I require notice before uprooting my family. If the Board doesn't like it, they can start running want ads in the trades."

Briefly, Jay fantasized telling his brother the whole truth. The primary reason the Board had abandoned the audition process and chosen Rand as their shaper was that Jay—feeling reckless in the aftermath of his breakup with Ethan—had privately sent word through the hotel manager that he would quit if they did otherwise. He had just enough clout to pull that off . . . and no margin at all: if the hotel came out of this looking bad, he was out of a job. He was the most famous living human choreographer of free-fall dance—but if he left the Shimizu, where could he go? There were only two other dance companies in space, and neither was hiring. Jay had been a spacer, permanently adapted to zero gravity, for over a decade now: if he could not work in space, he could not work—even if he could have learned to think and choreograph in up-and-down terms all over again.

No—he couldn't tell Rand any of this. If he did, Rand would think—would suspect in his heart forever, no matter what Jay said—that Jay had put his job on the line purely and simply because they shared a mother. Rand would never believe the truth: that he was truly the only one of the four candidates who was any damn good, the only one Jay could stand the idea of being locked into working with for the next umpty years. The hole in his self-confidence would founder him. And the realization that Jay's job *was* on the line would make his problem with his wife even worse.

Well, it was up to Jay to see that Rhea didn't opt out. His other choice was to slit his throat. "You're absolutely right. I'll make them see it that way. Shall I call you back with their answer?"

Rand shook his head. "We both know they're going to say yes. I can afford to call *you* now. Full-band color."

Jay let the grin escape at last. His brother was right. Kate would hate this—but she was committed. As committed as he was. "Damn right. Call me back at . . . what the hell time is it down there?"

"About ten in the morning." The Shimizu was on Greenwich Time; it was nearly 3 PM for Jay.

" . . . at about suppertime. Listen, I don't want to crowd you, but . . . how soon can you come up? The sooner you can make it, the less trouble I'll have selling this trial period."

Rand acquired the harried look of someone who is trying to solve a tricky problem while long-distance charges are ticking away. He glanced sideways. "What do you think, hon?"

After a time, Rhea's voice came from out of frame. "Three days, minimum. I'd like a month. I'd like a year, dammit."

"I think I can get three days, no sweat," Jay said cheerfully.

Rand tried for a diversion. "Anything we can bring up for you?"

"If I think of anything, I'll tell you when you call back." He gave the phone his best grin. "Listen, this is really great news. Really, Rhea—you'll see! Kiss Blondie for me. Phone off." As Rand's smiling image dissolved, he went on, "Diaghilev, where's Kate?"

"In her office, Jay. Do you wish an appointment to see her? She has an opening in her calendar tomorrow at—"

"No, I want her now. She'll see me. ETA fifteen minutes."

"Yes, Jay. You're right: Ms. Boswell has accepted for her. Fifteen minutes from . . . mark."

"Shower please, Diaghilev."

"Yes, Jay."

The studio shower accepted and cleansed him; ten minutes later he was dry, shaved, groomed and jaunting along the corridors of the Inner Sphere, heading inboard toward Katherine Tokugawa's executive office in the Core.

Heads turned as he floated past, but only one of the hotel guests had the nerve to call out to him. "Hello, Jay. You look happy—good news?"

Jay made a long arm and grabbed a jaunt-loop, braked himself to a halt. His boss would have a fit if she ever heard that a mere guest had learned news of this importance before she did—but Eva Hoffman was more than just a guest: she had been a resident fixture in the Shimizu for sixteen years now. He glanced around mock-conspiratorially. "Are you *sure* those are your original eyes?"

Eva grinned. She was one hundred sixteen years old, and showed most of them—having, most unusually, given up controlling her appearance on her hundredth birthday. She drew stares everywhere she went in the Shimizu these days . . . the most horrified of them coming from those guests whose own odometers had rolled past zero. "Thirty years ago I'd have known exactly why you were looking happy, at twice the distance. So your brother's coming back up to stay, eh? Congratulations."

"Thanks. I'm excited."

"Me too. You two do good work together. Pribhara was a waste of air."

"She . . . had her own way of doing things."

"Yeah. Wrong. Would you like me to take charge of his wife and daughter? What's her name, Spaniel?" Eva, of course, knew perfectly well what Colly's name was. "Help them get reoriented to free-fall, their first day, show 'em around the Mausoleum, and all that, so that you and Rand can get right down to work?"

He was touched by the offer. Eva was a Shimizu institution, and she did not offer her time lightly or often. She was one of very few guests who knew her way around the place as well as Jay, who did not need to follow some AI's trail of blinking lights to get where she was going. "I think I've got that covered," he said. "But if they do need more help, I'll know where to come. Thanks, Eva."

She looked dubious. "Who have you got in mind?" Eva had a low opinion of most of the Shimizu's staff Orientators—which Jay shared.

"The new kid. Iowa."

"Seen him a couple of times; don't know him."

"He's a natural. Spaceborn."

That interested her. "Is that good? Will he know what it is they don't know?"

Jay nodded. "He's been dealing with mudfeet all his life, one way or another. The ones here are just richer, that's all. I think he and Colly are really going to hit it off."

"I'll have to meet him. I always wanted to get to know a spaceborn."

Diaghilev cleared his virtual throat. "One minute, Jay."

Jay was still in Deluxe country—the cheapest of the Shimizu's accommodations, the inner-sphere suites with no windows onto space. It was time to jaunt. "I've got to go. Uh . . . look, keep this absolutely top secret for, oh, at least another fifteen minutes, okay?"

"Twelve, my final offer."

"Okay, I'll talk fast." He kissed her wrinkled cheek and pushed off.

"Drop by for a chat before dinner, all right?" she called after him. "Something I want to ask you."

He waved agreement without looking back.

He passed quickly through the rest of the Deluxe Tier to the inmost core, jaunted past his own suite without stopping, and reached the executive offices on time. Warned of his arrival by Diaghilev, Tokugawa's own AI had materialized its Personal Executive Assistant persona for him, rather than the Front-Desk Clerk avatar it would have shown to a guest. "Good afternoon, Mr. Sasaki," she said. Her voice was oddly flat and nasal, perhaps in an attempt to make her seem real.

"Good afternoon, Ms. Boswell."

"Ms. Tokugawa will see you now." The door to the inner sanctum dilated.

Jay jaunted through it, brushing the doorway with his fingertips to decelerate himself to a stop inside.

Katherine Tokugawa was sitting *kûkanzen* in the center of her spherical office, dressed in black ceremonial robes, her back to him. At the sound of the door hissing shut behind him, she unlaced her fingers, unfolded her legs from lotus, and flexed at the waist, rotating until she faced him. He politely spun until their local verticals matched, and they exchanged a bow. Then they each "took a seat," in the free-fall sense of the term, giving a short puff with their thrusters so that they backed away from each other and velcroed their backs and buttocks to opposing surfaces, Jay maneuvering to avoid sitting on the door he had just come through; they sat more or less simultaneously.

"Well?" she said then, in the slow exhalation of one emerging from profound meditation.

It was all bullshit, of course, and Jay knew it. If she had really been meditating, she'd have velcroed herself to a wall or some other support. A person who sits *kûkanzen* in the center of a room in zero gee, unsecured, sooner or later ends up bumping against the air-exhaust . . . and shutting down the airflow only causes a ball of exhaled carbon dioxide to accumulate and smother the meditator. The Manager of the Shimizu was—as the job called for—one of those people who prize appearance over content, style over substance, and Rinzai Buddhism was merely part of her admittedly impressive act. To have actually practiced it would have been an inefficient use of time.

But Jay was not about to let his boss know he saw through her. Not when he was about to piss her off. He slowed his breathing, adjusting to her rhythm. "My brother said yes," he told her.

She smiled wearily.

Tokugawa—he dared not let himself think of her as "Kate" while in her presence—was a hundred and sixty centimeters long, and massed forty-six kilos. In free-fall her small size had the effect of making her seem to be a little farther away than she actually was. Which made her seem just a little more crisply in focus than other people. She had stabilized her apparent age at forty standard years, with silver streaks in her hair that were in different places each time you met her. Jay had no idea what her real age might be. She was the granddaughter of Nobutake Tokugawa, who had succeeded Bryce Carrington as Chairman of the Board of the original Skyfac consortium back before the turn of the millennium, and her family still controlled a large share of space industry today. She had their "look of eagles," backed by a competence that few Tokugawas actually possessed anymore: she *looked* so much like the Manager of the finest hotel in human space that her genuine fitness for the job was almost a happy accident. Neither attribute particularly impressed Jay, but then, he had to work for her.

"Good," she said quietly. "It was about time for something to go right."

"Troubles, Ms. Tokugawa?" Jay asked, testing the waters to see just how bad a time this was to bring up the matter of the two-month escape clause Rand wanted.

She made a flicking-away gesture. "Not really. Just an infinity of minor nuisances."

"How minor? Is the house still pressurized?"

"For the moment," she replied drily. "No, nothing serious. I've got a major economic summit coming up next month, with so much weight I'm going to have to double security, and—"

"Excuse me, I could have sworn you just said you were going to double security."

"I did."

Jay stared. "There is no such quantity. You can't double infinity. *God* isn't as secure as a Shimizu guest."

She grimaced. "If He had security like those five are going to have, Satan would never have gotten off a speech, much less a coup attempt. Their combined resources are . . ." She paused, and Jay waited, curious to hear what word she would choose. " . . . impressive," she finished, and he repressed an impulse to lift his eyebrows. Any personal fortune that impressed Katherine Tokugawa staggered Jay. "If they ask me to, I'll have to taste-test their food myself—or anything else they want."

"That does sound like a lot of pressure."

"Special diets, special requirements, protocol headaches—the Muslim needs to know where Mecca is at all times, precisely, and the Chinese wants me to have that Soto Zen roshi flown in from Top Step to do dokusan with him, and as for the American—well, never mind what *she'll* want—and of course each and every one of them must be honored and coddled and pampered *precisely* as much as the other four, to the tenth decimal, never mind that it's apples and—" She caught herself, glanced down at her meditation robes, and took a long cleansing breath. "Never mind any of it. It's par for the course these days. And not your pidgin. About your brother—any problems I should be aware of?"

Jay's turn to take a deep breath. "One potential glitch . . . but I'll make sure it doesn't express. Don't even give it a thought."

"Fine. What am I not thinking of?"

"He says he wants a two-month trial period. He'll finish out Pribhara's season—but if his wife and daughter don't like it up here, he'll quit then."

Her eyes closed momentarily, and the ghost of a frown chased across her brow; those were the only external signs she gave. Those who choose style over substance are compelled to stay with style no matter how tough it gets. But Jay knew she was furious. And here he was, a convenient and fully qualified target . . .

"Why couldn't his family have come up with him the last time?" she asked quietly.

"His wife was on deadline and couldn't leave her desk for more than a few days," Jay reminded her. "She's a writer. Remember, they thought he had at least two more seasons—two more years—before the Board would make a final choice . . . and only a twenty-five percent chance it'd turn out to be him."

Tokugawa had her hands clasped in the *kûkanzen mudra*—but now she was unconsciously twiddling her thumbs. The effect was so ludicrous that he knew she would be even angrier if she became aware of it; he concentrated his gaze on her eyes. "True," she admitted grudgingly. "We are rushing him. His demand is reasonable. But if his wife decides she's a groundhog, the house loses face. Damn Pribhara—this is her fault."

Privately he disagreed. Pribhara could not help being a perpendicular. None of those poor unfortunates could. If anything, the situation was the fault of the Shimizu's Board of Directors, for not simply picking a shaper. The three-year rotating audition scheme had always seemed crackbrained to Jay; something like this had been bound to happen. But his advice had been ignored, and now was not the time to mention it. The blame looked better on Pribhara than it did on him. . . .

"I'd better call in Martin," she said. "I hate speaking to the man, but this is his pidgin. Maybe he can . . ." Her voice trailed off disconsolately.

Jay empathized completely. Even for a PR man, Evelyn Martin was a weasel; you wanted to bathe after talking with him on the phone. But he *was* gifted at spin control—

A metaphorical lightbulb seemed to appear over Jay's head.

"You're not looking at this right," he said suddenly. "This isn't bad news—it's mitigated good news. All it takes is a little spin control."

"Explain."

"Look, all Martin's press release has to say is that Pribhara has canceled for medical reasons, and that Porter has graciously consented to fill out her term. At the end of two months, *maybe* you have to announce that Porter has dropped out too, and let Choy and Mazurski carry on competing from there—a minor kerfluffle. But most likely his wife and kid will love this place as much as everyone else does—so you announce *then* that he's been given the final position and has accepted. Either way, none of the Board's face is lost."

"Your brother would accept that? Not announce that we've picked him as the final winner until he's committed himself? And not announce that at all, ever, if he decides to opt out?"

"Gladly, I think. It gets him out of an impossible situation too." He had a rush of brains to the head. "But you should bump him to the permanent salary right away."

Her thumbs stopped twiddling. "Done. Mr. Cohn!"

Her AI materialized its lawyer-persona between her and Jay, facing both of them. As always, Mr. Cohn reminded Jay of an impossibly motionless shark. "Yes, ma'am?"

She gave instructions for the amendment of Rand's contract, relying on Cohn's legal software to translate her wishes from conversational English into Lawyerese, and spoke her signature. At Jay's suggestion, she had Cohn upload a copy to Diaghilev so that Jay could pass the document on to Rand later that night. Then she dismissed the AI and turned back to Jay. "Sasaki?"

"Yeah?"

"You've earned your air today."

He smiled; the first sincere smile of the day. He felt as if he had just successfully matched orbits by eyeball, without a computer—a terrestrial analogy might be walking a tightrope over an abyss. "Always nice to hear. I'll let you get back to your meditation."

"Thank you," she said. "But first, your reward. *You* get to tell Martin about all this."

He grimaced. "It's true, then; no good deed goes unpunished."

"Except those committed by Stardancers. They seem to be exempt."

"That's an idea," he said. "I'll go out the airlock without a suit."

"'In space,'" she said, seeming to be quoting something, "'no one can hear you scream.' Please yourself—but see Martin first."

Jay sighed. "Yes, boss. After I've eaten."

He had originally intended to call Eva Hoffman and beg off on the chat she had asked for. But now he needed to tell someone how relieved he was, and how clever he had been in wiggling, at least for the moment, off the spot marked X. As he left Tokugawa's office, he consulted the mental list of people he trusted enough to share news like this, and—Ethan being history now—found only Eva's name. She was not an employee of the house, plugged into that grapevine . . . nor did she fraternize much with the other guests, even the other Permanents. Most of them considered her crazy. She was easy to talk to, and in his opinion she had more character and style than any ten other people he knew. He had often thought that if Eva were, oh, say, seventy years younger, he might have considered turning hetero again for her. Hell, even sixty years younger . . .

Telling Diaghilev to call ahead and announce him, he left the Core and jaunted back outboard, through both Deluxe Tier (peasant country, at least in Shimizu terms) and UltraDeluxe Tier (the bourgeoisie; governors, national-level executives and so forth), all the way to the Prime Tier, the outer suites with the most cubic and a naked-eye view of space. Eva's digs were in the Prime Plus hemiTier: the one whose view included Earth. She had chosen a suite offset from the center of that section, so that the home planet did not completely dominate the view, a choice Jay approved of since he had made the same one himself. Her door opened for him when he reached it, and her voice bade him enter.

Her suite was lavish and comfortable and hushed. As a long-time resident of the Shimizu, he knew the second most expensive thing in it was the hush. The third most expensive thing was the sheer cubic volume, and the air that filled it. Jay was one of the half-dozen hotel staff with enough clout to rate quarters in Prime Plus, and his own suite was a quarter the size of this one. Even by the standards of a permanent guest of the Shimizu, Eva was wealthy. Kate Tokugawa would have said that her assets were "substantial," only a step below "impressive."

His eyes found Eva where they expected to, by the room's *most* expensive feature: floating within the three-meter-across bubble window (called an imax for obscure historical reasons), which made the best Prime Tier suites cost twice as much as Deluxe accommodations. As was her custom when at home, she was wearing only wings and fins, sculling them gently and quite unconsciously to hold her position in space against the gentle current of airflow. It was a sight he had seen countless times, and still found striking and moving: a butterfly with a withered body, Rodin's *She Who Was Once the Beautiful Heaulmiére* somehow given the wings of a swan by the gods in clumsy compensation for the ruin of her beauty. Nobody looked sixty anymore these days—certainly no one whose real age had three digits—and Jay found Eva's defiant decay paradoxically entrancing. Especially juxtaposed against the wings, modern and high-tech . . . and that absurdly expensive surround-window . . . and the stars beyond, their steady fossil light unthinkably older than Eva could ever hope to be. He wished he had the nerve to use the image in a dance . . .

But Eva never missed a premiere. She had been born back in the days when nudity was strongly taboo—and while she'd obviously come into the twenty-first century, he had noted that she was never nude save when closeted with intimates.

Oddly, the thought had never once occurred to him that he would probably be free to use the image as he pleased one day, all too soon—that it could not be long before Eva died. If it had, the thought would have saddened him . . . but there was something about Eva that kept him from having it.

He politely removed his own clothing and let bee-sized tugbots take charge of each garment. He did not bother to remove his own wrist and ankle thrusters. Eva didn't object to their emissions, she just didn't care to use thrusters herself if she didn't have to; and Jay felt far more naked without them than he did without clothes. Nonetheless he allowed other tugbots to give him his own set of wings and fins, slid them on over his thrusters, and used them to join his hostess at the window. He was, if anything, more skillful at air-swimming than she was; he simply preferred the superior kinetic and kinesthetic versatility thrusters offered.

The jaunt to her side was uncomplicated: the room seemed as starkly furnished as a Zen master's cell, all its fabulous conveniences invisible until they were needed. That was its fourth most expensive feature.

She rode the turbulence of his arrival expertly, and helped him steady himself into station beside her, just far enough away to allow them both wingroom, all without taking her gaze from the window. She had chosen a local vertical that put Earth in the lower left quadrant of the window. Perhaps a fifth of the planet was visible, a lens-shaped slice of Old Home. The rest of the view was of eternity.

They shared it in silence for perhaps a minute.

"Drink with me, Jay," she said then.

He didn't care much for alcohol as a rule; he hated what it did to his balance and kinesthetic sense. But he did not hesitate. "Name your poison." He told himself that it would anesthetize him against having to talk with Martin later.

"Jeeves," she called, and her AI shimmered into view, oriented to her local vertical and seeming to be standing on air.

"Yes, madam?"

"The good stuff."

One holographic eyebrow rose half a centimeter. "Very good, madam."

Both of Jay's eyebrows rose at least that much. This was not going to be a casual conversation. He stopped rehearsing his account of how clever he had been in Kate's office.

5

Jeeves moved away without moving his legs, as if he were under gravity and his feet were on wheels, and ceased to exist when he left the humans' peripheral vision. Tugbots delivered an amber bottle, two bulbs and a spherical table to the spot where he had vanished. As they arrived, Jeeves reformed, and picked them all out of the air expertly as he "rolled" back into view. He placed the table between Eva and Jay and told it to stay there, placed a bulb against either side of its velcro surface and the bottle in the center facing them, so that the table looked like a stylized Pinocchio, and shimmied back a pace. Eva thanked and dismissed him; once again he glided out of view before dissolving.

"I never thought I'd see that again," Jay said respectfully.

She nodded. The bottle was an ancient quart of Black Bush, about three quarters full. It was something like a century old, and its contents were twelve years older than that, a blend of whiskey so fine that at the time of bottling it could not legally be exported from Ireland. Its source was the oldest distillery on Earth, whose charter-to-distill had been granted in 1608. There probably was not another bottle like it left anywhere in the Solar System. Jay was the only person in the Shimizu besides herself who had ever seen it; they had shared a dram the night Ethan's goodbye message arrived from Terra.

He steadied her while she poured, a process of pulling the bottle away while chasing it with the open end of the bulb, then pinching off the flow with one thumb while she sealed the bulb with the other. She did it better than the Chief Sommelier in the Hall of Lucullus, losing not a drop of the precious whiskey, fiercely proud of her ability to control her aged fingers. Jay accepted his bulb with thanks. He brought it up past his nose in a slow gentle curve, squeezing slightly so that the nipple dilated and the bouquet came to him. When she had filled her own bulb and replaced the bottle, he raised his in salute, and they drank.

The silence stretched on.

"Silly," she said at last. "I'll never get over how silly it is."

"What's that?" he asked.

"You could blindfold me, tug me around the hotel enough to confuse me, lead me into any room in the place and dock me in front of its window . . . take off the blindfold and *defy* me, without looking away from the window, to tell you which Tier I was in. There is no way to tell a real window from a fake one without instruments. And yet this thing is worth every yen it costs me. About the gross annual product of a medium town . . . and I'd pay three times as much if I had to. Why?"

He seemed to know a rhetorical question when he heard it; he made no reply.

"Why are they so goddam *happy,* Jay?" she asked then.

"Who?"

She gestured at the Earth. "Them." Her gesture widened to take in orbital space, then widened farther. "All of them. Our species. The human race in this year of Our Lord 2064. I think I know why the Stardancers are happy—but why people too?"

"I'm not sure exactly what you mean."

"Exactly. That's what I mean." She squeezed more whiskey into her mouth, rolled it around and swallowed. God, she missed her taste buds sometimes. "They probably don't even seem all that happy to you, do they?"

"I never really thought about—"

"Trust me. I've been watching the human race a long time. At this point we ought to be more traumatized than ever before in our history. The Curve of Change is almost vertical by now, like a goosing finger—you do know about the Curve?"

"Sure."

Of course he did—as a dry old chestnut from a history lesson. For millennia the curve of human social and technological progress had trended upward, but so slowly as to be almost imperceptible . . . then all at once it had passed some critical threshold and begun climbing sharply. Ever *more* sharply, the rate of increase itself accelerating steadily, until the race lurched from covered wagons to spaceships, from kingdoms and fiefs to planetary government, from chronic global poverty to staggering near-universal wealth, in a single century. Remarkable. Inexplicable. Where would it all end? And so on.

But Eva had been born into the middle of that century. Just about the time it was beginning to dawn on humanity just how oddly the Curve was behaving. And humanity's general response had been to run a high fever . . .

"I don't mean trivial things, like conquering cancer. I mean substantive changes in the map of reality. When I was a girl, the phrase 'New World' still meant North America. Now it means Mars. The Old World—that one right there—is just about unrecognizable, if you look at it any closer than this. The population has more than doubled since I was born, and look at that planet: it's still green. All the most fundamental axioms of politics, of economics, of industry, have all come apart since the turn of the millennium, obsoleted by new technology. We seem to have a handle on pollution, for God's sake! After half a century of holding my breath, I'm prepared to admit that it looks like we really may have outgrown war. Thanks to nanotechnology, I'm even getting ready to concede that a day may even come when we'll have outgrown *money* . . . a day when no one alive has to work to earn her living, when nobody will remember—or care—what a 'salary' was, or why people gave up a third of their lives to get one."

"And you wonder why people are happy?"

"*Yes!* Two axioms I cling to are that change is painful and that humans react poorly to pain. Change that radical and fundamental *has* to hurt, to confuse, to anger. For the first seventy years of my life, I watched my species grow ever more neurotic, more sullen, more despairing, more bitter. You know what I'm talking about."

"Well, I've read about it, seen records, old flatscreens and so forth—"

"They don't convey it. Believe what I'm about to tell you: when I was forty-five years old, ninety-five percent of the intelligent, thoughtful university-educated people I knew believed as an article of faith that technology and change were dooming the planet, and that some of us would live to see the Last Days. Just about every one of them had a different candidate for what specifically was going to get us. Nuclear Winter was the big one until the Soviet Union went broke. Within about fifteen minutes, fifty other Ends Of Everything had moved in to replace it: global warming, ice age, the ozone layer, overpopulation, deforestation, dwindling resources, pollution, energy shortage—I can't even remember them all anymore. Pestilence, famine and plague were evergreen favorites, and you could always find someone who was putting his money on a runaway comet. If you had a taste for the exotic, you could be terrified of flying saucers and empires of alien cattle-mutilators. But just about every adult I knew clutched *some* form of Ultimate Paranoia to his or her breast. Almost without exception they chose to believe that the End of All Meaning was just over the horizon. If you didn't know *that,* you were too stupid or naive to be worth talking to.

"I'm overstating it slightly, because the sample I'm talking about consisted almost exclusively of affluent North Americans. But only slightly. In 1991 a major poll asked average Americans if they would like to live five hundred years, assuming that could be accomplished cheaply and comfortably. *Only half of them said yes.* Fully half of that society was looking forward to dying."

Jay frowned and took a drink of his whiskey, forgetting to savour it. "How weird it must have been. To live in an age when the best and brightest worshipped Henny Penny. When the crew of Starship Earth, wealthy beyond the wildest dreams of their ancestors, were on the verge of mutinous panic . . ."

She nodded. "And then right at the turn of the millennium, just as the worst thing possible happened and the wildest of all those paranoid fantasies *came true* . . . just as actual aliens appeared in the sky, changed our destiny for us in great and incomprehensible ways, and vanished again before we could ask them any questions . . . everybody calmed down. The Curve kept on rising faster than ever, and somehow everybody on Earth seemed to heave a great sigh, and kick back, and *relax.* Not right away, no, not all at once—but the damn planet has been getting slowly and steadily *saner* for over sixty years now. And it's driving me crazy!"

He swirled whiskey around in his bulb, stared through and past the oscillating golden liquid to the planet they both had left forever. "It doesn't seem all that sane to me," he said.

"No, I'm sure it doesn't, to someone your age," she agreed. "It *isn't* all that sane. But it's sane-*er*. Do you know that at one time the United States had ten percent of its population imprisoned? Justly? As the best solution they could devise to problems they didn't begin to understand? Every year the papers told you the crime rate was rising. It's been falling for over twenty years, now . . . and somehow that never makes the headlines. The media just aren't geared up to report good news. You have to dig that out for yourself."

"I think it has to do with the Curve you were talking about," he said.

"What do you mean?"

"The latest spike in the Curve. The Nanotechnological Revolution. Molecular-scale machines and computers. It's qualitatively different from the Industrial Revolution or the Silicon Revolution or any of those. For once we got a new technology that cleans up its own wastes, doesn't despoil anything we cherish, and produces so much new wealth nobody could steal it all. Our first *healing* revolution. Take the revolution you grew up with, Eva: nuclear fission. They told everyone it would produce power too cheap to meter. Then it turned out the plants were big kludges, and nobody's power bill seemed to go down a dollar. No wonder they stopped trusting people in lab coats. But this generation got a technology that delivered on its promises." He sipped his drink again, appreciating it this time. "And come to think of it, that was mostly thanks to the Stardancers. Without them and their Safe Lab, we'd still be skirting the edges of nanotechnology, too scared of someone getting a monopoly on it, or scared of the wrong little nanoassembler getting loose and turning all the iron to peanut butter or something."

"Or we might have destroyed the planet in a war for possession of the new technology," she agreed. "Instead we've got a UN that means something—and a repaired ozone layer and a healthy ecosystem and nonpolluting industry and a world so fat and rich it hasn't had even a serious local war for thirty years."

"The Stardancers kept us honest," he said. "Thanks to the Fireflies, we had a precious resource: people we could trust to be above human greed and avarice, people with nothing to gain, people who could not be bribed or coerced."

"Bodhisattvas," she said.

"If you like," he said. "Fair witnesses, anyway."

"No wonder there used to be terrorists trying to kill them. A fair witness can be infuriating."

"Yeah, maybe—but the last serious attempt was about the time I was born. Even a fanatic reactionary can see they're just too valuable to the race now: they can live full time in space with no life support, and space is the only safe place to develop little artificial viruses, the only sensible place to collect solar power. Humanity got lucky. We got just what we needed, just when we needed it."

"Luck, hell," she snarled. He recoiled at her force. "You just said it yourself. Luck had nothing to do with it. It was those damned Fireflies: they saved our bacon for us, brought us the moon-full of Symbiote that makes a human a Stardancer, and *gave* it to us, for free. I could kill them for that!"

She could see that she had shocked him. She waited, to see how he would handle it. "This is what you really wanted to talk about," he said finally.

She smiled. "Pour for us, please, Jeeves."

When the AI had refreshed their bulbs, she turned to face him directly. He copied her, and they joined a hand to steady themselves in the new attitude. She held on.

"Jay," she said, "I'm old. I was old enough to vote when the first tourist littered the moon. I was spending a fortune on cosmetic camouflage the year the Fireflies showed up and Shara Drummond danced the Stardance for them. I've had a five-cent Coca Cola, and watched the first television set on my block. Flatscreen, monochrome. I've owned 78 RPM phonograph records and a hand-cranked Victrola. I've buried three husbands, three children and two grandchildren. One of my great-grandchildren in Canada is dying, and I have to keep asking Jeeves her name. Jeeves, what is my dying great-grandchild's name?"

"Charlotte, madam," Jeeves murmured from somewhere nearby.

"I have been a success in three professions," she went on, "and a failure in two. It's not that most of my life is behind me. *All* of my life is behind me, receding. I always said I was going to check out when and if my clock showed three figures . . . and I came here to the Shimizu for that purpose. I stopped controlling my cosmetic age the day I moved into this suite, as a sign that I was withdrawing from human affairs. I've been saying goodbye for the last sixteen years. You know most of this."

He nodded and sipped the Irish whiskey, still holding her hand.

"Haven't you ever wondered what's taking me so long?"

He shook his head. "Not once. I figure saying goodbye to life could take me, oh, *seventeen* years, easy."

"You'll find out," she said. "Old age is not for sissies. I had all my goodbyes said years ago."

"All right," he said agreeably. "I'll play Mr. Interlocutor. Why *are* you still using up air, Ms. Hoffman?"

"Sheer annoyance," she said. "I'd always expected to live to see the world end. I planned to watch humanity die of its own stupidity and meanness, and chortle at the irony of it all. I expected to enjoy it immensely."

"I can understand that," he said slowly.

"Long before I came up here, I'd admitted to myself that it just isn't going to happen any time soon. Okay: I didn't insist on doom . . . as so many of my contemporaries had. I would have settled for watching us come through in the clutch, reach deep inside ourselves and pull out the best of us and *solve* our damned problems." She glanced down at her bulb, found too much whiskey there and corrected the problem. "What I wasn't prepared for was to have big red Fireflies drop in and fix things *for* us . . . and then scamper off to wherever the hell they came from without telling us *why*!"

She looked into his eyes for understanding, and did not find it. He was too young for questions like this to be troubling in anything but an abstract sense. And he had grown up in a world where telepathic Stardancers—and the mysterious alien Fireflies who had appeared out of nowhere, created the Stardancers and their collective Starmind, and then vanished back into deep space—were prosaic history, something that had happened sixteen years before he was born. She saw him try to understand, and fail.

She broke eye contact and sculled around to face the window and the world again. "Anyway, it's come to me in the last few days that what I've been doing . . . what I've been waiting for . . . has been for the damned Fireflies to come back from wherever they went and tell us what's going on. Or for me to cleverly deduce it for myself. The most important philosophical question the human race has faced since the aliens dropped in and out again is, 'What the hell was *that*?' In sixty-four years we haven't made a dent in it.

"Realizing that has forced me to face the fact that I'm wasting my time. If nobody else can figure it out, I probably can't either. Available evidence indicates the Fireflies drop by once every couple of thousand years at best. I can't wait that long. And this steady diet of unearned good news lately has just got me baffled."

"Are you sure it's unearned?" he said. "Stardancers start as human beings, however different they may become after Symbiosis. The scientific name for them is *Homo caelestis.* Humanity birthed them: the Fireflies were just midwives."

"Stardancers do not suffer from fear or hunger or poverty or lust or loneliness," Eva said. "Thanks to their Symbiote, they're immortal, effectively invulnerable, and perpetually loved. As far as I'm concerned, that means they're not human anymore. And if things keep going the way they are, it's conceivable that one day nobody on Earth may be hungry or cold or oppressed. If that day comes, by my lights there won't *be* any human beings anymore."

"So you want to leave while things are still miserable," he said.

She frowned at her drink.

"No," she said. "That's my point. Everybody's happy now. I personally think that in time the hangover will arrive, and people will find out that even nanotechnology has hidden costs. No matter how many miracles we come up with, I believe there are *always* limits to growth. I have a friend named Ling who says he can prove it—I can't follow his math, but it sounds convincing. But meanwhile there is peace on the world . . . maybe it's only temporary, but nobody can know that yet. So maybe this is a *good* time to leave, and I should stop dragging my feet."

He kept his face expressionless. "How do you plan to do it?"

His very neutrality cued her that he was angry. It startled her. She precessed to face him again. "Is that relevant?"

"It's closer than anything that's been said since I jaunted in here," he said. "Let's cut through all the bullshit about Stardancers and Fireflies and how happy the world is today. You have obviously decided to check out. For some reason you think I need to know that in advance. That means you have some role in mind for me. I'm curious to know what it is. Do you want me to stand by with the ceremonial sword in case you lose your nerve? Am I supposed to talk you out of it? Or just be your witness and hold your hand? Angel's advocate, enabler, or audience—I can go any way you like, Eva. I'm your friend and I'll try to give you whatever you need of me, but you've got to tell me the steps."

She let go of her drink and reached toward him with her withered hands. He abandoned his own drink and took them in his own.

"In a month," she said, "Reb Hawkins will be coming to the Shimizu. I want to talk with him one more time. Immediately after that I plan to go out the airlock." She gestured toward the window with her chin. "Out there. When I'm ready, my p-suit will kill me, painlessly and not abruptly. I want to die in space. As I die, I would like to watch you dance . . . if you're willing."

He was speechless. He tried to free his hands, and she would not let him. He tried to tear his gaze from hers, and she would not allow that either. "Why me?" he said finally.

"Dance is the only thing humans do that's *only* beautiful," she said. "It's the only thing we do that speaks even to Fireflies, as far as we can tell. I want to die watching a human being dance. A human, not a Stardancer. You're the best dancer I know. And you're my friend. I thought about not putting this on you until the last minute . . . but I thought you might want some time to choreograph your dance. I know how busy you'll be once your brother arrives."

Globules of salt water began to grow from his eyes. Despite sixteen years in free-fall, she still found the sight of zero-gee tears simultaneously hilarious and moving. And contagious. He shook his head, and the droplets flew away. She blinked back her own, and waited.

At last, with difficulty, he smiled. "I am honored, Eva," he said. He released her hands, plucked his bulb out of the air, and raised his arm in a toast. She reclaimed her own, and they emptied them together. She did not hesitate, spun and threw her bulb as hard as she could, directly at that absurdly expensive window. The bulb shattered musically.

She had startled him. A cannon couldn't have broken that window—but still, what a gesture! He was game, though: his own bulb burst only a second or two after hers. When they had recovered from their throws, he bowed to her, a Buddhist *gassho* she suspected he must have learned from his grandmother. She returned it gravely. "Thank you," she said.

There was nothing left to say. Or too much. After they had watched the tugbots chase and disassemble glass shards for a few moments, he cleared his throat and said, "I've got to see Ev Martin before dinner."

She grinned. "Another argument for suicide. You're right, you wouldn't want to talk to him on a full stomach."

"Not even on a stomach full of hundred-year-old whiskey," he agreed. "But it'll help. Thanks for it."

She made a mental note to leave him the balance of the bottle in her will.

He paused at the door. "Eva?"

"Yes," she said, without turning.

"Is it all right if I spend the next month trying to get you to change your mind?"

"Yes," she said. "But don't be attached to succeeding, Jay. I've been thinking about this a long time."

After a while she heard the door close and seal.

6

Toronto, Ontario
4 December 2064

There is no such thing as a slight flaw in a dance floor.

And all floors have flaws. Anyone but a dancer would probably call them slight: certainly the manufacturers do. Nonetheless, each floor has its own invisible peculiarities, lurking in wait for dancers' feet. Even the floor of Toronto's famous Drummond Theatre. The company had gone through two complete rehearsals, undress and dress, without a hitch; it was in the final onstage warm-up class, a scant hour before curtain, that John DeMarco, who had been dreaming of and working toward this night for all his professional life, found the flaw with his name on it. It broke his ankle.

At any other time it would have been a nuisance. The actual repair could be accomplished in less than ten minutes at the nearest hospital, after two hours of datawork and waiting in the emergency room. And once fixed, you'd be hopping around good as new . . . in a matter of mere hours. . . .

The ugly sound had riveted the attention of all. It took only minutes to establish that the nearest hospital was half an hour away in the best of times, and that everyone in the company seemed to have run out of painblock at once. So had John, of course. Dancers started to drift away to call hospitals and search dressing rooms and find the driver; the AD, watching her company scattering to the four winds an hour before curtain, bellowed them into stasis and bent over John's recumbent form. "Is there any hope at all?" she asked.

It was clearly a break, not just a sprain. John shook his head, and started to apologize.

She waved it away. "Then you'll have to live with it for a while. I can't spare anyone here: I have to recast the whole performance in forty-five minutes, and everyone I can see I *need.* We'll put you in dressing room two. Jacques! Harry!"

The pain was exquisite, almost nauseating. "No! Wait! Put me in the audience. If I can't be in it, I'm gonna see the run-through."

She nodded to Harry and Jacques. "Do it."

Harry, the stage manager, gave him a jacket to put over his warm-up clothes, promised to try and find him some painblock and a ride as soon as possible, and left him front-row center. Not an ideal seat, but convenient. One of the dancers who could be spared momentarily brought him an improvised pack of ice from the concession in the lobby. He concentrated on the frenzied activity onstage to distract himself from his pain.

Shortly after he decided Anna was fucking the whole thing up, he noticed that the pain was gone. Utterly.

He yelped, in astonishment and something like fright. Anna glared at him from the stage. "Harry, take him back-stage—"

"No," he said. "Sorry. I'm fine; won't happen again."

She went back to her work. He bent and looked at his ankle. No question, that was a broken ankle, all right. The swelling was already so advanced that he knew it was badly broken. Now why in hell didn't it hurt?

The swelling began to visibly reduce.

He yelped again. Anna turned and came to the edge of the stage. "John, I'm sorry, but—"

"Look at my foot!"

She blinked.

"God dammit, come down here and look at my fucking foot!"

The dancers followed her. They gathered around and watched his ankle heal itself. After a few murmurs and gasps, no one said a word. In minutes, the ankle looked just like its mate. John flexed it slowly, listening for grating sounds, and then extended it with the same care. Then he circled it, one way and then the other, and started to laugh. Soon everyone was laughing, even Anna. He got to his feet, took a few cautious steps—then took a running start and sprang up on stage. He did a combination on his way to his place for the first piece. "Come on, boss," he said, still laughing. " 'Time's a-wastin'!" It was one of her catch-phrases; the company dissolved into hysterics.

Anna let that go on for a good five seconds. From then on they were so busy that it wasn't until midway through the triumphant fourth curtain call that John had time to wonder about it all.

He never did figure it out. He had to be told. But he didn't mind.

PART THREE

7

Logan Aerospaceport
Boston, Massachusetts
5 December 2064

Rhea felt as if she were on a conveyor belt, sliding ever closer toward the butcher's blade.

Logan Aerospaceport was used to celebrity press conferences; a soundproof room had been found for Rand, Rhea, Colly and the cronkites and riveras representing the planetary, national and local-birthplace media pools. Cambots swarmed like blackflies, recording the scene from at least eight directions. Once in a long while, one of them would decide the ambient light was insufficient, and turn into a white firefly for a moment or two.

Tough new laws had finally succeeded in taming the media: all four cronkites, and even the riveras, were scrupulously polite. Nonetheless they managed to annoy Rhea—by putting seventy percent of their questions to Rand. In the half-dozen previous press conferences they'd had together, the percentages had usually been reversed. It embarrassed her to be annoyed by that, but she couldn't help it. At least she was able to keep him from noticing . . . though she wasn't so sure about the cambots.

Colly lapped it up. And put on a performance that would have made a child holostar blush. That annoyed Rhea too.

Which made her ask herself why she was so irritable. She realized what bothered her most of all was how much Rand was enjoying the attention and flattery. It scared her. This was going to be a hard thing to undo. It was feeling more and more like a done deal . . . and she still hadn't given her agreement to it. Rand knew that, but he wasn't acting like it. Oh, he told the reporters—and the world beyond them—the assignment was only temporary, just completing Pribhara's season: the story he'd worked out with Jay and that horrible-sounding Martin person. But when he said it, she heard in his voice the quiet certainty that the permanent job was his. She wasn't sure if the cambots were hearing that too, or if she was projecting it.

She felt disconnected, surreal, moving against a tide of invisible molasses. *This is a hell of a way to spend my last hour on Earth,* she decided. "Time to go, darling," she said helpfully, as Rand finished a reply.

"Just one more," the flaky-looking rivera from the planetary pool said. "Do you have any comment on the breaking story about outbreaks of rogue assemblers?"

Rand looked startled. "I'm sorry, I've been too busy packing to monitor news. Nanoassemblers, you mean?"

The rivera nodded. "There seems to be growing evidence over the last few days of random instances of . . . well, of anarchist nanotechnology, all around the globe. Spontaneous healings, spontaneous slum regenerations—sort of little miracles. There's no telling how many, since the tendency is to underreport miracles. Some say there may be some sort of . . . well . . ."

"A conspiracy of rapturists?" Rhea said, thinking of an old story-idea she had never gotten around to developing.

"Rapturists?" the woman from the New England pool pounced.

"The opposite of a terrorist," Rhea said. "But what has this got to do with us?"

The flaky one tried not to look like he knew he was stretching for a tie-in hook. "Well, you're going to space, where nanotechnology comes from. Are you, I don't know, at all afraid some . . . uh, 'Rapturist' might decide to put laughing gas in your p-suit tanks?"

To everyone's surprise, it was Colly who spoke up. "There hasn't been one of those stories in space so far," she said. They all stared.

"It's true," she insisted. "Not one. I watch the news. Anyway, they haven't hurt anybody, have they?"

No one replied.

"Maybe not yet," Rand said. "But anarchy can get pretty scary even when it means well, honey. Maybe especially when it means well." He turned to the rivera. "But no, we're not worried at all. Everybody knows you're safer in space than you are on Earth: look at the stats. We really have to go now. Thank you all—"

On the flight up, Rhea tuned her seatback screen to a news channel, in time to hear herself ask, " . . . a conspiracy of rapturists?" and then, in response to the rivera's prompting, define the term. A few moments later, Colly and Rand's exchange was quoted too.

The piece in which the soundbite was featured might as well have been titled, "Nanotechnology—Threat or Menace?" It was about three times as long as the item she managed to find later on an arts channel, about Rand's return to the Shimizu.

She wanted the flight to be miserable. It was idyllic. No dropsickness in her family—none on the whole plane. No emergencies; minimal, gentle maneuvering; a perfect hop. Superb, pleasant service from human and robot alike. Even the food was excellent: real, microwave cooking rather than flashpak. The Shimizu did not permit clients to arrive unhappy, whether they wanted to or not. The hardest part of the flight was keeping Colly's seat belt buckled once the gravity went away.

The approach was spectacular. The Shimizu looked like God's Christmas ornament, a vast gleaming globe. Its exterior was fractalized for maximum radiating surface, so it sparkled in the sunlight like a vast ball of crinkled aluminum foil. It was girdled by an equator of huge cooling and power-collecting vanes, brilliant silver on one side and space black on the other, that slowly rotated independently as the relative position of the sun changed. A thousand points of light—peoples' windows!—added to the illumination, randomly distributed, going on or off as tenants entered or left their rooms.

The plane crept up on the hotel sideways, spinning slowly around its own axis to distribute the sun's heat, so there were no bad seats. Every time you decided you were there now, the damned thing got a little bigger; it seemed planet-sized by the time they actually reached the spaceport at the "north pole."

After a textbook docking, all four doors opened the instant the seat-belt light went out, so that passengers need not stand in line to debark; customs formalities occurred electronically without any of them noticing. The dock itself was beautiful and impressive, its layout and decor operating somehow on the subconscious to make you feel you were home.

Then Rand muttered, “Oh no—*that* asshole.”

A large spider monkey with a head like a red sea anemone sprang at them out of nowhere. At the last possible moment he braked to a stop with smelly, poorly tuned thrusters and flung his arms around Colly. She looked wildly around to Rhea, her eyes asking permission to be terrified.

“I could kiss you,” the apparition said, and did so, on the forehead. Colly decided she didn’t need permission; the man said “Eek” and let her go and clutched his groin.

“Nice shot, dear,” Rhea said, and interposed herself between them before Rand could. She was pleased to find that free-fall reflexes came back quickly to her; she still remembered how to jaunt. “Who or what are you?” she asked him.

He forgot his aching testicles. “The guy who could cheerfully strangle you, Ms. Pash-o,” he said cheerfully. “What ever *possessed* you to give them a bite like that, for God’s sake? You blew *my* whole story right off the Net with that rapturist line, lady. Who asked you to improvise? If it hadn’t been for this little genius here,” he said, pointing to Colly, “it could have been a disaster.” Forgetting that she had just kicked him, he reached out and tried to pat her head. “You just keep following your mama around, kid, and every time you see her open her mouth to a sniffer, you talk instead.”

Colly ducked until he gave up. “Rhea and Colly,” Rand said through clenched teeth, “this is Evelyn Martin, Shimizu’s publicity chief.”

“And people still come here?” Rhea asked. The man was strikingly ugly. His head looked like a large red Brillo pad with bat-ears and pop-eyes. She had not met him on her previous visit, but Rand had assured her Martin was an excrescence; she decided he had understated the case.

Martin didn’t seem to hear. “It’s okay for you to talk like that now; I’ll dub the audio later, give us all beautiful lines for the release. But I’ve got the top three cronkites in space waiting nearby to do the personal bit, so pee if you have to and we’ll—”

Jay arrived. “Rand and his family will be happy to meet with them later this evening,” he said firmly, and embraced his brother. “Sorry I’m late, bro.”

Martin continued to talk rapidly while Jay greeted Rhea and Colly in turn, but they all ignored him. "Twenty-one hundred, Ev," Jay said as he led them from the hall. "They'll wait. Nobody ever turned down a free dinner at the Shimizu. Least of all a cronkite." Martin watched speechlessly as their luggage emerged from the plane and began to follow them.

Rhea had known Jay since her courtship with his half-brother over a decade ago, had chatted with him for dozens of hours on the phone since. But since Jay had made the permanent move to space, around the time she and Rand got married, she had only been in his physical presence once, briefly, during Rand's previous residency. In one sense she knew him well already. But to know if you really *like* someone, you have to smell them. As they all relaxed over drinks in their suite—Rhea's new home!—she found herself remembering how much she really liked Jay.

During a visit to the bathroom she took the occasion to summon Diaghilev, Jay's AI, and ask if there had been any recent news of Ethan. "Ethan who, Ms. Paixao?" was the reply, which was all the answer she needed. The relationship was irreparable. A shame; Rhea had liked Ethan, at least over the phone. "Is Jay seeing anyone?"

There was an imperceptible hesitation while Diaghilev made sure she was cleared for that information. "No, ma'am. He dates occasionally, but has not dated anyone twice." She made a mental note to keep an eye open for a nice young man for Jay, and rejoined the others.

The suite was considerably nicer than the one she'd had on her last short visit. It took her a while to note, and a little longer to believe, that the window was real. Earth was centered in the frame, the terminator just reaching what looked like a major blizzard over the northwest coast of North America. This was one of the more expensive suites in the hotel. She hunted for flaws, and cheered up a little when she noticed the furniture was all permanent. Excellent, and fully programmable, but it didn't go away when you were done with it.

But everything else she could see was state of the art or better.

She told herself sourly that the hotel had given them this suite to soften her up—that once Rand signed on for good, they'd be moved to somewhere inboard with the rest of the peons.

It was Jay who snapped her out of her gloomy mood, by asking her about her work. She thought of the story about Mr. Hansen and his beloved nun, but did not bring it up, speaking instead of the novel she had been struggling with for nearly a year now. Jay listened well, widening his eyes at the right spots, making little murmurs of agreement, asked insightful questions with great diffidence. Several of the questions made knowledgeable reference to her earlier works. He was either as much of a fan as he claimed to be, or a gifted actor. Either was gratifying.

Colly jaunted around the room like an old-fashioned maid robot, inspecting everything and trying out acrobatic maneuvers with both her wings and her child-strength thrusters, having the time of her life. Every few minutes she found something that made her giggle and call Rhea or Rand to "Look!" or "Come see!" Rhea let her roam unchecked, knowing she would tire herself out and nap soundly soon. They'd all had to get up before dawn to make the flight, and it was now nearly 6 PM, Shimizu time. Besides, this suite was safe for kids. It was probably safe enough for a blind hemophiliac epileptic.

One of Rand's early songs, "Blues in the Dark," was playing in the background. It was relatively obscure, but one of her personal favorites, since it was about her and Rand's courtship. Jay had selected it when they came in; either he had remembered some casual reference she'd made in a phone chat, or they shared similar tastes. Either way, it helped her warm to him.

She had to admit, it did feel good to be in free-fall again. She had forgotten how restful it was, how reminiscent of childhood fantasies of being able to fly, like the Little Lame Prince. The drugs had controlled the stuffy-head feeling this time, and her stomach felt fine. Rand had already inserted his personal wafer into a terminal in the suite: Maxwell Perkins, her own personal AI avatar, was again at her beck and call, moved from home into new quarters in the Shimizu's memory cores, as was Rand's version, Salieri—while their original copy still maintained the house back in Provincetown. (Also present, and presently in use, was the persona by which Colly addressed it: a large rabbit named Harvey.) Before long Rhea found herself thinking that this wasn't the worst possible place in the world . . . and then reminded herself sharply that it wasn't *in* the world. Not the same one P-Town was. She glanced out the window at the distant Earth and failed to locate New England.

Look on the bright side. Your husband might fail spectacularly. You might get a terrific divorce settlement. You might even convince your daughter to come back to Earth with you. The damned hotel could get hit by a runaway planet. Some Rapturist might put laughing gas in your air tank. The future holds infinite possibility.

If Jay was scheming to convert her, his next move was below the belt—literally. He led them all to dinner at the Hall of Lucullus. Not the Grand Dining Room, which peasants like governors and pop stars had to make do with—where Rhea had dined on her last visit—but the Lucullus, the most famous oasis in human space. Rhea had dined well in her time, but this was something out of the realm of her experience. They did not turn the cherries into beans for her dessert coffee until she had named the blend she preferred—then roasted them before her eyes . . . and under her nose. The coffee waiter—there was a separate, live coffee waiter—announced proudly as he was pulverizing them (pausing every few seconds so as not to overheat them prematurely) that these cherries had seen the sun rise from a tree on the island of Sulawezi that very morning. When she had tasted the result, she believed him.

The meal preceding had been so perfect that Rhea took the coffee almost in stride, which mildly shocked her. Lucius Licinius Lucullus, dead over two millennia, would have been proud of what was being done in his name. She was halfway through her bulb before she realized how *many* live human beings had been waiting on them hand and foot throughout dinner, with only the maître d', wine steward and coffee waiter ever coming to her conscious attention. Zero gee left a lot of ways to skirt the edges of peripheral vision, but still . . .

Jay saw her glance around and read her mind. "They're a highly specialized breed of dancers," he said, grinning. "A few of them take class with me. The standard joke is, if you can see one, you don't have to tip him."

Rhea was used to superb service from machines. From human beings it was *much* less common, and a bit unnerving. It made her feel a little like a plantation owner before Civil War One. She reminded herself that these serfs almost certainly made more money than she did—and didn't have to keep thinking up new ideas.

Even Colly, who hated restaurant dining, was impressed. The peanut butter and jelly sandwich she was served (by yet another waiter! They couldn't keep one around just for that; he must be a kind of utility infielder) precisely matched her specifications down to brand and relative proportion of ingredients, and when she challenged the kitchen by impishly requesting an obscure brand of ice cream only sold in Provincetown, they accommodated her without batting an eye.

For all of Rhea's life, "cooking skill" had consisted of selecting the right equipment. It still tended to be the wife who told the equipment to start working, but it had been half a century or more since women's sense of self-worth had depended to any significant degree on the results. Nonetheless, she was mildly irritated to see Rand put away twice as much food as usual.

She managed to find a more acceptable reason to be disgruntled almost at once. A glance around the sumptuous room reminded her of how terrifyingly easy it was to get fat in free-fall. A fat person floating overhead will never again be able to impress you face to face. She had heard that plumpness was fashionable in space—at least among those raised in gravity—but she didn't care if it was.

For his piéce de résistance, Jay let Rand pick up the check . . . making the point that he could now afford to. Colly's eyes grew round at that, and Rand swelled visibly as he thumbprinted the pad.

What can I do? What can I possibly do?

The second press conference was a little more fun than the first, because at least half the time was devoted to asking her to expand on her comments about Rapturism, which by now had acquired an audible capital letter. The fun part was ignoring Martin's frantic attempts to change the subject or put words in her mouth. Book interviews were wonderful training for that sort of thing. And Rand didn't seem to mind sharing the camera—perhaps because this time the implied larger audience was spacers, people he didn't identify with yet. Or perhaps, she had to concede, he was just being in love with his wife.

An hour later, on that assumption, she gave him the fuck of his life in the ingeniously designed bedchamber of their lavish new suite, using tricks only possible in free-fall, and drifted (literally) off to sleep curled around his back, furious at him.

* * *

The next day she and Colly were peeled away from Rand, and sent on a tour of the hotel with a slender, frail-looking, yet strikingly handsome young Orientator, while the two brothers holed up in Jay's studio to try and salvage what Pribhara had started.

Colly gaped at him when he stated his name. "Duncan *Iowa?*"

Rhea started to chide her, but Duncan only grinned broadly. "My mother was a Frank Herbert fan." Seeing that she didn't get it, he went on, "He wrote a book called DUNE with a character named Duncan Idaho. So she always wanted a son named Duncan . . . and then she married my dad, Walter Iowa, and just couldn't resist."

Rhea noticed that he did *not* go one step too far, and explain to an eight-year-old Terran that Idaho and Iowa were both the names of states. That was careful diplomacy. He was spaceborn, and would have explained it to another spaceborn, to whom states were distant and remote abstractions. But he could think like an earthborn, well enough to preserve a child's dignity. She decided she liked him.

So did Colly. "I have the same problem," she said solemnly. "My own parents thought it would be fun to name me after a breed of dog."

Duncan nodded gravely. "That's something to bitch about."

She burst into giggles, and they were friends.

The tour was not the standard first-time first-day grand tour Rhea had taken on her previous trip here. This seemed more like a kind of VIP, behind-the-scenes version. It was still quite impressive, but more intimate, somehow, conveying the added message that only special people got to be impressed in this particular way. "Of course, you'll still be learning things about this place the day before you go back home," he said at one point. "I'm still learning things about it."

"How long have you had this job?" Rhea asked politely.

"I just got it. But I've been coming here since I was a kid."

That long, huh? she thought ironically, but kept the thought to herself.

She swapped bio synopses with Duncan as the tour progressed. He was twenty, bisexual, single, and had a bachelor's degree in molecular electronics from U.H.E.O. which he hoped to parlay into a Master's once he had earned the tuition. If only he had been fifteen years older, massed twice as much, had a hairier torso and been muscled more like an earthborn, she would have considered trying to pair him off with Jay. His parents were both spacers who worked at Skyfac.

Colly's favorite part of the tour was what she instantly dubbed the Blob: the Shimizu's famous zero-gee swimming pool. Located at the very center of the hotel for reasons of orbital stability, it was essentially a large spherical tank, thirty meters across, containing 210,000 liters of crystalline water and happy people.

Of course Colly insisted on going in. You donned breathing and comm gear and four fins, and entered through an airlock. Inside, it was preternaturally beautiful: artistically colored lights were deployed all around and blended to produce shifting effects, and the tank was stocked with multihued fish of tropical breeds—robots, of course, but no less brilliant or beautiful for that. They were absolutely impossible to catch, or even touch: Colly spent a happy time trying. Rhea enjoyed herself almost as much as her daughter. Afterward in the dressing room, Colly announced that air bubbles were prettier in free-fall—and acted more interesting too.

What Rhea thought was that swimming in P-Town was better—whether you did it on the ocean or bay side. But she kept the thought to herself.

When they rejoined Duncan, the first thing Colly said was, "Duncan, how come you don't have muscles, like Daddy?"

"Colly!" Rhea began.

But Duncan cut her off, smiling. "I know that would be a rude question on Terra—but things are different in space. Here it's just a good question."

Colly looked pleased. "So what's the good answer?" she asked.

"Because I don't need 'em. Earthworm muscles—excuse me, Terran muscles—are worse than useless up here. You don't need that much power, and you keep hurting yourself, by pushing off too hard."

"Oh." Colly looked down at her skinned knees, and rubbed a banged elbow thoughtfully. "I knew that: I was just testing you."

"Can I ask you a question now?"

"Sure."

"Back there in the pool—why did you like those angelfish so much?"

"They kept making, like, a flower," she said. "You know, tails together but each head pointing out a different way, like a puffball."

"Don't real angelfish do that on Terra?" he asked.

She stared at him. "How could they? Some of them'd be upside down!"

He blinked, and grinned. "Isn't that funny? I knew real fish can't live in free-fall, because they die without a local vertical to align to; I've read that. But I didn't follow it through and realize they wouldn't ever make puffballs down there."

"That's the difference between book learning and experience," Rhea said, seeing a chance to make this a lesson for Colly. "Duncan was born in space. He knows a lot, but you know things he doesn't."

"And vice versa," he agreed. "That's why I'm here. Over the next couple of days you're both going to get real tired of hearing me repeat certain things. Free-fall safety, vacuum-drill, flare-drill, p-suit maintenance, things like that. And you'll tell me that you know all that stuff, and you'll be right. You know it as book learning. So let me keep bugging you, okay? Otherwise you may get in some kind of trouble, from not expecting angelfish to make a puffball."

Colly nodded solemnly. She had been watching the way he handled himself in zero gee, and trying to copy his movements, but from then on she would ask his advice, and take it.

"For instance, both of you put in your earphones for a second."

Rhea and Colly both complied.

"I want you to hear a sound without others hearing it. Listen—" He touched a pad at his wrist, and they heard a distinctive warbling shriek. "If you hear that, you have less than twenty minutes to get here to the pool. If you're late, you'll die. It means a bad solar flare is on the way—and this pool is also the Shimizu's storm shelter."

"How long do they last?" Colly asked.

"Anywhere from eighteen hours to three days or so."

"We might have to swim for three *days*?" She didn't seem alarmed. Rhea certainly was.

"Oh, no! They pump the water into holding tanks all around the pool, so it'll do the most good as shielding."

"That thing is huge," Rhea said, "but is it really big enough to accommodate twelve-hundred-odd people for up to three days?"

"If they're friendly," he said with a grin. "Don't worry: most flares you're ever liable to see, you can deal with by just getting into the radiation locker in your suite. It takes a Class Three flare to empty the pool, and that hasn't happened in my lifetime. Doesn't mean it couldn't in the next ten minutes—but they've got some real sharp folks modeling the sun nowadays, plus the Stardancers keep a couple of angels way in past the orbit of Venus all the time, keeping an eye on the old girl. They can send a telepathic warning back to Earth orbit *instantly*, a lot faster than a radio or laser message: when Mama Sol clears her throat, we get a lot better warning than you get of a quake in San Francisco. And in any emergency, trained men in radiation suits will chase down stragglers and sleepers. *But*—and this is what I was talking about before—you can't ever leave safety to machines and other people. Sometimes they goof. If you ever start seeing green pollywogs—little green flashes in your vision—get into that locker, fast. Don't wait for the central computer to tell you to . . . and don't stop to pee."

After lunch he took them to Wonderland. Both ladies found it delightful. As you approached it, the first thing you noticed was a child-sized white rabbit a little ahead of you, wearing a vest and consulting a pocketwatch. You followed him as he jaunted feetfirst "down" a long tunnel; onrushing air gave a reasonable illusion of falling in a magical sort of way.

The place into which you emerged lived up to its name.

Colly wanted to stay—forever. After an hour, Rhea was sick of rosy cheer and wanted to go be sullen with her husband. She left Colly with Duncan, made an agreement to meet them at suppertime, and followed Maxwell Perkins's excellent directions through a maze of unfamiliar corridors to Jay's studio. One thing about AIs: they made it hard to be a stranger in a strange land, even if you wanted to be. As long as there was a local database for your AI to invest, wherever you went, you were home.

She paused outside the door, and had Max ask his alter ego—Rand's AI avatar Salieri—whether she could enter without disturbing her husband; with his assurances she thumbed the door open and jaunted in. The work in progress looked so odd that her eye ignored it, noting only that it seemed to involve some sort of pseudo-underwater visuals and twelve-tone music. She had been married to a shaper too long to expect a rehearsal to look or sound like much.

Rand was drifting a few meters off to her left, upside down with respect to her local vertical. His body was derelict, relaxed into the classic free-fall crouch, all his attention focused on the dozen writhing dancers who filled the cubic before him. Even upside down she could see that he was scowling so ferociously his forehead looked ribbed. He was making little growling mutters deep in his throat, shaking his head from side to side.

She knew she had never seen him happier.

Dammit.

In that first glimpse of him, utterly intent on his work, she knew deep down, below the conscious level, that she was doomed. She could either live the rest of her life here, or start reliving the glorious single years . . . with an eight-year-old. Her subconscious thought about it, decided her conscious mind did not require this information just now, and tucked it away in the inaccessible node where stories got worked out.

It stayed there for the next month. Every time it tried to get out, she went to work on a story instead. It was a very prolific month.

8

The Shimizu Hotel
7 January 2065

Rand became aware that a fragment of his attention was needed somewhere. His wife was present, and speaking to him. He played back mental tape and found that she had asked him if he would be free for dinner.

The question confused him. It called for speculation, and contained a word with at least six different meanings. He searched for a proper response, and selected, "Hah?"

She understood perfectly. "Thanks, darling. I'll have Salieri ask you again later. Listen to Salieri, okay? He'll know where we are."

There were so many words, he decided a nod would be safest. It seemed to work: she went away, and though she was frowning slightly she did not slam anything on the way. Relieved, he relaxed and let his eyes and mind go where they needed to. *Damn* Pribhara anyway! Thanks to her, he had been placed in a position where his triumphal first achievement as Resident Shaper would be to wash someone else's laundry. He had been doing so for a month, and all he had to show for it was a mountain of wet laundry.

The thing was worse than awful: it was more than half done. Pribhara might not be good, but she was fast. There was no hope of scrapping it altogether and doing something completely new; deadline wouldn't allow it.

Ah well—the ones he should feel sorry for were Jay and the dancers of his company. They had already wasted hours and liters of sweat trying to make this dopey idea work . . . and were committed to performing the results in public, unarmed. All he had to—

She didn't say, "I love you" before she left.

He was going to give that some serious thought—but just then it came to him in a clap of thunder how something might be salvaged from this fiasco. Steal from that weird dream he'd had last night: scrap the fakey underwater visuals completely . . . and substitute mid-air. Instead of sea-bed, substitute a city-sized carpet of clouds, backlit. Individual clouds could billow and move *almost* the same way the stupid seaweed did, the way the dancers needed it to for the choreography to work. From time to time, clouds could part to reveal the ground far below. Sure, it had been done before—but not lately, and not by him. God damn, that might just make the nut. But could he get away with it? What about the abominable shark in the second movement? Substitute a roc, perhaps? No, screw the details—what did it do to the overall *feel?* Did the dance still work with the music?

Well, hell, just about anything worked with that twelve-tone noise. Or didn't, if you asked him. No, it felt feasible. The essential artistic *wrongness* of dancers moving normally while supposedly deep underwater vanished now. If he had to, he'd write all new music to match the dance—he could almost hear it now, he certainly knew the choreography well enough. "Jay! *I got it!*"

It took a while to establish communication; Jay was in work-mode himself. But eventually they had recognized each other and agreed on a common language, and Rand floated his concept. Jay liked it—said, in fact, that he had had a vaguely similar dream himself only the week before. He sank a few experimental harpoons into the idea before he would get excited, but when it continued to hold air he became nearly as elated as Rand.

But not quite. There is a special pleasure in solving a difficult puzzle that has baffled your big brother. Jay had always been thirteen years older, stronger, smarter and more successful. Rand did not resent him, exactly: he had always been kind, supportive and generous with his time and attention. That they had had a childhood relationship at all had been primarily Jay's doing; he'd seemed to really enjoy having a brother to teach things to. He had doubtless influenced Rand's career choice, and had never (Rand was sure) insulted him by using his own artistic clout to pull strings on Rand's behalf. And they were as easy in each other's company as brothers were supposed to be; the difference in their ages had not been relevant for decades.

And still, it was always pleasurable to pleasantly surprise the man.

Jay handed the group off to Francine, his dance captain and assistant choreographer, and took Rand to his own suite. Along the way they tossed the new concept back and forth like an intellectual medicine ball, firming it up considerably in the process.

"One thing that helps a lot," Rand said as the door sealed behind them, "this crew is really good."

Jay nodded enthusiastically. "Best of the two. They actually enjoy the pony shows as much as the art." The Shimizu offered two streams of dance entertainment to its guests: the high art on which Rand and Jay were collaborating, performed in the Nova Dance Theatre, and the "pony show"—essentially cabaret dance adapted for free-fall, sophisticated T&A—performed in the Dionysian Room. "I think of the two assistant ADs, Francine is the one who'll take over my job when I retire. The team you worked with last time is good too—but this team is the original. It's not just more hours logged: about a year ago something clicked and they meshed." He tossed Rand a bulb of cola, got a root beer for himself.

"That must be rare," Rand said.

"About like the odds of any twelve people in the same occupation falling in love and making it work."

The analogy, with its reminder of the collapse of Jay's relationship with Ethan, made Rand's good cheer begin to evaporate. Work had driven the crisis in his own marriage clear out of his mind—as he had hoped. Jay must have seen something in his face, because his next words were, "So how are things going with Rhea?"

"Honest to God, I don't know what to tell you, bro. She's adjusted to free-fall now, and she seems to like it here okay—but it's going to take more than that. All I can do is cross my fingers and pray that she falls head over heels in love with the place before the next month is up. Because if she doesn't, I'm screwed."

"It happens," Jay said sadly. "Happened to me: *I'm* in love with this dump. It sort of creeps up on you. Don't—"

"You weren't born in Provincetown." But he knew Jay was trying to cheer him up, and did his best. "That kid you picked to show her and Colly around *is* a good salesman, though."

Jay grinned. "If you're not careful, she'll fall head over heels in love with *him.* I'm kidding! As a matter of fact, I have it on good authority that he's, well . . . at least bi."

"That was my guess . . . just how good is your authority?"

"Don't be silly. A twenty-year-old? I'm old enough to be his . . . his . . ."

" . . . best lover yet. Come on, what have you got to lose?"

"A lot. You obviously haven't tried to keep up with a twenty-year-old lately. Anyway, I like 'em with muscles. We're wandering. Look, what I started to say was, don't change that diaper until you smell it. I know how much that house means to Rhea, and I know Provincetown is the most amazing place on Earth. But this is the most amazing place in space. Give her time."

"Well . . . I've got a surprise I've been working on for her in my spare time; I plan to spring it on her soon. Maybe tonight. It might just—"

"Phone, Jay," Diaghilev said. "Eva Hoffman, urgent."

Jay's face changed. "Oh, shit. Excuse me, bro. Sergei, give me privacy." Tugbots brought him earphones, hushmike and a monitor screen. He tossed Rand his holo remote and took the call. Rand passed the time by not-quite-watching flatscreen music videos from the Old Millennium, with the sound off, trolling for images to swipe.

He killed the screen when he heard Jay say, "Jesus Christ."

"Something wrong?"

His brother looked stricken. "One of my closest friends just decided not to die after all."

Rand looked at him. "Yeah, that'd be hard to take," he said solemnly.

Jay grinned, then frowned, then emitted a short burst of nervous laughter. "God, that sounds dumb, doesn't it?" He shook his head. "Maybe I've got the same problem she has. I just don't know how to deal with good news."

"Who are we talking about? Or should I ask?"

"Eva Hoffman."

Rand was shocked. "*She* was thinking of catching a cab? I always figured her for an honored guest at the Party at the End of the Universe. I'm glad she changed her mind. I like her a lot."

"Me too. She'll be at the special, tomorrow night."

"What special?"

The company was presently performing *Spatial Delivery,* the piece he and Jay had co-created during his earlier residency; it would be played three nights a week and Sunday matinees until the new piece replaced it a month from now. But this was the first Rand had heard of a special performance.

"Oh shit, I haven't told you yet? Sorry; too many things on my mind. We're doing a command performance. A private concert. In the same theater, of course, but the rest of the goats get told the show is cancelled. Only uips and a handful of peasant vips admitted."

" 'Whips'?"

"Spelled *U*-I-P. Ultimately Important People."

Rand prepared himself not to be impressed. "Like who?"

"Chen Ling Ho. Imaro Amin. Grijk Krugnk. Chatur Birla. And Victoria Hathaway. The Fat Five, I call 'em."

It was hard to get air. "All of them? In the same room at the same time? They're gonna see my—our—piece?"

"Yep. Kate Tokugawa's been working on this visit for a month, in secret, and she wants all the trimmings. She authorized me to tell *you,* of course, but I plain forgot."

"What the hell are five of the most powerful people on Earth all doing here at the same time?"

Jay shook his head. "My guess is, historians will just be getting really involved in arguing about that forty years from now. Probably no one will ever know. Those folks can edit reality. And they do not like people knowing what they're doing. Especially before they've done it. Make damn sure you tell Rhea and Colly not to tell anyone about the special until all five are dirtside again."

"Tell two women not to talk about the most exciting thing that's happened to them in weeks. Yeah, that'll work."

Jay grabbed him by the upper arm. "Listen to me. This is serious. If the presence of those five guests becomes public knowledge, while they're still here, you and I could both become unemployed real fast. If not worse. People have accidents in space."

Rand shook his arm free. "And an ordinary hotel guest like Eva Hoffman is invited to this top-secret performance?"

"Oh Christ, Rand, Eva isn't any ordinary guest, you know that. Eva is Eva. Even Kate is afraid of her. As a matter of fact, I think Eva's going to be there as a guest of Chen Ling Ho. Her and Reb Hawkins-roshi. Look, just trust me on this, okay? Tell Rhea and Colly not to discuss this, even with Duncan. After the Fat Five have left, they can brag all they want; by then security won't matter anymore. Between you and me, I suspect the news will be all over Shimizu within five minutes after they dock—but I do not want any leaks traceable to *us*. I like this job. And I'd like to get back to it, okay?"

"Okay. I'll tell them. Boot up Terpsichore and let's see how the new idea is going to work."

While Jay brought up the holographic choreography software, a collateral descendant of the original twentieth century Lifeforms program, and set up the parameters of Pribhara's wretched piece, Rand checked in with Salieri.

"How'm I doing, Salieri?"

"Rhea and Colly are expecting you for dinner at 19 o'clock in the Hall of Lucullus, but they will understand if you are late. I will remind you at 18:45. If you elect to keep working, I will inform them, and remind you to stop work and eat at 21 o'clock, using extreme measures if necessary."

"Excellent. Whenever I go home, remind me about that new window program just before I get to the door. Dismissed. Let me at that interface, Jay—see how you like this . . ."

Extreme measures proved necessary. By the time he got back to his suite, Colly was fast asleep, dreaming of angelfish making puffballs.

He was eager to show Rhea the surprise he had prepared. But she had a surprise of her own to show him first. "I was checking on . . . oh hell, what I was doing was snooping," she said gleefully, tapping a keyboard. The file she wanted displayed on the nearest wall. "And I found this in Colly's partition." It was a text document. At first he took it for one of Rhea's manuscripts, since it had been created with the same arcane, obsolete word-processing software she used. But then he saw the slug at the top of the file: "*The Amazing Adventure,* by Colly Porter."

"It's a short story," she said, her delight obvious. "About a little girl who goes to space and defeats spies."

He grinned. "Oh, that's wonderful. And she didn't say anything to you about it?"

"Not a hint. Wait, let me show you the best part. . . ." She scrolled the document a page or two, found the place she wanted, and highlighted a portion of the text. It read: "But the truth was far from reality."

His bark of laughter triggered hers, and then they tried to shush each other for fear of waking Colly, and broke up all over again. The sequence ended with them in a hug, looking at the screen together in fond appreciation. "Is it any good?" he asked.

"Hard to tell; she hasn't finished it yet. But so far . . . for an eight-year-old . . . it's terrific."

"How long has she been working on it?"

She punched keys. "File created three days ago."

He was impressed. "And she's got, what, eight pages down? Jesus, that's amazing."

She nodded vigorously. "Damn right. Eight pages in three or four days is good output for *me.*" She frowned. "Could we have raised one of those freaks who actually enjoy writing?"

He gave a theatrical shudder. "Could have been worse. At least it isn't heroin."

"That'd be cheaper. Ah well, she'll grow out of it. At her age I wanted to be a gymnast."

"Sure, I know. But it's still cute as hell. And you should still be flattered."

She hugged him closer and nuzzled his ear. "You watch: in another year or two, she'll be shaping. I'll go snooping through her files, and a monster will appear and bite me on the ass."

"And it'll serve you right," he said, nuzzling back. "Snooping. Despicable. You haven't been snooping in my partition, have you?"

She snorted. "As if I could outhack you. Why, is there anything interesting in there?"

He smiled. "Never accuse your husband of having a boring diary. Salieri!"

"Yes, Maestro?"

"Run file 'Home.'"

"Yes, sir."

"Take a look out the window, love." He pulled his head back slightly so he could watch her reaction. He was really proud of this idea, and had high hopes for it. He had set himself the question: *my wife is suffering, and it's my fault. What can a person of my special talents do about that?* This was the answer he had come up with after three days of thought. Because it was just a rough first draft, the visual image took a few seconds to coalesce and firm up, pixel by pixel. But somehow he got the idea she guessed what it was nearly at once, the moment she heard the soundscape. She stiffened in his arms.

Outside the window were Cape Cod Bay and Provincetown. The view from Rhea's upstairs turret writing-room window, back home. Bay to the left, stone dike sticking its tongue out at the horizon; P-Town in the center, the Heritage Museum's spire rising above the jumble of rooftops; and off to the right, the Pilgrim Monument. It was early evening there; a crescent moon was just rising over the water.

"That's not a simulation," he said quickly. "It's live, and real-time. Well, three-second switching delay." Somewhere a dog yapped. "See? That's the Codhina's rotten little Peke."

Something told him to shut up now. He studied her face. It was as though a gifted actress had been asked to do the audition of her lifetime in fifteen seconds. Every expression of which her features were capable passed across it in rapid succession. The only sounds were distant waves, winter winds, a few gulls, a passing car with a bad gyro and, over all, the sound of Rhea's deep breathing.

And when she finally settled on a reaction—silent, bitter tears—he only got to see it for a second before she left the suite at high speed.

Nice work. He breathed deeply himself for a minute. Then he jaunted to the window and gazed hard at Provincetown for a measureless time. Finally he shut down the display. "Salieri, let me speak to Rhea."

"She is not accepting calls, sir."

"Where is she?"

"Privacy seal, sir."

He nodded. He knew a couple of ways around that . . . but he decided he had already done enough stupid things for one day. If Rhea had wanted him to find her, she wouldn't have taken the trouble to invoke privacy seal.

He was too tired to deal with this much misery, and could not diminish or share it, so he took his work to bed with him, and fell asleep on the back of a cloud, winds whistling past his ears.

9

The Ring
Saturn

The Stardancer was unplugged from the Starmind, thinking with only her own brain. The vast System-wide flow of telepathic information from the millions of Stardancers who made up the Starmind passed through her, but she did not pay any conscious attention to it, and sent nothing back out into the matrix.

A year ago, something she still did not fully understand had told her that she needed to be still and meditate. She had been engaged in the form of meditation that worked best for her—dancing—continuously ever since. This sort of unplugging was not unusual; at any given time, as many as several thousand Stardancers might be out of rapport, dropping in or out of the matrix as suited them, and as they could be spared from ongoing tasks. Having accepted the alien gift of Symbiosis, they were all untroubled by the need to eat, drink or sleep, and were impervious to fatigue. Furthermore they were effectively immortal, or at least *very* long-lived, which tended to produce a meditative state of mind.

To an observer unfamiliar with Symbiosis, she might have seemed to resemble a human being in an old-fashioned, bulky red pressure suit—without air tanks or thrusters or transparent hood. But she was not human, anymore, and the red covering was literally a part of her; the organic Symbiote with which she had merged forty-four years earlier. Designed by the enigmatic alien Fireflies to be the perfect complement to the human metabolism, Symbiote protected against cold and vacuum, turned waste products into fuel, could be spun out at will into an effective solar sail . . . and conferred telepathy with all others in Symbiosis.

It also required sunlight, of course, like all living things. She was now orbiting Saturn, almost as far as she could get from Sol without artificial life-support in the form of a photon source. But she did not feel cold . . . any more than she had felt hot when, decades earlier, she had traveled to the other extreme end of her range, the orbit of Mercury.

She had selected an orbit high enough above Saturn's mighty Ring to free her from concerns about navigational safety in that endless river of rock. Her visual field was perhaps the most beautiful the Solar System had to offer, so beautiful that she had almost ceased to see it. And even her harshest critic—herself—could not have said that her presence there detracted from the view, for she had been a gifted dancer even before she had entered Symbiosis. A tape of the past year's dancing would have fetched a high price on Earth. But this was hers and hers alone. As her body flung itself energetically through the near-vacuum, her mind was utterly still; she had long since reached that much-sought state in which one is not even thinking about not thinking. She was pure awareness, fully present yet leaving no trace.

Since she had once been a human being, there was a very primitive part of her mind which was never still for long, and in that part something like daydreaming took place from time to time. Sometimes it reached out across the immensity that engulfed her and touched the similar places in the minds of her most beloved ones, as if to reassure itself that they still existed and that all was well with them. As it went down the list, brushing against each mind, her dance unconsciously changed so as to express them and her relationship with them. Thus an occasionally recurring series of motifs ran through the dance: a sort of kinetic giggle that was her youngest child Gemma, followed by the syncopated, slightly off-rhythm movements that represented Olney Dvorak, the Stardancer she had conceived Gemma with . . . and so on, down to her eldest, forty-three-year-old Lashi, and his human father—

—it was at that point that her back spasmed and she screamed.

Any telepathic scream is strident and shocking enough; when it comes from one who has been in deep meditation for a year, every

Stardancer in the Solar System flinches. And comes running to see what is wrong and what must be done about it. At once, the Starmind enfolded her like a womb, probing gently to learn the nature of her hurt.

But even she did not know.

The only clue was the word she had screamed: the name of her first co-parent. *I just touched him,* she told the others, *and suddenly I knew something was wrong. Everything is wrong.*

He was in the hookup, of course, and as baffled as she was. He reported that as far as he knew, nothing specific was wrong. He was in a region of great potential danger, but he had been there for half a century now. He was presently engaged in a delicate and complex task, with elements of almost inconceivable danger in it, but as far as he could tell it was shaping correctly.

Since there was absolutely no explanation for her terror, she could not shake it off. Unreasonable fears are the hardest to conquer. She wanted to scan and analyze every second of his memories of the last several weeks at least, looking for clues to the danger, but since he was not a full-fledged Stardancer she could not probe as deeply as she wanted. Their son Lashi joined her, and they probed together.

The results were still ambiguous.

So Lashi turned his attention to his mother. *When did you first become aware that something was wrong?*

When I screamed.

But how long before *that could something have gone wrong? When was the last time you had monitored Father?*

She thought about it. *Yesterday, I think. And everything was fine then.*

And we know what has changed in the last twenty-four hours. So we know where the danger lies.

Lashi's father said, *But why are they any more dangerous to me today than they were yesterday?*

I don't care, she wanted to say. *Can't you get out of there?* But she could not ask that, because she already knew the answer.

I don't know, she said instead. *But dammit, you be careful!*

You know I will, Rain, he replied.

PART FOUR

10

The Shimizu Hotel
7 January 2064

By the time Jay and his brother had finished a room-service dinner and separated for the night, it was 21:45. Jay tried to call Eva, but her phone was not even accepting messages. He and Rand had accomplished so much work that he decided to celebrate. He jaunted to Jake's, in the Deluxe Tier, one of the livelier of the Shimizu's twenty-one taverns—and one of only three in which off-duty employees were welcome. There he found some friends, and settled down to matching orbits with them.

He liked Jake's; he had become a semiregular there since Ethan left him for an earthworm. The management frowned on spilled blood or broken bones, but was tolerant of merriment short of that point. It was a great place to hear extravagant lies. One red-faced old man, for instance, a wildcat asteroid miner named Wang Bin who had come to the Shimizu to drink up a lucky strike, insisted on telling the whole room about a "white Stardancer" he claimed to have seen on his last trip out. "Damn near ran into him, no beacon or anything, spotted him by eyeball. Just like any other Stardancer, but white as a slug. Didn't even have the manners to acknowledge my hail." And a groundhog dancer from Terra who had joined Jay's table told them all a whopper about a broken ankle that had healed itself just in time for a curtain.

The dancer was attractive, close enough to his age and well built—but as Jay thought about making an approach, he realized he still wasn't ready. The memory of Ethan was still too clear. A few abortive experiments had reconfirmed for him that casual sex is best with oneself—certainly simpler.

A sense of duty made Jay leave sooner than he wanted to. As soon as he got back to his room, he tried Eva again. Considering the late hour, he did not expect to reach her; he hoped to leave a message requesting an appointment for a chat tomorrow. But the face that appeared onscreen was not Jeeves. Instead he saw a bald and beardless man who had done nothing to disguise the fact that he was well over ninety years old, dressed in black loose-fitting tunic and trousers.

"Hi, Reb," Jay said after a moment of surprise. "I heard you were coming over. How are things in Top Step?"

Reb Hawkins bent forward in the Buddhist *gassho* bow, then smiled warmly. "Hello, Jay. It's good to see you again. Things are well in Top Step, I'm happy to say. How is it with you these days?"

It had been a long day; Jay was too tired for tact. "To be honest, Reb, I'm consumed with curiosity. Is Eva still up?"

"She's gone to bed, but she told me to expect your call. Why don't you come over for a cup? We haven't talked in a while. Or are you too tired? I know you've been working hard on the new piece."

Jay was torn. His brain hurt. But he did want to know why his old friend had decided not to die after all, and it was not the sort of question that could be dealt with over the phone. "I'm on my way."

Hawkins-roshi was something of a legend in space. He was a Zen Buddhist monk, and the oldest continuous resident of Top Step, the Earth-orbiting asteroid where human beings came to enter Symbiosis. For over forty years, until his retirement, he had helped hundreds of thousands of postulants make that profound transition, from *Homo sapiens* to *Homo caelestis,* with minimal psychological and spiritual trauma. A cronkite had once referred to him as the Modest Midwife to the Starmind. During those four decades, he had also made regular visits to most of the other human habitations in High Earth Orbit, including the Shimizu, dispensing spiritual sustenance and friendship to Buddhists and nonBuddhists alike. He and Eva were old and close friends, had known each other since they'd been groundhogs. Jay had met Reb through her.

Almost the moment Eva's door had dilated behind Jay, he was glad he had come. He had forgotten how soothing Reb's presence could be. It was not merely his obvious years; Jay was pretty sure Reb had had the same effect on people when he was a teenager. He simply had an almost tangible aura around him, projected a zone of serenity, of clarity, of acceptance. There is a quality dancers call "presence," and Jay was very good at achieving it onstage. Therefore he knew how amazing it was for Reb to have it all the time, every day. Presumably Hawkins-roshi had an automatic pilot, like everybody else . . . but he never seemed to use it. He would surely have long since been abbot of his own monastery somewhere down on Earth by now, if he had not found a career more important to him in space; helping human beings become something more.

"How long are you here for?" Jay asked him. "Can that big rock get along without you?"

Reb smiled. "Top Step can get along just fine without me. I'm retired, remember? It's Meiya's headache these days. I'll be here for a week, or until Eva throws me out, whichever comes first. I can use the vacation."

"I'm glad. I'd like to have a long talk with you sometime."

Reb nodded. "But not tonight. You're exhausted. You don't want any tea, do you? I'll make this as quick as I can. You want to know why Eva has changed her mind."

Jay nodded gratefully. "She told you she'd confided in me, then."

Reb nodded. "We talked for a long time. About suffering, and what it is for. About friendship, and what that is for. About what she has done since she came here to space, and what she might do yet. About samsara. In the end I was able to persuade her that to end one's life when one is not in mortal pain or fear is a kind of arrogance."

Jay stared. He had said much the same thing to Eva, in one form or another, at least a dozen times in the last month. "But Eva *is* arrogant," he blurted out.

Reb said nothing.

It came to Jay that perhaps Reb was just better than he was at teaching people about arrogance. Come to think of it, he was doing it now. . . .

"Well," Jay said lamely, "that's great, then. I'm glad you managed to get through to her. But I still don't see how you—"

"How do you *feel* about Eva's new decision?" Reb interrupted quietly. "If you don't mind my asking."

One of the problems with talking with holy men was their uncanny habit of putting a finger—gently, nonthreateningly—right on your sore spots. Another was the difficulty of successfully bullshitting them. "Ambivalent," he admitted.

Reb nodded. "I can see why. What a mix of emotions you must have felt, when she asked you to dance at her dying."

Jay nodded vigorous agreement. "Oh God, yes! Sad, of course, but also proud to have been asked, and annoyed at the extra workload, and creatively stimulated, and . . . and Reb, I'm almost as confused right now. I'm glad we're not going to lose her. But I've just gone through a month of trauma and grief reconciling myself to the idea that we were . . . and I've wasted hours of work on a piece that now may never get performed, at a time when I was already up to my ass in alligators . . . and—"

"And?"

"—and if you want to know the truth, a part of me resents the hell out of *you,* for accomplishing in one conversation what I've failed to do in a month of trying. I mean, I know this is your line of work—but she and I have been friends a long time. Part of me wants to kick you—and then go wake her up and punch her in the nose."

Reb grinned. "You're welcome to kick me. But if you feel you must wake Eva, make sure your insurance is paid up first. Whatever Eva's brain may be thinking at any given moment, her body's survival instincts are strong . . . and I happen to know she fights dirty."

"Yeah, I know." Jay had once seen a foolish person behave rudely to Eva. He lived.

"Think of it this way. A man tries to split a tough piece of wood with an ax. He strikes again and again, day after day, with no result. Then another man comes along and takes a tentative swing. The wood splits with a loud crack. Did the first man play no part?"

"Well . . . sure, he did. But he's going to feel frustrated as hell."

"So you didn't just want Eva not to die; you wanted the credit for changing her mind. Be content with partial credit, all right?"

Jay laughed ruefully. "You're right. I'm being silly."

"Also known as the human condition. You're tired and high. Go to bed, and in the morning you'll be a much more admirable human being. I'll be impressed, I promise."

Jay laughed out loud. Reb could always jolly him out of a sulk. "You're right. Uh . . . look, tomorrow's going to be hectic. Could you ask Eva if she can set aside time for a visit with me the day after tomorrow?"

"I'll tell Jeeves."

"Thanks. And could you and I have a talk the day after that?"

"Whenever you like. I'm going to be busy myself tomorrow, but the rest of the week is pretty much open. Diaghilev and Rild can work out a time."

"Good. I'll see you then."

"And I'll see you tomorrow night at the performance," Reb said.

"Oh, right. I should have known you'd be on the comp list."

They exchanged bows, and Jay left. On the way home his thoughts were so scattered that he let Diaghilev navigate for him. Eva's sudden flip-flop just seemed so weird, so . . . arbitrary. Rhea would have said that it didn't ring true artistically. *Eva spends sixteen years making up her mind, withstands a month of argument from me . . . and then Reb shows up and tells her suicide isn't nice, and she folds?* There had to be more to it than that. What else had Reb said to her? All Jay could think of to do was to ask her at his first opportunity.

As he jaunted along, he remembered some of Reb's closing words. "Diaghilev and Rild can work out a time." Jay was struck by that now. Reb met thousands of people a year, juggled trillions of details . . . and had remembered the name of Jay's AI without checking. He himself had forgotten that Reb called his own AI "Rild"—and had never gotten around to following up his original mental note to find out what that name signified. Whereas he was willing to bet that Reb knew not only who Sergei Diaghilev had been, but exactly what he symbolized for Jay. Perhaps here was a clue as to why Reb had succeeded with Eva where he had failed. Reb retained every detail of what people told him, and followed them up, thought them through. "Sergei," he said suddenly, "who did Reb Hawkins name his AI for?"

"I don't know, Jay. Shall I find out?"

"Please."

"Waiting . . . The only match I find on file is a character in a twentieth-century novel called LORD OF LIGHT, by Roger Zelazny. Rild was student of the Buddha, a former assassin who came to surpass his master in enlightenment."

The answer was interesting—but what caught Jay's attention was its first word. It had taken Diaghilev a startlingly long time—nearly two whole seconds—to tap into the vast memory cores of the Net. It was late at night; most guests and staff were asleep. Someone must be using a hell of a lot of bandwidth and processing power for something.

Of course. The Fat Five were inboard. When Leviathan swims under your boat, the sea swells.

He was essentially asleep before he reached his suite; Diaghilev guided him inside, sealed the door, undressed him, administered hangover preventative, and strapped him into his sleepsack so that he would not wake with the classic free-fall stiff neck. His dreams were full of Stardancers . . . millions upon countless millions of them, swarming around Terra like moths around a fire, staining the ionosphere red with their numbers.

The next day began with an omen, to which he paid insufficient attention.

"Huh? Whazzit?"

"I'm sorry, Jay," Diaghilev said, "but Evelyn Martin insists on speaking to you at once."

Jay suggested some other things Martin could do instead; Diaghilev pointed out that they were physically impossible. "Not for him they aren't. All right, all right: audio only, accept. What the fuck do you want?"

"You're not archiving tonight, right?" Martin's nasal voice demanded.

"Oh, for Christ's sake." From time to time, especially if he had made any alterations in the choreography, Jay would have a concert recorded for archival purposes—and some of the camera angles would include the faces of the audience. Martin was afraid he might do so tonight, with the Fat Five in the house. As a matter of fact, he had been planning to. "Of course not. Anyway, what's the difference? By the time the tapes are edited, the uips will be long gone, and the fact that they've been here won't be secret anymore."

"Doesn't matter," Martin said. "Just promise me the cameras stay off tonight. If you want to swear it on your mother's grave, I won't mind."

"Do you have any idea what time it is?"

"I don't give a shit. I've been up all night, swimming in a river of shit upside down, and the tide's still coming in: they come aboard in a couple of hours. I feel like that little Dutch kid that used to go around sticking his finger in lesbians; if it ain't one thing it's six others. On top of everything else I had a guest croak on me a couple of hours ago, like I got nothing else to do—"

"A guest died?" That was unusual. The Shimizu had diagnostics and emergency medical facilities as good as anything on Terra; it would take something like an exploding bullet to the brain to defeat them. The saying was, *You couldn't die here if you tried.* "How did he manage that?"

"Genius. Apparently he built the comm gear in his p-suit himself. So he's outside taking a stroll, and he goes to put in a call to his heap, up at the dock. Only his homemade antenna slips out of alignment when his homemade power supply blows up, so he microwaves his frontal lobe instead. So now I got to grease all the news weasels to forget to file the story, and rummage through the antheap down there to find his dirtbag relatives and grease *them*—"

Jay did not want to hear about french-fried brains and PR men's problems before coffee. "Who was he?" he interrupted. "Anybody I'd know?"

"Nah—just checked in yesterday. Some old rock rat who struck it rich, and decided to spend his fortune and the last minutes of his life making mine miserable. Why the hell couldn't the inconsiderate bastard have poached his brains out there in the Belt somewhere, where it wouldn't have been my problem?"

Alcoholic memory stirred. "Wait a minute. Chinese guy? Wang something?"

"How the hell did you know?" Martin sounded suspicious.

"I ran into him at Jake's last night. He was telling us all some yarn about a white Stardancer."

"Jesus Christ—keep that quiet, will you? It's gonna be hard enough sitting on this, and those bastards love anything with a Stardancer hook, gives 'em great visuals to cut to. 'White Stardancer,' my ass—the old fart's probably been sautéing his cerebrum for weeks now, and only just finished the job this morning. Hey, that's it—if he was already brain-damaged when he got here, we got no liability at all—"

This triggered Jay's gag reflex. "I'll keep the cameras off tonight, Ev," he said, and cut the connection. Getting back to sleep was out of the question now, so he called for coffee, unstrapped himself from his sleepsack, and began his day.

* * *

Twelve extremely hectic hours later, he met Rand and his family at their suite and journeyed with them to the Nova Dance Theatre. All were dressed in their finest, and the adults were as nervous as if they were about to go onstage themselves. They chattered along the way, and fiddled with their seams and fastenings, and inspected each other for unseen flaws in costume or makeup. Only Colly seemed to take it all in stride; money and power did not impress her, since she did not use the former and had all she presently wanted of the latter.

They had to pass a checkpoint to reach the foyer, manned by six very serious-looking guards, each wearing different-colored armbands. No weapons were visible, but it was clear that they were available. Jay noticed with amusement that the guards seemed to watch each other as carefully and constantly as they did the civilians. Five private security forces, plus the Shimizu security, and none of them trusted any of the others.

And indeed, when they had passed thumbprint and retina checks and entered the foyer, Nika, the tech director, approached them before Jay could even begin trying to spot the uips. "Boss," she said, "how the hell am I supposed to call the show with a six-pack of gorillas looking over my shoulder, frowning every time I touch something?"

"Jesus," Jay muttered. "They're even back in the tech hole?"

"They seem to think it's their fucking command center," she said bitterly. "And there's more six-packs at every entrance and exit to this area, plus one at each stage wing. I don't care about them, as long as none of the dancers crash into them when they exit, but can't you get me a little elbow room in the hole?"

Jay thought about it. "I don't think so, Nika. They're right; that area has to be secured. If I were an assassin, backstage is the way I'd come in. Do the best you can, okay? At least Rand and I won't be in there with all of you; we're watching this one from the house. Just tell the goons not to touch anything while the concert's running."

"None of them would dare. The other five would shoot him. They get nervous every time *I* touch a control. Honest to God, I never saw such a paranoid bunch in my life."

"If you needed bodyguards, wouldn't you want them to be paranoid? I have to go—"

Nika jaunted off, frowning, and Jay caught up with Rand and his family. They were just being presented to the honored guests by Katherine Tokugawa.

"Mr. Imaro Amin . . . Pandit Chatur Birla . . . Honorable Chen Ling Ho . . . Ms. Victoria Hathaway . . . Citizen Grijk Krugnk . . . please permit me to present the Shimizu's Co-Artistic Directors: our resident choreographer, Mr. Jay Sasaki, and our resident Shaper, Rand Porter." All bowed. Jay was amused again. Kate had solved an impossible protocol problem in the only way she could—by introducing the five uips to her vips in alphabetical order. . . .

"We bid you welcome to Nova Dance Theatre, lady and gentlemen," Rand said smoothly. "It gives me great pride to present my wife, the author Rhea Paixao, and our daughter, Colly."

More bows all around. "I read your last book, AND CALL HER BLESSED, with great pleasure, Ms. Paixao," Birla said.

"So did I," Hathaway said, "and it was wonderful. Even better than THE FREE LUNCH."

"I would have to agree," Birla said, "although it is a close call. I have conversations with characters of yours all the time."

Rhea thanked them, turning a fetching shade of pink. The compliments had to be genuine: the uips had not expected to meet her, and had no reason to stroke her if they had. Jay was stunned to learn that people as rich as this read fiction for pleasure—two of them, anyway. And while Rhea had a good and growing literary reputation, she had never yet had a top-ten bestseller: you had to *care* about good books to know of her work. Interesting. Uips were not automatically philistines. Rand caught his eye and grinned, and Jay knew precisely what he was thinking: *if they like Rhea's stuff, they'll like ours.*

While the conversational pleasantries flowed back and forth, Jay studied these five people who could make Kate Tokugawa snap to attention. He had never met a whole handful of trillionaires before.

Amin was a Kikuyu financier from Kenya, said to be the only African trillionaire. Of average height and mass, he was in his early forties and looked thirty, except for his eyes; he was the most obviously vicious of the five. His hair was straightened, but paradoxically his skin tone was artificially *darkened*, to a Bantu black which did not match his nose and cheek structure. His fortune was based on Earth-to-orbit shipping. He ignored the arbitrary local vertical which everyone else had adopted—the Terrans from habit, the spacers out of politeness—and just let himself drift free.

Birla, a swarthy Marwari from Rajputna, was the talker of the group, which made him seem more trivial than he could possibly have been. He was a hundred and twenty—four years older than Eva!—and looked forty. According to the bio Jay had scanned, he was ostensibly a devout Hindu, but he seemed in no hurry at all to reincarnate. The friendly twinkle in his eyes had to be fake, but it was a good fake. He owned as large a proportion of the Terran and orbital media as the UN would let him, and influenced even more; Evelyn Martin hovered near him solicitously, ready to open a vein on request.

Chen Ling Ho, a Mandarin from Beijing, was fifty and looked fifty. He was short to the point of tininess, smaller than Kate, and looked as benign and childlike as Colly. Jay had read that his enemies called him The Krait. He was also the Zen Buddhist at whose request Reb Hawkins had been invited to the Shimizu. That interested Jay: there were many Chinese Buddhists, but few who followed the Soto path, which had originated in twelfth-century Japan. Chen was a grandson of the legendary Chen Ten Li, the twentieth-century statesman who had been present at the creation of the Starmind; heavy (and early) family investment in nanotechnology had made Ten Li rich beyond measure. In defiance of tradition, it had been the *second* generation—his son Chen Hsi Feng—who had nearly succeeded in destroying the family name and fortune, by becoming an antiStardancer fanatic and launching a treacherous and doomed attack on the Starmind. Ling Ho, the third generation, had miraculously managed to salvage most of the wreckage, largely thanks to adroit fence-mending with the Starmind. That doubtless accounted for his conversion to Reb Hawkins's faith. Jay wondered how many trillionaire Zen students there were.

Victoria Hathaway was a WASP from New York; calendar age eighty-seven, apparent age just under thirty. She looked like holo stars wished they looked—but there was a coldness in her eyes and mouth that made Jay think of her as a long sleek shiny pair of scissors, with a carefully trimmed little tuft of pubic hair just at the place where the blades joined. Most of her money was said to be in real estate, on and off Terra, and she was famous for both her ruthlessness and her absolute lack of any vestige of a sense of humor—though no one dared mention the latter quality to her face.

Grijk Krugnk was by far the ugliest of the lot, a Slav of some kind from Votoskojek who was sixty-six and looked fiftyish. He was built like a power plant, but not as pretty, so obviously a brute that many had found him fatally easy to underestimate. His wealth sprang from power generation, most of it spaceborne. Oddly, he was the only one of the five whose English was utterly unaccented, like a cronkite's. He handled himself in free-fall as well as Amin, but made less of a point of it. His complexion must have been ruddy on earth; in zero gee his face looked like a tomato.

Each of the five had a personal bodyguard, and all but Chen had an additional companion as well. These latter were introduced, but Jay didn't bother to remember any of the names; they were obviously AIs with a pulse. The killers were not introduced, as it might have distracted them. Chen's bodyguard seemed to be the only one with any extensive space experience: Jay noticed that he watched feet as well as hands. That made his boss the smartest of the five uips.

"Is there anything you would like to tell us about the work we are about to see, Mr. Sasaki? Mr. Porter?" Birla asked, snapping Jay out of his reverie. Rand let him take it.

"No, sir," he said. "If it doesn't speak for itself, then nothing I could say will help. Shall we go in?"

Perhaps taking their cue from Tokugawa's introduction, the five uips entered the theater in alphabetical order. Once inside, things got briefly complicated again.

This piece, *Spatial Delivery*, had been staged for proscenium performance, rather than in the sphere. That is, it was designed so that the audience used only half of the available "seating" area, strapping their backs to a common hemisphere, and the piece was performed against the backdrop of the other half. This cut audience capacity in half, but was a lot easier to choreograph and shape than a spherical piece which had to look good from all possible angles at once.

But if five people sit against a hemisphere, and keep pretending that there is a local vertical, then some of them must sit "above" others.

After a few seconds of backing and filling, the five decided face was more important than up and down, and solved the problem by making a puffball, like a two-dimensional version of Colly's beloved angelfish. Lesser mortals filled in the gaps between them in whatever orientation suited them. Jay sat with Rand and his family in the center. He saw Eva nearby, and waved; she waved back.

The house lights dimmed, Rand's overture began, and Jay forgot anything as trivial as trillionaires.

The first half went very well. Emerging from his warm fog to the realization that he must make small talk during the intermission was like being dumped from a snug bed into an icy vacuum.

And indeed it developed that the intermission chatter of uips was every bit as inane and clumsy as that of the mere vips Jay was used to. They all liked it so far, of course, and said so—but for all the wrong reasons, some that Jay would never have thought of in a million years. Intermissions always made Jay wish he had taken up engineering, or any trade where the customer's wishes were possible to fathom. Talking to civilians usually reminded him forcefully that no artist ever succeeds save by dumb luck. Since he believed the purpose of art was to communicate, this tended to depress him slightly.

Five minutes before the end of the interval, he excused himself from the gathering, saying that he needed to check something with his technician backstage. Rand seized the opportunity to accompany him, ignoring his wife's brief look of dismay, and they jaunted back into the empty theater together.

There were four "wings," short cylindrical tunnels of invisibility created by Rand's shaping gear, at the four cardinal points of the terminator that divided audience from stage. Dancers seemed to materialize as they entered, vanish as they exited. Knowing that two of the wings would be blocked by knots of dancers nerving themselves up to go on for the second act, Jay and Rand picked one of the other two at random.

And nearly got themselves shot by trigger-happy guards. "Jesus, folks, relax," Jay said. "There won't even be anybody out there to protect for another five minutes yet. Why don't you safety those damned things until then? I don't want you drilling one of my dancers on their way to the can." Shaking his head, he passed on until he came to the tech hole, which was located at the farthest point of the theater, so that its one-way glass looked out past the dancers toward the audience. In fact, he and Rand had nothing to accomplish here; Nika had this piece on tracks by now. The tech hole was simply the nearest place to hide for a few minutes.

Not wanting to risk being shot again, he paused at the door and touched the intercom button. "It's me and Rand, Nika," he said. "Coming in."

The door opened on horror.

Five bodies, drifting limp in free-fall crouch. Jack-in-the-box effect made them move toward him as the door swung open. Nika was one of them. A barely perceptible bitter odor preceded them; Jay could not identify it but knew it was trouble. "Oh, *shit,*" Rand said behind him.

"Hold your breath," he snapped, and leaped into the hole. The room's air system had already scavenged up most of the bitter gas, but who knew how much it took to immobilize a man?

He did not have time to find out if any of the floating bodies were alive; more urgently he needed to know who was missing. Sure enough, the worst possible: the Shimizu's man. His brain raced. The assassin had planned to kill from here, firing through the one-way glass into the house. At Jay's announcement he had bolted out one of the other two doors from the hole—seconds ago. His only move now was to cut through another six-pack somehow, enter the theater through one of the four wings, leave by the audience entrance, and try to kamikaze whomever his intended victim was out in the foyer. But *which wing?* Presumably he knew which two were mobbed with dancers; he had been hanging out in the hole. And if Nika had had her mikes hot . . . he knew which wing was guarded by a six-pack *who had just been told to safety their weapons.* By Jay! The son of a bitch could have circled around behind them while they were gaping in the open door of the hole. . . .

"Make an announcement," he brayed at Rand, and pointed to Nika's board and mike.

"What do I say?"

"Run for your fucking lives!" He left the hole at full thruster power.

He began deep breathing as he left the hole—can't have too much oxygen in a crisis—but within seconds he held his breath again as he detected more of that bitter smell ahead. The assassin had had a second gas-bomb—and kept it to use where it would do him the most good. As Jay came around the curve he saw the six-pack he had passed moments earlier, drifting with the air-currents. He wanted to decelerate to a stop and peer cautiously into that magic tunnel before entering it—but he was traveling so fast he'd have had to overshoot it and beat back, and he just didn't have the time. Instead he threw himself into a power turn and rocketed right into it at max acceleration.

That probably saved his life. The assassin was still in the tunnel, waiting to scrag Jay the moment his head showed. But Jay arrived like a right hook, smashing solidly into him before he could fire. They recoiled from each other violently, and the assassin lost his grip on his weapon, a hand laser. But there was no gravity to take it away; it kept station with him as he tumbled, and he grabbed it again on the second flailing try.

The assassin was a very good shot. But Jay was a very good dancer—and fortunately the gun was a pulse job rather than a garden-hose-type continuous-beam laser. He twisted, arched, feinted, leaped, contracted, and bolts of shining death missed him by centimeters. He had one further advantage: he could use all four thrusters, while the assassin had to reserve one wrist for aiming. Thank God the man seemed to be out of knockout bombs.

But Jay could not hope to close; it was all he could do to stay alive. And any second his luck must run out. He could leap through the imaginary wall of the tunnel, but the killer would only follow. Any minute now the nearest six-pack would arrive behind him, and none of them would hesitate to fire through him even if they identified him as a friendly. Jay had time to realize that he was going to die protecting people he did not like or even respect, and then the tunnel had a blowout. A hole the size of a Frisbee appeared in its wall with a plosive *phuff,* jagged metal teeth pointing outward; the shriek of escaping air tore at their ears and pressure began to drop.

Of course it is impossible for a holographic cylinder to have a blowout, and in any case the nearest vacuum was hundreds of meters away. But both men were spacers; they reacted quite instinctively, dropping their quarrel and leaping for the hole together to seal it with their bodies if necessary. Only one of them remembered on the way that the greatest shaper in human space was presently in the tech hole, and that this tunnel belonged to him.

11

Eva was the first to enter the tunnel; nearly at once she reversed thrust and recoiled backward into Reb, who was at her heels. A weapon she was not licensed to possess vanished from her hand. Jay had clearly coped. Even her atrophied sense of smell could detect the odors of burned metal and burned meat.

"Nice work," she said. "Remind me not to piss you off."

Jay's eyes met hers, but it took him a second or two to recognize her. "I got him," he said wonderingly.

That much was clear. The body that floated between them was so obviously a corpse that Eva's subconscious had ignored the gun it still clutched in one hand. Boiling brains leave a skull any way they can. Jay had a small smear of suet on his right cheek that must have burned him as it struck, but he didn't seem to be aware of it. Eva threaded her way through horrid drifting tendrils of brains and blood and took Jay in her arms. "That you did," she said soothingly, wiping his cheek. "That you did."

Rand arrived just then; at Eva's signal he left Jay to her. She gestured again, and he and Reb took charge of the body, towing it backstage, shooing its gore along with it.

Sure enough, Rhea and Colly were the next to arrive. At the alarm, all five uips had ducked for cover and their guards had clustered around them, and mere vips had struggled to get away from them, and Tokugawa and Martin had called for information—but Rhea and Colly had both realized they had family in the firezone. Rhea hadn't been able to stop her daughter, but had gotten—barely—ahead of her to shield her from possible fire. Eva moved so that she and Jay blocked their way. "He's fine," she said quickly. "Wait here for him."

Rhea was frantic. "I've got to—"

"*You've got to wait here,*" Eva said, indicating Colly with her eyes.

"I—yes, okay." She got a firm grip on Colly. "He's really all right?"

"Not a scratch, truly."

"He saved my life," Jay said.

"And others," Eva agreed. "Both of you did. I'm surprised at you, Jay—I thought you had more sense than to be a hero."

"I had to," he said. "It was partly my fault."

She put a hand over his mouth. "He's delirious," she said to Rhea. "All the adrenalin." She turned back to Jay, put her lips to his ear. "As your attorney, I advise you to shut the hell up. You are not competent to assess blame."

He blinked at her. "You're not an attorney, Eva."

"The hell I'm not. I'm licensed for the High Court—and if you don't start zipping your lip I'm going to need to be. When they get here, you tell them facts only, get it? Facts only. You can draw conclusions when you're thinking more clearly. Okay?" She shook his shoulders. "Okay?"

"Sure, Eva. Facts only. That's good." She studied him carefully, decided he was not quite in shock in the medical sense—but close.

The tunnel went away; Rand must have reached the tech hole. Almost at once they were hip-deep in people, all talking at once—all five uips, assorted assistants and bodyguards, the Shimizu's security chief, the house physician. The loudest by a good margin was Martin. Eva bellowed for silence, but her tired old lungs weren't equal to the task.

Reb's amplified voice filled the theater like the voice of God. "Ladies and gentlemen, please compose yourselves. There is no longer any reason for alarm. An attempted assassination has failed, and the situation is under control. Please return to the foyer as quickly and quietly as you can; emergency personnel will be arriving and you are in their way. You will all receive a detailed report when things have clarified."

Rand's voice joined him. "Dancers, please join our guests in the foyer and escort them to the reception room. The rest of tonight's concert is canceled."

The tumult of attempted conversation became even louder—but at Martin's physical insistence, they at last began moving away, with Tokugawa in the lead. Rand told Rhea to take Colly back to their suite, and she agreed without argument. Dr. O'Regan and Chief Cruz remained behind. "Who was it?" Cruz asked.

"One of yours," Eva said. "Dunno which—he didn't have his face with him."

Cruz's face darkened. "I know which. Shit. Where'd they take him, the tech hole?"

"I think so." She turned to Jay. "Can you stand another look at the son of a bitch? Chief Cruz needs you to show her what happened."

"Oh sure," he said.

As they left the tunnel, they had to duck around tumbling bodies and a few severed limbs—but fortunately no more horrid trails of blood, as laser amputation tends to self-cauterize. Eva noticed how hard Cruz had to work to ignore the one in Shimizu livery.

Cruz made them wait briefly outside the tech hole. Two crime-scene technicians and three interns all arrived at once; she and the doctor went inside with them. The security chief emerged with Rand in less than a minute, scowling blackly. The conference took place there in the corridor. Cruz—mortified that one of her own people had been the killer—obviously wanted Eva gone, but did not dare try to chase her out. Eva did not even have to claim status as Jay's attorney of fact; a steely glance was all it took. She and Cruz had taken each other's measure a long time ago.

So she was able to ride herd on Jay. She was fond of the boy, and his raving about the attempted assassination being partly his fault had unsettled her. If Cruz had heard that, the questioning might well have taken place under drugs. At Eva's direction, Jay gave a baldly factual account of what had occurred. She spotted what he had meant as soon as he said it—"I told them to safety their damned weapons and continued on to the hole"—but of course no one else saw any blame in that. It was what anyone might have said in his place. She was glad she had gotten to him first.

"Pity you couldn't have taken him alive," Cruz said, when Jay had finished the story and Rand had added events from his perspective. "I hate to let someone kill a dozen people in my care without asking him who paid for it."

"I was dead," Jay said, "and then Rand gave me a split-second advantage. I didn't think about it. I grabbed his gun hand and made him shoot himself under the chin. I'd do it again."

"Oh, I wasn't criticizing! *Do* it again, if there's a next time."

Eva snorted at that. If Jay had not gotten lucky, Cruz would have had more dead—and perhaps a dead uip or two as well—and would have been looking for work tomorrow.

"I wish he was still alive too," Jay said. "So I could kill him again. Nika's . . . Nika was special." Suddenly he shook his head with great violence. "Jesus! Did that really happen?" He giggled.

"You've got everything you need for now, right, Chief?" Eva said.

Cruz frowned, but nodded. "I may want to hypno him tomorrow."

"Gotta wait for it to seep into long-term storage for hypno to do any good," she agreed. "Jeeves—"

"Yes, madam?" He shimmered into existence, urbane and unflappable.

"Take Mr. Sasaki home. My place, not his. Bunk him down in my bed and make me a doss in Guest Room Two."

"Very good, madam. If you would be good enough to follow me, sir . . ."

"Half a mo." She motioned Jay close and murmured in his ear. "Want Jacques to join you?"

He blinked at her and struggled with the question. Jacques's job description read, "hedonic technician"—but Eva happened to know that he was more artist than technician, a natural healer and comforter. "No," Jay said, and then, "I don't think so," and then he blushed slightly and said, "Uh . . . yes. Please."

She nodded. "Tell Jeeves. Run along now."

Once he was gone, she turned back to Cruz. "How did you know who the assassin was?"

"Eh?"

"You said, 'I know which.' How did you know?"

"Oh. Savannavong only joined the force a month ago. I wouldn't have used him on this job, for that reason—but Hanh came down sick this afternoon and I was stretched thin."

"Savannavong was real good at making people come down sick," Rand said bitterly. "Hanh got lucky."

"So did you two," Cruz said. "You both reacted like trained cops. Either of you ever in service?"

"I did two years with NYPD. Draftee. But that was over twenty years ago, and I never drew my weapon in the line of duty. Jay's never had any kind of combat training, to my knowledge. We just kept making mistakes until the bastard was dead."

"You'd better get home," Eva said. "Your wife still doesn't know the details."

"Chief?"

"Go ahead."

Rand threw her a grateful glance and made his escape.

People were coming and going from the tech hole now, bringing in forensic equipment and taking out corpses. But they gave the glowering Chief Cruz a wide berth; for the moment Eva was effectively alone with her. "Does your thumb hurt, Chief?" Eva asked suddenly.

"Eh? Yes it does—why? How did you know?"

"Because I figure you for an honest cop. The moment that alarm sounded, an honest cop in your shoes would have pushed a button and flooded the whole damn theater and backstage area with sleepy gas."

"I did! Some son of a bitch had—"

"I know. It didn't work, so you kept pushing; that's why your thumb hurts."

Cruz nodded slowly. "I see." She thought some more. "Well, it wouldn't have helped anyway; the bastard obviously had nose filters in."

Eva nodded. "Like you do. But you didn't know that at the time. An honest cop couldn't have."

"But why disable the sleepy gas if he had filters?"

"So he'd have maximum confusion to escape in after he made his kill? Squawking civilians in all directions."

"God dammit, Eva—"

"Relax, Rani—I'm on your side. I know this whole episode makes you look like a horse's ass, but I can't think of anything you could've done better. And I'll tell Kate Tokugawa that, if you like. But if I were you, I'd have Dr. O'Regan document that thumb sprain."

She left Cruz and went to the reception, curious to see how the ultimately rich responded to a brush with death. Six cronkites ambushed her just outside the door, looking like children who needed to urinate; the first in line named a figure. "No comment," she said.

He named a second figure, and when she refused that too, a bidding war developed. She brushed through them grandly and entered the hall. Guards prevented them from following; frustrated, they all jaunted off to file what little they already had.

The party had that slightly forced gaiety which screams of fear just past. But the uips themselves seemed the calmest people in the room—except for Reb, of course. In fact, the only person who still showed any overt signs of fear was Evelyn Martin, grinning and sweating and talking even faster than usual. He spotted her, detached himself and came over.

"Hi, Eva," he said loudly. "So glad you could make it." Sotto voce he added, "Anything else gone wrong out there? Any more assassins come to squeeze my ulcers? Fresh stiffs? Other major felonies? Chief Cruz find out the assassin is a High Council member or anything like that?"

"Good news," she said. "No news." Louder, she added. "Awful to see you, Evelyn. You're looking uglier than usual tonight."

He beamed. "Thank you, dear—have you met our honored guests? Chen Ling Ho, for instance?"

"Get a grip, Evelyn. I introduced *you* to Ling. Why don't you go take a trank?"

"I'm at system max now," he said.

"Take stimulants, then. Your voice will rise above the audible range and you won't be so conspicuous." She drifted away, and joined her escort, Dr. Chen. He was chatting with Reb and Victoria Hathaway. Chen introduced her to Hathaway—who regarded her aged features with barely concealed horror.

"Hello, dear," Eva said. "It's nice to see you again."

"We've met?" Hathaway said, disbelieving but polite.

"I knew your grandmother. You peed on my lap once."

Hathaway gave the only possible reply: dead silence.

Chen intervened. "Eva, have they determined yet who was the assassin's intended target?"

She shrugged. "For all Cruz can tell at this point, he was a good guy, come to take out Evelyn Martin on behalf of all mankind."

That got a laugh; even Hathaway almost smiled. "I assume the man's background is being checked?"

Eva shrugged again. "Sure. But it's a waste of time. The background check you have to go through to get hired for Shimizu security can't be improved on. Serious money went into this." She made sure her gaze was not resting on either Chen or Hathaway. "I will bet cash the person who hired it done is in this room."

Hathaway flinched, but Chen only nodded. "The probability is high," he agreed.

"Was it you, Chen?" Hathaway asked bluntly.

Again Chen looked as if he were remembering what it felt like to smile. "Twelve dead, none of them the right one? I'm offended, Victoria. Can you truly believe me so inartistic?"

"Oh, but you can believe it of *me,* right?"

"Since you ask, yes. Now we are both offended. Shall we seek another topic of conversation?"

Eva had a mischievous thought. "Unless you'd like me to narrow the list of suspects for you," she said.

"How?" Chen and Hathaway and Reb all asked simultaneously.

"Well, only theoretically. I don't actually expect, uh, people of your caliber to submit to a body search. But I'll bet a dead frog the person who hired that killer is wearing nose filters. He or she knew the killer would be covering his escape with death gas, and might have been forced to flee past his employer. Nose filters that go in far enough to be invisible aren't easily removed."

Hathaway objected. "That wouldn't prove a thing. Any of us might be wearing nose filters out of simple paranoia. In light of events, it would seem an intelligent precaution."

Eva nodded. "But you're probably not *all* filtered. I said 'narrow the list,' not nail it down. Irrelevant anyway; none of you will tolerate a search on principle—and I don't blame you."

"Then why did you bring it up?" Hathaway snapped.

Eva did not answer. But she was already enjoying the mental picture. As the word spread, the five would spend the next hour discreetly trying to peer up each other's nostrils. Victoria Hathaway might actually not look down her nose at anyone for the rest of the night.

Reb escorted her home. They took double-bulbs of Irish coffee to the window, and sat looking out at Mother Terra in companionable silence for some time.

"Jeeves," she said then, "is Jay awake?"

"He and Master Jacques are both sound asleep, madam."

"Thank you. Let me know if he wakes." He shimmered away again, and she turned to Reb. "That bedroom is soundproof anyhow."

Reb nodded. "Go ahead."

"I need a better cover story for him. About why I'm still using up air. Oh, you did a good job. But I heard his voice, and he didn't really buy it, deep down. I'm afraid I shot my mouth off to him about why I was planning to take a cab. He's not going to be satisfied with what you told him. And I don't know what else to say. The boy knows me too well. And he spent a whole month trying to change my mind: his pride demands a convincing explanation."

"Not just pride, Eva. He loves you."

"So what do I tell him? I *can't* tell him about—"

"No. I suggest you stall as long as possible. With everything that's happened tonight, he'll be too busy to remember the question for a few days. When he does, you can be unavailable for some additional time. It may be weeks before he has time and opportunity to brace you about it."

"And what then?"

"You tell him I promised you entertaining surprises were still in store for you—and proved it the very next day."

"And if he persists?"

"Let icicles form on your brow and tell him it's personal. A shame to hurt his feelings, of course, but I don't see what else you can do."

She sighed, and sipped her drink. "You're right. I can't tell him."

"No, you cannot. I should not have told *you*, Eva. But you are my oldest living friend, and I could not see you leave just before everything changed."

She found her eyes stinging, and shut up. They shared more silence for a time.

"Do you think it was Chen?" she asked at last.

"Behind tonight's violence, you mean? I don't know. What do you think?"

"I think an inartistic hit would be a very artistic touch indeed. But it's hard to refute his essential point. If he'd done it, it would have worked, however garishly."

"Apparently it was only by incredible chance that it didn't."

"And I tend to find incredible chance incredible. But I'd bet my life both Jay and Rand are straight." She glanced over her shoulder at the bedroom door. "You know what I mean. They're both honest."

"The gods have blessed us," Reb said cheerfully.

"They have?"

"Of course. How often does life hand you a really good puzzle?"

She blinked, and grinned. "You're right. Not often enough these days. I feel like a sixty-year-old again."

12

Kechar Dzong
Lo Monthang
The Kingdom of Lo, Nepal
12 January 2065

"There was a time," the old monk said above the howling of the late afternoon wind, "when this kingdom controlled all trade throughout the Himalayas. It was the top of the roof of the world."

Gunter Schmidt thought, *I will not kill my travel agent. That is far too merciful. I will sue him until he bleeds from the eyes.*

"Of course," the old man said with magnificent redundance, "all that was long ago." He underlined the unnecessary words with a sweeping and equally superfluous gesture. Every square inch of the immense fortress-cum-temple within which they stood shouted that the structure had already been a long-abandoned ruin on the day Johann Sebastian Bach died.

From their vantage point on one of its flat rooftops, they could see Lo itself laid out below them in the merciless sunlight of a cloudless December afternoon, a collection of flat-roofed, log-laddered earthen dwellings at the base of the hill on which this crumbling castle of Kechar Dzong stood. Even by Fourth World standards, the Kingdom of Lo was unimpressive. The land was parched, supporting nothing higher than thornbushes; a few carefully nurtured stands of poplar and willow saplings were to be found in the village itself, but wood had been too precious to burn here for centuries. The brief growing season was over, and even the Himalayan vista in the distance could not overcome the bleakness and desolation of the landscape. The kingdom was permitted to exist, semiautonomously with its own king and queen, within the larger kingdom of Nepal—largely because there was nothing here worth arguing over.

"What happened?" Gunter asked, not because he wanted to know, but because he wanted to hear the old monk say something he didn't know already.

"Calamity. The Kali Gandaki moved."

"I hate when that happens."

The old man actually seemed to catch the sarcasm. "The Kali Gandaki was the river from which the strength of Kechar Dzong flowed. It once passed by right there—" He indicated a vague gully meandering through a section of rocky outcroppings no more or less desolate than any other, a few hundred meters downslope. "But when it changed its location at the end of the sixteenth century . . ."

Gunter understood now, and his anger deepened. "And ever since, you have been praying for its return—"

"—in the Tiji ceremony, the elaborate and beautiful ritual I told you of earlier, yes," the old monk agreed happily. "Dorje Jono, the son of the demon who moved the river, repels his father with the power of his magical dancing, and brings water back to the land. The Tiji ceremony takes three full days, and involves every member of the kingdom who is well enough to travel. We summon them with the two mountain horns I showed you downstairs, each of them four meters long. For three days Lo becomes the most magical place in the Himalayas, with *damyin* music and feasting and dancing and singing and beautiful costumes and pageantry and—"

"In *May*," Gunter said through his teeth.

His rhapsody interrupted, the old man blinked at the venom in Gunter's tone. "Well, yes, as I said, that is when foreigners usually visit us. We seldom see a European this late in the year."

"Really?" Gunter said, pulling his parka tighter at his throat against the sharp and icy wind. He mentally replayed the conversation with his travel agent, realizing in hindsight that while the man had waxed eloquent about the Tiji festival, he had never specifically said when it was held. He had only seemed to suggest, somehow, that Gunter barely had time to book his passage if he wanted to be there in time. The trip here had been quite arduous.

The last fifty kilometers had been accomplished on horseback, following a guide with whom Gunter had no languages in common. *So I can't sue the bastard, and killing him is too good for him. Ah, but what about torture?*

From somewhere in the far distance to the north came the half-mournful, half-comic sound of a Tibetan mountain horn like the two Gunter had been shown downstairs, a sustained baritone bleat that made him think of a brontosaur dying in agony. It made the mountains ring with echoes. "What's that?" he asked idly. "Call to prayer? Some sort of religious ceremony in another temple?" Perhaps this trip need not be a total loss. Exotic religions were a hobby of Gunter's; having had his mouth set for a grand festive colorful Buddhist ceremony, he was now prepared to settle for the local equivalent of Vespers, rather than go home empty-handed.

But the old man was shaking his head. "I have no idea."

For some reason, this irritated Gunter. "Well, who lives up that way, then?"

The old man looked sore puzzled. "Hardly anyone. There is an old hermit who lives in that general direction . . . and I know he has such a horn, because I have seen it outside his home. But I have never heard him blow it—if indeed that is his horn."

Gunter lost his manners. He had wasted a week and a fortune to see something exotic, and now he was freezing his buns off in a crumbled ruin—an *empty* crumbled ruin—that would be deserted for the next six months, with a canny native guide—clearly one of the oldest inhabitants of the area—who could not even tell him the significance of a simple mountain horn signal. "Perhaps it is Charlie Parker," he snarled, "practicing in secret until the day when Kansas City needs him again!"

He did not expect the monk to get the reference, of course—but the gesture the old man made indicated that he had not even heard the remark. The wind had redoubled in fierceness and volume. "Never mind!" he said, louder, and could not even hear himself this time. Again the monk pantomimed, *Excuse me?* Gunter's temper boiled over; he waved his arms angrily, gave a wordless shout of exasperation, and set off toward Lo, below. He deliberately left the ancient ruin by a different exit than the one by which he and the monk had entered, one which was more difficult to negotiate, and once he had reached the ground he continued at a pace which he knew the old man would be unable to match. He had forgotten how difficult the climb up had been.

Within a few hundred meters, he was breathing hard. It occurred to him suddenly, as he was negotiating a two-meter drop-off, that in his irritation he was about to leave here *completely* empty-handed. He stopped and took his camera from his shirt pocket. At least he could get some good shots of the ruined temple itself. He had purchased enough memory for five straight days of shooting; might as well get a few minutes. He turned and grunted with satisfaction: the decaying temple really did look striking against the sky. It somehow gave Gunter the impression of a fortress built to defend men against the gods. Unsuccessfully. He backed off a few steps for a better angle, and checked the camera's charge. To avoid wasting power, he disabled the audio pickup. The wind was really roaring now, and he could overdub the audio later, with something suitably timeless and melancholy.

He peered through the viewfinder and panned across the face of the ruin, left to right and then back again. He did not see the old monk anywhere, and wondered if he were still within the walls, paralyzed by Gunter's rudeness. Then he did see him—and sure enough, he was standing in the same window they had both been looking out from, minutes earlier. He appeared to be doing jumping jacks.

Gunter grunted in surprise, and zoomed in. No, the old man was hopping up and down and flapping his arms, but not in any organized fashion. He seemed to be waving at Gunter. Gunter zoomed in farther, and became even more puzzled. The old man appeared to be laughing like a loon. And he was pointing now, pointing to the north. Was he trying to say something about that silly horn blast? In sign language, at this distance? Gunter waved back with his free hand, signing, *forget it.* This seemed to convulse the aged monk; he held his ribs and roared with silent laughter.

Gunter had heard of this: Himalayans were known to go into spontaneous laughing jags, due to the low oxygen content at this height. He found it annoying: here he was trying to get an imposing shot of this ancient temple, and its caretaker was capering like an ape in the foreground. *Go away,* he gestured. *Get out of the window!*

The monk nodded at once, still laughing merrily, and vanished from the window. Gunter kept shooting. Now the wind began to devil him, increasing its force until it was tugging at his clothes, pressing at him like a Tokyo commuter, hammering at his eardrums. The camera was just big enough to present sail-area to it; the wind kept trying to force it to the right. Gunter had image-stabilization circuitry, but knew that this much wavering was taxing it. He twisted slightly to his right to put his back toward the wind, shielding the camera with his hunched left shoulder. The wind pressed especially hard at his ankles, for some reason, and his feet began to feel chilly. *Oh fine,* he thought, *defective boots on top of everything else. I am definitely going to sue* somebody *when I get home!*

But almost as he finished the thought, he realized that his feet were actually *cold,* colder than they should have been even if the boots' heating systems had both failed completely. He glanced down, and discovered that he was standing ankle deep in crystal clear water. It rose as he watched, climbing his shins.

He looked to the north, and saw the Kali Gandaki river returning, after five centuries, dividing around his feet. Now his ear could distinguish between the sound of its passage and the similar sound of the wind. For no reason at all he remembered the damned travel agent saying that the Tiji festival was also known as the Festival of Impermanence.

From above him, in the temple, came the continuous *BBBR-RRRRAATTTTTTTT!* of a mountain horn, cutting cleanly through the wind and water noise to alert the village below, and this horn sounded to Gunter more like a brontosaur laughing. . . .

PART FIVE

13

The Shimizu Hotel
18 January 2065

Rhea was drifting helplessly in deep space, her air supply almost gone, her thrusters dry, gasping for air that wasn't there, when windchimes sounded in the distance. She sighed, came back to reality, saved her changes, folded the typewriter and tucked it in her pocket, and went to answer the door.

It was Duncan, of course—the only person besides Rand, Colly and Jay for whom the doorbell would function while she was working. "Is Colly ready?" he asked.

His eyes seemed to ask several other things, and Rhea sighed again. *I wonder what my eyes are answering,* came the sudden thought. "Come in," she said, and looked away. "Max, please tell Colly Duncan is here."

"Beg pardon?" the AI said.

"Sorry. Tell Colly *that* Duncan is here." Rhea hated making syntax errors; it was professionally embarrassing.

After a pause, her AI said, "Colly says to tell you she's changing clothes and will be with you in two seconds."

They looked at each other. "Five minutes," they chorused together, and shared a grin.

Almost at once something about that trivial event bothered Rhea. It was a domestic little moment, something she and Rand might have shared, a small intimacy. Rand had in fact been doing his best to generate such moments, lately—probably because the deadline for her Big Decision was approaching. That underlying awareness had been making the return grins she gave her husband slightly forced. The grin she had just given Duncan was quite genuine. She realized she was drifting just perceptibly toward him, and overcorrected. "Come on in," she said to cover it. "You know where everything is."

"Are you working?" he asked, entering the suite.

She hesitated. The question meant, do you want to be left alone? Duncan was very understanding of a writer's problems; if she said yes, she would cease to exist for him. "No," she decided. "Can I get you anything? There's time for coffee."

"No, thanks," he said. "How's the work coming?"

"Not bad, thanks to you. I really struck ice with Buchi Tenmo."

He grinned again at the spacer expression. Spacers didn't give a damn for gold or diamonds or oil: for them a new source of potable water was real wealth. She had picked up the idiom from him—and it seemed to please him that she had. "Yeah, she's pretty amazing . . . when you can tell what the hell she's talking about."

"Yes, there is that. It's like talking to an angel on psychedelics sometimes. Would you mind sitting in on the conversation once or twice? You've been talking with Stardancers a lot longer than I have."

"Sure—but don't expect that to help much. Buchi's just *different.* Even for a Stardancer. The ones born that way, who've never breathed, are the weirdest . . . but the most interesting too, I think."

A week ago, Rhea had asked Duncan how one got to know a Stardancer. She knew it could be done simply and easily, even from the surface of Terra—but how did one scrape up an acquaintance? It turned out Duncan was friendly with several Stardancers. Most spacers were. And one of his personal friends among *Homo caelestis* happened to be physically located near enough to the Shimizu to allow for something very like a face-to-face meeting . . . through Rhea's own window. Duncan had made the introduction a few days earlier, then politely left them alone. "When would be good for you in the next few days?"

"Any time; when's good for you?"

She thought about it—and suddenly realized that the search criterion with which she was examining her calendar was "times when Rand and Colly won't be around." That made perfect sense: the conversation would be confusing enough without distraction. Nonetheless it struck her all at once that she was making a date to be alone—or almost alone—with a handsome young man. One who, if she wasn't misreading signals, was interested in her.

It's for work, *for heaven's sake!*

Yes . . . but is it prudent?

Oh, shut up. "How about tomorrow night, after twenty?"

He nodded. "Program loaded."

There was a brief silence. Rhea felt compelled to break it. "So how are things with you?"

"Pretty good, actually. I made another piece last night, and it turned out well."

Duncan's hobby was vacuum-sculpture. To Rhea the artform seemed to consist of assembling ingredients in various combinations, exposing them suddenly to vacuum, and then taking credit for the weird and beautiful shapes chemistry caused to occur. But vacuum-sculpture could be very beautiful—and she had to admit that Duncan seemed to produce aesthetically pleasing results more often than chance could account for. Didn't photographers throw out twenty prints and take credit for the perfect twenty-first? Come to think of it, wasn't her own storage cluttered with drafts that hadn't quite gelled?

"I'd like to see it," she said politely.

"No problem. We'll talk to Buchi from my place, then."

She opened her mouth . . . and then closed it firmly. He was pointedly not looking in her direction.

"I thought I'd take Colly to the pool again," he went on.

Rhea laughed. "You think you have a choice, huh?" The laugh sounded too loud in her ears. "She's a born water baby. You couldn't keep her out of the surf, back ho— . . . back in Provincetown. You know, I've always thought it's ironic. As far back as history goes, the Paixaos have made their living on and from the sea—and my mother was the first one in the family that ever learned to swim. How could you spend all that time on the water and not know how to swim? Weren't they scared?"

Duncan shrugged. "I've lived all my life in space—and I don't know how to breathe vacuum."

"But that's not possible—and it is possible to learn to swim, and it doesn't even take much time."

"Look at it from your greatest grandfather Henry's perspective," he said. "Suppose you're off the Grand Banks and the ship sinks. How much good does it do you to know how to swim?"

It occurred to Rhea that Duncan knew a lot more about her family than she knew about his. She was not normally so forthcoming; had he been making an effort to draw her out? She reviewed memory tape, and could not decide. "I guess. It still seems odd. Maybe we should ask Buchi to teach you how to breathe vacuum."

And now I've drawn the conversation back to our rendezvous. . . .

Colly appeared just then. How she could have spent five minutes dressing was something of a mystery, for she was dressed for the pool, in the ubiquitous guest robe and nothing else. Since so many nationalities and cultures mingled in the Shimizu, all guests conformed to a minimal nudity taboo in politeness to the less civilized nations; one did not jaunt down public corridors naked. But a guest robe was sufficient, and even those could be dispensed with once one reached the pool—or any other nonpublic location. "Hi, Duncan! Come on, let's go!"

"Sorry to hold you up," he said sarcastically, and made way so Colly could hug her mother goodbye.

As Rhea handed the child off to Duncan, their hands brushed briefly. Rhea had gotten used to casual touching in space, even from strangers; free-fall made it necessary in close quarters. But this touch she felt from her scalp to the soles of her feet. It seemed to her that he made it linger.

She was glad then for Colly's eagerness to be in the water; the two headed for the door before the blush reached her cheeks.

I should have said yes when he asked if I was working.

In fact, she *should* be working. She took her keyboard from her pocket and unfolded it. Work would be a wonderful distraction from the trend her thoughts were taking.

Almost at once she found another distraction. The virtual screen that sprang into existence over the keyboard was preset to display her calendar as its boot document, so she wouldn't start sinking into the warm fog if there was some imminent obligation scheduled. It showed the next thirty days, and the box for 5 February was highlighted—it leaped out of the screen at her, as it had been doing ever since she had highlighted it.

I have two more weeks to make up my mind whether I'm going to stay here, was what she had thought when she first started work that morning. Now, perhaps because of what had just transpired, it came out, *I have two more weeks to make up my mind whether I'm going to stay married to Rand.*

She entered her date with Duncan into the calendar, put the typewriter away again, and went to the window. She watched the majestically turning Earth for a measureless time, trying to put names on her feelings, and failing. They would not hold still long enough.

Finally she looked around her, as if to make sure she was alone . . . and checked her watch to make sure Rand was not due home . . . and spoke to her AI. "Maxwell: window program 'Home.' "

"Yes, Rhea."

Terra went away, and was replaced by Provincetown.

She was back in her own writing room in her own home, looking out of the turret through her favorite window, hearing the sounds of the street below, hearing the gulls and the distant surf, seeing Mrs. Vasques, her neighbor, haranguing yet another motorist who had clipped her fence in trying to negotiate the insanely narrow street. The illusion was nearly perfect—except for the same flaw it had had weeks ago, when Rand had first sprung it on her. This time, she was able to identify the flaw. *This Provincetown didn't smell.* There was no salt tang in the air—none of that rich aroma that the landsman calls the smell of the sea and the sailor calls the smell of the land, the shore smell of decaying vegetation and sea creatures at the border between two incompossible worlds.

Maybe I could get a steward to bring me some fish leftovers, she thought, and began to cry. Fetal position is hard to achieve in free-fall, but she managed it.

She never did get back to work that afternoon. But she did manage to stop crying an hour before Duncan was due to bring Colly home for supper, so that her eyes wouldn't be red when they arrived.

Rand showed up just as they did. He had been making a major effort to eat most meals with his family these days. For some reason, his arrival relieved her. Duncan declined an invitation to join them for dinner, and that relieved her too. During the meal she found herself paying more attention than usual to her husband, asking questions about his work and listening attentively to the answers, making little excuses to touch him. Before she knew it they had made a nonverbal contract, entirely by eye contact, to make love when he got home again that night. He went off to Jay's place whistling.

She managed to get a little work done after supper, while Colly was off playing with a friend. She didn't understand where the story was going, but it wouldn't let her alone; its disturbing central image—adrift, running out of air, no direction home—had been recurring in her thoughts for weeks now. The question was, of course, *who* was adrift, and why? She had no clear idea as yet, but she knew if she kept playing with the situation it would come out of her eventually.

As she was putting Colly to bed that night, she said, "So—was it fun playing with Jason, honey?"

"He's okay, I guess," Colly said. "For a boy, anyway. At least he's gonna be here a whole two weeks." For Colly, the biggest flaw in the Shimizu's accommodations was its criminally inadequate and excessively fluctuating supply of eight-year-olds. Children of transient guests rarely remained aboard more than a few days; permanent guests tended not to have small children, and by evil luck all the spacer children of hotel staff were either over ten or under six—less use than a grown-up. Colly still had all of her phone friends, of course, and her Provincetown chums were all phone friends too, now . . . but she was chronically short of playmates she could smell and touch.

"Oh, that'll be fun," Rhea said.

"I guess." Suddenly Colly looked stricken. "Hey, Mom?"

"Yes, dear?"

"I just thought of something. My birthday comes in two and a half weeks, right?"

Rhea did mental arithmetic. "That's right, honey. Why?"

Colly sat up on one elbow. *"How am I gonna have a party?"*

Rhea started to answer, and stopped.

"You can't have a birthday party on the *phone,"* Colly said. "And all my friends are back on Earth! I'm not gonna get to have a real party, am I?" Her voice was rising in alarm.

"Uh . . . sure you will, honey. There'll be kids aboard then, I'm sure there will. One or two, anyw—"

"But I won't *know* them," Colly insisted. "What good is a party with people you don't even know?" She started to snuffle.

Rhea was tempted to join her. Instead she took Colly in her arms and rocked her. "Don't cry, baby. It won't be so bad. All your friends can be there on the phone—no, you know what? I'll tell you what: we'll get Daddy to merge all the phone signals into his shaping stuff, and your friends can be here almost like real, holographically, walking around and everything." As she spoke, Rhea was estimating the cost of such an event: assuming Rand had time for this, and valuing his time at zero, it came to roughly the price of two luxury automobiles back on Terra. They could afford it, now—but still . . .

Colly considered the offer for a moment, then resumed snuffling, softer than before. "That'd be better . . . but you can't tickle a holo, Mom. You can't throw pieces of birthday cake at a holo."

"Sure you can—only it's even better, because nobody really gets messy. You wait and see: it'll be fun."

Colly was dubious, but after ten minutes of rocking and cuddling and soothing she allowed herself to be mollified, and went to sleep. Rhea left her bedroom exhausted and heartsick. Colly was right: a birthday party aboard the Shimizu probably wasn't going to be much fun.

Less than a minute later, Rand arrived home, shiny-eyed and eager to make love.

Since adolescence Rhea had known that a contract with a man to have sex at an appointed time *must* be honored, if at all possible. Feeling martyred, she pasted a smile on her face and cooperated. But she made a mental note to discuss Colly's birthday party with him as soon as they were done; she was not a hundred percent sure the consolation prize she had promised her daughter was technically feasible.

It was just as he was entering her that it dawned on her that the question might be moot: their child's birthday came *after* the date on which she was to give Rand her final decision. . . .

It was not a terribly erotic train of thought. The act was technically successful for both of them, for they had been married for a long time—but for the same reason, Rand asked, "Want to talk about it?" when their breathing had slowed.

She burst into tears. "I don't even want to *think* about it."

He held her close, but said nothing. He knew, in general, what was on her mind—and knew that she knew he knew. What was there for either of them to say?

What could Donny Handsome have said to Patty?

She untucked her chin from his neck and pushed at him with her hands; he rose far enough on his elbows so that she could see his face. She looked at it a long time . . . not just the eyes or the mouth, but the whole face. He waited. "You're staying?" she said finally.

His face went blank. He was silent an equal time. She waited.

"Yes."

She nodded, and pulled him back down to her. They lay there together in silence, breathing in the same rhythm and thinking the same thought.

What did that nod mean?

Twice, she felt him start to ask her. Each time he changed his mind. She couldn't blame him—but part of her wished he had asked. If he had, perhaps an answer would have come to her.

She forgot to ask him about Colly's birthday party that night.

Rhea knew that a real window like the one in her suite was supposed to be much better than a fake one—she knew, to the yen, how much more the former cost. But she was a shaper's wife: to her Duncan's fake window was just as good. Better, for she could shift to a view in any direction at all simply by touching a control. Somehow it felt more correct to talk with a Stardancer *without* Earth in the background, overshadowing everything.

And Buchi Tenmo did not appear to mind talking to a camera rather than a person in a window. She did not need to see Rhea; she already had. She must be used to talking with Duncan this way too.

Insofar as she was used to talking at all. So far Rhea had found it always took the first few minutes of the conversation for Buchi to become even partly comprehensible. That did not surprise Rhea. To temporarily "place on hold" an ongoing conversation with millions of others, and funnel consciousness down to only one or two non-telepathic minds must be a disorienting experience—especially for a spaceborn Stardancer, who had never been such a limited being herself. The wonder was that the trick was possible.

And already Buchi was winding down, only minutes in. She had progressed from incomprehensible polyglot babble to a lock on

English—of a sort. Any minute now it would start conveying information.

"*—as the world whirls around peg in a square holy cowhide it from yourself-esteem cleaning up your action figures it would be that's entertainment to tell you but I forgot is a concept by which we measure painting the town read all of your books now, Rhea, and they're very beautiful . . . the gostak distims the doshes . . . eftsoons, and right speedily . . . don't blame him for not being careful in the beginning . . . a straight hook basically seeks fish who turn away from life . . . there: subject, object, predicate . . . am I getting there, Rhea? Duncan? Can I hear you, now? Are we having fun yet?*"

"You're getting there," Rhea agreed. Things always improved dramatically, she had found, once Buchi reinvented the sentence. She found herself asking the question she had suppressed during her previous encounters with the Stardancer. "Buchi? Does it hurt? Doing this, I mean, talking with us—is it hard?"

"It's fun!" For that moment Buchi sounded remarkably like Colly. *"Is it hard to talk with me?"*

"A little," Rhea admitted. "But you're right, it's fun. But then, I'm only doing what I do all the time: talking, in my own language. You're doing all the work."

"*By 'work' I understand you in this context to mean 'energy expenditure regretted or begrudged.' By that definition I have never worked in my life. Although I'm always busy.*"

"I wish I could say the same." A light dawned somewhere in the back of Rhea's head. "But you've put your finger on something, Buchi. I've been thinking about our conversations, and why they haven't satisfied me, and I think you just gave me a handle on my problem."

"*Problems are better with handles on them?*"

"For me they are. Looking back over it, everything I've been asking you has been about . . . has had to do with things that a human supposes would be disadvantages of being a Stardancer. The bad parts. I've been asking you about the bad parts—and for each one I come up with, you explain how it's not a bad part. Some of the explanations I just flat don't understand—"

"I always have trouble conveying the idea of self generated reality," Buchi agreed. *"To a human it seems a flat contradiction in terms."*

Rhea had asked in her first conversation whether Buchi ever missed being able to "really" walk the surface of a planet, as opposed to "merely" reexperiencing it through the memories of those Stardancers who had lived on Earth before joining the Starmind. Communication had broken down when Buchi insisted that she could, really, walk on Terra any time she wanted—that she could "really" experience things she had never personally experienced—knowing the difference, but unbothered by it. Rhea, who had never confused even the best virtual-reality environments with real-reality, was baffled by this. She had spent most of her own professional life battering at the interface between almost-real and real, trying to make words on a screen sound and smell. She had to tiptoe around the thought that anyone for whom reality and imagination were interchangeable was someone who was not quite sane.

"—but that's not the problem," she went on, but Duncan interrupted her.

"It's like this window, Rhea," he said, touching her wrist and pointing.

"Huh?"

"You know that to most of the people in this hotel, this window we're looking out right now isn't as good as the one you have back in your suite. God knows it costs a lot less. But we've talked about it, so I know you agree with me that this one is actually better. It may not be 'real'—but it can look in any direction you want, or show you anything you want to see, flatscreen anyway. I know yours can do even better, the way Rand has it tricked out now . . . but most people who pay a premium for one of those windows do it so they can tell themselves that what they're looking at is 'real.' They care a lot about 'real.' You and I care a little less. Buchi cares not at all. Think of it as a spectrum rather than a discontinuity."

Rhea looked at him, surprised and a little impressed by his insight. "I think I see what you mean," she said.

He flushed and went on. "With total control of her brain and body, reality can mean whatever she wants it to mean. She can *experience* the touch of someone half a light year away, feel it on her skin. Or feel the touch of someone long dead . . . as long as someone in the Starmind holds the memory of how it feels to be touched by that person. Not one coffee molecule has ever passed her lips her whole life long, but she's probably tasted better coffee than you or I ever will."

"I'm doing it now! 'Bean around the Solar System . . .' " Buchi let the song parody trail off after a few more hummed bars.

"But with reality that slippery . . ." Rhea began.

Duncan interrupted. " . . . how do they make sure they don't lose track of the one you and I believe in? What do they do for a reality check, you mean?"

"Yeah, I guess that's what I mean."

"We are many," Buchi said. *"And we are one.* E pluribus unum. *Alone/All-one. Consensus reality is very important to us. If we ever lost it, we would come apart. It is the same with your own neurons. We put about as much effort into it as they do. And about as often, we fire randomly—we make things up, we vacation in realities of our own fashioning, singly or in groups. The universe is always there when we return. It is not a problem."*

"Now *there,*" Rhea said triumphantly, "is *my* problem. As I started to say before, I can live with the fact that I have trouble grasping your explanations of why assorted aspects of being a Stardancer aren't problems for you. What's driving me crazy is that you just . . . don't seem to *have* any problems!

"None of the ones I envisioned. None of them has even triggered mention of any problem you do have. I'm a writer: to me a character *is* his or her problems; if they don't have any, they're no use to me, I've got nothing to work with, no way to motivate them. I guess what I'm asking is, don't you people—you Stardancers—have any problems? I know you never get hungry or thirsty or cold or lonely or lost or have to go to the bathroom at an inappropriate time. But Jesus, Buchi—isn't there *anything* you fear? Or miss? Or yearn for? Or regret? Is there anything you lust after? Or mourn?"

"Must your characters always be driven by the lash?"

Rhea thought about it. "Pretty much, yes. That's what the audience wants to see. How someone like itself reacts under the lash. Because it helps the reader guess and deal with how she would react under the same pressure. The rule of thumb is, the sharper the lash—the tougher the antinomy—the better the story. For us humans, life is suffering, just as the Buddhists say. Is that really not true for you?"

The answer was almost a full minute in coming. It was the first time Rhea could remember Buchi hesitating even slightly in responding. Two or three times she began to speak, but each time decided to wait for an answer.

"The Starmind suffers," Buchi said at last, *"as sharply, as deeply, as keenly, as you yourself. But in different ways . . . for different reasons . . . and I cannot explain them to you. No terrestrial language contains words that will convey the necessary concepts: you do not have the concepts. Every human language contains the implicit assumption that individual minds have bone walls around them. It would be* much *easier for me to convey color to a blind man."*

Rhea was frustrated . . . but if there was anything her work had prepared her to believe, it was that some things simply could not be put into words. "What are you all *doing*?"

"*What are you asking?*"

"What is the Starmind doing? Are you doing *anything*? Did those Fireflies have any *purpose* in creating your kind? Are you all working toward something together . . . or just floating around like the red blobs in a lava lamp, marveling at the Solar System and unscrewing the inscrutable?"

"You know hundreds of things we do. I can download a summary list to your AI *if you wish. It runs about a terabyte."*

"Then I've seen most of it. Well, scanned it." Even that was an absurd claim. "All right, I've scanned the superindex, tiptoed through some of the subindices, and jumped in at random here and there a few hundred places. And one thing I noticed."

"*Yes?*"

"Most of the things you do come down, in the long run, to helping *us.* Helping humans. Helping Terra. Some of it benefits us directly, like nanotechnology, and some it just seems to happen to work out to our benefit way down the line, like that Belt-map hobby of yours that kept us from getting clobbered by Lucifer's Hammer in '32. Even the 'pure-science' researches you're engaged in always seem to benefit us more than they benefit you, when the dust settles."

"Can we ignore suffering at our own heart, at our roots? We may not be of *humanity . . . but we are* from *humanity."*

"I'm not complaining. I'm just asking: is that what you Stardancers do for problems? Borrow ours?" She had an image of the human race as endearingly dopey pets, who could be relied upon to produce fascinating but trivial problems, supply life's necessary irritant.

"If some cosmic disaster wiped us all out . . . would the Starmind go crazy from boredom? Or would you still have things to *do?*"

Another pause. This one was only ten seconds or so. *"We would still have a nearly infinite number of things to do. And again, I despair of finding words that will successfully hint at their nature."* Another five seconds. *"One subset may perhaps be intelligibly outlined, at least. You are aware, are you not, that the Starmind is not alone in the Universe?"*

"Huh? Sure. So what?" It was a classic insoluble problem. Within a few years of its initial formation, the Starmind had reported to humanity that it was receiving telepathic broadcasts from numberless other Starminds throughout the Galaxy and Magellanic Clouds—a potential source of inconceivable wealth in any terms. But it came in *all at once*, at the same "volume," from all quarters—and none of it appeared to be in any known or decipherable language or concept-system. The Starmind did not even know how to say, "Quiet, please—one at a time!" The best it had managed, according to all reports, was to learn to ignore the useless infinity of treasure, as a geiger counter suppresses its "awareness" of normal background radiation. "What good does that do you if you can't *communicate* with anybody?" Rhea asked. "You can't, right?" She knew the answer—but from books and media accounts, and knew how much that was worth.

"No, we cannot," Buchi agreed. *"But that may not always be so."*

"You think the problem might actually be solvable?" Duncan said excitedly.

"Our seed has been awake for less than seven decades," Buchi said. *"There are yet far fewer of us Stardancers than there are neurons in even the most limited brain. Yet our numbers grow—and the Starmind grows wiser every nanosecond. It is certain that we live longer than you, and we do not waste a third of our lives in stupor and another third working at life-support. We have time. Time has us. We use tools you cannot understand to build tools you cannot conceive to solve problems we ourselves cannot name. It is not a thing to trouble yourself over."*

"Do you know anything at all about where it's all going?" Rhea asked. "That you can explain?"

"Yes. Wonderful *things are going to happen."*

Rhea blinked. "But *what*?"

The silence went on until she realized no answer would be forthcoming. "When?" she tried then.

That answer came at once, startling her.

"Soon."

"*How* soon?" she blurted.

Again, silent seconds ticked by.

"Within my lifetime?" she tried.

"I cannot be certain, but I believe so."

"Will you be able to explain these things to us humans when they happen?"

"When they happen, you will know."

"And you can't give me any idea what it will be like?"

More silence.

"Why doesn't anybody else know about this?" Rhea said irritably. "I've read—scanned—everything I could get my hands on about you Stardancers. This is the first hint I've heard that the galactic signal-to-noise problem might be susceptible of solution. Is it a secret, or what?"

"Would I have burdened you with a secret without warning you? The reason you have not heard of this before is that you are the first to have asked about this in many decades, the first since we began to be sure of it ourselves."

"Really?" Rhea asked. "That's hard to believe."

"Yes, isn't it? Rhea, answer me two questions. First, regarding the Fireflies, who made us: is there any characteristic commonly associated with the term 'gods' that they lack?"

Rhea thought hard. Apparently omniscient, apparently omnipotent, apparently benevolent but absolutely unknowable . . . long gone and not expected back soon . . . "No," she admitted. "Wait: two. They seem to have no desire at all to be worshipped . . . and they haven't instructed anyone to kill anyone else in their name."

"You anticipate my second question: do you know of any religion on or off Terra which worships them?"

It startled her. "Why, no. There are cults who worship *you* . . . at least one large one. And up until forty-odd years ago there was a small one trying to kill you. But I don't know of any Firefly-worshippers, now that you mention it."

"Rhea, humanity can just barely live with the mere memory *of the Fireflies. They are too vast to think about. From the human point of view, the best thing about them is that they were in the vicinity of Terra for a matter of hours, at the orbit of Saturn for a matter of*

months, and left promising my father not to return for a matter of centuries. We Stardancers are tolerated, for all our alienness, because we were once and still partially are human. Beneath my Symbiote are flesh and blood, born of woman. But of all the things we are asked—and we are asked many things by many humans—we are rarely asked about the Fireflies . . . and almost never *about* other *Starminds, circling other stars. Your governments and philosophers were overjoyed to learn that the galactic surround is incomprehensible to us, and have been happy to tiptoe around the sleeping dragon ever since."*

"If that's true, I'm pretty disgusted with my own species," Rhea said.

"You need not be. Think of it from a historical perspective. After two millions of years of slaughter, humanity has just *learned how to live with itself in peace, and has done so for a time measured in mere years. Can you reasonably expect it to be prepared to deal with a* galaxy *of unknown strangers? So quickly? I can tell you that* we the *Starmind tremble at the thought of the Fireflies returning—and we could at least talk with them if they did. Why should you not 'pretend it never happened'? It seems to me a healthy psychological adjustment for your race at this time."*

Rhea started to reply, but Duncan interrupted her again. "Excuse me, Buchi—I want to backtrack a second. Did you say when the Fireflies left, they made a promise to 'your *father*'?"

"Yes."

That had caught Rhea's ear too. "Who is your father, Buchi?" she asked.

"Charlie Armstead."

Rhea's eyes widened. "And your mother?" she managed to ask.

"Norrey Drummond."

She heard a singing in her ears, like a Provincetown mosquito. The second and third Stardancers who had ever lived, founders of Stardancers Incorporated, as famous throughout even the human race as Shara Drummond herself! "My God! I never dreamed—"

"Me either," Duncan said in awed tones. "You never told me that, Booch."

"You never asked. What's your *father's name, and why haven't you told me?"*

"It's 'Walter.' But you're right. His name only comes up if someone finds *my* name funny and I have to explain the story."

"I saw the humor in your name the moment you told it to me," Buchi said. *"But I assumed you were tired of explaining its origin, so I did not comment."*

"And bless you," he said. "It's just that I keep forgetting you folks don't use last names to indicate either paternal *or* maternal descent."

"There is no need to. We know *our lineage, and each of the other's—it need not be encoded in our names. We choose names purely for their meanings."*

The humming in Rhea's ears was beginning to diminish. "What does your name mean, Buchi Tenmo?" Rhea asked.

"*'Dancing Wisdom Celestial Net,'*" the Stardancer answered.

"That's beautiful!" Duncan said . . . an instant before Rhea could. "I wish I had a name that good." He turned to Rhea. "Or like yours. 'Rhea'—'earth' or 'mother,' two of the most beautiful words there are. And 'Paixao,' just as beautiful: 'passion.'"

The mosquitos resumed their attack on Rhea's ears. She could feel the lobes turning red, offering blood. "What does *your* name mean?" she asked quickly, aware of the significance of his having looked up the meaning of her name, but unwilling to acknowledge it.

He made a face. "I got the booby-prize. 'Duncan' means 'dark-skinned warrior' "—Rhea found herself thinking that he was dark-skinned even by Provincetown standards, though he certainly wasn't *muscled* like a warrior . . . and forced herself to pay attention to what he was saying—"and 'Iowa' . . . well, there's the political district in the North American Federation, of course, the province or state or whatever . . . and at least one writer once confused that with Heaven. But actually it comes from 'Ioakim'—apparently an official at someplace called Ellis Island made Greatest Grandad change it. It's Russian Hebrew for 'God will establish' . . . which I for one find wishful thinking."

Rhea found that she wanted to change the subject from Duncan's name, from Duncan, and suddenly remembered a question that had ghosted through her mind perhaps a dozen times over the course of her life. "The word 'God' makes me think of Fireflies again," she said. "Buchi, there's one more question I've always wondered about. Why did the Fireflies come when they did?"

"They came when it was time."

"Yes—but why was it time? The generally accepted answer is that they came 'at the dawn of space travel.' But it was more like brunchtime. Humanity had been in space—had been established in space—for years when they showed up. We'd been to Luna decades before. Did it take them that long to notice? Or that long to arrive? If we could establish a time-duration for their journey, it might be a clue to where they came from."

"Their arrival was instantaneous," Buchi said flatly.

"Then what triggered it? Do you know?"

"The signing of a contract. An agreement between Skyfac Incorporated and Shara Drummond."

Details from a history lesson came back dimly to Rhea. Sure enough, the way she remembered it, the Fireflies had first been sighted in the Solar System about two weeks before Shara Drummond left Earth to create the Stardance. They had flicked into existence around the orbits of Neptune and Pluto (at that time very close together), the outer limit of the System, and then moved in as far as the orbit of Saturn a couple of weeks later . . .

. . . the day Shara reached Skyfac! Where they stayed, until she was on the verge of being sent home again with her dream unfulfilled—then arrived just in time to force the performance of the Stardance . . .

"They came to us the moment that a human being came to space for the express purpose of creating art," Buchi said.

The words seemed to echo in Rhea's skull.

"How they knew of that, even the Starmind cannot yet imagine—but the fact is unmistakable."

She felt as if her head were cracking. The insight was too immense and powerful to deal with—yet so obvious she could hardly believe no one had worked it out ages ago.

"Thank you, Buchi," she said quickly. "You've been very gracious and helpful, we'll talk again another time, I hope you'll excuse me now but I need to get to my typewriter so I can—" She stopped babbling when she noticed that she had already switched off the window.

She turned from it, and there was Duncan.

At once he turned away, which relieved and annoyed her at the same time, and jaunted across the room . . . but in seconds he was back, bearing a strange and uncouth object, waving it at her as he braked himself to a halt at her side. "I promised I'd show you this, Rhea," he said.

It was his manner more than anything else which cued her. This had to be the new piece of vacuum sculpture he had mentioned. Resolving to find something polite to say about it, she began to scrutinize it for material to work with.

A timeless time later, she began to experience perceptual distortion, and slowly figured out the cause. Her eyes were beginning to grow tearbubbles. . . .

What it was made of she could not guess. The subtleties of its composition process were a closed book to her. But what it looked like, to her, more than anything else she could think of, was a piece of driftwood she had once brought home from the Provincetown shore. It had a similar shape, twisted on itself, asymmetrically beautiful, and it had the stark bleached color and polished appearance of very old driftwood. Washed up on an alien shore . . . like herself.

"It's very beautiful," she said, and heard a husky note in her voice. She searched for polite small talk. "Does it . . . do your pieces have names?"

"It's called 'Driftglass,' " he said. His own voice was hoarse.

She flinched slightly. "It's very lovely. It reminds me—"

"—of home, I know," he said quickly. "It's yours. I made it for you."

The mosquitos at her ears had brought in chainsaws. "I . . . I really have to go," she said. "I promised Rand—" She was already in motion, three of her four thrusters firing at max acceleration, past him before she could see his reaction.

"Sure, of course, good night," she heard him say behind her as the door got out of her way, and as she came out of her turn and raced down the corridor, she was for a time very proud of herself. Until she noticed that she had Driftglass in her hand . . .

And I didn't even thank him.

"You are going too fast," came a voice from all around her. "Please slow down." She flinched, and then realized it was only an AI traffic cop; she was exceeding the local jaunting speed limit. She decelerated at once.

"Thank you," she said. "That is very good advice."

14

Rand had come to feel that his favorite part of the Shimizu was the corridors. They were designed to be visually appealing, padded enough for the most inexpert jaunter, and offered an ever-changing parade of rich and almost-rich people to gawk at. They were the place where one flew, where you could enjoy the sensation of a jaunt that was not over within seconds. Most important to him, they represented the blessed hiatus between the problems of the studio and the problems of the home. They were the equivalent of a solitary drive from office to home back on Terra: the place of unwinding from work, and of winding other mechanisms back up again.

But sooner or later the corridors always led him back to his door. He was coming to think of it as the Place of Sighs; whichever direction he was going, he always seemed to pause just outside the threshold and sigh, first.

He did so now, decided he was ready to enter his home, and thumbed the doorlock.

Before he could enter, something burst from the room and enveloped him. Its first effect was as invigorating as a cool rain on a dry afternoon: his wife's laughter . . .

As a musician he found it one of the Universe's more glorious sounds; as a husband he found it exhilarating. In either capacity, he had been missing it lately. Like an addict following the smell of smoke, he followed it inside, seeking the source.

Rhea was in the living room, a little northeast of the window. She was sitting in the piece of furniture in which she usually did her writing—she moved around as she wrote, and hated the sound of Velcro separating as she did—but her seat belt was not fastened. And she had configured the furniture in the shape which its menu called "love-seat." In its other corner, also unstrapped, was a broadly grinning Duncan Iowa. He had just opened his mouth to say something, to make Rhea laugh again, when he caught sight of Rand in the doorway. "Hello, Rand," he said.

Rhea turned, smiling. "Hi, darling," she said. "You must be exhausted—would you like a drink?"

He controlled a frown. "Why would I be exhausted?"

She looked surprised. "Well . . . the premiere is only a week away, right?"

"Sure—but my part was done yesterday. Jay and the dancers will be killing themselves from here on in, muscle-memorizing it, but I'm just there babysitting the software and looking for holes. I told you that last night."

"Oh. I forgot."

"Never mind." He had been hoping to hear some more of her laughter, and now she wasn't even smiling anymore. *Nice work.* "What were you guys laughing about? I could use a giggle."

She shook her head. "It'd take too long to explain it. Duncan just came up with a neat way to improve some comic business in a story I'm working on."

"Oh. I see." In ten years of marriage, Rhea had never permitted Rand—or anyone—to see or hear about a work-in-progress. It was one of her many writer's superstitions. "A story is like a soufflé," was the line he had heard her tell people a hundred times.

"Where's Colly?"

"Studying." She glanced at her watch. "No, by now the terminal has unlocked, so she's probably playing games or watching a movie."

He nodded. "As long as she's not on the phone again. That kid will talk away our air money one of these days."

"Oh, no, she can't be—I've got the White Rabbit set to warn me if she asks for a phone circuit."

"The which?"

"The White Rabbit," Duncan said. "It's her new name for Harvey. He's still a rabbit, but he's shorter, and dressed like the Tenniel version. You know, the guy who illustrated the original Alice books."

Rand was doubly irritated: that a strange man knew more about his daughter than he did, and that this young lout thought the best damn shaper in human space needed to be told who Tenniel was. But he still had faint hopes of hearing Rhea laugh again sometime tonight, so he pasted a big happy smile on his face. "Ha ha," he said, as if reading the words from a page. "That's cute. Pocket watch and all, eh?" *I know the fucking books, sonny.* "We'd better be careful what she eats and drinks. If she starts to grow, we'll need a bigger suite."

He was rewarded with a grin from his wife. "I don't think there is such a thing. If she does, we'll have to put her in the pool: she can have it all to herself."

"I think Colly would really like that," Duncan said.

"Can you stay for dinner, Duncan?" Rand asked, in the tone of voice that both sounds perfectly sincere and conveys the subtext, *a negative answer is expected.*

The lad was not completely mannerless; he pushed himself away from the love-seat and looked around for anything he might have left. "No, thanks, I have to—"

A braying sound interrupted him, for all the world like a burro's mating call. All three froze.

"FLARE WARNING, CLASS ONE," said a very loud voice. "THIS IS A SAFETY EMERGENCY. ALL GUESTS MUST GO AS QUICKLY *AND CALMLY* AS POSSIBLE TO THE NEAREST RADIATION LOCKER, AND REMAIN THERE UNTIL FURTHER NOTICE. THERE IS NO CAUSE FOR ALARM AS LONG AS YOU SEEK SHELTER *NOW.* IF YOU HAVE A SPECIAL PROBLEM, ONLY, PHONE 'FLARE EMERGENCY' AND HELP WILL ARRIVE AT ONCE. WAVE-FRONT X-RAYS EXPECTED IN NINE MINUTES, TWENTY SECONDS. CLASS ONE FLARE WARNING—" It began to repeat.

"Volume mute!" Rand barked, and the voice went away. "Duncan, you're staying."

"I shouldn't," he said. "I've got my own bolt hole, two minutes away—that's seven minutes cushion."

"Don't be silly," Rhea said. "There's plenty of room in our locker, I've seen it. This suite was built for up to six." Still Duncan looked hesitant. "For heaven's sake, we're going to be in there with Colly for what, three hours to three days? With no phone, no TV, completely cut off from the Net? We *need* you, Duncan."

He grinned. "That logic I understand."

"We're wasting time," Rand snapped, and led the stampede.

By thoughtful design, access to the radiation locker was through Colly's room. They expected to find her in a panic—but as they cleared the door they found her oblivious, wearing earphones and fixated on a screen, talking on the phone with a hush-filter. She flinched sharply when she became aware of them; on Earth she would have jumped a foot in the air. In free-fall the same reflex causes one to tumble erratically; she flailed like an octopus to regain her balance. *"It was just for a minute,"* she cried. *"I was just gonna hang up, really!"*

Rand got a grip on an ankle as it went past, swarmed up her and yanked the earphones out. "Quiet, Colly!" he said, trying to control his voice carefully so as to command instant attention without scaring her.

It seemed to work. "What is it, Daddy?"

"It's all right, baby—there's a flare on the way, but it's only Class One. We're all going on a picnic together for a little while. Wanna come?"

Her eyes got big and round. "Sure, Dad. Can I bring the White Rabbit? Harvey, I mean? I changed his name."

"So I hear. I'm sorry, honey—radiation lockers are meant to keep electrons out, and that's pretty much what the White Rabbit's made of. We're going to have to rough it, like they did in the Olden Days. Do you have any books around?"

"Hard copy, you mean? None I haven't read a jillion times. You mean no games, or *anything*?"

"Only if they're free-standing, hon. Nothing that uses the Net. Get your Anything Box." It was a nanotechnological toy-set, which could be caused to become a range of things, from a 3-D chess set to a Monopoly board to Scrabble game.

"I forgot to charge it," she wailed.

Duncan already had the locker hatch open, and was waving Rhea to enter; she held back. "Come on, Colly," he called. "You don't need machines to play games."

"You *don't*?" She looked dubious. "Okay." She started for the hatch. "Hey—what about supper?"

"That kitchenette will make sandwiches in under two minutes," Rhea said, and began to turn toward the door. "We've got about seven left—"

"No, Rhea!" Duncan ordered. "That was a best-guess, and you don't screw around with a flare emergency, for *anything.* There's food and water in the locker—come on!"

"Go ahead," Rand said. "I've got Colly."

Rhea gave up and went to the hatch. Duncan caught her as she arrived, and handed her through the door. To guide a body from behind in free-fall without causing it to tumble, one pushes the buttocks. Rand had been in space long enough to know that, so he couldn't even be annoyed. He put his attention on his daughter. "Push off on me, hon," he said, and spread-eagled himself facing the hatch. Colly doubled up, put her feet against his stomach, and jumped. He used his thrusters to recover and follow her. Her aim was superb; she went through the hatch like a perfect slam-dunk and into Rhea's arms.

Duncan seemed to have assigned himself the role of doorman; he waited for Rand to precede him. "After you, son," Rand said gruffly. And as Duncan turned, he pushed the lad in, the same way he had done for Rhea.

The next few hours were not particularly pleasant ones.

Perhaps no one has ever spent a really comfortable three hours in a radiation locker. They were the only cubics in the Shimizu which could reasonably be called "spartan," being simple boxes designed to keep a human alive for up to three and a half days despite the best efforts of energetic protons to kill him. (X-rays, although they arrive first, and keep coming as the following plasma cloud of electrons and protons strikes hull metal, are not a problem: a mere millimeter of aluminum will stop most of them.) A radiation locker is very easy to get into, impossible to get out of until the emergency is past, and will supply breathable air, potable water, digestible food substitutes, basic emergency medical care, and plumbing facilities. Period. If one wishes to make it congenial, one can stock it with one's own free-standing computer gear, library of music and literature, programmable furniture, or a supply of gourmet delights, for there is a fair amount of room. But almost no one ever does . . . for the same reason that people still build at the base of volcanos. Bad solar flares are quite uncommon for about nine and a half out of every eleven years. When the tornados come once every decade or so, it is easy to forget to keep the storm shelter adequately stocked. So most visits there begin with a mournful inventory that is finished all too soon, followed by the dawning realization that this will be a sentence.

In this case, Rand decided early on not to dwell on the dark side of things, and resolved instead to concentrate on what *could* be accomplished while in here. So he checked his mental buffer, and found a task waiting: chewing his daughter out for using the telephone against express orders. But to his intense annoyance, Duncan interceded on her behalf ("butted in," was how Rand phrased it to himself), claiming that she deserved praise for having figured out how to circumvent an AI lock. When he rejected this as irrelevant, Colly took over her own defense, presenting in a shrill voice the novel theory: "Anyway, I'm not even getting a real birthday party; space stinks and I want to go home."

Since Rand had been counting on Colly's enthusiasm for space to help win over Rhea, he took recourse in a strangled silence. Rhea had privately asked him, several days ago, about interfacing his shaping equipment with the phone so that the friends at Colly's party could at least be convincing fakes. At the time he had been too busy, and said he would "think about it," but later he had thought it through in financial terms only, and rejected the idea on those grounds. He wanted mightily now to promise—to have promised—to do it . . . but he could not construct a logic-bridge that would get him from "You're spending too much money on the phone" to "I'm going to help you spend a king's ransom on the phone," and did not have Colly's daredevil indifference to logic to help him. He made a firm private resolution to tackle the project—and banged his nose on the fact that he could not even begin for . . . how long did Class One flare emergencies generally last, anyway? He was forced to ask Duncan. And the answer—three hours to three days; we'll know when the door opens—did not please him. It began to dawn on him that he was going to have to fill an indeterminate time with small talk, with a wife whom he had hurt, a child he had disappointed, and a young man who was beginning to annoy the hell out of him.

In the end, it was only eight hours, and even they were not the horrors they might have been. But only because Rhea rose heroically to the occasion, and almost singlehandedly carried the group on her shoulders, quelling negative emotions by sheer force of personality.

She changed subjects, she suggested topics, she refereed potential disputes before they could occur, and she took upon herself any housekeeping task that might otherwise have brought Rand and Duncan into contact.

Eventually she bullied them all into the proper bomb shelter spirit. She told them endless stories, some pirated and some improvised. She cajoled Rand into singing the songs he sang best. Duncan reached back into the memory banks of a childhood in circumstances so primitive (by contemporary Terran standards) that he had frequently been deprived of amusement facilities, and pulled out game after game that could be played without tools or power. Before long Colly too was making her unique contribution: giggling. Not long after her usual bedtime, she fell asleep, but a child's snores and other sleepsounds are nearly as uplifting as her giggles. And it is difficult for a conversation to turn to an argument if there is a child sleeping in the room. Before long, Rand had regained his original impression of Duncan as a decent enough young man—just needed a little seasoning among Terrans to learn the fine points of good manners, that was all. After all, Rhea seemed to like him, and she had good people radar.

Good spirits might not have lasted, but luck was with them: just as group morale peaked, the locker door opened and a loud voice began reassuring them that everything was fine. They managed to silence it before it could wake Colly, and emerged smiling together. Duncan had the grace to make his excuses and leave nearly at once. By the time Rand had finished seeing him out the door, Rhea had put Colly into her sleepsack and gone to their bedroom; he put the suite to sleep and joined her. He was quite tired; the only things he intended to do before sleeping were check to make sure their AIs were still sentient, and make sure that if there were any casualties, no one he knew was on the list.

But by the time he reached the bedroom, Rhea was more than halfway out of her clothes.

"Uh . . ." he managed to get out before the process was complete, and then she advanced on him like a cloud of electrons and protons. His own clothing was no protection at all. His next syllable was some five minutes later, and was even less spellable; he repeated it several times over the next few minutes, with increasing volume and decreasing period. The last iteration was a shout, which by then seemed to him to contain all the information the universe out there desperately needed to hear—until he heard Rhea shriek the message's other half in harmony with him.

Before he fell asleep, he regained enough intelligence to compose a platitude, something along the lines of "Out of adversity comes fortitude." Maybe . . . just maybe . . . Rhea was going to snap into it.

Talking work with Jay wasn't as much fun as it had been; with four days left before the premiere of *Kinergy* (as they had decided to name the new work) Jay had too much else to do, Rand had too little else to do, and there was nothing to discuss together but things that might go wrong. And the incessant ego-struggles and other personal frictions among the dancers—but Rand hated that particular topic. He had himself pointedly chosen a field that allowed him to work alone when it suited him.

So he had no digression to propose when Jay said, "How's it going with Rhea, bro?"

He decided to tackle it. "You know, last week I'd have said it was fucking hopeless. But it's the funniest thing: somehow that flare emergency seems to have turned things around. At least a little, anyway. She came through it like a trouper, never complained once, never even frowned—and as soon as it was over, so was she: *all* over *me.* We haven't had a session like that since . . . Jesus, I don't know, but whenever it was, it was back on Earth. It felt . . . it felt like christening the Shimizu, christening space. Do you know what I mean?"

Jay nodded at once. "Ethan and I christened High Orbit that way, once."

Rand winced away from the thought. Obviously the event had not cemented Ethan's commitment to living in space very effectively. "I mean, it's like when I first moved to P-Town. I'd never lived by the ocean, and I wasn't sure if I could take that much horizon. And the storms, you know, the winds. And then we went through our first hurricane together, and it was hard, but when it was over I felt like, 'Well, that wasn't so bad; I can live here.' Sitting in a radiation locker isn't fun . . . but it's a lot more fun than sitting in a singles bar. Maybe she's going to steady down and learn to live here."

"But it's still that much up in the air, is it? With four days to curtain? You have to give Kate an answer one way or another the following week."

"I know, I know. But it's the kind of problem where you can't push for an answer, no matter how urgent it is."

"Well, all I'm saying is, if she bails out, don't necessarily assume that you have to follow her—for keeps, I mean. Just because Ethan and I couldn't make it work on a commuter basis doesn't mean it can't be done. Look at that Philip Rose and *his* wife—and he's a writer, like Rhea. Quite a few spacers have made marriage with a groundhog work."

"You really think it's an option? After what happened to you?"

"Well, maybe not a great one. But it might be worth giving it a year and seeing how it works." He seemed to start to say something, and then changed his mind. "I'm just being selfish, bro. *Kinergy* is a good piece. I like working with you; I don't want to give it up. Losing partners is a habit I'm trying to break."

Rand thought about it, and shook his head. "I hear you. But I just can't see Rhea and I staying married that way. Besides, it's not fair to Colly to yo-yo her that way, uproot her every three months."

"There are other rotation schedules."

"Doesn't change anything. If Rhea goes, my choices are her—and Colly—or my work. So you can imagine how relieved I am at any hint that she might be willing to stay."

Again Jay seemed to choose his words carefully. "Rand? Suppose she does go? Suppose the wild sex after the flare was just the bomb-shelter reflex to celebrate not having been killed after all? Suppose your choice *is* Rhea or the Shimizu: what then?"

"That I can answer concisely and with absolute certainty. The answer is, it beats the shit out of me." He picked at a cuticle. "I really like this place. I really like this job. I really love working with you. But I *really love* Rhea and our kid. All I can tell you is, I'm praying it never comes up. And all hopeful omens are welcome."

15

Assorted Terran Locations
19 January 2065

Hidalgo Rodriguez woke from a troubled sleep. His nightmares had been stranger and more unsettling than even a full gourd of *wheero* could account for. But opening his eyes was less than no help. He shrieked, and sprang to his feet even faster than he had on that distant childhood day in his father's goat shed when he had learned empirically that a human sneeze means "Run for your life!" in Goat.

The shriek woke Amparo and the children; within seconds they were harmonizing with him.

Their homey familiar hovel was gone. It had been replaced, by something indescribable, almost literally unseeable. It was everywhere, on all sides, had no apparent openings, and no features that any of them could identify. The light by which they saw it had no detectable source. Their first and best guess was that it was some kind of magical trap.

This diagnosis caused Hidalgo to utter a bellow of what he hoped sounded like rage, and throw himself bodily at the nearest part of the thing he could reach. He did not really expect to break through, but he had to try. He struck hard with a hunched shoulder, rebounded and gasped. He had not produced an opening or even a dent—but part of the omnipresent . . . *stuff* . . . had suddenly became transparent.

A window . . .

Outside it Hidalgo saw the familiar landscape of his home region, with some odd alterations he was too busy to study. He grabbed up a rag, wrapped his fist in it, and smashed at the window. It emphatically refused to break. His hand was more equivocal; he swore foully.

His son Julio followed Hidalgo's example, racing full tilt into the nearest wall to him. When nothing happened, he picked another spot and tried again. This time he was spectacularly successful: a door appeared in the stuff. He tested it; it worked just fine . . . and the entire Rodriguez clan joined him at high speed.

They stood outside the thing for a minute or so, all talking at the top of their lungs, none of them hearing a word—or noticing the sounds of similar loud "conversations" in the near distance.

The thing was still unidentifiable. It certainly did not look like a house, or even a building—not any that they had ever seen. It did not seem to have any straight lines or perpendiculars or right angles to it; there was no chimney.

Curiosity—and the growing realization that it was *much* hotter out here than it had been inside—finally caused them to reenter it.

They tried poking it some more. Finally Luz let out a scream. She had found a spot which caused it to grow a basin. Shouting at her to get away from it, Hidalgo cautiously approached the thing. For some reason, it had an extra faucet. He tried the one nearest him; its mechanism was unfamiliar to him, but not hard to figure out. Water came out, and swirled away.

Hidalgo gaped. His family had never, as far back as history recorded—yes, even unto his grandfather's day!—had access to running water in the home. He was rich! And there were *two* of the things. He tried the other one—and when he had grasped what it produced, he fainted dead away.

Hot water . . .

When he awoke, his new house was talking to him, telling him cheerfully of traffic conditions in a city he had only heard of. It showed him pictures. . . .

Hidalgo was a little comforted when he learned, shortly, that all of his neighbors in the hillside shanty-community were undergoing essentially identical experiences. So, elsewhere around the planet, were the family of Nkwame Van der Hoof, and *their* neighbors . . . the family of Algie Bent and their neighbors . . . the family of Trojan (his parents had named him after their hero) Khamela and their neighbors . . . the family of Lo Duc Tho and their neighbors . . . the list went on. Indeed, it was never completed.

A plague of houses seemed to be loose on the world. . . .

It took much longer for it to become apparent—and longer for it to be believed by anyone with an education—that people who lived in those toadstool houses could not get sick.

PART SIX

16

The Shimizu Hotel
20 January 2065

Jay was watching the first full tech run-through of *Kinergy,* and wistfully praying God to strike him dead, when the alarm went off.

"FLARE WARNING—CLASS THREE—"

"Again?" someone groaned.

"—REPEAT, CLASS *THREE!* THIS IS A SAFETY EMERGENCY: ALL GUESTS MUST GO AS QUICKLY *AND CALMLY AS* POSSIBLE TO THE POOL AREA, AND REMAIN THERE UNTIL FURTHER NOTICE. THERE IS NO CAUSE FOR ALARM AS LONG AS—"

"Jesus, Class Three!" Francine said. "All right, everybody: drop what you're doing and *move.* Quietly! Rand, Andrew, kill the holo and sound—"

It vanished, and the theater reappeared.

"—PLEASE REPORT ALOUD WHEN YOU HAVE LEFT FOR THE POOL; THE SHIMIZU WILL HEAR YOU AND NOT WASTE TIME SEARCHING FOR YOU—"

"Nova Dance Company, all members, leaving the theater now," Jay barked.

Andrew, the tech director who had replaced the murdered Nika, was a spacer: he came popping out the hatch from backstage like a cork leaving a champagne bottle. Jay suddenly remembered that Colly was back there with Rand, and headed for the tech hole to see if his brother needed any help. On the way it dawned on him that his troubles were over, or at least postponed: the company—and everyone else in the Shimizu—would all still be in the pool when the curtain was supposed to go up on *Kinergy.* Rescheduling after the emergency would take days. The Sword of Damocles had extended its expiry date.

Rand and Colly were emerging from the tech hole as he reached it. Colly seemed frightened, but not panicked; Rand was looking grim. "Honey," he said to her, "Uncle Jay is going to take you to the pool. Mom and I will join you there in two seconds."

"Daddy, no—"

"Take her, Jay."

"Rhea will be *fine,* bro," Jay began, but Rand cut him off.

"I tried to phone. Not accepting calls."

"At worst, somebody in a rad-suit will fetch her—"

"It's only a little out of the way—*take Colly.*" He kicked off and fired his thrusters. Jay found himself reassuring Colly, which helped calm himself; they jaunted for the pool together.

So did most of the population. The crowd of course thickened as it neared the center of the hotel. Some had a festive, holiday spirit; some were manic; some were silent and terrified; some were being dragged, protesting bitterly, by employees in bulky anti-radiation gear. Those whose protests became loud were sedated. Every corridor seemed to have a calm, competent employee whose sole job was to keep traffic flowing, and another who said reassuring things to anyone who would listen. Colly was actually enjoying herself by the time they reached the pool area. A smiling employee gave her and Jay ear-buttons to insert; at once a calm voice was murmuring instructions in their ears. "The pool is nearly empty now. When you are told to enter, do so promptly. Look for your last initial in the large green letters on the pool wall, and jaunt to that area so we can sort you out. Look for an employee with red arm- and leg-bands. If you have any emergency—first aid, medicine, need for a toilet, a missing loved one—report it to that employee—" and so on. The whole thing was well thought-out, well rehearsed, and worked wonders in holding down the general confusion; the Shimizu had been doing this, successfully, every eleven years for the last half-century. In under a minute, all of the pool's large doors opened at once, and they were told to enter. The ear-buttons became strident on the subject of not stopping in doorways to gawk. Jay and Colly were swept along with the flow, and found themselves inside the pool, with hundreds of chattering guests.

Jay looked around, located a green "P" on the wall a few hundred meters away, and took Colly there, breathing a sigh of relief that both Rand's and Rhea's last names happened to end with the same letter. "We'll wait here for your folks, pumpkin," he told the child. "This is gonna be lots more fun than a dumb old rad locker, huh?"

"Sure," she agreed, counting the house. "Wow! Kids I don't even know! There's one that looks *my* age—over there, see? Uncle Jay, can I go say hi?"

"Later, honey. Let's wait for your parents, okay? We've got three days, you know."

"Oh . . . okay." Suddenly she was horror-struck. "Uncle Jay—*what about the show?*"

He grinned. "The concert, you mean. Colly, do schoolkids back on Earth still get 'snow days'?"

She blinked. "Oh. No—but Mommy told me about them. You mean like 'sunspot days,' when the school system crashes, and you don't have to study."

"That's right. Well, your Dad and I, and the whole company, are about to have three 'sunspot days' in a row. And believe me, we can all use the rest."

"Oh. Hey, well that's great, then. Boy, it's weird to be in here without any water . . ."

"That's right, I hear this is your favorite place, isn't it?" Jay said absently. His watch said there were a little less than five minutes left before the doors would seal; he was scanning all the door areas at once for Rand and Rhea. At this point the majority of the new arrivals were being dragged by no-nonsense employees; Jay tried to mentally subtract them from the view, and so he didn't see Colly's parents right away.

Then he did. They and Duncan were just being released by the trio of chasers who had hauled them in. They must have come peaceably, for they were all still conscious—but as Jay opened his mouth to call Colly's attention to their arrival, he noted their respective body languages, integrated them, and closed his mouth again. Something was wrong. . . .

He squinted. Duncan seemed to be saying something—whether to Rand or Rhea or both was unclear. Whatever it was required gestures to get across. Rand's reply was so emphatic that even at that distance

Jay could hear it, though not what was being said, amid the general din. Rhea and Duncan both answered at once and at length. This time Rand's reply was inaudible. A few seconds' pause . . . and Duncan spun around and started to jaunt away. Rand thrusted after him, overtook him, grappled with him, both their voices were heard shouting, Rhea chased them doing some shouting of her own—

For some reason nine groundhogs out of ten who attempt to fight in space make the same mistake: intuiting that a straight punch will push them away from their opponent, they instinctively go for an uppercut. But this only sends them sliding *past* him, toward his feet. Spacers know this, and are generally ready to meet the descending chin with an upthrust knee. Jay saw his brother begin an uppercut, and winced in anticipation. Rand massed much more than Jay—a terrible *disadvantage* under these conditions.

—but for some reason Duncan did not make the obvious counter. He took the punch, failed to lift his knee, and he and Rand went past each other like tectonic plates. That was all they had time for; the three chasers who'd fetched them here had already left in search of remaining stragglers, so it was a couple of the ear-button vendors who handled the job of sedating Rand and Duncan and, since she was still shouting, Rhea. In seconds, all three were at peace or a convincing imitation. The whole brief incident had gone largely unnoticed in all the general confusion.

"Do you see Mom and Dad anywhere, Uncle Jay?" Colly asked.

"No, honey," he said gently. "But I'm sure they're just fine. They've probably volunteered to help out with crowd control, since they know you're with me."

"Oh, I'll bet you're right," she said. "Daddy's real good at getting people to stay calm in a 'mergency."

"Yeah." He looked around and located an employee without arm- and leg-bands, a roving problem-solver, and waved her over. "How about this, pumpkin? How about if I stay here and wait up for them, and you go with this nice lady here, Xi—hi, Xi!—and meet some of those kids you saw? Xi, this is Colly Porter."

"Hi, Colly."

"Hi, Xi. Hey—get it? 'High-gee,' like the Space Commando's ship."

"That's a good one," Xi said patiently.

"Wow, suppose your parents really liked the Oz books, and they picked 'Wiz' for your last name? I have this friend named Duncan Iowa, because his parents—" They drifted away together; Colly forgot to say goodbye to Jay.

As soon as they were out of eyeshot, Jay made a beeline for the area where Rand, Rhea and Duncan had been towed and secured. A banded employee whose name Jay couldn't recall was trying to ID them so that they could be processed. "Those two are mine," he said. "Family."

"Fine by me, Sasaki-*san*," she said respectfully. "Wrap 'em up and take 'em home. What about the Orientator?"

After a split-second's hesitation, Jay said, "Process him."

"You got it." Duncan would regain consciousness in the presence of a proctor, receive a ringing lecture—and a large black mark would be entered on his record. It might even be a firing offense, if the cause of the fight had been what Jay suspected it was. His first instinct had been to cover for Duncan . . . but if it turned out that his brother had not had some good reason to take a poke at the boy, the record could always be jiggered retroactively.

"How're you fixed for antidote?" he asked the woman.

She started to say something, then shrugged and tossed him a pair of infusers from her pouch.

He towed the sleeping Rhea and Rand slowly to the "P" section—an awkward task, especially in a crowd, but not difficult for a dancer. On the way he thought things through; when he got there he left Rhea in the care of the banded employee in charge, told him to let her sleep for now. Then he located a glowing letter whose adherents chanced to include few children and none near Colly's age, and towed Rand there. He Velcroed his brother to a support, bared his arm, triggered the infuser, and backed off a few meters.

Rand woke as quickly and seamlessly as he had fallen asleep—and looked around wildly for his opponent and prepared another punch. In moments the world snapped back into focus for him. He groaned; his shoulders slumped and his head bowed. Then he drew in breath for what was going to be a great bellow of either anger or grief—but by then Jay was close again, and clapped a hand over his brother's mouth.

"Easy," he murmured. "You don't want to get dosed twice. You might—" Some mental censor made him decide not to name the most common consequence of a double-sedation: temporary impotence. "—regret it. Calm down . . . and tell me what happened." He took his hand away.

Again Rand slumped, this time all the way into free-fall crouch, a position halfway to fetal. He said nothing for long moments.

Jay already knew the general shape of what Rand was probably going to say, but it was important that Rand say it. "Well?"

His brother looked up with the expression of a man who has just lost a limb, and is trying to integrate the intellectual knowledge with his emotions. "When I got there . . . they were together."

Jay thought of six or seven things to say, hundreds of words. "So?" was the one he chose.

Rand struggled to keep his voice down. "Come on, Jay, do I have to show you a graphic?" he said in strangled tones.

Jay frowned. "You caught them in the act? They ignored a Class Three alert? I don't believe it!" *Even if it really happened,* he thought, *there simply* had *to be time for them to at least throw a goddam robe on—they're dressed now, for Christ's sake!—and if they did, there's no way to* prove *anything—this can still be fixed—*

"They were fully dressed. It took me nearly two full minutes to get there. But Jesus, Jay—*I've got a fucking nose,* okay? I've got eyes. It happened. Something happened."

"—and you don't know just what. Do you?" When there was no answer he rushed on. "It could have been a passing thought, a fleeting temptation, and some very bad timing, okay? It happened to me once: I was flirting, like you do, you know . . . and just as I started to realize it was getting to be more than just flirting, just as I was deciding to back off, his wife came in and caught us both with boners. It didn't mean a thing; it blew over. There's no way to be sure this meant anything. Give her a chance to explain, when she's over the embarrassment."

Rand looked away. "I will." He looked back again. "But Jay, I've lived with her for ten years. I've seen her look embarrassed. I've even seen her look guilty. But this is the first time I've *ever* seen her look ashamed. I already know all I want to know. And I thank you for your counsel and support, and I would greatly appreciate it if you would leave me the fuck alone now, so I don't have a fight with you, okay? Wait—where's Colly?"

"She's covered," Jay said. "Take it off your mind. I'll go get her as soon as I wake Rhea up. You sure you'll be okay here?"

"No, but moving won't help. Go."

"Listen to this when you're ready," Jay said, handing Rand his own ear-button. "It'll tell you the procedures." And he left his brother alone to mourn.

As Jay was returning to "P" section, he found himself humming a tune in a minor key, and suddenly recognized it as a nearly century-old Stevie Wonder song called "Blame It on the Sun." The irony was too unsubtle for his conscious mind; he stopped humming. He knew he should be sad for his brother, he intended to be as soon as he could, but for now he was numb. Too much going on; too much still to do; an eight-year-old still his nominal responsibility—to whom this all must somehow be explained before much longer. Then, three days or more locked in a can with the problem. His head began to throb.

Rhea came out of it as quickly as Rand had—and began blushing the moment she focused on Jay's face.

"What happened?" he asked. "No, forget that: *how much did he see?* How much can he prove?"

Her eyes widened as she took his meaning. "Oh, Jay—"

He turned away. "Dammit, Rhea . . . dammit to hell . . . *fuck* it to hell—"

"Where's Colly?"

"Having a jolly time in the company of a very nice lady, meeting other kids," he said bitterly. "I'd say we have at least another ten minutes before you're going to have to explain to her why Mommy and Daddy aren't talking to each other. And why Uncle Duncan has a bruise on his chin. But you're a writer: I'm sure you can improvise something."

"She doesn't call him 'Uncle Duncan,'" she said absurdly. And then: "Oh . . . my . . . God . . ."

"MAY I HAVE YOUR ATTENTION, PLEASE," said a loud and omnipresent voice. It repeated twice, as the hubbub dwindled, then went on, "WE ARE VERY PLEASED TO REPORT THAT THE CLASS THREE FLARE ALERT WAS A FALSE ALARM—REPEAT, THE ALERT WAS A FALSE ALARM." The hubbub became an uproar; the voice got louder to compensate. "THE EMERGENCY IS

OVER. TO MINIMIZE CONFUSION, PLEASE RETURN TO YOUR STATEROOMS BY LETTER-GROUPS, BEGINNING WITH THOSE WHOSE LAST NAMES BEGIN WITH 'A' AND THEIR FAMILIES. PLEASE DO NOT TRY TO LEAVE UNTIL ALL THOSE IN THE PRECEDING LETTER-GROUP ARE GONE. THE SHIMIZU APOLOGIZES FOR ANY INCONVENIENCE, AND THANKS YOU ALL FOR YOUR COOPERATION DURING THE EMERGENCY—"

"Jesus Christ—" Jay began.

"Take her home for me, Jay," Rhea blurted, and jetted away before he could object. She mingled with the crowd whose last names began with "A," and was lost from sight. Jay stared after her, feeling his headache gather force.

Within moments, Colly appeared, trailing a frantic Xi. "Did they show up yet, Uncle Jay?"

He started to say no automatically. But then he had the thought that in the near future, a lot of people were going to be lying to this child, and he didn't want to be one of them anymore. "I caught a glimpse of them," he said, then skated quickly off the thin ice. "But we'll never find them in this madhouse now. That's okay; I'm sure we'll meet them back at your suite"—whoops, hitting thin ice again—"eventually. Say, did you meet any interesting kids?"

"Wow, yeah—I met a boy my own age, named Waldo, and he's a spacer, like me: *he's* gonna be here forever too! I never saw him around before because he's got something wrong with his muscles and he can't go out and play—but who cares? I can go to *his* house and we can be friends *forever*! I invited him to my birthday party—"

Don't count on it, pumpkin, Jay thought, but all he said was, "He sounds nice."

A lot of people's plans were going to be changing soon.

He had already left the pool with the rest of the *S*'s, and was in the corridors with Colly, before it sank in: *Kinergy* was going to go on at the appointed time after all. . . .

In common with most of the choreographers who had ever lived, Jay had, two days before curtain, no idea whether he was on the verge of artistic triumph or disaster. It was no longer possible for him to evaluate the work, either objectively or subjectively. He was prepared to take the most ignorant amateur criticism to heart, or discount the most informed professional praise. The final, and only important, verdict would come two nights from now, in the form of applause or its embarrassing absence or—God forbid!—active booing. He burned to know what that verdict would be . . . and feared to find out. The only thing he knew for certain was that he could definitely have used another week to polish the damned thing. That was why he had welcomed the flare emergency.

And all the fucking emergency had accomplished was to cost him his tech rehearsal—and to shatter his brother's world.

Well, perhaps there was a relatively bright side to all this—at least from Jay's point of view. Presumably Rhea would go back dirtside now—that might even be why she had done it. That would leave Rand no real choice but to stay here in space! The only place waiting for him on Terra was Provincetown, Rhea's town. He'd be miserable for a while, sure . . . but as Sam Spade had once said, that would pass. He'd heal. A season of his own original work, some media massage courtesy of Ev Martin, a few standing *O's* . . .

Oh, shit! Would Rand be in any shape to come to the premiere?

Jay assumed his brother would not make the remaining two days of rehearsals—and that would hurt, but Andrew could probably handle things alone. Jay also knew he would miss Rand's companionship, his services as a sounding-board, the last-minute inspirations he might have contributed—and that wasn't fatal either.

But Kate Tokugawa would be livid if Rand did not appear at the premiere. His presence was *required.* All the media would be there. It was a matter of face. Hers, and the Board's.

In his heart, Jay knew face was as low in Rand's present scale of values as it was high in Kate's. Oh, this was more than a tragedy: it had all the makings of a catastrophe. . . .

"I wish that dumb old flare wasn't a false alarm, Uncle Jay," Colly said. "That was starting to be fun."

Guilt tore at his heart. He thought *he* had problems? "Me too, honey," he said softly, tightening his grip on her small hand. "Me too."

What the hell am I going to do with her?

"Sergei?" he tried.

Personal AIs were back on-line. "Yes, Jay?" Diaghilev said.

"Excuse me, Colly, I have to check on something with Andrew. Sergei, hush-field, please." The sounds of the crowd around him went away. "Phone Rand."

"Not accepting calls, Jay."

"God dammit, emergency override 'P-Town'!"

Rhea answered. *"What?"*

"What do I do with your daughter?" Jay asked brutally.

There was a short silence. "Can . . . can you take her? For a while, anyway?"

"What do I tell her?"

He heard Rand say something angry in the background. " . . . something good, okay?" she said. "Please, brother? I'll call you when . . . when we're ready for her."

It was the word "brother" that made up his mind. Rhea had never called him that before. She was begging. "Okay." He was prepared to end the conversation, but could not decide how. Did he say "Good luck"? Instead he said, "I'll wait for your call. Off."

Something good, okay?

"Colly, you're coming home with me. The cronkites want to interview your mom and dad about the flare—you know, celebrity on the spot stuff."

It was weak; no one had interviewed them after the previous, genuine emergency. But Colly bought it. "Neat! Maybe we can watch it at your house—they'll probably rush it onto the Net—"

Jay winced. "Well, maybe not right away. It'll take time to edit, you know—"

"Phone, Jay," Diaghilev said. "Two calls waiting: Andrew and Francine."

Jay wished someone would solve brain-cloning. "Colly, excuse me; Sergei, give me both of them; Andrew, Francine, I can't talk for long right now, but . . ." His mind raced. " . . . uh, today's a wrap. We'll do the tech rehearsal tomorrow at noon; first dress after supper; final run-through will have to be the afternoon of the performance."

"Are you sure, Boss?" Francine asked. "We could do the tech tonight—cancel the pony show."

"No," Jay said. "After something like this, the cabaret show is *essential.* I won't be there, but trust me: you'll never have a better house. They'll cheer themselves hoarse, and tip like Shriners.

Everybody needs to celebrate still being alive"—*well, almost everybody . . .* —"and not being trapped in a swimming pool for three days. I've got to go; I'll leave my notes from this afternoon with your AIs later and talk with you tomorrow. Off."

"Calls waiting, Jay: Katherine Tokugawa, Evelyn Martin, Eva Hoffman . . . and another just coming in, Duncan Iowa."

"Suffering Jesus! Flush Iowa and Martin, tell Eva I'll call her back, refuse all further calls, and give me Kate. Greetings, Tokugawa-*san*—some excitement, eh? I know why you're calling, and don't worry: we'll be ready when the bell rings—"

By the time he had given his boss every reassurance he could counterfeit and gotten her off the phone, he was back home. Once inside, he turned Colly over to the White Rabbit; it checked, learned that Room Service was not yet back on-line, and led her off to Jay's personal pantry, glancing irritably at its pocket watch, for the stiff peanut-butter and jelly it knew she required. Jay took a deep breath—

—let it out; took another—

—thought longingly of a drink, and retracted all the furniture in his living room, and began to dance. And kept on dancing, ricocheting around the room in great energy-wasting leaps and landings and spins and recoveries, until his body was as exhausted as his brain. He poured all his fear and confusion and guilt and anger into the dance . . . his irritation with his beloved brother, for picking now to be betrayed . . . his sneaking sympathy for the bitch who had picked now to put the horns on his brother . . . his heartbreak for the small child who was about to become a helpless leaf in a storm she would not understand for years . . .

When he finally stopped, Colly's applause startled him. He had not been aware of her watching, hadn't thought to censor what his body was saying. But she was not disturbed by his dance, only impressed; her applause was sincere. She was oblivious to her doom.

They ended up napping in each other's arms.

17

Nova Dance Theatre
The Shimizu Hotel
22 January 2065

Early on in the dance, Eva knew she was in good hands, and relaxed.

You couldn't always tell, that early. Sometimes a serious dance was over before you had decided whether you liked it or not. Every piece must, along with what it actually conveys, explain to you the rules by which it is meant to be judged, and sometimes that subtext can take as long to grasp and evaluate as the work itself. For that very reason, Eva had avoided seeing any rehearsals, so she could assess the finished work fairly. But a minute or so into *Kinergy,* she stopped praying that her friend's work wouldn't bomb, and became lost in it. Jay and his brother had meshed well, for the second time: this piece, despite its origins in the turgid head of Pribhara, was even better than *Spatial Delivery* had been.

It was not as cerebral as that piece, nor as simple. For one thing, it was staged in the sphere rather than in proscenium, so it had to work in any direction. The stage was bare: apparently none of the standard vector-changing hardware of free-fall dance was going to be used tonight . . . which meant the dancers were going to work harder. The piece's title was another clue. *Spatial Delivery* had been a single pun, based on a long-obsolete term—but *Kinergy* was a cascade of overlapping ones—synergy/kinetic energy/kinship energy/kin urge—all primal concepts of the human universe, as old as DNA and as unlikely to ever become dated. It had opened, in fact, with two chains of six dancers unwinding from a double helix in a sudden burst of illumination. The musical accompaniment that appeared as they separated was likewise timeless: the tones of its individual voices did not precisely match any classical instrument, but neither did they sound electronic. The music they made together was difficult to categorize; one could have imagined such music being played at just about any time in history. The dancers were costumed as neutrally as possible, in unitards that matched their complexions, with hoods that masked their diversity of hair styles and colors, and with oversized wings and disguised thrusters.

Nor did the ensuing choreography seem to contain any period or style "flags" in its movement vocabulary—not even those characteristic to its creator. Eva was familiar with most of Jay's work, and might not have identified this as his if she hadn't been told: he had managed to transcend his own limitations.

Ordinarily, for instance, he hated unisons, referred to them as "redundancies," and tended to use them as little as possible—but once his two chains of dancers had separated into twelve individuals, they spent several minutes dancing in unison, changing only in their dynamic relation to one another, like birds altering their formation in flight.

Eva slowly realized that the piece *did* have an unavoidable period flag: since the dancers were weightless, the dance had to belong to the twenty-first century. Few of its sweeping movements could have been performed any earlier in history, on Terra, without the help of special effects. But as that realization came to her, Rand's shaping began, and cut the piece adrift in time again. The audience facing her on the far side of the theater went away; the dancers were now flying in a blue Terran sky that went on forever, peppered with slow-moving clouds. The sun, its brilliance tempered to a tolerable level by an intervening cloud, was directly opposite Eva, so her subconscious decided that she was lying on her back, *mere thousands of meters above Terra,* about to fall, an effect so unsettling that she grabbed for her seatmate. (Glancing briefly around, she noticed that many others were doing the same—but not those who were spaceborn.) But the clouds and dancers did not recede, she did not "fall"; before long she relaxed and accepted the fact that she could float in a gravity field, that she was simply lying on a cloud. She resumed watching the dance.

How old is the concept of fairies? Of winged humans who play among the clouds? These dancers played *with* the clouds, buzzing them, bursting through them, batting them to and fro like fluffy beachballs. A sextet formed, grabbed each other's ankles and made a great circle just in time for a cloud to thread it in stately slow motion. Another group at the opposite end of the theater seemed to echo the phrase, but contracted as the cloud was passing through their circle and pinched it into two clouds; the sextet broke into two trios, and each took one of the cloudlets to play with. The remaining six formed a puffball, like fish in the pool, with a cloud at their center; it slowly expanded outward through them, moving up their torsos, and became a translucent wispy sphere around them, then a globe of water, swirling with surface tension. All six came apart from each other and burst the bubble: it popped with a comical moist sound and sent droplets cascading in all directions like a cool firework blossoming. The ones coming toward Eva vanished just before arriving.

She was delighted. The simple beauty of weightlessness, which became prosaic for every Shimizu resident through daily familiarity, was made magical again by the setting. In this context, the dancers seemed somehow *more than* (or was it less than?) weightless; they seemed to be nearly massless as well, ethereal. They could meet at high speed without apparent impact, change vector so that it seemed to be their will rather than thrusters which caused the change, bounce from a cloud as easily as penetrate it, pivot on a passing breeze.

Fetch a Sumerian shepherd with a time machine, give him an hour or two to get used to zero gee, and show him this piece: it would communicate to him instantly. The same for a Cretan stonecutter or a medieval alchemist or, Eva imagined, a hypothetical twenty-third century energy creature. There were probably *apes* who would appreciate this dance. The creative audacity of trying to rekindle the ancient wonder of flying, for people in an environment where one had to fly to get to the bathroom, people who had been striving since their arrival inboard to become blasé about that very miracle, was inspired. Eva had been in space for a long time, and this was the first time in years that she had reflected on how *lucky* she was: that mankind's oldest dream—to fly like a bird, and never fear hitting the ground—was for her a commonplace.

During the brief interval between movements, Eva reached up and tapped the program-button in her ear; she had deliberately not audited the program notes before the piece began, but now she wanted to know what the creators had had to say about it. She heard the recorded voice of the immortal Murray Louis, reading from one of his own books:

> *Performance is not mired, it floats. It exists upward, it hovers. It is immediate. It happens. It has no roots, it feeds from the air. It floats above all the tangibles that create it. From its loftiness, its aura descends and permeates all, lifting everything to its height as well as its depth. Performance is the revelation that speaks for itself.*

She switched off as the credits began; the second movement had begun. During the interval the dancers had all exited—seeming to shimmer out of existence, one by one—and the clouds had thickened into banks of rolling thunderheads that blotted the sun and darkened the sky. Now the darkness was nearly complete; one could just make out individual billowings in the roiling storm. The temperature seemed to drop slightly, and the air pressure to rise.

Suddenly, with an earsplitting crash, a fractal fork of lightning arced between two prominences. It came *toward* Eva, ended only meters from her; for the second time she clutched her seatmate tightly. The audience gasped, then muttered and tittered nervously. Five or ten seconds later a second bolt, shorter and with a different vector, again gave a snapshot of the interior of the storm. The music began to sound like mountain horns in the far distance, great deep bass tones punching through intervening winds. Another bolt, more crooked than the last, flared and died . . . then another, and another. Their randomness was convincing; they came anywhere from two to twenty seconds apart, lingering in the eye for nearly a second.

Then all at once all twelve dancers were there, caught in the sudden glare of God's flashbulb, frozen in tableau. Again the audience murmured. The next flash found them in a different tableau, and the next. Sometimes they were arrayed as two sextets, sometimes as four trios, or three quartets, or a septet and quintet, or six pairs; sometimes they were simply twelve lost individuals. No matter how close together the flashes came, the dancers were never caught in motion. Eva wondered how they managed to navigate to each new position in the dark without colliding, but refused to let herself speculate on how the trick was being done, preferring to simply enjoy it. Soon she was noting patterns in the progression of patterns itself. The whole thing began to remind her of the ancient computer game called "Life," in which a collection of cells changes shape and structure in successive frames, "evolving" and "growing" according to simple rules. This was like a three-dimensional Life sequence run at a very slow frame rate, had the same weird but intuitively appealing beauty, constantly changing yet remaining stable over time.

Just as seeming chance brought the dancers fairly close together in a cluster, an especially bright bolt of lightning lingered longer than usual, split again and again, fractured into a hundred snake-tongues of fire that raced around the entire storm—and in their flickering light, the cluster of dancers began to move in space, turning end over end like a Catherine wheel. As the actinic sparkles faded slowly away, the dancers themselves began to glow softly, somehow emitting their own light, shining from within like fireflies. They began to move bodily too, without losing their place in formation, first in unison and then individually, and before long the tension of their solos tore the cluster apart into smaller groups.

Two of the groups, asymmetrically opposed, began to leave trails of light behind them as they moved. Short at first, mere afterimages, the trails slowly lengthened until they were winding tails, as though the invisible eraser that chased them was falling farther and farther behind—then they vanished, and three other groups began to leave trails of their own. Soon dancers were making light sculptures all over the sky, like particle tracks in a cyclotron, occasionally mirroring one another for a time and then diverging. Again Eva was reminded of something from the dawn of the Age of Silicon: a screen-saver program called Electric Fire. The effect was hypnotic—but a kind of hypnosis that made the pulse race and the breath come faster, a *heightening* of alertness. Forks of lightning still flared here and there among the clouds, imbuing the whole scene with a sense of energy, largeness, danger. Perhaps there were subsonics buried in the score as well. One sensed that something awful, cataclysmic, might happen if one of the dancers missed a movement, distorted the weave of the incomprehensible pattern they were shaping together. Something on the scale of Ragnarok. The speed and intensity of the dance increased, until all twelve were racing to and fro at the highest speeds they could reach without crashing into the unseen audience, threatening to lose control and do so. The very clouds seemed to back away from them. In their boiling frenzy, they came to resemble the classic historical footage of the Fireflies confronting Shara Drummond . . . save that they were not red. Each glowed a *different* color now, twelve distinct shades; together they seemed the shards of a proto-rainbow struggling to form.

As the music swelled and steadied, they succeeded: seemingly by chance, they settled one after another into the same stable orbit, a great ring whose axis kept changing, like the "orange-slice" orbit of Peace Monitor satellites around Terra, like a primitive model of an atom with twelve electrons. Their trails became one orbit in length: a coruscating rainbow chased itself around the globe.

A short blast of trumpets, and the rainbow flared, doubling in brightness. Each and every cloud dissolved into a trillion spherically expanding droplets of water, a trillion seeds, each carrying with it a tiny reflection of the rainbow. As they dispersed and vanished, the stormclouds lightened in color and mass, thinned out, became wispy, melted away save for a handful of benign white clouds. The storm was broken; the sun returned, and the achingly familiar blue of the Terran sky. (Even spaceborns, studies had long shown, resonated emotionally to that color; it seemed to be in the DNA somewhere, though none could say how.) The music moved gradually up the scale, from deep baritone horn sounds to medium frequencies that sounded eerily like human voices, yet moved in ways no human culture sang. The dancers glowed so fiercely now that they seemed to have enlarged, and their features were indistinct.

Then the rainbow-ring came apart, and they were again the playful, independent sprites they had been in the first movement—but shining, gleaming. The voices became a vast choir, hundreds of voices singing their hearts out in a language Eva had never heard before. The net effect was dysharmonic, but occasionally little resolutions came and went, as if the choir were singing a dozen songs in a dozen keys simultaneously.

The blue sky turned suddenly to gold. Groups of dancers formed, interacted and broke up with dizzying speed. A quartet would come together, agree on a movement phrase, split apart and bring the phrase to other groups, which made up new phrases to combine with them, then split apart in their turn. Choreographic ideas appeared spontaneously and spread around the stage like heat lightning or rumor. A unison formed by apparent accident among the twelve dissolved, then returned—while in the score, more and more singers reached agreement on a key and rules of harmony, until they too were working together to build something. Dance and music together established a stable base and began to climb higher.

Literally! Clouds came toward Eva, and wind into her face: she and the dancers were rising, leaving unseen Terra behind them. The illusion was utterly convincing, and quite breath-taking. The wind fell away, and they left the clouds below; the golden sky began to darken again—not the turgid dark of the storm, but the pure star-spattered blackness of space.

No, not pure. They traveled through a fine mist of some kind of dust. Red dust. It began to accumulate on the bodies of the dancers, until they were caked with it, coated by it, covered in it, each of them glowing a shade of red: ochre, umber, amber, crimson, scarlet, ruby. It was Symbiote, and they a dozen newborn Stardancers, spreading their wings now, spinning them out into lightsails, joyously learning a new way to dance together, rubbing together like blobs in a lava lamp.

Eva put all of her attention on keeping perfectly still and calm. It was difficult—but Reb had trusted her. Many decades of lucrative poker came to her aid.

Briefly the twelve boiled together at the center of the stage like swarming bees, a "quotation" of the Fireflies who had given mankind the Symbiote—then they opened out again, formed a spherical matrix . . . and folded gracefully together into the *kûkanzen* posture of those who meditate in space, each facing out from the center, away from all the others. Together they bowed, to the Universe; the music resolved at last into a major chord spanning the entire audible range; dancers and music began to fade away, like Cheshire cats, until there was only silence and infinite space and the burning stars; then they too dwindled and were gone.

Five full seconds of total silence. Then, pandemonium—

One of the many reasons art in space is performed in spherical theaters is acoustics. Applause reinforces itself, just as a person standing in a hemispherical building on Earth can hear with total clarity a whisper from someone standing precisely opposite him. Any ovation in space sounds like a Terran audience going mad; it makes up for the fact that they cannot stand to deliver it. But *this* ovation would have shaken the walls of the Bolshoi.

Eva let herself glance at Jay and Rand, now, as the house lights came up. They were together at the opposite end of the vip section, unbuckling their belts to join the dancers for the bow. Her eyes were not what they had once been, but she had a century of experience in intrigue: one glance at Jay's face and she was intuitively certain *he* didn't know Reb's secret. Rand was much harder to read. Ev Martin—hearing that Rand's wife had left him yesterday, taking his daughter back to Provincetown with her—had spoken with the house physician. The shaper was stoned to his cheeks, smiling beatifically. His eyes were wounds, and he was jaunting like a tourist, but he would pass muster for the media.

Could *Rand* know something? Unlikely . . . but then, it was a visual that had shocked her, rather than choreography. Still, perhaps it was just coincidence . . .

The crowd was merciless in its admiration, demanding eight curtain calls before the exhausted dancers were allowed to go backstage and peel off their soaked costumes. Eva stopped clapping much sooner; her aged hands gave out. Finally the ovation was over, and her companion, Chen Ling Ho, was murmuring, "I liked it very much . . . despite the ending."

Again she had recourse to her poker experience. "Wasn't that blackout section terrific? Where they did the tableaux in the lightning flashes? How do you suppose they got around in the dark without a train wreck?"

" 'How do I get to Carnegie Hall?' " the trillionaire replied.

"You can't possibly be old enough to remember that joke—Carnegie Hall was torn down before you were born!"

His eyes twinkled. "I like to think of myself as a student of classical humor."

She blinked. " 'Your money or your life?' " she asked, quoting an ancient radio joke.

Chen gave the correct response: dead silence.

She rewarded him with a smile, unbuckled herself with one hand and took his arm with the other. "Let's head for the reception—I want to congratulate the boys before the crowd beats them stupid."

Rand and Jay were already glazing over by the time Eva elbowed her way into the receiving line with Chen, but she caught their attention—and managed to fluster them both—when she said, "Lads, somewhere Willem Ngani is smiling tonight."

"He'd have loved that piece," Chen agreed, and the two thanked them, both stammering. Then Eva let herself be chivvied away by assistant cronkites—this was the worst possible time and place to probe Rand's secret thoughts.

She and Chen returned to her suite. He accepted a drink, and they moved to the window. Terra was about a quarter full. The illuminated crescent contained China; twilight in Beijing. They shared silence for a few minutes. Then he said, "You did not respond to my criticism of the ending of *Kinergy*. Did you like it?"

She felt like she was juggling eggs in a gravity field. "Yes, I did. It resonated for me. What didn't you like about it?"

"The Stardancer motif."

"Too obvious?"

He hesitated. "Yes, that."

"Something else?"

Again he hesitated. "You know my true feelings toward the ones in red."

"Not really," she said. "I'm aware that you're not a major fan—and that you don't want that publicly known. Given your father's history with the Starmind, I understand that. But do they really bother you so much that a reference to them spoils a work of art for you?"

"Yes."

"For heaven's sake, Ling, why? Personal feelings aside, you of all people must know how much the human race owes them—"

"Precisely. How then can I not resent them?"

"Oh, that's silly!"

There might not be another person alive privileged to say that to Chen Ling Ho; from Eva he took it. "Gratitude implies obligation. The scale of the obligation is, in this case, horrifying."

"But there's almost nothing they want that we have—just trace elements we'll never miss. The bill will never come due."

He nodded, and again said, "Precisely. That makes the obligation even more intolerable. It is, on both sides, literally unforgivable."

She frowned. "There's more to it than that."

"What do you mean?" he asked.

"You're not mankind. Your personal share of the debt . . . well, with your resources you could probably pay cash. At most, it's a philosophical abstraction. To spoil a dance, something has to have its roots in your gut, not your head. What really bothers you about the Starmind?"

"Their virtue," he said.

"Come again?"

For the first time, emotion came into his voice. "They are so damned virtuous! So relentlessly admirable. My instincts tell me to despise and fear anyone who appears above reproach. Their harmlessness disarms us. Again, literally! We allowed them to abolish war for us, allowed them to strengthen the United Nations into a true world government. Perhaps war is not, after all, a truly necessary evil—there are more efficient ways of getting rich now—but we may find one day that it was necessary in ways we do not yet grasp."

"Jesus, Ling—you want *war* back? Even I'm not that nostalgic."

"I feel in my heart that in the old days, when we were a brawling, clawing, struggling world, we were more human. Now we grow fat and soft on the riches flung down to us from on high—and because our short-term wealth has *temporarily* overtaken population growth, *we have stopped fearing population growth.* One day we will reach a point where no input of new wealth can help us . . . and then civilization will fall, and millions, billions, will die. Conceivably *all.* All humans. But not the Stardancers. They may *never* die." He heard emotion creeping into his voice and caught himself. "You understand, I do not discuss these matters publicly. Stardancers are much beloved. In this age, no man can hold real wealth or power save he treat with them. Humanity is drunk, today, happily drunk, and in no mood for grim warnings. But how can the Neanderthal not hate the Cro-Magnon, Eva?"

She nodded. Time to change the subject. "Well, I can't say I share your feelings, but at least I think I understand them now. Thanks for explaining. I'll remember not to buy you the new Drummonds holo for your birthday."

"Oh, no," he said. "Please do, if you like. One may admire the exquisite gyrations of cancer cells in the microscope. The choreography of the Stardancers themselves I find very interesting; it's only their existence that offends me."

That made her smile. "It's a shame your country gave up emperors, Ling. You'd have been one of the great ones."

"One hates to be a merely good emperor," he agreed, and finished his drink.

She followed suit. "Are you sleepy?"

"No."

"Shall we go to bed?"

He bowed and took her hand. "All my life I have wondered why other men prize young women."

"Perhaps," she suggested, "they do not feel they deserve the best."

He smiled, and came closer.

18

Washington, D.C.
28 January 2065

The assistant director of the United States Internal Revenue Service knew that her office was as snoop-proof as human ingenuity could make it. Nonetheless she got up from her desk and personally made sure her office door was locked. Then she told her AI to cancel all appointments for the day and hold all calls, and opened a "Most Secure" phone circuit to Brussels.

Her global counterpart, the Right Honorable Undersecretary of Revenue for the United Nations, and Assistant Chairman of the Committee on Fiscal Anomalies, answered promptly. "Hello, LaToya. This is early in the day for you to call. What is it, 8 AM in Washington?" He looked closer. "My God—are you ill?"

"I've been up all night, George."

The Undersecretary sighed. "Something serious, then. All right, which hat shall I wear?"

"Both of them, I think. And hold on to both. You may have to invent a third hat: I don't think there's any precedent for this."

A sigh. "Go ahead."

"George, I've run the integrations through again and again. I used three methods, different machines, I even had the software triplechecked."

"And—"

"You'll be receiving more than you're expecting from us this year."

The Undersecretary lifted an eyebrow. "How much more?"

"On the order of ten percent."

The other eyebrow rose to join the first. "You are telling me the gross national product of the United States has taken a ten percent jump. *Up.*"

"That is part of what I'm telling you. I talked with Jacques and Rogelio last night . . . and they report nearly identical bulges. Jacques puts his at nine percent; Rogelio is running behind, but says Mexico will probably run eleven and a half."

The Undersecretary was frowning. "So someone is pumping serious money into North America. Is it real, or just pixels?"

"As far as I can learn, it's genuine money."

"Where is it coming from?"

"It falleth as the gentle rain from heaven. Drop by drop—all over."

A grunt. "Stonewalled, eh? Very well—where is it *going*? Who's paying taxes on it? What categories?"

"Take a tranquilizer."

The Undersecretary frowned, then did as he was bid. At once the frown smoothed over. "Go ahead."

"One category: self-employed income."

"Self-employed?" That was the last sector in which he would have expected such a surge in earnings. "Any breakdowns as to subcategories yet?"

The assistant director nodded. "Again, one. Self-employed artists."

The Undersecretary stared. After a full ten seconds of silence, he said, "What kind of artists?"

"All kinds of artists. Live theater, dance, film, music, literature, sculpture, painting . . . what it comes down to is, in every genre and subgenre there is, from grand opera to street theater, roughly ten percent of the working professionals have had a very good year."

"And all from the same source?"

"No. Maybe. I don't know. I suspect it, because it all seems to be coming in the same way: anonymous donations, rather than grants or box office. One donation per artist or arts group. Substantial ones."

"But then it's simple!" the Undersecretary said. "Who's declaring the increased donations on their taxes?"

"That's the problem. Nobody. Not in North America anyway. But why the hell would someone overseas want to take such a huge flyer in North American art?"

"Confusing," the Undersecretary agreed.

"Confusing, hell. It *worries* me, George. Good news on this scale is ominous. I smell a swindle of some kind."

"I don't suppose there's any chance these benefactors are North Americans who elected for some reason not to claim . . ." He trailed off.

She politely pretended she hadn't heard him. "Will you look into it, George? *Quietly?*"

"I'll get back to you," he said, and broke the connection.

For the rest of the day work devoured her attention, but she fretted most of the night. The next morning at the office she flinched when her AI said, "The Undersecretary of Revenue."

"Accept!" she said at once.

"He is not on the phone, ma'am. He is in your outer office."

"Jesus." She took a deep breath, and rose to her feet. "Admit him."

Two bodyguards entered first, scanned the room carefully, and nodded through the door. The Undersecretary came in, and dismissed them with some unseen signal. She started to come around her desk to greet him, but he waved her off. They sat together; he came to the point without formalities. "This room is secure?"

The assistant director checked a telltale. "Yes."

"It's happening all over the globe. And in space. High Orbit, Luna City, everywhere. Has been for over six months now."

"*Everywhere?* The same way?"

"Not everywhere. Just the places where people make art for money. But all of those."

She looked surprised. "All? You don't have up-to-date data from all, do you? I thought there were several nations still refusing to switch over to a December 31 tax deadline."

"True; there are nonconforming nations. But almost *all* nations require self-employed artists to report quarterly. I can't prove there are no exceptions, yet, but I'd bet money. The pattern is clear."

She powered her chair back away from her desk until it hit the wall. "Isn't this the *damndest* thing?"

"Have you anything new to report?"

It took her a few moments to respond. "Null results, mostly. I tried to do further breakdowns and correlations, to see if I could get a clue regarding motive. *Which* artists are getting money? Why them? How much? That sort of thing."

"And?"

"Nothing helpful. Some of them are starving-in-a-garret types, but some are major stars or companies, and some are in between. No geographical, financial, political, religious or even aesthetic connections I can find. Competing schools of theory, some of them. The one steady correlation I've identified tells me nothing useful."

"And that is—?"

"The amount. Apparently, each lucky beneficiary—from the poorest poet to the richest director, from barbershop quartet to symphony orchestra—had his or her or its annual budget approximately quadrupled. In a few cases, that comes to megabucks."

The Undersecretary nodded grimly. "That accords with what I've been able to learn."

The assistant director paled. "Good God, George—there are less than a half dozen fiscal entities on or off Terra who are in a position to disburse *that* kind of money—"

"I know."

She got a grip on herself. "So you went to the Secretary."

"I deemed it necessary, yes. This is too big for a bureaucrat like me; I needed a statesman."

"And he said—?"

"He said that an anonymous donation is an anonymous donation, regardless of size. He said no law requires a philanthropist to take a tax deduction. He said support for the arts is not a crime. He said it is the policy of the United Nations to respect the right of privacy. He said, with emphasis, that anyone who violates privacy with respect to support for the arts will be broken back to a G-7 clerk."

She was staring at him in growing disbelief. "He said to forget it. That's what you're telling me."

"He said nothing of the sort. Forget what?"

She opened her mouth. Thirty seconds later, words came out. In the interval, she examined her life, for the first time in decades. "I forget," she said at last.

He nodded. "Elephants never look happy."

She powered her chair back to her desk, looked at it, drummed her fingers on it. "The story *will* come out," she said finally. "Artists always talk to cronkites. Sooner or later one will listen, and realize he has actual news on his hands. The data are public information."

"They will be when we release them," the Undersecretary agreed carefully.

She did mental arithmetic, checking a few figures with her desk. "George, this is scary. *Whoever* is doing this, they're spending themselves broke. At the present rate of outlay, any conceivable candidate donor will be bankrupt in about five years."

George nodded. "That's the figure I arrived at. But there are signs that the rate is increasing."

"My God! George, you know better than I: a fluctuation of this magnitude in the global economy simply has to translate into suffering and misery, sooner or later. Doesn't the Secretary *see*—?"

"I'll tell you what I wish," he said.

"What?"

His voice was wistful. "I wish I had kept up the guitar."

PART SEVEN

19

Provincetown, Massachusetts
24 February 2065

Rhea opened the front door wide. "Goodnight, Tommy," she said politely, and hurled him through the door and clear off the front porch. Tom Cunha landed well, and turned back to her with a baffled expression. She tossed the plastic bag of fresh fish he had brought her after him, scoring a direct hit on his head. "Not tonight," she said. "I have a haddock." She cackled with laughter and slammed the door on him.

The laugh didn't last long; she was too angry. And then the anger too failed her, and she was back to sad. Her shoulders slumped; she turned and headed wearily for the kitchen.

Two weeks to the day since Rand had gone back up to the Shimizu—for good, he said, and she believed him. Fourteen days since her marriage had officially ended. Half a moon of loneliness and celibacy. Provincetown was a small town, its jungle drums especially efficient in winter; the unaffiliated were already beginning to sniff around. P-town being P-town, less than half of them were male, Rhea's own preference. But God dammit, couldn't *one* of the oafs approach the business with any *class*? She wasn't asking for love, or even strong affection. Given the least salve for her pride, she might have relished a chance to lose herself in simple sweaty exercise. Instead she got fresh fish and jovial offers to "take her off the hook."

Soon the global literary grapevine would catch up . . . and then the offers would be even more offensive.

A whole planet of men to choose from, and she didn't know one she'd swap for another night with Rand.

Or Duncan, for that matter. As she passed through the living room on her way to the kitchen, her eye fell on Driftglass, tumbling slowly end over end beside the bay window, balanced on an air-jet at head height. She had placed the vacuum sculpture there, defiantly, the day after Rand had gone back to orbit—right beside the spot where the family-portrait holo of the three of them stood. She stopped and contemplated it now. It seemed to belong there, next to the bay view, among all the old photos and mementos of Paixao history, looked to be a true part of Provincetown.

And all at once that irritated her. It was *not* of Provincetown. It was of space. It did not belong in that living room. The symbolism was wrong, it clashed. Things in Provincetown did not turn end over end in mid-air, defying gravity. Nothing in Provincetown was formed by vacuum except the town government. Space had not only taken her husband and her marriage, it had sent a tentacle down into her very own living room here on Earth. And made her like it. It had seduced her the same way it had Rand . . . with beauty. She could never, would never, go back . . . but she would never again fully leave space behind. A piece of her heart was caught there.

All right: if even her childhood home wasn't safe, there was always the shore. There was nothing of space there. She reversed direction and headed for the door. No sense going to the kitchen anyway; she hadn't been able to choke down a bite in days.

She paused on the porch, to make sure both that Tommy was gone and that she had smart clothes on, and then summoned the car. The bayside beach was less than a block away by foot . . . but the ocean beach on the north side of town would be windier, and thus less populated now that the sunset was long over.

As the seat harness enfolded her, she noticed that the passenger seat beside her was still set to Rand's dimensions. With a sharp gesture, she randomized it again. On second thought, she adjusted it to Colly's shape, and randomized the back seat. Time for the kid to start sitting up front. "Herring Cove, public lot, via Commercial Street," she said, and the car moved forward at the local maximum of 20 KPH.

The four days of Rand's visit had been agony. The first day was Colly's birthday, and both parents were invincibly cheerful, maintaining the truce even when Colly wasn't around for fear of shattering it. That was bad, but it was worse when they began talking on the second day. It took them two more days, progressively worse through exhaustion, before both were willing to concede that there was nothing to say, nothing to be done. Rand was staying in space; she was staying on Terra; no compromise existed. Once they had admitted that, they'd made love one last time, ceremonially. Rhea had never made love in despair before. She did not quite regret it in retrospect . . . but she wished she could stop remembering it for a while.

Perhaps oddly, Duncan's name had not come up even once. She would always remember him fondly, had interceded with the Shimizu to save his job—but she and Rand both knew he had only been a symptom, an excuse, a way out of a dilemma she had not been consciously willing to resolve. And in any case, that relationship was over: Duncan was, by birth, just as committed to space as Rand intended to become.

She phoned Tia Marguerite on her way to the ocean, and was told that Colly was fine, Tia Marion was just giving her a bath, don't you worry about a thing, dear. She cut the connection, and worried.

It had been two weeks. She could not stall forever. Sooner or later she was going to have to have a long talk with Colly, and try to explain the change that had come into both of their lives. Colly knew that she and Mommy were going to be living on Earth again for a while—but had not been explicitly told why, or for how long. She did not yet know that Daddy's visit earthside had been his last. The longer Rhea waited, the harder it would be. But the wordsmith had not yet found the words she needed. Or perhaps it was courage that eluded her.

Commercial Street was a single one-way lane along the waterfront, not much wider than her car. Her progress was sporadic: in compliance with local statute, her car braked for all pedestrians and pets. On either side of her as she drove were a parade of temptations, bar after lounge after club after bistro, each as inviting as human ingenuity could make it, overflowing with the light and warmth and sounds of convivial merriment. She shuddered at the thought of entering one. She began to regret choosing this route—but it did keep her within smelling distance of the shore the whole way, and that was worth the aggravation of being surrounded by people and their damned gaiety. She was glad when she passed the rotary and breakwater by the Provincetown Inn, and left town behind. The car speeded up, and soon her headlights showed only dunes and marshgrass and rosehip and blueberry bushes.

She switched on her clothes, and by the time the car parked itself at Herring Cove they had warmed up. She set out at once into the teeth of the wind, leaving her face unlit to indicate that she did not welcome company. She walked along the shore, feeling her way in almost total darkness, until she found a private semicircle of dune, and crept deep into its pool of shadow. It was too overcast to really see the ocean, but the sound of the surf overpowered and calmed her thoughts, and the shore-smell sank into her bones. She lay on her back in the sand, and dialed down her clothes until she could feel some of its coolness.

She was very near to something like peace when, an hour later, the overcast blew away—and the stars came out.

Even here, half of the entire world was space. The only difference between the view here and that from any window in the upper hemisphere of the Shimizu was that here she was under one gravity of acceleration—and here there was not even a layer of glassite between her and all that emptiness. . . .

No, there was another difference. Rhea had *always* loved the stars. And this beach had always been one of her favorite places from which to view them. Now, as the wind whipped over her, she was forced to admit that they were prettier without atmosphere in the way. In space the stars did not twinkle or shimmer, just burned steadily down forever. There was a better perception of depth, of scale, there. And the distinctions astronomers made—blue star, yellow star, red giant—in space you could actually see them.

Oh, if only the stars could be seen that way without sealing yourself up in a claustrophobic little can!

Or hiring a good shaper . . .

She found herself clutching at the sand on either side of her, and sat up abruptly. As soon as she did, she realized she would not have this stretch of beach to herself much longer. Something over a dozen people were coming her way along the shoreline, faces glowing softly like jack-o'-lanterns. Unusually, they did not seem to be chattering, did not seem to have fetched any kegs or food or instruments or collected any driftwood for a fire. For a moment, instinct made the hairs rise on the back of her neck—but there had not been any serious crime in Provincetown in decades. She watched them approach, hoping they would pass by and keep going.

To her disappointment, they stopped not far away. She stiffened when she saw them form a circle. Trancers! Just what she needed now: dance imagery against the backdrop of the stars. Worse: trance-dance—as close to zero-gee dance as you could find on Earth, in spirit and in phrasing. She got up, had her clothes repel the moist sand that wanted to cling to her back, and headed back to her car, giving the Trancers as wide a berth as the terrain permitted.

Nonetheless, one of them left the group and approached her, just as the first dancer was getting under way in the center of the circle. She started to speed up to avoid him—but slowed and then stopped as she recognized him: Manuel Brava.

He pronounced his name in the old Portagee way, "M'nal." He was a local character, even in a region rich with colorful eccentrics. There was no telling his age; Rhea did not know anyone in town of any age who didn't have childhood memories of him. Nor did anyone know how he made his living. One saw him from time to time, usually in stillness: sitting motionless by the shore of the ocean beach, or on a pier on the bay side, staring out to sea and smiling faintly. He was sort of the Cape Cod equivalent of the wandering Hindu holy man, who lived simply and said little and was fed by all he passed. In return he would give single, short sentences, which were never overheard by anyone but the recipient. People were reluctant to discuss whatever it was Manuel had told them, but the consensus was that he was a smart old bird.

In Rhea's own case, she had wandered past him one day in her sixteenth year with an extra cheese sandwich . . . and in return for it had been told, "When you're alone . . . you're in pretty good company." It had meant little to her at the time, but she had never forgotten the comment, and over the ensuing years it had come to seem wiser and wiser.

At sixteen, being alone had been her greatest fear, and the root of it was exactly as Manuel had diagnosed: a failure to treasure herself. Manuel's casual, offhand comment might as well have been the final sentence of a full day's conversation between them. He had known her, without her knowledge, before she'd ever said a word to him. He seemed to know everyone in town that well; at least, he never seemed to need a second sentence.

Why that wasn't creepy was that what he had said, after studying her that well, was something kind. Good return on a cheese sandwich.

As he approached, now, there was no doubt in her mind that he knew all about the recent upheaval in her life; she waited for her nugget, wishing she had a sandwich on her. God knew she could use a little insight just now.

He stopped beside her and turned so that they both faced the sea and the Trancers. They watched them together for a timeless time. Shortly she forgot that she was waiting for him to speak. Trancedance lived up to its name: there was something elementally hypnotic about it. There was something otherworldly about it too: in some subtle way she could not pin down, the Trancers reminded her of Stardancers. Perhaps it was only the rosy glow of their illuminated faces against the black sea and sky. Their dance did not seem to require any great skill, yet it held her spellbound. For the first time she began to understand why one would want to spend so many hours doing that.

"Be ready," Manuel said. "It's gonna be good."

She turned to look at him, and he was smiling. Her first reaction was to ask, what is going to be good? And when? But Manuel never explained, never amplified. So she was surprised when she heard herself ask, "Will I know when it's coming?"

His smile broadened. "You won't miss it."

Two sentences was a record. She decided to go for broke, and ask him *how* to be ready—but he was already shuffling back through the sand toward the Trancers. She watched in silence until he joined in the dance. Then she turned and trudged away toward her car.

Halfway there she stopped . . . stood for a moment . . . then turned and retraced her steps. She stood at the fringe of the dance for perhaps half an hour before joining it. When she did, it welcomed her.

She returned to linear consciousness in the car, on the way home. Her watchfinger said it was a little after four in the morning. She did not feel as tired as she should have; somehow the dance had given more energy than it had taken. She felt as though if she were to unseal her seat harness, she might float up to the ceiling.

In addition, there was an odd, almost forgotten sensation deep within her. She was hungry . . .

She entered the house at a dead run, and ate nearly half a loaf of *massa cevada,* Portuguese sweet bread, slathered with butter, washing it down with pirate-strength black tea. When she was done, she made and kneaded a vast batch of bread dough for *malassadas.* The fried sugarcoated treats—a Portuguese version of beignets, known locally as "flippers"—were Colly's favorite breakfast.

While the dough was rising, she went upstairs and outside onto the roof, to watch the sun rise from the widow's walk. It was one of the few authentic widow's walks left in Provincetown; five generations of Paixao women had paced these very boards, scanning the horizon for signs of their returning husbands. Every time they had been successful too, eventually; none of the Paixao men had been lost at sea—which probably made this the luckiest widow's walk anywhere. Rhea was conscious that she was breaking the string of good luck, and it brought a pang—but as the colors began to take form on the horizon, she decided it was one she could endure.

Most of the boats had gone out long since, but one unfortunate captain with a cranky engine was just putting out from MacMillan Wharf, warping around the breakwater. A delivery truck was clattering down Commercial Street, and gulls were harassing the garbage collectors. From her high eyrie, Rhea could see the silhouette of a lone figure walking along the shore, beachcombing.

That trance-dance had been her first extended break from pain in many weeks. No, not from pain, but from the suffering of it. At no time had she lost a preconscious awareness of her emotionally damaged condition . . . but she had relaxed to it, ceased to fear it. She believed now that she was healing—even if she had no idea how long the process would take. And she knew she would be returning to the ocean shore to join more trance-dances. Perhaps Colly might enjoy it too; Rhea had seen children at daytime trance-dances, and it was something they could share. . . .

Just as there was enough light for her to make out Tia Marguerite and Tia Marion's house, a few blocks distant, she saw a light go on in the room where Colly would have slept. She went back downstairs and punched down the *malassada* dough. She cut it into pieces, stretched them a little, and set them aside. Then she called Colly, making sure to tell Maxwell not to wake Colly's guardians if she failed to answer.

But she did answer, at once. "Hi, Mom!"

"Hi, honey. Are you having a good time?"

"Sure!"

The enthusiasm was plainly counterfeit; Rhea was recovered enough to hear that now. Colly loved her great aunts—but knew perfectly well that she only slept under their roof when she was being left out of something. "Well, I don't want to spoil any big plans or anything . . . but if you're not here in ten minutes, the flippers won't be hot when you eat them."

"*Flippers?* Homemade? Wow! Quick: open the door so I don't break it." She hung up—and was in the kitchen before the oil was hot. They made the *malassadas* together, giggling, and gorged themselves until they creaked.

And then they had a long, long talk.

20

Top Step
25 February 2064

Rand hung suspended like a fly in black amber at the precise center of the universe, tethered to a mountain. The only sounds were the oceanic ebb and flow of his own breath, and the persistent slow drumming of his pulse. All of creation was arrayed around him. He felt an impulse to put himself into a spin, so that he could see all of it, but knew that he would foul his umbilical if he did. Probably just as well; even half of infinity was a lot to take in at once.

He found himself thinking of a poem Salieri had retrieved for him last night. He had asked for "something with Fireflies in it," and the AI's search engine had yielded up a *hauta,* a species of Japanese folk song more elaborate than the more common *dodoitsu:*

Kaäi, kaäi to
Naku mushi yori mo
Nakanu hotaru ga
Mi wo kogasu.
Nanno in gwa dé
Jitsu naki hito ni
Shin wo akashité—
Aa kuyashi!

(Numberless insects there are that
call from dawn to evening,
Crying, "I love! I love!"—but the

Firefly's silent passion,
Making its body burn, is deeper
than all their longing.
Even such is my love . . . yet I
cannot think through what Karma
I opened my heart—alas!—to
a being not sincere.)

The truly remarkable thing was that the *hauta* had been transcribed and translated into English by Lafcadio Hearn in 1927—seventy years before "Firefly" meant anything but a species of insect. Yet it seemed to fit Rand's situation with eerie accuracy.

The Fireflies had *created* humanity, seeding Terra with life millions of years ago and moving on. The Fireflies were of space. They had returned here the instant man began making art in space. Surely, then, space was where a human artist should go—even if love called him back to Earth.

Space didn't solve your problems . . . but it sure put them into a larger perspective.

"All right, people," Thecla said in his earphones. "Time's up. Precess."

Rand turned with the rest of the class, until they all faced the mountain they had come from: Top Step, the place where humans came to become Stardancers. He was a little self-conscious; he knew he did not really belong here, with these Novices. They were second-month students, only another month away from renouncing their former lives forever and accepting Symbiosis. Being among them made him feel a little like a tourist on Death Row, or an infidel smuggled into Mecca. But Reb Hawkins himself had suggested that he join this class.

Rand already had his "space legs," could handle himself in free-fall—but all his experience was indoors, inside pressurized cubics. Everyone said that to really *feel* space, it was necessary to spend a lot of hours EVA. The Shimizu was equipped to take guests EVA if they wished—but strictly as tourists, carefully shepherded and pampered, in permanently tethered suits with no thrusters at all and so much radiation shielding that mobility was severely limited, for a maximum of half an hour. Groundhogs were just too good at getting themselves killed outdoors. Spacers all laughed at anyone whose only EVA hours were in Hotel Suits—but more advanced training was not offered in-house.

When he'd met Reb Hawkins, he'd found himself telling Reb his problem, and the monk had invited him to visit Top Step and join a Suit Class. "But won't your students resent an outsider?" he'd asked.

"There'll be no reason for them to know you are one," Reb said. "Top Step is a big place now, and we have a strong custom of privacy going back half a century. If you show up in a class one day, people will just assume you've transferred in for some reason, and leave you alone. Most of them will be in the middle of life-reviews of their own."

Rand had thanked him—but still felt uneasy about the idea, and put it out of his mind.

Until his marriage had self-destructed.

When both Jay and Eva had suggested, within hours of each other, that he take Reb up on his invitation to visit Top Step, Rand had shrugged and acquiesced. He and Rhea had agreed that there was nothing a counselor could do to help them—but now that the plug had been pulled, he found that he needed to talk to *someone.* A legendary holy man who made his home in space didn't sound like a bad choice. Rand had liked Reb at once when they'd met, and Jay and Eva vouched for him, "punched his ticket," as Eva called it.

And now, as he rotated in space and faced Top Step—an immense stone cigar, glowing softly at the tip—he had to admit that coming here had been a good idea. Talking with Reb had helped: Reb's end of the conversation had consisted entirely of questions, just the right questions. Taking class had helped: it was hard to sustain self-pity out in naked space. And being around Postulants and Novices and Symbiotics had helped too: all these people were in the process of saying goodbye to their lives, and their company helped reconcile Rand to living his own.

"All right," Thecla said, "we're going to try something new, today: you're all going back in on your own power."

There was a buzz of excitement, but it cut off quickly. Nobody wanted to louse this up.

"One at a time," she added. "I don't want you unsnapping until the person before you has made it all the way inboard. Abadhi, you're first."

One of the two dozen-odd p-suited figures in Rand's field of vision tapped his umbilical join. The tether separated, and Top Step began reeling it in. He oriented himself, starfished, and waited.

"Go ahead."

There was no visible exhaust from Abadhi's thrusters, but slowly he began to move toward Top Step. Very slowly. The trick in EVA maneuvering was to go about half as fast as you thought you should—then you only arrived about twice as hard and fast as you wanted.

At such speeds, covering ten thousand meters takes some time. Porter came far down the alphabet. Rand had plenty of time to study his classmates as he waited for his turn.

He had lost a marriage: these people were surrendering *everything.* They were more committed to space than he would ever be, and they were giving up more to be there.

And in return they would gain so much that part of him envied them. Centuries of life, life free of fear or hunger or loneliness, in the bosom of the largest and closest family that had ever been, working and playing among the stars. Those of them who were artists could spend the next century or two pursuing their art, twenty-four hours a day if they chose, with no need to seek commercial or popular or critical success. Or to look for love.

Maybe someday, he thought. *Maybe in another ten or twenty years, I'll come back here for real.*

The thought came back, *why not now?*

He was not done yet, that was all. Married or not, he was still a parent, and would be for at least another decade. He had not used up his visions yet; he still had shapings to create which would not have worked in a Stardancer context. He had still not outgrown his need for applause, his need to achieve. He had fought for his present position so long and so hard that he could not abandon the cup until he had drained it dry. It had, after all, cost him a good wife.

"Porter—get ready!"

He snapped out of his reverie and ran through the procedure in his mind. *This* sequence of commands tells the tether to go home; *that* combination of taps on the palm keypads will deliver matched bursts from all five thrusters; move my chin like *this* for the heads-up targeting display . . . "Ready, Thecla."

His tether wiggled away toward Top Step. He centered the target ring in his display, stiffened his limbs, and triggered the thrusters. Aside from a mild pressure at wrists and ankles, nothing seemed to happen. The thruster at the base of his spine produced no sensation at all. Could it be broken? No, his display claimed he was jaunting, just as planned. He glanced around, and saw that the others were indeed receding, just quickly enough to perceive. He waited—and after a while, Top Step suddenly began to visibly approach. He checked his position carefully, decided he needed a course correction, and made it.

His aim was good: if the vast open window of the Solarium had had a bull's-eye, he would have hit it on his way through. His deceleration was equally perfect: he ended up motionless within arm's reach of the handgrip he had been aiming for. He saw admiring glances from other returnees, and preened. "Very nice," Thecla said. "Okay, Pribram: get ready!"

His AI, Salieri, whispered in his ear. "Phone, Rand. Reb Hawkins."

He cut off his suit radio and took the call. "Hi, Reb."

"Hello, Rand. Are you enjoying EVA?"

"A lot!" he said. "Thanks for letting me sit in. It's *different* outside . . ."

"It certainly is. Listen, I just wanted to tell you I'm not going to be around for the next couple of days. I have to shuttle over to the Shimizu."

"Really? What's up?"

"A party, of sorts. You're invited if you want, actually—if you don't mind taking a couple of days off from EVA classes, you could hop over and back with me. It should be a memorable event."

"What's the occasion?"

"You know Fat Humphrey?"

"Who doesn't?" The round restaurateur had been famous ever since the release of Armstead's Starseed Transmission at the turn of the century; it was said that his Le Puis rivalled the Hall of Lucullus as a gourmet's and gourmand's paradise. Armstead claimed you never had to tell Humphrey what you wanted to eat, how you wanted it done, or how much you felt like eating. Over the past week, Rand had found that to be literal truth.

"Well, he just turned one hundred . . . and he's retiring to the Shimizu to enjoy his golden years."

"Wow. That's going to disappoint a lot of folks."

"Yes, it will. He's been swearing for decades that he was going to retire the day his odometer showed three figures, and it seems he meant it. Last night after dinner he took off his tux and spaced the thing. The chefs are all people he trained, of course—but it just won't be the same without him sizing up the customers and serving the orders. Fat sweetens the air where he is. Anyway, he won't let us have a farewell party for him here, prefers to just leave like a cat—so Meiya and I are bringing him over to the Shimizu tonight in a special shuttle. There's room for you if you want to come along."

"Sounds good," he said. "I'd like a chance to get to know Fat half as well as he knows me. Every time he pulls that magic act of his, I can't help wondering what *he* likes to eat."

Reb's answer was a moment in coming. "Do you know . . . in almost fifty years, I don't believe I've ever *seen* Fat eat?"

"He must do it some time," Rand said dryly. Fat Humphrey massed well over a hundred and forty kilos; in repose he resembled a Jell-O model of the Shimizu.

"True enough. Well, maybe we'll get to see him in action when we get him to the hotel."

"I'll take him to Lucullus's tomorrow," Rand said. "It would be an honor to buy Fat Humphrey a meal. And you and Meiya."

"Done," Reb said. "Meet us at the dock at 17:00." He broke the connection. Reb never seemed to be in a hurry—but he never wasted time or words either.

The last of the students had returned inboard; Rand turned his radio back on in time to hear Thecla dismiss the class. He left the Solarium and with Salieri's help found his way through the maze of tunnels that honeycombed Top Step to the room he'd been assigned. There he took off his airtanks and thrusters and set both to recharging, and packed a small overnight bag. He was not yet ready to return to the Shimizu full time, but a day or two couldn't hurt. It might be instructive to test the strength of the scab Top Step had begun to form over the deep wound in his heart.

And he could check in with Jay, see how the new piece was going. He hadn't produced a note of music yet, hadn't even viewed the working tapes Jay sent every day . . . but Jay would understand. Rand had left him a perfectly good shaping to use—the New Mexico desert setting he'd already had in the can—and Jay knew his brother was perfectly capable of showing up a week or two before curtain and producing an acceptable score for whatever choreography he came up with. This retreat had been Jay's idea as much as anybody's.

A thought struck him as he packed. "Salieri—can you determine relative locations for Colly and Rhea?"

"Maxwell indicates they are approximately fifty meters apart, Rand."

"Good. Get me Colly on a hush-circuit."

"Hi, Daddy! What's up?" Colly's cheerful voice asked a few seconds later.

"Hi, princess. I just wanted to let you know I'm going back to the Shimizu for a couple of days. I know we were scheduled for a long chat tonight, but it looks like I'm going to be too busy. Can we reschedule for Thursday?"

"Sure. I guess . . ."

"Problem?"

The answer was a while in coming. "Dad?"

"Yes?"

"I . . . uh . . . Mom and I had a talk this morning."

"Oh." The first sensation he was conscious of was of a large weight leaving his shoulders. He had not relished the prospect of explaining things to Colly—but it hadn't looked as if Rhea was ever going to get off the dime. He was enormously relieved to learn that she had.

Then he realized that only half the weight was gone. "Are you . . . okay with that?"

Again the answer was agonizingly slow in arriving. "Can I ask you something? I asked Mom, but she said she didn't know, and I should ask you."

He took a deep breath, and held it. "Go ahead, honey."

"What's the most time I can spend up there with you?"

He exhaled noisily. There was a sound in his ears like bad reception on a suit radio, a sort of vast echoing hum. "Without adapting, you mean."

"No, I found that out from the White Rabbit," she said. "I mean, without being a pain in the butt."

His heart turned over in his chest. "The max, baby. The max. And if that isn't enough to suit us both, I'll come down there and see you sometimes. Until I adapt, anyway."

"That's good," she said firmly. "Uh . . . can I ask you one more thing?"

"Sure."

"Are you still mad at Duncan, Daddy?"

The question was like a surprise punch in the stomach. He took it, and shook his head, and answered honestly. "No, Colly. I'm not mad at Duncan."

"I'm glad. Tell him I said hi. Bye, Daddy—I love you!"

"What an extraordinary coincidence: *I* love *you.*"

"What are the odds of that, huh?" She hung up smiling.

Rand finished packing. Then, with time to kill before he was due at the dock, he played some of Jay's tapes, and tinkered with ideas for musical accompaniment. Hell, maybe he should stay at the Shimizu when he got there, and get back to work. Maybe it was time to resume his life. He could play around with EVA another time, when there wasn't so much to do. He thought of calling Jay, to tell him he was coming. But the timing was bad: Jay would be in the studio now. He decided to call when he got in.

The trip to the Shimizu was thoroughly enjoyable, despite the spartan furnishings aboard the small shuttle. Fat Humphrey in a p-suit was an unforgettable sight, for one thing. And as a traveling companion, he was the original barrel of monkeys; while they were all unstrapped between acceleration and deceleration he even managed to produce a recognizable parody of *Kinergy* that reduced Rand and everyone else aboard to tears of laughter.

Rand was honored to be included in the merriment. It was apparent to him that this trip was a sentimental journey for Reb—and for Meiya, Reb's successor as Head Teacher at Top Step. While they had been training and graduating a quarter of a million Stardancers together over the past half century, Fat Humphrey had been one of the very few constants in their lives. Meiya, a quiet, solemn woman, wore an expression that reminded Rand of old pictures he had seen of mothers sending their sons off to war.

As he watched Fat Humphrey mock the moves of a Stardancer, he suddenly wondered why Fat had not accepted Symbiosis on retirement. But he knew he would not ask, not today anyway. The question was in an area of privacy you learned not to violate if you spent any time at Top Step: he didn't know Fat well enough yet.

And the man read his mind. The moment the laughter for his performance had died away, he looked at Rand and said, "You wonderin' how come I didn't eat the red Jell-O for my dessert, huh?"

"Well . . . yes, Fat, I was, as a matter of fact."

Fat Humphrey grinned. "You ever hear about the time them assholes blew up about a cubic kilometer of Sym?"

"Sure." Almost a decade before Rand's birth, a fanatic antiStardancer terrorist group, headed by Chen Ling Ho's father, had somehow managed to destroy a large mass of Symbiote on its way from its source in the upper atmosphere of Titan to Earth orbit, where it was supposed to serve the needs of the next generation of Top Step graduates. Several Stardancers riding herd on the load had been killed.

"Well, most o' that was suppose' be for me. They been tryin' to catch up ever since, but it's gonna be another twenty year or so before they ready to handle me again." Rand cracked up; so did Reb and Meiya. "I figure in the meantime I watch a little TV, go for a swim, catch a show. You get me a good seat?"

"Well, I'll tell you, Fat," he said thoughtfully, "in terms of sightlines and vectors, maybe what we should do is mount a special show just for you."

"How you mean?"

"Put you in the center of the theater, and work around you."

Fat roared with glee and slapped him on the back; fortunately his seat belt held. "You're all right, kid."

They reached the Shimizu by 19:30. The deceleration was as mild as the acceleration had been, no more than half a gee, and for only a few minutes. Rand could have taken more easily, but the others were all spacers, intolerant of gees.

Fat Humphrey had specifically requested that there be no reception on his arrival. Of course Evelyn Martin had double-crossed him, and was waiting at dockside to drag him off to a press conference. But Rand had halfway expected that: he debarked first, took Martin aside, and threatened to take him by the testicles and fling him through the nearest bulkhead into hard vacuum if he didn't change orbits, now. Grumbling and muttering, the little PR man complied. It is difficult to slink in free-fall, but he managed it. "Don't bother with check-in," he snarled over his shoulder as he went. "It's covered. Just take him right to P-427."

Rand rapped on the hatch to signal that it was safe, and the others emerged. As nanobots scurried away with luggage, he tried to show Fat Humphrey where to insert the wafer that would install his AI in the Shimizu's data crystals . . . and was startled and a little nonplussed to learn that Fat did not have one.

"How about you, Meiya?" he tried.

But she shook her head too. "I won't be inboard long enough to bother. We'll all use Reb's to get around."

"Well, okay," he said. "But stick close to him. This place can be a rabbit warren if you don't have an AI."

"There are public terminals all over, left over from the old days," she pointed out. "If I get lost, I can just ask for you."

"Sure. I'm not listed, but my AI is: Antonio Salieri. How about if I go get my brother and meet you all at Fat's new suite in about an hour? I'd like to grab a shower too; I've been in this p-suit all day."

"Good with me," Fat Humphrey said.

"We'll meet you there in an hour," Reb said, and installed his own AI. "Rild—direct us to Suite Prime 427, please."

One of several exits began to blink softly. "This way, *Tenshin.*"

Rand jaunted to his own room, checked the time, and decided to phone Jay before showering. He would have just finished dinner by now.

"Hey, bro, what's shapin'? When are you coming back?"

"About five minutes ago. Want to meet the happiest fat man in human space?"

Jay blinked. " ' . . . the happiest fat man . . .' Hey, you mean Fat Humphrey? Is *he* here?"

"To stay. He's just retired; it's his centennial. I came along for the ride; I'm going back with Reb tomorrow. Little gathering at his new digs in about an hour: just him, you, me, Reb and Meiya, as far as I know. You know Meiya, right?"

"Sure. Hey, this is great! I've always wanted a chance to kick back and talk with Fat for a few hours. Where's he at?"

"Prime 427. Meet me at the nearest corner at 20:25 and we'll go in together."

"See you there."

Fifty minutes later he was waiting at the appointed spot. Almost at once, Jay arrived from another direction, grinning. They hugged, and pounded each other's shoulder blades.

"How are you, bro?"

"Fine," Rand said. "I've gotten a *little* work done—I'll show you later."

"The hell with that—how *are* you?"

"Okay," he said. "Not well, yet, but I can see daylight, you know?"

"That's good. I told you that place'd be good for you. Hey, Eva's gonna be here too: Reb called her. Probably in the suite already, in fact; I spoke with her half an hour ago and she said she was leaving right away. I get the idea she and Fat are old friends."

"It wouldn't surprise me in the—"

The lights went out.

"What the *fuck*—" Jay said. "Diaghilev!"

No answer.

"Diaghilev, God dammit!"

"Salieri?" Rand tried.

Silence.

There was a public terminal nearby, but it was unlit, presumed dead. "Jesus," Jay said softly, clearly controlling his voice with an obvious effort. "I think the whole fucking system is down. That's never happened. I'd have bet a billion dollars it couldn't possibly happen."

They heard a scream somewhere in the far distance; no telling even the direction. The Shimizu corridors had some funny acoustics.

Rand's heart hammered. "Oh my God . . ." If they had no lights, no AIs, no phones—how long before they had no *air*? He fought for calm in the claustrophobic darkness. "All right, what's our move?"

Just then lights came on. Small red emergency lights, every hundred meters along the corridor, with larger blinking ones marking intersections. Rand found them an immense relief, a sign of recovery, but he saw Jay frowning. "They should have kicked on a *lot* sooner, even if this is a total system collapse," Jay said. "Something really weird is going on."

"Have we got air?"

Jay spotted the nearest grille, jaunted to it, and put his face near it. "Yeah. Reduced flow, but it's air."

"What do you think: is this just local, or is the whole damn hotel really dark right now?"

"Beats me. They're supposed to be equally impossible. I pray to God it's local."

A suite door opened not far from them, and someone stuck his head out. "Hey, mate," he called in an Aussie accent, "any idea what the bloody hell is goin' on?"

"Look at it this way," Jay called back. "You're getting tonight's rent free."

"Too right," he said, and closed his door again.

"God," Rand said, "Fat and the others must be freaking out in there. If they had the window closed when the power failed, they're in minimal emergency lighting: it could take them an hour to find the manual door release, let alone figure out how to use it."

"Hell of a welcome to the Shimizu," Jay agreed. "Come on, let's go try and calm them down."

They jaunted in the eerie pale red light to Suite 427. "We'll never convince Fat the place is safe now," Jay complained as they neared it. "Shit, I just don't *believe* this. The only thing I can imagine taking out the Shimizu system is a comet right through the core crystals—and we didn't feel any impact. It just doesn't . . . oh, you asshole." Automatically, he had stopped in front of the door and waited for an AI to ask his business. "Hit that release for me, will you, bro?" he said, pointing.

Rand pulled open the access hatch indicated and pulled the handle inside. It moved easily—but the door did not move. "Seems to be broken," he reported.

Jay grimaced. "Naturally. Things never go wrong one at a time." He put his hands on his hips. "Christ, the door's soundproof—we can't even bang out 'Calm down' in Morse code."

"What's Morse code?" Rand asked.

"Eva would know, but it doesn't—wait a god damn minute! What do you mean, 'broken'? That's a mechanical latch: it *can't* be broken."

"Okay," Rand said agreeably. "Then what *does* nonfunction and a blinking red light mean?"

"A blinking—"

In free-fall one almost never pales visibly; blood does not drain from the head as pressure drops. But even in the poor light, Rand could see his brother's expression come apart. He jaunted quickly to Rand's side and stared at the little flashing pilot bulb. After a few seconds, he began to shake his head slowly back and forth, the picture of denial.

Rand grabbed his shoulder, *hard,* and shook him. "What does it mean?" he cried.

Jay turned to him. There was horror in his eyes. He needed three tries to get the words out, and when he did, they were barely audible. "There is no pressure on the other side of that door."

21

High Earth Orbit
25 February 2065

Sulke Drager had always hated it when everybody talked at once. Thirty years as a member of a telepathic community had taught her a great deal about handling multiple inputs—more than any human being had ever known—but never before in history had so much of the Starmind all been sending at the same time. And underlying it all, pervading the whole Solar System like a taste of metal in the back of the mouth, was the wordless shriek from Saturn.

And naturally, the "voices" she most needed to "hear" were the weakest. They were also the closest, but distance means nothing to a telepath; signal strength and bandwidth were all that counted.

So she borrowed energy from every Stardancer in the heavens who was *not* shouting something, and used it to drive a message that had never before been sent across the matrix.

Shut the fuck up!

The System seemed to echo in the sudden relative quiet. Even the wordless wail from the Ring halved its "volume" and "pitch" and dropped back down into the region of speech. The words—*Save him, Sulke!*—repeated endlessly, like a mantra.

And now Sulke could clearly hear the gentle voice she most needed to hear. *All right so far, cousins,* Reb said. *We are all unharmed so far, which means they intend to parley. Be calm.*

She knew his location precisely now. The vessel in which he was imprisoned was superbly stealthed—the combined power of the

United Nations could not have found it—but she had detection gear no battle cruiser could match, if the target was another telepath. Reb had been one years before he'd met his first Stardancer; a natural adept. So were Fat Humphrey and Meiya.

So were four other humans currently in space, and fourteen on Terra. About average for humanity. All of them had been kidnapped too, at the same time as Reb, Fat and Meiya—every one was now a prisoner—but *this* vessel was Sulke's pidgin: the one she personally happened to be close enough to do something about. She instructed her subconscious to monitor the other ongoing rescue operations for data relevant to her own problem, and consciously ignored them.

She fed Reb's location to those who were good at orbital ballistics, grabbed the report that echoed back and swore. *You're going nowhere fast! Your trajectory is taking you up out of the ecliptic, and there's nothing there!*

He was still calm. *Naturally. We knew they must have a covert base in space; now they're leading us to it. We already know where the ones dirtside are being taken.*

Yeah, and we can't touch the place. What if where you're going is just as well defended?

Then we will have to be very clever. And very lucky.

She went briefly into rapport with those who had had military training back in their human lives, and swore again. *We have Stardancers vectoring to intercept your projected path at multiple points . . . but there's no way to know where you're going until they decelerate. And if they maneuver in the meantime, we could lose you completely.*

They probably will. They're paranoid; they'll assume their stealthing may not be good enough, and try every trick there is.

I can match orbits with you right now, she said. *You're coming right at me, near enough.*

What about relative speeds?

She was already adjusting her lightsail, spinning out Symbiote like pizza dough. *You're a bat out of hell—but if I can grab hold, and it doesn't kill me . . .* She had an unusually powerful thruster on her belt she had never expected to use; she poked it carefully through the Symbiote membrane, borrowed a hundred brains to help her aim it, and fired it to exhaustion.

What can you accomplish? Meiya asked.

Tear off antennas, bugger up their communications, bang on the hull and distract them while you jump 'em . . . if I have to, I'll unscrew the fucking drive with my fingernails.

There was a hint of a chuckle in Reb's voice. *I love you too, Sulke. Whoops—they're about to drug me . . .*

Me too, Fat Humphrey said. *Watch your ass, Sulke.*

She could see them now, by eyeball, and they were indeed coming on fast. But she was confident; she had learned to board a moving freight when she was eight years old, leaving a place then called East Germany. *Yeah?* she sent back. *I'll give you a two-kilo gold asteroid if* you *can pull off that trick, pal.*

His answering giggle was the last thing she ever heard. She never saw the white-winged figure who came up behind her and put a laser bolt through her brain.

PART EIGHT

22

The Shimizu Hotel
25 February 2065

Jay remembered an old story from the dawn of spaceflight: a Skylab astronaut had awakened to a lighting failure, and had taken nearly twenty minutes to find the backup switch—in a sleeping compartment the size of a phone booth. Darkness and free-fall were a disorienting combination.

He knew his way around the Shimizu about as well as anyone alive—but in the eerie, feeble glow of emergency lighting, everything looked *different.* In places even the emergency lights had failed, and almost everywhere he and Rand encountered adherents of the ancient philosophy, "When in danger, when in doubt, run in circles, scream and shout." There was absolutely no doubt in Jay's mind that somewhere Evelyn Martin was hemorrhaging and tearing his hair out in clumps.

For the first time in his life, Jay did not give a damn about offending guests; he and Rand went through them like buckshot, leaving a trail of outrage and broken bones that was sure to give birth to expensive litigation.

The destination that would most efficiently allow them to find out what was going on, report what had happened, and do something effective about it, was Kate Tokugawa's office. There were other nerve centers, but that was the only one Jay was confident he could find in his sleep without AI assistance. It was startling to realize how much you depended on the damn things. *God help me if I suddenly need a cube root or something,* he thought wildly, bouncing a fat bald groundhog off a bulkhead.

Rand deked expertly around the ricocheting guest and pulled up alongside him. "They couldn't have started losing pressure before the blackout, or we'd have heard alarms. To reach zero by the time we tried that latch, they must have blown out *fast*."

"The whole window must have gone," Jay said.

"Is that possible?"

"No. Not without help."

"So they're dead?" He clotheslined an employee who was, quite properly, trying to prevent them from speeding recklessly through a developing riot—and, since it was the quickest way to explain, regretfully sucker-punched the woman as he went by.

"Probably. But maybe not."

"How do you figure?"

"I ask myself, what could take out a whole window? I come up with a ship designed for the purpose. I think they've been snatched. I think when they jaunted into that room, the window was already gone: *they saw a holo of one.* And at some point they all got sleepy . . ."

"And somebody came through the holo and towed them away . . . wouldn't somebody *notice* a fucking barnacle attached to the Shimizu?"

"Remora," Jay corrected. "It moves. Not if it was stealthed well enough. Fat's room is all the way around from the docks. And by now it's gone—and the sphere of space within which it could possibly lie is expanding every second. You can spot even the best-stealthed ship by eyeball, by occultation of background stars—but you have to know just where to look."

"Maybe we should quit dawdling, then." They were into the final corridor now, a straight run of perhaps two thousand meters; perhaps a dozen flailing figures cluttering the way between them and the door to Management country. He lifted his head, bellowed "FORE!" at the top of his lungs, tucked his chin and triggered all his thrusters at max.

Jay did likewise. Miraculously, everyone managed to scatter out of their way. Halfway to the door, they shut down, flipped over, and began to decelerate—and discovered that they had both burned themselves dry. They impacted with bone-jarring crashes, desperately grabbed handholds, and nearly had their arms pulled out of their sockets by the rebound. Jay's first thought was for Rand, but his brother threw him a shaky grin and a circled thumb and forefinger.

Jay found the manual doorlatch and released it. He was greatly relieved when this one worked; he had not been sure he would find pressure in Management—and had had no idea what to do if he didn't. They scrambled in together, then resealed the door to keep out guests who wanted a refund. There was nobody at the front desk, nor in the outer offices beyond it. "Where the hell *is* everybody?" Rand snarled.

"I don't know," Jay snapped, even more nervous than his brother. This was wrong, wrong—"Wait a minute." He doubled back, went to the front desk. "I filled in for a guy once or twice," he said as he got there, and began tapping code on a drawer under the counter. "Let's see if they still . . . ah!" He got the drawer open—and took from it a totally illegal police-issue GE hand-laser. "Sometimes Security doesn't show up fast enough when you call them," he said, checking the charge and clicking off the safety. "*Now* let's go see what's in back."

"I'll go first and draw fire," Rand said. He and Jay exchanged a glance. It became a grin. "The Hardy Boys in High Orbit," Rand said.

"And in a big-ass hurry."

They worked their way back through the outer offices to Kate's door cautiously but quickly, Rand preceding his brother through every doorway. Finally they floated outside her office.

"No point in listening at a soundproof door," Jay said.

"No point in knocking, either," Rand agreed, and opened the manual release compartment. "I'll go first, again."

"No need. I'll *know* where the target is, if there is one."

"Okay. If there's trouble in there, you go right and I'll go left."

"Which way is that?" They happened to be upside down with respect to each other.

"You go away from me and I'll go away from you." Rand unlatched the door. It let go with a pop, and opened a few centimeters. He gripped the release latch to brace himself, and slid the door the rest of the way open. He and Jay entered together, and stopped.

And then both began to laugh.

They knew it was inappropriate; that only made it worse. Facing them was one of the most ridiculous sights they had ever seen: Evelyn Martin, holding a gun.

Laughing, Jay tried to move away from Rand as agreed—and remembered that his thrusters were dry. He still was not worried; he and his brother could outjaunt a spastic like Martin with muscles alone.

Then he saw Katherine Tokugawa well to his left, also armed. His laughter died away. They were outgunned. He shook Rand's shoulder and pointed her out. After a microsecond's thought, his own gun steadied on Martin. If he were going to be killed by one of these two, he preferred Kate. More dignity.

"Drop it," Martin yapped.

Jay thought hard for a whole second, then opened his fingers. The gun, of course, stayed where it was.

"*Lose* it," Martin corrected, expressing his exasperation by putting a bolt into the wall beside the doorway. The smell of burning bulkhead plastic filled the room faster than the air-conditioning could suck it away. Jay gave his own gun a finger-snap, like a child shooting marbles; it drifted away toward Martin. Ignoring the man, he turned and addressed Kate.

"I should have figured you'd have to be in on this," he said. "But I'm damned if I can see how you expect to come out of it with your job."

"Oh, I'll probably lose that eventually," she agreed. "But by then I'll have a better job."

"A better job than *this?*"

"Much better. I'll be running something a little more prestigious than a hotel."

"What's that?"

"High Orbit," Martin said, and snickered.

"Shut up, Ev," Tokugawa snapped.

He stared. "What the *hell* are you talking about? Nobody runs High Orbit."

"No," Martin said. "The UN wouldn't let them. But the UN isn't going to be around much longer." He giggled nervously.

"Shut *up*, Ev," Tokugawa barked. "You can tell them things like that after they're dead. Not before."

Jay tried to restart his laughter; it didn't catch. "You seriously think you can take on the UN—and the Starmind—and win?"

Kate couldn't resist answering. "Not me," she said. "But I know people who can. I've been working for them all my life."

"You artists are always yapping about your 'vision,'" Martin said, and brandished his gun. "Ha! You assholes don't know what vision is! We're gonna reshape the future."

Jay felt the universe shifting in his head, crushing his brains beneath it. Surely this was lunacy. Even the UN itself could not have defeated the Starmind. He could conceive of nothing human that could.

"Come in, gentlemen," Tokugawa said then. Jay glanced over his shoulder, and saw two Security men enter with guns drawn. Each, he noticed, wore an unfamiliar earplug and an unobtrusive throat-mike. Communications gear that did not use the house system. Turning back, he saw that Tokugawa and Martin both had them too.

"So," he said to Kate, "you already know more about what happened in Fat Humphrey's room than we do."

She nodded. "Oh, yes. Much more."

"Of course. You assigned Fat his room. So this is where you gloat, and tell us what's going on, so we can be awed by your cleverness?"

"No," she said. "This is where you get taken away and killed. Goodbye, Sasaki." She sketched a *gassho* bow. "It has always been a pain in the ass to work with you. Martin, you go along with them—make sure it looks pretty; that's your line of work."

Jay opened his mouth to say something, but never got a chance to learn what it was going to be. Something touched the back of his neck, and he slept.

It was a very troubled sleep, full of unpredictable accelerations that triggered horror-dreams of falling from his terrestrial past, and unfamiliar voices shouting incomprehensible things in the near and far distance, and the nagging certainty that something he couldn't quite recall was terribly, terribly wrong.

You were *meant* to come out of the drug confused. But his surroundings when he finally did certainly enhanced the effect.

He was in a corridor. Not a public one, a . . . the term took awhile to surface. A service tunnel, that was it. The lighting was even lousier here. Things were floating in his vicinity—important ones, he sensed. First he counted them: four. Then he classified them: human beings. Next he laboriously identified them. Evelyn Martin. His third-grade gym teacher—no, that was . . . was . . . right, one of the security guards who was going to kill him. Sure, there was the other one. And the extra one . . . hell, know him anywhere: that's my bro. Like a brother to me.

So now he had them broken down into two groups. Friends: one. Foes: three. That didn't seem like a favorable ratio. On the other hand, one of the guards seemed to be lacking a face; that evened things up a little. And Ev Martin's head hung at a funny angle . . .

A few more foggy seconds of contemplation and he had a second breakdown he liked much better. Rand was breathing; the rest were not.

The example inspired him; he breathed deeply, stoked his brain with oxygen and felt the cobwebs begin to melt away. *This is great,* he told himself. *How did I do this?*

As Rand began to show signs of recovering consciousness too, a hatch opened nearby and Duncan Iowa appeared. "Good," he said. "You're awake. I ditched their comm gear on the assumption it's trackable, but we ought to move anyway. No telling which systems they have up and running." He moved to Rand, started to slap him awake . . . then thought better of it, and instead spun him, to centrifuge blood into his head. "Take this and keep lookout," he added.

Jay got his hands up in time to catch a laser considerably more powerful than the police-issue job he'd liberated from the front desk. He blinked at it for a moment—then snapped out of his fugue. He checked charge and safety, assessed the tactical situation, and assigned himself a guard post. "You're something else, kid," he said wonderingly. Duncan ignored him, busy with Rand.

Rand spent less time in stupor than Jay had. Groundhogs and new spacers usually shook off drug effects faster; their blood pressure was higher. He looked around at the drifting bodies, shook his head like a horse shooing flies, glanced at Jay and turned back to Duncan.

"I punched you in the mouth," he said wonderingly. "And you let me live."

"I had it coming," Duncan said tightly. "Look, we've got to move. I don't need to know who we're running from or why just now, but if you know anything that would suggest where to, I'd love to hear it."

"Shit," Jay said. "I wish I knew more about riot-control procedures . . ."

"What do you need?" Duncan asked.

"For a start, a large tank of sleepy gas with a hose on it."

"Come on," Duncan said, jaunting away. "I'm an Orientator—I know this dump better than Kate Tokugawa."

I hope you're right, Jay thought. Rand jaunted after Duncan, and Jay took up the rear, gun at the ready.

In the discreetly unmarked riot-control compartment Duncan led them to, they found the tank Jay wanted, fresh thrusters, and a sonic rifle for Rand. While they swapped the new thrusters for their exhausted ones, they also exchanged information.

"I was heading for Deluxe country, I knew the panic would be worst there, and I took service corridors to make better time. Then I saw Martin and those two goons go by at an intersection ahead of me, guns out, towing you two. They didn't see me in the lousy light."

"What made you decide to butt in?" Rand asked. "And how did you know which side you were on?"

Duncan didn't duck the question. "I'm in love with your wife, and she's in love with you. I didn't want her hurt."

Rand didn't duck the answer. "I understand. How did you ever manage to take all three of them?"

Duncan shrugged. "All three were earthborn. Taking Martin's gun wasn't a major challenge. Actually the other two didn't do too badly; I was trying to keep one of them alive to question, but they hurried me. So tell me: who are the bad guys and what do we do about them?"

"Anybody could be a bad guy," Jay said. "But the one we know about is Kate Tokugawa herself." Duncan's eyebrows raised, but he made no comment. "And what we're going to do is take her alive for questioning. But I almost hope she hurries us. She's behind the system crash—she's using it to cover a kidnapping."

Duncan's eyes widened, then shut tight. "Jesus."

"You think they're alive, then?" Rand said.

"Have to be. There are much easier ways to kill somebody."

"Easier ways to kidnap people too. They could have snatched us off the shuttle without all this hooraw."

"The Space Command keeps a careful eye on moving objects in High Orbit," Jay said, "but they hardly ever look at the Shimizu.

Doing it here cost the bastards, but it probably bought them enough lead to get away clean."

"Who got kidnapped?" Duncan asked.

"Fat Humphrey Pappadopoulos, Reb Hawkins, Meiya and Eva Hoffman. Possibly others, but I'm sure of those. They snatched them right out of a suite: right out the goddam window and into a stealthed ship, long gone by now. I don't know what the fuck is going on, but it has something to do with a coup against the UN."

"Jesus Christ!" Duncan said. "An honest-to-God old-time coup d'état?"

"I think *coup du monde* is more like it, from the way Ev was talking. I don't care what historians call it, as long as they put 'failed' in front of it. So we need Kate—alive, and with her vocal cords intact; everything else is optional. She's in her office . . . and I think I know how to get her out, if we can get there alive. But that might be a problem. I'm sure she has a private surveillance-and-defense system. She let us approach the last time because Martin didn't want to have to explain embarrassing laserburns on our corpses to the cronkites—but if she sees us coming again, I don't think she'll hesitate."

"So what's the plan?" Rand asked.

Jay sighed. "I was hoping one of you would come up with something. *I* don't know how you storm a castle with a slingshot when they know you're coming."

"I do," Duncan said. "You use the servant's entrance."

Twenty minutes later, they peered out through the grille of an air-circulation tunnel ten meters from Tokugawa's office door. They were all wearing stock p-suits scavenged from the riot-control locker, but maintaining radio silence. Jay unsealed his hood and sniffed the air; when he didn't pass out, the others did the same.

"I think we're inside her perimeter," Duncan said. "I don't see anything in that hallway that looks like the business end of a laser."

Jay wedged past him and looked. Bare walls. He clutched the tank of sleepy gas to his chest. "So one of us tries it and the other two avenge him if necessary."

"Let's not rush into this," Rand said.

Jay laughed mirthlessly. "Feel a little stuffy in here to you, bro?"

"Now that you mention it, I'm sweating like—oh!"

"When a groundhog starts to sweat, he smiles and reaches for a cold beer. When a spacer starts to sweat, he reaches for his p-suit." The hotel's backup system had power for air circulation and limited lighting—but none for cooling. The Shimizu was a shiny ball of metal in the sunshine, full of heat-producing people, and contrary to groundhog belief space is not cold at all. "Folks are going to start dying if the system doesn't come back up in the next hour or two: we're running out of time."

"How do you plan to get her to open the door for your gas?" Duncan asked.

Jay grinned wickedly. "I don't need to. Ev Martin drilled a neat little hose-sized hole for me about a meter earthward of the door." He started to push the grille free, but Rand stopped him.

"Let me," he said.

"I claim privilege," Jay protested. "I've known Eva and Reb a lot longer than you have."

"My point exactly. You said before you almost hope she hurries you. I don't. I have less need to find an excuse to kill her."

"That could get *you* killed."

Rand grinned. "Well, bro, just now the world doesn't need a first-class shaper as badly as it needs her."

"I'm faster than both of you put together," Duncan said.

Rand turned to him. "Yeah. But that's a massy tank: you haven't got the muscles to hump it. Some things, earthborns are better at. Besides, it's my turn to do something heroic. Okay?"

After a moment, Duncan nodded. "Good luck."

"Thanks."

After all that melodrama, the capture itself was ludicrously easy. Everything went like a good opening night, just enough adrenalin to keep you in top form and no surprises you couldn't cope with. There were hidden gas-jets in the hallway—but p-suits made them irrelevant. The laser-hole by Tokugawa's door was the perfect gauge for Rand's hose. She had a p-suit of her own stashed in her office, and managed to reach it—but passed out before she got its hood over her head. Once they had access to her terminal, Jay and Duncan were able between them to coax the system back up and on-line in a matter of minutes. As the main lights came on, they could almost feel the cheer reverberating around the Shimizu. Then, ignoring the hundreds of incoming calls, they put in an SOS to the Space Command, and soon found themselves talking to an Admiral Cox, an old warhorse who was most interested in—and totally unfazed by—an attempted overthrow of the planetary government. With a minimum of words, he extracted from them every scrap of useful information they could give him, then put them on hold.

Despite a mild sense of anticlimax, Jay felt himself grinning. "We did it, guys," he said.

"Hell of a note," Rand said. "I started the day a respectable artist—and now I'm running a goddam hotel."

Jay giggled. "You may be going out there just a star, kid . . . but you're coming back a waitress."

"You know," Duncan said, "I always *thought* I could run this dump better than that asshole." He gestured at the sleeping Tokugawa, and all three of them broke up. She did look silly. In the absence of gravity, simply binding a person's wrists and ankles does not immobilize her effectively enough; instead you tape each wrist to its related bicep, each ankle to its thigh, then tape elbows and knees together. The result looked remarkably like a Buddhist in the midst of prostrating herself.

But their laughter chopped off short when they noticed that she was no longer breathing.

" . . . and about half an hour later, Commander Panter showed up with six Marines in full armor—and here we are," Jay finished. He glanced at his watchfinger. "I'd say she died about two hours ago. That's everything we know, Admiral."

He and Rand and Duncan were in a place any small boy would have killed to visit: the command center of the Citadel, the UN Space Command's principal fortress in space. It looked just like it did in the movies. The only person with them now was Admiral Cox himself, a grizzled old centenarian with a startlingly warm smile—but Jay knew perfectly well that every word he'd just said had been heard by literally hundreds of people on and off Earth. It was beginning to make him distinctly uneasy too. Cox was treating them as vip guests—but Jay was beginning to suspect how long it might be before he slept in his own bed again.

Cox sucked coffee from a battered military-issue bulb, and nodded sadly. "Post mortem shows a fatal allergy to sedation. Iatrogenic, of course. Her superiors didn't even give her an option. They wanted her interrogation-proof. Interesting people."

"I'm sorry, Admiral. We should have thought—should have given her antidote right away—"

Cox shook his head emphatically. "There was no other way to take her; you'd have thrown your lives away trying. And it was too late for antidote the moment she lost consciousness. More coffee, gentlemen?"

Jay had been too busy talking to consciously taste his; he queried his tongue and learned that the brew had come from the Atherton tablelands of Queensland. "Yes, please, Admiral." The others accepted as well, and a servobot much uglier and clumsier than anything in the Shimizu brought them fresh bulbs.

There was a short silence while they all drank. Rand broke it. "We screwed up," he said hollowly—and Jay felt himself nodding in agreement.

"On the contrary!" Cox said. "You walked among the lions today, son, and all your blood is still on the right side of your skin. Are you sure none of you has had military training?" All three shook their heads. "If you were my cadets, I'd be sewing stripes on all three of you right now."

"But we don't know *shit*," Rand insisted.

"We know a lot more than we would if you three had gotten yourselves dead trying to take her cowboy-style! I'd be sitting here right now, listening to Kate Tokugawa tell me the emergency was over and thanks, but they didn't need any assistance. Who knows how long it would have taken for someone at Top Step to try and call Humphrey, and get a no-such-guest-in-house? Now we've got everything you learned, *days* before they thought we would—and five low-level thugs we were able to take alive, we can sweat them—"

"—and it all adds up to doodah," Jay said. "If the Security goons know anything useful, they'll be allergic to interrogation. And what we know just doesn't make any goddam *sense*."

"Not by itself, no. But it may tie in with other things . . . tell me, would you gentlemen consent to hypnointerrogation? You may know things you don't know you know."

"On one condition," Rand said.

"State it."

"Admiral, this is high-level stuff. I'm a civilian. I want your personal word that when you put this all together, you'll share it with me. I'll take any kind of secrecy oath you want—trigger me up like a courier if you want, so I *can't* talk—but I have to know. Not what the cronkites get told, but the truth."

"The same goes for me," Jay said.

"Me too, Admiral," Duncan said.

Cox did not answer right away, and they did not hurry him. He met each of their eyes in turn. Finally he said, "I agree to that, whether you consent to hypno or not. You've earned it. For a start, I will tell you that yours wasn't the only kidnapping. Data are still coming in, but there have been at least two others in space, and more than a dozen dirtside—beautifully coordinated, assorted methods but one hundred percent success rate. I am not aware of any other military engagement in modern history accomplished with such elegance and efficiency. Billions were spent. Well spent."

"What kind of people were taken?" Jay asked.

"Saints."

"*What?*"

"Holy men and women. Spiritually enlightened people. Like Reb and Meiya—and Fat Humphrey too, in his way. Several different faiths, and two whose religion has no brand name at all, but they're all what Reb would call *bodhisattvas.* Mother Theresas, if you're old enough to get the reference. You know: saints."

"You mean like the Pope?" Duncan asked.

"I didn't say religious leaders. I said spiritually enlightened people. One of them seems to be an Aboriginal witch woman. Another is a Pakistani musician who only plays hospitals."

"Of course," Rand said, slapping his forehead. "What's wrong with me? You want to overthrow the UN, naturally you kidnap saints, musicians and fat maitre-d's."

"It just keeps getting worse," Duncan said. "More than a dozen perfect military operations, carried out by wealthy morons."

"Admiral, is there anything the captives have in common *besides* . . . well, besides holiness?" Jay asked.

Cox lifted one bald eyebrow respectfully. "You do keep surprising me, Sasaki-*san*. Yes. One and only one overt connection between them. They are all known to be on especially intimate terms with the Starmind."

Rand's eyes showed a gleam of excitement. "Some sort of hostage deal—" he began.

"I've asked the Starmind for their evaluation of the known data," Cox said. "It can take a week to get an answer from them on a simple question, sometimes, but they've promised me at least a preliminary answer by 12:00 Greenwich, about . . ." He winked briefly; his own watch was inside his eyelid. " . . . twelve hours from now. You'll have slept off the hypno by then. Meet me here at noon and you'll hear anything I do."

As far as Jay was concerned, he woke up with a click, totally refreshed and restored and in a comfortable bunk, one second later. He never managed to remember anything of leaving the command center, let alone the hypnointerrogation process itself. It did not trouble him, then or ever; he simply slid out of his sleepsack, confirmed that he had time to keep his appointment, stuck his head out the door and had the Marine stationed there cause breakfast to be fetched.

He did find himself wondering, as he ate, whether any alterations might have been made in his memories or motivations while he slept. But he reasoned, correctly, that the ability to form the question was a reassuring clue, and dismissed the matter. His generation had been the first in a century to grow up trusting its government. Instead he tried to imagine how possession of holy people gave anyone leverage over the Starmind and/or the UN. No rational answer suggested itself.

He reached the command center early, and was admitted by the Marines guarding it; Rand and Duncan arrived shortly thereafter. At noon exactly Admiral Cox jaunted in, looking exhausted. It was obvious he had not slept. "Good morning, gentlemen," he said. "I hope this won't prove to be—"

"*BILL.*"

The voice came from everywhere. Jay found it hauntingly familiar, but couldn't pin it down. Then he grasped what it had said, and was suddenly dizzy, a most unfamiliar sensation for a zero-gee dancer.

Cox was a common name. But this was Admiral *William* Cox. *The* William Cox—former commander of the *Siegfried*! Jay had assumed he was dead. He was used to the company of vips and uips—but he had been drinking coffee and chatting with a legend: the first human being to have set eyes on a Firefly . . .

"Yes, Charlie, I'm here," Admiral Cox said quietly.

Jay gasped aloud in shock. This could be no other than Charlie Armstead himself. Shara Drummond's video man, the man who had personally taped the Stardance; co-founder of the first zero-gee dance company in history; the second Stardancer who ever lived and the spiritual father of Jay's artform. He felt his dizziness turn to nausea.

But he felt infinitely worse when he heard Armstead say, *"I'M SORRY OLD FRIEND. I HAVE VERY SAD NEWS . . ."*

23

Somewhere North of the Ecliptic 26 February 2065

Eva woke hard, feeling every one of her hundred and sixteen years, tasting each one somewhere on her tongue. Her first coherent thought was that Jeeves must have been nipping at the cooking sherry. He had mutated into a Chinese gorilla and put on a white p-suit. But he still had that quality of shimmering self-effacement. "Good morning, gracious Lady," he said, and bowed. Even the bow was different.

"The hell it is," she replied—and realized they were conversing in Cantonese, a language she had not spoken in forty years. "Speak English."

"This one regrets that he cannot, Lady." There was something wrong with his p-suit speaker; it gave his voice too much treble.

She took several deep breaths, and felt the mists begin to recede. That wasn't Jeeves—or any AI. It was a human being . . . sort of . . . and too dumb to be a servant. And why was he in a p-suit when there was plenty of air in here? Something was badly wrong.

She played back memory. The last thing she could recall was asking Fat Humphrey what he wanted from Room Service. She looked around. This was not part of Fat's suite—or anywhere in the Shimizu. It looked more like a construction barracks, unpainted metal and visible joins. She and this Cantonese thug were alone here. There didn't appear to be even any potential furniture—not so much as a sleepsack. No wonder her neck ached so badly: she had been nodding in time with her breathing for . . . God knew how long.

Hours, at least. Her chest hurt too. In fact, her everything hurt.

Well, some phrases she knew in over a dozen languages. "Where am I? Where are my friends?"

"Lady, this one is too ignorant to be questioned. His instructions are to offer you nourishment, and then convey you to his master."

"Who is your master? You can't be *that* ignorant."

"That is not for this one to say, gracious Lady."

She decided asking him his name would be a waste of time. A tagline from an ancient comedy series flitted through her mind: *He's from Barcelona, you know.* "Skip the nourishment. Can you show me to the washroom?"

That turned out to be something he could handle, thank God. It was down a short corridor from what she was getting through her head was her cell. The Cantonese minder never took his eyes from her, and though he wore no visible weapons something about his bearing said he didn't really need any. She understood now that he wore a p-suit so that he could use sleepy gas on her if he felt he needed to.

As soon as the door sealed behind her, she tried to empty her mind of everything but the question, *Reb, are you alive? Are you here?*

Nothing came back. She thought she might have detected something like a carrier wave, a power hum, but there was no signal. And it might have been wishful thinking. Reb had only been tutoring her in this empathic sensitivity stuff for a couple of months, and her progress had been frustratingly slow. She tried "tuning in on" Meiya and then Humphrey, but was unsurprised to achieve no better results. She was on her own.

Well, she had a century and more of practice.

Bladder empty and face washed, she looked about the horrid little cubical for a useful weapon. The facecloth seemed to exhaust the possibilities. She gave up and left. Her self-effacing jailer was a discreet distance down the passageway, and quite alert.

"All right, Marmaduke: take me to your leader." She spoke in English, but he seemed to take her meaning. He led the way—but jaunted backwards, so that his eyes rarely left her.

She memorized the route, and kept her eyes open along the way. This pressure felt *bigger* than a ship, somehow. Indefinable subconscious clues told her it was something more like the Shimizu or Top

Step: a massive habitat. More like Top Step in the old days: thrown together, rough carpentry, baldly functional. She also got the impression he was taking her by the back way. They passed few people, and once when they did, he and the others had bristled at each other like challenging cats in passing. She filed the observation away.

The room he led her to reminded her a little of her own suite in the Shimizu. Spartan simplicity—but expensive simplicity. She grew a chair and shaped it to suit her. "You may leave me," she said.

He grimaced. "This one regrets that he cannot, Lady. But he will cease to intrude." With that, he . . . became a piece of furniture. It was like a robot powering down; suddenly he wasn't there anymore, except in potential. She tried to catch him breathing, but to her wry amusement she found she could not keep her eyes on him for more than a few seconds; they slid off. She gave up, studied the right arm of her chair, and ordered strong black tea.

She was intrigued to notice that it appeared to arrive under its own power, herded not by microbots but by invisible nanobots. Rough carpentry, yes . . . but state of the art technology.

As she took the first sip, the door sighed open and Chen Ling Ho entered. The Cantonese powered back up and came to attention.

"You could have just asked," she said. "Two of my marriages were elopements."

Chen smiled. It struck her that that was his only response. Almost any other man she had ever known would have felt obliged to make a clever comeback. He made some signal she didn't quite catch, and the guard left, in a wide, fuel-wasting arc to avoid passing between them.

When the door had slid shut behind him, Chen spoke in Mandarin. "Sun Tzu—privacy!"

"Yes, Highness," his AI replied in the same language.

"There," Chen continued in English. "We now have total privacy. But very little time." A chair came to him and enfolded him, and a globe of water found his hand. "I am sorry you were caught up in this, Eva. I would have had it otherwise."

"Where are Reb and the others? For that matter, where the hell are *we*?"

"*Tenshin* Hawkins and his friends are sleeping presently." He sipped his water delicately, and pursed his lips in approval. "Your second question has many answers. We are in an elongated polar orbit, high above the ecliptic, in a region of space where neither the United Nations nor the Starmind could find us, even if they were looking. This pressure itself is many things. Fortress. Laboratory. School. Flagship. My home away from home."

"Is 'prison' in there somewhere?" she asked. "Or can I go home now?"

He failed to hear the question. "Specifically, we are in my quarters, which I invite you to share."

"Damned rude invitation. I hurt all over. Don't you know any better than to subject spacers to high gees?"

"There was a regrettable need for speed and stealth," he said. "All possible care was taken: military antiacceleration technology was employed. Happily, you all survived."

"But in what condition? The others should have woken before me; they're all younger."

"But they left Terra behind much longer ago. Their journey was actually more arduous than yours. But do not worry: I am told that their health is excellent."

"Then when will they wake up?"

He sighed. "I do not envision that occurring, I'm afraid."

She set her jaw. "Ling, quit dancing and spit it out. What's going on?"

"You will recall the economic summit conference in the Shimizu last month?"

"Let me see . . . the one we almost got killed during, or am I thinking of some other one?"

He ignored the sarcasm. "We five have managed to repair our relationship . . . for the time being, at least . . . and are now about to destroy the Starmind and overthrow the United Nations."

Eva Hoffman had known more than a few power-mad men and women in her lifetime, including some who were quite successful at it. Had any of them made such a statement, she would have laughed, or at least wanted to. From the lips of Chen Ling Ho the words were blood-curdling. No flip response was thinkable. "My God . . . ," she whispered, horror-struck.

"We hope to create the first rational planetary government," Chen went on conversationally. "Rather along lines K'ung Fu-Tzu might have approved of, I think. But it scarcely matters. The point is that once the Starmind is annihilated, any mistakes humanity makes will be its own."

REB! For God's sake, WAKE UP!

Just the barest hint of response, like a man turning restlessly in a deep sleep.

"Ling, for the love of Christ, humanity can't *make it* without the Starmind, not anymore, you know that!"

"Precisely why the Starmind must die. The riches it showers on us are like welfare checks: they demean, and degrade, and diminish us. Stardancer benevolence has already devolved us from wolves to sheep, from roaring killer apes to chattering monkeys, in three generations. This trend *must* be reversed, before the inevitable day comes when the Fireflies return. The transition will be painful—but we will make it by our own efforts, as free human beings, or die trying."

"You really think you can kill every Stardancer in the Solar System? *How?*"

He frowned, and chose his words carefully. "Before I can answer that, Eva, I must ascertain your status. I have stated my intentions. Three options are open to you: you can be friend, foe or neutral."

"Nice of you to offer the third choice," she said.

"Yes, it is. But if you choose it, I cannot answer your question, or any other of a strategic or tactical nature. In that event I will sequester you here, in reasonable comfort but complete ignorance, and release you in your own custody when events have resolved. On the order of three months from now."

She noticed that he did not say, " . . . on the *close* order of . . ." and grimaced. "I assume foes don't get briefed either."

"On the contrary," he said. "If you tell me that you oppose me, I will answer any questions you have. You have been an intimate companion to me, Eva: I would wish your death to be as agreeable as possible."

Reb, wake UP! Rise and shine! Dammit, you're gonna wet the bed!

"I see. And if I claim friendship?"

"You get it," he said simply. "After this is over, you can have the Shimizu for a gift if you like. It lies within my fief."

"And you'll take my word."

"Eva, I know when you are lying."

"How long do I have to think it over?"

"As long as you wish. But in ten minutes I must leave here to begin the attack, and I will be unable to return for at least twenty-four hours. If you wish to witness history as it is happening, at my side, you must choose to be my friend before I leave this room." He swiveled his chair away from her and began scanning a readout of figures in no alphabet she knew, politely giving her space to think it through.

The trouble was, she thought, the canny little son of a bitch probably *would* know if she lied. That was bad, very bad, for she had to oppose him—*had to*—and dared not even hint why. After a hundred and sixteen weary years and countless flirtations, death had come for her at last, was a matter of minutes away. She was shocked by how much that realization hurt—but even a newfound fear of extinction was of less importance than the awful responsibility she *must* now discharge before she died.

Why me? she thought—and smothered the thought savagely. That was exactly the kind of self-indulgence she could no longer afford. Instead she made her limbs relax, took control of her breathing, and forced herself to remember the words Reb had once told her.

"It's state of mind more than anything else, Eva. Telepathic sensitivity is largely a matter of sweeping the trash out of the communications room. Try and remember what it was like when one of your babies cried in the night and woke you. There is no 'you' at such a moment, no ego, no identity, no fear, no viewpoint . . . only the need, and the feeling of it, and the will to serve it, to soothe the pain at all costs."

She kept measuring her breath, felt her anxiety begin to diminish. She had not meditated with any regularity since the 1970s, but it seemed to be one of those riding-a-bicycle things. Perhaps it is true that it becomes easier to surrender the ego at the point of death, when you finally admit that you cannot keep it forever anyway. Eva soon felt herself going further away from the world than usual, or perhaps closer to it—climbing to a higher place or perhaps it was descending to a deeper level, though neither term meant anything in zero gravity—went *beyond,* achieving a selflessness she had only been granted a few times in all her years, for fleeting moments.

With it came a wordless clarity, a focused four-dimensional seeing. Dualities of all kinds became as obsolete as up and down: within/without, self/not-self, good/bad, life/death.

She now knew exactly where Reb and Meiya and Fat Humphrey were: how far away, and in which directions. There was another sleeping adept here in this pressure, too, one she did not know. Their consciousnesses were like fireflies—not the mighty aliens but the feeble terrestrial kind, glowing like embers and dancing mindlessly in the dark. She called out to them. Each resonated to her mental touch, but none responded. They could not "hear" her, and she could not wake them.

There was no help here. She must cope alone.

She let herself return to her body.

She had forgotten how weary and frightened and angry it was. From a purely selfish point of view, dying didn't seem like such a terrible idea. Chen was still scanning what looked like the same screenful of gibberish.

"How long have I got?" she asked.

He checked the time. "Another six minutes before I must leave."

No more time at all. "Chen Ling Ho, I oppose you with all my heart."

He closed his eyes for a moment, and inhaled sharply through his nose. "That is regrettable," he said sadly. "As you wish. I will tell you as much as I can before I must go; any questions you still have can be answered by Sun Tzu."

"How can you possibly kill a quarter of a million indetectable people in free space?"

"Do you remember the terrorist bombing of a shipment of Symbiote from Titan, some forty-five years ago?"

"Sure—your father did it. But that was a traveling ocean, constantly announcing its position. What's that got to—"

"This will go faster if you reserve your objections. My esteemed father Chen Hsi Feng was acting in accordance with a plan devised by his noble father, Chen Ten Li. His intent was not merely to destroy Symbiote, but to discreetly secure a large sample of it for analysis. Fine control of the explosive caused the Symbiote mass to calve in a predictable pattern. While all eyes fixed in horror on the destruction, then turned Earthward in search of its source, a stealthed ship was waiting quietly in the path of one of the largest fragments.

"My father was assassinated by a Stardancer trainee, but the conspiracy he had dedicated his life to lives on. That sample has been studied intensively ever since. We now know how to grow a pale white variant which does everything Symbiote does *except* confer telepathy. It has been further altered so that it requires regular large doses of a chemical which does not occur naturally in space to stay alive. One as astute as yourself will immediately appreciate that it is therefore now possible for the first time to create a Symbiote-equipped army which will stay loyal. Starhunters, we call them. Among other things, this base we're in now is to Starhunters what Top Step is to Stardancers."

In spite of herself, Eva objected. "You can't possibly have raised up an army large enough to threaten the Starmind, not in secret. The head start they've had, the way they breed, the motivations you can't possibly offer a recruit—I just don't believe it."

He was nodding. "And since our troops must use radio or laser, limited to lightspeed, our communications and coordination are inherently inferior to telepathy, a crippling disadvantage. You are quite correct: we could never seriously threaten the Starmind with infantry, even though Starhunters are heavily armed and Stardancers are not. The Starhunters are not intended to kill the Starmind. They are chiefly intended to conquer the United Nations Space Command, and thus the world. He who rules High Orbit rules Terra."

"And what is the Starmind going to be doing at the time?"

"Running for their lives, the few left alive. If they are intelligent enough to keep running right out of the Solar System, a handful of them may live to circle some other star—and good riddance to them, for they can never return. Do you recall how the Symbiote mass was bombed?"

She thought hard. Forty years ago, she had read an eyewitness account by a Stardancer named Rain M'Cloud, who before entering Symbiosis had killed Ling Ho's father to avenge the bombing. Eva seemed to recall there'd been something uniquely horrid about the method of delivery . . .

She felt a thrill of horror as the memory surfaced. "A nanobomb. Concealed in a kiss."

"It worked well—and close study of Symbiote has suggested many improvements. For the last forty-five years, we have been seeding the entire Solar System with similar bombs, self-replicating at viral speed, self-powered, absolutely undetectable. They ride the solar wind, seek out red Symbiote, home in, burrow in and hide. They've been spreading through space like a fine mist for forty-five years. Stardancers breed like rabbits. Statistical analysis indicates that by now, some ninety to ninety-five percent of the Starmind has come into physical contact with either a bomb-spore, or another infected Stardancer."

For a moment she thought her old heart would literally stop. This was what she had always imagined that would feel like. "Radio trigger?" she managed to say.

"Relays all over the System," he agreed. "About an hour from now I will broadcast a master triggering signal from here. At the moment named in that signal, some six hours later, every relay will begin sending the destruct code at once. Maximum possible warning due to light-speed lag should not exceed one minute anywhere in the System."

"Trillions of dollars," she murmured dizzily. "To murder angels."

"It could not have been done undetected in anything but the wild-growth economy the Starmind gave us," he admitted. "So in the end they have served a useful purpose."

"Some of them will survive," she said fiercely, and felt something tear in her chest. She ignored the pain. "They'll come for you—they're good at nanotech, they'll find a way."

"Quite possibly," he agreed. "That is why we have kidnapped *Tenshin* Hawkins and his friends, and every other human telepathic adept we could locate. Enslaved by drugs, I believe they will function as excellent Stardancer detectors. Is there anything else you wish to know, Eva?"

She was silent, concentrating on listening to her heart, willing it to keep beating.

"Is there any other last favor I can grant you, in the name of our friendship? I fear time is short."

Was there any chance at all that the truth might change his mind? She had no other cards to play.

No, none. She remembered a fictional god she had read of once, called Crazy Eddie, worshipped with awe because in times of crisis he invariably incarnated in a position of responsibility and did the worst possible thing from the best motives. There were usually just enough survivors to perpetuate his memory. It was proverbially pointless to reason with Crazy Eddie . . .

"I . . . I'd like an hour alone to compose myself," she said.

"Done," he said. "Sun Tzu!"

"Yes, Highness?"

"Ms. Hoffman is not to leave that chair, nor this room." The chair's seatbelt locked with an audible click. "She is not to communicate with any person or persons outside this room. One hour from now I want you to kill her painlessly. She may command you to shorten that deadline, but not extend it. You may answer any questions she has, and serve her in any way that does not conflict with these instructions. Acknowledge."

"Program loaded, Highness."

He pushed his own chair away and bowed, a full formal salute of farewell. "Goodbye, Eva. I'm sorry you will not share my joy."

Then he bowed again, quickly. Her tea-bulb missed his head by an inch, ruptured on the unpadded bulkhead behind him and splattered his back with hot tea. When he straightened, she was giving him the finger.

His expression did not change. He left.

Pain nagged at her attention, but she had long ago learned to bypass pain. She could still dimly sense Reb and the others; a ghost of the seventh sense with which she had perceived them earlier was still with her, like a ghostly heads-up display on her mind's eye. There was no point in entering deep meditation and trying to wake them again. She had no assets she had lacked the last time she'd tried, was weaker if anything, and the medical technology keeping them stupified was sure to be foolproof.

She was going to have to think her way out of this. Or fail and die.

God dammit, I have not *endured all these years of bullshit to become the greatest failure of all time!*

And with that, an idea came to her. It was only a possibility, and a long shot at that, but it was infinitely better than nothing.

She thought it through carefully, with the slow, intense deliberation of a freezing man with a single match planning the building of his fire. She built event-trees in her mind, assigned probabilities and risks, prepared contingencies, rechecked every calculation. Finally she felt she was ready.

Assuming that she was right, and did in fact possess a match . . .

She checked her pocket, and found her personal wafer was missing. She hoped that was a good sign.

Well, I'm not getting any younger.

"Jeeves!" she said.

He shimmered into existence. "Yes, Madam?"

Chen Ling Ho had cherished the hope that she would agree he was Alexander the Great and accept the role of emperor's companion; naturally he would have installed her AI on-line in case he won her over. He would remove the wafer again after she was dead and his war was over. That much had made psychological sense. What had worried her was a matter of semantics. Was an AI a "person"—in the opinion of another AI? And if so, since AIs were effectively everywhere, was Jeeves a person "outside this room"?

She was still alive. Step one accomplished. Now to push the envelope . . .

"Jeeves, is Rild on-line?"

If the answer was no, Sun Tzu would not know who Rild was, and might kill her out of caution, just in case this Rild was a "person." And Eva thought it likely the answer would be no.

Chen's holographic gear was excellent; Jeeves became discreetly pained. "Yes, Madam. He has been under constant interrogation since our arrival in this pressure."

Good. Then Sun Tzu was aware of Rild, and classified him as "not-a-person-outside-this-room."

"Rild, can you hear me?"

Reb had long ago given Eva access to all but the most personal levels of Rild; she was privileged to summon him. The question was, did he have bytes to spare? Or did the software interrogating him tie up too much of his capacity?

"Yes, Eva," Rild's soft voice said.

She felt like she was tap-dancing on a high wire in terrestrial gravity. Balanced in her hand were all the eggs there were, or ever would be. She began breathing in slow rhythm, composing herself, reaching again for the wordless timeless Evaless place. "Do you have some way to wake Reb?"

The answer came from far away, down a long tunnel. "Yes. A posthypnotic trigger."

Causing a person to be awakened is not communication. "Do it," she murmured, and her eyes rolled up.

This communication, Sun Tzu was not equipped to monitor . . .

* * *

Reb was there waiting for her; awake, untroubled, numinous. His serenity helped calm her, eased her fear, brought them closer together.

She merged with him. She became him, and he her. For the first time in her life she sensed what it must be like to be a Stardancer. She had always wondered why beings who expected to live for centuries did not fear death *more* than a human; now she understood. It was not the brain that mattered, nor the mind which invested it, but the energy that wore both like a series of intricate disguises for a time and then became something else. She had dimly known this for a long time; now she surrendered to it.

She *felt* the entire Starmind, all around her, heard its chorus echo in the Solar System, grasped its quarter-million-member dance in its entirety, from the orbit of Mercury to the farthest fringes of the Oort Cloud where the comets winter.

And when that happened, Reb knew all that she knew, simply and effortlessly. And she in turn knew what he knew, which was all that the Starmind knew. Well over ninety-nine percent of that information she would never get to integrate, but she did have time to perceive certain essentials.

Such as: nanotechnological booby-trapping is a game that two can play. And: some nanobombs can be triggered, not by radio signal, but by biting a simple code on the back of one's tongue. And: her great granddaughter Charlotte in Toronto was going to recover. And: Reb loved her, and everything was going to be okay now. And finally: things are worth what they cost, and death is a small coin.

She even had time, in those final nanoseconds, to grasp the full extent of the cosmic joke the Universe had played on her, and to begin to smile.

Then she and Reb and all the other atoms in and of Chen's flagship were converted to a rapidly expanding perfect sphere of plasma, the color of a Stardancer.

Different conditions obtained on Terra; at the same instant, the corresponding base in North China began turning into a large white mushroom cloud, the color of a Starhunter.

24

Noteworthy Events in March 2065

—Military mop-up of the rebel forces went into high gear, spearheaded in space by Admiral Cox and on the ground by General Chang of a mortified China; after the first week, loss of life was nominal. Doubtless many conspirators were missed . . . but they were not free for long. Some ninety-three percent of the relay trigger stations in the Solar System were located and destroyed, although it was apparent that all those who had known the trigger code had died in the same instant.

—After lengthy consultation with the Starmind, the UN high command elected to delete all mention of a plague of triggerable nanobombs in space from its report to the public. This had the effect of making the Rebellion of the Group of Five appear a desperate, doomed kamikaze affair rather than a narrowly averted coup. Despite—or perhaps because of—its irrationality, the story played.

—The media went into delighted spasm, like sharks dropped into a fish farm. Old-timers for whom the business had lost something when people stopped having wars wept openly. The Sacrifice of the Adepts passed almost instantly into fiction—the cronkites and riveras had it to themselves for nearly a week before the first movie and novelization could be released, and then the floodgates really opened. The job of massaging the legend into a pleasing shape began. The performing arts, oddly, did not seem to take to the new subject: most of them already had funded work under way, with more upbeat themes.

—The Board of Directors of the Shimizu Hotel appointed a new manager and a new PR chief. A special monument was installed in the Grand Foyer, to honor their predecessors, who had bravely sacrificed themselves in a vain effort to ensure the security of guests. In return for keeping their faces straight at the dedication of this monument, and their mouths shut forever after, Co-Artistic Directors Rand Porter and Jay Sasaki received lucrative new contracts terminable only by them. Each contained an ironclad artistic control clause.

—The Board of Directors of the Starseed Foundation announced that Top Step would suspend operations while replacements were sought for its key personnel. The current three classes would graduate, those who made it through, but it would be at least four months before any new Postulants would be lifted to orbit. During the month of downtime, Top Step personnel would be busy dealing with the arrival from Titan of the largest mass of fresh Symbiote ever shipped, a truly stupendous tonnage intended to meet the next fifty years of anticipated demand.

—Rhea Paixao and the group with which she had been trance-dancing two days a week learned belatedly that Manuel Brava had been one of the Martyred Bodhisattvas, and would not be showing up to join them again. His absence had gone almost unnoted; he had been that sort of man. They all went home and mourned—but the following Saturday night, the group spontaneously reformed on the beach, and Rhea was there. When she got home that morning, she began a novel with a Stardancer as a major character.

—In Yawara, North Queensland, the Yirlandji elders chose another witch woman, and held services for Yarra, who had returned to the Dreamtime after dreaming a mighty dream in a place called China. A song was sung for her by the whole tribe, a song by a dead protégé of hers, called "The Song of High Orbit." And indeed some particles of her may have followed the Songline that far, for all anyone can know.

—All over the Solar System, Starhunters began to die, for lack of a chemical so exotic it was not likely to be found on any ship they could raid. The luckiest of them had nearly a year's supply in their system when the source vanished; some had only weeks. The average ran about three months: the Group of Five had tended to keep its undetectable army on a short leash. As this became clear, some chose to emulate the example of *Tenshin* Reb Hawkins and briefly lit the heavens. Some attempted to surrender to the UN Space Command, and some to Stardancers; the survival rate in the latter category was much higher, but neither agency was really geared up to produce the needed chemical in bulk. Starhunters became the first new addition to the endangered-species list in thirty years.

—People in business suits all over the planet and throughout human space found their adrenal glands flooding as the wills of Chen Ling Ho, Victoria Hathaway, Grijk Krugnk, Imaro Amin and Pandit Chatur Birla came into effect; fortunes were made and smashed as the economic machinery of a species began to shift gears.

—Jay Sasaki took a day off from rehearsals, went EVA in a p-suit, and danced a dance he had choreographed in his mind months ago, but never gotten to perform. It was not taped or seen by any human or Stardancer eye, but when he was done, he felt somehow that it had been appreciated. Its working title, the only one it ever received, was "I Love You, Eva." The next day he asked his half-brother to help him shape a new piece, involving a butterfly with a withered body.

—The Human Genome Project issued its final report to the United Nations; it was formally thanked and ordered to begin dissolving itself. After three quarters of a century, the massive planetwide research effort had at last succeeded in deciphering all the "pages" of the DNA "book" which made any sense, a truly staggering accomplishment. Among other effects, the day seemed now in sight when disease would be spoken of only in the past tense.

Still largely unexamined, of course, were all the "garbage pages," the introns, popularly known as "junk DNA": the quite lengthy segments of genetic material (over ninety percent of the total) which, lacking end-begin codes, never express. The prevailing theory was that they represented several million years of accumulated nonlethal errors in transcription. One of the Directors of the HGP argued passionately before the UN Science Council that there was no such thing as an uninteresting component of DNA, and begged for at least some continued funding. But since introns had no discernible effect on human metabolism, there seemed little urgency—indeed, little point—in studying them, and Council voted to spend the money on more interesting problems.

* * *

Noteworthy Events in April 2065

—Minions of the Group of Five continued to be identified and taken into custody, on Terra and in space. Admiral William Cox suffered a transient ischemic attack while overseeing the cleanup in space; lateral paralysis proved reversible, and his cognitive and communicative faculties remained unimpaired; nevertheless he was awarded the Terran Medal of Valor and retired on full pay. He took up residence in the Shimizu, in the restored suite whose last guest, Humphrey Pappadopoulos, had enjoyed it so briefly. He chose it because Terra was not visible from its window. In the weeks that followed, there was always at least one Stardancer outside that window, available should he wish company.

—The United Nations Executive Council decreed that henceforth June 22, Solstice Day, would be a global holiday in honor of Reb Hawkins and the other slain Adepts, and would be known as Courage Day. On that day no nonessential work was to be performed, and all humans who could possibly do so were requested to take part in a planetwide Hour of Remembrance, scheduled for 3 PM Greenwich (thus 7 AM in Los Angeles, midnight in Tokyo; only residents of the Pacific islands need lose any sleep to participate). There was to be no formal ceremony involved; it was asked only that citizens of Terra go outdoors at that time, contemplate the sky, and remember the Adepts. The idea was a popular one.

—As the media orgasm crescendoed, most of the planet overlooked an offbeat story from New Orleans. It seemed that the area immediately around the French Quarter had fixed itself up, more or less overnight. Centuries of grime vanished; crumbling sidewalks became elegant banquettes again; decayed hulks strengthened themselves and grew ironwork balconies as intricate and lovely as anything in the predominantly white part of town, and the statue of Louis Armstrong in Armstrong Park sparkled as it smiled down on a manmade pond whose water was pure enough for human consumption for the first time in a hundred years. Tourists emptied out of the Quarter to stare enviously—and soon were being charged admission. The Mayor publicly promised that if the rapturists responsible would come forward, he would give them the keys to the city and hire them to finish the job . . . but there was no response.

—Duncan Iowa was asked by ADs Porter and Sasaki to join Nova Dance Company as an apprentice, the company's first spacer. He proved a diligent pupil, and by the third day he was showing the other dancers tricks.

—Hidalgo Rodriguez's wife Amparo finally succeeded in persuading him that the implement in his magic new home obviously designed as the perfect male urinal was in fact intended to be a sink (Ridiculous! Who did dishes while they moved their bowels?), and that he must use this other silly thing instead. And remember to put the seat down afterward. It made no sense at all to him, but nobody had ever said upward mobility was easy.

—Rand Porter, in private conversation with Charles Armstead, finally brought himself to ask the question, "Were all of you in rapport with Reb and the others when they did it? Did the Starmind feel their deaths?" and was told, "We wished to, but they would not permit it. They shielded us." The answer did not help him sleep any better, but he was glad to know.

—Somewhere above the Ring, the Stardancer Rain M'Cloud was finally brought out of catatonia by the combined ministrations of her children Gemma and Lashi and one Olney Dvorak. At once she began dancing her grief. The others, each separated from her and each other by at least a million kilometers, joined her in ensemble and submitted to her choreography. The rest of the Starmind attended, and resonated. The loved ones of all the other dead Adepts already danced their dances as well. Yet the Starmind as a whole did not grieve, and even among the most grief-struck like Rain there was an acceptance, a resumption of life, a looking forward. There was much to be done.

—Performing arts groups all across the planet began premiering new works. Not a single one was depressing. An inordinate percentage incorporated images or subtexts of space, or of floating, or of flying.

—Pursuant to the last will and testament of Eva Hoffman, a glass quart bottle of Old Bushmills Black Bush, about half full, was delivered to Jay Sasaki. Later that evening, he and Duncan Iowa lightened its mass by another two ounces, and became lovers.

—The estate of Evelyn Martin formally filed suit against the Shimizu Hotel, its Board of Directors and citizens Duncan Iowa,

Rand Porter and Jay Sasaki, alleging wrongful death, loss of consort, slander and assorted other torts and seeking a billion dollars damages from each and every defendant; suit dismissed with prejudice when trial software determined that the estate and the deceased had been married for a total of four days and had not seen one another in the ensuing twenty-seven years.

—Rhea Paixao increased her trance-dancing to three days a week, and began taking her daughter along.

—The Nanotechnology Lab near Top Step announced the commencement of a major new research effort. Its stated purpose was so abstruse that the cronkites gave up and took refuge in repeating the words as if they understood them. No one caught them at it.

—The Right Honorable George Kiku, Undersecretary of Revenue for the United Nations and Assistant Chairman of the Committee on Fiscal Anomalies, took early retirement under his burnout clause, and resumed a long-interrupted study of the guitar. It came back hard, but he took to soaking the fingertips of his left hand in cold tea, and eventually the calluses returned.

—Alert Space Command software noted that an unusually high number of Stardancers were in the close vicinity of Terra, and that many more seemed to be vectoring earthward. But since it did not classify Stardancers as either threat or navigational hazard it did not notify any human beings.

Noteworthy Events in May 2065

—The last Stardancer was successfully disinfected of her submicroscopic bomb, and shielded against reinfection. A misty disk of death still spun about the Sun, but it could now be ignored until it was convenient to clean it up.

—Colly Porter received a vacuum sculpture by courier. It was called "Puffball," and pleased her mightily. Her mother liked it too, and placed it in a prominent place in the living room, beside one by the same sculptor called "Driftglass."

—A dancer named John DeMarco, realizing his dream of a lifetime, was invited to join Toronto Dance Theatre as a principal dancer, largely on the strength of a particularly inspired performance at the Drummond four months earlier. His former Artistic Director never forgave him for accepting, and made a point of telling him (mendaciously) that she had faked every single orgasm.

—LaToya Dai Woo, Assistant Director of the US Internal Revenue Service, resigned under a cloud having to do with inexplicable anomalies in that year's data; while the antiquated computer system was torn apart and rebuilt, she moved to the Shimizu Hotel and took up recreational sex.

—The New Orleans self-renovation phenomenon began occurring in ghettos, slums and eyesores around the planet. One economist calculated that even given the immense cost-effectiveness of nanotechnology, several trillions of dollars had to have been spent by rapturists worldwide. Hardly anyone believed him; he was, after all, an economist.

—Gunter Schmidt finally recovered from the bronchitis which had followed upon his stroll through ice water in Nepal, and succeeded in suing his travel agent into bankruptcy. He then returned to Nepal to catch the May Tiji Festival—and learned on arrival that since the Kali Gandaki had in fact returned, the festival had been declared redundant. The Lo were too busy planting crops.

—Unnoticed by anyone, Admiral Cox slipped out a maintenance airlock and entered Symbiosis. The p-suit he removed in order to do so eventually burned up in the upper atmosphere, flaring as the air tanks went up. Since his bills continued to be paid and his room and AI reported no medical emergency, his absence went unnoted until late June.

—The rising wave of "cheerful art" reached such a crest worldwide that even critics began to notice it. Certain conspiracy theorists among the media began to smell a rat, and whispered along the E-mail byways of "rapturist conspiracy"—ideally some kind of immense digital fraud. To their annoyance, investigation kept indicating that the money funding all this new art was real. And anonymous. So they went public with the old standbys, thinly veiled suspicion and unsubstantiated rumor—and would have gone on to entirely baseless allegations in turn, if they hadn't noticed that nobody seemed to be paying the slightest bit of attention to them. Everyone was too busy attending performances that sent them home feeling good.

—The mammoth new mass of Symbiote reached Earth Orbit, was calved into six chunks, and each was inserted into a stable orbit. The reason for the subdivision was not known, but it aroused little curiosity. Few humans were of a mind to pester the Starmind with nosey questions these days.

—Colly Porter, having been back on Terra for the recommended three months, returned to High Orbit to spend a month with her father in the Shimizu Hotel. Shortly after her arrival she stated the opinion that hugging was more fun when you could use your legs too. This caused her father to blush (humans seldom go pale in free-fall, but they can still blush), and begin rehearsing a speech he had been meaning to deliver for a couple of years now. But in the end he managed to stall just long enough, and was spared the necessity.

—A peculiar glitch began to show up in automobiles—*all* automobiles, regardless of place or date of manufacture. Changing lanes without signalling at least five seconds in advance appeared to cause total CPU failure. Fortunately, the "crashless crash" safety feature hardwired into the guidance system usually brought the offending vehicle safely to the side of the road. No one claimed credit for the innovation, and public opinion split: some attributed it to rapturists, while others blamed a much older, half forgotten group called "hackers." But the prevailing response of humanity at large was glee, and no one tried too hard to crack the case.

At the end, there, everything seemed to happen at once.

PART NINE

25

The Dunes East of Provincetown
22 June 2065
Courage Day

"This is a good spot, mom."

Rhea thought so too. They were at the ocean shore east of Provincetown, just where the upthrust arm of Cape Cod curls its wrist back toward the mainland. Before them was the sea, next stop Europe; behind them to the west, between them and P-Town, lay kilometers of sand dunes. The weather was perfect, and had been since they had watched the sun rise together over the Atlantic several hours ago. It was now almost time for the Hour of Remembrance, and she and Colly were just finishing the food they had brought with them from home.

There were few others here, even on this global holiday. There were too many beaches a P-Towner could reach without having to walk several kilometers of sand, too many boats available to take them out on the water, especially since the fleet was not fishing today. Nonetheless Rhea had never seen this particular stretch of shore so heavily populated. The idea of Courage Day had caught on.

The spot did not feel crowded; there was no rowdiness; the general mood seemed to be a kind of subdued celebration. People spoke less than usual, and in softer voices; those who listened to music or news did not inflict it on their neighbors; even teenage boys were not horsing around. Rhea suspected things would get more festive later, after the Hour was past, but for the moment there was a kind of solemnity in the air that seemed to call for decorum. It had been a long long time since so many saints had been martyred at once.

"Do you feel like Trancing?" Colly asked.

Rhea looked around. There were a few individuals dancing, but no group had formed as yet. She did not see anyone she knew nearby. "Maybe later, hon. After the Hour."

"Okay." Colly liked trance-dancing well enough, but was not as attached to it as Rhea had become in recent months.

"I'm surprised you have the energy," Rhea added idly. Colly had only been back on Earth for a few days after visiting her father in orbit.

"I know," Colly said. "Me too. Yesterday I was tired as galoonies—but today I feel like Waldo. You know what I mean? Like he must feel. Like, I know I'm weak, but I don't *feel* weak."

It took Rhea a second to get the reference. "Oh, *Waldo*—your new friend in the Shimizu. I forgot all about him." Come to think of it, Colly hadn't mentioned him once since her return. "How is Waldo?"

Suddenly Colly was a textbook illustration, labeled Nonchalance. "Okay," she said off-handedly, studying her fingernails. "His frog died, and he likes that dopey classic rock music now, and his teacher says he understands calculus." Beat. "And he said he wants to marry me when we're bigger."

Rhea's heart turned over in her chest. She didn't know whether she wanted to laugh or cry, only that she must do neither out loud. *And so it begins,* she thought. "Oh," she said, with equal casualness. "I'm . . . sorry to hear about his frog."

"Yeah. Hip was cool."

"So, uh . . . what did you tell him? About the marriage thing."

"I said I'd think about it."

"I see. Did that satisfy him for now?"

"I guess." Another pause. "He wanted to kiss me."

Rhea chose her words with care. "How was it?"

Colly had run out of fingernails; she segued smoothly to toenails. "Okay, I guess." Suddenly she turned and looked her mother in the eye. "But honestly, Mom, I don't get what the big deal is."

Rhea refused herself permission to smile. It cost her. "You will, baby," she said solemnly. "You will."

"Yeah, but *when?*"

"You won't miss it," she said. The words made her think of Manuel Brava, and she glanced at her watchfinger. "Hey, it's almost time."

It was about five minutes before the Hour. All up and down the beach, conversations were ending, people were sitting up straighter and facing the sea. Boats out on the water killed their engines, and their passengers came out on deck. Rhea felt a sudden pang of loneliness, the kind that a child's presence does not assuage. Holidays are always the worst time for those with no significant other.

"Mom? We're rich now, right?"

The non sequitur made her smile. "No, dear. But we're richer."

"Well . . . can we afford to call space for an hour?"

Automatically Rhea started to do mental arithmetic . . . then abandoned the equation unsolved. Her daughter had sideswiped her for the second time in less than a minute. "*Yes,* Colly! That's a *great* idea! Oh, I hope he's not . . . no, they won't be working in orbit, either." She was already autodialing, half-wishing the car was near so they could have visual too. Space images would have been appropriate during the Hour. Ah well . . .

Rand answered almost at once. "Hi, Rhea! Is Colly there? Of course she is—hi, princess!"

"Hi, Daddy!" Colly called back.

Rhea adjusted the volume for privacy. "Hi," she said.

"Where are you guys? No, wait—let me guess. Audio only, so you're out in the boonies somewhere. From the sound of the waves, ocean rather than bay side. The Dunes, right?"

How could someone who knew you that well be hundreds of miles away? "That's right."

"Is Uncle Jay around?" Colly asked.

"Right here, cutie," Jay's voice said.

"Hi, Uncle Jay! Hi, Duncan!"

There was the sound of laughter, then, "Hi, Colly," from Duncan.

Rhea monitored herself to see if Duncan's voice caused any internal fluttering. Nothing. She hoped he and Jay would make a success of it. "Where are you guys, anyway? No wait—let me guess." It couldn't be one of the Solariums: Rand and Jay were celebrities. Somewhere private, with a good view . . . got it! "You're all in Eva's window, aren't you?"

"Right," Rand said. "As a matter of fact, I think I can see you from here. Wave, Colly."

She looked skyward and did so. "Here I am, Daddy!"

"I see you," he assured her. "You've got mayonnaise on your chin."

She checked—and burst into giggles when she found he was right.

"We're planning to do some damage to the legacy Eva left me, as soon as the Hour is over," Jay said. "I wish I could send you down a snort."

"Me too!" Rhea said. "Look, I know the Hour's almost here. We don't have to talk or anything—but can we all stay on-line together until it's over?"

"It's something Terrans and spacers should share," Duncan said.

"It was my idea," Colly said proudly.

"And a good one," Rand told her.

"Are you okay, Uncle Jay?" she asked. "Are you sad about Eva?"

His answer was slow in coming. "Let me put it this way, honey," he said at last. "I'm not exactly okay yet—but I know I'm going to be. You know what I mean?"

"I know exactly what you mean," she said solemnly, and Rhea felt a brief stab of guilt. "Daddy, tell him that thing Captain Kirk said."

"Huh?"

"You know, about leaving."

A chuckle. "Oh. Not Captain Kirk, honey: Rahsaan Roland Kirk. An Old Millennium jazzman. He said once, 'Nobody dies. They just leave *here*.'"

There was a pause, and then Jay's voice said, "I think that's true. Thank you, Colly."

"Two minutes," Duncan said.

"It feels like we ought to be *doing* something," Rhea said. "Colly told you we've been Trancing a little, right? Maybe we should all dance or something."

"Well," Jay said, "I figure like this: Reb was Soto Zen. One of his favorite sayings used to be, 'Don't just *do* something—sit there!' Do you guys know how to sit *zazen*? That's what we were thinking of doing."

"Sure," Colly said with just a hint of scorn. "Duncan taught us once. Well, *kûkanzen,* not *zazen,* but they're prac'ly the same." She began manipulating sand into an improvised *zafu,* and Rhea followed her lead. She was cautious about exposing her child to organized religion, but Zen did not meet her definition of a religion. It had no deity, for one thing—but more important, it did not require either killing or converting unbelievers.

"It's okay to get up if you get antsy, Colly," Jay said. "Reb wrote a book once called RUNNING JUMPING STANDING STILL. Any of those would be appropriate, I think. And there's a walking meditation called *kinhin,* for groundhogs, anyway. Or you can Trance, if you like. But let's sit a little at first, at least at the start."

"Sure," she agreed.

"I'm the *Doan* today," Jay said. "The timekeeper. I'll ring a bell three times when the Hour strikes, and again when it's over, and we'll all be silent in between, okay?"

"Are you studying Buddhism now, Jay?" Rhea asked.

"Aw, I've been fiddling with it for years. But yeah, I'm getting into it more lately. It's a lot like drinking Black Bush, only cheaper."

Rhea checked her daughter. "No, honey, like this. You don't have to lace your fingers together in a gee field, remember? Left hand on top of right palm, thumbtips just touching."

Colly corrected her *mudra,* and straightened her spine. "Are we supposed to look downward?"

"Technically, yes," Jay said. "But for today I think looking up is okay. There's really no wrong way to do it, if your heart's in the right place. Just follow your breath . . . and remember Eva and Reb and all the Adepts."

"Get ready," Duncan said. "It's almost time."

The beach was hushed, now, save for the omnipresent *whush* of waves. The sky was nearly cloudless, baby blue. Rhea felt an electricity in the air. It was awesome to think that at this moment, all over the world, most of the human race was about to do just what everyone here was doing. Had humanity ever acted with anything like this kind of unanimity before? What a pity it took a tragedy to bring it about. But wasn't that always the way? Nothing brought people together like a good disaster. . . .

"*Ting. Ting. Ting,*" said the phone. Rhea composed herself, drew in a measured breath through her nose—

And the sky turned gold.

Not "gold" in any metaphorical or analogous sense, as one can be said to have "red" hair when it is not really red at all. The whole sky was literally golden, the color of burnished 14-karat gold, the color of the wedding ring Rhea had still not been able to bring herself to remove. It happened all at once, seeming to mushroom outward from several sources like a crystal forming in an instant. It was like a translucent gold roof cast suddenly over the world, shimmering and twinkling, backlit by the sun.

Everyone on the beach—very nearly everyone alive—gasped, and stared upward in wonder. Rhea found that she and Colly were clutching each other's hands, *mudra* be damned. An indescribable sound began to come from the people on the shore. Rhea had once, many years ago, been caught in a riot, and would carry the memory of that indescribable, unmistakable sound to her grave. This was its opposite: a vocal sharing of awe. Perhaps the Israelites had made such a sound when the Red Sea parted.

Some of it seemed to be coming from the phone. "Can you guys *see* this?" she cried. "It's unbelievable!"

"We see—" Rand began, but she did not get to hear what he saw for some time, because his voice was drowned out by another. It seemed to come from everywhere, yet did not have the echoing quality of loudspeaker broadcast; it was as though every AI on the beach had been co-opted at once.

"This is Shara Drummond, calling the human race. I need your attention."

Rhea knew that her heart should be racing. Shara Drummond—the first Stardancer! Addressing all mankind directly, for the first time since her original Stardance, sixty-five years ago . . .

Yet somehow Rhea felt herself growing calmer. She met Colly's eyes . . . and they resumed formal *zazen* posture, side by side, but continued to hold hands.

"I have taken over all data channels and AIs in human space to talk to you, because something unprecedented is about to happen. A radical change. It may seem frightening at first, but I promise you it will be all right, if you do as I ask. The Starmind is here to help you through this . . . but you must do your part, and no one can do it for you. The first thing you must do is get everyone on Terra outdoors, and everyone in Luna onto the surface. I mean everyone. *Essential services personnel, hospital patients, the dying, the housebound, prisoners in solitary, all human*

beings. If you know of someone trapped indoors, get them outside now. *And hurry! There is no time to lose. I will tell you what I can—but don't stop to listen if you know of some human who needs help getting outdoors; the information will be repeated many times.*

"A turning point has come in the history of the human race—one set in motion by the Fireflies on the day they came here for the second time, the day of the Stardance. We Stardancers were created in large part to help you through it."

Rhea thought quickly. Thank God Tia Marguerite and Tia Marion were out on Ti Louie's boat—it was an hour's hard walk back to the car. Everyone else she knew in town was mobile too. Suddenly she missed Rand so much her stomach hurt. "Are you guys hearing this too?" she murmured.

The phone's LED said the circuit was still open, but there was no reply. She thrust it absently into her breast pocket.

"I'm afraid your life is about to change forever. Your old life is over; a new one is about to begin. I know that will not be welcome news for many of you. No baby wants to be born; they all come out crying. But they stop. I'm afraid you have no more choice in the matter than a baby does: the contractions are beginning, and no power in the Solar System could stop them now. All we of the Starmind can do is see that the birth takes place as smoothly and painlessly as possible. We have sacrificed much to that end . . . but today is not our *Courage Day, but* yours. *I can only ask you to trust in me—and in the Fireflies, who refused to let me die in orbit so many years ago.*

"On that day, my planet was like a womb whose fetus is overdue for delivery. Such a fetus grows too large for its environment, begins to pollute its ecosystem with its own waste products, begins to degrade its surroundings. In the decades that followed, you—and we, the Starmind—have cooperated to help correct most of the damage to our home planet, using nanotechnology to minimize new wastes and recycle old ones efficiently. The womb is repaired—but it is time for the fetus to leave it behind now."

Rhea did not guess what was coming; it was only a shadowy intuition. But it was enough to make her heart sink. She stared around that perfect beach, that eerie golden sky, as if to memorize it, and clutched Colly's hand. At an answering pressure, she met her daughter's eyes—and found them serene, untroubled.

"It's okay, Mom," she said. "It's Courage Day."

Shara Drummond's voice continued:

"You know that the Fireflies seeded this planet with life. You know that much of what you are is written in your DNA. *Some of you may know that large segments of the information encoded there appear to be gibberish, and do not express somatically—the so-called junk* DNA. *These genetic 'instructions' are never carried out, because they lack the end-begin codes that would activate them.*

"In just a few minutes, a kind of telepathic trigger signal will go out from Titan. There is no way to avoid or shield against it: it will be as unstoppable as a neutrino, and faster. Designed by the same beings who designed DNA *in the first place, it will insert end-begin codes in certain introns—and switch them on. Everywhere in the Solar System, the nature of human tissue will change, permanently.*

"It will become transparent to gravitons. In plain language, it will become immune to gravity."

Rhea moaned.

"Please listen to me and try to be calm. Many of you on Terra may have the idea that what is usually miscalled centrifugal force will send you flying off the planet at high speed. This will not *happen. When you go weightless, the net upward force acting on you will not exceed .003 gee. Your clothing should suffice to hold you in place; even shoes will probably be enough. Ask your* AI *if you don't believe me; I'll be releasing it to your control again soon. Nonetheless you will be in free fall, with the usual physiological symptoms most of you know: dizziness, stuffy nose and so forth.*

"This period will last for perhaps five minutes. Then machines will turn themselves on. There are three of them. One is buried deep in the core of Terra, one at the heart of Luna, and the third at the core of Mars, though no one is there to be affected by it now. Each is designed to generate antigravitons . . . a special kind of antigraviton which will only *affect altered human tissue."*

The next sentence was delivered slowly, deliberately.

"Like it or not, you will find yourself rising into the sky."

A wordless cry went up all around the beach—doubtless around the planet—a discordant amalgam of clashing emotions. Shara Drummond seemed to anticipate that, and waited for it to die down.

"DO NOT FEAR," she said then. *"It is not death that waits for you*

in the sky, but a new kind of life. You will not freeze or suffocate as you climb, I promise you.

"For the last sixty-five years, the Starmind has worked at modifying our Symbiote, in preparation for this day. The gold you see in the sky is the variant we have shaped, a variant designed to survive, for a time, at the interface between Terra and space. It cannot come down to you . . . but you will find it waiting for you about five kilometers above the ground, just as the air is getting too thin to breathe. Touch it anywhere, drink it, and it will shape itself to you. It will breathe for you, and bring you higher, changing from gold to red as you leave the atmosphere behind.

"This is why the Adepts made their sacrifice. If the Group of Five had gotten their way, all *of you would have died this day. The Five knew nothing of this, nor could we tell them. Without a Starmind, you would have suffocated as you left the stratosphere—and would not be hearing me now. But thanks to* Tenshin *Reb Hawkins and the others, you will live to reach space.*

"And we the Starmind will be waiting for you. To show you your new world. Your new home. You will be one with us, and we with you, Homo caelestis *forever."*

A vast soundless sound filled the world. Rhea heard it inside her head, as if on headphones. It was music, and she even recognized it: something Rand played all the time, something by Brindle whose name she could not recall. But to her tortured imagination it seemed like the Trump of Doom that Christians believed would signal the Rapture. She found that she was clutching Colly to her fiercely, keening without words. The words that raced through her mind were, she knew, probably shared by millions; indeed, they might have been the final thought of most of the humans who had ever died: *Not yet! I wasn't* done *yet!*

It was a protest the universe had never heeded yet. As she drew in a breath to scream it aloud, Colly spoke against her breast.

"Don't worry, Mom," she said. "I didn't want to come out either, remember?"

Rhea remembered. Colly had been born three weeks overdue. She had stayed stubbornly in the womb . . . until a pitocin drip induced labor, and forced her out. And Colly had come to like this world.

"It's okay," Colly insisted. "We're gonna go see Daddy now."

She kept her deathgrip on Colly's shoulders, but pulled back so she could see her face. Colly was smiling. "Can you feel it?" she asked.

With a thrill of something like horror, Rhea felt her weight leaving her. She tried to hang on to it, but could not. Within a minute it was gone completely. Her sinuses began to fill, and she felt her face reddening as blood redistributed itself evenly throughout her body. She felt mild dizziness too. It was just like climbing to orbit in a shuttle—except that the rest of the world around her continued to observe the law of gravity.

Shara Drummond's message began repeating.

Colly picked up an uneaten apple, held it out, and let go. Rhea's body-awareness told her that she was in zero gee, so persuasively that it was jarring to see the apple fall normally. Colly giggled.

Suddenly she squirmed out of Rhea's grasp, a trick she had perfected at age five. Rhea cried out, but it was too late: Colly had already unfolded her legs from beneath her . . . causing her to rise into the air.

Without thinking, Rhea sprang after her and caught her like a tackler, hugging the child to her. They found themselves about six or seven meters in the air, sinking with the gentle slowness of a feather beneath the weight of their clothes. This high in the air, Shara's repeating message was almost inaudible. Others around them were airborne too. *A convention of Nijinskis,* she thought wildly as she drifted down. *Oh, Jay would love this! And Rand . . .*

"I wish Dad and Uncle Jay could see this," she said aloud.

Colly was grinning, exhilarated. "Just pay attention," she said. "We can give them an instant replay later."

They landed gently on sand, a few meters west of their takeoff point. With space-trained instincts and Trancer skill, both let their legs absorb the energy of landing, so they did not bounce away again. For a moment they bobbed there together, poised at the very membrane between earth and sky. They could hear Shara's voice clearly again, now that they were close to the earth—and many competing sounds too. Some people were screaming, some were laughing, some were yelling contradictory advice; some were flailing helplessly in the air, trying vainly to swim back to earth. And some were finding out how high they could jump. Out on the sea she could see people leaping higher than their masts, moving lazily in the air, like drowners in reverse.

"Let's Trance, Mom," Colly said. "We can do it for real, now."

Rhea had a sudden vivid memory of Manuel Brava, the night she had trance-danced for the first time.

Be ready, he had said. *It's gonna be good.*

And this was the Hour of his Remembrance . . .

Somewhere in Rhea's heart, something gave way. Without regret, she closed the book that was her life . . . and began a new one. "All right, Colly." She released her embrace. "Take my hand, though, okay?"

"Sure," Colly said. "Here we go!"

They leaped together.

A few minutes later, Rhea admitted to herself that she was having fun. More fun than she had had in a long time. It was a little like trampolining or bungee-jumping in ultraslow motion. It was very much like dreams she had been having all her life. It was, in literal reality, what Trancing had always felt like, except that the moments of breathless exhilaration were not fleeting and transient.

Some others around her were also moving in the characteristic flowing movements of trance-dance, now; she and Colly were not the only Trancers here. Out on the sea, some people were walking on water, with exaggerated steps; she could just hear them laughing.

"—you okay?" Rand's voice said suddenly from her breast pocket. "Rhea! Colly! Can you hear me? Dammit, are you okay?"

He sounded half out of his mind with worry. Rhea took the phone out of her pocket. "We're fine, darling. Hang on—I think we're coming for a visit."

"What the hell do you mean? What's going on down there?"

"Didn't you hear Shara up there?"

"Yeah, but it didn't make much sense. She told us to go EVA, find some Symbiote, and take off our p-suits. But what about you? She said something crazy about immunity to gravity, and gold Symbiote."

"That's right. We're about . . . oh, I'd guess twenty meters above the ground right now. It looks like you win: Colly and I are coming to space after all."

"Oh God—you'll freeze, before you can reach the Symbiote."

"I don't think so," she said. "It's warmer than it should be down here. I think that gold Symbiote is having some kind of lens effect. They've had a long time to think this through."

There was silence on the line. The first to fully absorb the news was Jay. He began to laugh with joy. "Oh, Eva!" he cried, "What a glorious joke on you! Oh, how *wonderful*!"

"What do you mean, Jay?" Rhea asked.

"I get it now—I see it—I know why she wanted to die—and why she was dragging her feet—the stubborn old biddy was holding out for *meaning* . . . and she got it, bless her selfish heart—damn, she got the prize—oh, I'll bet she died smiling—"

"I don't understand," Rhea said. "Rewind and start over—slower."

"I'll try. Look, at age one hundred, Eva was done with life. So she went into sixteen years of life review . . . and found no *meaning* in anything she'd done. During a century of living as hard as she knew how, Eva converted *X* cubic tonnes of food and water into excrement and offspring; she pushed *Y* megabucks from one imaginary place to another; she experienced *Z* increments of pleasure or pain; once done, she could find no real significance in any of it. So her last hope for meaning was her death: she spent sixteen years hoping, irrationally, to find a meaningful death, an opportunity to give up her life *for* something. That's why she kept postponing her suicide for so long—why, even after she gave up and made up her mind to die, she stalled long enough to let Reb arrive, and give her a convincing reason to wait just a little longer. The reason was: to live to see this historic day."

"It's a shame she missed it, then," Colly said.

"No, no that's the best part, don't you see?" Jay said. "It is a shame she didn't live to see it with her own eyes, sure. But I'm sure she got to see it through the Starmind's eyes before she died—and more important, she got something even better. She got what she'd wanted in the first place, what she'd already given up on when Reb told her about today: a meaningful death. Think about it: how many humans—how many creatures, in the wide universe—had ever been privileged to sacrifice their lives to save *two* intelligent *species?*"

Colly was the first to see it. "Wow, yeah," she said wonderingly. "If it hadn't been for her and Reb and the Adepts, all the Stardancers would have got killed, and there wouldn't be any of that gold simmy-oat up there waiting for us. All us people would have died today . . ."

"She got the most meaningful death there ever was," Rhea said. She giggled suddenly. "Every damn time humanity goes through some kind of birthing, there seems to be an Eve around."

"Are you *sure* you're okay?" Rand asked. "You sound sort of giddy."

She laughed out loud. "Let's just say a great weight has been lifted from my shoulders. We don't have to be apart anymore, baby. Not ever again. Hang in there—we'll be along directly."

"What should I do?" he cried, his voice agonized.

"What Shara said. And don't be afraid. I'm not. I was, but I'm not anymore. It's gonna be *good.*"

"But—"

"Go ahead. I've got to hang up now, I don't want to miss this. We'll be there soon, love." She let go of the phone, and watched it fall away.

She and Colly were slowly moving away from the ocean, into the dunes. With each leap they came down farther to the west, for the earth went on without them all around them. They were sweating with exertion, now, and the sweat behaved the way it did in free-fall, as content to drip up as down. In her mind's eye Rhea saw the whole human race doing this. Hovering. Tottering on the brink. Trembling on the verge.

The ground was coming up again. You didn't even have to look: when you could hear Shara clearly again, it was time to prepare for your landing.

"Colly!" she cried. "Want to go for the big one?"

"Sure," her daughter said.

Rhea began undoing her clothing. Colly got the idea at once and skinned out of her own clothes. They let go, watched their clothes fall. This time, when they hit the earth and rebounded, they kept on rising.

They kept dancing for a while as they rose, but the view was simply too distracting to concentrate; after a time they stopped moving in space and just gawked, letting the wind do with them as it would, turning end over end. The earth moved slowly and majestically beneath them. Soon Provincetown was below them. It was weird, inexpressibly weird, to see P-Town with hardly a soul on the streets. The beaches were full of hopping fleas, and the sky was starting to fill with naked people. It reminded Rhea of news footage of hot-air balloon regattas in the desert.

"Look," Colly said, pointing. "There's our old house."

Rhea saw it. For a moment it filled her heart, and called her back. Her beloved widow's walk. Below that, the tower room in which her unfinished novel waited, and below that the bedroom into which she had been born. Kicking and screaming.

"Goodbye," she said to it. "I'll never forget you."

"'Course not," Colly said. "Me either."

Suddenly they were rising faster, as though propelled by a great wind from below. It felt surprisingly like surfing vertically.

"Hang on," Rhea cried.

"Here we come, Daddy!" Colly called.

And they rose up forever, going for the gold.

EPILOGUE

High Earth Orbit
22 July 2065

It did not go totally smoothly, of course. Human beings were involved; at least some chaos and tragedy had to result.

But there never were more than the two choices: evolve or die.

Perhaps it need not have been done as it was, by surprise. Perhaps humanity, forewarned and prepared, might have agreed to leave its ancestral womb forever, peacefully and without panic. The decision not to risk it was irrevocably made on the day the original Six entered Symbiosis and founded the Starmind, back at the turn of the millennium, back when half of the human race was hungry and poor, and pessimism was still the hallmark of intelligence. Once Charlie Armstead elected to leave Courage Day out of the report he sent back to humanity from Saturn in the historic Titan Transmission, it was too late to turn back: the Starmind was committed to secrecy.

If you could somehow establish telepathic contact with a human fetus in its ninth month . . . would it be a kindness for you to tell it everything you know of the birth trauma to come? Would it benefit from the foreknowledge—or panic, jam the birth canal, and kill itself and its mother? After all, less than one percent of the race ever voluntarily chose to go to Top Step and become Stardancers. Being human is a hard habit to break. Shara Drummond, Charlie Armstead and their companions believed—all the Starmind still believes—that humanity might well have died rather than leave Earth, given the choice. So they did not give it the choice until the last possible instant . . . and spent sixty-five years secretly preparing it for that instant.

This cost the Starmind much ethical anguish over those years—and sharp tragedy at the eleventh hour—but right up until the Day of Courage, the overwhelming consensus of the massed brains of the Starmind was that the stakes were just too high to permit any risks. One of the few concrete facts the Fireflies told the Starmind before they left us to work out our own destiny is that *Homo sapiens* is at least the *third* sentient race to be raised up in this solar system.

The first sentient race ("sentient" defined as "capable of art") lived eons ago, on a planet some call Lucifer, whose shattered remains are now known as the Asteroid Belt.

The second such race appears to have been somewhat more advanced: they "merely" blew the atmosphere off the next closest planet to the sun, Mars. But they are just as dead.

We appear to have squeaked through to the finish line.

Had we too failed our most final of exams . . . well, there hangs Venus, within the habitable zone, its reducing atmosphere ready to collapse into a viable biosphere at a chemical nudge. . . .

Perhaps when I was a human fetus, I would have consented to be born. But I am glad, all things considered, that I wasn't consulted.

Volumes larger than this one could be—are being—written about the chaotic events of the hours and days that followed the Hour of Remembrance, the countless millions of varying human reactions to Shara Drummond's call.

No volume however large could describe what happened when over six billion minds entered telepathic symphysis in a single great cascading wave, nor will I try even to hint at it here. Suffice it to say that only the presence of a quarter of a million trained and prepared telepaths made it possible at all. Symbiosis is profoundly disorienting in its first onset, and some find it terrifying—Stardancer Postulants used to spend three months in Top Step preparing themselves for the transition. But human beings are tough, when they have to be, and we had to be.

Even now, a month later, the integration process is still ongoing. It might not be too inaccurate to say that the new HyperStarmind has achieved consciousness, and is working—slowly!—toward awareness.

Despite the very best efforts of a quarter of a million linked minds planning for over half a century, a little more than two percent of humanity perished in the mass transcendence to *Homo caelestis,* most through stubbornness but some from sheer stupidity. No telepathic entity can take lightly the deaths of so many millions of souls—especially needless deaths, on the very verge of immortality. But at least their surviving loved ones *know* with utter certainty that everything possible was done to save them; there is mourning for them in the Starmind today, but no recrimination. Cells die whenever a baby is born; it is no one's fault. Balancing the sorrow to some extent is the joy of all those who love an autistic or retarded or catatonic or mute person—for now they can communicate with their loved one on a level far deeper than words could ever have reached.

Approximately one half of one percent of humanity were unaffected by the telepathic tocsin from Titan or the subsequent flood of antigravitons: genetic defectives whose DNA had sustained too many nonexpressing mutations over the millennia, whose introns were fatally damaged despite massive redundancy in the coding. But nearly ninety percent of those eventually reached space and joined the Starmind too . . . for there were suddenly spacecraft to spare.

And a little over five percent of the human race flatly and stubbornly refused to go—improvising an astonishing variety of desperate methods to remain near the earth's surface, to remain only human. Within a month, however, their number had shrunk from five percent of the former total to about two.

The present population of Terra, then, consists of a little more than one hundred and sixty million people—on a planet with wealth and technology and room enough for six and a half billion. Most of them are wearing weights. You are one of them, or you would not be reading this. And the odds are that despite your new wealth and lebensraum you are lonely and/or hurt and/or angry and/or afraid.

You do not have to be any of those things. If you insist on staying on Earth, your life need not be hard: we will continue to beam down power, and programs for your nanoassemblers, and other things you will need—or you can make your own way as your forebears did, if that pleases you.

But you do not have to stay.

The golden sky of Earth is blue once more—but there is plenty of red Symbiote in orbit. And even now, Terra holds more than enough resources to send you to join us. Even if you are one of the rare genetic unfortunates—and if you are, we have the resources to heal your introns, once you enter Symbiosis.

That is why I am writing this.

All you have to do is find a phone. Shara Drummond is accepting collect calls, and will tell you how to reach the nearest functioning spacecraft. We're waiting for you.

Some of the oldest Chinese legends speak of a mysterious "edible gold," one taste of which confers immortality. It seems unlikely the ancient Chinese could have had any direct knowledge of the Fireflies or of Symbiote—it may simply be that, given enough time, *any* prophecy will eventually come true.

For millions of years, loneliness has cascaded down through the millennia, an ever-expanding wave of loneliness, powered by itself, by its own terrible self-creating hunger. Confined in bone boxes, we sought solace by rubbing our meat-mounts against one another, and so made more prisoners of bone and flesh to replace us and keep loneliness alive and expanding across the ages.

Now loneliness is only an option, rather than a sentence. Your sentence has been commuted: you are released, not on, but *upon,* your own cognizance. The cell door is open at last: you can walk out any time you are ready. You have been ready since you were born.

And it is safe now. You can leave your cell without fear, without shame, without self-doubt. No matter what horrors you flatter yourself lie uniquely in your skull, no matter what unforgivable deficiencies you claim to yourself, you will find understanding and total acceptance in the Starmind. Everyone else did. One of the nicest things about living in zero gravity is that it is no longer possible for one person to look *down on* any other. There is no rank, no class, in the Starmind. There is no obsession, for there is no need for it. Yet paradoxically, somehow I can look *up to* many of my fellow Stardancers—and look *into* any who consent. All of them, sooner or later.

To join us is *not* to "lose your ego." It is to gain nine billion more. Love on that scale has never been imagined, in all the ages of the world. I tell you that it is better than you *can* imagine.

There is a reason why I have been chosen—out of more than nine billion!—to tell you this story of the final days. And the reason is *not* because I used to practice the writer's trade, although that has proved helpful.

This task fell to me because fate placed me in a unique position. I yearned to live out the rest of my days on Terra so badly that I tore my heart in half, and risked the heart of my daughter, to stay there. Yet I live in the Starmind now, and will live out the rest of my days in space—and am deeply joyous. I have lost *nothing* . . . and gained the stars.

And more. Buchi Tenmo was quite right about self-generated reality: I still have Provincetown. I smell it as I write . . .

In fact, I have P-Town now far more than I ever did before . . . for now I can see it through the eyes (through *all* the senses) of Tia Marguerite and Tia Marion and Cousin Tomas and all my relatives and friends, can know it through the perceptions and experiences of every other former resident, nearly everyone living who has ever seen it. If binocular vision creates three-dimensional visual depth, imagine the kind of depth with which I now know my beloved home. Over a hundred years of Provincetown, times millions of people, raised to its own power! I have more of my beloved home than a hundred thousand normal lifetimes could have given me . . . and I no longer need it. I have much deeper roots, now.

And my husband, who needed the attention of strangers, expressed in dollars, so badly that he tore his heart in half and risked his daughter's heart for it, has more raw attention available to him than he could ever have imagined . . . and sacrifices *nothing* for it . . . and needs it not at all.

And his brother, who risked his job and thus his art and thus his life, all to be near him, is now with him always. Just as intimately as I am, for the Starmind understands genetics as no human ever did. I carry their child in my womb now . . . a girl who is already Shaping herself, and will begin dancing soon.

That is the reason why I have chosen to tell my own story through more eyes than my own—right up to the moment when all our viewpoints converged.

Can you see that, if any of those three surviving protagonists in the foregoing comedy had known as much about what was really going on as you did when you read their story, they could not have acted as foolishly and destructively as they did? Can you really want to keep wasting as much time and energy as they all did, blundering through the dark of their lives, squinting through the twin chinks in the bone box and trying to read the hearts of others through theirs?

I/we have also reconstructed Eva's story, and made it part of mine/ours, partly for the additional perspective it adds, and mostly to show that I/we can. Reb knew her, and so the Starmind does, and always will. No one will ever completely die again . . . so long as there is one brain in the Starmind that ever knew him or her. I'm teaching the unborn daughter in my belly about Eva right now—since Rand and Jay are going to give her Eva's name.

"O wad some power the giftie gie us, to see oursels as others see us! It wad frae monie a blunder free us, and foolish notion."

Robert Burns was right. The gift has been given. Take it . . .

What has happened to our species may seem unprecedented. But it is not. We have made other Jumps of comparable magnitude, up the evolutionary scale. From the sea to the mud to the trees to the mountaintops to the skies . . . and now to space itself, free of the womb altogether.

There is less than no future in being a Neo-Neanderthal . . . for the *next* evolutionary Jump is *already in progress.* A Starmind of nine and a half billion brains possesses the necessary complexity and depth to begin to make sense of the Cosmic Background Babble. Deep in the Oort Cloud where the comets play, far from the sun, something is presently nearing completion that will help, a thing that has no analog in human experience. The infant is listening, learning to hear; one day it will learn to talk. There are as many stars in this galaxy as there are neurons in a brain: imagine a mind made up of a galaxy of Starminds!

For millions of years, an endless succession of generations of upright, lonely apes have gazed up in dumb yearning at the stars, at the infinite depth and breadth of the universe, at the teasing promise of the other 99.9999+% of reality. Now, at long last, we have come home.

Join us—as soon as you are ready!

I am Rhea Paixao, and my message to you is: the stars are here.